2015
PUSHCART PRIZE XXXIX
BEST OF THE
SMALL PRESSES

EDITED BY BILL HENDERSON
WITH THE PUSHCART PRIZE EDITORS

Note: nominations for this series are invited from any small, independent, literary book press or magazine in the world, print or online. Up to six nominations—tear sheets or copies, selected from work published, or about to be published, in the calendar year—are accepted by our December 1 deadline each year. Write to Pushcart Fellowships, P.O. Box 380, Wainscott, N.Y. 11975 for more information or consult our websites www.pushcartprize.com. or pushcart press.org.

Acknowledgments
Selections for The Pushcart Prize are reprinted with the permission of authors and presses cited. Copyright reverts to authors and presses immediately after publication.

Distributed by W. W. Norton & Co.
500 Fifth Ave., New York, N.Y. 10110

Library of Congress Card Number: 76-58675
ISBN (hardcover): 978-1-888889-72-7
ISBN (paperback): 978-1-888889-73-4
ISSN: 0149-7863

For
Maxine Kumin (1925–2014)
and
Peter Matthiessen (1927–2014)

INTRODUCTION

Here's how stunning news arrives at Pushcart. I open a letter from Contributing Editor Tom Paine: "I'm writing to you about a young writer named Emma Duffy-Comparone. She was born with an emotional radar that borders on the psychic as it does for all true writers, and luckily, she also has the ability to pluck a word from the air that is just perfect. . .but most of all she is a lyrical writer of exceedingly musical prose. . ."

That's the kind of excitement that can lift you out of your chair on a grey winter day and it duplicates many of the nominating letters from our Contributing Editors. Tom mentioned several of Emma's stories– from the *Mississippi Review, American Scholar, The Southern Review, The Sun, Iowa Review* in print or forthcoming and enclosed her first published tale "The Zen Thing" from *One Story*–it became the first-ever-first-published story to be featured as a lead in thirty-nine years of Pushcart volumes.

The joy of editing the PP series for almost four decades is discovering writers like Emma. This edition includes many new talents besides her. Indeed, I recognize only a few names from the current pantheon of established authors in this edition. All of this newness gives me mighty hope for the future. And since all writers reprinted in Pushcart volumes become lifetime Contributing Editors we expect to be new and vital for quite some time.

But our thanks extend to the past also. Thousands of editors and writers have helped keep this series thriving. Back in the early 1970's Stuart Brand's small-press-published *The Whole Earth Catalog* was an inspiration to millions. It billed itself as an "access to tools" of all sorts–books, medicines, bikes, shelters, etc. And drew its inspiration from thousands of people who helped.

Brand's idea of asking many people to help out was borrowed by Pushcart in 1976 for the first *Pushcart Prize.* At that time, twenty-six distinguished founding editors assisted us as did hundreds of little magazines and small press book editors with nominations. Over the past thirty-nine years "the people who helped" listing on our masthead and back pages has grown to almost 950 for each edition. " Access to literature" might be our motto, and our gatekeepers are readers everywhere.

For this edition I honor two of those gatekeepers–Peter Matthiessen and Maxine Kumin who both died earlier this year.

Maxine Kumin was co-editor of poetry for PP37. Amazingly she volunteered for the job, which all past guest editors know is an impossible position–four thousand poems to consider and only a few dozen to honor. As I do with all editors I warned her the pay was pathetic and influx immense. But despite being ill she persisted and she made an excellent selection.

Since 1963 Maxine and her husband Victor ran a hardscrabble New Hampshire agricultural establishment they dubbed with suitable irony Pobiz Farm. They were helped in this endeavor by their three children. From Pobiz Maxine issued streams of essays, novels, short stories, children's books and poetry, twenty poetry collections in total including her Pulitzer Prize winning *Up Country* (1973) about life in their tumble down acres, and her last book *And Short the Season,* just published by W. W. Norton & Co. Along the way she served as Poet Laureate of the United States 1989-1994.

Maxine loved animals. I first met her during a poetry reading sponsored by Joan Murray, editor of *The Pushcart Book of Poetry,* at New York's Baruch College. Joining her were Billy Collins, C. K. Williams, Lucille Clifton, Gerry Stern, and Grace Shulman. We talked for a bit before the event and I proudly announced I'd just bought a Portuguese water dog as a Christmas present for my wife. "No good. You should have found a rescue at the animal shelter," snapped Maxine in her usual direct fashion.

Maxine was an evangelist not only for animals but for the sound of poetry. When she taught at Tufts, New England College, and The Breadloaf Writers Conference she insisted that her students memorize 30-40 lines of poetry a week–Hopkins, Housman, Moore. It was an unpopular chore but she insisted on it. The sound of poetry was everything to her.

When Maxine was herself a student in her early 20's in a local workshop she and classmate Anne Sexton dedicated a telephone line so they could recite to each other and appreciate the sound and sense of their daily compositions.

Maxine was a wonderful poetry editor, a faithful donor to our endowment and a Contributing Editor over many years.

Peter Matthiessen was another "person who helped". For many years he donated generously to our endowment, but perhaps the greatest donation was the example of his life. In 1953, Matthiessen, a Yale graduate, joined his lifetime friend George Plimpton in Paris. Peter had gone there, like many before him–myself included a decade later–to write his great novel. The glory of Hemingway and Fitzgerald still lingered in Paris. Peter's trip was financed by the CIA, who hoped he would mingle with the local leftists and keep tabs. Later he would admit to an astonishing innocence in accepting CIA cash but at that time of Soviet threat it seemed a righteous cause. In fact, the CIA grants helped start *The Paris Review*. Later, his unsuspecting friend Plimpton was outraged when told the source of his income.

Soon *The Paris Review* staff got rid of the CIA and worked from a tiny office in a larger French publishing firm (they weren't allowed keys to the office and had to climb in and out of a window for access and egress). Eventually *The Paris Review* operated from a table at the Left Bank Café de Tournon and from an old grain barge moored in the Seine.

Years later *The Paris Review* moved itself to George Plimpton's New York apartment and today is a granddaddy of all small presses. Peter's pal Plimpton was a stalwart supporter of the Pushcart Prize and opened his apartment many times for gala celebrations of this series.

But Peter Matthiessen's influx extended far wider than his cofounding of *The Paris Review*. In more than thirty books of fiction and non-fiction he was a journalist, environmentalist, Zen priest, novelist, professional fisherman and explorer in Asia, Australia, Africa, New Guinea, the deep oceans and the Florida swamps. He was the only author to be awarded the National Book Award in both non-fiction and fiction. Through books like *The Snow Leopard, In the Spirit of Crazy Horse, Killing Mr. Watson, Men's Lives,* and the just issued *In Paradise* Peter crossed genres and showed all of us how passion for literature trumps all.

As Alec Michod wrote in a letter to *The New York Times,* "Forget MFAs kids, read, study, emulate Matthiessen."

In exact opposition to the spirit of Peter Matthiessen is the contemporary attitude toward writing. Books are dubbed (by publishers) "units" and in mass-market distributors they are treated like widgets. To magazines authors are mere "content providers" to fill in the space around ads.

The proliferation of vanity presses–*Create Space, iUniverse, Archway, AuthorHouse*–often run as profitable sidelines by commercial presses that now accept only sure thing celebrity memoirs, diet fad titles and formula fiction–are encouraging a deluge of junk writing. Authors no longer aspire to greatness. Why bother? You can't sell your effort to the commercial girls and boys so why not shell out a bit to the vanity people and at least have your book to hold, as sloppy as it is.

As agent David Gernert stated in a recent *Poets & Writers,* "the business of publishing words–of putting stories and ideas in front of the public–is rapidly trending toward the unprofessional. . . bad looking, typo-ridden, a looming disaster. . ."

In a recent *New York Times* Op-Ed, Timothy Egan nailed it–he pointed out that educators are attempting to harness creativity and corporations are trying to own it. Apple even has a creativity app. "Creativity needs messiness, and magic, serendipity and insanity."

That's where small presses come in. We aren't about skimming profits from authors' dreams. We don't encourage dullness and depression of spirit. As *Publishers Weekly* noted in reviewing last years PP (with a star and a box): "With large publishing houses facing an uncertain future, *The Pushcart Prize* is more valuable than ever in highlighting the unique voices thriving in America's small presses."

Every year I ask our co-poetry editors to write about their editing experience. This year Claudia Rankine and Eduardo C. Corral helped out by selecting poems from a massive array.

Eduardo C. Corral is a CantoMundo fellow. His work has been honored with a Discovery/The Nation Award, the J. Howard and Barbara M. J. Wood Prize from *Poetry,* and writing residencies to the MacDowell Colony and Yaddo. *Slow Lightning,* his first book, won the 2011 Yale Series of Younger Poets competition. He's the recipient of a Whiting Writers' Award and a National Endowment for the Arts Fellowship.

"For months I traveled with Pushcart-nominated poems. Each time I flew in a plane or rode in a bus, I'd pull out a bundle of poems from my messenger bag. I underlined memorable lines. I dog-eared pages. I whispered stanzas. I circled stunning similes–I read until I arrived at my destination. Here's a joyful confession: I never tired of reading Pushcart-nominated poems. Again and again I was surprised, moved, thrilled, and intrigued by the range of voices and approaches. No single school or aesthetic dominates these days. If you want pared down beauty, you will find it. If you want a baroque gaze, you will find it. Reading for the Pushcart Prize anthology was an immensely enriching experience. I want to thank the editors and the writers who nominated these poems. I want to thank the poets for writing these poems."

Claudia Rankine is the author of several collections of poetry. Her newest book *Citizen: An American Lyric* is just out from Graywolf. *The Racial Imaginary: Writers on Race In the Life of the Mind* is forthcoming from Fence Books. She teaches at Pomona College where she is Henry G. Lee Professor of English. Recently she won the Jackson Poetry Prize, and the Morton Dauwen Zabel Award In Literature from the American Academy of Arts and Letters.

"Reading for the Pushcart Prize is bit like driving a long distance; it takes time and you see many things you expect but the surprises are delicious. I read poems that I immediately wanted to share with a friend; I was reminded of journals that I had stopped reading but clearly should start reading again and I was introduced to new poets and journals. Time seemed to be the governing theme in many of the best poems–the state of our times, the passing of time. It was an honor to be part of the process."

My profound thanks to all of the people who helped this year and in the past. And as always, my deepest appreciation to you, honored reader. Thank you for keeping the faith.

Bill Henderson

THE PEOPLE WHO HELPED

FOUNDING EDITORS—Anaïs Nin (1903-1977), Buckminster Fuller (1895-1983), Charles Newman (1938-2006), Daniel Halpern, Gordon Lish, Harry Smith (1936–2013), Hugh Fox (1932-2011), Ishmael Reed, Joyce Carol Oates, Len Fulton (1934-2011), Leonard Randolph, Leslie Fiedler (1917-2003), Nona Balakian (1918-1991), Paul Bowles (1910-1999), Paul Engle (1908-1991), Ralph Ellison (1914-1994), Reynolds Price (1933-2011), Rhoda Schwartz, Richard Morris, Ted Wilentz (1915-2001), Tom Montag, William Phillips (1907-2002). Poetry editor: H. L. Van Brunt

CONTRIBUTING EDITORS FOR THIS EDITION—Steve Adams, Dan Albergotti, Dick Allen, John Allman, Idris Anderson, Antler, Philip Appleman, Tony Ardizzone, Renee Ashley, David Baker, Kim Barnes, Ellen Bass, Claire Bateman, Bruce Beasley, Marvin Bell, Molly Bendall, Pinckney Benedict, Bruce Bennett, Marie-Helene Bertino, Linda Bierds, Diann Blakely, Marianne Boruch, Michael Bowden, John Bradley, Fleda Brown, Rosellen Brown, Michael Dennis Browne, Ayse Papatya Bucak, Christopher Buckley, E. S. Bumas, Richard Burgin, Kathy Callaway, Bonnie Jo Campbell, Richard Cecil, Kim Chinquee, Jane Ciabattari, Suzanne Cleary, Billy Collins, Jeremy Collins, Martha Collins, Lydia Conklin, Robert Cording, Stephen Corey, Eduardo C. Corral, Lisa Couturier, Michael Czyzniejewski, Phil Dacey, Claire Davis, Kwane Dawes, Chard deNiord, Jaquira Diaz, Stuart Dischell, Stephen Dixon, Jack Driscoll, John Drury, Karl Elder, Elizabeth Ellen, Angie Estes, Ed Falco, Gary Fincke, Robert Long Freeman, Ben Fountain, H. E. Francis, Seth Fried, Alice Friman, Sarah Frisch, John Fulton, Frank X. Gaspar, Christine Gelineau, Gary Gildner, Elton Glaser, Mark Halliday, Jeffrey Hammond, James Harms, Jeffrey Harrison, Timothy Hedges, Robin Hemley, Daniel L. Henry, David Hernandez, William

Heyen, Bob Hicok, Kathleen Hill, Jane Hirshfield, Jen Hirt, Edward Hoagland, Andrea Hollander, David Hornibrook, Christopher Howell, Andrew Hudgins, Maria Hummel, Joe Hurka, Karla Huston, Colette Inez, Mark Irwin, David Jauss, Bret Anthony Johnston, Nalini Jones, Laura Kasischke, George Keithley, Brigit Pegeen Kelly, Thomas E. Kennedy, David Kirby, John Kistner, Judith Kitchen, Richard Kostelanetz, Maxine Kumin, Wally Lamb, Don Lee, Fred Leebron, Sandra Leong, Dana Levin, Philip Levine, Daniel S. Libman, Gerald Locklin, Jennifer Lunden, Margaret Luongo, William Lychack, Paul Maliszewski, Matt Mason, Dan Masterson, Alice Mattison, Tracy Mayor, Robert McBrearty, Rebecca McClanahan, Davis McCombs, Erin McGraw, Elizabeth McKenzie, Brenda Miller, Jim Moore, Micaela Morrissette, Joan Murray, Kent Nelson, Kirk Nesset, Michael Newirth, Aimee Nezhukumatathil, Celeste Ng, Risteard O'Keitinn, Joyce Carol Oates, William Olsen, Dzvinia Orlowsky, Alicia Ostriker, Alan Michael Parker, Benjamin Percy, C. E. Poverman, Kevin Prufer, Lia Purpura, James Reiss, Donald Revell, Nancy Ritchard, Atsuro Riley, Laura Rodley, Jessica Roeder, Jay Rogoff, Rachel Rose, Mary Ruefle, Vern Rutsala, John Rybicki, Maxine Scates, Alice Schell, Brandon R. Schrand, Grace Schulman, Philip Schultz, Lloyd Schwartz, Salvatore Scibona, Diane Seuss, Anis Shivani, Floyd Skloot, Arthur Smith, Anna Solomon, David St. John, Maura Stanton, Maureen Stanton, Paul Stapleton, Gerald Stern, Pamela Stewart, Patricia Strachan, Terese Svoboda, Mary Szybist, Ron Tanner, Katherine Taylor, Elaine Terranova, Susan Terris, Robert Thomas, Jean Thompson, Melanie Rae Thon, Pauls Toutonghi, William Trowbridge, Lee Upton, G. C. Waldrep, Anthony Wallace, B. J. Ward, Don Waters, Michael Waters, Marc Watkins, Charles Harper Webb, Roger Weingarten, William Wenthe, Philip White, Jessica Wilbanks, Marie S. Williams, Eleanor Wilner, Bess Winter, S. L. Wisenberg, Mark Wisniewski, David Wojahn, Carolyne Wright, Robert Wrigley, Christina Zawadiwsky, Paul Zimmer

PAST POETRY EDITORS—H.L. Van Brunt, Naomi Lazard, Lynne Spaulding, Herb Leibowitz, Jon Galassi, Grace Schulman, Carolyn Forché, Gerald Stern, Stanley Plumly, William Stafford, Philip Levine, David Wojahn, Jorie Graham, Robert Hass, Philip Booth, Jay Meek, Sandra McPherson, Laura Jensen, William Heyen, Elizabeth Spires, Marvin Bell, Carolyn Kizer, Christopher Buckley, Chase Twichell, Richard Jackson, Susan Mitchell, Lynn Emanuel, David St. John, Carol Muske, Dennis Schmitz, William Matthews, Patricia

CONTENTS

THE ZEN THING

fiction by EMMA DUFFY-COMPARONE

from ONE STORY

Each year, like a shifty circus in a truck, the family unpacks itself for a weekend on a beach and pretends to have a good time. This summer they are in Rhode Island, on Scarborough Beach. Everyone is staying at the Sea Breeze Motel down the street. Expectations are low. It is the kind of setup where doors open to a courtyard, which is carpeted. In the middle of the carpet is a pool. In the middle of the pool, submerged, are a bikini bottom and a bloated swimming noodle, which has somehow drowned like a piece of plumbing pipe.

Billy, Anita's brother, who is thirteen and has Down syndrome, has spent the morning dipping a red bucket into the pool and watering all of the plastic plants with it: the scheffleras in the corner, and a few palms slouching under the exit signs. He wears an industrial measuring tape clipped to his bathing suit and has measured the diving board several times and the circumference of the doorknobs to their rooms. Anita adores Billy.

"He's really into maintenance these days." Anita's mother sighs. "And breasts."

Anita and her boyfriend, Luke, have driven down from Maine for the day. Five months ago, after their two-year affair, Luke left his wife for Anita, and they fled to a friend's empty cabin in Harpswell, where they have been staying ever since. Luke is twenty-five years older than Anita and was her art professor. As it is with this kind of thing, Anita is finding the narrative of an affair much more reasonable than the living of it, which is, when you get right down to it, a clusterfuck. She is twenty-three. Her period is late. It is an unfortunate and terrifying thing, much

19

like the eight beers Luke has taken to drinking each night before he calls his daughter, Matilda, who is eight, and who, because he cannot bear to tell her, and because his wife is certain he will come back, still thinks he is on a business trip.

Everyone is supposed to meet in the courtyard and head down to the beach, which is across the street and over the rock wall. There are a dozen plastic lawn chairs by the pool that have yellowed like teeth. Anita's grandmother is sitting in one of them. She is dressed all in white—pants and sweater and shoes—and is breathing heavily. She is staring at Luke. Since his haircut, which makes him look like an Irish cop, he seems to be grayer than ever, especially around his temples.

"You look like that actor," Anita's grandmother says to him. She has already said it twice.

"Oh, I doubt it," Luke says, but she nods. She has already complimented his eyes and his chin. She doesn't know he is married, or really anything about him at all. Her husband, Frank, is there too. When Frank speaks, he leaves little white spots on the shirt of whomever he is talking to, and he says, "I was going to say the exact same thing," after anyone speaks. He and Anita's grandmother are eighty years old. They met five years ago at Fresh Seafood, where Anita's grandmother worked as a cashier. They were both living in mobile homes at the time, but Frank's was a double-wide, and so they decided to move in there. Everyone is glad for it, especially Frank, who seems to have no family to his name whatsoever and will now, he knows, have his ass wiped by Anita's parents when the time comes. He has already asked Anita's mother, who is a nurse, to be his medical power of attorney. Everyone is pretty sure Frank is gay, and possibly black, though Anita's grandmother, having never had any experience with either, is unaware of this.

"You okay, Gram?" Anita asks. Her grandmother has been moaning and belching all morning.

"I've got, you know, the dysentery," she says. She is reattaching her Italian horn pin, which Anita has always thought looked like a penis.

"It's just diarrhea, Ma," says Anita's mother. "Not the trenches. Stop eating all those goddamn fried scallops." Anita's mother is turning sixty next month and is not doing well with this. She has been talking a lot about death lately, and her own father, who left the family when she was eleven and years later got drunk, drove up an off ramp, and was killed before Anita's mother got around to forgiving him. Once a week she has been going to Boston to see a psychic, which, Anita knows, has less to do with death and more to do with Anita. The offense, however, is unclear: the affair or simply moving out of the house. Now that both of her daughters are gone, Anita's mother says, she has no one to talk to, and Billy, God love him, sometimes makes her want to get the gun. She also still gets hot flashes, which she calls HFs, and which make her stop whatever she is doing, unhitch her bra, and whip it out of her sleeve like a rabbit from a hat.

"She's a complex woman," is all Anita's father has to say about any of it.

He is still having difficulty processing that his daughter is having sex with a man five years younger than he is. Anita knows this because her mother told her so. She can't blame him, really.

Theresa, Anita's sister, has been applying suntan lotion to her chest with one finger, careful not to smear her bathing suit. She is wearing sunglasses that are too big for her face, which seems to telegraph just how expensive they are. Theresa is thirty-one, and after a decade of casting about in cocaine and low self-esteem in Chicago, she has suddenly pulled a life together for herself. She has moved back East with her new husband, Trey, who makes lots of money reselling life insurance policies. He has several life-size oil paintings of George Washington in the house.

"They change hues depending on the time of day," Trey explained earlier.

"That must really be something," Anita said.

Trey makes many dishes with truffles and drinks only German wine. He is considering pursuing a Ph.D. in economics at Brown. Or Columbia or Harvard or Dartmouth. He is also a Libertarian, and though no one really understands what that means, they know it is scarier than a Republican. Theresa and Trey have one child, Francine, who is two and apparently has a lazy eye, though no one knows what Theresa is talking about. The corrective surgery is scheduled for next month at Mass Eye and Ear.

They are all making their way across the street and beginning to climb over the rock wall because Anita's father does not want to pay the ten dollars to park for the day. Luke hands the beach bag to Anita and helps her grandmother navigate a boulder.

"Thank you, Luke," says Anita's mother. Anita can tell by the way she looks at Luke that her mother is mourning for Ben, Anita's boyfriend of seven years, who lived down the street and came over for dinner almost every night. Anita's mother has written Ben several letters and has told Anita that, though she knows it is inappropriate, she hopes sometime he can come over for dinner. She has no idea that Anita cheated on him for several months at the Best Western two blocks from the house. Neither does Ben, who emailed Anita last week to say that he is still in love with her. She has been thinking about this situation more than she would like to admit. She has been trying to remember what was so bad about him in the first place. True, he pronounced *supposedly* "supposably." He gave her noogies sometimes. Once, when she asked him if he found her attractive, he said, "I like the buttons on your jacket." Still, when she is fifty, he will be only fifty-two.

"Isn't he lovely," her grandmother says of Luke, who is wrapping his arm around her hip, which is as fat as ever, and hoisting her over the wall. Anita nods. He is. Sometimes she cannot believe she is finally with him. Her friends are all excited for her. They consider it a fairy tale, and while Anita agrees that it is remarkable, they were not with her in Maine, in December, trying to start a fire with used Kleenex, while Luke sat on the kitchen floor and asked her over and over if children of divorced parents ended up in mental institutions. They have not been there when he goes for long jogs in the dark, so long that she sometimes drives around looking for him, like last night, when she found him on the side of the road, sitting on half of a blue buoy, sobbing into his hands.

Anita's father is already down on the beach, setting up umbrellas. His technique is to stick the pole in the sand and then hit it hard with a hammer. Billy loves to help with this. He has taken out his tape measure and is measuring the pole and their father's feet. Her father is the only one with truly olive skin, but when he sits down, his stomach fat folds on itself, and so it has tanned in a marble effect. He is a good-humored man, though lately he has the slouching look of someone who considers himself slightly cheated by his life. The few times he has met Luke, he has been cordial. Last month, Anita's parents invited Luke and Anita over for dinner, where everyone talked about the Gulf War except Anita, who smiled and knew little about the Gulf War because, Jesus Christ, she was two.

The family is setting up its own stations, laying down blankets and unfolding beach chairs. Anita's mother grabs the hammer from Billy, who has been offering to check people's reflexes with it, and throws it into the rocks. Luke is still lagging with Anita's grandmother and waving his arms in the air the way he does when he is talking about something that excites him. He is the most earnest person Anita has ever met. He is gentle and curious and frequently undone by factual tidbits from the BBC. Luke quotes Rumi sometimes about how "love is a madman" and says anyone who doesn't get that can go fuck themselves. Sometimes, he just stares at Anita and sighs. She loves this, but when she considers his fifty thousand dollars worth of credit card debt, or the beer bottle caps strewn across the floor of his car like scabs, or the picture of his wife and daughter that fell out of his wallet when he went to pay for gas this morning, Anita marvels at how quickly she has fucked up her life.

Anita walks toward Luke and her grandmother. Anita can see crabs popping in and out of holes, lugging their fiddles. Even crabs have baggage, she thinks. It isn't anything new. Anita's grandmother points to the afternoon moon, stuck in the sky like a specter of a plate. "Remember when you used to think there were fish on the moon?" she says. She pats Anita's arm.

"No."

"You thought the craters were lakes. You were always talking about all the fish on the moon, even though I told you there weren't any."

"Okay, Gram," Anita says.

The women are all helmeted in beach hats. Anita's grandmother eases herself into a chair that someone has set up for her. She is still wearing shoes and socks. Frank is already helping himself to one of the sandwiches Anita's mother has packed in a cooler. Frank has a colostomy bag, which Anita imagines strapped like an animal to his body. Though she knows not everyone will end up with one of these, for her it has come to represent, like a piece of postmodern art, everything that is horrible and grotesque about aging. Anita watches Frank chew in an unseemly way, and then she imagines the remnants of the tomato and cheese sandwich sitting hot and runny under his shirt. When Luke is his age, Anita will be only fifty-five, which is something she has taken to weeping about in the bathroom after Luke has fallen asleep. She has never been good at the Zen thing. She has, since she can remember, anticipated the deterioration and death of everyone she loves. Now, she realizes, her parents and her husband (if he ever gets divorced) will all be in a nursing home at the same time. Maybe she will be able to get a group rate. Her own mother is fifty-nine and seems very, very young. She still gets her period sometimes, for Christ's sake. For a minute, Anita tries to imagine her mother married to Frank instead of her father, but it seems too fucked for words.

Anita's father and Trey are standing down where the sand is wet, talking about insurance options, and Luke has wandered over, carefully sidestepping a castle, his hands in his pockets. She watches him bow his head as he starts to listen, trying to get the gist of things, nodding occasionally. She knows that even if he has no idea what they are talking about, he will figure it out and say something intelligent. It is one of the reasons she loves him. He is wearing running shorts that they bought yesterday at Goodwill. They have a patch that says "England" on the front, which is probably covering some scary stain. He looks good in them, though, Anita notices. He looks good in everything.

Anita's mother sits down, oblivious to the pubic hair that is crawling halfway to her knees. Anita tries to catch Theresa's eye, to share a joke about it as they always have, but Theresa is busy with Francine, whose diaper is already packed with sand.

"What did I say about that?" she is saying. "What did I say?" She has turned into an important, scolding mother. Anita liked her sister better when she wore a Budweiser bikini and made great mix tapes, when they stayed up late watching movies and scratching each other's back for ten minutes apiece.

"It's the beach," Anita says to Theresa. "There's sand."

"Yeah, well," Theresa says, standing up and adjusting her bathing suit. "I'm trying to be a parent, here." She glares at Luke, but Anita pretends not to notice.

"Why don't you two play rummy?" Anita's mother says and digs into her bag for a deck of cards. "I love having my girls around me."

Anita sits down on the blanket. Francine toddles off toward Trey, and Theresa sits down, too, picking grains of sand, one by one, off her arm. She is most likely afraid they will interfere with her tan. Her diamond is a sparkling mouse on her finger.

"So, are you painting these days?"

"Sort of," Anita says. Her canvasses and brushes are in the trunk of her car. She has not touched them for five months. She has found herself too anxious to do anything except clean the kitchen. She is going to apply to grad school in the fall, no matter what happens. She has promised herself this much.

"How's the job?" Theresa asks. Theresa doesn't have to work anymore, though she has a way of making this seem a natural thing, as if everyone has forgotten that she worked at a gas station for seven years.

"It's temporary," Anita says. Until she and Luke figure out where to live, she has been bagging groceries at Hannaford's Supermarket in Brunswick. She is not even a cashier yet. She makes eight dollars an hour. She works forty hours a week, because Luke is still sending almost all of his paycheck to his wife. He hasn't worked that part out yet. He hasn't worked any of the parts out yet.

"Of course it's all *temporary*," Theresa says. "That much is clear."

"Who wants a soda?" Anita's mother asks.

"Not me," Theresa says. "I am trying to get to one hundred and forty pounds. As much as I try, I just *cannot* get there. It is maddening." Anita has no idea who Theresa is anymore. She never used to say things like *maddening*. She used to say things like *donkey cock*.

"I don't want to hear that," Anita's mother says. "You are a beautiful weight." She is wearing mirrored sunglasses. She thinks they hide the fact that she is staring at people, but it is obvious because her mouth hangs open a little when she does it. Anita knows she is watching Luke.

Billy runs over and lands on his knees, his cheeks creamy with sunscreen. He crawls over the blanket toward Anita and gives her a long hug. He is strong and weighs almost two hundred pounds, and she falls back onto her hands.

"I love my Anita," he says.

"I love you too, Billy," she says and gives him a squeeze with one arm. He clings to her, licking her ear, pressing his mouth to her neck and making sucking sounds. He is laughing. "Okay, Billy," Anita says.

"Billy, people want personal space," Anita's mother says. "Not everyone needs a hickey."

"Give me those lips," Billy says, now holding Anita's face close. He is wearing braces. "You have such cake lips, baby. Let's kiss."

"Jesus Christ," Anita's mother says. She stands up and pulls his arm. "Stop that, Billy."

"It's okay, Mom," Anita says.

"He's been watching YouTube videos about kissing. He's obsessed with love and everything. He's, you know, working out his sexuality."

"That's embarrassing," Theresa says. She looks disgusted. She is not good with Billy, who has, Anita knows, always repelled Theresa a little, though she tries her best to hide it. Lately, this suits her more than ever. She has a strip of zinc on her nose, and her chest is pink. She looks severe and matronly.

"What's going on?" Anita's grandmother asks.

"Nothing, Ma," Anita's mother says. "Go back to sleep."

"What a sweet boy," Anita's grandmother says.

Frank is eating the second half of his sandwich. His hands are trembling. Billy makes him nervous. When he comes near, Frank's lips jump around like crickets.

"Are you going to let him hump everyone in sight?" Theresa asks.

"Don't be like that," Anita's mother says.

"You've got to discipline him," Theresa says.

"Oh, really?" Anita's mother says. "Jesus Christ, I'm doing what I can! You try this." She throws her arms out and motions all around her. "You try dealing with all of this every goddamn day!"

"Fine."

"You're burning," Anita's mother says. She points to Theresa's chest. "There and there."

"So are you," Theresa says.

"I am not," Anita's mother says. "I'm having a fucking HF, all right?" She throws her beach hat onto the blanket and starts marching toward the water. Her hair is flattened to her head, as if in a net. Billy scrambles to his feet and follows.

"What's an HF?" Theresa asks.

"A hot flash," Anita says. "Give her a break."

"*You* give her a break." Theresa stands up, too, and points to Luke, who is telling a story to Anita's father and Trey. Everyone is laughing, and he seems encouraged by this. "Mom calls me every other day in tears," Theresa says. "You're killing her."

"You're a little too much, you know that?"

"What do you think you're doing with what's-his-name?"

"You know his name."

"Do you think you're in a novel, Anita?" Theresa says. "Look at your life." With that, she brushes off her ass and staggers across the sand toward her husband.

Luke is coming back now. He is pulling his shirt over his head. "Your dad wants to go bodysurfing," he says. He looks exhausted but not unhappy, which is, Anita realizes, how he has looked for the past five months. But there is also a pain in his eyes that frightens her. He hands her his shirt, and she starts to press it to her face but stops. With Ben she could show affection, but with Luke she feels off-color and conspicuous.

"You okay?" he asks.

"Fine. You?"

He nods. "You're a poem," he says. "You going to swim?"

"Okay," she says, and takes off her dress. He stands back and makes a little shape of an hourglass with his hands. Then he walks to the cooler. "Hey, Tim," he yells down to her father, who is standing by the water. "Want a beer first?"

Anita's father shakes his head and pushes his hand through the air. "No thanks!"

"It's eleven," Anita says.

"So what?"

"I know you do this at home, but don't do it here."

Luke shuts his eyes and pinches the bridge of his nose. He stays like that for a while. "Please," he says, finally. "I don't need this right now." Then he starts down the beach.

Trey and Anita's father are limping into the water, clapping their hands and hooting. The waves are bruised with seaweed. Billy is picking up tufts, like wigs, and throwing them. Theresa has waded as far as her ankles, holding Francine. Anita's mother floats in the water, just a head and two feet, looking out to sea.

Anita stands in the sand. Her grandmother and Frank are both asleep under umbrellas. They have matching hairdos, and their skin is white and sunken, their mouths pulled in. Ben used to joke that if he looked quickly, he couldn't tell them apart. She finds a bottle of water in a bag and drinks from it. She is light-headed and can feel a zit on her chin, tender and zippy, like a spring bulb. She sits down in her mother's chair in the shade and looks across the beach, which is quickly filling in around her. She watches children crouch and slap their hands in the tide pool that is winding across the flats. All the women, breasts heavy and tired in their suits, pull wagons and strollers across the sand and begin to set up shop. Everything is a production. There is sunscreen. There are so many toys.

Luke and Trey and Anita's father are bodysurfing. She watches the men stand and wait for the waves, then leap in front of them and swim hard until they're driven under the water. As a child it had alarmed her, watching her father wash ashore like a corpse. He is the best surfer, but Luke is good. He is a strong swimmer. She watches him crawl out of the froth and adjust his shorts. He has a way about him that is younger, even, than Trey. A few little girls run into the water near him, dragging boogie boards by their leashes, and Anita wants to shield Luke from them. But this is silly, she knows. He thinks about Matilda all of the time.

Frank has woken up, and so has Anita's grandmother. They are flushed in their acrylic sweaters and smack their lips together in a groggy way. They look lost and small.

"Oh, dear," Frank is saying. He is looking down at his waist. "Oh, no."

"What is it?" Anita's grandmother asks. She is peering over his chair and looking down. Anita decides, then and there, that if he has an erection she will kill herself. She will find a lot of rocks and put them in her pockets. Late period or not.

Her grandmother is standing up now. Frank is moving around in his chair.

"What's wrong?" Anita asks.

"Get your mother," Anita's grandmother says.

"What is it?" Anita has stood up.

"It's his bag," she says.

Anita jogs across the sand, darting between towels, and calls for her mother, who has walked out of the water and is now talking to Theresa and tugging at Francine's toes. "Ma," Anita says. "It's Frank."

"What?"

Anita knows her mother does not like Frank. She thinks he is a phony and a taker. "Something about the colostomy bag," Anita says. "I didn't want to look."

"Oh, why doesn't he just die already," Anita's mother says.

"Ma." Anita laughs.

"I'm all set with this day, I think," Anita's mother says, and starts trudging toward the chairs.

Anita's grandmother is in tears, flapping a Kleenex in the air. "Oh," she says. "Oh."

"Relax, Ma," Anita's mother says. Anita knows her mother hates this kind of thing, even though she is a nurse. "Let's see what's going on, Frank." Frank pulls up his shirt past his nipples. Anita's mother gets some napkins and a bottle of water. "Let's just clean it up a little, and then we'll get some soap from the bathroom." Anita stands aside. She does not know whom she pities most. She thinks about bodies, the failed mechanics of them, the rot and stink. The second infancy. "It's fine," Anita's mother says. "The seal wasn't tight, that's all. Everything is fine. Ma, Jesus Christ, go sit down."

Theresa has come over now, and Billy, who has put a crown of sea-weed on his head. Anita winks at him. "What's going on?" Theresa asks. She has not gone in the water. She doesn't like to swim.

"Frank's colostomy bag leaked or something," Anita says. "Mom's taking care of it."

"Heinous," Theresa whispers. "You want to deal yourself that hand?"

"Shut up, Theresa," Anita says.

Billy has pushed to the front of the action and is looking down at Frank. He has pulled out his measuring tape. "Thank you, Billy," Anita's mother says. "But I don't need your help." Billy doesn't move. He is staring. Then he begins to laugh. He laughs and claps his hands. He starts to fidget and then run in place, shrieking with delight. Anita's grandmother is moaning, covering her face with her hands.

"Oh, what a fucking scene," Anita's mother says. "Where's your father? Get him out of the water. I can't do everything here." Billy is now running around the blanket, whipping a handful of seaweed in the air. "Poopy belly button!" he cries. "Poopy Frank!" He stomps back to the blanket for another look.

Theresa walks over to him. "Stop it, goddamn it!" she yells, and hits him across the face. There is the sound of wet skin. It is something between a slap and a punch. Everyone is quiet. Then Billy begins to sob.

"Classy, Theresa," Anita says. Her mother is still kneeling in front of Frank, dirty napkins in a fist. Her mouth looks blurry. She has licked off her lipstick, which she has worn every day since Billy was born.

Billy is hysterical now, holding his cheek and wailing. "I hate you," he cries, pointing at Theresa. "I hate you!"

"You people," Theresa says. She bends over, grabs a towel, and folds it. Then she throws it back on the blanket.

Anita goes to Billy and tries to calm him. Anita's father has arrived now, and Trey and Francine. "Get our daughter out of here," Theresa says to Trey. "Be useful." He backs away, mouth open. People up and down the beach are turning now to look at Billy, who is shrieking.

"It's okay, pal," Anita says, putting her arm around Billy, but he shoves her back.

"Go away!" he cries. He is standing with his feet tight together. He points with both hands at Theresa, like pistols. "I kill you!" he cries. "I kill you and you!" Billy points to Frank and Anita's grandmother, then Anita's mother and father, then Trey and Francine, and then Anita. It is time to go.

Anita can hear radio static, and somewhere the dull clatter of plastic pails. She watches the silver waves fold over each other, a man sprint a kite into the air, and behind him, Luke, who is walking toward the family.

Water is dripping from his arms, and as he reaches Anita's side he is breathing hard from the cold. When Billy points his fingers at him and makes a lippy, popping sound of a gun, Luke grips his heart and falls to his knees, gasping. Anita watches him as he crumples sideways onto the sand, twitching his feet until they lie still. Billy stares. So does everyone else, including Frank, who is clutching a floppy sunhat to his waist.

Then Anita laughs.

Nominated by One Story, Lydia Conklin

WHAT THE BODY KNOWS

by JONI TEVIS

from ORION

> *I will say to the north, Give them up, and to the south, Do not withhold; bring my*
> *sons from far away and my daughters from the end of the earth.*
> —*Isaiah 43:6*

Waiting outside the Fairbanks train station, I had the feeling the whole thing could fall through. When our guide Carl showed up, we shook hands, slung our gear into his van, and headed up the Haul Road before anyone could stop us. We were bush leaguers, my husband David and I, lugging grocery bags full of canned stew, Chef Boyardee, boil-in-bag rice. All night Carl drove as the sun shone through burn-over black spruce, the sky glowing an apocalyptic red behind charcoal trees. A blur of jolt and jounce, the silver pipeline always leaning over my shoulder, big rigs barreling toward us, skidding on gravel. Midnight, and after midnight. Could he stay awake? Past four a.m. by the time he pulled into Coldfoot and killed the engine. We made camp beside the skinny airstrip and crashed into sleep.

I had tried to prepare—trained, researched gear, plotted distances—but as the little plane surfed and dropped in the thermals, I saw that it wasn't enough. "What made you want to visit the Refuge?" the pilot asked, and my throat closed. Cliffy mountains on either side, and below. Snow caught in their creases. And marks where hooves had struck stone. "Got a bee in my bonnet," I said, and as soon as I heard the words I wanted to take them back. Why did I want to go? I wasn't sure. More than just curiosity, although I did want to see what all the fuss was about. Wanted to see a place with a bounty on its head, a place outside my ken, a place with no trees or roads or (now, midsummer) darkness. In the cockpit, a locket swung from a knob, and a picture of the pilot's kids covered a dial. He belonged here, not me. But the truth was, I had to see the Arctic National

31

Wildlife Refuge for myself; if we waited, I somehow knew that it would be too late.

The plane touched down on a flat place littered with bones, and after we unloaded our equipment, the pilot slammed the door and took off, making for a cleft between mountains.

Time to inflate the raft, rope down the gear, and go. If you fall in, point your feet downstream, and protect your head from the boulders with your arms. Let the current carry you into a side channel where it will be shallow enough to stand. Six inches or more and you'll be swept off your feet. Carl tells us this as we're separating our stuff into dry-bags with HULA HULA and GOLDEN EAGLE and KONGAKUT inked on the sides. I'm trying to hide how nervous I am. I'm a decent swimmer, but white-water scares me. And after all, this is what I've signed up for, scrounged and plotted and saved for. We're 140 miles south of Bird Camp, with only one way to get there. No road but the river, and two weeks to reach the edge of the world.

Perched on the raft's edge, one leg wedged beneath the taut rubber roll and the other splayed for balance, I clench the paddle in my hands and shove. Into glacial till opaque with runoff, so cold I can feel my bones inside the dead meat of my hands and legs. I squint in the bright sun on the water, looking straight ahead as David and Carl banter in the back of the raft, their words blurry in the steady stream of wind and water.

At night (I need no flashlight) I write in a notebook with a waterproof pen, a frail stay against the onslaught of detail that threatens to swamp me. Can you draw up Leviathan with a fish-hook? Not here, in this place out of time, where the sun never sets and our passing leaves no mark. Everything tends north: following the river, we paddle from the mountains, where the current is swift and deep, to the plateau, where the Upper Marsh Fork and the Canning join to make a wide trunk, to the coastal plain, where the water spreads out thin and silted, draining into the ice-clogged ocean. Along the way, we spot shorebirds and raptors, caribou and earwigs; see the riverbank strewn with the tracks of many beasts. Moose scat like marbles. Cast antlers beneath low, stiff bushes. We spend hours on the river, soaked and shivering, and one night when we haul out I ask David, "Have you ever been so cold you think you're going to puke?"

"Here," he says, "have some tea."

A friend who'd visited the Refuge years before spoke of the place reverently, but with few specifics. "The landscape there is . . . deceptive," he said, and as we paddled the river, I saw that he had spoken well. I'd sweep my eyes across the rolling green tundra and would have sworn the place was deserted, until caribou or musk oxen emerged from a line of bright-green willows. Things were sewn up in seams there, and sometimes we saw the animal itself, but more often we saw its mark, which we read as best we could. On our day hikes, I'd consult my field guides, noting what I'd seen and when, but soon realized that science was not enough for me to make sense of the place. I needed something more, something like magic.

The river shapes us and our days. We sleep on its banks, drink it in chalky quarts, dip our cook pot into it to boil our noodles, soak our feet in the raft's self-bailing bottom. We bear right when we can and read the water ahead, trying to dodge the shallow places that send us swinging, or the shelves where water pours strong over submerged benches and snagging there means getting dumped. Water slides quick against ice banks sharp enough to slice your hand. Pay attention! The mountains don't move and neither do you, paddling hard for hours in an unwieldy current, and when finally you stop, you can't tell how far you've come. Sun high in the sky but it's nigh on midnight. Time to make camp; time to eat, macaroni and cheese mixed with canned chicken, a chewy, salty feast. Open a can of spinach and cram it down, dark juice and all.

The doctrine of signatures, which once dominated medical thought, holds that a plant's appearance reveals its use. Nettle has milky sap, so it's good for lactating women. Pine needles resemble front teeth, so a tea made from them promotes healthy gums. This is the same idea behind what anthropologist James Frazer calls "sympathetic magic" in *The Golden Bough*, his landmark study of belief and ritual. The key tenet of sympathetic magic, he says, "is that like produces like . . . an effect resembles its cause."

So if shape indicates purpose, what to make of the Alaska cotton blooming outside the tent? I roll it between my fingers; downy and insulating, it could be a stay against cold, or with its white hair, a bulwark against early death. That's not far off, my field guide reveals. Nursing caribou rely on it for protein, their milk-warmed colts staving off weakness and wolves, at least for a little while.

Like produces like, and certain images repeat themselves. The vole track pressed into the gray riverbank sand is shaped like the grizzly's, but smaller. A willow twig swaying in the wind leaves a jagged scribble, and the gull above us teases the jaeger by flying up and down, up and back. The fine mat of grass roots is lank and brown as musk ox hair; clouds over the Brooks Range pile themselves into a second set of mountains in the sky. As I stand there on the bank, the river leaps along, slicing a new channel for itself, carrying ancient meltwater and grit, catkins and leaves, swelling after rain, tugging the valley this way and that. I cup my hand and drink, wipe grime from my face. Make me different, is the thought I can't put into words. I don't want to be the same after this trip. Bolder, maybe, less concerned with things I can't control. I turn a blue cobble over in my hands; it's honeycombed with chalky white, fossil coral. Individuals do best in community, it says. I tie it to a line and guy out the tent in case of rain.

We're rocketing down the river, balanced on the edge of the raft. Dig deep and pull, front to back, torquing with the belly and not the arms, making for deeper water on the right, the banks blurring past, mountains above them unmoving, and then we're caught. On a boulder the size of a recliner, solid in the current. The river pushes the back of the raft; we're perpendicular to the bank now, and the water's lifting my side of the raft higher. If it flips, we're all going in, and the current is strong enough to sweep us all downriver. I'm riding high, trying to press myself and my side of the raft down, wrestling water as Carl works the paddle, trying to dislodge us. The riverbed is too deep to touch, but he searches the side of the boulder we're stuck on and leans against it with all his weight, and then the blade slips against slick stone, the raft moves a tick, he keeps pushing until the aluminum paddle bends double and breaks, and then we're over the hump, sliding down the other side.

Soon after, it's time to make camp. We unroll the tent and spread it flat, thread the poles through their sleeves, and pop the ends into the grommets. Home appears, a bright-orange dome tucked into a stand of willows. We've done this so many times now that we don't need to speak; one step follows the next. It feels good, knowing exactly what to do, unzipping the door and laying out the sleeping pads, bags, books we're reading. The sun warms the nylon wall where we tuck the bear spray. Everything we need and nothing we don't, wallets forgotten in a dry bag with LYNX on the side.

I crawl out of the tent to fill my water bottle, stepping over the mountain avens growing just outside. A small plant with a white, daisylike flower, the aven means good camping, and legend calls it "the blessed herb, which stops the devil from entering." Here's home for a while, a dry place on the tundra. We share it with wolves, one of whom surprises me as I crouch by the river. He locks eyes with me, evaluates, decides to move on, and lopes easily away along the gravel bar. In the pause after he's gone, I hear the hum of billions of mosquitoes. One clings to the outside of the tent, clapping her front legs.

Brooding over these things, eyes scanning the tundra, I sense something strange taking root deep within myself, an insistent wriggle of thought I dare not speak aloud.

This is midsummer, a powerful, auspicious time. The line between waking and sleeping is porous now, dreams more real than waking, hours of paddling front to back, front to back, staring at layers of cobble-striped light, sun vinegary on thin water. The clearest sign is the absence of a sign.

Clouds race across the sky, and a rain-smear hovers over the mountains, but we hear no thunder. You see her too, don't you? The lone caribou staring at us from the gravel bar. The hawk floating overhead. Look at these piles of yellow hay drying in the sun, left by arctic voles or maybe ground-dwelling birds, and it seems vitally important that I find out which. Sometimes I'm breathless with the sense of time tumbling past, but when paddling we're caught in a moment that never ends. The shallow current tugs us north, the wind off the Arctic Ocean presses us south, and we're caught, vertical needles pointing straight up at the coppery sky.

Old accounts, written by sober men employed by the U.S. Navy to map the coastal plain we're traveling, tell of mirages so sharp that the men see their distant camps hovering above the horizon. The angle of the light and the curve of the earth made their far-off colleagues seem to walk upside down, heads to the tundra and feet treading thin air. The accounts speak of driftwood polished and old, and survey markers that turn temporary, tundra working the concrete loose by freeze and thaw, heaving the heavy plugs free. One afternoon I could swear we're alone when a herd of thousands of caribou appears, crosses the river in front of us, then vanishes. They leave hoofprints in the dark sand, snatches of hollow hair, and a scent like beef jerky in the air. I'm the only one who can smell it.

Months later, we'll watch her pale bones appear on a dark screen: skull, vertebrae, and sacrum, what lasts longest of any of us. It's then that I'll realize what I sought in the Refuge is as close and unknowable as my own belly. Images taken during the earliest days of gestation show a shape that looks something like a tongue. Nubbled, bumpy, a crease where the spine will be. While I craved spinach and liver, her brain knitted together. While I paddled and paddled against the wind, shouting with rage and strain, her body was rocketing through a whole host of changes, and I hardly knew.

Praised and cursed be the thread-legged horde, filchers of blood, for keeping us always in the moment. They hatch before the snow melts, rise in clouds from the tundra, drive caribou onto snowfields; they are ever with us, their hum as constant as wind on the river. We wear head nets while eating, snaking spoonfuls of grub under the mesh as fast as we can and extricating our hands, bitter with DEET and pimpled with bites. They bite through our pants, our shoes, our neoprene socks; they bite through our head nets where the fabric brushes our temples. At night, we unzip the tent door and roll in quick, then set about killing the dozens that swarm inside. Yet without the mosquito, the jaegers and longspurs and buntings would starve, and the wolf and the bear. They're the wide base of the food pyramid here, billions of pounds of protein on the wing.

We paddle past midnight and sleep until noon, and one bright morning brings me my grandmother, gone and buried under Ohio turf these many years and yet now, somehow, seated across from me at a table covered with a white cloth. We're at a banquet, and the air between us hums with the low talk of other guests; later there will be a keynote speaker, but right now I'm telling her about some apartment my sister wants to rent. An ordinary conversation. *I am so happy we can sit here and talk like this*, I tell her, and she smiles. We hug each other and I wake, shaken; I could swear she's visited me.

The light and water and cold shake loose everything I carried here with me—the cities of my adulthood, then the small town of my girlhood, and now the farm country of my childhood, vast ripples of green and gold, and stubble after plowing. Dark earth. My grandmother lived all her life in that place. She worked hard, borrowed trouble, made the best of what little she had to do with. And foresaw things, both bad and good, before they could rightly be known. Her husband's sudden death, yes, but also children, and other things I can never now ask her.

Later, after watching a herd of musk oxen vanish into a stand of willows, I find a twist of soft underwool, *quiviut*, snagged on a bush and tuck it into my field guide to save. It would have been better, maybe, if I had left something in its place—not necessarily to pay for what I took, but to acknowledge a certain reciprocity. The Dena'ina, a native tribe from central Alaska, teach that "when a person harvests a medicinal plant in the mountains, besides speaking correctly to it, he should also leave a small gift, such as a thread or match or bit of tobacco, in place of the plant." What should I have given? A bone, a hank of my own hair? A pinch of loam from a fallow field, a thing that might, over time, become part of here? We pass clumps of dwarf fireweed, also called river beauty, whose purple florets are just starting to open. When the last blooms fade, people say, you've got four weeks until first snow.

By this point in the trip, we are keeping it very real. We've been on the river ten days without showering, and the coastal plain is so flat, there's not even a hillock for privacy. Between these physical demands and the conversations we have, we've become a band of three with our own lingo of inside jokes and games. We roll down the river singing songs from our youth, like "Eye of the Tiger," "Purple Rain," and our anthem, "Beat It."

Michael Jackson goes to work in that song. He sings it all—lead, backup, and the off-beat *hee-hee*s. But Eddie Van Halen plays the guitar solo, thirty seconds so indelible I bet you could lay it down right now. We did, barreling downriver, Carl howling the guitar line, David singing the rhythm, me whapping the side of the raft. It starts guttural and ends in a keening scream, and by now, twenty-five years after its creation, it's spread across the world, gone circumpolar, like some lichen species. Four verses and a chorus: Some fights you win outright, others by avoidance. And then the knock on the door. They've come for you.

It's not the song so much as the contrast it provides, the gap between Michael Jackson and this wild place. It's a way to be silly, a relief from the cold and exhaustion, and a distraction from the fear we seldom speak aloud. We're paddling the Canning, the boundary between the protected-for-now Refuge and the disputed "1002 area"; we make camp on the Refuge side and gaze across the river. It's quiet now, except for the current and the gulls, but what's coming? What can we do about it? Right now, here's what we can do: bear right, dig hard to slide past that gravel bar, and suck down enough air to sing the next word.

We sing other songs too, but keep coming back to this one, and as we repeat its lines they turn almost tangible, calling up a feeling of warmth on my shoulders, hills sliding past, spray on my arms. I am not going to drown while singing "Beat It." Here's how the body calms the mind: perform a repetitive task, repeat a familiar litany. In the old days, people built bonfires on Midsummer's Eve and danced around them until dawn. The only fire we have is the hissing Jetboil, but after we scarf the day's last meal, we jig around the raft to get our blood moving and howl till we're hoarse at the floating sun.

Without trees, the mountains seem disproportionately high, and when we go hiking, land that looks smooth and unbroken turns out to be boggy, tooled with gullies and seeps. So I find myself looking down, at things small enough to focus on, and find lichen in amazing profusion. While David and Carl read, I go a-hunting for powdered sunshine, rippled rockfrog, and fairy puke. Here's elegant orange lichen splattered across a stone, but no frog pelts or rocktripes. Nor pixie cups, tiny club lichens that look like miniature goblets. Their species name, *pyxidata*, comes from "the Latin *pyxis*, 'a box,' maybe because the tiny cups looked like miniature containers," muses the writer of the wonderful *Plants of the Western Boreal Forest and Aspen Parkland*. "A pyx is a box in a government mint in which sample coins are kept to be tested for purity or weight. Are the tiny scales in the cups of this lichen fairy coins?" I recognize rim lichen from back home in South Carolina. Flat and bluish-white, it's called "manna" by some. According to my book, "local people believed that it fell from heaven, and in times of famine they followed the example of their livestock and used it as food."

Lichen gnaws stone, making earth from raw quartz and flint. It grows slowly, sometimes as little as 0.02 millimeters per year—a hand-sized patch can be a thousand years old—and scientists studying lichenometry can uncover details about glaciation and what the planet's climate used to be like. Lichen reveals the air of the past, too, taking heavy metals into itself and dispensing hidden knowledge to those who know how to ask. Fabulous secrets, kept since the world was young, and I step over them, leaving them behind as I bounce across the tussocked plain, eating of bitter dock and looking for ragged paperdoll and granulated shadow.

Something here sings to the body's stony bones and wrinkled veins, pulls at the blood's piling tide. The iron-rich stones wipe clean the details of the life I somehow used to know, with its rooms and its light bulbs. Why had I stayed indoors so much? Why had I believed it mattered what people thought of me? Taste how sweet is this chalky water straight from the river. Feel how good is this sleep in the blessed bag. Do you see it too, the plateau sliced into red books of shale, tangled branches of a rough-legged hawk's nest, fox tracks? Sometimes my own name sounds strange to me. How could I need it here?

Eventually, we'll register for gear at the baby superstore, staring gobsmacked at the wall of wipes and rubber nipples and nail clippers kitted out with tiny flashlights. If only we were outfitting a trip to the Arctic, I'll think. At least then we'd know what to pack.

Memories of the truck stop at Coldfoot will come flooding back to me, suggesting the many ways that a journey like ours could go wrong. A framed collage of disaster snapshots hung on the wall next to the pay phone. Big rigs jackknifed in a ditch; tow trucks loading a mangled SUV. Someone had pasted dialogue bubbles to the glass. Beside a crumpled Tahoe: "Will my insurance cover this?" A man chaining a big rig's undercarriage for a tow: "Relax, I'm a doctor." Gallows humor, exactly what you need when you're halfway to Deadhorse. In for a penny, in for a pound; if the inclines don't get you, the frost heaves will. But what can you do? You can't stay here.

And so we'll tick our boxes, take our chances, and exit the store to face the mystery of what's to come.

* * *

Our last day. From afar they look like animals, but up close I see they're oil barrels, dozens of them, black and rusty. It's jarring; for two weeks, the only human-made things we've seen have been what we carry with us, until we come across these barrels, left from exploratory drilling twenty years ago. Across the plain, in the distance, beads of light burn above Prudhoe Bay. Too easy to imagine drilling platforms here, gashes ripped by wide tires, a rime of frozen smog. I turn away from that and out to sea, the yellow grassland running up to the edge and falling away.

Piles of dry wood mark the tideline in silvery drifts. Here, where land begins, bear tracks mark the soft beach, and I step aside with an unconscious deference. These are barren-ground grizzlies, Carl tells us, smaller and less numerous than their Kodiak cousins, but hungrier. There are no streams jumping with salmon here, and they have to make do as best they can. The beach is littered with skull pans and vertebrae of long-dead caribou, stained dark by the sand. The Arctic Ocean, what we've been making for all along.

As for that deep-seated fear of being swept downstream: Cast it off, along with your grimy clothes, and run naked into water so cold it shorts out thought. Ha! Dog-paddle out to the nearest chunk of ice. Slap it, bob in the water, and swim back to shore, sand yielding underfoot. Stagger out onto dry land and rub down with a little towel; stand bare-skinned on the damp sand, baying with joy. "What a rush!" I holler, heart booming in my chest. "What a rush!" Warm rays of sun on your back as you towel off. An arctic fox's bushy white tail. Telemetry station, steel pipe listing to one side; underfeathers from a snowy owl. And atop the rise, a graveyard with markers cut from silvery wood. It had been edged with a low fence once, but now the palings lie on the ground, worked loose by animals or frost heaves. The wooden markers are dry and sound, and the characters carved on them read plainly:

NASON

DIED

FEB. 10 1933

ANGOPKANNA

DIED

MARCH 23 1936

JIM O CAROOK

BORN

MAY 19 1933

DIED

SEPT. 4 1934

An old whaling camp, Carl says, and I try to think what it might have been like for the people who lived here, keeping snug in sod-built homes, eating strips of blubber from bowheads they'd caught, bearing babies and trying to raise them right. We stand in the wind, looking out over the ocean stretching north clear to the Pole.

Maybe the closer you get to the top of the world, the greater your risk of madness. Move beyond the life you once knew and into a new place that breaks with the past. Into this new body, arms lean and trembling, palms black from the paddle shaft, feet fluent in the safe path hid between stone and current. Into this place where the very stones grow bread, speak of ancient warm seas, crack open where yarrow sprouts. Cups smaller than a baby's nails hold precious samples waiting to be tried; I assay the value of a thing by bathing it again and again in glacial melt, exposing it to sunlight for weeks at a stretch.

And in the pink sky at three a.m., the sun's pale bubble floats. We lie on the grass at Bird Camp; we'll leave in the morning. Early July, and spring is just beginning to green the grass stems, though the wooly lousewort's already blooming. All of it passing away—rivers carrying mountains out to sea, lichen eating stone, the spinning earth hauling the long darkness closer, one minute at a time.

Morning. Coastal fog could have given us another day, but the air was clear, and the pilot skidded to a landing right on time. We loaded our gear and climbed inside, and the Beaver lifted, banking over the shallow lagoons lousy with loons, rising over gleaming braids of the Canning delta, the double lines that meant caribou trails, grizzlies' brown humps. I grieved to go, and all that afternoon's long drive back to Fairbanks I felt sensitive as a peeled egg as we skidded past hillsides of purple fireweed, gorged on gigantic Boo Boo Burgers dripping with teriyaki sauce, drove through roostertails of road dust. On the radio, Bob Marley sang "Redemption Song," and I worked hard not to cry. *Won't you help to sing.* Our last hours together, our band of merry singers about to split. *All I ever had.* And somewhere along that busted road another heart started beating beneath my own ribs.

The fluorescent lights in the all-night grocery store hurt my eyes as I hunted a pregnancy test to confirm what I already knew. We said goodbye to Carl and watched his van disappear into traffic. Something had ended.

And something begun. Back in South Carolina, her heartbeat pounded like wave after wave of skirling wind. Like that Arctic wind, coming from a far distance and hauling with it the chill of great change.

I believed that landscape to be far behind us, but during the lengthening nights I dreamed it close, seeing again the hills and divots I'd quietly named First Raft Put-in, Prince's Purple Meadow, Mew Gull Bombing Range. Sunny Draw Piled with Hay. Campsite Where I Told David My Suspicions. Last Place, Which I Mourned to Leave. The Gwich'in call that coastal plateau Sacred Place Where Life Begins.

Those musk oxen we watched in the bright midnight must now, early February, stand in clusters in the howling dark as wind scours the snow from low places in the tundra and they feed on the grasses exposed there. Soft underwool streaming in the gale. So are you, my child, eyes opening and closing in the black. A glow, now and then, toward which you turn your face. I do not know when to look for you, but what I imagine is a time belonging to no hour.

In *The Golden Bough*, James Frazer tells of people from Bombay to Transylvania who believed that unlocking doors and opening windows would help a woman in labor. Back then, men would unbraid their hair, uncork bottles, unlid pots. David and I prepare as best we can. If it would help to unsnarl the extension cords, straighten the garden hose, unclasp necklaces and lay them flat, we would do it. We crave something useful to do, a song whose every word we know by heart.

It will begin after midnight, the old stories say. As the time draws near, I dread nightfall, and every sleep is surrender. I long for the constant sunlight we had in the Refuge, but it's winter now, and darkness falls early. Here in our bed, David sleeps beside me. He will do what he can, I know, but mostly I'm in this alone.

Or so I think. When the pain begins, I know what to do: set it aside to get more sleep, rest I will need for the work this day will require. At the time appointed it shakes me awake and wracks me with cold, and I say, *There you are, my enemy, my fear. Let me wrestle you as with a lover.* One at a time. This I can do. As the wrenching starts, low in the belly. As it catches and strengthens and pulls me into itself, tight. More, more. As I climb the steep side of the wave, and higher. Breathing through my throat, ah. Pain a burning cold that builds on itself and burns out from the marrow. Caught upon the tines of it. Whirled into a dense core. No words for this, but a moan and huff. A gleaming, blinding center, glaring as sun on ice. And from the peak of it to slide down the far side. It wanes and I wax, aware of myself again, laughing at how it took me. And here comes another, crawling up my belly to my heart.

They come, they come, a few breaths apart, then two, then one. My body wringing like a twist of cloth. We gather our gear—towels, Vaseline, *Joshua Tree*, a snapshot of a two-lane highway—and go. David drives the car down the road. It was not this tidy, but to leave it unwritten is worse. The story diffuses into the air, leaving flashes of images behind: squinting in the sun. A harsh birdcall. Swirl of rock flour in the cook pot. In the moments between I become aware of the seat belt snug under my belly, fluorescent lights in empty offices, bare sidewalk. Five a.m. on a Monday. And then: yellow grass. A mosquito cloud rising from the tundra to find a haunch and settle. I have done this, have fattened with life and split, my labor inseparable from the place where I first divined its coming. This is the difference between spirit and flesh, the idea of a place and its reality. Beyond the mind lies the visceral: what the body knows. I have taken pleasure in the steaming mug of tea, sun on my back, springy earth pressing my feet. Look: a miniature forest of tiny golf clubs, short as a knuckle. And this: a gnawed antler, half-buried, tooth marks like little ditches in the bone. It lasts a long time, until the others take what they need, and its calcium turns into a vole nestling, from that into an owl's eggshell, and from that into a thieving fox's belly, where kits overwinter in the stretching dark.

Slow. I walk down a hall. I lie down and relax a muscle at a time, neck to shoulders to back to belly, and the pain comes in wave after wave that I slip up and onto and over and down, up and onto and over and down, and when I glance over to gauge my progress, I see the same bedside, the same cutbank as before.

When the final press comes I'm ready. "What we came twenty thousand miles to get is worth saving," Starbuck says to Ahab, the chase hard upon them. Starbuck, always too careful. Doesn't he know? When the time comes, you have to give it all; hold nothing back. Ahab knows this, and so do I. Breathless with the relief of finding, at last, the long-sought one, and after all the rolling of line and sharpening of points, anticipation and dream, nausea and swelling, ready now to stare and throw. I strive with my work as with an opponent outside my body, and wrestle myself to the mat. Can't sit without help but I'm strong, feral, working through a body that doesn't feel like mine, a curl of muscle and sinew, cut loose from a narrating mind. I lose speech during this re-peated action; spells fill the space. What strange glow marks this seam between life and death; one hand takes the other and grips.

Pray for those who labor, the old ritual says, for danger holds them, and they must give themselves up to it, moving outside of thought into a place that splits them clean open. I drag myself forward a stroke at a time, by turns crabbed and lean with the strain, making for a place meant not for dwelling but for witnessing things beyond time's usual span. Eyes squeezed shut, I reach out and slap the slick of a broken berg, bobbing in an icy humor that blanks out thought and burns all over. With numb toes, I push off the bottom and make for land, blind-stumbling and staggering, choking with cold, gasping up and out and onto the beach, falling onto something that knocks the wind out of me, a solid thing that is not an idea but a fact on its way to arriving, a fact that sings I BE in a rising stream of notes that is a cry.

And then I laugh and laugh, David will tell me later, but I have for-gotten that. I remember only her here, warm and slick, holy dirt smear-ing her crown, clinging to a scalp that pulses with life. Soon, the midwife will wash and wrap her, but for now we hold tight to each other, curded with the river I drank to swell our first shared blood. She was with me all along. Child from far away, my daughter from the end of the earth.

Nominated by Orion

WHY WE MUST SUPPORT PBS

by BOB HICOK

from FIELD

"I didn't think of it as killing them," the executioner
from the late eighteenth century said to Charlie Rose,
still wearing a hood, his axe resting on the wood table
I've assumed is oak. "I don't know how to put this:
it's as if I loved them in the moment I swung, loved them
and wanted to offer them peace." Charlie Rose was smiling,
excited. Even more than usual, the joy of an otter
seemed to be swimming through the long river of his body
when he put a hand on the man's memoir and said,
"But then something happened that made you question
your entire existence up to that point." It was hard
to see the man all in black on Charlie Rose's black set,
as if midnight were speaking, saying, "Yes. One day
I looked down and there was the son I'd never had
staring up at me from the block, I could tell
by his eyes, this was my boy, this was my life
flowing out, reaching beyond the sadness of its borders."
"You knew this," Charlie Rose said. "I knew this,"
the executioner replied. "Even though you'd never been
with a woman." "Never. I was all about career." "You knew
because the eyes tell us something." "Because the eyes
tell us everything." "And you couldn't go on." "No.
I couldn't go on." They changed gears then and honestly
I drifted off, half-dreamed I'd arranged a tropical
themed party on a roof without testing how much dancing

45

and vodka the roof could hold, people were falling
but still laughing, falling but still believing
there was a reason to put umbrellas in their drinks,
that otherwise their drunkenness would be rained on,
rained out, when I heard the executioner say, "We
were running and running. Finally we made it the border
and I put my arms around my son and told him, you have a future
but no pony. Get a pony." Charlie Rose smiled
like he was smiling for the otter, for whatever is lithe
and liquid in our spirits, and repeated, "Get a pony."
"That's the last time I saw him," the executioner said.
"And that's why you've refused to die." "Yes."
"To keep that moment alive." "Yes." "And you believe eternity
is an act of will." "Yes," Mr. Midnight said. "Will.
Will and love. Love and fury."

Nominated by Field, David Hernandez, John Allman,
Ed Falco, Elton Glaser, Mark Irwin,
David Jauss, Fred Leebron

MADAME BOVARY'S GREYHOUND

fiction by **KAREN RUSSELL**

from ZOETROPE: ALL STORY

I. FIRST LOVE

They took walks to the beech grove at Banneville, near the abandoned pavilion. Foxglove and gillyflowers, beige lichen growing in one thick, crawling curtain around the socketed windows. Moths blinked wings at them, crescents of blue and red and tiger-yellow, like eyes caught in a net.

Emma sat and poked at the grass with the skeletal end of her parasol, as if she were trying to blind each blade.

"Oh, *why* did I ever get married?" she moaned aloud, again and again.

The greyhound whined with her, distressed by her distress. Sometimes, in a traitorous fugue, the dog forgot to be unhappy and ran off to chase purple butterflies or murder shrew mice, or to piss a joyful stream onto the topiaries. But generally, if her mistress was crying, so was the puppy. Her name was Djali, and she had been a gift from the young woman's husband, Dr. Charles Bovary.

Emma wept harder as the year grew older and the temperature dropped, folding herself into the white monotony of trees, leaning further and further into the bare trunks. The dog would stand on her hind legs and lick at the snow that fused Emma's shoulders to the coarse wood, as if trying to loosen a hardening glue, and the whole forest would quiver and groan together in sympathy with the woman, and her phantom lovers, and Djali.

At Banneville the wind came directly from the sea, and covered the couple in a blue-salt caul. The greyhound loved most when she and Emma were outside like this, bound by the membrane of a gale. Yet as sunset fell Djali became infected again by her woman's nameless terrors. Orange and red, they seemed to sweat out of the wood. The dog smelled nothing alarming, but love stripped her immunity to the internal weathers of Emma Bovary.

The blood-red haze switched to a silvery blue light, and Emma shuddered all at once, as if in response to some thicketed danger. They returned to Tostes along the highway.

The greyhound was ignorant of many things. She had no idea, for example, that she was a greyhound. She didn't know that her breed had originated in southern Italy, an ancient pet in Pompeii, a favorite of the thin-nosed English lords and ladies, or that she was perceived to be affectionate, intelligent, and loyal. What she did know, with a whole-body thrill, was the music of her woman coming up the walk, the dizzying explosion of perfume as the door swung wide. She knew when her mistress was pleased with her, and that approval was the fulcrum of her happiness.

"Viscount! Viscount!" Emma whimpered in her sleep. (Rodolphe would come onto the scene later, after the greyhound's flight, and poor Charlie B. never once featured in his wife's unconscious theater.) Then Djali would stand and pace stiff-legged through the cracked bowl of the cold room into which her mistress's dreams were leaking, peering with pricked ears into shadows. It was a strange accordion that linked the woman and the dog: Vaporous drafts caused their pink and gray bellies to clutch inward at the same instant. Moods blew from one mind to the other, delight and melancholy. In the blue atmosphere of the bedroom, the two were very nearly (but never quite) one creature.

Even asleep, the little greyhound trailed after her madame, through a weave of green stars and gas lamps, along the boulevards of Paris. It was a conjured city that no native would recognize—Emma Bovary's head on the pillow, its architect. Her Paris was assembled from a guidebook with an out-of-date map, and from the novels of Balzac and Sand, and from her vividly disordered recollections of the viscount's ball at La Vaubyessard, with its odor of dying flowers, burning flambeaux, and truffles. (Many neighborhoods within the city's quivering boundaries, curiously enough, smelled identical to the viscount's dining room.) A rose and gold glow obscured the storefront windows, and cathedral bells tolled continuously as they strolled past the same four landmarks: a tremulous bridge over the roaring Seine, a vanilla-white dress shop, the vague facade of the opera house—overlaid in more gold light—and the crude stencil of a theater. All night they walked like that, companions in Emma's phantasmal labyrinth, suspended by her hopeful mists, and each dawn the dog would wake to the second Madame Bovary, the lightly snoring woman on the mattress, her eyes still hidden beneath a peacock sleep mask. Lumped in the coverlet, Charles's blocky legs tangled around her in an apprehensive pretzel, a doomed attempt to hold her in their marriage bed.

II. A CHANGE OF HEART

Is there any love as tireless as a dog's in search of its master? Whenever Emma was off shopping for nougat in the market, or visiting God in the churchyard, Djali was stricken by the madness of her absence. The dog's futile hunt through the house turned her maniacal, cannibalistic: She scratched her fur until it became wet and dark. She paced the halls, pausing only to gnaw at her front paws. Félicité, the Bovarys' frightened housekeeper, was forced to imprison her in a closet with a water dish.

The dog's change of heart began in September, some weeks after Madame Bovary's return from La Vaubyessard, where she'd dervished around in another man's arms and given up forever on the project of loving Charles. It is tempting to conclude that Emma somehow transmitted her wanderlust to Djali; but perhaps this is a sentimental impulse, a storyteller's desire to sync two flickering hearts.

One day Emma's scents began to stabilize. Her fragrance became musty, ordinary, melting into the house's stale atmosphere until the woman was nearly invisible to the animal. Djali licked almond talc from Emma's finger-webbing. She bucked her head under the madame's hand a dozen times, waiting for the old passion to seize her, yet her brain was uninflamed. The hand had become generic pressure, damp heat. No joy snowed out of it as Emma mechanically stroked between Djali's ears, her gold wedding band rubbing a raw spot into the fur, branding the dog with her distraction. There in the bedroom, together and alone, they watched the rain fall.

By late February, at the same time Charles Bovary was dosing his young wife with valerian, the dog began refusing her mutton chops. Emma stopped checking her gaunt face in mirrors, let dead flies swim in the blue glass vases. The dog neglected to bark at her red-winged nemesis, the rooster. Emma quit playing the piano. The dog lost her zest for woodland homicide. Under glassy bathwater, Emma's bare body as still and bright as quartz in a quarry, she let the hours fill her nostrils with the terrible serenity of a drowned woman. Her gossamer fingers circled her navel, seeking an escape. Fleas held wild circuses on Djali's ass as she lay motionless before the fire for the duration of two enormous logs, unable to summon the energy to spin a hind leg in protest. Her ears collapsed against her skull.

Charles rubbed his hand greedily between Emma's legs and she swatted him off; Emma stroked the dog's neck and Djali went stiff, slid out of reach. Both woman and animal, according to the baffled Dr. Bovary, seemed bewitched by sadness.

This strain of virulent misery, this falling out of love, caused different symptoms, unique disruptions, in dogs and humans.

The greyhound, for example, shat everywhere.

Whereas Emma shopped for fabrics in the town.

On the fifth week of the dog's fall, Charles lifted the bed skirt and discovered the greyhound panting up at him with a dead-eyed calm. He'd been expecting to find his favorite tall socks, blue wool ineptly darned for him by Emma. He screamed.

"Emma! What do you call your little bitch again? There is something the matter with it!"

"Djali," Emma murmured from the mattress. And the dog, helplessly bound to her owner's voice—if not still in love with Madame Bovary, at least indentured to the ghost of her love—rose and licked the lady's bare feet.

"Good girl," sighed Emma.

The animal's dry tongue lolled out of her mouth. Inside her body, a foreboding was hardening into a fact. There was no halting the transformation of her devotion into a nothing.

III. WHAT IF?

"If you do not stop making poop in the salon," Félicité growled at the puppy, "I will no longer feed you."

In the sixth month of her life in Tostes, the dog lay glumly on the floor, her pink belly tippled orange by the grated flames, fatally bored.

Emma entered the bedroom, and the animal lifted her head from between her tiny polished claws, let it drop again.

"If only I could be you," Emma lamented. "There's no trouble or sorrow in *your* life!" And she soothed the dog in a gurgling monotone, as if she were addressing herself.

Dr. Charles Bovary returned home, whistling after another successful day of leeches and bloodletting in the countryside, to a house of malcontent females:

Emma was stacking a pyramid of greengage plums.

The little greyhound was licking her genitals.

Soon the coarse, unchanging weave of the rug in Emma's bedroom became unbearable. The dog's mind filled with smells that had no origin, sounds that arose from no friction. Unreal expanses. She closed her eyes and stepped cautiously through tall purple grass she'd never seen before in her life.

She wondered if there might not have been some other way, through a different set of circumstances, of meeting another woman; and she tried to imagine those events that had not happened, that shadow life. Her owner might have been a bloody-smocked man, a baritone, a butcher with bags of bones always hidden in his pockets. Or perhaps a child, the butcher's daughter, say, a pork chop–scented girl who loved to throw sticks. Djali had observed a flatulent Malamute trailing his old man in the park, each animal besotted with the other. Blue poodles, inbred and fat, smugly certain of their women's adoration. She'd seen a balding Pomeranian riding high in a toy wagon, doted on by the son of a king. Not all humans were like Emma Bovary.

Out of habit, she howled her old courtship song at Emma's feet, and Emma reached down distractedly, gave the dog's ears a stiff brushing. She was seated before her bedroom vanity, cross-examining a pimple, very preoccupied, for at four o'clock Monsieur Roualt was coming for biscuits and judgment and jelly.

A dog's love is forever. We expect infidelity from one another; we marvel at this one's ability to hold that one's interest for fifty, sixty years; perhaps some of us feel a secret contempt for monogamy even as we extol it, wishing parole for its weary participants. But dogs do not receive our sympathy or our suspicion—from dogs we presume an eternal adoration.

In the strange case of Madame Bovary's greyhound, however, "forever" was a tensed muscle that began to shake. During the Christmas holidays, she had daily seizures before the fireplace, chattering in the red light like a loose tooth. Loyalty was a posture she could no longer hold.

Meanwhile, Emma had become pregnant.

The Bovarys were preparing to move.

On one of the last of her afternoons in Tostes, the dog ceased trembling and looked around. Beyond the cabbage rows, the green grasses waved endlessly away from her, beckoning her. She stretched her hind legs. A terrible itching spread through every molecule of her body, and the last threads of love slipped like a noose from her neck. Nothing owned her anymore. Rolling, moaning, belly to the red sun, she dug her spine into the hill.

"Oh, dear," mumbled the coachman, Monsieur Hivert, watching the dog from the yard. "Something seems to be attacking your greyhound, madame. Bees, I'd wager."

"Djali!" chided Emma, embarrassed that a pet of hers should behave so poorly before the gentlemen. "My goodness! You look possessed!"

IV. FREEDOM

On the way to Yonville, the greyhound wandered fifty yards from the Bovarys' stagecoach. Then she broke into a run.

"Djaliiiiii!" Emma shrieked, uncorking a spray of champagne-yellow birds from the nearby poplars. "*Stay!*"

Weightlessly the dog entered the forest.

"Stay! Stay! Stay!" the humans called after her, their directives like bullets missing their target. Her former mistress, the screaming woman, was a stranger. And the greyhound lunged forward, riding the shoals of her own green-flecked shadow.

In the late afternoon she paused to drink water from large cups in the mossy roots of unfamiliar trees. She was miles from her old life. Herons sailed over her head, their broad wings flat as palms, stroking her from scalp to tail at an immense distance—a remote benediction—and the dog's mind became empty and smooth. Skies rolled through her chest; her small rib cage and her iron-gray pelt enclosed a blue without limit. She was free.

From a hilltop near a riverbank, through an azure mist, she spotted two creatures with sizzling faces clawing into the water. Cats larger than any she'd ever seen, spear-shouldered and casually savage. Lynxes, a mated pair. Far north for this season. They were three times the size of the Bovarys' barn cat yet bore the same taunting anatomy. Analogous golden eyes. They feasted on some prey that looked of another world—flat, thrashing lives they swallowed whole.

Gazehound, huntress—the dog began to remember what she'd been before she was born.

Winter was still raking its white talons across the forest; spring was delayed that year. Fleshless fingers for tree branches. Not a blade or bud of green yet. The dog sought shelter, but shelter was only physical this far out, always inhuman. Nothing like the soft-bodied sanctuary she'd left behind.

One night the greyhound was caught out in unknown territory, a cold valley many miles from the river. Stars appeared, and she felt a light sprinkling of panic. Now the owls were awake. Pale hunger came shining out of their beaks, looping above their flaming heads like ropes. In Tostes their hooting had sounded like laughter in the trees. But here, with no bedroom rafters to protect her, she watched the boughs blow apart to reveal nocturnal eyes bulging from their recesses like lemons; she heard hollow mouths emitting strange songs. Death's rattle, old wind without home or origin, rode the frequencies above her.

A concentrated darkness screeched and dove near her head, and then another, and then the dog began to run. Dawn was six hours away.

She pushed from the valley floor toward higher ground, eventually finding a narrow fissure in the limestone cliffs. She trotted into the blackness like a small key entering a tall lock. Once inside she was struck by a familiar smell, which confused and upset her. Backlit by the moon, her flat, pointed skull and tucked abdomen cast a hieroglyphic silhouette against the wavy wall.

The greyhound spent the next few days exploring her new home. The soil here was like a great cold nose—wet, breathing, yielding. To eat, she had to hunt the vast network of hollows for red squirrels, voles. A spiderweb of bone and fur soon wove itself in the cave's shadows, where she dragged her kills. When she'd lived with the Bovarys, in the early days of their courtship, Emma would let the puppy lick yellow yolks and golden sugar from the flat of a soft palm.

Undeliberate, absolved of rue and intent, the dog continued to forget Madame Bovary.

Gnawing on a femur near the river one afternoon, she bristled and turned. A deer's head was watching her thoughtfully from the silver rushes—separated, by some incommunicable misfortune, from its body. Its neck terminated in a chaos of crawling blackflies, a spill of jeweled rot like boiling cranberries. Its tongue hung limp like a flag of surrender. Insects were eating an osseous cap between the buck's yellow ears, a white knob the diameter of a sand dollar. A low, bad feeling drove the dog away.

V. REGRET

Regret, as experienced by the dog, was physical, kinetic—she turned in circles and doubled back, trying to uncover the scent of her home. She felt feverish. Some organ had never stopped its useless secretions, even without an Emma to provoke them. Hearth and leash, harsh voice, mutton chop, affectionate thump—she wanted all this again.

There was a day when she passed near the town of Airaines, a mere nine miles from the Bovarys' new residence in Yonville; and had the winds changed at that particular moment and carried a certain woman's lilac-scented sweat to her, this story might have had a very different ending.

One midnight, just after the late April thaw, the dog woke to the sight of a large wolf standing in the cave mouth, nakedly weighing her as prey. And even under that crushing stare she did not cower; rather, she felt elevated, vibrating with some primitive species of admiration for this more pure being, solitary and wholly itself. The wolf swelled with appetites that were ancient, straightforward—a stellar hunger that was satisfied nightly. An old wound sparkled under a brittle scabbard on its left shoulder, and a young boar's blood ran in torrents from its magnificent jaws. The greyhound's tail began to wag as if cabled to some current; a growl rose midway up her throat. The predator then turned away from her. Panting—*ha-ha-ha*—it licked green slime from the cave wall, crunching the spires of tiny amber snails. The wolf glanced once more around the chasm before springing eastward. Dawn lumbered after, through the pointed firs, unholstering the sun, unable to shoot; and the wind began to howl, as if in lamentation, calling the beast back.

Caught between two equally invalid ways of life, the greyhound whimpered herself toward sleep, unaware that in Yonville Emma Bovary was drinking vinegar in black stockings and sobbing at the exact same pitch. Each had forgotten entirely about the other, yet they retained the same peculiar vacancies within their bodies and suffered the same dread-filled dreams. Love had returned, and it went spoiling through them with no outlet.

In summer the dog crossed a final frontier, eating the greasy liver of a murdered bear in the wide open. The big female had been gut-shot

for sport by teenage brothers from Rouen, who'd then been too terri-
fied by the creature's drunken, hauntingly prolonged death throes to
wait and watch her ebb out. In a last pitch she'd crashed down a column
of saplings, her muzzle frothing with red foam. The greyhound was no
scavenger by nature, until nature made her one that afternoon. The
three cubs squatted on a log like a felled totem and watched with grave
maroon eyes, their orphan hearts pounding in unison.

Still, it would be incorrect to claim that the greyhound was now feral,
or fully ingrained in these woods. As a fugitive the dog was a passable
success, but as a dog she was a blown spore, drifting everywhere and
nowhere, unable to cure her need for a human, or her terror at the
insufficiency of her single body.

"Our destinies are united now, aren't they?" whispered Rodolphe
near the evaporating blue lake, in a forest outside of Yonville that might
as well have been centuries distant. Crows deluged the sky. Emma sat
on a rock, flushed red from the long ride, pushing damp woodchips
around with her boot toe. The horses munched leaves in a chorus as
Rodolphe lifted her skirts, the whole world rustling with hungers.

In the cave, the dog had a strange dream.

A long, lingering, indistinct cry came from one of the hills far beyond
the forest; it mingled with Emma's silence like music.

VI. A BREAK

The dog shivered. She'd been shivering ceaselessly for how many days
and nights now? All the magic of those early weeks had vanished, re-
placed by a dreary and devoted pain. Winter rose out of her own cavi-
ties. It shivered her.

Troubled by the soreness that had entered her muscles, she trotted
out of the cave and toward the muddy escarpment where she'd buried
a cache of weasel bones. Rain had eroded the path, and in her eager-
ness to escape her own failing frame, the mute ruminations of her
throbbing skeleton, the dog began to run at full bore. Then she was
sliding on the mud, her claws scrabbling uselessly at the smooth sur-
face; unable to recover her balance, the greyhound tumbled into a
ravine.

An irony:

She had broken her leg.

All at once Emma Bovary's final command came echoing through
her: *Stay*.

Sunset jumped above her, so very far above her twisted body, like a heart skipping beats. Blood ran in her eyes. The trees all around swam. She sank further into a soggy pile of dead leaves as the squealing voices of the blackflies rose in clouds.

Elsewhere in the world, Rodolphe Boulanger sat at his writing desk under the impressive head of a trophy stag. Two fat candles were guttering down. He let their dying light flatter him into melancholy—a feeling quite literary. The note before him would end his love affair with Emma.

How shall I sign it? "Devotedly"? No . . . "Your friend"?

The moon, dark red and perfectly round, rose over the horizon.

Deep in the trench, nostalgias swamped the greyhound in the form of olfactory hallucinations: snowflakes, rising yeast, scooped pumpkin flesh, shoe polish, horse-lathered leather, roasting venison, the explosion of a woman's perfume.

She was dying.

She buried her nose in the litterfall, stifling these visions until they ebbed and faded.

It just so happened that a game warden was wandering in that part of the woods, hours later or maybe days. Something in the ravine caught his eye—low to the ground, a flash of unexpected silver. He dropped to his knees for a closer look.

"Oh!" he gasped, calloused hands parting the dead leaves.

VII. THE TWO HUBERTS

The greyhound lived with the game warden, in a cottage at the edge of a town. He was not a particularly creative man, and he gave the dog his same name: Hubert. He treated her wounds as those of a human child, with poultices and bandages. She slept curled at the foot of his bed and woke each morning to the new green of a million spring buds erupting out of logs, sky-blue birdsong, minced chlorophyll.

"Bonjour, Hubert!" Hubert would call, sending himself into hysterics, and Hubert the dog would bound into his arms—and their love was like this, a joke that never grew old. And like this they passed five years.

Early one December evening Hubert accompanied Hubert to Yonville, to say a prayer over the grave of his mother. The snow hid the tombstones, and only the most stalwart mourners came out for such a grim treasure hunt. Among them was Emma Bovary. From within her hooded crimson cloak she noticed a shape darting between the snowflakes—a gray ghost trotting with its lips peeled back from black gums.

"Oh!" she cried. "How precious you are! Come here —"

Her whistle crashed through the dog's chest, splintering into antipodal desires:

Run.

Stay.

And it was here, at the margin of instinct and rebellion, that the dog encountered herself, felt a shimmering precursor to consciousness— the same stirring that lifted the iron hairs on her neck whenever she peered into mirrors, or discovered a small, odorless dog inside a lake. Suddenly, impossibly, she *did* remember: Midnight in Tostes. The walks through the ruined pavilion. Crows at dusk. The tug of a leather leash. Piano music. Egg yolk in a perfumed hand. Sad, impatient fingers scratching her ears.

Something bubbled and broke inside the creature's heart.

Emma was walking through the thick snow, toward the oblivious game warden, one golden strand of hair loose and blowing in the twilight.

"Oh, monsieur! I, too, once had a greyhound!" She shut her eyes and sighed longingly, as if straining to call back not only the memory but the dog herself.

And she very nearly succeeded.

The greyhound's tail began helplessly to wag.

"Her name was Deeeaaaa . . . Dahhh . . ."

And then the dog remembered, too, calloused hands brushing dead leaves from her fur, clearing the seams of blackflies from her eyelids and nostrils, lifting her from the trench. Their fine, sturdy bones clasped firmly around her belly as she flew through evening air. The rank, tuber-like scent enveloping her, the firelight in the eyes of her rescuer. Over his shoulder she'd glimpsed the shallow imprint of a dog's body in the mud.

With a lovely, amnesiac smile, Emma Bovary continued to fail to remember the name of her greyhound. And each soft sound she mouthed tugged the dog deeper into the past.

It was an impossible moment, and the pain the animal experienced— staring from old, rumpled Hubert to the absorbing, evanescing Emma— did feel very much like an ax falling through her snow-wet fur, splitting down the rail of her tingling spine, fatally dividing her.

"My dog's name is Hubert," Hubert said to Madame Bovary, with his stupid frankness. He glanced fondly at little Hubert, attributing the greyhound's spasms in the cemetery drifts to the usual culprits: giddiness or fleas.

Writhing in an agony, the dog rose to her feet. She closed the small, incredibly cold gulf of snow between herself and her master.

"Sit," she then commanded herself, and she obeyed.

Nominated by Zoetrope: All Story, James Reiss

PLAYING AT VIOLENCE

by PACIFIQUE IRANKUNDA

from THE AMERICAN SCHOLAR

On a fall afternoon a few years ago, inside my dorm room at Deerfield Academy, I started hearing gunshots. I had been warned that in America people hunt with guns. I comforted myself with this thought at first, but the sounds went on and on and grew increasingly familiar. *It can't be hunting,* I thought. *Why would anyone be hunting on the grounds of a Massachusetts prep school?*

I threw my door open and rushed outside the building, but I couldn't hear the sounds anymore. I saw students chatting and laughing as if everything was normal. Was I just dreaming? I went back inside the dorm. Walking down the hallway, I heard the sounds again. *Oh, it must be a student watching a movie!* I thought and returned to my room, closing the door. *Idiot!* I laughed at myself—where was I going to go anyway? I had just come to America, and I could hardly find my way around the campus. Even if the gunfire had been real, I would have had no idea where to run.

As I sat at my desk, the sounds brought back images from my home village in Burundi. This disturbed me. Finally, I covered my ears. From time to time, I would uncover them, hoping the movie had ended, but the sounds went on and on. *A movie of gunshots and nothing else?* I wondered. *What type of movie is that?*

As dinnertime approached, students started emerging from their rooms, and I joined them in the hallway. "Were you just watching a movie?" I asked one of my dorm mates.

"Oh, I'm sorry! Was it loud?" he said.

"No, no!" I said. "I just was curious to know what movie you were watching."

"It wasn't actually a movie," he said. "I was playing video games."

Huh, I thought. I did not ask for an explanation. At the time, I didn't know what video games were, only that they made noises that sounded like gunfire.

There was a time when silence reigned all over my village. Rivers were loud, but their rhythmic sounds were part of the silence. People worked in their fields with hoes. There were no cars, no factories. I imagine that to Westerners that time and place would have resembled the Stone Age. Planes flew over the village, but never more than once a week. There was another season that broke this silence. It was the time of crops growing. From the early stage of the seeds' sprouting, parents would send their kids into the fields to make noise and chase away the birds that ate the seedlings. This went on for a month, and after that the silence would come again. I enjoyed the quiet, but it did not last. Another season erupted and broke all the silence. It was the season of war. It came in the fall when I was four, and it lasted for more than a decade.

In this new season, just as in any other, some things died and others were born. Everything was transformed. When the militia attacked a village, it left behind the remains of the dead—people and animals—and the houses in ruin. People moved from their houses to live in the forests. New words appeared—*ibinywamaraso* ("the blood drinkers") and *ivyamfurambi* ("deeds of the wrong first born")—and new expressions: *kamwe kamwe ku ruyeye ku rwembe* ("one after another, gently on a razor"). This slogan and others like it said not to worry if you did not kill many people. The secret was to keep killing.

This new season made children my age wish they had been born blind and deaf so they couldn't see their houses being burned and their mothers being raped before being killed, or hear the sounds of bombs or their parents screaming and crying. But at other times, you wished you had the eyes of a hawk and the ears of a deer, so that you could distinguish, in the dark, a black stump with branches from a man dressed in black pointing a gun, or a thin string tied to a mine from a long blade of grass lying across your path. These were times when you needed to know that the sound of raindrops falling on leaves wasn't that of militiamen approaching on tiptoes. For a while you wished for something, and after another while you wished for the opposite. You learned to cover your eyes in the day; you learned to see in the dark.

In the hallway at Deerfield, the boy, whom I'll call Luke, went on talking about video games, as we waited for our classmates to join us for dinner. Almost everything Luke said was so confusing that I asked him: "What do you mean by saying you killed so-and-so?"

"Well, my enemies. Paci, how often do you play video games?"

"Actually, what are they?"

The other students looked at each other and smiled.

"Come on, Paci!" Luke led me to his room. He took up a little device in his hands and turned on his computer. He pointed at the computer screen, at images of people with guns. "Once you press this button, they start moving and you hunt them, see?" Out of the computer's speakers came the sound of shooting, the sound of war.

"You'll have to play with us, Paci!"

I faced the computer but lowered my eyes. I didn't want to offend him, but I didn't want to watch what was happening on the screen. Instead, I watched his fingers moving, handling the device.

"What are you doing with this thing?" I asked, pointing at the little device in his hands.

"I'm playing! That's how you play!"

"So you're actually doing the shooting?"

"Yeah! Here, you try it."

"No, no. Thanks. Let's go to dinner."

In the seventh year of war in Burundi, I went to a public boarding school by the shore of Lake Tanganyika. At that school and many others, returning students hazed incoming ones. Although the rigor and form of hazing differed from one school to another, the objective of hazing was the same everywhere: to embarrass new students. Usually a group of returning boys and girls would gather in a circle around a new student, ordering him or her to tell vulgar jokes. This worked best with girls, who would often start crying halfway through a joke and be doubly embarrassed. Some new boys enjoyed telling dirty jokes, but all boys were embarrassed if they were made to cry in public, and if you were a boy, no matter how tough you were, you were unlikely to leave the center of the circle without wiping your eyes. Every word—every gesture—was treated as an insult by the hazers, and the penalty was for one of them to rap his knuckles on your head. If you were a girl, you often had to do more than tell a dirty joke. You might also be commanded by one of the boys, "Date me until I fall in love with you!" The hazers would tell you to caress the boy who had said those words. And then that boy would scream and call out, "She is harrassing me! Please stop! Stop! Leave me alone! Leave me alone!" Other times the boy would make noises as if he were having sex and say things like, "What a whore!"

A person was assigned especially to haze me. His name was Chrysostom. Most of the hazers wanted to inflict only psychological pain. Chrysostom was different. If, for example, you saw a new girl cradling her breasts in pain, you knew that she had been hazed by Chrysostom.

I met him on my first day at that school. He came up to me and yelled, *"Kinyuzu!"* The name designated a new student who, according to the rules of hazing, did not deserve a proper name.

I did not reply.

"Why don't you open your mouth and say, 'Yes!' "

I kept quiet.

Chrysostom looked puzzled, as if I had done something not only incomprehensible but absolutely stupid. He then laughed ironically and called me by my proper name. "All right, Pacifique."

"Yes," I said.

"Are you surprised I know your name?" he asked.

"Well, yes, because we just met," I replied.

"Do you know my name?"

"No," I said.

"Because mine is too unimportant to know, but yours . . . You're a big shot, huh?"

Chrysostom was short but strong. He had a thick, muscular neck, and when he laughed, the muscles around his neck would get bigger and bigger as if air were being pumped into them. He was the boy who could get away with offending anyone, no matter how strong the other person was. Students would tell you: "Unless you intend to kill him, you should not try to fight Chrysostom." Whether you started the fight or he started it, it was for you to end it. You had to accept humiliation and ask for mercy. Otherwise the fight would never end. He would never quit.

From the moment we met until the end of the year, Chrysostom never let a day go by without spending some time with me. He made me his closest friend, in his special way of companionship. He always wanted me to tell him jokes, but he also made sure I did not go to sleep without being beaten up. Unlike others who often were not interested in jokes but only in inflicting humiliation, Chrysostom would listen to my jokes and would laugh when they amused him. If someone else had beaten me up, he did not need to beat me again. I only needed to go see him and tell him I had already been beaten, and then tell him jokes.

There was a particularly vulgar joke that hazers found funny, so new students told it often. The joke went like this: two children are playing outside their house on a sunny afternoon. It is a hot day, and their parents are napping—windows wide open. All of a sudden, funny noises come out of their parents' room; they are making love. One child runs over, looks through the window, and calls to his sister: "Mom and Dad are fighting!" The other child joins the first at the window. After a while, the children begin to cry. As they cry, the sister watches Mommy grabbing Daddy's shoulder, and then she shouts, "Go, Mummy, go!" The brother grabs his sister, and a real fight begins—the kids are taking sides. After the parents have "come to peace," they hear their children fighting outside. They rush out and separate them and angrily question them, and the kids reply, *"But you were also fighting!"* This was the punch line.

When I told this idiotic joke to Chrysostom, he didn't laugh. After a moment of awkwardness, he asked me, "Were the kids *seriously* fighting?"

"The story goes that they fought to their bleeding," I said. *Then* he broke into laughter. If there was anything related to violence in a joke, Chrysostom always wanted to hear more about it.

Another interesting thing about Chrysostom was that he wanted to tell me stories, too. He told me he lived in Bujumbura Rural, a province where a group of militia called the FNL (Forces nationales de liberation) camped. He would tell me how he enjoyed watching the FNL combatants—whom he called friends—fighting with government soldiers. Though he never said that he himself killed or had fought for the FNL, in his stories he sometimes used "we." He would imitate the sounds of different guns and would keep doing it for such a long time that his voice would get hoarse. He repeated one story often. He never seemed to remember that I had already heard it. He laughed while telling it as if it were new every time.

"Back home, my friends, the FNL," he would start. "You know the FNL, right?"

I would nod.

"When we catch people . . . oh it is so funny . . . the soldiers . . . those for the government . . . oh dear! *Ntakintu kiryoshe nkico, wohora ura-raba!* Nothing else on earth could be more amusing! You know how a cat, when he catches a mouse, you know how he can play with the mouse knowing that the mouse won't go anywhere? It is just like that. Oh, boy!" Then he would laugh and laugh. The muscles around his neck would swell. When he stopped laughing, he would go on: "We ask them questions, you know, and when they hesitate . . . You know, in the eyes!" He would stretch out his arm and point his long fingernails at my eyes. "And then after . . ." He would interrupt himself with laughter again. "The FNL would never waste their bullets, you know, they would use a rope, you know, even a shoelace, and put it around their neck, and . . ." Saying this, he would grab my neck and squeeze it. "And . . . strangle the idiots!" Then, as if hit by an electric shock, he would release my neck and fall backward onto his bed, and laugh so hard that tears came from his eyes. "I miss home! I very much look forward to vacation."

I could see he was absorbed by his story, as if he were right back there strangling someone. He did not realize that I was shivering the whole time.

"What do you do on vacation?" he would ask me. For me, going on vacation did not mean going to my family's house, but rather joining my mother and brother in the forest, where we hid from Chrysostom's friends, the militiamen he always told me about. I could not tell him this, of course. I would change the subject.

I tried to please Chrysostom, hoping he would stop abusing me, but he was not aware of what I felt. I would take him to a restaurant, buy him soda and cookies, but it was like caressing a stone. He would often put his arm around my shoulders, and we would walk around while I told him jokes. He would listen very carefully and would laugh and even give me a high five. Students who saw us walking side by side thought we were the best of friends. In fact, Chrysostom himself seemed to think I was his best friend. When he learned I was going to another school for my remaining years of high school, he told me: "I will miss you! You are very sweet. I do not feel I will have someone else to spend time with and have fun." And I could see in his face that he actually meant it.

It was an interesting friendship, but I am glad that it ended.

That evening at Deerfield, on the way back from dinner, Luke asked me to go play war video games with him. "No," I said. "I have a lot of work to do." I did have work to do. But I had other reasons for staying away. I thought that the boys who played the video games probably took drugs, that they were gangsters who pretended to be innocent.

One evening, I was having trouble with my computer, and I went to Luke's room to ask him for help. I found him in the midst of shooting imaginary people. After he fixed my computer, he asked me if I wanted to watch him play for a little bit. I said I did not and tried to explain: "You know, I've seen the real thing. So I'm not really interested. I'm sorry."

"Wait, you . . . How?" He stopped playing.

"There was a war back in my country," I told him. "I was little when it started, and I grew up in it. So I saw a lot of that."

"Wow!" he said. He asked me to tell him more. There was excitement in his face, which surprised me, and frightened me a little. When I first came to school in America, I assumed that I would never talk about the war in Burundi. Doing so might refresh my bad memories. And wouldn't the other students think that I was violent myself? Besides, who would want to hear about such horrible things?

He wanted me to tell him about the war. I said I would tell him some other day, knowing that day would never come. It would have been like telling jokes to Chrysostom. Was this boy like Chrysostom? Was he addicted to violence, too? "And thanks so much for fixing my computer," I said and quietly left his room.

Over the next few months, I realized I was wrong about Luke. He and my other dorm mates who liked playing violent video games weren't gangsters at all. They were just young, inexperienced, innocent. It took me some time to realize that the shooting wasn't real to them. They were just playing. For them the games were "mindless," as one friend told me. Many kids at the school played the same kinds of games. So there was nothing unusual about Luke. He was just doing what many American kids did. I felt relieved, but I was also puzzled by what seemed to me like an odd sort of entertainment. How could violence so easily be turned into a game? How could companies invent such games in the first place? And how could parents buy them for their children?

I lived through 13 years of civil war. I know that violence can become almost a culture in itself, and that it twists not all but many of the people who are trapped in it. Of course, not all the children who grew up in the war became violent. How you responded to your own resentments, whether you seethed with thoughts of revenge, how your parents, neighbors, and friends responded to the bloodshed—all of these things helped determine your own taste for violence. I was lucky. Many others were not. Maybe Chrysostom was a particularly sadistic case. I don't really know. Maybe he would have been a bad guy wherever he grew up. But he was not born violent, and certainly the war helped shape him. I don't know what happened to him as a child, but I imagine that since he himself grew up in that season of war in Burundi, he probably underwent a transformation and adapted the way a plant adapts. Violence in my country and in neighboring Rwanda and Congo had a similar effect on soldiers and militiamen, and especially on children drafted into armies or rebel militias. I remember how Nyandwi, a schoolmate and a neighbor who had joined one of the militias, hunted my family. When we escaped from him, he killed his own sister, apparently out of nothing more than frustration. I recall how Nyandwi, when he was no longer a militiaman, would proudly tell stories of how he killed 30 children with machetes in a single night. It was how his militia colleagues had initiated him, he explained.

I remember how Gilbert, a neighbor and Nyandwi's friend, enjoyed telling similar stories of when he was in the militia. How every one of his reactions, when he was back in the village, was violent and how he always laughed after he had done something violent. How he would heat a nail and stab the feet of his sisters to find out the truth if he suspected they had told him lies. To many young people, violence became easy and fun. It became one of their hobbies, as it seemed to have become Chrysostom's hobby. It is hard to allow yourself to imagine that you could become one of those young people, but you have to admit that you could, when you remind yourself that the children who are twisted by war were once lovely three-year-olds who smiled and charmed with their innocence.

I think back to the season of war and remember how we fled deep into the jungle, far from any people. That was how we managed to survive, by hiding, by turning our backs on the rest of humanity. Those parents who sent their children into the jungle to protect them from the bloodshed—they would have envied the peace that Luke and others like him took for granted. Most of all, they would have envied the fact that these lucky children did not know the true devastation of war. That they only played at violence.

Nominated by The American Scholar

WINTER ELDERS

fiction by SHAWN VESTAL

from ECOTONE

They materialized with the first snow. That was how Bradshaw would always remember it. He was standing at the living room window, listening to Cheryl shush the baby, when he saw specks fluttering like ash against a smoky sky, then caught sight of someone on his front step, though he hadn't noticed anyone coming up the walk. He could see about an inch of a man's left side at the window's border—an arm in a dark suit and a boyish hand holding a book bound in black leather. He knew instantly that there was another suit and another leather-bound volume out there, a companion to complete the pair: missionaries.

Bradshaw opened the door and blocked the frame. Body language was everything. Announce it—*you're not coming in.* On the step were two kids in suits, short hair, name tags. One was tall—taller than Bradshaw, maybe six foot four—and the baby fat on his face had begun to jowlify. The shorter one was younger, with avid eyes and scraped cheeks.

"Brother Bradshaw?" the tall one asked as he looked into the house. "Hi, we're here from the Church."

"I can see that."

"We're just wanting to check in, see if there's anything we can do for you."

"You could clean out my gutters," Bradshaw said. "Or rake the yard."

The little one chuckled, but the tall one looked up at the gutters, spilling over with leaves and twigs. The falling snow had thickened.

"Don't think we won't," he said.

His name tag read *Elder Pope.* He would not drop his smile or avert his eyes. There was something stubborn in him and, deeper, the sense that he was proud of his stubbornness. Bradshaw was impressed, a little.

"After you're done you could change the oil in my car," Bradshaw said. "So long as you're just wanting to help."

Elder Pope nodded softly, and pointed with his chin toward the inside of the house.

"Maybe we could come in and discuss your list of chores," he said.

"Right," Bradshaw said.

The littler missionary—his name tag read *Elder Warren*—said, "Could we just talk to you for a few minutes about Jesus Christ?"

"You could not just talk to me for a few minutes about Jesus Christ," Bradshaw said, pushing the door closed slowly against Pope's cheer. "I'd like it if you stopped coming here. Make a note back at the coven."

Through the window in the door, Bradshaw saw Warren turn to go, but Pope stayed, staring for a few seconds.

Bradshaw was twelve years out of the Church and not going back. For a long time, a new set of missionaries had appeared every few months, cloaked in fresh optimism. Each time, Bradshaw's hunger to disappoint them had deepened, until he finally asked them to remove him from the Church rolls for good. To kick him out. It had taken months, but they finally sent him a letter of excommunication, revoking his baptismal blessings and eternal privileges as a member of the Church of Jesus Christ of Latter-day Saints. The letter read like a credit-card cancellation, and he and Cheryl had made much fun of it. "You're out!" she would say and wrap her arms around his neck, and though he was glad to be out, too, her reaction made him defensive, and he would feel a germ of insult stick and grow. Now, staring at the place in the storm where the missionaries had vanished, he wished he'd asked what brought them back this time.

He heard the baby crying and went to check on him. He found Cheryl bouncing the boy gently, whispering, "And then the pig decided to become a happy pig and spread happiness into the world . . ."

"Who was it?" she whispered.

"Missionaries."

"You've got to be kidding," she said, bugging her eyes while she swayed and rubbed the baby's back.

"I'm not kidding."

Bradshaw leaned toward the boy and whispered, "Hello, Riley. Hello, Brother Bradshaw."

Cheryl pulled the boy away.

"Don't," she said. "That's not funny."

She was always serious now. Ever since the baby. *Earnest*. Riley was nine months old, and Bradshaw wondered what had happened to his partner in cynicism. They used to be in complete agreement about this if nothing else: Everything was such bullshit. Everything was so ridiculous. They had been bloodhounds for any trace of sentiment, any note of sincerity, upon which to pounce mockingly; after parties, they competed to do the best eviscerating impressions. New parents, all wide-eyed and self-absorbed, had been a specialty of Cheryl's. Such bullshit, people and their human mess. Now Bradshaw felt abandoned, adrift in his own head and swamped with hot-eyed exhaustion. The boy had started sleeping most of the night, usually waking just once, fussing and whimpering until Cheryl nursed him back to sleep. Bradshaw knew he had it easy by comparison, but still he felt flocked by trouble. Besieged. Once awakened, he would lie there for an hour or more, mind fixed on his current aggravation—an argument at work, something Cheryl had said, some spot of tension with the world. He would dream his constant dream of putting people in their place. Sometimes he lay on his side and watched the boy's head bob as he nursed, and Bradshaw would feel once more the pressure that had arrived with the child—a relentless sense that he was not up to this. That he was not made to be a father.

Coming home from work four days later, Bradshaw swung his car into the driveway, and the headlights washed over two spectral shapes in the grainy dusk. The missionaries. Pope had his hand wrapped around a rake shaft, talking to Warren, who was looking up and nodding. The snow had melted, and gluey brown leaves had been raked into a pile.

The open garage door spread a fan of warm light, but the house was dark. Cheryl and Riley were at her sister's. Bradshaw slammed his car door and only then did Pope look up, lifting his arm in an exaggerated wave, as though he were on a dock greeting a steamer.

"Brother Bradshaw!" he said. "Good evening."

Warren raised a hand briefly. He wore his embarrassment like a shawl.

Bradshaw stepped off the driveway onto the wet lawn, cold air like metal in his sinuses. The rake had been in the garage. They had gone into the garage.

"I bet you never thought we'd take you up on it," Pope said, smiling even as Bradshaw grabbed the rake handle and jerked. Pope held firm for a second, smile widening—in surprise or malevolence, Bradshaw couldn't tell—then let go, sending Bradshaw backward one step. Pope shrugged.

"Sorry," he said.

Warren laughed, snuffling behind his hand. Did he say something? Something to Pope? Bradshaw stared, seething. Breath crowded his lungs, and his vision tightened and blurred. Pope smiled patiently at Bradshaw, lips pressed hammily together. It was the smile of every man he had met in Church, the bishops and first counselors and stake presidents, the benevolent mask, the put-on solemnity, the utter falseness. It was the smile of the men who brought boxes of food when Bradshaw was a teenager and his father wasn't working, the canned meat and bricks of cheese. The men who prayed for his family. Bradshaw's father would disappear, leaving him and his mother to kneel with the men.

Setting the rake against his shoulder, Bradshaw ground the heels of his hands into his eyes. When he opened them, red spots expanded and danced across his vision. The missionaries faded, then clarified.

"Brother Bradshaw?" Pope said.

Bradshaw wanted to swing the rake at Pope's head. To watch his smug eyes pop as the tines sunk in. Why could he not just do it? He never could. Finally, he simply pointed toward the road, eyes averted, finger trembling. As they left, Pope said without looking back, "We'll be praying for you, Brother Bradshaw."

Bradshaw threw down the rake.

"Don't pray for me!" he shouted. "Don't you *dare* pray for me!"

He stopped when he saw his neighbor, Bud Swenson, standing at his mailbox, a handful of envelopes.

Later, after Cheryl returned, he sat on the floor with Riley, trying to get him interested in stacking wooden blocks. It was Tuesday of Thanksgiving week, and Cheryl was making pie crusts. She came in and watched them a moment, and when Bradshaw looked up, wooden block in hand, he was startled to find her on the verge of happy tears. It reminded him of the way his mother would get in Church, swept up in the spirit.

"I still can't believe you want to do the whole Thanksgiving thing," Bradshaw said. "With a baby."

"I know," she said. "But I want to. I feel like we're finally a family."

"We are finally a family," he said. "But so what?"

When the boy was born, Bradshaw kept waiting for it to happen. The flash of light. The surge of joy. Some brightness shining through the visible world. He had been so sure this would be it—the moment that he felt what everyone else seemed to feel, what his mother felt, what all the other Mormons felt, what people in other churches felt, what even people like Cheryl felt, people who were hostile to the very idea of religion: some spirit in the material. The thing behind the thing. Cheryl called it "an animating force."

"There has to be something, doesn't there?" she said. "When you really think about it? Something larger than us?"

Sometimes he thought she was right, and sometimes he thought she was wrong, and the fact that he could not decide had given him a sense that he was failing a fundamental duty to believe. In something or nothing. He had always been that way—back as far as he could remember, his mind fixed on the yes or no of it, and always shifting. He recalled wondering, when he was baptized at age eight, why all these spiritual people needed a mime show like baptism. Instead of anything transcendent, he had felt awakened to the concrete moment—the water in the font, the thick wet of the baptismal garment.

As a teenager, at Church camp, he had watched as the boys and girls stood up at testimony meeting and swore they had faith in the Lord, that they had a testimony this was the true Church. They wept and trembled, one after another, and soon he stood too and choked on his tears, swore he had been given a testimony. It was as though a bright beam of joy was pulsing from the heavens into the core of the earth, threaded directly through him. But by that night, he felt it fading, and within days it was gone. He told himself that what had happened was not genuine, that he had simply been weak, swept up.

When Riley was born, the moment assaulted him in its earthbound reality—the blood and mucus under the bright lights of the delivery room, the boy's pinched eyes, magenta skin, clammy hair, and that cord, that bunched gray-red tube of matter and fluid. It arrived like an undeniable announcement—this moment is the one thing. His son struck him not as an angel or a spirit, but as an animal, a creature who would die without his care, a creature who would die, a creature bound to other creatures. Bradshaw pressed the scissors and the blades separated the boy from his mother.

Later, Cheryl told him she'd been overwhelmed by something she could not define. "Just some kind of . . . whatever," she said, and laughed.

In the first days of it, when they would find themselves up at 3 a.m., waiting for Riley to stop gurgling in the bassinet, she would talk about it.

"Isn't it crazy?" she said, in a whisper of wonder. "It really is a miracle. It really is what people say."

She waited for him to answer. A pale parallelogram of summer moonlight lay over the closet door; he could smell cut grass outside, the cool of a sprinkler. What could he tell her? That he felt like he was being filled with life and drained of life all at once? That he had not imagined the consuming force of it? That he ached for the way he used to be filled with himself, only himself, all Bradshaw?

The day after Thanksgiving, it snowed almost a foot. Everything rounded, muffled. Snow balanced in strips along fence tops and tree limbs; footsteps left deep wells across lawns. It snowed another five inches overnight, and the next day dawned bright and icy. That afternoon, Bradshaw shoveled the walk for the third time in two days. His neighbor Bud Swenson's German shepherd, Jake, a genial but bloodthirsty-looking dog, came over to be petted. He and Bud shouted pleasantries and shared weather statistics. Bradshaw heard footsteps squeaking and scrunching around the corner. Later he would think he had sensed the missionaries' appearance before they appeared, trudging down his street since half the sidewalks were unshoveled.

Bradshaw took Jake by the collar, bent down and whispered in his ear, "Go get 'em, boy. Sic 'em, Jakie," and the dog braced. Bud called, "You're not telling him any of my secrets are ya?" and laughed, and Bradshaw ignored him and watched the missionaries approach. They did not angle toward his walkway, but kept to the road, and as they drew closer Pope raised a hand and shouted, "Hello, Brother Bradshaw," and Bradshaw said, "Sic 'em, boy!" Jake shot off, barking ferociously, while Bud shouted at him to stop.

Pope scrambled back, slipping, but Warren stood in place. He held out one hand, palm down, and said, "Hey there. Good boy. Good boy. That's a good boy," in a soothing voice. The dog stopped a few feet from Warren and kept barking.

"Hey, there, you're a good boy," Warren said.

He brought his other hand from his coat pocket and presented it, palm up. The dog stopped barking. His tail began to wag. He stepped toward the missionary and started to eat from his hand. Bradshaw stared. His stomach splashed like a boisterous sea. Warren patted the dog on the head, and the dog looked back at Bradshaw, tongue out, tail whipping the frigid air.

Bud called, "Come here, dammit," and glared at Bradshaw. The dog obeyed. Pope and Warren stood looking back and forth between Bradshaw and Bud, and when Bud shook his head and went toward his house, the missionaries turned and approached Bradshaw. He thought what he was feeling then—ribs like hot, heavy irons in his chest—was despair, true despair in the face of the grinding, unbeatable world.

"Missionaries always carry dog treats," Pope said, smiling once again.

Bradshaw said, "Look . . ." and Pope stepped to him, face bright with cold.

"May I ask you a favor, Brother Bradshaw? I know this sounds crazy, but could we possibly come into your home for a moment and warm up? That's all—just warm up? We're awfully cold right now, and my companion here is in worse shape than me."

Warren shivered, and his bright nose dripped. Bradshaw felt weakened by the demand. What kind of person was he, that he wanted so badly to say no?

"Okay," he said, turning and heading up the walk. Inside, they stood on the entry rug, in coats and hats, ringed by a dusting of snow.

"I'll be right back," Bradshaw said, and went to the baby's room. Cheryl was sitting by the rocker, reading a magazine while Riley napped. When Bradshaw told her what he'd done, she rolled her eyes and said, "It's your mess." He returned to the living room and saw the missionaries standing there, still bundled up. They seemed small. Young.

"Why don't you sit down for a second?" Bradshaw asked.

Warren dragged a glove across his nose. Pope unzipped his coat and pulled off his hat. They unsheathed and sat down on his couch, and Bradshaw sat in a chair.

"Don't get any ideas," he said.

"Well," Pope said. "I wonder if I might ask you just one question."

Unbelievable. "You might," he said.

Cheryl had moved to the dining room. He could hear her clicking on a calculator, tearing off checks.

"I just wonder if you've ever read the Book of Mormon all the way through and prayed about it?" Pope said. "Just gave it one real chance."

The question shocked Bradshaw. He'd come to feel that it wasn't what Pope was up to, after all. That he was here for something else. "I don't . . ." He couldn't figure out how to begin. "No, I haven't. I mean— you know what I think about when I think about the Church? The

73

stupid seagulls." Bradshaw hadn't really thought about the seagulls in years. "How those bugs were eating all the pioneers' crops and great clouds of seagulls came and ate them up. Right? In Salt Lake? Saved everybody from starving? Divine intervention?"

"What do you think about it?" Pope asked.

"What a bunch of bullshit it is. I mean, birds eat bugs."

"I had some relatives there for that," Warren said. "Ancestors."

"Yeah? Okay. Whatever. Let's just say it's a nice story. A nice little *tale*."

Pope seemed confused. "Just keep an open mind, is all I'm saying."

"That'd be a bit too open for me," Bradshaw said, and now he was feeling better, kind of energized. "I mean, actually, that'd be way, way too open."

The gears in Pope's smile slipped. Bradshaw continued, "Really, guys, that book is no more an ancient record than I am the Duke of Scotland," and the air in his lungs felt good again. "Maybe *you'd* like to keep an open mind to a few things. The historical record, for instance . . ."

A gate unlocked inside him. The beasts trampled out.

"I mean, right there on the first page or two, you've got a guy named Sam. Sam!" he said. His voice felt harsh and spiny in his throat. He was thinking that he'd really start—really blast every story about Joseph Smith, about the "translation" of the Book of Mormon, about everything. Make the stupid fuckers see.

"Sam! Sam! Just some Central American dude, two thousand years ago, named Sam! Not Quetzalcoatl or some shit. Sam!" He couldn't stop saying it. Fury tightened his scalp, the sockets of his eyes.

A long wail came from the back bedroom. Bradshaw stopped and realized how loud he'd been. He looked at Warren gazing forlornly at his hands. Pope kept his eyes on Bradshaw, looking resigned and sad. Bradshaw heard Cheryl stand and walk to the nursery. Hard, angry steps. He sat hot faced and trembling, embarrassment seeping in. The baby stopped crying, and still no one spoke.

Cheryl walked into the room, gently rocking the boy.

"I don't want you people in my house," she said, in her quiet-baby hush. "My husband can't seem to tell you that, but I'm telling you now. If you come back again, I'm going to call the police. I'll get a restraining order."

Warren said, "Yes, ma'am," and Pope's eyes bored into the floor. They rose and shuffled toward the door. Drew on their coats and hats. Warren stepped out, but Pope stopped and looked at Bradshaw.

"I just want to say, before I leave you alone," he whispered, "that I know the gospel is true. I know it. I know that it is true because God has told me it is true, and not because I'm special, or different than anyone else on this earth, but because He loves us all, all of us, all His children, and He will give us this knowledge if we ask Him for it. I promise you that, Brother Bradshaw. I swear it."

Pope, flushed and wet-eyed, ducked his head and left. Bradshaw felt an emotional swell that recalled that day when he had stood before the others at Church camp and wept. It was not that Pope was right and he was wrong, and not that Pope was wrong and he was right. It was that Pope had something he could not have, and he would spend his life not having it.

The snow refused to stop. Berms piled head high. Enormous icicles grew down from gutters to the ground. Bradshaw was shoveling the walk one night when he heard someone shout, "Hello!" He looked up and saw two shapes across the street, passing out of the street light and into the gray mist. One tall, one short. Both turned their shadowed faces to him as they passed.

The next night, dropping cans and newspaper into the recycling bin, he thought he saw a figure move behind a tree in his side yard. He walked toward it, stepping into calf-deep snow in his slippers. He thought he heard the soft crunch of a footstep.

"Pope!" he whispered harshly. "You better not let me find you out here."

Bradshaw's words billowed before him.

"I will make you wish you'd never been born."

Silence, but for the radical drumming of his heart.

"You're going to be in a world of hurt."

These were things Bradshaw's father used to say when he was angry, and they were things that Bradshaw had fantasized about saying to others, as his stronger self. His fantasy self.

"I swear to God I'll stomp a mudhole in your ass."

Bradshaw's father had only mentioned God when he was issuing a threat. His mom had dragged them all to Church on Sundays, to the tan brick ward house on Main Street. Everyone could tell his Dad wasn't a part of it, just by the way he stared out windows or into walls. After his mom died and he lived with his father in a downtown apartment, they stopped going to Church altogether. When the men from the ward came on Sundays to visit, his father wouldn't answer the door. They would sit inside, hold their breath, and wait for the footsteps to disappear down the hall.

"Pope," Bradshaw whispered, shivering, feet and legs soaked. "Pope."

Snowflakes began to fall. Bradshaw looked up into the purple sky, the glowing winter night. Snow plunged and swerved downward, and he felt drawn upward into a dark heaven. He was weightless. He would never stomp a mudhole in anyone's ass.

The next morning, before work, Bradshaw walked to the pine trees in the side yard—the huge, sixty-year-old tree and the littler pine tucked against it. The snow was sunken with footprints, drifted over by snow, crisscrossing, back and forth. He could not tell where they came from or where they were going.

Riley woke the next day with a fever, cranky and wailing. Bradshaw tried to take his temperature under his arm, but he wouldn't stay still.

"Maybe we ought to try the rectal thermometer," Cheryl said.

"Maybe *you* ought to try the rectal thermometer," Bradshaw said. He put his hand on the baby's forehead. "He doesn't feel *that* hot."

By the time Bradshaw returned from work, the boy was blazing: 101, 102. He wouldn't take breast or bottle. His diaper had been dry for hours. He was radiant in Bradshaw's arms. Cheryl looked as if she hadn't left his room all day—still in her sweatpants and T-shirt, fretful and pale.

"This is getting worse, right?" Bradshaw said.

"I think so. I'm not sure."

Bradshaw cupped the boy's head in his palm. It felt like a stone on a riverbank, some noon in July. Riley wouldn't stop whimpering and fidgeting, rubbing his soft fingers around his face. Cheryl tried to give him a dropper full of pink Tylenol, but he spat it out.

"What did the doctor say?" Bradshaw asked.

"Come in if it gets worse."

"This is worse. I think it's worse."

"We should go. Shouldn't we go?"

Bradshaw drove slowly on the snow-packed roads, leaning forward with both hands on the wheel. About halfway there, three large snow-flakes landed on the windshield and melted.

"It can't snow anymore," Cheryl said. "It can't."

At the hospital, the ER nurse said, "Oh dear, this little guy's de-hydrated," and they hooked him up to an IV. The sight of the needle invading his son's arm, of the dry skin cracking his lower lip, made Bradshaw feel helpless—proof that he was being tasked beyond his capabilities. Cheryl hustled around the room, checking the diaper bag for wipes, watching Riley's skin color, rushing out to the nurses with questions. Bradshaw sat beside the boy, sliding crushed ice into his mouth. Soon, Riley was cooler and calmer, but the doctor wanted to keep him overnight, so Bradshaw left to get toothbrushes and underwear.

Outside, new snow was piling onto old. Cars stuck at stoplights, spin-ning as the lights went green. Bradshaw drove slowly along the busy arterial. When he got to his neighborhood, he built up as much speed as he could before turning onto the unplowed street, but he immedi-ately bogged down. Halfway up the block, he spun to a stop and sat there, breathing loudly, mind hurtling—the boy would be okay, no thanks to him. But Riley's illness, his frailty and animal need, had sent an exact message: if the boy died—not now, he was not dying now, Bradshaw knew—Bradshaw would die, as well. Not that he would kill himself, though he thought he would, but that he had become some-thing else entirely, a new being who would only exist so long as his son existed. If the boy died, Bradshaw would become a ghost. He sat in his car as his breath fogged the windshield. He would never be free. He tried to slow his breathing and could not.

He climbed out, locked the car, and started walking the five blocks home. The storm blew sideways. Flakes clung to his eyelashes and nos-trils. Trudging clumsily in his snow boots, he was exhausted by the time he reached his house, dark and unlit. He started up the sidewalk, and a voice came from the darkness. "Hey there, Brother Bradshaw."

Bradshaw stopped. He looked at his house and couldn't see Pope anywhere.

"Sorry to surprise you like this," the voice said.

It was coming from the edge of the front patio, from the two metal chairs they never used. Bradshaw stared, narrowed his eyes. He thought he saw a shape in one of the chairs. He took several slow steps toward it.

"Pope?"

"Who else?"

Now the shape seemed to be standing. He could hear Pope smiling. Bradshaw was glad he had returned. Furiously thrilled. He took another step, and noticed that someone had cleared the snow from the fake rock where they hid the spare key. The fake rock lay overturned, a bowl filling with snow.

"I need to come in, Brother Bradshaw."

"You're not coming in."

"I need to come in."

The shape and the voice seemed to separate.

"Where's your partner?"

"He's home. Sick," Pope scoffed.

"What are you doing out?"

"Knocking on doors." The shape hung before him, straight ahead on the walk, grainy, slowly growing into Pope in the weak light. "Doing the Lord's work. But I'm awfully cold now, Brother Bradshaw. I need to come in."

"You're not coming in."

Pope held up the spare key between the fingers of his glove.

"I'm coming in. You know it. You do. It's just another thing you're not letting yourself believe right now. But you know it. In your heart."

"Nobody knows shit with their heart, Pope. That's not what the heart does."

Pope sighed, a long weary breath that turned smoky in the air. "People are always telling me no, Brother Bradshaw. All day long. Do you have any idea how discouraging that is?"

He turned toward the door, and Bradshaw lunged, wrapping his arms around Pope's torso. It didn't feel like something he'd actually done—it didn't feel like anything he would ever do. He scrabbled for the key, but Pope twisted and fought. Hanging on from behind, Bradshaw drove him onto the snowy sidewalk, feeling his rib cage expand with every breath. Pope fought to his knees, and they lumbered and lurched, and Bradshaw found his right hand suddenly, accidentally, clamped over Pope's mouth, bony chin snug in his grip.

"Okay," Pope said, relaxing. "All right."

Bradshaw's body wanted to do it. That was how he would always remember it—his body did it without him. His muscles twitched and fluttered with desire. His bones gathered and heaved backward. The sound was horrendous—a crack like a tree limb splitting—and Bradshaw felt it in his muscles and bones, in his own neck.

He sat back as Pope slumped onto his face, rear in the air like a sleeping toddler. Bradshaw breathed and breathed, watching each white cloud rise. Pope didn't move. Snow soaked through Bradshaw's pants. He stood. He noticed he didn't feel surprised. He hadn't expected this, but now that he was in the middle of it, it didn't feel unexpected.

"You're not coming in," Bradshaw whispered.

He leaned over and removed the key from Pope's glove, and used it to open the front door. He went in, took off his boots and coat, and began turning on lights. He walked the house, flipping every switch, every lamp, the bathroom lights, garage light, pouring on light. He stood in the blazing yellow of his front room window and gazed at the dark shape in the snow. He raised a force field around his mind and kept everything outside of it—wife and child, mother and father, the idea that the sun would rise on him ever again. He thought: I could eat a whole chicken. Or a pizza. The snow fell and fell on Pope, and Bradshaw watched it and thought: I'm either damned or I'm not, but I am *starving.*

He went to the kitchen. He found ham and turkey and Irish farmhouse cheese in the fridge, and made a thick, chewy sandwich. Lots of mayonnaise. No vegetables. His mouth was dry, and he had a hard time choking down the first bite.

"Not coming in!" he said, spraying crumbs and bits of half-chewed meat.

It was a delicious sandwich. He took another bite, but it turned impossible in his parched mouth, and he spat it onto the counter, a fleshy lump. He'd have to clean this up before he called the police. "A *hell* of a sandwich!" he said. He was holding it in both hands, staring at the empty places he had bitten away. He walked toward the front of the house. He had a vision of himself welcoming the officers. His demeanor would be pitched perfectly. Just the way Pope would do it. It would be no time for smiling. Whatever he said would be believable.

Nominated by Kim Barnes

A TAB OF IRON ON THE TONGUE

by SANDRA LIM

from THE ACCOUNT

Each time you see a full moon rising,
you imagine it will express
what your life cannot otherwise express,
that it's a figure of speech.

This really means watching yourself
turn something unknown into
something manageable.

As human tendencies go, this one is not
so terrible, and possibly winsome, besides.
Say *November*, and you name
the death working itself out in you,
season after season.

Call the bed you lie down into each night
a *raft* or an *island*, depending on
whether it's love or work you're running from.

Every moon has so much to say
about the unsolvable losses.
When it disappears behind a cloud,

filled with its own shining intentions,
it's an important translation.

When Schoenberg pointed out
the eraser on his pencil, he said, "This end
is more important than the other."

Nominated by Maureen Stanton

IF IT WERE ANYONE ELSE

fiction by LINCOLN MICHEL

from NOON

A bald man buddied up to me in the elevator, but he was no buddy of mine. He was much older than me, yet more or less exactly as tall, not counting my hair. He was holding a brown paper bag over his crotch.

"Does this go all the way to the roof?"

I made a big show of putting my newspaper down and turning my head.

"What the hell do I know about the roof? What would I do all the way up there?"

We stood still as we moved up the building.

"Just a friendly question." He licked the bottom of his mustache with the tip of his tongue. "Hey, do you like candy beans?"

There was no one else on the elevator; then the doors opened, and a woman in a green pantsuit stepped in. She looked at us and moved to the other corner.

"Who doesn't?" I was angry.

The man opened up his paper bag and dug around. He offered me an assortment in his palm. I took three of the red and four of the purple ones.

I got out two-thirds of the way up. The building I worked in was very tall, more or less exactly as tall as the tallest building in that part of the city, not counting the antenna. I often forgot how tall the building was because I kept the office blinds half-closed. If I opened them, I would get unnerved by the eye-level workers looking back at me from the building across the street. My company occupied four floors of the building, but they weren't consecutive. Between the lowest floor we owned and the third-highest floor we owned, there was a snack company. I had been working at my company for some time. I currently worked on the top floor of the floors we owned, but I had worked on the lowest floor, and also the floor above the snack company. I had never worked on the floor that was two floors above the snack company and one floor below my current floor.

The snack company often had sample bowls set up for new products they were testing. I liked to go down there when I thought I could get away for a bit.

The older bald man was sitting in a red leather chair near the elevator. He turned and smiled up at me as I pressed the down button.

"How was the roof?" I said. "Did you find what you were looking for?"

"Oh, I couldn't get all the way to the top. I got pretty close though. It was real nice, even not quite at the top. You could see the park and everything." He was nodding his head agreeably.

"Do you have business on this floor? Those red chairs are for people who have business on this floor."

We had four red leather chairs around a coffee table in the hallway. There was also a tall, thin plant that I was pretty sure was plastic.

The man looked up at me with a cautious smile.

I looked at him in his ugly, unbuttoned suit. The top of his head shined under the fluorescent light. I must have shown my disgust on my face.

"OK," he said with an exaggerated frown. "I get it. You've got work to do. Maybe some other time."

I didn't live in the city proper, I lived in one of the outer boroughs. You couldn't see it from my office window, on account of all the tall buildings. The buildings were much shorter in my borough.

I spent a lot of time traveling over and under water. There were a lot of bridges and tunnels connecting my borough and the city. I didn't like going through the tunnels. Sometimes the subway would stop deep underground and I'd close my eyes and try to think of something other than water rushing in and drowning everyone in the car.

I'd taken the blue bridge on the subway to get to work. After work, I walked back on the brown bridge. It was a nice day and the bridge was crammed with people. There were lots of children throwing scraps of food over the railing and down into the water.

About halfway across the bridge I thought I saw the bald man and I turned quickly and tried to duck. A biker was biking past me and shouted out. He started wobbling but didn't tip over.

"You're going to kill everyone!" the biker shouted back.

A few people yelled at the biker while he was yelling at me.

I stayed crouching down for a few moments.

There were millions of people in the city, but you just never knew.

I thought I saw the bald man again that evening. The man I saw was shouting in my direction from up the street, but he had a fedora pulled down low on his head and I wasn't sure.

I stepped into a new cookie shop that had opened on my corner. Before that, it had been a macaroon shop and when I had first moved in a cupcake shop. But it had originally been a cookie shop. Things always come around like that in this part of the city.

I was wrong about the man on the street. He must have been shouting at a cab. The bald man I'd been ducking from was inside the cookie shop. He had a whole stack and a two-thirds empty glass of milk.

"Wow," he said. He jumped out of his chair. "Now this is a coincidence. This has to mean something, right?"

I thought about leaving, going to the scone shop next door, but I didn't want him to think he had that kind of power over me.

He got up beside me at the counter.

"Hey buddy, I got an idea. Do you like ball games?"

The woman at the counter was asking me about my order. Her eyeballs rolled in their sockets.

"Sure," I said. "Everyone likes ball games."

"Let's go to the ball game. You and me. Just two guys watching a ball game. What's wrong with that? I got an extra ticket."

I didn't look back at the man, but I felt his hand pressing down on my shoulder. I could tell he was going to keep bothering me. He was like a lost mangy dog I'd accidentally fed scraps to.

"Just this once." I sighed. "One ball game."

The man slapped his hands together and walked toward the door.

"Not now. I want to finish my snack. I came here to have a snack."

The man had the door open and he started to close it.

"We'll miss the first inning," he said. He looked surprisingly annoyed, but then he cheered up. "That's OK. The team never gets going until the second or third. OK. Yeah. I'll be here when you're done."

He led me to a damp parking garage deep underground and unlocked the doors to a beige sedan.

The man looked at me and started to say something, but he stopped himself. He faced forward and turned on the ignition.

"Let's just take it slow. One day at a time."

We drove up the slanted cement.

"I only thought we could go to a nice ball game. Let's listen to some rock 'n' roll."

We were still a few floors too far underground. Then the static broke into clear guitars as we drove onto the level ground.

There were bits of trash all over the floor of the car, old snack wrappers and the like.

"This is a pigsty. Do you live in here? How old is this car, anyway? It still has a tape deck. They don't even make tapes anymore!"

His face and head started to turn a reddish color, and his knuckles turned white on the steering wheel. I saw his chapped lips count quietly down from ten.

"What do you think about our bullpen? " he said after a minute. He tried to smile. "Let's talk about the bullpen."

The ballpark was in yet another borough. The road was flat all the way there. It was a brand-new ballpark that had cost the team and the city a lot of money. It was nice and open. The breeze could come in and out, and there were all different types of food and snacks being sold, even sushi. It had all the modern amenities. There were always lots of families and old friends walking around. I went to this ballpark pretty frequently with clients for my company. I never knew where the seats my company bought for us would be. Sometimes the clients and I were way at the top, overhanging the field. Other times we were down low, almost level with the players.

When the man and I pulled up, there were no other cars in the parking lot. There was no one walking up and down the stadium. It was just quiet and the man and me in a dirty old car.

He turned off the gas and hung his bare head.

"The game must be tomorrow," he said after a bit.

I gave a laugh. I reached out and placed a hand calmly on his damp, bald head.

"Isn't this just perfect? You dumb schmuck! Harass me all day and take me to an abandoned ballpark."

He got out of the car and then I got out after him.

The man tore his suit jacket off and rolled it into a ball. He pressed this against his mouth to yell into.

Gray pigeons walked around us, knocking their heads down at fossilized pizza crusts. It was quiet and peaceful.

I got up behind him and grabbed his shoulder. He dropped the jacket on the pavement.

"Hey," I said.

We were getting somewhere now.

Nominated by Noon, Mike Newirth, Marc Watkins

ANNIE RADCLIFFE, YOU ARE LOVED

fiction by BARRETT SWANSON

from AMERICAN SHORT FICTION

1· THE BOSE WAS UNDER THE BRETON

Chalk drawings smothered the driveway. Crude flowers, bad stars. The new owners had planted a wall of dense shrubbery around the yard, a landscaped way of saying *Fuck Off.* A toddler-sized boulder still sat at the edge of the driveway, the street numbers stenciled in spray paint to its side. Arla leaned against her spavined Taurus and cupped a hand over her eyes. 1565 Deepmire Circle.

Stuck to the door's beveled glass window was a Post-it note covered in wonky cursive, a child's scrawl. Or a serial killer's. Or a child serial killer's. It was unclear how the adjectival functioned here. Could be a killer of children, or a child who killed. Maybe it was both. *Breathe out the poison.* This was something Dr. Klar, at their Thursday sessions, urged her to repeat. "Go ahead. Breathe out the poison."

> *Hello House-Sitter (Jeannie forgot to give me your name?!), Thank you, thank you, thank you for saying yes on such short notice. The key is under the mat. Yes, we are THAT obvious (har-har). You're welcome to whatever's in the fridge. Darwin's food is under the sink. Cup in AM, half-cup in PM. Don't look behind the Breton print, that's where we keep the safe (Egad!!). OK, Jeannie said you were good, so we trust you.*

Plus, Tom wired the house with surveillance, so look up and wave. JUST KIDDING! Annie's recital's in Buffalo on Sunday, which = home Tuesday. Nationals! We can't believe it. OK. Thanks, again. Seriously, though, don't look behind the Breton . . . OK, OK: JK!

–The Radcliffes.

Reflection in the door's glass: a Joan Jett haircut, a *seriously?* expression. And behind her: groomed lawn, plus helix of sprinkler water, plus paperboy, plus Swedish autos parked in long driveways, plus chubby teen boy in short-shorts jogging down the street. Amend that: ill-advised short-shorts. All of which equaled that sort of *Ozzie-and-Harriet* happiness she could recognize like a smell.

She reached for her overnight bag. Rib-cracking that Jeannie, her most recent client, had apparently given Arla a positive review. It had been Jeannie's husband who had pushed her against the dryer in the basement, returning to retrieve the kid's flippers and snorkel a day after the family left for their holiday. Smiled carnivorously at her, uttered smutty blandishments. His name was Mason or Buck. She couldn't remember. Something lumberjacky. Something rural. A name for the plains. He had given her a bruise.

Dr. Klar said her paramours functioned as a form of escapism not unlike her procurement of certain Ziploc baggies. That's what he called them. Her "paramours." As if all her trysts were committed in chintzy chateaus, she and her lover sipping Beaujolais. *No, no, amour. We'll eat the croissants après the lovemaking, oui?* Dr. Klar was heavy-set and wore lots of tweed, looking always as though he were holding back a burp.

On Thursdays, he would sometimes rest his chin on his fist and say, "If I can be candid, Arla, I think you might be prone to self-mythology." She still hadn't heard back about her book, *Character Theory of Finite Groups.* She had been told that university presses took eons to respond. She imagined the black-and-white author photo: dark cardigan, horn-rimmed glasses, a fierce fuck-it-all expression. Then chided herself because who the fuck cared what she looked like in her author photo. Imagined, instead, the critics calling her work "revolutionary" and "seminal." Too close to *semenal*? Imagined comparisons to Scarry, Acker, and Sontag.

Standing on the welcome mat, she futzed with the keys. Plan was to swallow the contents of a Ziploc baggie. Plan was to sit in front of the TV and study the campy anthropology of TLC and Bravo. Then shower, then raid the liquor cabinet for a Glenfiddich or Glenlivet—any Glen, really—and fall asleep on the couch.

Housesitting at her old house. If she were in front of her class, lecturing to those bovine-eyed college freshmen, she'd say, "'A plausible impossibility is preferable to a possible implausibility.' That's Aristotle. What do you guys think he meant by that?" To which students would lift their eyebrows, as if to say, *What the?* #wedontgetit. Her students had been amending their statements with more hashtags than usual lately. *Could I maybe have an extension on my paper?* #ithinkimightbepregnant. *Would you read a draft of my essay?* #iknowthissoundsmillenialbutifigetanotherbplusimgonnaselfharm.

"Come on, guys," she'd say. "What do you think our Greek polymath meant by that?"

One boy, with the scraggly beard and tilted ball cap, who'd spend the whole two-hour class looking at her tits, might say, *Uh*, rubbing his nose, *means anything's possible?*

In block-letters, she'd write a syllogism on the board:

MAJOR PREMISE: Arla Conters, PhD candidate in Applied Semiotics, your instructor for Intro Ethics, gets paid peasant wages by this illustrious university to teach you how to think. She housesits in the suburbs on the weekends to afford her coffin-sized studio in Wicker Park, where she lives with Mr. Bojangles, her parrot, who has cancer.
MINOR PREMISE: The house she grew up in is in Kenilworth, one of those suburbs. (Yes, parrots get cancer).
CONCLUSION: Arla Conters might have to housesit her old house.

Wouldn't tell them that she posted fliers in the Kenilworth Public Library. Wouldn't tell them that sometimes, after consuming the contents of a Ziploc baggie, she'd drive out of the city and take the exit for Lake Avenue and let muscle memory direct the car to Deepmire Circle, where she would drive at a glacial pace up and down the street, trying to peer inside the windows of her old house, to see what had become of it and whether some brave family had taken residence there, even after everything that had happened. Wouldn't tell her students that when Jeannie had called her about a friend who needed a house sitter on short notice, and when she said, "Sure, no problem," and took down the details on a sodden bar napkin, she nearly wept at the sight of that address.

On last semester's evaluations, one student wrote:

> Arla (who insists we call her that, Arla, instead of Miss Cond-ers, because, she says, gender-based titles are "vulgarities of overthrown paternalism"–#shereallydidteachmealot), some-times wore fishnets and goth makeup to class because she thought we'd "pay more attention to [her] lectures on post-structuralism if [she] dress[ed] up like a character from *Twi-light*." If we didn't do our homework, she'd threaten us with hexes. She seemed very troubled. I really did learn a whole lot, though.

Through the front door, she expected to find the same mudroom from childhood, all their shoes lined up: Dad's high-tops, Mom's sandals, her own Chuck Taylors, doodled with Bic-pen hieroglyphs–strangled stick faces, the lyrics to "All Apologies"–and Daphne's pink Velcro sneakers, which Arla wanted to keep, even though Mom wanted to donate every-thing to Goodwill after the accident.

But the mudroom was now the kitchen, and the kitchen was twice the size it had been. Its appliances were glinting and catalog-bought. Here was a chrome Kohler sink. Here was a stainless-steel fridge, sur-feited with gag magnets and kooky family photos. In a Polaroid, the Radcliffe father stands outside of a touristic restaurant with his shirt pulled up over his turgid belly, pointing with disbelief at its size. An-other: the Radcliffe mother in a pirate costume, her hook-hand threat-ening the neck of the teenaged daughter, an auburn-haired girl with a freckled complexion who was wearing fairy-wings and a bug-eyed ex-pression of mock terror.

Looked through the bay window. The backyard was bombed out, the trees anorexic and darkly scorched–struck by lightning, maybe, but still standing. Something about the singed bushes and the toasted tree trunks evoked the aura of nuclear wasteland. Strange that the note hadn't mentioned this. Had there been some ghastly accident–a mishap with fireworks? A defective grill? The lawn was leprous with patches of burnt grass. Out here one summer, when she was twelve or thirteen, Dad spent the whole night after dinner trying to catch fireflies in mason jars, which made Daphne and her mother laugh as he lunged awkwardly across the yard. Standing at the patio door, a five-year-old Daphne said, with stoic dismay, "Daddy's not a very good catcher." Around bedtime, Dad ferried the jars to her and Daphne's shared bedroom, arranging them on the nightstand, explaining breathlessly how they could be used as nightlights. Intermittently, the bugs would incandesce, bathing her and her sister's faces with Vermeer light. "They'll die in there," she scoffed, and pulled the covers over her head. But Daphne pealed, "Coooool," and said, "Thanks, Daddy!" Hours passed before Arla huffed out of bed, propped open the window, and climbed onto the roof to smoke a gasper and let the insects go. When she crawled back inside, Daphne was awake, holding the other jar out to her, saying, "Do mine too, Arla."

Opened the sliding glass door. The sky overhead photogenic: blue expanse marbled with bathwater clouds. The air was marinated in chlorine. There was the swimming pool. Same kidney-shaped depression. Same high-board ladder. The pool's surface was circuited with sunlight. The Radcliffes had purchased new patio furniture, replacing the wrought-iron table and chairs that used to overlook the deep end–the table that had been ritually overburdened by clean towels and plastic rafts when her own family lived here.

During her fourteenth birthday party, while all her other girlfriends lounged by the pool, Arla and her best friend, Autumn Petrarch, had stolen away to her second-story bedroom, where they pilfered sips from a bottle of schnapps, which Autumn had smuggled past the parents in a hemp rucksack, and as they sat on the polar shag carpet, they laughed full throatedly at their boldness, and could hear the chirpy babble of the other girls by the pool coming through the window, and when everything became funny, they swerved down the stairs, through the patio door, out to the hot deck, which scorched the soft pads of their feet. They scurried past the stereo that sat on the edge of a deck chair, its taut cord stretching to an outdoor socket. It was late afternoon and complex systems of shade moved across the yard. Sun-glinted and undulant, the pool was an oval of chemical jelly. Some of her friends did bad handstands in the shallow end. Others saw who could hold their breath the longest. Daphne shrieked by the side ladder with her eyes pinched shut, calling out "Marco!" again and again, reaching out for someone to bring an end to the game's required blindness. Through the cataracts of flavored liquor, Arla saw the world as a rococo blur of the senses. Loose movements. Delayed shouts. Everything was hysterical. She wobbled to the stereo and put on that summer's anthem, Tupac's "All About U," causing her friends to squeal and scamper up the shallow end's submerged steps, a dozen of them emerging in vivid swimsuits to boogie unselfconsciously on the hot deck, leaving Daphne alone in the pool. Tupac blared through the tinny speakers. Daphne called out, "Marco! Marco!" Autumn and Arla twirled at the edge of the deck, all limbs and exuberance, until there was an atmospheric shift, the ground betrayed her–she tripped over something? the stereo cord?– and the music abruptly stopped and the pool momentarily glowed and her sister's body went rigid in the shallow end. Then the sound of twenty girls screaming. Arla got up. Her knees were bleeding even though she couldn't feel them. She went to the pool's edge, her legs bent, as if she were about to jump in.

With her students last semester, the day before spring break, she discussed the problems of selfless action: "What's a paradox?"

Blank stares, a cough that sounded stage-directed.

"Paradox is like 'jumbo shrimp.' Get it? A self-negating idea? OK, so why is a selfless action a paradox?"

"I might be totally wrong here." This was the Mennonite girl from Indiana who wore Princess Leia braids and dressed as if she were an extra in a production of *Our Town*. "But do you like mean that selfish ends always motivate us? That we only perform selfless actions so that we end up feeling good about ourselves? #thereasonwhycharitable-foundationsalwaysincludethephilanthropistsnames #asinthebillandmelindagatesfoundation."

"Yes. Absolutely. Anytime I do good things for others, I feel good about it. It's as much about me as it is about them. In this sense, any act I do willingly satisfies my desire to do it, thereby rendering it at least partly selfish. OK. So, tell me: can you think of any truly selfless action?"

"So but wait," another student asked. "What about the Holocaust? Like those emaciated guys who would give their parcel of bread to the skinnier guy next to them?"

"I'm not saying that that action isn't good. I'm just saying it's not entirely selfless. The giver is either consciously or unconsciously thinking about Adonai as he's relinquishing his rye-crisp. And if the motivating animus of his charity is his own eternal salvation, then he can't be said to be operating from selfless premises."

Someone else said, "What about risking your life to save someone from a burning building?

Now the boob-ogler in the ball cap joined in. "Uh, but doesn't your martyrdom make you like the potential object of societal praise? Before you run into the building, don't you know you'll be a local hero?"

She watched her more talkative students slowly enact the argument, the idealists against the nihilists, which made her feel like a second-rate disciple of Ayn Rand. The rest of the class displayed various configurations of boredom. One student yawned. Another's head was bowed, as if in prayer, sneaking glances at a smart phone.

"Kant would say that an action is only worthy if it's performed out of duty to moral law, rather than out of practicality or desire. John Stuart Mill would argue that the proper course of action is one that yields the greatest aggregate happiness among all sentient human beings, regardless of the worthiness of the motivation. But if my desire is to be charitable or morally good, then am I actually adhering to Kant's idea of duty? And if I martyr myself, am I abiding the greatest happiness principle? Wouldn't my sacrificial death cause more pain to others?"

The EMTs later told her parents that the water had still been dangerous. That it was a good thing she hadn't jumped in.

OK, so on second thought, maybe not wait to raid the liquor cabinet. Went back inside, through the sliding glass door. First, better set an alarm in case she dozed. Good, good. OK, now where was the baggie? On the breakfast island were her keys, the note, some random change—the items sounded like something from a Joni Mitchell song. Oh, Joni—how many girls did you made weak and stupid? Still, "A Case of You" was a song she could get behind. "A Case of You" was her jam.

OK. The baggie was here. In. Her. Hand. Her dealer said two was enough and that three was a trip. She laid four tablets on her tongue and chewed them up. Tasted bitter and acidic, like turpentine—down, down. The cupboards were full of Williams-Sonoma porcelain—large mugs, big bowls, outsized dinner plates—but such items could no longer serve as accurate semions of class or politics, because of course the entire semiotics and hegemonic heft of America's late capitalism was now predicated on the rather flimsy premise that—tumblers! There they were. She shuffled to the fridge for ice cubes—Hello, Fat Daddy! Hello, Mama Pirate!—and, now, where was the liquor cabinet, to the left of the—Darwin! Here, kitty, kitty. Better feed him now. Food was under the–OK, woozy now, her dealer wasn't lying–sink. And my, my, my. What do we have–blue. Sixty dollars a shot, Johnny Walker Blue. Don't mind if I. The stereo was in the living room. She needed some Joni Mitchell. The Bose was under the Breton. The phrase sounded like code for something exigent and evil. Paging Dr. Klar, paging Dr. Klar: Your patient says, "The Bose is under the Breton." *The Song of the Lark.* A pretentious name. All it was was a beautiful girl holding a scythe. A pretty painting, though. She peeked behind it because why not. No safe. #thefamilywholivedherewashidingnothing. But, wait–on the CD rack. *Blue.* She and Dad had danced to "My Old Man" on the patio on the third anniversary of Daphne's accident, when Dad had skipped work, and she stayed home from school, and they spent the whole day listening to twinkly music by the pool, which was where she somehow found herself now, by the Radcliffe's pool, climbing the felt rungs of the high board ladder, a brimmed glass of Johnny Walker in her loose hand. The narcotics lent the yard a pixelated finish, as if everything had been treated with food coloring. Dad didn't blame her for what happened. She was standing on the pebbled board, rough like a cat's tongue against her cold feet, leaning over the edge, her reflection shattered and shifting on the pool's surface. She often wondered whether Dad would have rather it had been her who had been in the water. The Bose in the living room was blasting Ms. Mitchell. To her students: "The only selfless action is one that's unintentional." Her dealer wasn't bullshitting. #thisbaggiewasserious. Paging Dr. Klar. Someone was calling out to her. The glass was gone from her open hand. "Hey, Lady! Don't!" The Bose was under the Breton. A woman holding a scythe. A killer of children or a child who killed. *Breathe out the poison.* The board let go of her feet.

2· THE TREATMENTS

As he approached MERCY GENERAL, the totally bald boy skipped down the sidewalk, whistling "Don Giovanni." He then sashayed down the hospital's flagstone walkway, which was flanked by peonies, and pretended that the flowers were impoverished plebes who had lined his fiefdom's thoroughfare, just to watch him pass. In his head, he spoke to them with haughty sophistication, a tyrant attempting to quell a peasant coup: *Why must you crowd me, rabble? Be gone with you, needy sycophants. Filth! Slime! OK, OK, JK, guys, JK. Sheesh, take it easy. You guys are goofs. You guys seriously crack my ribs. We coo, guys? But seriously, bonhomies, how about letting your highness pass? How about letting a little guy squeeze through so he might visit his ailing father?* Then ambled happily through the automatic doors.

In the boy's ergonomic backpack were slabs of frozen meat. Every Monday, Wednesday, Friday, Gordon did his Care for Another meal program, which was sort of like Meals on Wheels, but because he was only twelve and couldn't drive a car and was thus ineligible to volunteer for M.O.W., he decided to establish his own program, which essentially consisted of his ferrying vacuum-packed Salisbury steaks and chicken Kievs to the neighborhood geriatrics on bike or by foot, after school, pro-bono. He had only four clients but had been saving up his post-tithing profits from his weekend lemonade stand to afford a full-color ad in the *Tribune*, which he thought would be a much more efficacious way to promote his start-up charity than simply doing cold calls via the White Pages, which had been his initial strategy before realizing that it wasn't exactly the brightest star in the whole marketing-strategy Orion.

On Tuesdays, he had Remedial Debate, which was like a step down from Model U.N., which he tried out for and didn't get accepted into, which of course made him feel the Bleakest of Coffins for like three weeks–that is, until he got the idea to petition the Donald K. Deepmire Middle School's Extracurricular Activities Board to let him start a Getting-the-Word-Out-About-the-Total-Fun-and-Literary-Genius-of-C.S.-Lewis's-*The-Chronicles-of-Narnia* Club, whose members now totaled a number of two, and which met before school on Mondays and Fridays.

On Wednesday afternoons, before Care for Another, he took the el to Mercy General and rode the rickety elevator up to Oncology to be with Dad during his treatments. Wearing an avocado-green bandana that Gordon bought him when his hair started to fall out, Dad would lie back on a huge La-Z-Boy with oven mitts on his hands and wine coolers on his feet, lest the treatments do some serious radiational damage to his nails, and while plugged into wheezing machines, Dad–being Dad, which = atheist, which = sad–would say something about how the school was in violation of the First Amendment for letting his son start such a club, and promised that if these weekly poisonings weren't at that minute withering him away to an impotent husk of a litigator, he'd fire up a legal brief so exacting and severe that it would make the boy's Yeshua-loving school principal squirt his khaki shorts. But then Gordon said that he didn't even bring up Christianity at the club meetings, because mostly they just talked about Mr. Lewis's subtext and how supremely cool lions were.

Because sometimes, if he was being completely honest, the simple things–like lions or Congress or the existence of gypsies–totally astonished him. Like how utterly weird it was that human beings had to sleep, how everyone had to, like, hurl themselves into unconsciousness for eight hours every night, that it was like a requirement for living, lest you be raccoon-eyed and grumpy, all zombie-like and weird. Or how migrating birds looked like arrows, as if all their shrill cheeps were just code for: *This way, this way!* Could they really be talking to him, the birds? Or maybe like God was, through them? Or through the trees, maybe? During big storms, the crowns of trees nodded like the heads of horses dashing in full sprint, like a friend tilting his head conspiratorially down an alleyway, as if to say, *Psst, yo man, check this out.* It was as if he and the world were in cahoots, coconspirators, they were pulling a heist–*I won't blow the whistle, Mugsy, get us cheesed!* And, gosh, how hard everyone was trying to stay in the game, to really let it all hang out. Like, *par exemple*, Dad. Mom gone, a tumor in his kidney, but still Dad went to Mercy General and completed the treatments without complaint. Still Dad wore his plastic Groucho glasses/nose/mustache while he made Gordon breakfast before school, just to make Gordon laugh. Said things like, "This morning I shot an elephant in my pajamas. How he got into my pajamas, I'll never know." Which cracked the boy's ribs. OK, Dad was still an atheist. And, technically speaking, Dad probably wasn't going to play Canasta with St. Peter at the pearly gates when his ticker ran out of double As. Which was scary. Would say things like, "Faith is for people who need it." Would trash the Bibles the boy gave him every year for his birthday. Would say, "Gobs mess you," whenever the boy sneezed.

The Mercy General elevator dinged on the thirteenth floor, Oncology Department, and Gordon hopscotched down the tile hallway–two feet on black squares, one foot on the white–and then zoomed real fast and did a hopping cartoon stop in the doorway of the chemo room, hoping to get a laugh out of Dad.

Inside, urine-colored light spilled through the dull hospital window, making Dad, who was sitting in the huge recliner, look jaundiced and obscene, making the whole situation seem way too dramatic, like a weepy symphony should be playing, like he and Dad should say stuff in hushed tones like those bad actors on the soap operas they watched on Saturdays whenever Dad was feeling dizzy.

"My God, these tubes! These wires! What are you doing to this man?" Gordon said. He said this every week.

Then Dad said, as always, "They're draining me alive!"

Then Gordon laughed, not because it was funny anymore, but because Dad was playing along, which meant he was OK. Dad's forearms were snarled with a highway of tubes.

Gordon walked over and sat in the open recliner next to Dad. "Shall we do a post-mortem?" Dad asked.

"On what? School?" Gordon said.

"Tell me about biology."

"Mrs. Vinka said birds using cigarette butts to build their nests because the nicotine works like an insecticide and keeps out bacteria was an example of evolution."

"And what'd you say?"

A little monitor beside Dad beeped. A nurse entered the room and gave the boy an obligatory smile. She patted his glabrous scalp.

"I said that evolution was only a theory. And that Mrs. Vinka should have explained that to the rest of the students."

"And she said that evolution isn't a theory?"

"Well, yeah, I mean, no. She didn't say that. What she said was the best science we have supports evolution."

"And you told her about fossil records."

"I said that fossil records increasingly show that no animal has ever switched from one type of animal into another type of animal."

The machine beside Dad clanked and wheezed. His throat was forested with long, crunchy hairs, his face looking gaunt and rime-caked, like that of a parched refugee. Another nurse came in and put fresh wine-coolers around his feet.

"And this supposedly strengthens the case for creationism, is what you're telling me?"

Gordon shrugged.

"You want to know what I want to know?" Dad asked.

"Why regardless and irregardless mean the same thing?"

Dad laughed. His laughter was booming and sonorous, more like he was yelling. It was good. It was good to make Dad laugh even when they were arguing. Two sparrows zipped past the hospital window. Outside, the sky was the washed-out blue of nursery blankets.

"You think God created the heavens and the earth in seven days?"

"Six days, but yeah."

"And that He impregnated Mary without intercourse, immaculate conception is what they call it at that Sunday school you insist I let you go to?"

"Uh huh."

"So, he did all of this, but you don't think he could hardwire the genetics of animals to switch from one species to another? That's what you're telling me?"

"But—"

"Bah," Dad said, which was what Dad said when he didn't have energy to talk anymore. And then he started coughing. Gordon couldn't tell whether this was real, since sometimes his father would bend over and start hacking just to make Gordon feel bad for him, just so Gordon would stop pestering him about hermeneutics.

After the treatments, Dad drove Gordon to his Care for Another appointment with Mr. Cavanaugh, who always ordered chicken Kiev and would regale Gordon with stories about the war. As Dad listened to NPR, Gordon leaned his head against the window, his breath fogging up the glass in little botanical designs, which momentarily erased the montage of homes and gas stations and prairies that scrolled by outside.

"OK, think about it this way," he said, turning to look at Dad, whose eyes looked dark and withered, like used teabags.

"Cub—"

"Just wait. I didn't even say anything yet."

"Cub, it's been a long—"

"But just say I'm wrong, then what do I lose when I die? Nothing, right? So I lived my life believing that Jesus was God, and then I die and there's nothing but dreamless sleep, like you said. Like the TV powers down, the screen just goes black, you said. But say *you* are wrong—"

"Hey, Cub—"

"And of course I'm not trying to say that you're going anywhere for sure or anything, I'm not like saying anything about tridents and lakes of fire, it's just that—"

"Do you really think that's a good reason to believe in something?"

Dad glanced over at Gordon, whose bald pate was pale and nicked with cuts. Every couple days, the boy used his father's Gillette to make his statement of solidarity.

"Is what a good reason?"

"That if I don't believe in God then I'm going to hell?"

"Well."

"Well? Then what about your God's free will, Peach-Pants? That I supposedly have free will and can choose whether or not to believe in him, yes? Isn't that what your precious Mr. Lewis says–"

"Dad–"

"–In *The Problem of Pain*. Don't think your daddy hasn't read what's on your nightstand, Lean-Jeans. But how is it free will when I'm threatened by eternal burning if I don't believe in him? Isn't that a kind of celestial hostage? Why should I believe in something that holds a gun to my head? And if booking a ticket to heaven is the only reason why anyone believes in God, then that's just plain selfish, isn't it? Why would you want to believe in that?"

The car flew past a strip mall, a Western Union, and a Dairy Queen. Soon they were on Riverside Drive, two blocks away from the townhouse with the rotting front porch into which they had moved after Mom left.

"He is love, only love, Dad. All you have to do is believe in love."

"You're quoting the Beatles?"

"David said, 'Commit your ways to the Lord, trust Him, and He will act for you.'"

Dad palmed his forehead and adjusted the bandana. "Why isn't the very fact that your mother has left us for greener pastures and that your poppa has terminal non-Hodgkin's evidence enough of–"

"Dad."

"–and even if that bastard does exist, don't you think he's got some explaining to do? I want him to explain–"

"*Dad!*"

"What?"

"You're bleeding."

A rivulet of blood was slowly running down his swathed temple. They pulled into Mr. Cavanaugh's driveway, and, unsure of what to do, Gordon rested his head against Dad's shoulder. In the stranger's driveway, in the idling car, they listened to Terry Gross interview a secret service agent from JFK's detail, the one who was trained to jump in front of the bullet, but who, at the critical moment, didn't.

Standing on the stoop, the boy unlocked Mr. Cavanaugh's door, using the key hidden under the bristly GO AWAY mat, and waltzed through the foyer, which was overhung by a huge chandelier that sent geodes of light swirling across the floor, making the boy feel like he was in the school gymnasium, two-stepping under a disco ball during a slow dance. At the other end of the front hallway was a grandfather clock with gold Roman numerals, which clanged every fifteen minutes like something out of Poe and gave the boy the Bleakest of Coffins. He attempted to moonwalk through the front hall, looking over his shoulder for Mr. C, whom he usually found in the den, watching *Maury* on TV. He did a quick trot and then a sock-slide into the kitchen where he saw a Threat Level 4 Safety Violation–i.e., the burner was still on. An empty pan that had probably been boiling water was now cooking nothing on the stove. He turned the dial to OFF and shuffled through the family room, toward the patio.

Mr. C was snoozing on a deck chair, in the parallelogram of shade the purple awning made, and opened on his chest was a water-wrinkled *Playboy*, whose front cover featured a blonde woman covering her mouth with lurid nails, as if to say *Oopsy*. Gordon snatched the magazine off Mr. Cavanaugh's chest and tossed it inside, where he wouldn't be tempted to look at it. Beneath the magazine was a pair of binoculars, so Gordon turned toward the thin forest at the back of Mr. C's lot, through which he could see the neighbor's swimming pool and high dive. While Mr. C claimed to be an "amateur ornithologist," Gordon had once caught the old man ogling the neighbor woman–Mrs. Radcliffe–tanning topless on her patio. For reasons that passed understanding, Mr. C referred to her breasts as "yabohs," as in, "What, what, you can't blame me! Look at those yabohs."

Back inside, standing at Mr. Cavanaugh's sink where he was rinsing kale for a salad, the boy looked out the window at the backyard forest, which was split by a shallow, stone-pocked gully that demarcated the Cavanaugh and the Radcliffe properties, and saw, through that mess of tree trunks and cross-hatched branches, a woman stumble from the Radcliffe house.

3. TELL ME IS IT REALLY LOVE

Jogging down Deepmire Circle in blaze-orange Daisy Dukes, Jake Willing decided that the first thing he'd say if a police officer pulled up and collared him about violating the restraining order Annie Radcliffe and her family had placed against him last week was that he was just out here on a run and must have gotten lost. True, he was supposed to

100

maintain a three-block perimeter around the Radcliffe residence, but couldn't the officer see his Dri-FIT Nike running shorts and matching forefend T-shirt? Jeez, he'd say, heaven forfend a guy go for a post-prandial jog in this town without getting an unconstitutional pat down, he'd say. He was just trying to shed some weight, officer. You know, stay tip-top. Trim off the floatie of blubber that spilled over his beltline. What his mother so endearingly called his life preserver. What his friends Munchie and the Beave poked during passing hours at school, yelling, "Dough-Boy!" OK, OK, the truth? The truth was maybe that he was out here running because he was planning to try out for the Reese-Meyer-Shannon High School wrestling team in a couple weeks, since scuttlebutt had it that the swiveling and mellifluous Annie Rad-cliffe, his ex-girlfriend, was now dating Travis Blokum, the Roman-nosed stud on varsity, who wore a letter jacket and had the distinction of being the only sophomore at Reese-Meyer-Shannon with a full beard. Jake thought if he could just crossface cradle Travis Blokum during a public match, Annie's family might drop the restraining order against him and he could win her back.

Occasionally glancing over his shoulder to see whether any squad cars had pulled up, Jake Willing trotted down the cracked gravel of Deepmire Circle, pretending to do a cardio workout rather auspiciously called "The Maximum Body Plan," which he read about in *Men's Health*, a glossy periodical to which he had only recently subscribed. His older brother, Marty, had proposed that the reason Annie Radcliffe didn't like Jake anymore was probably because Jake was a twerpy little pussy who didn't know the first thing about seducing a woman, which was why Jake had started doing mountain climbers and suicide sprints up and down the Morning Falls subdivision every afternoon after school–i.e. to get ripped–i.e. to redress the considerable paucity of self-confidence demonstrated by his wearing way too much GAP–i.e. to win Annie back. Marty was twenty-three and lived in Los Angeles, where he worked as a spokesman for something called the P90X At-Home-Gym, and sometimes, when he was up late watching TV, Jake saw his older brother in the P90X infomercials, pumping iron to smooth jazz under a caption that didn't really promise anything but simply an-nounced: TEN POUNDS OF MUSCLE IN TWO WEEKS!

"Plus," Marty said, over the phone, "you probably crowded her. Did you crowd her?" Only if crowding her meant composing for her tons of Petrarchan sonnets, writing them with special calligraphy pens on parchment paper, and then stuffing these poems through the vent of her locker both before and after school. Only if crowding her meant driving her and her friends to the Brookside Mall on Saturdays because he honestly liked Theresa and Marsha, even if they did give him guff about his flatiron chinos.

Jake rounded the cul-de-sac at the end of Deepmire Circle, passed the yard with the snippy white dog, and started back toward the start of the subdivision. His stride was hampered and trudging, as if he were shin-deep in snowdrifts. This was his eleventh lap around the neighborhood, but he had decided to keep running until a) the cops showed up, in which case he would haul ass for the trees behind the Radcliffe house, near the pool; or b) the owner of the rusted Taurus that was parked on the street in front of Annie's house emerged from the front door. He couldn't remember whether Travis Blokum drove a Taurus.

Annie had dumped him last month. On Facebook. "It's over," she wrote. She posted this status update to her Timeline, and within an hour, over half of the Reese-Meyer-Shannon sophomore class had "liked" it. Annie's friend Theresa replied by posting a homemade photomontage of Annie and Jake's relationship–Instagram pics of "A&J eating wings at Chili's," "A&J skiing at Sunburst Mountain," and "A&J snuggling on a paisley basement couch"–all of which was tracked by Boyz II Men's "It's So Hard to Say Goodbye to Yesterday," and on which Travis Blokum had commented, writing, "So fucking lame." Sitting in the ambient blue glow of his laptop, with tears running down his face, Jake thought, *Whatever Travis Blokum, you're the one who's fucking lame.* He almost posted that. But then he just tried to Gchat Annie.

JAKE WILLING (4:23 PM): is this for real? *it's over?*

ANNIE RADCLIFFE (4:43 PM): i'm sorry, jake. but ive been talking to theresa and marsha, and they say your not mysterious enuf 4 me. We talked about it @ lunch and they say I need someone whose got more whatdoucallit mystique. someone whose brooding. who broods.

JAKE WILLING (4:43 PM): i brood! i can totally brood! like sometimes ill just sit in my closet with the lights off, listening to the oldies like third-eye-blind on my ipod, and i think about how bad it is in the congo. or like about sudanese orphans, and get really sad.

JAKE WILLING (5:37 PM): you still there

ANNIE RADCLIFFE (6:45 PM): ur too nice for me, j. marsha thinks we need to spend time apart to discover ourselves, to establish tru identities and i agree. i just think i need to Xperience some other guys before i lock myself into a longterm high school relationship. weave already gone to 2 dances together.

JAKE WILLING (6:45 PM): annie . . .

JAKE WILLING (6:57 PM): wtf, annie. this isnt fair

JAKE WILLING (7:13 PM): i dont care what T or M say. Ur the stars of my night sky, annie.

In his despair, Jake took his phone into the closet and called his brother. "She posted the whole conversation on her News Feed."

"Listen, dippy, you need to shrug this shit off. Just do the workouts I gave you and all the hot chicks will be all on your nuts like fucking barnacles pronto."

"Maybe I'll go over to her house tonight and do that floating luminary idea I was going to use to ask her to homecoming."

"How the fuck did we bathe in the same genetic bath, is what I want to know. You sound like a fucking dandy, J. Like a little dandy in a petticoat who calls out for his governess whenever he soils his pantaloons, or some shit. I hate to tell you this, brother, but this thing with Annie has gone the way of the dodo."

First, he drove to Hobby Lobby and procured the necessary materials: luminary bags and glow-in-the-dark paint. After having acquired these supplies, he stopped at Men's Wearhouse and purchased a new tweed suit with leather elbows, which he thought would accurately convey the full breadth and measure of his brooding mystique, something he hadn't sufficiently exhibited while the two of them were together.

And so that night, around midnight, he snuck out of his house and drove over to the Radcliffe residence. He tiptoed across the dark backyard with the same expression as a bad cat burglar, and proceeded to skulk around the swimming pool, which glowed a muted blue and sent a shifting web of metallic light across the underbellies of the backyard's trees. On the patio he arranged the luminary bags at intervals, and on the pool deck he wrote "Annie Radcliffe, You Are Loved" in glow-in-the-dark paint. After dashing to his car to retrieve his boombox, he cued up Whitney Houston's "How Will I Know" to accompany the mesmeric aerial display he was about to surprise Annie with. And so, after checking the Windsor knot of his new silk tie in the little compact mirror he removed from his suit pocket, he cleared his throat and lit the first match. He ignited the luminary bags, which began to levitate like huge lightning bugs, passing the second-floor bedroom windows of the Radcliffe residence at a languid, dreamy pace. He hit play on the stereo and let Whitney's dulcet soprano draw Annie to the window. The lanterns coasted lazily between the trees, revolving to showcase every crimp and crevice of their shape, shrinking as they ascended. He heard someone walk out onto the eastern balcony. "Jake? Is that you?" Annie asked, sounding groggy and nonplussed. He smiled to himself. "What the hell are you doing?" she asked. "I'm winning you back," he said. And just as Whitney climbed an arpeggio and asked the listener how she could ever ascertain whether some nameless "he" really loved her, Jake noticed in his periphery that the sky was for some reason getting lighter, brightening, and actually beginning to warm his face, causing him to turn toward the now crackling woods, the oaks and willows of which were festooned with torrents of fire, great bouquets of flames, such that the whole sky above the Radcliffe residence was soon like something out of Dante, the heat and diabolic roar of which drew Mr. Radcliffe, Annie's father, to the opposite bedroom's balcony, where he stood totally naked, his form emblazoned by the fire, his dong much longer than Jake's, dangling there like a bent yam. "You little fucker! You little fuck! My lawn!" Sirens sobbed in the distance, and soon the fire trucks arrived, and brave, meaty men–guys who looked like grown-up versions of Travis Blokum–hosed down the trees. Sulfur perfumed the air, and specks of ash eddied across the yard, dissolving blackly in the pool like carcinogenic snow. Mr. Radcliffe, disturbed by the intensity of Jake's feeling for his daughter, decided to press charges and get a restraining order, and Jake spent the night in the Kenilworth Police Department's holding cell where, still wearing his Men's Wearhouse three-piece, he tried very diligently not to weep.

He was actually working up a warm shellac of sweat. He ran down Deepmire Circle for the twelfth time in what had to be less than an hour, but on this lap, as he bounced past the Radcliffe residence, he espied through the big, smudgeless front windows a wan, womanly figure drifting from room to room. Annie, he thought. Maybe Annie's home alone. He hauled ass up to the northern fringe of the property, looking for her parents' cars in the driveway. No dice. But what was the story with the decrepit Taurus? What if someone was in there right now trying to do unmentionables to Annie, acts involving corded rope and Vaseline? Or what if it just was Travis Blokum? Still, it was equally possible that it could be a pervy psychopath. It had only been a year since the Smiley Face Killer had murdered those boys in the next town over, burying their bodies in the forest and leaving cheerful graffiti on the trees. But what if something was happening right now to Annie, and he was hanging out here like a shrinking boner doing nothing? He was standing alone in the empty road. The sky overhead was that weak blue of late afternoon, an hour when the traffic finally quiets and you can hear the grackles screeching in the trees. His pulse was in his ears. Someone down the street shut off a lawnmower, and he looked left and then right in the conspiratorial manner of criminals. It wasn't impossible that something horrible was happening to Annie right now, but it was just as possible that the Taurus was Travis's or some other friend's. And yet if he didn't do anything and Annie got hurt, or was held down and got entered on a quilted bed, he'd never forgive himself. He briefly imagined a man with tattooed forearms pulling Annie's hair. But if he got caught on the Radcliffe property, it could mean further compromising his brother Marty's reputation, plus Mom and Dad's, both of whom were so embarrassed about his legal troubles that they had stopped attending their trivia nights at the Super Center and now spent their evenings at home, quietly watching reruns of *Unsolved Mysteries* and *Mad About You.* It could mean picking up litter by the side of the highway. It could mean jail time, or so said that district attorney with the walrus mustache, who told Jake he was lucky, since a restraining order was pretty much a slap on the wrist compared to the mandatory minimums for trespassing and arson. He saw himself wearing a rumpled orange jumpsuit, talking to his mother on a phone, through a pane of smudged glass.

Then he heard it. The splash. He ran across the Radcliffe lawn, each step closer to the house yielding a commensurate gush of bowel-tightening fear, and hid behind tree trunks as he approached the front door in a serpentine pattern. Finally, he cupped his hands over his eyes and peered through the front room's windows, looking for evidence of foul play. He imagined gag balls and leather swings. He imagined a sadistic séance. He imagined a pentagram painted on the walls with Annie's blood.

But no. The house was empty. Zilch. Nothing. He sprinted around the side of the garage, nearly slipping on the undone coil of hose, and entered the backyard, where all the trees were still black, charred and spindly, where meager patches of dead grass memorialized his botched attempts at romance. The surface of the pool was crimped with concentric rings expanding outward from whatever had disturbed it. A girl. Annie. Sinking. Face down. In the pool. Hair fanned out like an anemone. Breaching the three-block radius around the Radcliffe property had been a serious ethical no-no, but coming into any physical contact whatsoever with Annie Radcliffe was explicitly interdicted by the restraining order and was punishable by up to six months in jail. But there was no time. There was no choice. He shouldn't even be thinking about this, he thought. Annie wasn't even trying to surface on her own. Her body was slowly drifting toward the pool's pump and filter, bobbing a little, helplessly. Hopeful that everyone would later see his crimes as acts of valor and forgive him for this, for everything, he made a running start, took a deep breath and, failing to kick off his sneakers, jumped in.

4· A GOOD VANTAGE

Danger, Will Robinson, Gordon Weatherly thought. Here was something odd. Through the lattice of the backyard's trees, Gordon saw the thin, limping woman waltz across the Radcliffe patio in a white sundress and bare feet. Her head oscillated loosely from left to right, like a marionette whose strings had been cut. Butter-blonde hair curtained her face. Like Cousin It. Like that freaky girl who climbed out of the TV in that one scary movie that gave him the Bleakest of Coffins. Definitely wasn't church-approved viewing material. The woman veered toward the swing set and then tacked quickly back toward the sun-stippled pool. Her movements were abrupt and gawky, as if rehearsing the steps of a Fossean number. Before she and Dad split, Mom and Gordon used to do Fosse whenever Dad would come home from court and pontificate about civil rights. While he and Mom lurched and spun across the kitchen, Dad would smile and say, *OK, OK, very funny.* And Mom and Gordon would say, *We can only relate to your arguments through freestyle interpretative dance!* Then they'd get down on the linoleum floor together and laugh and laugh while Dad fixed himself a highball and muttered something about taking the dog for a walk. Despite what she did to Dad, Gordon still fiercely missed Mom. She lived in Arizona now. They Skyped on Sundays, after church.

From this distance it almost looked like the woman in the Radcliffe backyard was chasing an unseen toddler or something.

He stood at the window above the sink. Shreds of kale glistened in the wok. It was still ten minutes before the Kiev would be done. Something wasn't right about this. He ran to the patio where Mr. C was still snoring raggedly, and he pilfered the binoculars, running back to the sink where he had a good vantage. Here was a birch tree. Here was the roof of the Radcliffe house. He panned the binoculars slowly from left to right, looking for the woman. A smear of glittering blue—the pool—consumed his vision, and then, like a slide coming into focus, he could make out the high board's ladder and the woman's legs. She was climbing the ladder at a belabored, injured-seeming pace. The way she moved was sort of like she was in a dream but the rest of the world was awake, or something. He could faintly hear music trickling from the Radcliffe house, a plaintive voice.

Through the binoculars, Gordon saw the woman sway at the edge of the board, her arms outstretched beatifically, one hand clutching a glass, the other's fingers twittering, as if casting a spell. She leaned far to the left, but then quickly righted her weight, which caused the board to nod emphatically. Gordon smelled something burning as he dropped the binoculars, which rumbled into the sink, and ran through the house, past the Grandfather clock erupting into a metal clangor, and dashed onto the lawn, not stopping until he made it to the leafy fringe of the forest, through which he could just barely make out the woman bent over the edge of the board, which for some reason prompted him to yell out, "Hey, Lady! Don't!"

She turned around, but in doing so, took two steps off the board. Her sheer dress inflated with the wind of her fall.

5. ONE LAY AT A TIME

The world seethed. Her body was being cast in a mold of cerulean jelly. Opened her mouth. Screamed bubbles. Her arms and legs were stage props, ligneous objects without will or want. There was a viscous quality to the water, a cushy plushness that bore her body up despite its insistent weight. The water was opulent and blue and uterine-warm. Time began to slow. Percussive thumps swelled in her ears, an aortic cadence that she could not recognize as her own.

People were wrong about death. There was no airy soul's emergence from the body, no wisp of vapor borne aloft. No light-drenched ascent into a cherub-chocked sky. No sepia-stained montage of life's glories and whores. Gories and Horrors. Tories and hordes. Sheesh. Maybe this was the end? This hastened unraveling of words from their whirly counterparts? Worldly guard her hearts? When phrase no longer denoted objectification, when signifier was irrevocably severed from dignified? When you can't say what you mean, median and mode? What do you think, bug-eyed boy in a Nike headband, pleasant surprise, swimming toward me now with action-hero tenacity? Fun to play Cirque de Soleil in this chemical jelly, right? Like we're amoebas in a petri dish, no?

Do the lead man's bloat. The dead man's float. Here, watch me. Why so glum? You're rather cute, you know that, in a husky, Dr. Klarish, sort of way. The ladies are really going to fall over sideways for you one lay. Take it one lay at a time. Because time is of the. Time is of concupiscence. Easy, fella, watch where you put those paws, we just pet, save Tibet, meet Joan Jett. Is that your dick in your pocket or are you just happy trails to you until we met again on my own going down the only road ever known like a drifter I was ban a terrible beauty is the center cannot hold on to what we got it doesn'tmakeadifferenceifyoumakeito rnotwegotiteachotherand

Hanging in midair over the limpid blue pool, Jake Willing saw tomorrow's headline: AREA HERO SAVES EX-GIRLFRIEND FROM DROWNING, GIRL TAKES HIM BACK.

With a star athlete's post-game insouciance, he spoke to the imaginary reporter in his head. "Well, John, you know I really, really appreciate everything everybody has been saying about me and what I did yesterday. It wasn't an easy decision. What with the restraining order and the guilt and everything, I knew I was looking at some bleak statutory consequences if something went wrong out there, if my determination and will faltered. But Annie's my girl. Sure, we've had a fair share of tiffs and squabbles, but what storybook romance doesn't, am I right, John? You know, guys like me, we try and prepare ourselves for these situations–physically, emotionally, spiritually. Since I met her in fourth grade, I've been spiritually preparing to save Annie from danger at the critical moment. Am I superhuman? Am I capable of acts that defy logic and physical laws? Do I think I'm the only one who could have saved her? No. But the difference is that I–unlike other puny-hearted Reese-Meyer-Shannon wrestlers who will go unnamed–put myself *in a position* to save her. That's the difference between the real heroes and the poseurs, John. The difference between infatuation and true love. The difference between a selfish boner and a selfless hero."

He soared over Annie's body, misjudging his deckside launch into the pool, and hit the gleaming water, disappearing in a violent crystalline burst. The water was gelid, scrotum-shrinking, and he sank, encased in bubbles, eventually opening his eyes to the chlorinated burn of the water, searching for his One and Only. The hissing ended and the water cleared, which was when he saw Annie's body, floating like a Degas ballerina near the deep end, her gauzy dress undulating out behind her. Her hands reached for nothing. Threads of blood unspooled from her nose and mouth, the red strands dissipating into a thin pink mist, all of which compelled him to swim with piscine agility, his legs fluttering, his arms chopping, until he was finally gaining ground, until he was nearly there, which was when he reached out and wrapped his arms around her chest, making a Superman pose while kicking, and kicked until both of their heads surfaced. Oxygen was a revelation. Coins of sunlight winked through the mesh of overhanging trees. He took in huge delicious gulps of afternoon air. A faraway lawnmower droned in minor key. A lark on a limb made two even calls.

He lunged for the side ladder, grabbed it, and used it as leverage as he pushed Annie's bottom—which was plump and a little softer than he remembered—over the pool's tiled wall, laying her body on the deck. He climbed out and knelt down, bending over to perform mouth-to-mouth. Blanched tongue emergent from a blue-lipped maw. Wet hair doodled over her face. He remembered this from health class, when Mr. Stinewell, the sinewy, leather-tanned gym teacher with the combover and the halitosis, taught all the students the proper compression to ventilation ratio for CPR, which was like 15:2 or maybe 20:4. Shit, he couldn't remember. And where to put his hands? They had used foam dummies in class, and the dummies were just torsos, they didn't even have legs. They didn't have eyes that stayed open even though they were dying. Had Mr. Stinewell said to put the hands between the tits, on the xiphoid process? Or below them, on the diaphragm? Shit, didn't matter, just move.

Annie. Annie.

He couldn't see anything. His eyes gritted against the afterburn of chlorine. The full tableau of deck and pool and grass and trees and Annie was a smudge of water-blurred colors. 1-2-3-4, 1-2-3-4. Breathe.

He sat up in anticipatory silence, waiting for signs of revival. He thought he smelled barbeque. He was all breath and animal motion. Down he went again, compressing, grunting as he jabbed at her sternum, the imbrication of ribs that housed his girl's failing heart. He rose again and sat back, but soon realized that there was a boy beside him now, a wordless boy with a Hare Krishna haircut who had probably just emerged from the copse of burnt willows behind the pool, and who was now gesturing for Jake to get out of the way, hunkering down next to Annie, arranging his hands expertly over her xiphoid process and delivering blunt compressions with what Jake could only describe as surgical precision. The boy leaned over her mouth and didn't kiss/breathe her like Jake himself had but gracefully couriered air into her throat, trying to clear the passageway of water via the force of his expended breath. Jake watched the little guy administer a revival while becoming growingly aware of the slant of the sun on his back, and the eerie, oneiric silence of the neighborhood during this non-hour of evening, during which he and a bald seraph (he was convinced) tried to rescue Annie. His eyes were beginning to clear. He realized he was still down on his knees and that his bare knees were hurt and abraded. Night was falling, and the backyard grew dark. All around the pool deck, he saw faint traces of glow-in-the-dark paint beginning to surface on the cement, his neon yellow words slowly developing like images in a Polaroid. *Annie Radcliffe, You Are Loved.* He had decided on the passive voice to demonstrate the true nature of his heart, that his love for her was pure and entirely without ego. In the gradual sprawl of the evening's partial dark, he looked back at his True. His girl. His Annie.

Wait, what? What the hell happened to Annie? Did people look like especially older when they were unconscious? A kind of Benjamin Button effect or something? A kind of camera adds ten pounds = death adds ten years type of thing? Who was this lady? This thirty-something lady with deep crow's feet, whose breasts sagged old-lady-like, lucent in her dripping shirt? Raccoon stains of mascara below her eyes? Who was this woman? Who had he saved? And he had kissed her, hadn't he? Which meant that he had cheated on Annie. Not that they were even together anymore, true, but it was also true that he had kissed another woman when he claimed to remain totally committed to Annie and only Annie. Jesus. Was he really thinking about this at a time like this? Sad-eyed woman going blue and cold on the Radcliffe deck and here he was thinking about what Annie would think of him for doing something she probably didn't even care about. Who was this woman, anyway? What was her name? He had touched her butt, lifting her out of the water. Which, given that she was dying in front of him, made him feel sort of weird. Not pervy or anything. But something else. Something better. His hand zinged with feeling. He was newly aware of himself here, as he kneeled on the deck, cold and dripping in the growing dark. He had been so convinced this woman was Annie. Jesus. Fuck. What was wrong with him? If he could delude himself into thinking that this woman was Annie, maybe he was capable of convincing himself he loved Annie when he didn't really even know her. What did that mean? *Whoa, deep, Jake,* he imagined his brother Marty saying. *You're a regular Kierkegaard, man.* Suddenly, Jake realized the boy had been staring at him with a kind of beatific equanimity, saying, "Please help me." So Jake did the one thing he could think of, and held his hands out to the totally bald boy, hoping that the child would know better than he what to do.

7. HERE

Three weeks before the funeral, five weeks before holding the last meeting of his *Chronicles of Narnia* club, six weeks before saying good-bye to Mr. Cavanaugh and cooking the old man one last chicken Kiev for old time's sake, seven weeks before hopping on a plane and moving to Arizona and starting his new life with Mom, Gordon scampered through the front door, calling out, "Dad! Dad! Guess what? I figured it out!" and nearly slipped on the foyer's rug before breathlessly racing down the hallway to find his father standing up from the kitchen table at the sounds of his frenzied arrival. "What? What is it?" Dad asked. Gordon loved that look on his father's face, a hybrid of boyish expectancy and paternal concern. In those moments it was like he was able to see his father as man and boy both. It was like he could finally understand that grown-ups were just as scared of the world as he was.

The boy stopped and stood in the doorjamb, between the family room and kitchen, still wet with pool water, and waited. He waited for his father's face to grow with worry, enjoying it, knowing that in a few minutes Dad would be laughing and swelling with pride about everything that Gordon had just done—leaving Mr. Cavanaugh's house and sprinting through the gully; entering the neighbor's yard to help an older kid give a woman CPR; watching a spurt of pool water geyser out of her mouth, like from a whale's blowhole, and watching, too, as the woman came back to life, her eyes wide and white, and immediately started crying, saying, "I'm sorry, I'm so, so sorry," which made Gordon grab her hand and tell her that everything was OK, it was nothing, which inspired the older guy to grab the lady's other hand and say the same, and the three of them stayed there just like that, just that way, all before Mr. Cavanaugh called an ambulance and the woman went to the hospital, and the older kid thanked Gordon one last time before jogging home like nothing had happened, prompting Gordon to jog home too, past the MORNING FALLS sign, past the Ruby Isle Pharmacy, past lit windows in which mothers rocked babies, in which families ate meals, and past the yards where fathers taught their sons to throw tight spirals, which made Gordon speed up, desperate as he was to get home and tell his father what he had learned, which was this: it didn't matter what Dad believed, because even though horrible things happened, good things happened, too. Like, *par exemple*, wasn't it good that Dad was still here, that he and Gordon still had time? Time to take the dog for long walks? To recite lines from Monty Python at the grocery store, to make the cashier lady laugh? To point at cool-looking clouds? To point out possible girlfriends for Dad? To go for long car rides? To order Shaky's while studying for history? To talk about how awesome FDR was? About how Taft blew chunks? To look at old photos of Dad from high school and laugh at his sideburns? To listen to Coltrane, wear sunglasses, and groove their heads like cool cats? To

113

read Shakespeare together in bad British accents? To play chess and checkers and Parcheesi? To talk about the divorce? To talk about Mom? To cook dinner? To wear Groucho masks, do deadpan, and try not to laugh? To imagine for a second that there wasn't a God? To imagine for a second that there was? To leap out of faith? To leap into it? Because wasn't that good, Dad? That they still had time? That it wasn't over? That for some reason—despite this, despite everything—they were still here?

Nominated by American Short Fiction, Benjamin Percy

CITY HORSE

by HENRI COLE

from THE THREEPENNY REVIEW

At the end of the road from concept to corpse,
sucked out to sea and washed up again—
with uprooted trees, crumpled cars, and collapsed houses—
facedown in dirt, and tied to a telephone pole,
as if trying to raise herself still, though one leg is broken,
to look around at the grotesque unbelievable landscape,
the color around her eyes, nose, and mane (the dapples of roan,
a mix of white and red hairs) now powdery gray—
O, wondrous horse; O, delicate horse—dead, dead—
with a bridle still buckled around her cheeks—"She was more
smarter than me,
she just wait," a boy sobs, clutching a hand to his mouth,
and stroking the majestic rowing legs,
stiff now, that could not outrun
the heavy, black, frothing water.

Nominated by Threepenny Review, Philp Levine, Joyce Carol Oates

THE ICE COMMITTEE

fiction by DAVID MEANS

from ZOETROPE: ALL STORY

It was late afternoon. It would soon be dusk.

"I don't think I ever told you the one with Captain Hopewell in it," the man named Kurt was saying.

"Don't start. For God's sake, you'll jinx us for sure," the man named Merle said. "Just get me thinking about that one and it'll jinx us."

"This one's isn't going to jinx us. If you knew the story, you'd know that," Kurt said, and then for a few minutes both men sat silently and mulled over everything they'd discussed on the nature of luck over the course of the last few months as they'd wandered up and down Superior Street, shaking a cup for spare change, scraping for odd jobs, whatever it took to gather enough for some booze and a scratch lottery ticket. They'd agreed that to talk too much about good fortune just before you scratched would decrease the odds of it coming, because luck had to bend around the place and time of the scratch, establishing itself in relation to your state of mind at that particular moment. You either scratched in a deliberately calm, quiet moment, or in one of great emotional intensity. Scratch a ticket on the sidewalk in front of the Hope Mission—or worse yet, inside the lounge, with all that dusty grief—no chance in hell. At your mother's grave on a pristine winter day, after paying your prayerful respects and laying some flowers against the tombstone, about fifty/fifty. Out in Lake Superior on the deck of a good ship under a gloriously crystalline sky, sixty/forty. On the deck of the same ship in a hundred-year storm with slush ice forming on the lake, just after hearing the news that your old man's died, ninety/ten. Back at your mother's grave in the fall, at dusk, having survived the hundred-year storm, sure thing. Best to clear the head of all expectation and settle into a state of not-caring as you look out with silent and blissful longing at the lake.

"You haven't heard this one, so it's not going to hurt our chances if I tell it," Kurt was saying, leaning back on the bench. "It won't change the odds any more than if I were to start talking about that dream I have of buying a decommissioned ship, either here or down in Cleveland. Dry-dock the fucker, put in a Jacuzzi and a pool table and a wet bar—all that stuff," he said, and then the older man, who sat formally with his hands on his knees, reached up and adjusted the lapels of his coat.

"You just planted a seed in my mind about you buying that retired ship, which is just as much of a jinx, me thinking it."

"So you're saying I shouldn't talk?" Kurt said.

The lake in front of them was unusually calm for this time of year, a burnished glean that stretched out to a single vessel, far out, heading to the horizon. Behind them, to the right, the bridge sat with its hundred-ton counterweights up—the span down—waiting stubbornly to be relieved of its burden. The port of Duluth was dead, the chutes and conveyers empty. With the exception of the ship out on the water, nothing seemed to move.

"As we've discussed ad infinitum, you should hold off talking too much about fortune—good or bad—until we scratch the ticket," Merle said, shaking his hands in his sleeves and twisting his cuff links into position. He had a long, gaunt face and sad, still periwinkle eyes.

"Well, Captain Hopewell was a hopeless asshole," Kurt said. "Can I at least say that?"

Ships and 'Nam, 'Nam and ships—that's all the kid's got, Merle thought.

"Whatever you say, Professor."

"I didn't say a word," Merle said.

"But you were thinking something and I know what it was," Kurt said. He stood and walked down to the shore to examine, for the second time that afternoon, the dead flies and grime that marked where the water—no tide, nothing resembling a tide—had receded during the hot, dry summer.

The ship had disappeared over the horizon, heading on what seemed to be an upbound tack that would pass to the south of Split Rock Lighthouse and Isle Royale, then charting a course to the Soo Locks (*likely the Poe Lock*, Kurt thought, *yeah, the Poe—it's the only one that could handle a boat that long*), down through Lake Huron, down the St. Clair, past Detroit, across Erie, up the Welland Canal, across Lake Ontario, through the St. Lawrence Seaway—four hundred slogging miles—and out to sea. It was easy to imagine the urgency that would fill a ship this time of year as it shoved through the locks, searching out the sudden serenity of the seaway with the land close on both sides, and then, leaving it behind, entering the Gulf of St. Lawrence and, finally, the open Atlantic. That's how it worked. You boarded in the spring, hung from the sides and painted the hull, scrubbed the deck and worked your ass off bolting and unbolting hatches, hardly paying the water much notice, until one day, as you stood on the deck having a smoke, the vastness of the open sea flashed you like a girl with her skirt blown up, exposing a beautiful secret, and then you fell back to the boredom—the hatches, the decks, the dust in the holds. It opened and shut on you, the sea did.

"Hopewell, you busted my ass!" Kurt shouted. "You were a vintage Nova Scotia stoic."

"Again, I have to say, I've heard everything I want to hear about Hopewell," Merle said, studying his friend. Kurt was rail thin, dressed in an old flannel shirt and a canvas jacket that hung loosely from his wide shoulders. All the drugs he'd taken had given him a saintly gauntness, as if he'd starved himself for some grand purpose, and his eyes— when he wasn't squinting—had a shifty dart that somehow made him look younger than his fifty-three years.

"Come on, just tell me a little bit, just a word or two to confirm you know the story," Kurt said, slapping his sides and hopping, lifting off his toes. "I think we agreed that it's OK if it's a new version that has good luck in it."

"Well, if you insist," Merle said. "You told me you were working an old scrap heap. 'Due for the heap,' you said. It was flying a Portuguese flag and had a captain named Hopewell. Then you asked me for another word for *hard-ass*, and I suggested you use the word *stoic*. You said, 'Yeah, *stoic*, that's the right word.' You called Hopewell 'a vintage Nova Scotia stoic,' like you just did a minute ago, and then you told me the story."

"I could've told you a hundred fucking Hopewell stories. I have a bunch of them," Kurt said. "And *stoic's* a word I knew before you taught it to me."

" 'Nam was in it," Merle said.

"I'd say half my stories have 'Nam in them. That doesn't prove to me you've heard this one."

"Well, it had a Captain Hopewell in it, and it had 'Nam in it, and it had a ship that was due for scrap."

"Did it have a guy named Billy-T—my buddy who enlisted with me in Benton Harbor?"

"Did we not agree that we'd refrain from telling stories that might in some way involve luck? Did we not agree, at some point?" Merle said, pounding his walking stick into the dirt.

"Look, just humor me and confirm that you've heard it, and I'll shut up—but if you haven't heard it, then I think I should talk because I feel like talking, and you know if I don't talk when I want to talk there's a possibility that the tension from not talking might jinx us just as much as me telling some kind of story that has the wrong type of luck in it. Was there a guy named Billy-T? If Billy-T was in there, you heard the story before, in which case I'll let it go."

Merle reached up, pinched the dimple in his tie, curled his palm over the end of his stick, and—shaking violently—tried to stand. "Jesus, kid. Don't blame me if this scratch is worthless. I have my own desires to talk, but I also have the wisdom to hold my tongue."

He gave up the effort, sitting again, and watched as Kurt took a chug of beer, wiped his mouth, lit a cigarette, and scuffed his feet as he prepared to tell the story, working it over in his mind (presumably), trying to remember if he had indeed told Merle the entire thing from beginning to end, or if he'd given just an abbreviated version with the end left out.

"I was working as a low-life maintenance monkey on an old heap, a coal burner out of Cleveland flying a Portuguese flag. I guess I told you that, and maybe I told you that we were heading on a northerly course into some nasty weather. You could feel in the roll of the ship that someone was in for a dose of bad luck," he said, and then he waited for Merle to cut in on him, to warn him again about jinxing the ticket, but the old man had his head back and his eyes closed, nodding softly, so Kurt went on, saying, "I've told you about how it felt, the sense that the water wanted to drag someone to the bottom, and maybe I've told you how I hit Hopewell on occasion with my 'Nam shit as a way to get out of deck duty, and how most of the time he'd just listen and then tell me to get back to work. But this time was different. For one thing, against protocol, the bastard came in and ate with us at our table. The captain and his guys usually eat in a different galley, but I guess he'd noticed a disgruntled tension in the crew. Not that we'd ever mutiny. I mean, it was a good-paying gig. Mutinies are out of style. Anyway, the way I used to deliver it was to put in as much lingo as I could, but keep it vague, too, if you know what I'm saying, and try to ride a balance, because a 'Nam story has to sound crazy and true at the same time. And that day, with that storm churning under the hull, I knew I had to touch some part of Captain Hopewell that he didn't think I could get to, so I softened him up with some random details—the weird, pink flechette powder that dusted our fingers; PSYOP choppers pumping the sounds of crying babies down on the gooks to drive them to a crazy surrender. I worked these details until Hopewell's face went tight and his mouth screwed and the stick up his ass seemed to nudge against his brow. Then I knew he was truly hearing me.

"I told him that when I turned eighteen I was sure I'd be drafted and wanted an advantage on which service I'd join, so I enlisted on the buddy program with my best friend, Billy-T—we went over to the recruiting office in Benton Harbor and joined together. Anyway, I could see that Hopewell's eyes were drifting to the porthole, and I felt I had to get to the point, so I jumped right into it and told him how me and Billy-T found ourselves in the hot and heavy in Hue, street-to-street, real-war shit, and how Billy-T—who had a serious lisp—called in airstrike coordinates on the radio net. Mortar rounds coming in all around us, and these shit-can field phones we were using . . . 'Hell, don't get me started on that,' I said to Hopewell. 'Don't get me started on the arms we had over there. For a while we were using—and most folks don't believe me when I tell them this—fucking Remington rifles. I swear, wood stocks, single bore, flint action. You'd break one of those down and you could hardly get it back together because the so-called follower spring in the clip would fuck you up.' I added as much of that bullshit as I could to keep Hopewell's eyes from the porthole, and then I swung back to the main story again, making sure he understood that we weren't used to streets. We were used to a guy taking point with no line of sight. Hue was all line of sight, if you dared to look. You know the deal—put a helmet on your bayonet and stick it up over the wall, watch it get nailed with fire, just a hunk of Swiss cheese when you bring it back down. (Then some Wisconsin newbie would go ahead and do the same.) I told Hopewell, 'See, man, Billy-T was a short-timer, down to the end of his tour, just a few days from home. Streets have corners, you understand, angles, doorways, churchyards, windows, walls to press all that bullshit luck and chance down into sense. Anyway, point being, he called in the coordinates and we waited for air support to come in and solve the problem. That's how we worked it. Get into tight shit and let air support come in close, and then duck down and wait for the napalm heat. We hated them the way you'd hate any savior. They saved your life and took it at the same time, if you know what I mean.' "

"Well, I don't really know what you mean." Merle pounded his stick down. "But I think you should stop right now. I'd venture to say that in this case the redundancy might somehow nullify the jinx. The fact that I've heard this story so many times, and that I find it so boring and even incoherent, and therefore didn't listen to a word you just said, might somehow nudge the odds in our direction."

He shifted through memories in an attempt to locate the original version of Kurt's story, which he'd heard during one of their first afternoons together—still in that honeymoon stage, trading lives with a feverish desire, like lovers in bed—as they sat in what would become their spot near the port, smoking and drinking themselves into a stupor, listening to the roar of the chutes, feeling warm and cozy while the port—whose activity had dwindled down to a trickle in the last few years—suddenly, with the arrival of a ship, seemed grand and substantial. Kurt had explained that the crews on those boats still headed up-bound on the Fort William/Port Arthur tack, with top hampers still screaming in the wind, and plates and frames still groaning and flexing against the slush ice blowing in from the east, and their captains still had to contend with the dictates of the Ice Committee of the Lake Carriers' Association, a bunch of business suits in a fancy office in the Rockefeller Building in Cleveland, who gathered bullshit weather reports and used maps and charts and half-assed guesswork to make a call on when the upper lakes could be broken out for the new season.

As Merle had listened to Kurt's talk in those early days, some buried professorial part of himself would rise to the surface as he struggled to make intellectual connections between these ragged memories and his own life. Sitting there with the younger man he could remember what it had felt like lecturing to a class about those souls who—armed with their faith and a hardcore fortitude to put up with natural forces—had risked it all to make a buck, bartering their way along the shore and exploiting the natives one way or another, tapping into the great flex and yaw of capital as it moved between the hinterlands and the cities. A deep knowledge of sequential events, a gloriously full understanding that once allowed him to speak with complete authority, had since fractured to shards—Charlemagne and the Algonquins; Huron villages, bleak and shabby by French standards; Father Jamet; Brother Duplessis; Saint Lalemant; Ennemond Masse—that drifted and cleaved with those from

121

his own personal history: his wife, Emma; his mother-in-law, Gracie; his son, Ronnie; and two dozen men from the Holy Order for People on the Edge Mission, who'd lived out their days before the big, ocular presence of the lake as it pushed against the hardscrabble town, which boom-and-busted its way forward, its grand old homes clutching to the high, terraced land with surprising optimism, seeming to turn a blind eye to the lack of forgiveness in a landscape of mainly stone and ice.

Another time—staggering drunk along Superior Street, holding each other up, arms over shoulders—Kurt had admitted that he didn't see it as a matter of bad luck on Billy-T's part, but rather as bad luck turned to good luck because he'd gotten out of deck duty using Billy-T's death, and it had been rough duty because, approaching Taconite Harbor, the hatches had to be unbolted, ten bolts per hatch, and then he was one of those who'd be lowered down in something called a bosun's chair, nothing more than a slab of wood under your ass and an iron bar coming up through your crotch. They'd stopped in the middle of the street, face to face, and Kurt had admitted that Billy-T had most likely lisped the coordinates, and some poor radio operator in forward air control had misheard a number over the net and set the bomb down too close, blowing a few of the men away, including beloved Billy-T himself. The fact that Kurt was able to use the story to get out of deck duty had saved his life because a deck monkey (that's the phrase he'd used, weeping softly) had been killed that night—"And it wasn't me," he said, "it wasn't me. The dock at Taconite is only four feet wide, with a rim of wood along the edge to stop you from sliding, and it was glazed with ice as we came in, and the kid who took my place had done what he was supposed to do, keeping his eye on the line at all times, hauling and hauling, until he went right over the edge."

Then a few weeks ago, walking up to Indian Point Park with nothing to do and no money to spend, just whiling away some hours together, Kurt had admitted that Captain Hopewell hadn't really bought the story he'd told about Billy-T, and had simply been weighing the ramifications of sending a man top deck who was in such a sorry state of mind. "The salty old bastard was thinking about all the paperwork involved if this stupid deckhand, this shaky kid, were to go overboard. Then they'd have to drop the chains and wait until an official search was made and it would take days, and a few fucking days cut from the manifest would cost the company a fortune," Kurt had said, weeping again. "Captain Hopewell saw that I was just one more goofball 'Nam vet, way over his head when it came to his responsibilities."

On the bench, opening his eyes, Merle watched Kurt go down to the shore for a third time, to dip his shoe in the water. It might not matter what either of them said right now, the older man thought. Every big port like this one had a kid just like Kurt, a kid with sea legs on land and land legs on sea, a kid whose life had ended in country, somewhere in the Highlands, or in Khe Sanh, or in Hue, or in Saigon, as a member of Tiger Force, or as a gunner on a Chinook, depending on which version he decided to tell that day. And there was always an old coot whose life had ended in middle age, beginning with a fight over—*over what? he couldn't really remember*—that had resulted in the broken vase (a wedding present), and then another fight and a broken Hitchcock chair (another wedding present), and then another and a broken jaw (*Emma, oh my dear sweet Emma!*). He felt the deep shame of the memory: the clutch of her long, elegant fingers around her chin and her beautiful, deep, sad, brown brown eyes as he'd glanced back one last time before striking out, moving his feet over the ground day after day, until it seemed he'd walked (and he had, for God's sake, he had) the upper shore of Superior, across the border into Canada, and then back down, finding his way to the Hope Mission.

He was on his feet when he came out of it, shaking violently again, leaning all his weight onto the handle of his stick.

"You think the ice is coming soon?" he said.

"Christ," Kurt said. "Now you're gonna jinx the fucking ticket. Don't start talking. I heard that one, anyway. Ice, a bet, and a winner. For God's sake."

"I didn't say a word," Merle said.

"You said enough just by asking me if I thought the lake was going to freeze up soon. That's the one *you* drag up every time we scrounge enough to scratch. That's the one *I've* heard a million times."

"I didn't say a word," Merle said. But he wasn't sure because the memory was so strong. The warmth of the mission lounge back when he still had a little bit of his professorial bona fides. Cigar smoke bluing the air, catching the wedge of sunlight as it came through the room, thickening the afternoon while outside in the street the cars hissed through the slush and Jimmy Klein held court in the big leather chair with the split seams along the armrests. An old-timer—at that time—at the mission, his lips cracked and dry from five years of sobriety. Five dry years that had given him a wizened, sharp aspect that made the other men highly uncomfortable.

"You see, the tradition of the ice betting pool goes back a couple hundred years, to when this was a small port," Merle had explained. "Long before supertankers. Back when ships ran on coal and had a beam of something like fifty feet " His voice was stiff and authorial. (All the other men in the lounge that afternoon were now dead. Red Jason, an old Iron Range train switchman. Dead. Slappy Jack, a tool and die maker with a carbuncle on his neck. Long dead. Jimmy Klein. Long, long, long dead.) The men absently took studious poses, leaning forward with an unusual attentiveness.

"In any event, a man named Frank Lashway, who was about as deep in the drink as you can get, claimed he had a sure bet on when the ice would break. He put down the third day of March and went so far as to say it would break at three in the afternoon. Folks said, 'Lashway, you're sure on that?' and he said, and I quote, 'I'm sure on it. It's not a guess.' Lashway said, 'I got myself a vision on it,' and they said, and I quote, 'You got a drunken vision,' and he said, 'Well, a vision's a vision.' And please understand that all this is factual history; you can find it in the Kitchi Gammi Club archives. They ran the betting pool, at least for upper class folks, the ship owners and steel mill operators and the like. So a man named Lashway put his bet down on the third day of March."

"Where'd he get the money to bet?" Jimmy Klein had asked. And then Slappy Jack, grunting and moaning, had said, "It don't fucking matter where the wager came from so long as there was a wager in it, you dumb shit, because the point of the professor's story isn't about the amount of the wager; hell, it could've been the shirt off his back for all it matters." And Klein, taking a puff, had said, "Hell, it matters how much because without a big wager there's not much to the story at all. He could've been one lucky bastard who pulled a date out his ass amid a million guys pulling dates out their assess and he just happened to hit the nail and so we're hearing the story. Otherwise, he'd've just been lost like the rest of them. So what I'm saying is that the amount of the wager should mean something, because if it was a big one, his house, his wife's house in Wisconsin, something along those lines, then the story goes beyond just a guy with a lucky guess and becomes something else."

He'd gone on like that until, finally, Merle had cleared his throat, stroked his chin, gazed through the smoke, and said, "We shall say he wagered his house, one he hadn't seen in years but knew still existed, on a hundred-acre farm down in Green Bay, and that he wagered a draft horse and a plow and a new gizmo for shucking corn, just for the sake of my story, if that helps, because the wager—-and I'm agreeing with your argument, Jimmy—should matter, in theory; so if it helps you to appreciate my story, put a big wager in there. Whatever the case, the third day of March came and it was cold, cold as hell, and the harbor was still jammed, not a hint of thaw, not a hint of breaking up, and so on and so forth. The record indicates, at least as well as I could find, that Lashway went out on the ice. Just about the entire town of Duluth gathered to watch him pick his way over the drifts along the shoreline, and out to the smoother surface beyond. About a quarter mile out, he stopped and began chopping with an axe, just his elbow flipping up and down until there was a crack. Not a boom, but a single, loud, electric snap—you can imagine this, can't you?—and the ice started to break, and of course Lashway was sucked into the water and therefore released from the burden of the wager, so to speak, not knowing if he'd won or lost. And he did win, you see, but he didn't know it, so perhaps theoretically he didn't."

The men had mumbled and grunted, puffed smoke, looked solemnly at the television set. They'd often heard this type of story: preposterously out of tune with reality, but still as true as anything, mirroring their own desperation. ("Any one of us might've done the same," Slappy Jack had said. "You have to admit that, don't you?") It wasn't the image of someone out there on the ice that had struck home. It wasn't the ice breaking up around his boots. They'd all felt such stupefying forces. What resonated through them—as they waited, paused, spit into the spittoon, smoked, watched television, shifted, adjusted cuffs, squeezed balls, flicked bitten fingernails, listened to the clock vibrate by the check-in desk—was all that cash the guy would never collect. Finally Klein had said, "Fix the goddamn set," and got up to twist and fiddle the rabbit ears, spreading them wide; and as he reached around behind to turn the control knob, the picture drew into a tighter screw formation, and the same faces—one after another—rotated over and over, up to the edge of the screen and into eternity.

"If I win some cash I'm gonna head back to Benton Harbor and see how things squared away in my absence," Kurt was saying. "And I'm not talking about this penny-ante scratch, but a big payout on a big ticket. Because if we win this one we should go buy a bunch of big-pot tickets. Because if this scratch is a winner it means we did something right, and if we don't make use of that fact it'll just be more of the same." He was speaking from a squatting position and gesturing at the lake, which was now glossy and deep silver in the fading evening light, the color of mercury.

"I believe we should wait a few more minutes," Merle said from the bench. The cold was seeping through his trousers and into his aching knees. "I think we agreed that we wanted to see at least one star appear, or the moon. Some indication that there's something beyond the sky. I think we said that."

"I'm getting too goddamned cold to wait," Kurt said. Then he began talking about a girl he'd known in Chicago, shortly after he'd returned from the war. He'd taken her for a spin along Lake Shore Drive, up to the old fairgrounds, where he found a place to park. Then some punk kids had surrounded the car and broken a bottle on the fender, and he'd gotten out with a crowbar in hand.

He was still talking, but Merle had stopped listening; it was another threadbare story that Kurt told himself day after day after day to get a grip on a postwar rage so tremendous it had seemed mesmerizing.

"You'll come back, won't you?" Merle said. He was struggling to stand again. He wanted to be standing when the kid scratched the ticket.

"How's that?"

"If you go to Benton Harbor, will you come back here?"

Over at the bridge a warning bell began to clang, and the great gears were moving and the weights sliding down, as the span rose for one last ship. They listened to the gurgle of the turning screw and the murmur of the engine and then, a minute later, two woefully long signals from the vessel's horn, announcing its departure.

Kurt winced and took Merle's hand in his own and said, "I'll come back, believe me, you know I will. And anyway, it wouldn't be good luck to say I wouldn't, would it? At least not now, not here."

The ship appeared in the channel, looming over the wall, a giant supertanker—painted gray and white—about the length of a football field. They could hear the slap of wake and the glug of exhaust coming up from the screw.

"That'll be the final one for the season, I'd guess," Merle said.

"You and your ice again," Kurt said. "That boat's a thousand-footer, too long to fit the locks in the St. Lawrence. It's trapped in the lakes." He slapped his hand anxiously against his coat pocket.

"I believe this is the right moment," Merle said. "According to Saint de Brébeuf, or maybe Lalemant, the Huron played a dish game—I think it was called—with five or six fruit stones painted black on one side and white on the other, and they repeated this word *tet* that influenced the play, so maybe you should say 'tet' as you scratch it." He watched the ship leave them behind. "They played for the recovery of the sick, I think. The game was prescribed by a physician, but it was more effective if the sick man requested it."

"Oh, Jesus, if it'll save me from one of your historical lectures, I'll scratch this fucker right now," Kurt said, pulling the ticket—shiny and silvery in the dusky light—from his coat pocket and slapping it against his palm. From his other pocket he took a coin, and then, saying, "tet,

        tet,

             tet,

                  tet,

                       tet,

                            tet," he walked to the water and began to scratch, watching as the numbers appeared one after another. He scratched while the darkening sky—purple dissolving to black—seemed to harden the surface of the lake, and the town, behind them, seethed in the deep silence of loss, another day burned out in the fury of decline. He scratched as if he knew in his heart (and he did, he really did) that within hours the cold air, having gathered itself, would drive down from the plains of Manitoba and Saskatchewan, pound past the Knife River, sweep the length and breadth of the lake with an intensity that would seem a personal affront to both of them, as they lay in their beds and reexamined the afternoon from all sides, wondering what they'd done wrong, and how they could avoid the jinx the next time.

Months later, deep in winter, they would go back yet again and deliberate and ponder the moment they'd scratched the ticket. It was all in good fun, reconsidering the past. After all, both men had long since demolished a sense of linear time; it was gone, buried under the losses that had been compiled. But on occasion, in moments of drunk or high hope, they'd take a shot and try to arrange the order of things and make declarations so out of proportion to the realities of their lives that they would trigger fits of mutual hilarity. Merle might say that he was thinking of returning to teaching, that he yearned for the days in front of a class, with all those eager kids leaning into notebooks, scribbling away, taking down every fucking thing he said. Then Kurt might say that he was just going to forget fucking 'Nam and live in the moment, right now, right here, and put all his shit behind him, and Merle would pause for a long, long time—sometimes hours, sometimes days—and, in a highly pontifical voice, with his finger to his chin, he'd say, "The likelihood of you forgetting what happened in 'Nam and seizing the day is about as high as the Huron rising up from the dusty corridors of history and reclaiming their rightful place in the progression of civilization," and then they'd fall into spasms of laughter, kicking the sidewalk with their heels, and Merle would do a crazy, arthritic dance that made him look light on his feet. These were the glorious moments between them, when the burdens of their respective regrets seemed to merge and disappear, and it was because of these purifications that they were still together, still hanging on.

Snow was falling around them. Silence draped the town. The lake was a white shawl beneath a bowl of stars, pure and clear. Kurt had his arm around the old man, helping him walk, and then impulsively pulled him close and felt his frailty, the bones coming up against his skin; and all at once they were aware of the sorry picture the two of them must've made, shuffling through the drifts and hugging to keep warm.

"If we win the next one," Merle said, his voice airy and dry, "I'll find Emma, for good, and apologize and tell her I'm a new man and buy back the land I owned down near the Au Sable, where I was going to build a fishing cabin." And Kurt, without skipping a beat, said, "And I'm going to locate Billy-T's sister, who I always loved, and set her up really good with a house and the works, and see if we can make a life together." Then they heaved out of the drifts and into the center of the road, where the plow had cleared a smooth patch of ice, and began to laugh, falling into routine. It was a clean, open grace that appeared and disappeared with just enough regularity to keep them together, and it would end when the world ended, or perhaps it wouldn't.

Nominated by Zoetrope: All Story

BREAKING IT

by MARY HOOD

from THE GEORGIA REVIEW

Both conservationists and the wireless industry continue to press the Federal Communications Commission for some response to concerns that millions of migratory birds fatally collide with mobile phone towers every year.
—Matthew Lasar, arstechnica.com

From boredom, a way to keep me alert on a daily walk on a path I have traveled for years, I set quests. This day I noted things blue. Nothing manmade. I saw at first nothing that qualified. Blue is my hardest color. On these familiar hills, keeping up my pace, making my eyes work, too—surveying, hoping for large, then beginning to narrow and study, not sure I could collect ten blue and natural things in a three-mile path: sky could only count once and nothing I was wearing counted, even though my shirt was organic cotton chambray. Quest as a game taken seriously strips irrelevancy just as a real pilgrimage does—nothing I cherish and winnow with my eyes is mine, nothing I claim with a conqueror's glance is real estate; I was just passing time on the surface, with a little shallow seeking for what would get me through.

The game of color quest is a habit, and I mentally "play" it even though today I was walking with others, not alone, meandering a bit with young mamas pushing babies in strollers, and pausing from time to time to whistle back Willie the dachshund from someone's garden, or to call greetings to lakeside neighbors working on their docks. The air was stinging warm, and filled with pollen from the pines. Large-grained, this pollen crusted the drying edges of puddles. Too large-grained to make us sneeze, it ground in the eyes, gilded the young leaves on the trees and the toes of our trainers.

Blue is hardest for organic. Ten might happen in high spring, if you allow into the acceptable range all lavenders, purples, and whatever blend that tiny iris was under the lichens on the red clay cutbank where winter had sheared the edge sharp again and left the huckleberry roots dangling. Summer blue can be counted all in hydrangeas—every cottage at the lake seems to have them—but anti-hydrangists would argue such blue is not organic, but rather only a litmus blue—even though it is a response of the plant to acidic soil conditions. Still, why blame the plants, which can't help it? But they *are* cultivars, like petunias and window-box plantings—which don't count, I've decided. I make the rules and amend them toward difficulty, so the game is not a cakewalk but a challenge.

When I first moved to the woods, I learned a new wildflower each week for as long as I could find them. I backslid in winter; the next year, I had the pleasure of many of them to learn again.

In fall, in wilder years, I got lucky and found half the list with fleabane, asters, monkshood, skullcap, and gentian—but not lately. Not since the developers widened the lanes and installed the new landscapes.

Spring blues are difficult but not impossible: already I had seen birdfoot violets, confederate violets, henbit, Quaker ladies, blue-eyed grass, periwinkle—escaped from old cabin sites, does this last one count? Never mind, there was the throat of a sunning lizard, electric blue and dazzling, and the last little drying-up iris cristata, Asiatic dayflower, spiderwort, and . . . there! . . . that eyespot on the butterfly's wing, the tenth blue of my walk, and I still had half a mile to go. I won! The dog barked as the butterfly lifted and glided and was gone.

Our cavalcade paused for a wailing baby, offered adjustments and consolations, then moved on again. Our party was in different order now on the old road, which had rain-narrowed between vast tadpole-twitching ditches. I was in the rear, having paused to listen to the laughter of a pileated woodpecker somewhere down toward the lake where the dead pines stand.

I was no longer seeking blue as we rounded the curve, and that was when I saw it—the others didn't, instead looking through and beyond the new home's yard toward old, real trouble: those dead pines. A slow and capricious beetle horde had bored, bored, bored them to death, and the Corps of Engineers had decreed that we must clear-cut that whole section, and soon, or they would do so and bill us. Some trees were on community land, some on the right of way, some on lots whose homeowners lived in town. Weekenders. Those who got a letter from the Corps were talking about it. My land was not lakefront. My one huge old pine with beetles had outlasted the siege, outlived the blight. For a time I had been able to lay my ear against the bark and hear them creaking, chewing, drilling. There had been some resin spires—like turkey timers—but the massive old tree had inner resources, and survived. It did not have to be cut.

"The Corps always says soon, or else, or never," one of them grumbled, and that was what they were talking about, exactly there and then, when I saw the eleventh blue of my walk, almost eye-level, like a joke, a taunt, a toy, or a scrap of bright blue tarp. A bird? A blue bird? A bluebird. Wings spatchcocked flat, the whole thing was mounted like art in a square of new hog wire. I've seen birds fly through wire fences. I used to love watching them. They always flew through. Perfect timing. Some birds can even fly through chicken wire—little sparrows diving through, shooting through, making a game of it, bulleting and sifting back and forth, cleaning up crumbs the chickens overlooked, sweating the small stuff.

I did not tell the others what I had seen. I prayed they wouldn't see it. A bluebird dead in full flight was suddenly a larger tragedy than that whole grove of beetle-blasted pines, even though the Corps of Engineers would issue no edicts. The other walkers waved and went on around the curve, while I turned toward home, up the hill. But I slowed. I couldn't go on. I went back. I wanted to see that blue again.

I just stared for a moment. There is a law—I believe it is a good law—against messing with songbirds. But there is no law against looking. This was the real thing. Freshly plumed for mating, not one bad feather. Ultramarine. Beyond the sea. Something Montezuma would have worn to prove he was straight from the sun.

The law forbids even touching one feather. That's the law, and I broke it. The fence broke the bird. The owner of the new cottage had paid for this new fence with its greenish medicinal-smelling posts, setting new limits, seining out trespassers from its dog lot—but no dogs yet, just plain air, where the bird had flown all spring unfolded, untrespassing, untrammeled. The homeowner, the absent landlord, was not home, would never need to forgive this trespasser. He'd never see it. The natural world would resorb this bird before the homeowner's next visit, probably before the first payment on the new fence. This is not about blame, or some would fall on the bird, who in the first sweet surge of urge focused his eyes and wit past the edge of light and shadow into some dark hollow where his life-bonded mate counted down until he returned to free her from nesting work for her turn in the sky. Not to touch him, to leave him there, because of law? To hang like a doll jacket drying? Lolling like crucified Christ? Spread-eagled . . . or spread-bluebirded? Law or mercy in those ruined woods—my choice. And what choice, what mercy, to bury the dead in such a case? The female on the nest would never know what happened.

My hand to the fence, a slight pull as though picking ripe fruit, and then . . . the perfect wings shut, and then . . . into my pocket. Wings folded right back close, unbroken. Only the neck, quirked, lolling. I walked home. It was uphill. After consideration, I laid him away in the dark. I kept nothing. I offered prayer.

Did she wait long in her nesting cavity? Patient but harking? When would she have gone to seek, risking what they had begun, but not forsaking it, simply driven by hunger and thirst? Would she have found him, had I left him hanging? Might she have perished too?

Since then, the number eleven is blue. In my mind, the number eleven is blue.

I can't unknow it, what I saw that day. I can't unknow what we have learned about the cell tower millions—migrating songbirds similarly stopped cold, midflight. Imagine counting that high. Every one of them with a right by law to be unhindered, untouched by human hands, and no law—but every bird—broken.

Nominated by Stephen Corey, Rebecca McClanahan

MONOLOGUE DURING
A BLACKOUT

by KARA CANDITO

from JUBILAT

What about a zebra?—suppose
you had to come back as a zebra,
    knowing you'd spend your life
                trampling the savannah with the desperation
    of an *Open During Construction* sign?

Once, stepping off a plane
onto the blacktop of an ancient city
    where my father was born,
                I smelled burning garbage and understood
    anything can happen. Often,

it doesn't. The rain stops. We are not
washed away. I do not
    glide down five black flights
                to greet the electric truck. But when
    the air conditioner aches on again, how
blunt, how exquisite. No, I don't
    want to be famous. Yes, the radio—
                a man with the voice of a woman sings
    about a woman. The sky,

you said, is darker now. Would you
call white a bright color? Would you
    like Bach better through headphones?—

                    I mean the seismic privacy of tiny, angry
          gods beating your middle ear. I mean

          to make you dizzy. Here,
run your thumb along my chin
          while two workers shimmy down
                    a high voltage poll and everything
          that can pass between two people—
pleasure, shock, surveillance—
          the static of it—private or public—draws shut
                    like curtains across a first class cabin.

          What I thought in the dark,
forget it. A group of zebras is called
          a harem. We call them black.
                    We call them white.

Nominated by Jubilat, Karla Huston

SAY

fiction by JOE WILKINS

from THE SUN

Let's say we have a man and a woman.

Let's say they're riding in some old Chevy pickup, windows down, prairie earth wheeling past. Let's call it Nebraska. No harm to say some old Chevy. No harm to say Nebraska.

Though, to be honest, judging by the cheatgrass spiking the ditches, those four cow skulls nailed down a fence post's crooked length, and the great bluescape of sky, it might be Wyoming, or Montana, or a Dakota—any of those dun-colored, too-wide-open, go-crazy-you're-so-lonesome places in the middle of America.

But we'll say Nebraska. We'll say the Chevy's a faded green and has a beat-up topper on the back. We'll say the plates are nearly mudded over, the engine cranked up to a high whine. We'll say some things fell through back home, and they've heard there's work in Fort Collins. We'll say they've been on the road a long few days. We'll say that in the cramped cab of the Chevy they're close enough to touch, but they're not touching.

He drapes one hand over the wheel, reaches the other out to her, palm up, like he's trying to make a point, like he's trying to come to the point—but she's not listening. We don't even have to say that. You can see it in the way her gaze has gone as flat and vacant as these plains. See the sunburnt angle of her jaw? That quick tremble of her lip? For her sake let's say that, finally, he shuts up.

He smokes cigarette after cigarette, each one burning down faster than the last, and as the miles streak by, she has retreated to some dark place behind her eyes. It's probably fair to say they've had it hard. Not

135

only the four hundred flat, aching miles they've come since sunup in Sugar City, but his drunk father, her drunk father, the job he walked out on and wishes he had back, the two semesters she tried at state college and will pay for until she's thirty-seven, that thing he did so long ago in the night, that man who grabbed her wrist, the friend who loved him and whom he treated cruelly, the sister she let make her own mistakes. Yes, it must be said, like you or me or anyone—like everyone— they've had it hard. You can see it in the sharp wing his elbow makes, the way she shuts her eyes for miles and leans her head against the shuddering window glass. And, just to top it off, let's say the cassette deck is broken. So for hours it's been either silence or silence. Nebraska and silence. Yes, it's been a hard goddamn day.

But let's say—and it could happen, I promise you—she opens her mouth and begins to sing: *Ain't it just like the night to play tricks when you're trying to be so quiet?* Say, down the next dry hill, he can't help but offer up: *Freedom's just another word for nothing left to lose, / And nothing ain't worth nothing, but it's free.* Yes, let's say that, despite it all, they begin to sing. It's not so hard to imagine, is it? Not so hard to see them barreling down the road, the sun-washed wind in their faces, these getting-by tunes on their lips? *Out with the truckers and the kickers and the cowboy angels, / And a good saloon in every single town.*

Oh, I know, it most likely goes the other way. But, listen, I'm simply telling you that the ending's not yet written. Maybe she won't get out at that gutted Gas-N-Go in Osceola. Maybe she won't wait until he's gone to take a piss and then cross the street and turn the corner by the dollar store and simply walk away. Maybe two days later he won't meet that hatchet-faced man in a roadside bar. Maybe he won't strain bad whiskey between his teeth and clench his fist. Maybe the economies of entropy and regret won't have their way. Not today.

I'm holding on here with foolish hope. I'm telling you they sing their way through Osceola, then turn south to miss that storm boiling up over the Sandhills. I'm telling you they stop on the grassy banks of Little Dry Creek and splash a bit of water on their necks. Telling you they make McCook by nightfall and stop at that cut-rate motel he knows and split a quart of beer while they watch moths arc and spin around streetlights like kinfolk of the stars.

I'm saying that this night they undress and pull the comforter from the bed and sweat against one another and roll away to sleep as naked and tired as stones.

I'm saying, in the frog-loud Nebraska night, in the pure dark of the Middle West of America, they dream.

And his dream is of sunburn and off-brand cigarettes and a black, watery silence she dives into and through and pulls him from, and with his tired arms he greets again the light. And her dream is of all the things she has ever forgotten lined up on a country porch, and only after she has touched and blessed each one can she race down the steps and slide into the front seat beside him for the ride to the river.

I'm telling you—just trust me for a moment, won't you?—that she wakes and hears him already in the shower, and she rises and drapes one of his shirts over her small shoulders and begins again to sing. *And I remember something you once told me / And I'll be damned if it did not come true.*

I'm telling you they sing. Listen. Hear their cracked voices whirl and ring.

Nominated by Daniel Henry, Jennifer Lunden, Robert Wrigley

CALLING ALL GODS

D.A. POWELL

from THE KENYON REVIEW

Because I stand with my great unknowing yap and pray for speech.
Because I would open my body like a rasping bellows and have you
    fill it.
I do not know your name.
That's the zigzag lightning I know.
And that's the stout oak taken down by wind.
But what else am I to call you when you take me up in your
    embrace.
You've always touched me with a stranger's hand.

What is language outside the body but dry echo, the reflected
    want.
I stood on the embankment where the midges fussed about the
    water.
The black wings took them.
The dark celebration overtook its congeries.
No other voices but the frogs. No other sermon but the
    swallow's call.
Why did you not enter me there with all the others.
Oh, didn't you just. Oh, didn't you give and thrust.
But spoke no word.

No one man can be all things. That's why we need the river's
    indecisive swell.
I, of course.

I wait for you, the evening.
Abandoned boathouse hallelujah.
I have come to speech. I have turned to kiss your face.
I find your face in every corner of the congregated night.
And I am filled with tongues.

Nominated by Renée Ashley, David Baker, Kevin Prufer

MY WHITE HOUSE DAYS

by THOMAS E. KENNEDY

from NEW LETTERS

> *I am more inclined to apologize for writing about great events, which touched me not at all, than for tracing again the tiny snail tracks which I made myself.*
> —Hubert Butler

I used to be able to tell about this straight out. Not that I was proud of it, but neither was I ashamed. Years ago, I had what used to be referred to as a nervous breakdown. I tried to kill myself. When I broke down, I decided it was because of secrets, and I didn't want any more secrets. Then I began to heal and didn't want to talk about the breakdown any longer, tended to gloss over that period of my biography.

At the time, late summer-early fall of 1963, I worked in the White House—in the Executive Office Building, now referred to as the old EOB, which housed *inter alia* the office of the vice president. JFK was president. I worked as a stenographer for the White House Communications Agency—WHCA, responsible for the president's travel. You might think you see where this is going—1963, responsible for the president's travel—but it's probably not what you think.

In the office with me were two sergeants major, a WAC master sergeant, and a bird colonel, the director. The colonel had a ruddy face and white hair, a bushy white mustache, and I never heard him speak, only grunt—it seemed an elegant grunt. The WAC master sergeant was the colonel's secretary, and the two sergeants major were like Dupond and Dupont, probably in their late thirties, early forties. They must have done something, though I don't know what, other than sit around. I was a nineteen-year-old PFC. The sergeants major were nice enough, but I thought maybe they were watching me—I thought everyone was. We all had top-secret security clearances. Some had crypto clearances. We wore civilian clothes—suit, white shirt, necktie. I lived with two other young guys in a private row-house in Alexandria, Virginia—at 213 Tennessee

Avenue—a buck sergeant, handsome guy, about twenty-five and a corporal of maybe twenty-two. Neither of them worked in the EOB. I didn't know where they worked—something referred to as "the garage"—and they were in cryptology, about which I was not to say anything, not even the word "cryptology." I didn't even know what it meant. I was told not to say anything about the WHCA—not how many people worked in the offices, not what their ranks were or the rank of the director. If you said something, shot your mouth off, it could bring you trouble.

One time, I heard the one sergeant major say to the other, "You know, what's his name—the staff sergeant in the garage? Somebody overheard him last night playing lounge lizard in the Mayflower bar. Trying to impress some bimbo, telling her he spends every morning in a meeting with The Boss."

"Oh, he did, did he?" The other sergeant major picked up the phone and said, "Get me personnel." Then, "You know that staff sergeant in the garage? Yeah, that one. Cut him orders for the farthest outpost in Vietnam. Immediately."

I didn't really know what Vietnam was. This was a year before the Gulf of Tonkin Resolution, two years before the first official battle of that long war, but at my former base—a casual company for soldiers not yet assigned anyplace, where I had been waiting for my security clearance—a lot of the guys were drawing orders for Saigon.

"What's Saigon?" somebody asked. "Where's Saigon?"

"Where's Saigon?" said SFC Roche, who wore a combat infantryman's badge from Korea. "You don't want to know."

Thinking about that staff sergeant who was punished for his flannel mouth with a posting in Vietnam, I wondered if the sergeants major were just putting on a show for my benefit, to make me understand they played hard ball here. That creeped me out even more than the thought that it might have been true. Mind games were scary.

I had an ID card that allowed me past the guard at the gate of the White House grounds every morning. The guard usually did a double take when he saw the name on my ID—T. Kennedy. He got ruffled because my suit and white shirt and tie didn't show I was a measly PFC, and I guess I looked vaguely like a Kennedy. Hell, I was a Kennedy. When I had to go somewhere, I would call the motor pool and say,

141

"This is Kennedy at White House Communications. Would you send a car, please?" and I could practically hear the guy on the other end of the phone leaping to his feet as he yelped, *"Yes, sir!"*

But I *wasn't* a Kennedy. Not that kind, anyway. The son of the vice president of a small chain of banks in Queens, I had just been through twelve years of Catholic boys school. The two sergeants major were enthusiastic about baseball and wondered aloud within ear-shot of me if they maybe could overnight in my family's house, which was near Shea Stadium, when they went to a ball game there. I could not even begin to tell them that it was out of the question, because . . . I didn't know the because of it. I didn't yet understand my father was an alcoholic and my mother was depressed. We just *never* had anybody in the house. My father seemed a kind of important guy, his picture in the local newspaper sometimes, and my mother used to teach school. They were good people, but we *never* had anyone home. That's just the way it was. So I did not know what to say to the sergeants major when they wondered out loud whether they could stay at my house when they went to baseball games at Shea, implying that in turn they could get me rides on Air Force One and on the presidential train. They even gave me a handful of the cheap PT109 tie clasps that The Boss used to have his people hand out.

Another thing I didn't understand was that I was about to have a nervous breakdown, was already having one. A person who has a nervous breakdown is the last to know. The top-secret security clearance I had just been through precipitated the onset of it, although all the elements leading up to it were already present.

Each day the alarm clock jarred me awake in my bed in the little room in the private row house at 213 Tennessee Avenue. I did not want to rise, but I knew if I didn't get up I could go to jail because it was a crime not to go to work when you were in the Army. One time before I went to bed, I took a whole bottle of a non-prescription sleeping medicine— SLEEP EZ—washed down with half a pint of cheap rum, expecting not to wake up, but I did.

I had breakfast—coffee and a Pall Mall and apple juice, which was cheaper than orange juice. Then I took a bus along Tennessee Avenue into D.C. and walked up to the gate, showed my ID card, and went into the EOB, took the elevator up to the WHCA offices. I sat at a desk behind the colonel's secretary, the big tough-looking WAC. The desk was antique and ornate, said to be from Lincoln's presidency. A few times a day a captain or light colonel came in and dictated something to me. I took it down in Gregg shorthand and typed it up on an IBM Executive typewriter. I don't remember the contents of those documents, only that they didn't seem anything to be secretive about. Maybe they were in code. I remember once a captain chewed me out for not locking a cabinet of documents marked top secret. Sgt. Major Duncan said, "Come on. Give the kid a break."

At lunch time with a big skeleton key, I let myself into a side room that had a refrigerator and formica table you could eat at. I had my own key; it felt good in my pocket, substantial, from Lincoln's time, historical. I made a couple of sandwiches from the supplies I bought— bologna, white bread, mustard, piccalilli relish—and washed them down with a glass of milk. I didn't have much money for food. The pay for a PFC was about eighty-eight dollars a month then, and I got a differential because I lived off post, a food and rent allowance, but it wasn't much, and I more or less lived on *baloney* sandwiches with an occasional six-pack and radishes for snacks.

If I traveled in uniform on a plane, I got half fare, and once or twice a month I flew to La Guardia airport, which was a mile or two from my home. Aside from the single gold stripe on my sleeves, the only decorations I had on my uniform were the little metal shield of the Adjutant General's Corps, worn on the collar, and the marksman's qualification insignia with tiny appended bar that said "rifle" on the right breast pocket, but because I worked in the White House, I also had been given a colorful porcelain badge with the seal of the President of the United States, about the size of a demitasse saucer, worn on the left breast pocket—over the heart, I guess.

The first time I flew from Washington in uniform was the first opportunity I had to wear that presidential seal on my uniform blouse, and I was eager to display it. I carried my uniform into work in the EOB on a clothes hanger, because I would go directly to Dulles at five, and one of the sergeants major saw the seal on my breast pocket.

He swiveled his chair from his antique wooden desk, raised the toe of his shoe to where it almost touched the porcelain seal, and said, "You know, I wouldn't even wear that thing on the plane. Might start people asking questions."

So I took it off and buttoned it inside the pocket.

At Dulles, I thought about going into the men's room and putting it back on, but then I thought what if I was being watched? Or what if someone saw a young PFC with the presidential seal on his blouse and reported it? Maybe I would get sent to the farthest outpost in Vietnam. In a way, I would rather be in Vietnam than where I was, but I didn't yet know what Vietnam was. I just wanted to be in Orleans, France, where I had learned I would have been posted if I had said no to the White House posting. This was voluntary. If only I had said no to it.

That Saturday night I joined my neighborhood pals who hung around at Walter P. Shea's Bar & Grill on 90th Street and Roosevelt Avenue in Jackson Heights. An eight-ounce glass of beer cost a quarter, and I stood at the end of the bar with my buddies—Lenny O., an apprentice plumber, Kenny L., a sophomore at Fordham, Danny D., who delivered for a drug store that he used to steal condoms from, Nickie, a St. John's freshman with a football scholarship, Johnny Rak, a house painter, Bernie M., who worked in an asbestos factory, a few others. I felt at home in Shea's, away from the pressure that was building in my mind, knocking back Schaefer Beer and listening to the jukebox, where you could get three songs for a quarter: the Four Seasons' "Walk Like a Man," Ruby & the Romantics' "Our Day Will Come," Bobby Vinton's "Blue on Blue" and "Blue Velvet," Elvis Presley's "The Devil in Disguise," the Crystals' "Da Doo Ron Ron," Martha & the Vandellas' "Heat Wave," and my favorite, Barbara Lewis' "Hello, Stranger," which always made me think of Anne, a girl I was in love with the summer I was sixteen.

We young guys sat at the far end of the bar, and the adults took the end near the door. They didn't like us very much, the adults. That night Danny D., a tall wiry blond kid, had a black eye which he hid behind wrap-around plastic sunglasses and sat in the middle of the bar, closer to the adults, and for some reason he had a long-stemmed yellow rose in his hand.

One man—a big, fleshy guy with a beaked lip—must have felt like Danny was invading the adult territory and snapped at him, "Whattaya hidin' behind those shades?"

Always quick-lipped, Danny shot back, "Cost you a bean to find out."

"You look like a bag of beans yourself."

"And you look like forty miles of bad road."

Just like that they were on their feet boxing, but Danny was lighter and quicker than the big guy. Every time the man threw a punch, Danny ducked, slapped him in the face with the flower, and laughed like Woody Woodpecker. The man was frantic with rage until Mr. Shea broke it up, threw Danny out.

He came down the bar to us and said, "You boys don't behave your-selves, you can get the h-e-two-sticks outta here, too!"

I was already beered up, myself—and for some reason, I flashed my White House ID card. "Oh, yeah!" I said. "Well look at this. I get into the freaking White House with this card."

"Yeah, sure," he said. "That and fifteen cents'll get you on the subway."

I showed the card to my friends. "It's true," I said. "I get into the White House every single day of the week." They didn't seem impressed. Maybe they didn't believe me. In a sense, I didn't believe in it myself. I wanted to be impressed by it. I wanted to believe that it was wonderful, but I didn't really think it was. I only *wanted* it to be wonderful.

The problem was perhaps symbolized in that identity card, in the surface of identity, in the uniform I wore, or didn't wear, in the decorations on that uniform, the chevrons, the AG badge with its stars and stripes, the dog tags that jangled on a drain plug chain around my neck with letters and numbers stamped into the metal—my name, my service number, the letter "A" for my blood type and "RC" for my religion—Roman Catholic.

After I dropped out of college, volunteered for the draft, and had done my basic infantry training in the Army, I received orders to report for AIT to Fort Benjamin Harrison in Indianapolis, to the Adjutant General School (known as TAGSUSA) to be trained for twelve weeks as a stenographer. I hated the idea of learning stenography, which seemed less than masculine, although both my parents assured me it was an excellent profession for a young man. They trotted out examples of men they knew who had been stenographers and who went on to top executive positions. Buddy Kent, for example, who was now executive vice president of Borden Milk. I was not convinced. However, I could not deny that I was good at it. Very good.

One morning I was called out of class and invited into an office in which four or five men in civilian clothes sat. Suits. Narrow dark ties. The shades on the windows were drawn down, and I was asked a number of unusual questions, only four of which I remember:

"Do you like baseball?"

"I only follow the World Series."

"Who won last year?"

"Uh . . . I don't recall."

"Would you kill for your president?"

I thought for a moment. Dealing with the priests, nuns, and brothers had taught me how to answer questions not necessarily truthfully but so as to reflect good intentions tempered by humility.

"I would like to think I would," I replied.

The men looked at one another, nodded soberly. Then the man who seemed to be in charge, a jug-eared, narrow-faced man who turned out to be one of the sergeants major—Duncan—looked into my eyes and said:

"PFC Kennedy, how would you like to work in the White House?"

It is difficult to say how things *might* have been, but had I responded, say, as Bartleby, the Scrivener, "I would prefer not to," my life—at least the near future of it—might have been decidedly different. I might not have broken down, might not have spent time in a locked ward with men who were truly insane, might not have derailed for several years. But who is to say? All of the elements of my crack-up were already present—my good but alcoholic father, my good but closed-off home (as the homes of alcoholics, I later learned, often are), my good but depressed mother. . . . Then there was that priest who had pried into my secrets and told me, when I was fifteen, that I was already on the way to being seriously sexually perverted because I masturbated. He assigned me a penance so heavy that I could scarcely be expected to perform it, thus adding to my sense of guilt and making of me an apostate. . . . So all the elements were there, but it needed a catalyst to combine them and cause my melt down.

Sergeant Major Duncan's question had been posed and required an answer. The way that I had been reared through twelve years of Catholic boys school and my formative years as an American in the McCarthy 1950s had taught me not to look into my mind and see what I thought, but to look into my mind, try to discover there what I was expected to think and to respond accordingly.

In the army, I had hoped to be stationed in Europe after my Advanced Individual Training because I was taken by European literature. It did, in fact, turn out that my orders, already slowly grinding through the machinery toward me as I approached the last two weeks of a twelve-week training course, were for Orleans, France. I had, in fact, studied French for three years in high school and had read Camus, Gide, Maupassant, Jacques Prévert, a little of Rimbaud, and a bit of Balzac, Voltaire, Montaigne. . . . Those orders for France reached me when I was in the casual barracks going through repeated security grillings. I looked up Orleans—located on the Loire River on the site of Genabum, a Celtic city burned in 52 B.C. by the Roman General Gaius Julius Caesar; in 1429, Joan of Arc put an end to a long siege of the city by the English. I saw a picture of the communications base there, which was in a Renaissance building that looked like a castle. I went to personnel and tried to accept the orders for France only to be informed that my file had been blocked for special assignment. Then I worried that I would be punished for that attempted treachery.

But none of these things was yet known to me, and Sgt. Major Duncan's question remained to be answered. I looked at him with his jug-handle ears and narrow face, and having seen in my mind what all the priests and patriots expected me to say, my face lit up, and I exclaimed, *"Wow! Yes! I would be honored to serve my president!"*

The snag originated during the first security interview. It seemed to be a routine interview—that is, it would not be like the later ones, with wires from a polygraph machine cuffed to my fingers and fixed around my chest to measure my breathing rate, pulse, blood pressure, perspiration, and arm and leg movement in units of the zigzag markings on graph paper feeding along a conveyor belt. The first time, my answers were only recorded on a pad by a middle-aged man wearing civilian clothes who had introduced himself to me as Major something. His questions seemed ordinary enough that I don't remember them—until he asked:

"Have you ever engaged in normal sexual relations with a woman?"

Suddenly I was back in confession with the priest. But I had what I thought was the right answer—that is, the answer they wanted, not the answer that Jimmy Carter would give to a *Playboy* interviewer about fifteen years later when asked about adultery (*In my heart? Yes.*)

With mild indignation, I said, *"No!"*

The major looked up from his pad at me and asked, with slight incredulity, *"No?"*

147

The trap had snapped shut. I had exposed myself to the suspicion that I was a rat who smelled strange bread in women. There was no going back. I blushed. "No."

His eyes were on me, then dropped to his pad, where I imagined his printing in all caps the word RISK. "Have you ever had *abnormal* sexual relations with a woman?"

A "normal" nineteen-year-old might have asked with leering enthusiasm, "What's *that*?!" I had no idea what was entailed in abnormal sexual relations with a woman. I knew, however, that in my heart, regardless of what they were, I *wanted* them.

But my response was a neutral, "No."

I was terrified of what the next question might be. For I was convinced the answer would reveal that I was well along the road, as that priest had assured me, to sexual perversion: *Do you masturbate?* Followed by, *How often?* And, *What do you think about or picture when you masturbate?* (All questions that sick fuck of a priest had asked.) It would not have occurred to me that I could simply refuse to answer, simply say, *That's none of your business! Back off Jack!* I was a good Catholic boy and a good American, and this was official business.

But no. Of all the questions asked me, again and again, about my sex life, or lack thereof, that was the one question that was *not* asked: Do you masturbate? Of course, I was a sheltered kid. I had not guessed that it is normal to masturbate. That it is probably abnormal *not* to masturbate. But because of that priest, I was unable to interpret the absence of that question in these security procedures in that obvious manner. And I had no one to discuss it with.

None of my friends admitted to it. Frankie Monofski had tried one summer night, hanging around the park. He asked the group if they regularly had wet dreams. It was a trick question which, when answered negatively by most of us, led to, "I don't either. That's because we jerk off regularly." I think he was honestly trying to open a discussion that nobody wanted to have, and it led to him being ragged, his earning the nickname Jerkoffski, and frequent taunting questions, "Still doin' your daily exercise, Jerkoffski?"

So I had no one to discuss it with.

My father was an alcoholic. My mother was depressive. And I was a secret deviate.

Next question: "Have you ever," the major asked, while I held my breath, "had sexual relations with a man?"

This, at first, startled me. But now I was on firmer ground. *"No!"*
"Have you ever had sexual relations with an animal?"

It is so easy now, nearly fifty years later, to comprehend how bizarre, how absurd these questions were. How unnatural. How perverse. How abnormal. How invasive, transgressive. How, well, puritanical the sexual foundation of our society was. Not to mention the revelations since then about the sexual behavior of politicians, priests, and a certain FBI director.

But back then, for me, a boy who had gone to Catholic boys schools for twelve years and felt compelled to go most Saturday afternoons to mind-control sessions known as the Holy Sacrament of Confession (now disguised under the name of "Reconciliation") without which one was doomed to an eternity of the tormenting flames of hell—back then it was *not* easy. Not for me anyway.

Apparently my top-secret security clearance file was flagged, because about every other week for the next four months, I was called into the personnel office where, behind the closed door of a windowless room, I was hooked up to a polygraph and asked questions about my sexual behavior. Sometimes the interviewer was a major, sometimes a lieutenant-colonel, but always in civilian clothes. The first question posed—after the perfunctory start-up questions of name, rank, serial number, etc.—was always, "Have you revealed to anyone the fact that you have been submitted to a polygraph test?" A question that terrified me, that precluded me from discussing what I was undergoing with anyone.

The sex questions were always the same (indicating, I think now, how limited the erotic imagination of bureaucrats is):

- *Have you ever had normal sexual relations with a woman?*
- *Have you ever had abnormal sexual relations with a woman?*
- *Have you ever had sexual relations with a man?*
- *Have you ever had sexual relations with an animal?*

One of the colonels—they were always colonels now—told me that I should not feel singled out by these questions. He assured me these questions were posed to everyone (which I interpreted as everyone stupid enough to say that he had never had normal sexual relations with a woman). Another colonel revealed to me that because I was nineteen—had only just turned nineteen—it was not *so* abnormal that I had not yet had normal sexual relations with a woman. If I were twenty-one, however, it *would* be abnormal. I'm sure he thought he was being kind. But what I heard was that I had two years to get laid or else forever be condemned to the hell of abnormality.

Meanwhile, I was living in the casual barracks, taking casual temporary assignments in various offices around the base at Fort Ben Harrison. The other men came and went quickly, and I had no time to befriend any of them. Most drew orders for Saigon.

One week I was assigned to an office staffed by two civilians—a man of perhaps fifty and a woman with a Kentucky accent who could have been any age, late thirties to mid-fifties, wore a lot of lipstick, jangly jewelry, a low-cut blouse, and dress slacks tight around her ample hips. One day when I got out of my desk chair, she hopped into it and, her voice oozing mock sensuality, drawled, "Oh, PFC! This chair is *so hot!*" And rubbed her bottom around on it with an ecstatic expression on her pudgy face. I blushed so fiercely that sweat began to pool on my forehead and in my eye hollows, and the man, pipe between his teeth, cackled.

I thought, *What?! Do they know what I am being questioned about? Does everyone know? Is it a subject of cackling gossip?*

It was summer now, a thickly humid July, the air full of slow-moving fat black flies that got into your ears and your nostrils and mouth and food. Many days I didn't have any work to do, which suited me fine. I read a lot—Joyce, Camus, Dostoyevsky, Steinbeck, Orwell, Huxley, Kerouac. . . . Sometimes the casuals who shipped out to Saigon left paperbacks behind in their metal wall lockers or wooden footlockers—Cheever, Robbins, Wylie, Updike, night-standers. When I had money I took the bus into Indianapolis and wandered around. Once a Negro pimp in a pork-pie hat and a trim mustache approached me in the bus terminal and asked if I wanted something *fine.*

"How much?" I asked.

"Two dolla for the girl, two dolla for the baid."

The way he pronounced "bed" sounded like "bad," and I was afraid of disease, afraid of being rolled, afraid of being watched. Maybe this would be considered abnormal sexual relations with a woman.

Instead I walked. There was a servicemen's club run by elderly ladies who baked cookies and brewed coffee, and the club had a stack of old *New Yorkers.* I sat back in an armchair and read the short stories, three or four in every issue. The Brass Rail, a bar in town, served soldiers who were at least eighteen; sometimes I went in there for the air conditioning, to be in the cool dark with a cold bottle of beer, but usually I didn't have enough money. More often I just walked, around the Circle, at the center of which was a jutting pillar known as the Soldiers and Sailors Monument. The pillar was set on a mounded circular base that housed a war museum with exhibits like "Boots Taken from a Dead Japanese Soldier."

One time, as I made my circuit of the Circle, a middle-aged man in a seersucker jacket and open-collared shirt came up to me and said, "Let's go have a beer then, shall we?"

What? Was this a test? Was I being watched? If I said yes, would he peel off his seersucker jacket to reveal bird colonel insignia on his collars? Hah! Gotcha!

Another time a visibly pregnant woman with a very young face and a southern drawl asked me, "Soldier, would you buy me a glass of milk?" I was so lonely I longed to be with her, just to hold her, but feared that would constitute abnormal relations with a woman.

Sometimes when a whole bunch of guys had shipped out, I was all alone in the casual barracks. One such night I came in, flipped on the light, and found a brand new copy of *Playboy* on my bed. *Playboy* was an expensive magazine, and this looked crisp and new. You didn't just look through a *Playboy* once and throw it away. Why would anyone leave it on my bed? But my bed was the only one made up in the whole barracks—all the others were stripped to the springs, striped mattresses rolled up on them. I went into the latrine and washed my hands, threw water in my face, gave whoever it was time to take the magazine away, but when I came back it was still there. Tentatively I picked it up, peered into the shadowy corners of the room, stuffed it into my shirt, and hustled over to the TAGSUSA office building where there was a bathroom with a lock on the door, and I latched myself inside with the magazine, opened out the centerfold picture and spent half an hour with Carrie Enwright, Miss July 1963.

Walking back to the barracks along the empty dusty dirt path, my eyes glazed like a passionate young Cavafy hero, though troubled by the fact that my passion had not been spent with another human being but with a two-dimensional image on paper with a glossy finish, I pitched the magazine into a trash can. In the barracks, sitting on the edge of my bed, face in my palms, it occurred to me that someone was watching me. That the trap had been baited, I went for the bait, and they had watched me from somewhere, following and recording every move I made. It was all part of an orchestrated plan to make me reveal myself, to pry open my skull, just as that priest had done four years earlier, but these pryers were coming from a different place: The priest said, *You must not;* these bureaucrats said, *You must, or else you're strange.* It was all bait to get into my head by watching how I responded. The *Playboy* on the bed. The Negro pimp. The man who invited me for a beer. The pregnant woman.

Already sweaty from the humid night, I sat beneath the naked light bulb of the shadowy barracks and began to sweat even more; water oozed out on my forehead, down my face, beneath my arms, slid down the gutter of my spine, soaked my hair. I was afraid to undress, afraid to get under the sheets. The barracks were unlocked. Anyone could come in. Watch me in my sleep. I thought about taking a shower, but then remembered that the nozzle in the showerhead that morning had made me think of a camera lens. It occurred to me there might be cameras everywhere. Listening devices. I didn't sleep at all that night. Lay on top of my made bed with my eyes open, fully dressed, alert to every creak of the wooden structure.

Next time I was interviewed in the windowless room with the polygraph wires cuffed on my fingers and wrapped around my chest, the colonel sat in shadow, while I was in the lamplight, and he had a new question:

"Have you ever kissed a girl?"

"Yes."

"How many times?"

"You mean, how many girls? Or how many times with each girl?"

"How many girls?"

"I think . . ." I scanned backward in memory. The first was Evelyn when I was fourteen. Who was the second? Anne—oh, Anne! She was so pretty. When I was sixteen. I *loved* her. Took her to the Wintergarden with money I earned after school to see *West Side Story* with a full orchestra, Leonard Bernstein conducting. Then there was Nancy, the same year. Who else? Rita, a year later. "I think about four or five."

"Did you kiss them on the mouth?"

"Yes, I . . ."

"Okay," he said and held up his palm to signal that was enough. "Would you provide the full name and address of three of them? So that we can verify this?"

I remembered my mother having told me that some neighbors told her that an F.B.I. man had come asking questions about me. I would not like Evelyn or Anne or Nancy or Rita to know that I had told I kissed them. And what if they denied it? This was the only time that I rebelled against the questions, the demand for information. I said, "I was taught not to kiss and tell."

The colonel was silent for a time. Then he asked, "When you kissed these girls, did you want to do more? To . . . have sexual relations with them?"

"Yes. I . . ." I could remember with Anne Tarnière, a French Canadian girl, especially with Anne. She was so pretty and kind, with long auburn hair and small and slender. She was fifteen, I sixteen, and it was 1960, and we were at Rockaway, Beach 98. I remember holding her hand and walking out into the surf with her, plodding out in the hot sun against the rough cold push of the breakers, the way she looked at me, smiling, as though I were worth something. And that night on her front porch how she leaned into me as we kissed, our bodies tight against each other, and I was hard and knew that she could feel it, and still she pushed against me, and I looked down over her shoulder and told myself to lay my palms against her bottom, but my palms did not move.

"I thought it would be disrespectful," I told the colonel. But actually I knew I was just afraid. I *couldn't* cross that line.

"Was it," the colonel asked, sounding suddenly inspired, "was it because of religious convictions?"

"Yes," I said. "Yes." It was a lie, but at that moment I so thoroughly wanted to believe it that the polygraph probably didn't register it as a lie.

That was the last security interview. In late August, I was called in to personnel and informed that my top-secret clearance had been approved, and I had orders to report to Washington in a week.

But as Humbert put it—*Lolita* had been abandoned in a footlocker by a soldier departing for Vietnam—the poison was already in the wound and the wound wouldn't heal. I still felt that I was being watched, doubted.

In the row house at 213 Tennessee Avenue in Arlington, when my roommates were present, listening (I wanted them to hear), I phoned a girl I knew in New York. She was not a girlfriend but a pretty girl I

153

knew slightly—I think she was puzzled why I was calling her—and spoke for a long while with her, inviting her out to dinner the following weekend. She thanked me but said she was busy, and I pretended not to hear —"Well, see you then!" I said, and started worrying that the lines were tapped.

The corporal had a fiancée, and the buck sergeant played the field. He used to tell us as we drank beer and snacked on salted radishes in the kitchen about his encounters, told in considerable detail, which made me feel even more observed. Was I being watched right now to see how I responded to his tales of a girl putting her hand into the unzipped fly of his pants, taking him in her palm? Were *they* watching me? Or was someone else watching? Was that mirror a window to the next row house? Behind which was a man with a tape recorder, a camera, focused between my legs to see if I was hard? Was I *supposed* to be hard?

One late October weekend, I flew to LaGuardia, took the bus from the airport to our quiet tree-lined street and let myself in the side door of our house with the key my mother had given me when I was eight years old. How proud I was, as a boy, to have a key. "Don't lose it," my mother said. I never did. If I close my eyes, I can still see that key, still feel it in my palm. It seemed a key to warmth, to safety, to my family.

Inside, my father was sleeping on the sofa, snoring loudly, muttering in his sleep. The reek of whiskey exhaled from his mouth, hung in the air around his body. My mother was already in bed, her door shut. I sat in my room, and it occurred to me I no longer wanted to live. It did not occur to me that I had reached an impasse, as a religious and patriotic boy, where my religion was saying to me that I was a sinner if I did and my country was saying to me I was an abnormal man if I didn't. I had already read Joyce's *A Portrait of the Artist as a Young Man*, but had not yet comprehended how clearly it explained my situation.

I took the blade out of my safety razor, turned up my cuffs, and examined my wrists. With the tip of my finger, I located the pulses. The right one felt stronger. With the corner of the edge of the blade, I carefully sliced into the pulsing vein. The blade stung as it cut in. I did not want pain. I wanted only death. I wanted only to be released from life. To go to sleep and never wake up. I looked at the tiny cut in my flesh and felt like a failure, a prisoner of life.

In the bathroom, I looked into the medicine cabinet. There was not much of anything there. Then I found an unopened bottle of Bufferin. Thirty-five tablets.

Take Bufferin. Stop sufferin'.

I swallowed all the tablets, one after another, washing each down with water from my pale-green, translucent-plastic toothbrush glass. Then I slipped into bed and drifted off.

Crawling along the hallway runner, I awoke, vomiting, ears ringing, and two ambulance men were reaching down to help me into a stretcher. At Elmhurst General Hospital, my stomach was pumped. A nurse and doctor put a tube up my nose and down my esophagus all the way through to my stomach, saying, "Swallow. Swallow. Swallow." From time to time I choked the tube up, so it came out my mouth, and then it had to be withdrawn through my nose and inserted again. "Swallow. Swallow. Swallow." I vomited and vomited. I vomited on myself and on them.

"I'm sorry," I said to the nurse and the doctor who were administering the tube.

"We're sorry, too," the nurse said gently.

Afterward, the nurse asked what I had taken, and I told her, exhausted, murmuring. "Could they have killed me?"

"Yes," she said. "If you had held them down."

In a wheelchair in the lobby of the emergency room, I waited for military transport, wondering what would happen now. My mother's sad gray eyes were focused downward. I wished she would take my hand, touch my face. My father tried to explain it to himself as a joke— I guess so that he might laugh it away. "Good move, son!" he said, grinning with his false teeth beneath his red-gray mustache. "This will get you out of the Army for sure!" Within a year, he would be dead, fifty-eight years old.

That night I spent in a ward at the U.S. Army General Hospital in Gettysburg, Pennsylvania. A locked, Disturbed Ward, the wooden walls of which were painted mint green. Scattered about the ward recreation tables were silent men in blue uniform pajamas. I took a seat.

One very tall, broad patient suddenly rose and cried, *"Oh, no! My eyes! Won't go back in my head!"* He shuffled heavily over to a square wooden pillar and began slowly to beat his head against it. A large black orderly hurried to him and said gently, "Hey, man, you goin' to hurt yourself. Come sit down now. Everything *okay.*"

I looked at the man seated at the table beside mine to share the sadness and fright of the moment; a burly dark-skinned man with a low brow peered intensely back at me from his deep dark eyes, and asked, "You ever been in the shower at Fort Riley, Kansas? I could swear I seen you in the shower at Fort Riley, Kansas."

Looking to the table on the other side, I saw a tall gaunt gray-faced man. Hardly moving his mouth, with an expressionless face and a clear, quiet voice, he said, "All I know is someone's tryin' a kill me."

Another man, thin and short, asked how strong my eyeglasses were and if he could borrow them. "You know I get high when I wear very strong glasses. Get really high!"

Next day I was walking in formation with the other nuts along the basement hallway to breakfast in my blue nuthouse pajama uniform when Sergeant Major Duncan appeared. Quietly, he motioned me aside. He looked embarrassed, told me he was there to debrief me. Debriefing consisted of my signing a piece of paper. I don't recall what it said. Perhaps that I promised not to tell about the polygraphs, promised not to tell about anything. In my pocket I had the antique skeleton key to the EOB WHCA kitchen, and I returned it to him.

"I'm sorry, Sergeant Major," I said.

"We're sorry, too," he said, fitting the form I'd signed into his briefcase. Without looking at me, he nodded curtly and was gone.

On November 22nd, 1963, I was still in the hospital. Standing in the orderly room where a television set was mounted at the top of the wall, I watched Walter Cronkite take off his glasses and say into the camera, "It is official . . . President Kennedy died . . . some thirty-eight minutes ago. . . ."

They say that everyone alive on that day remembers where they were. That's where I was. I thought of the ruddy-faced, white-mustached colonel, the two sergeants major, the WAC master sergeant and wondered if they took any of the blame for it. After all, the White House Communications Agency was responsible for the president's travel. That's how close I was to history, although I never even saw JFK, only glimpsed LBJ one time—in fact, bumped his arm when I rode on the elevator with him. I didn't even know who he was until Sergeant Major Duncan told me afterward. "Are you aware that you just bumped into the vice president of the United States!" But I had been walking with my eyes fixed to the ground.

Three weeks later I was discharged from the hospital and from the Army—an honorable discharge for "a pre-existing medical condition aggravated by military service."

Those few weeks I was in Gettysburg army hospital, I was treated by a psychiatrist named Dr. Fisher, who had himself been drafted into the Army. The treatment went surprisingly well and quickly. Dr. Fisher—*Captain* Fisher, he had two silver bars on his collar—was interested in me because I was well read. I revealed to him my fears that people had been watching me, observing me.

"Well, they probably were," he said. "Just because you're afraid of being watched doesn't mean you're *not* being. Of course, they were watching you. That's what they do."

He recommended that I read Thomas Wolfe, and I did. *Look Homeward, Angel* was great but—I thought and still think—overwritten. Maybe that's why Dr. Fisher was sympathetic to me. In a sense *I* was overwritten, myself.

But in "the scrupulous meanness" of Joyce, especially in his *A Portrait of the Artist as a Young Man*, I found the explanation of my dilemma, the need to release myself from religious and nationalistic rhetoric and to pursue what I could discover by immersing myself in the place where word meets spirit:

—*Look here, Cranley, Stephen said. You have asked me what I would do and what I would not do. I will tell you what I will do and what I will not do. I will not serve that in which I no longer believe, whether it call itself my home, my fatherland, or my church: and I will try to express myself in some mode of life or art as freely as I can and as wholly as I can, using for my defence the only arms I allow myself to use—silence, exile, and cunning.*

I am a writer, an agnostic apostate, an expatriate living in Denmark for over thirty years now, and I once, many decades ago, tried to end the burden of secrets that had become my life.

Nominated by New Letters, Gary Gildner, Paul Stapleton, Claire Bateman

GEESE

by ELLEN BRYANT VOIGT

from GRANTA

there is no cure for temperament it's how
we recognize ourselves but sometimes within it
a narrowing imprisons or is opened such as when my mother
in her last illness snarled and spat and how this lifted my dour father
into a patient tenderness thereby astounding everyone
but mostly it hardens who we always were

if you've been let's say a glass-half-empty kind of girl
you wake to the chorus of geese overhead
forlorn for something has softened their nasal voices
their ugly aggression on the ground they're worse than chickens
but flying one leader falling back another moving up to pierce
   the wind
no one in charge or every one in charge in flight each limited
   goose
adjusts its part in the cluster just under the clouds
do they mean together to duplicate the cloud
like the pelicans on the pond rearranging their shadows
to fool the fish another collective that constantly recalibrates but fish
don't need to reinvent themselves the way geese do
when they negotiate the sky
                      on the fixed
unyielding ground there is no end to hierarchy
the flock the pack the family you know it's true if you're
a take-charge kind of girl I recommend

house plants in the windows facing south
the cacti the cyclamen are blooming on the brink
of winter all it took was a little enforced deprivation
a little premature and structured dark

Nominated by David Baker, Diane Seuss, Marianne Boruch, David Levin

THE MOTHER

fiction by LATOYA WATKINS

from RUMINATE

The Visits done died down a little bit now. Some still come. The rustlers like this one sitting in front of me. They still asking bout Hawk. Bout how he come to call hisself the Messiah. Bout who his daddy is, but I ain't got nothing for them.

I look out the window I keep my chair pulled up next to. Ain't no sun, just cold and still. Banjo lift his head up when he see my eyes on him, but it don't take him long to let it fall back on his paws. He done got his rope a little tangled up. Can't move too much with it like that, but he can breathe and lay down. He alright. I'll go out and work out the knot when I can–when this gal leave.

It's cold out there, but I ain't too worried bout Banjo. He got natural insulation. I'm the one cold and I'm on the inside–supposed to be on the inside cause I'm a person. I ain't got no insulation though. This old house ain't got none neither. The window is rickety and wood-framed. Whole house is. Whole house ain't no thicker–no stronger than a big old piece of plywood. Ain't nothing to separate me from the cold wind outside but the glass and the pane. This gal sitting there shivering like white folk ain't used to the cold. Everybody–even me know white folks is makers of the cold. And this one here white as the snow on the ground out there. Ain't a whole lot of snow out there. Not enough to stick–to keep these wandering folks like her out my face. I wonder if the snow reached Abilene fore Hawk and his white folks left life for good. Fore he crucified hisself and took all them other people with him. Wonder if he left this world clean.

"Trees on the outside my window naked all the time," I say, and I pretend in my mind I was raised here and not on 34th. Just pretend I been on the East side all along. On the East side where good-time whoring didn't never catch, even if being strung out on drugs did. Where snow come to cover up the dirt in places where grass don't never grow, like icing covering up chocolate cake or brownies or anything dark and sweet. The East side. Where you be happy poor and don't try to pretend you can whore your way out. I just pretend in my mind I was brought up poor and wasn't never no whore.

"Ma'am?" the girl say like I done confused her. Lines come up on her forehead. Make all them big freckles look like they shifting. Like she got skin like a sow. Skin that got a life of its own and move and breathe and filthy. She run her hand through her stringy, red hair. White folk hair. I pray to Jesus she don't leave none of it in my orange, shag carpet.

"Some folks see green in the summer. But come this time of year, everybody trees look like them out yonder." I nod my head at the window. I want to make sure she get a good look at the naked, flimsy trees out there. "Like they naked. Like they poor," I say after a while.

"Oh. Yes," she say, nodding her head and letting her eyes open real wide like she recognize something I just said. She lift up her head a little bit to look past me—to look out my window. "But won't you let the dog in? He's so small for the cold." I don't say nothing, but she say something else after a while. "Joshua's father, Ms. Hawkins. I asked about him. Remember?"

I sigh real loud. I want her to know that what she asking me to talk bout don't come easy. I'd rather tell her my momma was a junkie whore just like her momma, and the little two-room shanty the government help me rent now would've been a mansion in the sky for either one of them. I want to tell her I was fourteen and pregnant when Butch Ugewe come to the Hitching Post and saved me. Made me his. A honest woman. I want to finally tell somebody—anybody—how momma ain't put up no fight. How all Butch had to do was offer her a little bit of under-the-table money to make me his. But I can't.

I shrug my shoulders. "Everything different when you traveling through places," I say, thinking bout where I growed up and how pretty everything looked on the outside. How the womens what lived in Ms. Beaseley's whorehouse on 34th was poor and throwed out by the world, but couldn't nobody tell it by looking at them on the outside. Men couldn't even see the ruin of the place they was in once they got past Ms. Beaseley's nice lawn and long country porch. The painted up women with twice-douched snatches covered up all the ugly they was pushing theyselfs into.

I move my eyes away from the window and put them on the girl. She got a long bird face and her teeth stick out a little too far for her tiny mouth. I can tell by the way the sides of her mouth drooping down, she ain't used to being in a place like mine. I don't want to make her feel more uncomfortable, so I don't say nothing bout the pregnant looking roach crawling slow up the wood-paneled wall behind her head.

"I reckon peoples be just like them trees, you see?" Her face blank. I can tell she don't see. "Everybody got a season to go through being ugly and naked." I laugh a little bit.

"Yes, ma'am," she say. Then she sigh and let her eyes roll halfway round in the sockets. "We all have problems, but can we–"

"That enough heat on you?" I ask. "Can't never keep this old lean-to warm. That enough heat on you–" I stop myself from calling her "miss". I want to spank the back of my own hand. She younger than me. Probably bout by twenty years or more. Still, I want to make sure that the old electric heater sitting on the cracked and splintered floor near her feet humming is doing what it's supposed to do. Sometimes it blow cold air instead heat like it's supposed to. I want to make sure it ain't freezing her.

She look confused bout my question. Them lines in her head get deeper, and she start shaking her foot a little. She want her story for the paper. Want to find out if I think my son was God like them folks what was following behind him in Abilene.

Last time I saw him, Hawk told me he was the real son of God, and Jesus was a scud. Told me he was the truth, and me and the rest of the world best believe it. Dust storm was swirling outside like it was the end of things that day. He walked into my life after all those years. All I could wonder was how he found me. Walked in and spread his arms like a giant black bird and said "Woman, you are the mother of I am."

I shake my head. "Hawk was always a good boy. Always. After Butch died, he helped me raise hisself for as long as he could. He did everything he could to make sure we was tooken care of. Hawk wasn't but nine, but he sure learned to do what he had to do."

Hawk asked me bout his daddy when he was still a little boy. I told him it was Butch, and Butch denied it right in his face. Later on, after Butch was dead and my legs was back to welcoming mens all night long, I told him bout Mary and Jesus and me and hisself. Tucked him into bed, and he looked up at me like I was something. Everything was still in the house that night. No tricks, no Butch, no drugs. And I wanted him to be still and special and good, so I told him the same story I heard as girl. Same story the preacher shouted over the pulpit some Sundays when Ms. Beaseley would drag every whore in the house down to Good Shepherd's Baptist Church. Cept I made him the star. "Truth is you dropped right out the sun to my arms," I told him. "I was just a girl. Ain't know nothing bout mens and babies. You special, Hawk. You special. God your daddy. You special." I wanted him to be normal. I ain't want him to be no whore son. Folks would've judged him for what I was.

When Hawk first died, the papers and stuff ain't bother with me too much. Reckon wasn't really no way for them to know who I was. I hadn't been his momma since I gave him up. But after his body went missing from out the morgue last week, all kind of stuff done printed in the paper. Newspapers coming to get my story—to know bout Hawk and me and how everything happened. Some of them say I can make money and be rich, but I want to be where I am. I want be happy poor. I tried most of my life to whore myself rich. I don't want to pretend. I'm gone be where I'm at.

Fore his body went missing, it was all scandal. It was a story printed in the paper bout him messing with a little girl up there in Abilene. Say he was charged with aggravated sexual assault on a child cause he used some kind of doctor instrument to see if the little girl had some kind of cancer in her woman part. Paper say he was doctoring them Abilene folks and ain't have the right training. Had his own community—own world out there. He was God and made soap and growed food, and them folks gave him everything they had so he could have more than they did. Hawk got thirty years in prison that I ain't never know bout for doctoring on that little girl. Least that's what the paper say. Called it some kind of rape or something. Say he made all them folks kill they-selves, so he wouldn't have to do his time.

Now though, since they can't figure out what done happened to his body, they printing stuff bout proving who he really was, eye witness accounts of his miracles, and the search for his real daddy. I can't tell them nothing. I don't know what to think. All I know is I don't talk to the big ones. I only let them small timers come through my door. They don't come promising nothing. They want to hear me.

The lady look at the pad she been writing on. "Yes, but Butch Ugewe wasn't his biological father, right?"

I try to dig back to stuff I remember from church and Ms. Beaseley talking. She was like some kind a madame preacher. Always saying the world need whores so the good Lord can have folks to save.

I finally smack my lips and say, "Shoot. Baby, you gone have to forgive me. Bonanza bout to happen." I get up slow cause my body don't move the way it used to. I cross over her legs and say scuse me, making my way to the TV. I push the button on the thing, and it make a loud popping noise that make the girl jump a little bit. "Ain't no need to be afraid, chile," I say, making my way back over her legs. "Things old round here. We all got our ticks."

She sigh. "Yes, but Butch Ug–"

"You a God-fearing woman, umm . . . what's your name, baby?" I ask, and wait for her to tell me her name again.

She look at me like she don't know what to say. Then she say, "Rhoda. Rhoda Pearson, and I was raised Catholic." She kind of tilt her head up a little like Catholic is more better than regular God-fearing.

"Oh," I say, and I don't know what else to say cause I don't know much bout them Catholics. "Y'all go by the Bible?"

She nod her head and shrug her shoulders at the same time. Her lips is straight across like a line drawed on a stick-figure face. Like she don't know what that got to do with anything—her religion.

I think bout my last conversation with Hawk. He talked bout earthly fathers and his heavenly one. "Well, you know in one them books, Matthew, I think, when everybody get to begetting somebody else?" She nod her head. "Well, Hawk told me that ain't had nothing to do with Jesus momma. That's all bout Joseph. The step-daddy."

"That's right. The genealogy in that book is Joseph's," she say, nodding her head. She interested in what I got to say now.

"Well, if the Jesus, the one you and half the world think was the Messiah, and his disciples ain't care nothing about who was and wasn't his real daddy, why we always trying prove DNA and mess today?"

She laugh a little and then sigh. She sit the pad down on her lap and look at the old TV I got sitting on top the big floor model. Bonanza going and she act like she into it.

This one chubby. She got brown hair, and I know it's shedding soon as she walk in. Got strings of it all over her shirt, and it don't look healthy at all. She holding her little notepad close to her chest like it got secrets about the world in it. When she sit down on the couch, the plastic I keep it covered with sound like it's screaming. She look around the

164

room until she land her eyes on me. Look like she trying to place the dates on my old-time furniture.

"It ain't antique," I say. "Just old. Stuff ain't nobody else want no more."

She smile and nod her head. I sit down in my rocking chair next to the window.

"I hated to hear about your son's death, Ms. Hawkins," she say. I wave her words away with my hand. She keep going. "I hate for any mother to lose her child. I'm a mother myself, Ms. Hawkins," she say, grabbing at her breast with her chubby hand. "Miscarried four times before my son was born. I know what it's like to lose a child." Her eyes look sad like she want me to be sad with her. She looking at me hard. I wave my hand at her again.

"I hadn't seen a hair on Hawk head in years fore I saw them surrounding his place on the news. I loved him. Mommas always love they boys. But Hawk been gone from me longer than two weeks."

"I take it you all weren't close," she say, looking at me from the corners of her eyes like she done found out something important, or I done gave the best gossip of the day.

And I think on it for a minute. The last time I saw him, I cooked for him. Smothered pork chops, collards, sweet potatoes, and hot water cornbread. It was the first time I had cooked for him since fore drugs took hold of me. Fore I lost him—for they took him. He wouldn't eat the pork chops. Said they don't do that at the House of Joshua. Said they don't do a lot of other things. They don't bathe with regular bath soap. They make theirs out of lye. Said pork chops and real soap is grounds for excommunication.

He brought a white man to my house that day. Short, stocky something. His skin was bout as pale as the off-white paint on my wall, and he was bald at the top but had his hair swooped over like he wanted to hide it. I wanted to tell him his head was slick as a table even with that hair swooped over, but I had seen too many white, bald, swooped heads to let my tongue go like that. He didn't never open his wide rubber lips—not the whole time he was here. Just stood there like some kind of midget bodyguard.

He told me I looked good. Said he could see clean in my spirit, and I ain't apologize to him bout leaving him to be with myself. For never coming to get him when them white folks took him from me. I ain't tell him I was sorry for letting him go out into the world ten years old and full of my lies. I ain't apologize bout nothing.

Apologize for what? Hawk ain't end up so bad. Turned out better than he would've if I wouldn't have messed up. Foster family what got him, kept him. Made him go to school. Made him stick with it. He went to school for theology. Found hisself in there, he said. Sat at my table and tossed words I ain't understand around like a empty grocery bag, blowing in a dust storm. Seeing him that day with his midget driver and bodyguard and being served by them white folks like he was sweet Jesus hisself made me feel good bout saving him from being a whore son.

Sat at my table and told me he found his daddy. I wanted to find out who he found. Wanted to know who his daddy was myself. All his life I had tried to look for signs in his body. Something to tell me which one of them mens that had me made me have him. Looked at his height. Even that day, his tall body swayed when he walked through my front door. He had to bend–kind of fold hisself just to get through. His eyes was like two light chestnuts, but his skin was dark as pure brass. He was a big, muscular man. Look like he could crush you without trying.

Hawk stretched out his hands like he was bout to be pent up on a cross and asked me in his thunder voice, "Woman, would thou like to be saved? Set free?" Then he told me his story bout being my savior–savior to all mens and womens. Savior of the world. Told me he had place for me in paradise. Told me he wanted me to come to Abilene.

"We was close enough," I finally say to chubby. She write on her pad.

"What was he like as a boy, Ms. Hawkins?" she ask, smiling. I see some green stuff in her teeth, and it make me smile too. I don't say nothing bout it. Just sit there smiling back at her.

I shrug my shoulders. "Hawk was a regular boy. Wanted what regular little boys want. Went where regular little boys we–"

"I know, I know, but he had to be different in some kind of way, Ms. Hawkins. There must have been something significant about him. He led all of those people in Abilene. Most of them followed him for more than twenty years, and a lot of people say they saw him perform miracles. People died for him, Ms. Hawkins," she say, holding her hands out in front of herself, letting them shake a little like she having a fit. She finally drop them back down to her lap and sigh.

"Was he anything like his father, ma'am?" she ask.

I look at her long and hard. She just a little younger than me. Look like she probably in her late forties or something. Got a round pie-face like a trick used to come see me when I was still a little girl. He didn't never seem to mind my young naked bottom on the nasty bare mattress. I always imagined him going back home to nice clean sheets. Leaving me dirty and ruined and spilling over with his seeds. Now I imagine him as her daddy.

I let myself smile. "You from here, young lady?" I ask. And she look like she don't want to answer, but she do.

She nod her head and smile. "Been away most of my adult life though. Never wanted to write for the *Avalanche*. Too small. Everything about this place is small," she say, looking around my den. "Alas, I am here. The winding roads of life, huh?"

Her eyes land on the only picture hanging on the wall. The eight-by-ten frame is crooked and dusty. I haven't touched it in years. She got questions in her eyes. The black woman in the picture smiling with her hand halfway covering her mouth, and a white man touching–look like a soft touch–the side of her face and looking at her with love in his eyes. A dark image in the background blurred out of focus, but it look like a child playing in the background.

"May I?" she ask, pointing at the picture, standing up like she gone walk toward.

"Gone," I say. "If it tickle your fancy." I turn my head and look out the window. Banjo resting on his paws, tied up to the tree. I think about maybe putting a blanket out there, so he won't have to lay on top of the snow. He old and tired and ain't barked to complain bout being tied up. Tied up to that tree is all Banjo know though.

"Oh, it's the photo that came with the frame," she say out loud, and then she laugh a little bit and start making her way back to the couch. "So is he? Is–or was your son anything like his father."

"You anything like your father?" I ask. Her eyes get wide, and she look down at her hand.

"I suppose I used to be. He's nothing like himself these days. Alzheimer's. He . . . , she trail off and sniff. "He dies some everyday." She look sad, and I feel kind of sorry bout pushing her, but I know her kind. She want her story. She'll cry to get it.

"Guess we all got a little bit of our daddies in us. If we dig deep enough we find that. Hawk ain't no different. He was his father's son."

"Who was his father, Ms. Hawkins? If you don't mind my asking." She add the last part on kind of quick.

I shake my head cause now I can't get the picture of my old trick out

167

of my head. I see him on top of me with Alzheimer's. He drooling on my face and calling me a strange name.

"I was Hawk daddy after Butch was gone. After I was gone, he had a foster daddy. I'm sure he had pieces of all us in him," I say.

"Yeah, but I meant . . . ," she say and just stop talking. She tilt her head to the side and smile. "Yeah."

Hawk told me that Jesus was scud and his disciples was tricked. Told me I couldn't get to heaven if I didn't go through him. Called hisself the "Great Mediator." Called God El Shaddai; said El Shaddai told him I was pure as a virgin, so he choosed me. Said that white man, who name was Troy, was the one true disciple of the one true Messiah. I laughed at him and that white man that day.

"Woman, my family are those who do the will of my father," he said that day, looking at me all serious. "All real men like this one," he said, pointing at Troy. "Woman, these men have cast their homes, their businesses, and their people aside. Everything to follow the one true Messiah." He was nodding his head and poking his lips out like he used to do when he was young–when he in trouble and wanted to cry his way out.

I asked, "You mean for me to believe you Jesus hisself, Hawk?"

He just shook his head. "I mean for you to believe I am Joshua the Messiah. Jesus was a scud. We–my Father and I–we chose you from the beginning. I mean–we mean," he said, pointing to Troy and up toward the ceiling, "for you to believe the truth. To carry it. To live it."

This one is a homely looking thing. Look like a baby–mutt baby. She mixed. Black and white, I think. She ain't got no pen and pad, but she done bought a official looking white woman with her. Woman look like she FBI or something. Got a real straight face and a long thick body. Something like a giant or a angel or something out of this world. Coal black hair pulled back in a bun. It look wet. I want to thank her for at least tying it up fore coming here. But her face–the way the bones in her cheeks all high and tight make it look like she can't smile if she want to, like she evil and mean, and I don't want to say nothing to her. She ain't the one here for the story though. I can tell by her empty eyes. It's the young'un–the mutt want the story.

She look bout fifteen–a tall fifteen. Look like white trash with drops of black up in her. Hair that dirty blonde a lot of mutts born with, and it's long and stringy and kind of thin for her kind. She don't look right with the FBI lady. Make me think bout Joshua and the last time he was here with his midget bodyguard. They looked lopsided just like these two. Cept with them it was they builds. These two gals is lopsided in other ways. They lopsided in what they got. One get to be all white and one don't. Anybody can look at them and see that.

The young'un look like she belong here—here on the East side with the poor black folks. Look like one of us, so out of all the wonderers that been in here asking bout my boy, I offer her a cup of water. I don't want to offer her FBI agent nothing, but I gone head and do it. The young'un say yes, but, just like I knew she would, FBI say no. She looking around like she expecting to see a roach or something, and I kind of want to tell her that they don't go to crawling till I turn the lights off for bed. I want to tell her they like bed bugs, cept they don't want me—my blood. They want the crumbs I drop that been dropped down to me.

She look at the young'un and nod her head toward me, and the young'un open her mouth and say, "We aren't really supposed to be here. Ms. Gertrude risked her fostering to bring me here."

FBI Gertrude reach out her hand and let it slide from the top of the girl head all the way down to her shoulders, and I hope she don't leave no hair on my couch. "It is really not a problem, Chloe," she say, and I realize she ain't American. Sound like she from somewhere hard and cold like Germany or Russia. I had a trick that had been to both places, and his body always felt like popsicles. He was hard and rough, and I couldn't never do nothing good for him. "You have been through so much already. Gertrude only want to help." Then she do something that surprise me. She spread her lips and smile like it hurt.

The young'un smile back at her fore she look back at me. "I need you to tell about Joshua Hawkins. They printed your name in the paper, and Ms. Gertrude—she's my foster mother since everything happened—"

"Maybe you should tell her what happened, child," Gertrude say.

The girl ignore her and say, "I'm Chloe Hawkins, ma'am. Joshua was my father." She say her words with a straight face like I'm posed to know. Like I been expecting her or something. But Hawk ain't say nothing bout no kids when he come here three years ago. Ain't say nothing bout no wife either. Matter-of-fact, Hawk ain't really say nothing bout hisself. I look at her skin and know she carrying somebody blackness. She tall like Hawk, and her eyes sit big in her head kind of like his.

"Oh," is all I can say. I don't feel nothing like I think a grandmother would. I don't feel nothing like wrapping her up and warming her from the world. I want to though. Want to feel how I forgot to feel with Hawk. Want to want to go bake a tray of cookies or a pie or something like that. But I don't. Just sit here and wait for her mouth to guide me. "I had twelve brothers and sisters," she say, letting her eyes drop to her lap. "They're all gone now. Died with my father and mothers. I was with Gertrude. They placed me there after . . ." her words just stop.

She look down at her hands and start bending her fingers back like she want to pop or something. She look back up, and her eyes shining different cause they got tears in them. She sniff and sigh, and I know.

"You her, ain't you?" I ask, looking in her eyes. They chestnuts like Hawk's. They just like his. His eyes was the first thing I noticed when I slid him out my snatch like piss. They was brown and nutty, and I knowed nothing that beautiful didn't come from me. I wanted to pop them out and save them—hold them close to my heart. I loved his eyes. They was always his very best thing. They was always the thing I wanted to save from seeing the whore in me.

"You the one he got in trouble bout touching," I say. "You my grand-baby?" I ask.

She nod her head and sniff hard. The water in her eyes start to spill on out, and Gertrude rub her back. "I know he wasn't certified or any-thing, but he would never hurt me. Not the way they say. He was good doctor. All he eve–"

"It is okay, Chloe," Gertrude say, spitting a little on the last letter of each word she say. "Remember what the doctor says. Do not make excuse for him. The only way to face it–"

"Stop it, Ms. Gertrude," she say loud enough to cause the lady's eyes to get wide but still soft enough to not be disrespectful. "Just stop it. You've got to stop hating them. I can't get past them. They were all I knew." Gertrude nod her head and look at me. Chloe look at me too. "They took me from home after the whole thing got out–after the mole leaked it. They took me, and now I don't have a home anymore."

"Yes, you do, Chloe. You are with Gertrude," Gertrude say real fast and sloppy like she got to hurry and get it out. Like if she don't hurry up Chloe won't understand that she want to be there for her.

"I know," Chloe say real soft. "But I want my family. I want them to rest in peace and not lies," she say, the words spilling out her mouth like fire ants from a stepped on nest. "I want to follow the truth. I believe my father was him—the Messiah. He lives. I don't care what people say. How they want him to look. He—"

"Okay, Chloe. Okay," Gertrude say, nodding her head.

Chloe smile and rest her back in my couch. She trying to get comfortable, and I want to tell her that the springs poking out ain't gone let her. I want to tell her I had that old couch since Hawk was a little boy. I done screwed on that couch. I done shot-up and throwed-up on that couch, but I don't say nothing. I let her try to find her place in it.

"Please, ma'am," she say without looking at me. She looking at her hands in her lap. "My father was the son of El Shaddai. I know that. But there have to be witnesses in the world. I'm a witness. But you have to tell them—tell them who his father was." she say, looking up at me. Her eyes filling up like a glass under the faucet. "Tell all these folks so they can finally know. Tell them so they can be saved too."

I think bout Hawk and El Shaddai and God and this little half-something gal sitting in front of me. She want the story—acting like she need it. And Hawk was a good boy, and his story was really the only thing he ever asked me for. Wanted his daddy and to know I wasn't perfect like I kept telling him. Wanted to know the truth bout hisself, and I ain't had no way of knowing myself. He went on out and made his own truth, and I ain't got half a right to take that away from him.

All them skinned knees and unfixed lunches and bullies and growling stomachs and me high or on my back or not there flash fore my eyes. And his last visit do too. The one where he bought the white man with him. How he left with tears in his eyes cause I laughed when he asked me to come follow him in Abilene. How his lips quivered like they did when he was six months bout to cry. How he was asking me to be the momma of God cause I had told him when he was little I was. How I struck a match to my cigarette and laughed in his face. I see it all, and I know Hawk wasn't never confused. He knowed I was a junkie whore and ain't know who his daddy was, but he wanted me to be something else. He wanted me to be what I said I was.

He went out and made me the momma of God. I laugh a little, thinking bout people following an old junkie whore, bowing to her like she pure and righteous and clean. Like she the momma of God. I look in Chloe lonely, lied to eyes, and I wonder. They the same eyes as Hawk's. I wonder if Hawk would've done that exam on her if I told him his momma was a whore when he was little. Wonder if he would've been a messiah if he seen the truth back then. Wonder what would've happened if I'd of popped out his eyes after he slid into the world.

I open my mouth, thinking bout what Hawk made me. What I want him to be.

"Baby, I ain't knowed no man when Hawk was made. Matter-of-fact, I called him Hawk cause it seem to me he dropped right out the sun into my arms," I say. "And if you want me to, I'll tell the world."

And that little girl smile so wide it feel like the sun shining on me for the first time ever.

Nominated by Ruminate

THE NEWS CYCLE

fiction by DANIEL TOVROV

from ZYZZYVA

Doom comes in cycles here. Right now, everyone is preparing for the end. Resumes are being sent out wildly, clips are being saved, contacts are being pressed for leads; no one is actually working. The *Global Financial Times*, it seems, is about to fold. Jeremy Black, from the Politics desk, has been tape recording editorial meetings and forwarding every email from management to his personal account. He plans on writing a book about the company once the end finally does come. There certainly isn't a shortage of material. In little more than two years, the *GF Times* has become a textbook example of how not to run a newspaper. Jeremy's worried he'll be sued, which is probably true, but I don't think the parent company (whichever it is) has the resources for any sort of robust legal effort, even with its alleged cult money. Jeremy, one of the few J-school grads here, has good instincts and solid information, so the company wouldn't have a case. Plus, we'd all go on record against the paper, especially for Jeremy, whom we all respect. This place has screwed each of us so many times; who wouldn't want payback? After getting fired, Pierre Ruine, formerly the commodities reporter and one of the best journalists we had, tried to expose *GF Times*'s dirty secrets through various trades and blogs. Lucky for those of us still employed by the paper, Pierre failed to ruin any reputations; no one wanted the story. He finally gave up the fight once his unemployment kicked in. That was six months ago, and Pierre's now in Istanbul researching crude reserves in the Near East. Jeremy says his book will be "a polemic on journalism in flux, vis-à-vis New Media," with the *Global Financial Times* as the paradigm of the industry's failed attempts to maneuver an undeveloped landscape. It's a book that needs to be written, although it's less sexy than Pierre's attempted exposé. Jeremy says I need a backup plan, too, before it's too late. But I'm not worried. I've seen this before—the doom, that is. Everything will be fine. Anyway, I'm too focused on my Syrian Proxy War story. If this really is all coming to an end, that needs to go out ASAP. It's an important piece, I sincerely believe, and it's good. I did good journalism, despite all the obstacles that management put forth, and if the paper does come crumbling down, this piece could land me my next job. Even if it doesn't come crumbling down, this piece could land me another job. And for that reason the story needs to go out before it's either scooped or before the situation on the ground changes and renders it irrelevant.

Things have been escalating. According to opposition sources, 129 civilians were killed across Syria on Monday, making it the single bloodiest day of the uprising to date. In Homs, eighty-eight civilians were crushed to death when heavy shelling by government artillery caused an apartment building to collapse. In the city of Aleppo, fifteen people were killed in a clash between protestors and regime forces, while roughly twenty refugees were shot trying to cross the border into Turkey. Last week, here in the office, fourteen new reporters were hired. I walked in one morning and saw all fourteen of them huddled around Hoa Tsu, who was giving his spiel on Search Engine Optimization and the Holy Google Algorithm. Hoa sat at his desk and they encircled him like reeds on the edge of a marsh. Each had been given a new reporter's notebook and a black ballpoint and they were taking notes as Hoa demonstrated how to write a headline without verbs in it. Most of them were straight out of college; they all looked like babies. I'm not much older, sure, but I at least have a few lines on my resume. I've worn down some shoe leather. I've paid *some* dues. In this business, there are rules that must be learned. Journalism exists for a reason; it's a necessity like food or shelter, neither of which those people in Homs have right now. Journalism isn't about page rank or web stickiness or slideshows. But at least now there will be some asses at some desks. Maybe this place won't be so goddamn quiet anymore. Newsrooms should never be quiet. We moved into this office that used to be *Newsweek*'s. It's oval-shaped, with editors' offices on the edge of the loop and clusters of desks forming an inner circle. The carpet is a pale blue and is stained with *Newsweek* coffee. There are TVs mounted on the wall above each desk cluster, but they remain off because the cable hasn't been installed. Our move was an experiment in wishful thinking. Before, the *GF Times* only had enough reporters to fill a quarter of the desks. We had been in a tiny office on the twelfth floor of a crumbling wedding-cake-looking building on Wall Street. The building was built in the 1920s, and, according to legend, on Black Tuesday brokers jumped to their deaths out of our windows. That office provided all the space we needed at the time. But then we moved and soon the empty desks got filled. Not all of them, but a lot more than we thought, especially once the Continuous News desk was created. I was cycled into the second shift on the Continuous News desk (or, CND, as it quickly became known), but only for a month, mercifully, and then I was allowed to go back to the World desk. It was hard to write about Syria while trying to generate web traffic, so I had to stay late (till at least 1 a.m. while on the second shift) to work on my piece, which made reaching my contacts in the Syrian opposition even more difficult. Rebels aren't easily reached by email. My piece was about Iranian Quds—the Revolutionary Guard's notorious Special Forces division—clandestinely fighting on behalf of the Assad regime. According to my sources, Iranian snipers had been suppressing protestors across the Damascus and Idlib provinces, an indication that the Syrian situation was evolving into a Mideast proxy war (especially if the rumors about the opposition's new Saudi weapons were true). I had finally received a photo of what was likely a Quds operative disguised in a black Druze prayer robe when the Arab League ratified its United Nations-backed six-point peace plan. The main tenet of the plan threatened to get President Assad and opposition leaders into the same room (in Istanbul) for negotiations, which, if things went well, could swiftly kill my article. Luckily, that didn't happen, and soon Hezbollah death squads were crossing Syria's southwestern border. A spokesperson for Hezbollah declined to comment on the report. That article went out with the name Omar al-Bashir in the lede instead of Bashar al-Assad. Bashir is the president of Sudan, and Internet commenters delighted in the error. (Nasty comments are better than death threats, which I had been receiving recently for an article about the People's Mujahedeen of Iran, a cult-like, pro-American terrorist/refugee group; although, when a reporter gets death threats, it usually means he's doing something right.) Ayusha Balasubramanian, normally a talented copy editor, has been letting a lot of errors slip through. She allowed three different spellings of Moammar Gadhafi in one piece, for example, including the ridiculous "Qathafi." Ayusha, who started a week before me, hasn't received her paycheck this month, and she's been distracted. They pay us monthly, which is already fishy, and this isn't the first time it's happened to her. Nor has she been the only victim of a *Global Financial Times* "accounting error." Once, they paid me $700 less than I was owed. They made it up on the next paycheck, but what if I had been short on rent that month? When I went to talk to Enrico Condenado about it, he told me, "Everything will be fine." Enrico, our sole HR employee, was sitting at his desk with large, noise-cancelling headphones on, and he didn't notice me until I sat in front of him. He acted surprised when I told him about my check, but he was quick to add that the accounting office has been swamped—"with all the personnel changes, you know?"—and that the error would be fixed as soon as it could. When I asked if I could talk to accounting—located in a different building, its address left off our pay stubs—he said he'd do so for me. He really has us reporters' backs. I left his office feeling alright. The next day he sent out a memo saying we were no longer allowed into his office without scheduling a meeting at least one day in advance. Well, if everything isn't fine, it will be. CND traffic is picking up. Hits are approaching October numbers, which means big advertisers will be coming back soon, along with some revenue. Until CND cracks the latest Google algorithm changes, we can float by on the cult money. Hoa is getting close. Last week, an article about a family court judge in Texas beating his developmentally challenged teenage daughter with a belt (with video!) was the top result for three unique search terms ("Texas judge daughter video," "Texas judge beats daughter," and "Judge William Brown") for four hours, bringing in tens of thousands of hits. As soon as it dropped down to the second search result, CND published five more pieces—"Judge William Brown's Phone Disconnected," "Texas Judge's Wife Also to Blame for Abuse," etc.—the last of which was linked to by a popular Christian blog and is *still* on the Most Popular Articles sidebar (along with "Scrunchy, the World's Cutest Bulldog," "Virginia Earthquake: Funniest Twitter Reactions," "China's Dog Meat Festival [PHOTOS]," and "Sex Robots: Are They a Threat to Prostitutes?"). Right now, the *GF Times* can get big exposure on stories like that: small, local scandals that the major news outlets take longer to find. Hoa is the king of finding hot search terms like "Texas Judge Beats Daughter" before they are trending nationally. On bigger stories, the important ones, we get no traction whatsoever. Elections in the U.S., for example, get no readers, but neither does celebrity gossip or even bikini beach-body slideshows. For a time, we could get lucky, but then

176

Google changed the algorithm and all of our tricks became useless. Traffic dropped by seventy-five percent overnight. A week later, eight desks were empty again. Those of us left were called into the editor-in-chief's office one by one and told that if our hits weren't doubled by the end of the month our contracts were void. It really felt like the end. Not just for us reporters, but for *GF Times in toto*. There were other signs. For the first time ever, Francis DeSales, the founder and CEO, could be seen walking around the news floor. For a while, we thought him a phantom, but there he was, stalking the bullpens, sitting on the edge of section editors's desks, chatting like an old friend. It was terrifying. One morning we would show up to the office and the doors would be locked. We just knew it. But somehow, we all got our hits up and the company stayed afloat. That cycle's happened three times since I've been here: *GF Times* spams Google, Google catches on and changes up, *GF Times* constricts while management punishes us—either with mandatory night and weekend shifts, new desk assignments, or hit quotas—Hoa breaks the new algorithm, hits go up again, and then back to the start. At the same time, advertisers sign on and drop off, bonuses are given, and then paychecks aren't paid, fresh reporters are hired then contracts expire. Jeremy, from the Politics desk, has been able to survive the bad times by writing flattering, aggrandizing articles about Ron and Rand Paul. To protect his reputation, Jeremy published them under a pseudonym, which no one bothers him about so long as he's getting hits. The Pauls have a relatively small but cult-like following—devotees who (when not stockpiling guns in their doomsday bunkers, no doubt) read and share *every* article that mentions the libertarian congressmen; if it's favorable, it goes up on RonPaul.com. "Fred Romaine" has three pieces there now. I wonder if he'll include that in his book, because what Jeremy is doing sure as hell isn't journalism. But one Ron Paul article takes an hour to write and unburdens Jeremy for the rest of the day so he can do something meaningful. During the last Great Google Downgrade, I got lucky twice. First, a lunatic in Belgium attacked a bus stop with a hand grenade, killing two and injuring six. The assailant also blew off his own arm, which lay photogenically next to a *pomme frites* cart. Normally, that's not a big story, but the attacker had brown skin, so leading headlines with "Terrorist?" in them generated a nice amount of traffic. The story was somewhat difficult to follow from New York, but because I was allowed to copy-and-paste the body of my original story and repost it with a new, slightly updated lede—examples: "a third man now is in critical condition after . . ." or "police are looking for a second suspect in Liege, Belgium, where . . ."—I was able to pump out stories faster than our competitors and siphon off some extra traffic that way. The man turned out to be a local, and not a terrorist. Just a guy who snapped. It turns out that brown people are actually quite common in Liege, a fact that became another article. The second lucky break was when a Christian pastor was hanged as an apostate in Iran. His name was Youcef Nadarkhani and he led a congregation of thirty from his basement church in Rasht. Iran's religious police arrested Nadarkhani during a Christmas-night raid. Nine others were arrested but eventually released. The Gilan district court found Nadarkhani guilty of converting Muslim men over the age of thirteen, a crime under Ayatollah Khomeini's founding fatwas. Despite international pressure, Tehran went ahead and sentenced him to death, drawing scorn from world leaders and 150,000 unique page views for me, a personal record that was rewarded with a twenty-five dollar gift card to Starbucks from the *GF Times*. That's what people want to read about. Muslims persecuting Christians. "They don't want to read about Iranians training Syrian militia in a desert somewhere," Jeff Pulaski, our editor-in-chief, explained to me. I was sitting on the couch in his office, right leg crossed over left, trying not to be distracted by the garbage barges billowing black smoke out his large window. Pulaski had my story in front of him. The first few pages were painted in red ink, but apparently he gave up editing halfway through. Pulaski came to us from Bloomberg by way of MSN and entered with grand plans of hard-hitting news and capable senior editors. We were so excited. Before Pulaski, Nathan Charan, a man who'd never written an article before co-founding the company with DeSales, ran the newsroom. When Pulaski was hired, we thought things were finally headed in the right direction. They weren't. I was sure my story was dead. "We can't just write a straight news story. We have to differentiate ourselves. What's the angle?" he asked me in his office. "That Iranian black-ops are likely murdering Syrians," I told him. He turned his monitor so I could see it. There were colorful graphs and pie charts, the bars and slices growing and shrinking by the second. "Look here," said Pulaski. "The most popular articles on the site this second are '5 Facts You Didn't Know About Horse Meat' and 'Victoria's Secret Models Without Makeup: Natural Beauties or Just Plain Average? [PHOTOS].' Now, the merit of the topics aside, these are great articles. The reporters took a popular story—one a current scandal, the other something always popular—and found a new way to tell it. We don't have to do 'Congress Considers

Official Horse Meat Ban.' Let the *New York Times* have it. We can't compete with them. Someday we will, but until then we have to find our niche with every story." "But the *Times* doesn't have my Iran story yet," I said. "That's not what I'm saying," said Pulaski. "Take your Christian pastor story . . . That was good because you played up the persecution angle in the hed." The *Times* didn't run that story, either, but I didn't say anything. "If you want to run with this Iran-Syria story, it should be six grafs, not six pages, with two expert quotes." Outside, a Staten Island ferry chugged into harbor. I tried to explain the implications better. Syria was becoming the sectarian war everyone feared it would. The fighting could last for years and disrupt the whole region. A separation along religious lines could draw Syria's neighbors into the conflict, not to mention that it would open the door for radical groups like Jabhat al-Nusra or other al-Qaeda affiliates. "Al-Qaeda in Syria . . . Now that's a lot sexier than Iran in Syria," said Pulaski. He began brainstorming. "'5 Signs Al-Qaeda Has Infiltrated Syria,' 'Is al-Qaeda Targeting the Syrian Regime?,' 'Al-Qaeda Gov't Next for Syria?'" I told him I'd work on it and left his office. Hit-baiting headlines aside, the sectarian violence angle was something I could work with. Many of my Iran sources could still be used in one way or another. My article could still be salvaged. Especially when, that same night, a band of Shabiha militia murdered 108 Sunni villagers in the Houla region, including thirty-four women and forty-nine children. Believed to be under the order of the Assad government, the Shabiha, or "ghosts," arrived after nightfall. Dressed in all black, their faces covered, the attackers reportedly entered civilians' homes one by one, rounding up and executing entire families. According to eyewitnesses, many of the women and children had their throats slit, while the men were subjected to "summary executions." The Shabiha, like President Assad, are members of the Alawite sect, and the massacre was an indication that the regime sought to amplify partisan tension with the hope of splintering rebel groups along religious lines. The official Syrian Arab News Agency stated that "armed terrorist groups" were responsible for the attack. Accurate reports of ground activity in Syria are impossible due to the government's proscription against foreign journalists, which, in at least three instances, has been lethally enforced. No one at *GF Times* has to worry about that, though. How can we expect them to pay for us to go into the field when they can't even afford to turn on the TVs? And there are rumors that we're behind on our rent. That's probably why Misha Gibelov, Amanda Phan, and Carl Bell were all moved from the

Markets desk to CND yesterday. All of them are capable and passionate business reporters, and the logic of the move is transparent. The three will never adjust to writing "continuous news," and they'll be fired. CND has implicit hit quotas that just can't be reached by anyone with integrity. Misha and Amanda and Carl will try their hardest to get their hits up while not losing their souls, and they'll fail. The thing is, their hits *will* go up—their hits can only go up from what they were getting writing about foreign markets—and *GF Times* will thereby profit in the short term. Then, once the three are fired, the company can hire three cub reporters at a lower pay rate, and with even flimsier contracts. CND has been growing in this manner for a while now. Once those three are gone, there will just be two of us left who saw that old office on Wall Street. Everyone else is wholly part of this new *GF Times*. Ayusha Balasubramanian was let go, it turns out. Nadine Svenson said Enrico stood over Ayusha while she packed her desk into a box and then escorted her out. She kept asking, "Why? Why?" and he mumbled something about editorial etiquette, left her in the lobby, then turned around and walked away. It won't be long until Jeremy and I are finding our niche in CND, and then being cycled out ourselves. No. They need someone to do just enough real journalism to make the front page look respectable. I'm just hoping to be here long enough to get this proxy war story out. After my meeting with Pulaski, I started over. I've worked the piece and reworked it, found new and opposing sources, explored the angles, and I actually think it's a better piece. A sectarian conflict would be detrimental to the uprising, so the opposition has been denying all instances of religiously charged violence. "This is a revolution, not a civil war," they keep saying, over and over. Whatever it means, it's a good pull quote. But the facts on the ground, as far as they can be interpreted, tell a different story, and the experts at the Washington think tanks foresee a splintering among the rebels as the next logical phase. After that, the proxy war begins. The conflict starts anew. Iran and Hezbollah will join the regime's camp, while the Saudis, Turks, and Jordanians—maybe even with Israeli air support; it's all getting very muddled—move to the side of the opposition. And al-Qaeda is right there in the nut graf, for all of Google News to see. So, maybe it's not actually a better article. It's just different; analysis instead of investigation. So what? It's going to come out fine. As long I don't have to rewrite it again. I gave the latest version to Alberto Sviluppo—a scandal-happy CNN dropout who just came on as the new Front Page editor—and he's making God knows what edits. His highlighter has been squeaking all afternoon. If he doesn't finish soon, the article will have to wait until Monday. It'd be nice to run it as a weekend feature, but it's Friday and Francis DeSales has just called everyone into the large meeting room in the center of the oval for an unscheduled pizza party. This is unprecedented. Jeremy flips on his tape recorder and slides it into his pocket. All of the new hires are high-fiving one another, but I know where this march leads. "It's going to be fine," Jeremy says, putting an arm around my shoulder. "Your hits are on the way up." He must mistake the look on my face for dread, but I'm really thinking about Syria. There's one day left before the Arab League peace plan officially fails, at which point the country is doomed, finally, completely. "Everything is fine," Yemeni envoy Lakhdar Brahimi said today. "We have been assured by the Syrian government that the ceasefire will take place as scheduled. Red Crescent convoys are standing by on the Jordanian border and are prepared to deliver aid to internally displaced people." But neither side will lay down their arms unless the other does so first. It's already too late for my article, no matter what it becomes. In Damascus, the Free Syrian Army bombed a number of strategic targets, including a military barracks, a mosque, and a hospital. Black smoke curls over the presidential palace and floats west toward the sea. The city of Homs is just rubble now, and bands of Islamist marauders roam the countryside. The walls of Aleppo, once the glimmering capital of the Amorite empire, have crumbled. The country could only circle around the drain for so long before it plunged into chaos. It's Yugoslavia all over again. The country will break up into smaller pieces, and those pieces will carry on in the same manner. When Jeremy and I walk past Pulaski's office, the door opens and Pulaski walks out with DeSales, Nathan Charan, and Enrico Condenado, all somber-faced. What the fuck does anyone know about what will happen in Syria anyway? It's an endless cycle. A pizza party? Jeremy and I walk in before our bosses, and take a seat at the table. The room is already full of people standing around, eating off paper plates. Nadine and Laura are together, laughing. By the large, black television screen, John, from the Travel desk, is saying something to the guy with the thick glasses. I don't know his name. He's been around a few months, hired to cover Autos, which he can do from CND occasionally. All the new employees are still snuggled in a group around the pizza boxes, while Hoa has positioned himself behind DeSales and the rest. Alberto walks in and takes a seat across the table from me, next to Serge Hadžić. He shrugs at me, and turns to talk to Hadžić about possible headlines for a profile on a Washingtonian who

181

ate his family. So that's that. The room is full now. I don't recognize half of these people. Marcus Finger takes the last empty seat, which is next to me, on my left, and says, "Do you know what this meeting is about?" in a way that makes me think he knows. "The jig is up," he says. Under the table, a printout is slipped onto my lap. I look down. It's an article from the *Christian Post:* "The Second Coming Christ Cult." Official confirmation at long last. According to the article, a Korean expat preacher named David Kang has amassed a quiet fortune calling himself the Messiah. Two of the lieutenants of his church are named as Francis DeSales and Nathan Charan. The *Global Financial Times* is only mentioned within a long list of assets allegedly used to launder devotees' life savings after they are willingly handed over to Kang. Even on just a cursory read, one can see it's a great work of journalism. Yet, about us, it asks more questions than it answers. "It's done," says Marcus. "Sit back and enjoy the show."

DeSales calls for attention. The room hushes. "Ladies and gentlemen," he begins, "today is a historic day for the *GF Times.*" He is smiling. Charan, standing behind, hands DeSales a slip of paper. "I'm very happy to announce that, today, we are launching ten new sites!" He pauses. Everyone is silent. "Each site will be a small, niche publication. They are independent entities, but will be guided by the same standards and practices driving this company now. The new sites are the *International Fashion Times*, the *World Tech Times*, the *Global Hollywood Report* . . . you get the idea. Here," he says, handing the paper leftward, "I'll pass this around. We plan on hiring twenty new reporters immediately to staff the new pages. Hoa Tsu, whom you all know and love, will be overseeing the whole operation." "Congrats, Hoa!" yells an enthusiastic new hire. "Yes, congrats," continues DeSales. "The new publications will be staffed from the ninth floor of the building, for which we have just signed the lease." Charan applauds. "But until we finish the hiring process, we'll be sending many of you upstairs to begin generating content. Section editors will give you your new assignments after the meeting. Until then, enjoy your pizza. And congratulations, everyone!" When the meeting breaks up, the new reporters jockey for the last slice. Nadine asks, "What happened to the paper with the names on it?" and Jeremy winks at me, pointing to his pocket. As I walk back to my desk, Pulaski comes up behind me and taps me on the shoulder. He asks if we can talk in his office. When I sit down, he asks how my Syria proxy war story is going. He must also misread my face, because he tells me everything's going to be fine. It's only a temporary move. I'll be back on the World desk in no time.

Nominated by ZYZZYVA

APPROACH OF THE HORIZON

by LOUISE GLÜCK

from THE THREEPENNY REVIEW

One morning I awoke unable to move my right arm.
I had, periodically, suffered from considerable
pain on that side, in my painting arm,
but in this instance there was no pain.
Indeed, there was no feeling.

My doctor arrived within the hour.
There was immediately the question of other doctors,
various tests, procedures—
I sent the doctor away
and instead hired the secretary who transcribes these notes,
whose skills, I am assured, are adequate to my needs.
He sits beside the bed with his head down,
possibly to avoid being described.

So we begin. There is a sense
of gaiety in the air,
as though birds were singing.
Through the open window come gusts of sweet scented air.

My birthday (I remember) is fast approaching.
Perhaps the two great moments will collide
and I will see my selves meet, coming and going—
Of course, much of my original self

is already dead, so a ghost would be forced
to embrace a mutilation.

The sky, alas, is still far away,
not really visible from the bed.
It exists now as a remote hypothesis,
a place of freedom utterly unconstrained by reality.
I find myself imagining the triumphs of old age,
immaculate, visionary drawings
made with my left hand—
"left," also, as "remaining."

The window is closed. Silence again, multiplied.
And in my right arm, all feeling departed.
As when the stewardess announces the conclusion
of the audio portion of one's in-flight service.

Feeling has departed—it occurs to me
this would make a fine headstone.

But I was wrong to suggest
this has occurred before.
In fact, I have been hounded by feeling;
it is the gift of expression
that has so often failed me.
Failed me, tormented me, virtually all my life.

The secretary lifts his head,
filled with the abstract deference
the approach of death inspires.
It cannot help, really, but be thrilling,
this emerging of shape from chaos.

A machine, I see, has been installed by my bed
to inform my visitors
of my progress toward the horizon.
My own gaze keeps drifting toward it,
the unstable line gently
ascending, descending,
like a human voice in a lullaby.

And then the voice grows still.
At which point my soul will have merged
with the infinite, which is represented
by a straight line,
like a minus sign.

I have no heirs
in the sense that I have nothing of substance
to leave behind.
Possibly time will revise this disappointment.
Those who know me well will find no news here;
I sympathize. Those to whom
I am bound by affection
will forgive, I hope, the distortions
compelled by the occasion.

I will be brief. This concludes,
as the stewardess says,
our short flight.

And all the persons one will never know
crowd into the aisle, and all are funnelled
into the terminal.

Nominated by Threepenny Review, Mark Halliday, Philip Levine

THE FICTION WRITER

by MARIBETH FISCHER

from THE YALE REVIEW

> *The past don't control you . . .*
>
> – *Bob Dylan, "Ye Shall Be Changed"*

Even now, I see her hands and forearms covered with ink—phone numbers, dates, reminders about meetings, words she wanted to remember. And once, sitting at the bar at Smitty McGee's, she swung around on her stool, lifted the hem of her skirt and showed us her leg, covered to mid-thigh with writing: notes about the novel she was working on; a song lyric she'd heard while driving. Another time, over coffee in the morning, I saw words from the day before imprinted on the side of her face. I knew how she slept then, hands tucked under her cheek. I didn't mention that the words were there and later, after she saw herself in the mirror, she said, "Why the hell didn't you tell me? Geez, would you let me run around with my dress stuck in the back of my underwear too?"

"It was barely noticeable," I laughed. The ink had been smudged, like faint bruises.

I'm still not sure why I didn't tell her she had writing on her face—it *is* the kind of thing you'd want your friend to let you know. It seems fitting that I didn't, though, for this is how I'll always remember her: words literally pushed into the pores of her skin.

Writing a story on her body so that her body had a story.

In the end, this was all she was—a story we would tell repeatedly. Each time, we would embellish it more, highlighting certain moments, habits, things she used to say or do.

Like stripping an old car for salvageable parts: that's what we would do to her life.

It's what she had done to ours.

She showed up one rain-drenched autumn Saturday at the monthly meeting for the writers' guild I had started. I was out of town that weekend, but I heard about her the minute I returned. "This woman—Natalie (that's what I'll call her)—is *amazing!*" my friends gushed. "Wait until you hear her writing!" She'd just signed a two-book deal with Random House, had directed the San Diego Writers' Center for two years, had taught with Pam Houston at the Aspen Writers' Conference *and* . . . "She wants to join *our* writers' guild."

"Why?" I laughed. "What's she doing here?" Here: this emptied-out Delaware beach town two and a half hours from D.C., with its closed shops and restaurants and "See you Next Summer!" or "Thanks for a Great Season" signs taped in dusty windows.

Her mother had a house one town over, Natalie was going through a divorce, she had revisions due on her novel, and the beach in the winter seemed the perfect place to write.

Years before, I had moved here for a similar reason, my then-husband out of a job, our marriage disintegrating, the excitement of publishing my first novel with a major publisher dissolving into the reality of book sales and numbers, none of which were good. I walked the gray beaches for hours that first winter, slowly coming to terms with the end of my marriage and feeling my way back to the novel I would finally sell a few weeks before Natalie came into my life.

I met her for the first time in the local bookstore. She was sitting in an armchair by the fireplace, laptop balanced on her knees. I had pictured someone thin and pretty; a woman in jeans and a turtleneck and sexy reading glasses; a cosmopolitan, *writerly*-looking woman. But Natalie was overweight and sloppy, and though it was late November and cold, she wore wrinkled Bermuda shorts and running shoes, a man's flannel shirt. Close to forty, the same age that I was. Her wild curly hair uncombed. No makeup. Words in black ink written on the backs of her hands.

Relief washed over me. *I'm thinner*, I remember thinking. *Prettier.* But it was small consolation. I felt unsettled by this woman, and scared. I'd gone out of town for one weekend—*one!*—and returned to find myself, if not replaced, then set aside, or so I felt. It is my single greatest fear, and though I'm not sure where this fear comes from or why, I do know that because of it I have worked incredibly hard in my friendships and marriages and as a teacher to make myself indispensable: if I'm not, no one will need me. And if no one needs me, no one will want me.

I could disappear one day and no one would notice.

I think of those entertainers who twist balloons into myriad shapes: a dog, a lion, a flower. It is what I have done with my life, twisting myself into whatever shape I needed to be, giving myself away like a party favor to make someone else happy. There is nothing normal about this, nothing even remotely okay, and yet it is the very quality, I believe, that has allowed me to succeed as a fiction writer. I am good at cannibalizing my life for the sake of the characters' lives; good at disappearing completely into whoever I need to become so that *they* might step from the pages more real, it often seems, than I ever was. And yes, of course, it is a double-edged sword. So quick am I to step into another's shoes, to intuit someone else's needs or desires, that I have no clue about my own. For years, when my therapist asked what I felt, what *I* wanted, I would panic. I don't know, I would tell her, aware only of what *she* wanted, which was that I feel *something*.

Natalie's appearance deceived me that first day. Had she looked more like me physically, would I have known how similar she and I actually were? Could I have foreseen the lengths to which we'd go in our efforts to become indispensable to each other? Could I have understood that all those months when I was looking at her, I was looking in a mirror?

She too was terrified of disappearing.

Until one day she did.

Within a month of her arrival, our writing group was meeting weekly instead of monthly. Natalie's idea. She and I took turns facilitating the sessions. She was a wonderful teacher. She began each meeting by reading the "Guidelines of Writing Practice" from *A Writer's Book of Days*, by Judy Reeves, the woman with whom Natalie had run the San Diego Writers' Center. *Trust your pen*, the rules advised. *Go with the first image that appears*. It has been over five years now since Natalie disappeared, and I still read these guidelines at the start of each class: *Be willing to go to the scary places that make your hand tremble and your handwriting get a little out of control.*

Be willing to tell your secrets.

Natalie suggested, too, that we read poetry, and she'd start each class by reading out loud a poem. It is another thing that, five years after her disappearance, we continue to do.

"I would never have started writing poetry if it wasn't for Natalie," my friend Gail told me recently. "I almost e-mailed her the other day to thank her."

Something in me constricted. How can you even *think* of e-mailing Natalie after what she did, I wanted to ask. But I thought of how our writers' meetings, which had never attracted more than a dozen members, swelled to twenty, then twenty-five, after Natalie joined us. The bookstore where we met wasn't big enough. Natalie suggested we have two writing groups a week, then four.

More people kept joining. Most were retired. They had lived entire other lives, had careers as administrators, lawyers, schoolteachers, secretaries. They'd owned companies, raised families. Finally, though, they were doing what they'd always wanted to. Gus began writing about his experiences in Vietnam for the first time. Sherry started the memoir she'd been yearning to write for years. Daniel, who had never written before, never thought he could, wrote about the last time he saw his father. Daniel's voice wobbled as he read, his hands shook. The writing was beautiful. When he finished, Natalie nodded, said thank you, turned to the next person. She didn't offer praise or criticism or encouragement. That wasn't the point.

All that mattered was the writing and the reading, the telling of the story or poem or paragraph. Everyone had a story, Natalie believed, and every story was important, and she taught the rest of us to believe this too. The participants in the writing group stopped apologizing for their work, and when they read it out loud they slowed down, stopped covering their mouths with their hands. You could see their confidence in the flourish of a metaphor, in the way their faces softened when everyone sighed with amazement and recognition as they read a paragraph that was so true the entire group seemed to feel the words physically in their own throats. It was as if Natalie's belief that they were real writers somehow allowed them to be.

And isn't that what writing, friendship, *love* is about in the end? Belief?

Throughout that fall and winter, Natalie taught classes for free. She volunteered to bartend at our holiday party. She organized a literary reading for Valentine's Day. We drank Emily Dickinson Cosmos and

Raymond Carver Martinis, and Natalie read from her forthcoming novel about a woman teaching writing in a small beach town. Snow fell past the windows into the water of the bay. Our candlelit reflections wavered in the dark glass. People flocked around Natalie, wanted to know when her novel was coming out. We decided to hold a reading every month. She helped me organize the two-day writing conference our writers' guild held each year; she started a book club. Our membership continued to increase.

Indispensable. The two of us met every morning in coffee shops to work on the novel revisions we both had due; we ran the writing groups together, went to Smitty McGee's every Thursday night to hear Randy Lee Ashcraft, in his jeans and cowboy boots, with his great voice and sexy smile, sing Johnny Cash and Jimmy Buffett songs. Natalie and I sat at the bar and talked: about our Catholic-school upbringing, our divorces, the characters in our novels, people in the writers' guild. I laughed often during those months, laughed more than I had in a long time, maybe since graduate school nearly two decades before. Until I became friends with Natalie, I don't think I realized how alone I'd become. How serious. The year I met her, my third divorce had just been finalized; my seven-year-old nephew had recently died, and a part of me I could barely acknowledge, much less feel, was reeling with shame and disbelief because this wasn't how I'd wanted my life to be. Natalie just rolled her eyes, jokingly referred to me as "grief girl," ordered us another shot, and plunged forward into the next plan: an idea for a class, another novel, a guy she thought I should date. She made me feel normal again. And fun. Alive in a way I hadn't been.

We talked, too, about my friend Kent, with whom Natalie had begun to fall in love. Kent was a contractor who played music in the local bars and was working on a CD. Natalie told me about the night they sat on the deck of a newly built house that Kent was trying to sell. There was no electricity yet. He'd brought peanut butter for her, her favorite kind, which she ate by the spoonful as they sat in the dark listening to the rain and taking turns naming songs with the word *rain* in the title. She told me about the night he sat on a curb in the darkness and cried, told her things about himself he'd never told anyone. They had two- and three-hour phone conversations, talking until their phone batteries died or until one of them fell asleep listening to the other's voice.

Although they seemed perfect, I was surprised. Kent is sort of rock-star good-looking—thick brown hair, sharp chiseled features, tanned muscled arms—and there was Natalie, disheveled and overweight in her frumpy khaki shorts and flannel shirts. I loved that Kent could see beyond the superficial, though, loved that he loved Natalie for the reasons that mattered: she was smart, talented, and fun.

That they were such an unlikely couple only made their story seem that much more real somehow. Twice Kent had been engaged to gorgeous, talented women; twice he'd broken off the engagements. It made an odd kind of sense, then, that it would be someone like Natalie, someone who didn't fit any of Kent's expectations, with whom he would finally fall in love, falling hard in a way that sometimes scared me. I didn't want her to hurt him, and I feared she would. The sale of her novel had been huge: "Let's just say there are a lot of zeros in the number," she would laugh when talking about her book advance; her agent was one of the top agents in the field; her editor worked with writers who were already anthologized in literature texts. Natalie would outgrow Kent, I thought. She wouldn't need him as much as he needed her.

I didn't share these fears with Natalie as we sat in various cafés or at the bar at Smitty McGee's. Mostly, we talked about the books we were writing and reading. Natalie had a story forthcoming in *Redbook;* an essay to be published in the "Modern Love" column of the Sunday *New York Times.* She encouraged me to send work to these same places, told me to use her name as a recommendation. She knew everyone, it seemed, in part because of her work at the San Diego Writers' Center, in part because of her longtime friendship with X, a staff writer for *The New Yorker,* whose first book had been on *The New York Times* best-seller list for almost as long as *The Da Vinci Code* and whose second book seemed destined to stay there just as long. Natalie often spent weekends with X in New York, had accompanied him to the National Book Awards in November wearing a six-hundred-dollar yellow bra—her first splurge with the book advance from Random House. The next day she showed us X's picture in *The New York Times*, pointed to a place just outside the frame: "I can't believe they cut me out of the shot!" She described how she'd hoped to talk to Joan Didion, but could only say hello before Joan was whisked away. Joan's book *The Year of Magical Thinking* had won the nonfiction award, so of course everyone wanted a piece of her.

In January, X's editor, while having lunch with Natalie and X and listening to Natalie's descriptions of life in our off-season resort town, suggested she write an essay for *The New Yorker* and call it "Letter from the Beach." Natalie did, subtitling it, "Searching for Bob Dylan in the Land of Jimmy Buffett." The essay was both beautiful and sad because that's what beach towns are in the off season. She talked about how here, in this place where she couldn't find a good jukebox and none of the local musicians knew any Bob Dylan songs; here, where everybody was married to—or dating—someone else's ex and most of the stores and cafes that *did* open mid-week were closed by three or four in the afternoon; *here*, she wrote, I found *a place that felt more like home than so many places I'd lived.*

By this time, she was talking about buying a small house on the beach with some of the book advance. It became a campaign of sorts among members of the writers' guild to get her to promise that she'd stay. She never did, and I wonder now if it's because she knew she couldn't.

She read a section of the "Letter from the Beach" at another of our literary readings, and again I watched as people flocked to her, asking when the piece would be published, and could they have a copy of it now. We were excited. *Our* little town was going to be in *The New Yorker. We* were going to be in *The New Yorker.*

She sent it to X's editor, who loved it.

Loved it enough to agree to a second essay, this one about searching for Dylan in New Orleans, where Dylan was playing during Jazz Fest.

It has been over five years since Natalie left, and still some days as I'm driving to work or sitting in a cafe, as I am now, and a Dylan song comes on the radio—*How does it feel to be without a home / like a complete unknown*—I find myself trying to once again pinpoint the moment when I started questioning Natalie's good luck. It's not that I didn't believe her—that she was friends with X and had a two-book deal with Random House and was writing for *The New Yorker* and *Redbook* and *The New York Times.* I believed every bit of this. I'd seen her teach; I'd read her writing. I had no reason to *not* believe her.

And isn't that what writing, friendship, love is about in the end? Belief?

Still, I began to doubt. Not whether Natalie was lying, but was she exaggerating maybe? Had X's *New Yorker* editor really *asked* her to write the "Letter from the Beach"? Or was she simply confident, believing so much in herself that the rest of us couldn't help but believe in her too? All I knew was that John Updike and Margaret Atwood and

Calvin Trillin had written for *The New Yorker*, and it didn't make sense that the editor, even if he were her friend X's editor, would not only commission one essay by an unknown writer but would also, before that essay was completed, commission a second, agreeing as well to cover Natalie's expenses in New Orleans. I wondered, too, about the fact that her novel was due out at the same time as mine, yet she hadn't gotten the galleys to proof. When I asked her, though, she was nonchalant. "For what they're paying me, I imagine they're just taking extra time with the whole thing. Hell, I would."

It sounded reasonable. And Kent and I had heard her on the phone with both her agent and her editor, discussing revisions, laughing, at one point arguing about something one of them wanted Natalie to revise, which she refused to. "Why did they pay me so much if they were just going to change everything?" she said after she hung up. Then she was quiet for a long time.

And so I dismissed the tiny pricks of doubt I increasingly felt. Why *wasn't* it possible that the editor at *The New Yorker* was willing to take a chance on an unknown? Why *wasn't* it possible that she was friends with X, that she'd met Joan Didion at the National Book Awards or sold her first novel for nearly a million dollars? "Isn't that the reason we become writers?" Richard Russo says in the epilogue of Jennifer Finney Boylan's *She's Not There*. "Our understanding that all sorts of implausible things turn out to be true?"

I thought about the writer Donna Tartt selling her first book, written when she was still in college, for a million dollars. Or my friend Marisa's first novel selling in twenty countries and being optioned for a movie with Sarah Jessica Parker. The divorced mother living on welfare who wrote *Harry Potter*. A good friend from graduate school getting a phone call on April Fool's Day from Oprah, who was phoning to say that she'd just chosen my friend's second novel for her book club. April Fool's Day, for god's sake.

Weren't these things as much a part of the fiction writer's life as the solitary hours staring at the computer, struggling to find words? Wasn't this normal in a way? We not only created dreams; we believed in them. How else to keep doing what we did?

Kent accompanied Natalie to Jazz Fest for the *New Yorker* article. They missed their connection in Houston and ended up driving six hours to New Orleans. Near midnight, she phoned from the SUV they'd rented.

"We're looking for a truck stop," she laughed. "It's fucking perfect, isn't it?" And it was, and right then I knew where her *New Yorker* piece would begin; in a truck stop in the middle of nowhere in the middle of the night on the way to find Bob Dylan.

"It was magical," she kept saying when she described that trip to us. *Magical.* Her face shone when she talked about it, whenever she wrote about it. And she did. Constantly. She wrote about listening to a Lucinda Williams CD as she and Kent drove past the ruined homes that had been damaged in Hurricane Katrina, about the symbols spray-painted on doors: a mark to indicate the house had been inspected; another to indicate that a body had been found. She wrote about driving to Jackson, Mississippi, and on the way back stopping at the crossroads where Highway 61 meets Highway 49, where the great blues legend Robert Johnson supposedly met the devil and sold his soul in exchange for the ability to play guitar.

Sold his soul.

The words echo.

Natalie worked on her "Searching for Dylan" essays all spring. She read paragraphs of them to the writing groups, e-mailed or read them over the phone to me and Kent. Randy Lee started playing Dylan songs for Natalie, ending the nights with "Knocking on Heaven's Door" or "Lay Lady Lay." People brought her articles about Dylan, someone brought her a copy of Martin Scorsese's *No Direction Home.* She teased me mercilessly for saying "A hard rain *is going to* fall," instead of "a hard rain's *a-gonna* fall. "You're kidding me, right?" she said. "Please tell me you didn't say *is going to.*" She made me practice. "*A-gonna,*" she'd laugh. "Repeat after me: *A-gonna.*"

One night that spring, Natalie, Kent, and I drove to a small town on the Maryland-Delaware border to meet Randy Lee for dinner. On the drive we listened to a bootlegged Dylan CD from 1970. Dylan and Johnny Cash. The windows of Kent's van were open, and it was a perfect May night, the sky pink over acres and acres of green-gold farmland. I watched as Kent caught Natalie's eye. Her dark curly hair was blowing across her face. She was smiling. She looked beautiful.

We stayed out until the bars closed, talking with Randy Lee about books and music, about what it meant to make a living as a writer or a musician. It wasn't easy, we agreed, but we loved our lives, loved that we spent our days doing what made us happy.

It's a memory I come back to often. The four of us talking about how we loved our lives.

"I don't think she expected it," Randy Lee said after Natalie disappeared. "How happy she would be here."

Although Kent and I lived next to each other, I no longer saw him much, and when I did Natalie was there. I never saw them hold hands or kiss, but they'd glance at each other across a room or a table, and this shimmering look would flash between them, as if they had a thousand secrets. They were planning to live in New Orleans the following winter, Natalie had confided. He was going to accompany her on the book tour. She suggested I meet them in different cities. "You can read with me," she offered. She often invited me to join them, but I felt ill at ease, and more and more, I began to decline.

The discomfort was more than just the feeling of being a third wheel, though like so many things about Natalie, it wasn't anything I could name, exactly.

"Kent told me not to tell you this," she confided once as we sat at Smitty McGee's, "but Kate's getting John Irving to blurb my book." Kate was her editor. The *John Irving* barely registered.

"Why would Kent tell you not to tell *me*?" A tight feeling in my throat.

"Oh, he just worries that it's hard for you, all this attention *my* book is getting." She paused. "I mean, before I came here, *you* were the big-deal published author and I know I've stolen some of the limelight." She laughed. "But I told Kent you were the least jealous person I'd ever met."

Gratitude to her. A feeling of betrayal from him.

Another time she told me, "Gus wrote the most amazing thing today." She paused. "I told him to show it to you, but he said he wasn't comfortable . . ." Natalie would see in my eyes or on my face whatever it was—hurt? fear? confusion?—and she'd punch my arm and say, "Oh, don't worry, he sang *your* praises too."

"People are always confusing us," she said another day when we took a break from writing. "I swear, you could show up at my writing class and if you just gained a few pounds, they'd think you were me." She inhaled sharply on her cigarette, then blew out a long stream of smoke. "Hell, let's just merge our names." She laughed. "Marinat. What do you think?"

Some days, it seemed not that we were the same but that she had actually *become* me, only better: more fun, more talented, more successful. Her book had sold for nearly a million dollars; Random House was planning a huge, thirty-city book tour. And *she* was running the guild now; *her* classes were the ones everyone wanted to take. My closest friend was now the love of *her* life.

In retrospect, I realize that I should have felt frightened at her suggestion that we merge names, but I remember being flattered. The equation seemed so simple: People loved Natalie, I was like Natalie; therefore, people would love me too. I would not disappear.

How could I have known that already I was beginning to?

I forget the details of the argument, but I questioned Natalie in front of one of the writers' group participants about something she had forgotten to do that she had promised she would. It wasn't a rebuke so much as a nudging, and so I was unprepared for her reaction. "How *dare* you question me in public?"

We were in the bookstore. Customers glanced warily at us, then moved quickly away.

"All I meant –" I started to say, but she whirled on me, eyes blazing with tears. Immediately I felt awful. She was right: I shouldn't have said anything in front of someone else, shouldn't have said anything, period. "I didn't –" I began again, but she wouldn't let me finish. "Bullshit, Maribeth." She was shoving books into a canvas bag, and when she turned to face me, she was literally quivering with rage. I had no sense of boundaries, she said. I was inappropriate, unprofessional, filled with negative energy, and so jealous it was pitiful. And everyone knew it.

"But I *brag* about you," I said. And I did. "I'm proud of you, Natalie." I still was then.

"Believe that if you want." Her lip trembled. "But I don't need you" – she spat the word—"to be *proud* of me." She walked out.

Her words unsettled me. I thought of those pinpricks of doubt I'd tried to push away. Maybe I *was* jealous. And everyone knew? Which meant what? That they were talking about me? *Pitying* me? I felt like a fool. But I was also frightened. The writers' guild was my job, and I needed it. I didn't have a huge book advance, not even close. And the people in the guild—they were *my* friends, weren't they?

Of course, I apologized to Natalie. Repeatedly. But she refused to listen. It made no sense. Shouldn't this have been a minor disagreement? I kept assuming that eventually we'd move on, but we never did, not completely, for in questioning Natalie, no matter how inconsequential my question might have seemed, I had unknowingly betrayed her, broken an unspoken pact.

In *The Art of Fiction,* John Gardner talks about the "suspension of disbelief," the term Coleridge used to describe the reader's willingness to believe—no matter how improbable the events and characters might be—that the story is real. To do this, the writer must continually provide the reader with accurate and precise details that act as a kind of proof while at the same time tell the tale with such confidence and authority that it seems crazy *not* to believe it. And anything—a discrepancy in time, a detail that doesn't ring true, a scene that lacks the precise description needed in order to see it—anything that breaks this suspension of disbelief has the possible effect of making the reader suspicious of the story or, worse, of putting the book down, no longer willing to believe its premise at all. Like waking from a dream. No matter how hard you try to get back to it, you can't; some part of your mind is aware now that it isn't real, that it never was.

It's easy to see now. In rebuking Natalie for whatever task she had not completed, I broke the suspension of disbelief: for that single instant she was *not* the famous novelist with the million-dollar book deal but an ordinary person who had made a mistake. By criticizing her publicly, I had undermined her. Worse, though I didn't yet understand this, I had exposed her.

She began sending e-mail after e-mail, ten, fifteen, a day, written at six in the morning, at two in the afternoon, ten at night, one in the morning. She recounted mistake after mistake that I had made that she had "forgiven." "If you're honest with yourself," she wrote, "you'll admit that you are threatened by me." And "Your jealousy is painful for *everyone.*" No longer sure what was real—I *had* been threatened by her at first, hadn't I? I *had* doubted her—I kept apologizing.

Groveling is the word I would use months later when I described those weeks to Kent.

My voice felt strained, my skin stretched too tight across my face, my smile fake. Because I didn't understand exactly what I had done wrong, I had no idea how to make it right. I worked even harder. To please her. To please the other guild members. *Your jealousy is painful for everyone.* My conversations with Kent grew awkward. I noticed that some of the writers' group members no longer looked me in the eye. I felt sick inside. Shattered. The grief I had never allowed myself to feel about my nephew's death came pouring out. I found myself falling apart for no reason, sobbing uncontrollably once when a flight was delayed.

In June, Natalie started a class, "The Year We Become Artists; the Year We Become Ourselves." *This summer become the writer you are, tell the story that needs to be told, become yourself,* she wrote in the course description. The class filled. We had a waiting list. Natalie mentioned teaching it again in the autumn, but for the first time since she had arrived in our town, something in me sank at the prospect that she would still be here.

Tell the story that needs to be told, become yourself.

I had no idea what this meant except that more and more it seemed to me that ever since Natalie had come into my life, I was losing that life, that she was literally stealing it away. It made no sense, though. How could I even suggest that I didn't trust this woman who donated her teaching stipends back to the guild? I didn't trust this woman who volunteered hours each week to the writing workshops we held? I didn't trust this women whom so many people wanted to be around, this woman with whom Kent had fallen in love?

It sounded laughable, even to me. Natalie had everything I could possibly want: a successful writing career, important friends, students who idolized her, a man who was in love with her. Why would she want *my* life? Jesus. She didn't need me. *I* needed her. Of course, I couldn't see then that I'd had many of these things long before Natalie came to town—which is the irony of trying to make yourself indispensable, of transforming yourself into what you intuit someone else needs you to be: it is the other person who actually becomes indispensable to *you*, for you have given yourself away so completely that without that other person there is no you left. As the poet Carl Phillips writes in "The Messenger," "What happens, I think, is we betray / Ourselves first—our better selves, I'd have said once—/ And the others after . . ."

Natalie still hadn't received her book galleys. The essay due to appear in *The New York Times* was pushed back to another date. The library where Natalie was leading a book discussion asked for her résumé. A simple request, but Natalie was livid, again writing two- and three-page e-mails about how she refused to work for any institution that wanted to censor her; they were violating her freedom of speech; on and on. I began to suspect that maybe she didn't have a résumé because maybe nothing about her was true.

I learned from a friend of Kent's that Natalie had "lost" her credit cards en route to the New Orleans Jazz Fest, that Kent had charged everything on his cards—the-two-hundred-dollar-a-day SUV with the GPS system, the five-star hotels. Months later, he would tell me how, when he tried to convince Natalie that they didn't really need a *five*-star hotel, she'd rolled her eyes and told him, "I hardly think we're breaking *The New Yorker*'s budget." Three months later, he still hadn't been reimbursed and now, *now*, The New Yorker was "footing the bill" for her to go to Europe to catch Dylan in concert over there—for the final essay in the "Searching for Dylan" trilogy.

Trilogy?

And then Bob Dylan phoned Natalie, in response to a letter she'd sent him about *The New Yorker* articles. Immediately Natalie phoned Kent. "You're not going to believe who just called." Her voice was shaking, Kent said. He had been in Lowe's buying appliances. *Lowe's*, for god's sake. And Natalie was talking on the phone to Bob Dylan? Bob fucking *Dylan*?

When Kent hung up, he told the appliance guy, "Bob Dylan just called a friend of mine."

The appliance guy looked at him. "*That* Bob Dylan?" he finally asked.

"Yeah, *that* Bob Dylan," Kent said.

The phone call led to another, then another. Apparently, Dylan invited Natalie to New York to sit in on a recording session, sent a limo to pick her up. She ran into Bono in the hallway. And then, apparently, Dylan and Natalie were friends, and sometimes while Natalie was at Kent's, Dylan would phone her, and Natalie would "talk to him" for ten, twenty minutes. "I stood right there, listening to her," Kent told us after Natalie was gone. "I *smoked* Kents once," Dylan apparently said on one of these occasions. "And I still could if I had to."

"Bob Dylan was jealous of *me*?" Kent would laugh when he told the story later.

Of course, people would laugh at *us* after Natalie left. How could we have believed this? How could we have been so stupid? *Bob Dylan*? Calling Natalie on the phone? A million-dollar book deal? *The New Yorker*? Hell, there wasn't even a word for *that* level of gullibility.

None of this, though, was what finally tipped Kent off, he told me. It was that Natalie would ask him out to dinner, then realize she'd forgotten her money—again. It was the four-page e-mail she sent from a friend's BlackBerry while hiking the Appalachian Trail—thirty-eight miles *in one day*. She talked about surfing but never had any sun on her face. The stories got too improbable. She and Bob—it was just Bob now, not Bob Dylan or even Dylan, but *Bob*—were going to meet in Europe; did Kent want to come?

I wonder now whether the stories became so outrageous because she was exhausted by them, by trying to juggle so many lives/lies. Did she want to be found out?

"We invent ourselves through our stories," her "friend," the writer Pam Houston, wrote in *Cowboys Are My Weakness*, "and in a similar way, the stories we tell put walls around our lives."

Two days before Natalie and Kent left for their "*New Yorker*–paid trip to Europe," he phoned. "I need to talk to you." He hesitated. "If I'm out of my fucking mind, tell me."

"It's about Natalie, isn't it?"

He exhaled a long breath, then blurted, "I think she's a pathological liar. Or crazy. I don't think anything about her is real."

The minute he said it, I knew it was true.

Kent had been up all night, he said, debating whether to talk to me, had stood with his forehead pressed to his window, trying to see if any lights were on in my apartment. A part of him had been relieved, he said, that there weren't. What could he possibly say? What if he was wrong about Natalie? He knew nothing of my own doubts. He still thought she was my best friend.

"I've wanted to talk to you too," I told him. "But what if *I* was wrong? You were *in love* with her." It struck me then how painful this must be for him. I thought of all their plans—to live in New Orleans the following winter, to go on the book tour together. I thought of that night on the deck of his house when he fed her spoonfuls of peanut butter and they thought up songs about rain.

"Wait, wait, I was *what*?" he said.

"You were in love. Everybody –"

"That's a lie," he exploded. "It's a huge, fucking lie."

"But you—you were always together and on the phone and –"

"We were friends. *Friends.* Who else thinks this?"

"People in the writers' guild and . . . *everyone*, Kent." It was a small town.

He told me about her "friendship" with Dylan then, about how Natalie had sent Dylan a copy of Kent's CD and Dylan thought it was good, had offered to let Kent use his studio out in L.A. "I fucking believed her," he said. I nodded. She had offered me dreams as well: *Redbook, The New York Times.* "Make sure to use my name when you send them your work." I had. I thought, too, of how her editor—her famous editor–had told Natalie that she'd be willing to read my next manuscript. How she wanted Natalie and me to write a text on fiction writing.

The morning felt like those games where you search a picture for the objects hidden within it: a toothbrush in a tree branch, a pencil in the umbrella spoke, a shoe masquerading as a flower. The objects are there all along, but until you understand what you are searching for, you can't see them. So it was that day. The picture of who Natalie was dissolved and all I could see were the broken truths and half-lies that had been there all along.

The phone call from Kent was followed by a string of phone calls: To her "agent," who had never heard of her. At Random House, where she had been offered that "sexy book deal—let's just say there are a lot of zeros in the number," there was no mention of her in their database. Her "editor" had never heard of her. Kent emailed X. He'd never heard of her either.

We didn't bother contacting Dylan.

I was shaking when I made the first phone call to her agent, terrified even then that Kent and I were wrong and the agent would demand to know who I was and would later tell Natalie, who would never forgive me. There had to be a mistake, I kept thinking. Why would Natalie do this?

When I hung up the phone after the last call, my heart was still racing. I grabbed my keys and headed for the beach, not caring that it would be packed with tourists, not caring that parking would be impossible, not caring about anything except the fact that I needed to move, to walk, to think. The world felt unknowable and alien that afternoon in a way that even my nephew's death a year earlier hadn't made it. I thought of how Natalie had shown up at Smitty's with a cake and candles on what would have been my nephew's birthday, and I wondered now if this too had just been another part of the lie, the elaborate game? Had she used even this—a child's death? I didn't know what was real. Had she ever been my friend?

I wanted to feel angry, even hurt, but mostly I felt a kind of stunned disbelief. The part of me that ran the writers' guild knew that she was teaching classes under false premises, that people believed they were taking a writing workshop with a published author. I would need to cancel her class, reimburse the participants, but what would I say to them? To her? Later, I would phone my brother, who was a lawyer, unsure if there were legal issues. Everything Natalie had done for the guild had been as a volunteer though, and I now suspected even this was part of her scheme: we'd been so busy being grateful that we'd never asked for a résumé, for proof that she was who she said she was. I stared at the waves crashing onto the beach, then pulling back, the constant give and take, and I felt bewildered all over again. I thought of all Natalie had done for the writers' guild, of all the people she had helped. *Why*, I kept wondering. But the word was like the waves, endlessly repetitive, one *why* leading to another and another after that. By the time I finished walking, hours later, I knew that *why* didn't really matter. Perhaps Natalie was mentally ill in some way or maybe just so insecure that she couldn't fathom being loved simply for who she was, but either way the whole charade seemed pointless and awful all at once, in part because of my own complicity in it. I wondered if we *would* have loved her without the big promises and big plans, and I suspected that maybe we wouldn't have, and I didn't know what that said about me. About Kent.

At some point in the afternoon, Natalie phoned to tell me that Kent had cancelled the trip to Europe. She was crying. "I don't understand," she sobbed. "I just—Oh, Maribeth, why would he do this?" There was nothing fake about the pain I heard in her voice, and I wondered if she really had convinced herself that they were in love. I felt mean, pretending to be her friend when I knew the truth. It *was* like letting her walk around with her underwear tucked in her dress. But she pleaded with me to go to Smitty's. "Just us, I just want to talk girl crap."

I told her I would. I wasn't ready to confront her yet. I didn't know what I'd say. I didn't know how I felt.

At the bar, she tried to talk about other things besides Kent, though now and then her eyes would fill and she'd say quietly, "I don't understand." And then she'd get angry. "It's just so . . . so unprofessional to cancel at the last minute." She talked about her agent, the one who had never heard of her, about how everyone at Random House was really excited about the revisions she'd just completed. She kept looking at her phone. "I'm waiting for X to call," she said.

I found myself believing her, forgetting that I'd talked to "her agent," who had never heard of her, and that there was no editor, no friendship with X, no novel, no seven-figure deal, no *New Yorker*. Not even a college degree. The university she'd attended had no record of her either.

"What is description after all / but encoded desire?" Mark Doty asks in one of his poems. I understood that Natalie was describing not the life she had but the life she desired, and she was describing it so well that even though I knew it was all a fabrication, I continued to believe that world existed. In a way, as long she kept describing it, it did.

Which is what fiction writing is all about.

When I think of that last night that Natalie was in my life, I think of how when reading a book that I love, a book whose story I can't bear to have end, I read more and more slowly, trying to draw it out, trying to make it last. This is what I did with Natalie's story: even after I knew the truth, a part of me didn't want it to be over.

I told Natalie what I had learned about her on a bright July morning in the upstairs room of the local library, where she had just finished leading the weekly writing group. She had begun the class as she always did, by reading the guidelines from Judy Reeves's *A Writer's Book of Days:*
    Tell the truth.
    Be willing to tell your secrets.

I waited until everyone left, then nervously said something about how grateful I was for all she'd done for the writers' guild, and how I hated that we had to have this conversation. Finally, I just blurted it out: "I talked to your agent, to your publisher, to X."

As I spoke, her lips quivered as if she were about to cry, but before I could finish the sentence, she disappeared. I don't know how else to describe it. She was still standing there, but her eyes went blank, her pupils dilated, her face turned pale and expressionless. It was like watching someone sinking under water, her features becoming blurry, almost indistinct, her movements mechanical. I kept talking to her. "I wouldn't have cared if you didn't have a novel published. No one would. God, Natalie, people loved you." Was this true? I wanted it to be. But it didn't matter. She was already gone. When she spoke her voice was small, squeezed into a tight fist. "Okay," she kept saying. "Okay." I kept talking, though I'm not sure what I wanted: an explanation, maybe? An apology? Perhaps just a sense of who Natalie really was underneath all the lies. But she just kept repeating "okay" in that same robotic voice, not looking at me, not looking at anything.

I left as she was gathering her books. It was the last time I would see

Natalie for three years—when I would literally run into her on a bitter March night outside one of the bars, and she'd grab me hard and whisper over and over into my hair, "I'm so sorry, I'm so sorry."

I almost believed her. Until a few weeks later, when a private investigator contacted me: Did I know a woman named Natalie? A famous writer? She had apparently just gotten a publishing contract for 1.7 million dollars . . .

Another two years would go by, and now her name is Laura, and again, there is a forthcoming novel that sold for a huge amount and numerous articles soon to be published. Now and then, someone new to the writers' guild asks, "Do you know Laura ——? She lives in town, and she's published all kind of articles in magazines like . . ." and they'll rattle off a list of national publications. I nod and say I knew her years ago, which is also a lie, because of course I didn't know her at all.

And yet, in an odd way, I understood her.

As a fiction writer, I know how to create entire lives from mere words. I think of how I too have taken, stolen, appropriated details from my life, from my family and friends, and given them to a character. It sounds benign, for these are just details, after all, but what else are our lives made of? I know how easily fact can become fiction. I know that what never happened often lives a ghost life alongside what did and sometimes seems more real because it is imagined so fully, each detail exact. "Is the true story the story that is made or the story that is forgotten?" Helen Humphreys asks in *Afterimage*.

I no longer know.

I see "Laura" now and then in the Starbucks, writing on her laptop, and it occurs to me anew what an odd profession fiction writing is, this sitting alone day after day, creating lives and worlds out of bits and scraps of other lives. It's not just creating, though, which, again, sounds so benign. We start to care about these fictional characters, perhaps we fall in love with them a little, we worry about them and wonder what will happen to their lives. We see them more clearly sometimes, understand them so much better than we do our own selves or the people we love. What does it mean, I wonder, to feel so intensely about something, someone, that isn't real, while around us people are dying in wars, losing jobs and homes, burying, as my sister did, a child? What does it mean to care about, to invest in—for months and years at a time— something that doesn't even exist? And how, if it is okay to do this—and I find ways to justify the writing of fiction every day, for it is what I do, what I teach others to do—can I feel such irritation with Natalie? Is what she did all that different in the end? She appropriated bits and scraps of our lives, of my life specifically, and she created a character that became real not only to her but to the rest of us. That character, fiction or not, affected people, changed people, in many ways for the better.

And when the story ended, she moved on and invented another.

I want to find this sad. I want to be angry. I remind myself that Natalie cost me friendships, that she betrayed Kent and stole the thousands of dollars he had spent in New Orleans, those dollars that "*The New Yorker* would reimburse." Many days I do feel these things. But I also know that when someone asks me, "Do you know that writer, Laura ——?" I also feel, albeit begrudgingly, a kind of admiration.

Because for the nine months that Natalie was in our lives, she *was* a big-time author whose life was about to change in wonderful, dramatic ways. She *was* a wonderful teacher and Kent *was* in love with her and she *was*, as Randy Lee said, happy. And I *was* a woman who was fun and spontaneous. *Fun.* A word that had been gone from my life until Natalie brought it back to me. During those nine months, Kent believed that Bob Dylan had listened to his music and liked it, and because Kent believed he became confident in ways he'd never been, played music better than he ever had before. The members of the writers' guild began to see themselves as writers, began to believe that their stories mattered. And so they did. And I can't help it: I find something beautiful in this capacity to believe so fervently in the stories we fabricate that we *become* what we dream.

This is not to say that Kent and I don't berate ourselves for being so gullible. Even after five years, we still wonder how, *how* we could have believed she was writing for *The New Yorker* and John Irving was going to blurb her book and she was good friends with Dylan—Bob Dylan. But the real question, the one we are perhaps afraid to ask, is why Kent and I betrayed each other by believing the things Natalie said about *us*, and why, despite the growing improbability of her stories, did we dismiss our own gut feelings and betray ourselves?

"You know the saddest lies / are the ones we tell ourselves," Lucile Clifton writes in her poem "1994." But what, I still sometimes wonder, is the difference between a lie and a story? And I think of how, despite my three divorces, I still believe in love, and despite the fact that nearly two hundred thousand books are published in the United States each year, I still believe my novels will not only get published but *noticed*. Mostly, I think of how, against all logic, I believed, truly believed for nearly a decade, that my nephew, born with a *terminal* illness, would not die. Were—*are*—these lies I was telling myself?

Or stories?

Stories, the only thing that allowed Scheherazade to survive for a thousand and one nights.

Stories, the only thing that allows *anyone* to survive loving someone she will one day lose.

It's in this—in my own belief in the improbable—that I feel closest to Natalie now. I know what it is to want so much for something to be true that you literally try to will it into existence.

The suspension of disbelief.

This is the job of the novelist. To make the fictional world seem so real that for a while we believe it is.

Belief.

What else is writing but this?

What else is love?

Nominated by Lisa Couturier

ALBION

by PHILIP LEVINE

from THE THREEPENNY REVIEW

On narrow roads twisting
between the farms, if farms
these were and not fallow
fields set off by stone walls
too low to keep anything
in or out. I'd been told
that when the west wind raged
local spirits—all the ghosts
of the unmourned—gathered
on the hilltops where no one
dared to go. We parked
in a little meadow shaded
by ancient birch and sycamore
going silver and gray under
the noon sun. Hand in hand
we climbed until the under-
growth separated us and she—
more nimble than I—took
the lead, and I followed until
the trees thinned out. The only
sound besides our breathing
was the silence. Beyond the first
clearing a stone wall stumbled
up and over a steeper rise.
Once there we saw the land

itself became confused as to
where to go. What, I thought,
could possibly be waiting
beyond still another grove
of birch and sycamore?
That was forty years ago
or more. We were still
young or young enough,
and new to the adventure,
so of course we kept going,
not in the hope of finding
Celtic arrowheads or human
skulls purified by time
and weather, or bronze relics
of lives we knew nothing of,
or what was actually there:
the exhausted chalky soil
of this depleted island
my father fought for. High
above, the clouds moved
against a pure blue sky
or perhaps it was the sky
that moved and everything
else stopped, like the two
of us, listening. Listening
for what? I ask myself now.
Call and response from bird
to bird or the sough of wind
stuttering through the trees,
the voices of a forgotten past?
I can't recall how long we
stood there nailed to the spot,
hand in hand, expectant,
as though anything
could tell us where we were.

Nominated by Joan Murray

THE PROSPECTS

fiction by MICHELLE SEATON

from ONE STORY

Huge and eternally hungry, the prospects carry trays overburdened with food, with mounds of spaghetti trailing off chipped plates, with cheeseburgers and stacks of peanut butter sandwiches, with bagels, crackers, sweaty boxes of milk, with cookies, brownies, ice cream. The prospects are eager to gain. All morning long, through history and English and shop, their bellies have groaned with want, their growing bones have ached. The cafeteria ladies with their hairnets and ample bodies just laugh and shake their heads at the sight of so much food. Every day they ask the same thing: *How can you boys eat so much?*

In stuffy classrooms and chatter-filled hallways, the prospects move like sloths. They shuffle. They slouch. They doze or turn sleepy gazes to the blackboard, out the window, at the floor. Only at lunchtime do they come alive. Hunched over their trays, baseball caps backward, the prospects tuck in. They eat steadily without pause. The prospects wear low-slung jeans and fat sneakers, and tent-like T-shirts bearing slogans. On Fridays, the prospects wear grass-stained game shirts. Next week is the last week of the football season and already the college coaches are gathering, writing, phoning, texting, sometimes visiting.

The recruiting coaches who do visit bring with them the aura of a big campus, where they govern teams cheered and chanted over, and players written about and talked about on TV, interviewed by sideline reporters, who are always women and always blond. And yet these coaches never smile. They peek into the cafeteria, and stare at the prospects without expression as though what happens next is a formality, a foregone conclusion. The prospects continue to eat, to grin at the lesser mortals around them, to steal food from a buddy's plate and fling it on a neighboring table. They pretend they are not being watched.

The prospects know their own potential. The prospects have exaggerated their weights and heights. Their blocks and tackles, their receptions and touchdowns have been captured on DVD and emailed to campuses in every state. Their foot-speed has been carefully clocked. They can run forty yards in five seconds, or four and a half seconds. Never six seconds. Six seconds is too slow. They bench 250 or they bench 300. They swallow gel caps filled with supplements nicknamed Nitro and Xplode. They drink protein shakes tinted green with algae. The skin on their biceps, on their chests, on their shoulders is crisscrossed with silvery stretch marks. In foggy suburban bathrooms, they stand shirtless and sweaty and flex all their muscles at once, flex their biceps until the skin is pulled tight, until the muscles cramp; they flex their chests looking for striations in the pecs; they look straight into the mirrors and speak to a phalanx of invisible microphones and to a roomful of reporters, also unseen, and respond to questions unasked, about plays and games and moments yet to unfold. The prospects speak with great sincerity in an unbroken chain of clichés as they teleport themselves away from manicured lawns and department store fashions, away from top forty hits of love and loneliness, away from rules and curfews and virginal girlfriends and parental control, and boredom and bad grades and into the imagined world of college football, where they will live among tens of thousands of students, where the roster of players is a hundred deep, with players who travel in packs, eat together, work out together, attend all the same classes, and throw their own parties, replete with binge drinking, casual vandalism and spontaneous sex. This is a world in which the players as a group occupy a status outside and above everyone else on campus, a world that will be partially but carefully unveiled to the prospects in one of several on-campus visits, each one a tacit promise of future freedoms and successes, if only they can get in, get the offer, the scholarship, the free ride, the three-quarters free ride or even the half free ride with optional no-show job attached. The prospects won't consider anything less.

But for now the prospects still live at home, in football-fervent cities and towns, among the hollowed-out factories, the vacated office parks, under the care of their parents, the unemployed and over-mortgaged, the downgraded part-timers, the patriotic, the doggedly informed, the God-fearing and peace-loving, the green-thinking and Internet-surfing, but most of all, the hopeful, the would-be triumphant, meaning those who hold lottery tickets and buy wrinkle cream, those who cruise the self-help section of the bookstore in earnest, those who are working on themselves, re-evaluating their weaknesses, tweaking their resumes, evolving into some higher state, while watching TV shows in which the nobody rises over several weeks to become a big star, those who believe that talent and luck can coincide, those who had the mystifying good fortune to birth a child of monstrous size, who has collected admiring letters, signed letters, from famous coaches in distant states. And in these homes, each prospect is still a boy who seems to ingest his body weight in food five or six times a day, who views a pizza or roast chicken as an appetizer, a boy who can down a quart of milk while standing at the open refrigerator door, a child who cannot look both ways before crossing a road, who cannot be trusted with the car or the television remote because he has no impulse control, no sense that others also exist. Yet, this child seems tailor-made for the triple-XL world he will inhabit, a world of super portions, mega churches, and 56-inch plasma screens, of catastrophic storms, runaway fires, tandem tornadoes, of taxpayer-funded stadiums and billion-dollar television-rights deals, swollen CEO salaries and severance packages, a world in which the ones with an early push are the only ones who survive.

The prospects believe in their own celebrity. Like starlets, like politicians embroiled in scandal, like criminals emerging from court, the prospects have learned to ignore the syllables of their own names. The prospects do not turn when hailed. They have cell phones they do not answer. They receive texts they do not read. They have learned to block out their fathers, their momsters, their siblings' sneering comments, the nagging of teachers, the pleading or pouting of girlfriends old and new, the looks of envy and disdain beamed toward them from all directions. They ignore everyone except the coaches who send letters promising a visit, coaches who don't visit, but who call frequently, almost nightly. The phone begins to ring at just past the dinner hour and continues until the last decent hour, at 9 or sometimes 9:30, rarely later than that. The prospects never stir to answer the phone. The mother does that, always the mother. The prospects lounge on lumpy rec room couches in finished basements, while thumbing consoles or working joysticks and staring at the flickering images they control. The prospects stomp zombies, they steer cars through tracks, they draw swords against Spartans. They invade, they pillage, they steal, they kill, they die. They wait for the gentle knock on the bedroom door, the shout down the basement stairs, followed by the plaintive announcement that coach so-and-so is calling. The prospects make a big show of not wanting to talk. They sigh loudly and curse softly as they shuffle to the phone. They answer questions about their grades, their classes, their games. They are polite, and reserved, never chatty. The prospects wait for the offer of a full ride, a partial ride, a scholarship large or small, but never ask for it. They listen to the hints, the chattiness, the faux friendliness, hoping to hear a whisper of actual need.

The best recruiters, those working as assistant coaches in the top programs with the biggest budgets, of course show nothing. They, like the prospects, function as a gravitational force that draws in every direction. They can afford to expend tiny amounts of energy to draw inordinate attention from all potential candidates.

And right behind them are the recruiters from the lesser schools, the also-rans, the schools in transition with losing records, the small schools in Division Two or Three, the schools with spare budgets and few scholarships. Recruiters from these schools are perpetually on the road, perpetually in sales meetings with disinterested buyers. Every day these men steer a rental car into several high school parking lots, and sign in at the office where they don visitors' badges and wait for the prospects in empty classrooms. These men wear golf shirts with a discrete college logo. They have trim waists and crisp haircuts and good posture, they have firm handshakes and carry large binders. They introduce themselves using the word coach and present business cards. Their resumes are stacked with credentials, with assistantships in high school and college programs, with associates degrees or undergraduate degrees in criminal justice or business administration. Some include the stats of their playing days in big programs, of yards rushing or defensive tackles, of completed passes or receptions, of touchdowns and wins and, yes, the losses, too, for the losses are never forgotten, nor are the missed tackles, the dropped passes, the broken plays, the lost leads, the miscues, mistakes, poor judgments. The imprudent risks of a lifetime never go away; they just add up.

These men are former college athletes who still bear the telltale height, the broad shoulders, the barrel chests and deep voices of top players, men who spend hours each day in a gym hefting weights while counting reps, or laboring mightily on a track, on a treadmill wearing earbuds, in a lap lane, on a squash court, men who play pick-up games of basketball, softball, tennis, who study the sports pages every morning, committing box scores to memory and snorting at the words of each columnist, who follow multiple teams in many sports, who shout at their television sets during games, and who gamble a little while pretending not to, and for whom the appetite for food and competition and exertion and adrenaline has not diminished and may never fade.

These recruiters are in their 20s, or in their 30s, or, rarely, in their 40s. They are salesmen who spend the winter months driving through an assigned territory, meeting, glad-handing, smiling, visiting homes, selling the program, the college, the athletic experience to multiple players at every position. For this, they may earn a salary similar to an assistant professor or they may earn a few thousand dollars per year along with a dining card that allows for free meals in the college cafeteria, or in some cases they are glorified interns, meaning that they are part-time stringers, hoping to catch on somewhere. These job titles contain an asterisk, a disclaimer, a notice of provisional status, a status far afield from the contractual agreement—sometimes totaling millions of dollars—that binds top head coaches to their universities. A recruiter in a small program is a man who stocks shelves and collects tip money for each delivered pizza and sells athletic shoes in a sporting goods store while sleeping on a friend's couch, or while sharing a studio apartment with six other men and three dogs, and whose resume is in the hands of every football coach, great and small, with whom he has had even the merest acquaintance. He is a man who once dreamed of greatness as a coach, but whose dreams have shrunk to one goal, that of a paid position at any program.

On rainy days these recruiters limp with little reminders of injuries, those tendons that popped in stride, or the ankle that was ground into the turf under a pile of bodies, or the collision in mid-air that cracked a vertebrae, a scapula, a femur, a collarbone snapped under the weight of a set of pads propelled by 315 pounds of lineman. Each man can narrate the whole scenario of his injury, can tell it with a smile that hides some other, more complicated feeling, that hides the vivid remembrance of lying out on the grass, on the turf, gulping for air and trying not to puke from the throbbing, the stinging, the skin tightening around the swelling, the others crowding around as the pain comes in waves, sharp and then dull and then in a long, shrill shout when the trainer palpates the hot skin, squeezing the accumulating blood and marrow, crunching the dislocated bits of tendon or cartilage between thumb and forefinger, and then waiting for the trainer to glance up with the sad and knowing expression, before giving the quick head shake that alerts everyone that this bone, this joint, this ligament, this

214

tendon, this body, this tool so carefully tended will never again be what it was just a few minutes ago.

Recruiters never talk about their own concussions, except in jest, about blacking out mid-tackle and waking up on the sidelines, about walking as though drunk while the horizon swims. These men never mention, and claim that they never think about, the thousand little hits that cause a slow erosion of brain cells, the fog that may already be dissolving their grace, their coordination, their speech, their memories, their identities.

And every few months, when another former player takes his own life, as the newspapers put it, that is to say when another former player shoots himself in the chest or jumps from a bridge or hangs himself in the shower leaving nothing but a note in clean type or shaky handwriting saying that it has all become too much, they know that what he means by too much is that the headaches and waves of nausea, the forgetfulness, the sudden rages, the inertia that fills his body with lead for days at a time has triggered a realization that these symptoms might not represent the usual vestiges of a storied career in sports. And afterward, after the body has been found and identified and after the skull has been sawed apart, and the spongy brain prised out, dropped into a cooler and sent to a lab in Boston, that's when the players who have become recruiters look in the mirror and look at each other and look to the newspapers for some report, some quote or fact, some reason to believe that it has all been a mistake, some reason to believe that they will be spared.

Ambitious recruiters always focus on the task at hand. They think about the next sale, the next smile paired with a handshake, the face of the next prospect who waits in an empty classroom, silent or smirking or staring blankly, the next boy who wants to be sold, wants to be offered, wants to be better than you and your stupid Division Two program, because Syracuse has been calling. And Nebraska. And good recruiting coaches know this, and they know how to smile at the entitled little pricks and feed them humility and collect them into the warmth of their own certainty. And when that fails, these grown men beg. And why not? It's just begging. A recruiter is a student of human nature who is also a performer, an instant responder to facial cues, tones of voice, inflections on syllables, an actor who comes into every conversation with a single objective in mind, a con man who says that he wants only the best for you and your son. Throw away the Lombardi clichés about preparation and the will to win, ignore the Bryant axioms about character and perseverance. No one becomes a college coach at any level without mastering the art of persuasion in a mother's living room, without learning to close a sale using charm, flattery, flimsy half-truths, desperate lies, and even tears.

The recruiting never ends, not after a winter of travel, not after coveted prospects sign letters of intent, not after spring football scrimmages start. Even then players from high school come to visit with their parents in tow. These boys stand on the sidelines, overawed and smiling, or disdainful or wary. They must be greeted, spoken to with interest. They must be encouraged, even at age 16 or 17, to imagine themselves here practicing on this field, wearing these uniforms, chanting along with these calisthenics.

At least spring football brings the recruiters to an actual field. It is a relief to hold a clipboard, to hold a whistle, to twirl the lanyard around two fingers until the whistle hits your palm, and then twirl it the other way. It is a relief to coach, even if the players are bitching and shivering, even if the quarterback is throwing wounded ducks because he can see his own breath and the receivers stop running halfway through every play, even if the place kicker is still hung over at 4 in the afternoon. At least it's outside in the open air, at least there are plays to run, at least there are players to yell at and cajole and teach. And when it's time to run plays at three-quarter speed, the recruiters bend down and rest their hands on their thighs and squint with great concentration.

Nothing else mimics the rhythm of a play, the burst of a whistle that sends each squad to the line, where they wait, silent and alert, squatting with fingertips on the ground, or squatting and upright, or frozen in a half stride but ready to move. The players fidget and adjust as they hear the audible, as they wait for the snap, at which point they move with urgency and precision or sometimes with confusion and panic. The coaches watch and then yell or laugh heartily. They, too, remember the weight of the helmet and how it made their necks ache, the stench of sweat-soaked pads, the sting on the shoulders after that first hard hit of the day, the feel of shuffling and pushing, of beating your man by a half step, of catching him with a forearm to the facemask, something to remember you by. At practice the old sensations return, like ghosts, and they are welcome.

Too soon every afternoon it is dark and time to go inside.

When not recruiting, these assistant coaches have many daily chores that include, but are not limited to: monitoring study halls for players on academic probation; counting the push-ups assigned to punish players who have wandered into meetings ten minutes late, or who have forgotten their playbooks or their formations or who have failed to recall their positional reactions to each formation; taking attendance in the weight room while spotting players who perennially lift above their weight class; collecting mid-term reports and shaming players who have blown off yet another calculus exam; trolling the dorms on bed checks to make sure the freshmen aren't killing themselves with drink; watching and cataloging the hundreds of DVDs sent in by prospects each month, by their coaches and parents; cataloging opponents' game films; conducting sorties to the admissions office in order to forge alliances with those who might approve questionable future candidates; thinking about, worrying about the next game, even if it's many months away.

At night they make the calls, ten or twenty of them, each one to a different living room in a different town or state, to a different kid who is also the same kid as any other, a kid who is bigger and faster than everyone on his team, a kid who is a marvel to those around him, and therefore well-schooled in the future that may be possible for him. These phone calls are paramount because a program cannot function without prospects, five or six or ten at every position, without players sitting at home yearning for another letter or phone call, praying for a home visit, dreaming about the chance to be a part of the team, even if they will never see a down of actual play.

And how dreary these conversations can be, conducted while pacing around a conference table alongside other assistant coaches dialing from cell phones, asking to speak to Trey or Demetrie or Deon, Marcus, or one of the infinite Justins or Ryans, the endless Tylers and Brandons, then inquiring in mock cheerful terms, but really by rote, How's it going and How are the grades, and Have you studied for the SATs and Are you going to take them again, and You really should think about that, and Did you bring up that D in math or English, and Stay healthy, and then getting off the phone as quickly as possible with some sort of clipped, *Hey buddy, talk to you soon.* Smiling, and chuckling while talking, but never getting chummy with the kid, asking but never answering questions, and never promising anything or pretending to promise anything, these are the tenets of every conversation. Because at some point, the recruiter will take a pen and draw a line through this kid's name and never dial his house again and never give a thought about where he ends up, whether another program takes him, whether his parents can piece together prep school tuition so that he can be a

217

prospect again next year, or whether he sinks from academia and into a part-time job painting houses or pouring coffee or selling meth. The recruiter will draw a line through two or three names per day, until only a few are left of all the hundreds that were in his binder. At that point, a coach with more authority will review the tapes and the notes and make a home visit to keep stringing the kid or kids along, before making a decision about a partial scholarship for one of them, a kid who could go either way, a bubble kid as they say, who is alive to the program at this point in December or January or in the first week of February as a hedge against a much better player at his position who still wavers between several offers.

By August, the best prospects have become freshmen players. They become jersey numbers. And at the start of any practice, they are likely to hear a head coach say to the assistant coach: *Just keep the animals moving.* And they do keep moving through two practices per day, a new drill every ten minutes, sprints, ladders, hitting sleds, ball handling, scrimmages. They are herded to the weight room, to the cafeteria, to meetings, to film sessions, to study hall, to class and back, their attendance taken at every step. They have been handed thick playbooks to be memorized, with new jargon, a soup of letters and code names for each position, each play and its many variations. At no time is a freshman player, a former prospect, addressed by the head coach. Coaches don't care about freshmen players, don't like them, and refuse to look at them. And so the kid who was seduced so carefully finds himself ordered to do push ups in a meeting because he cannot remember the correct field position of the strong safety in each one of a dozen possible formations, or because the practice video shows that he is the one player who stepped the wrong way three plays in a row, and who can't wrap up a tackle, whose torso is too weak, who is told again and again that he is too stupid to follow the simplest instruction. At home games, the former prospects stand on the sidelines in crisp uniforms, helmets in hand, and watch while others play.

These boys soon realize that the only players revered by coaches are those who play without injury, without pain, without fear, players who lack entirely the genetic urge for self-preservation, players who react without error, whose synapses spark without hesitation, players who fervently and unthinkingly obey, and whose bodies have also been gifted with speed. Very few players can excel under this standard and the rest fade into obscurity, also known as the scout team. Some grow frustrated and talk back to coaches and trainers, they mock the program, make mean jokes surrounded by snickering cohorts. Others strive only to see their bodies betray them, hamstrings and groin muscles overextended or torn, ankles turned on artificial turf, the all-too-common stingers, so named because of the icy pain that shoots to each hand when a hard hit pinches a player's spinal cord at the neck. A few bulk up and transfer to positions away from the ball, where they can do less harm. Some zone out and become depressed when they get one concussion too many, or when their impulses steer them into trouble and they flunk out or get arrested. Among them are the dogged over-achievers, the walk-ons, who ride the bench and make every meeting and hope to get some playing time, and who love the game, every bit of it, from breaking down film to charting plays to doing push ups, and who may already be dreaming of a second life as a coach. To succeed, these players know that they must emulate the elite players on the field and ignore them everywhere else, ignore their class-cutting, the binge drinking and pill taking, their reckless boasting, the rumored felonies—and those witnessed—at this or that off-campus party. It's the only way to survive.

The recruiters, too, must learn to ignore more than they notice, be-cause there is so much to ignore, such as the reports of cheating and grade-fixing encouraged by other coaches or the administration; the charges filed and then dismissed against a head coach for punching his wife, or propositioning an underage prostitute, or driving drunk; the threatened investigations by the NCAA for improper contact with pros-pects; the rumors of hazing incidents in which freshman players are stripped and beaten and pissed upon, or who have had beer and crushed sardines siphoned into their mouths before being driven out into the countryside, where they are dumped, drunk and lost and vomiting and crying for their mothers.

The program rewards selective awareness, which is also called loy-alty, dedication, and minding your own business. Besides, there are always the distracting phone calls to make, the scouting trips to distant counties, the home visits to influence the talented high school juniors who can be snapped up before other programs know about them. Be-cause even in a small program, success in recruiting leads to winning and winning is a balm that soothes moral uncertainty. One winning season can become two. A conference championship might lead to an offer from a larger program with a real salary, which means no more hefting paint rollers overhead in cavernous living rooms or on exterior ladders, no more driving a bus or a cab or tutoring English or selling scrap metal. Instead: practice schedules to draw up, and playbooks to memorize and endless coffee-fueled debates about the health status of injured starters. And with each successive sale, each lured prospect, comes greater value to the program, greater success, and trips farther afield and away from suburban New England territories and into larger markets, in New York and New Jersey where the high schools are three and four thousand strong, where the economic burdens are great and hope is slender but for the prospects. And then more championships, and more wins, and the travels to Florida and California. Even Texas.

That hope, that promise of the future is what keeps recruiters driving rented cars all over the state, makes them stay in motel rooms, eat take out, sell their school to these kids, makes them stand next to the men from other schools, better schools, and wait in empty classrooms—with the metal desks, the white boards, the faces of Presidents affixed to the wall—or sometimes in the cafeteria.

The recruiters stand in a line against the wall, where the air is thick with the smell of grease and salt, the yeasty smell of warmed corn ladled from a vat, canned carrots and microwaved hot dogs, the same food they remember from school when they ate everything all the time and dreamed about the future. They stand and listen to the chatter and watch the wary girls and stare at the prospects. They judge the boys, noting the cut and slope of a shoulder from across the room, and measuring the prospect's height even when he sits at a table, but certainly when he stands to carry a tray to the garbage can, and they can see when a kid pretending to be 6 foot 5 and 260 is in fact far smaller, too skinny, with a frame that will never carry the required 300 pounds that he would need to get into a big program. The recruiters know then that whoever is calling that prospect won't be calling for long, and may have stopped calling already. The kid is always the last to know on these things.

The recruiters who watch these former versions of themselves are already dead-eyed and bored senseless at the thought of spending even a minute in the company of another prospect, and yet they wait to drop into a deferential pitch, one that sounds equally convincing to the bubble kids and the studs, and not really even remembering the names anymore.

They do it because they must, because this is what the sport demands. Because football is a game, a game that is also a war, and a war that is also an industry, and an engine for alumni donations and merchandise sales, a vehicle for advertising and a broker of broadcast rights, a grantor of scholarships and contracts unguaranteed, a channel for pride and loyalty among strangers, and a purveyor of values that favor winning and domination and strength and bulk and speed and guts and violence repeated in slow motion, and pain dulled by pills but never erased, and cunning that always edges toward cheating, and complexity that requires computer models and hundreds of pages of coded plays and headsets and hand signals, and an injury rate well over one hundred percent, an injury rate that requires multiple players per position to be queued up and ready to play when—not if—the starters go down.

For that, a program needs prospects, thousands of them. It also needs men who will spend hours on the phone in cold calls, and months on the road making sales and notes and sleeping in their rental cars at night if the budget can't stretch to afford a hotel room. It needs men who are already addicted to the game, to its complexity and to the notion that they belong near a field, in a stadium, working alongside others who also love the game, and managing the plays and defenses for legions of fans who also adore the game. Each recruiter must feel that he deserves to be the one wearing a headset and thinking mightily about which risk to take on a third and long, on a fourth and two, on a first and goal with the last seconds ticking down and the players panting and twitching with nervous energy.

In order to harbor this fantasy, the recruiters drive to all the high schools in the state, and shake hands with oversized boys with substandard scores and overeager fathers. They will smile blandly and refrain from comment while a high school coach talks about a boy's frame and how it will likely support an extra 60 pounds of weight: *He could weigh three bills, this kid, easy. Just like the father. Have you seen the father?* The recruiters will nod at this while calculating how much more time they must stay here and how far it is to the next school where they will meet the next coach who is also the school's history teacher or the town's fireman. It's hard to keep them straight. And there the recruiters will meet more boys who look at them and rightly understand that driving around shaking hands is not the job of someone important, someone who makes decisions about actual scholarships and playing time.

All day every day the recruiters meet boys who ask: *When did you play?* The truthful answer is always startling. Perhaps that last down of football occurred in a major program in a bowl game, but it was a game that ended in a time before the great financial crash, before the election of the first black president, before Twitter, before cell phones could take pictures, before even that date in history we all call 9/11, which means really that it happened in grainy VHS—it might as well have happened in ancient Rome—meaning it might never have happened at all. At the moment the recruiters utter the date of their own graduation, they might look across the table at the prospect, and see a kid with a flabby middle, whose forty times are a joke, whose grades in English and biology and civics are so many dominoes set to fall, and who has no idea that every coach who visits him this term is fighting to get three other guys at his position who are faster, smarter and stronger by far than he is.

Or maybe they look across the table and see a kid who doesn't care about football at all, doesn't love the game. A handful of those kids get recruited, too, kids who don't care that they'll never play a down, kids who look at the whole program as a factory job. These kids take their free education and go on to some other field in finance or engineering or marketing, some field that has weekends and vacation time, a field where people can't be fired on a head coach's whim, or fired alongside everyone else because the team lost five games instead of four. The recruiters look at kids like that and pretend not to envy them.

In the early days of February, the convincing is mostly done. The top prospects have signed, and so have most of the others. In the end, there is only one kind of conversation to have with a kid who has received no other offers. On days like these, the recruiters wait while a kid is summoned from the cafeteria. They follow the high school administrator into a classroom, and tell the kid he can have a partial scholarship, maybe half of the school's enormous tuition fees will be waived. Sometimes the kid will hide his disappointment, sometimes he will make a show of saying that he's had a better offer, sometimes he says he has to talk to his parents, sometimes he accepts without thinking. It doesn't matter. This is his one option for a four-year college, whether he likes it or not. He is no longer a prospect, but a young man with obligations to the program, just like everyone else. In this moment, the kid looks right at the recruiter before him, and sees him for what he is: a bad salesman who will never be head coach; with bad knees, and frequent headaches, a guy who is no longer young, no longer ascending; a guy who is the last to know.

Nominated by Alice Schell

MY MOTHER TOLD US NOT TO HAVE CHILDREN

by REBECCA GAYLE HOWELL

from RATTLE

She'd say, *Never have a child you don't want.*
Then she'd say, *Of course, I wanted you*

once you were here. She's not cruel. Just practical.
Like a kitchen knife. Still, the blade. And care.

When she washed my hair, it hurt; her nails
rooting my thick curls, the water rushing hard.

It felt like drowning, her tenderness.
As a girl, she'd been the last

of ten to take a bath, which meant she sat
in dirty water alone; her mother in the yard

bloodletting a chicken; her brothers and sisters
crickets eating the back forty, gone.

Is gentleness a resource of the privileged?

In this respect, my people were poor.
We fought to eat and fought each other because

we were tired from fighting. We had no time
to share. Instead our estate was honesty,

which is not tenderness. In that it is
a kind of drowning. But also a kind of air.

Nominated by Davis McCombs, Michael Waters

THE TOWER

fiction by FREDERIC TUTEN

from CONJUNCTIONS

Sometimes his urine was cloudy. Sometimes gritty with what he called "gravel." Sometimes his piss flowed bloody and frightening. No matter how disturbing, Montaigne recorded his condition in his travel journal as coolly he did the daily weather. He was always in various degrees of pain, and he noted that too, but dispassionately, like a scientist in a white lab coat.

Even before he suffered from kidney stones and the burning pain that came with them, Montaigne had long thought about death, and not only his own. He had thought about how to meet it and if doing so gracefully would change the encounter. His closest friend, the man he had loved more than anyone in the world, was to love more than anyone in the world, had died with calm dignity. In his last minutes, in his last words, his dear friend did not begrudge life or beg for more time or express regrets over what was left undone or make apologies to those he might have or had offended or injured. Montaigne thought that when death approached, he would neither wave him away nor welcome him, but say to death's shadow on the wall, "Finally, no more pain."

I put my book aside when she walked in.

"I'm leaving you," she said. She had a red handbag on her arm.

"For how long?"

"For always."

"And what about Pascal, will you take him?"

"He's always favored you." I was very glad. I could see Pascal sitting in the dining-room doorway, pretending not to listen.

"Yes, that's true."

"Don't you care to know why I'm leaving?" she asked, petulantly, I thought.

"I suppose you'll tell me."

"I will, but maybe another time." She stared at me as if wondering who I was. Then she started to speak but was interrupted by a car-horn blast. I looked out the window and saw a taxi with a man behind the wheel.

"May I help you with your bags?" I asked.

"I'll send for them later, if you don't mind."

"Who will you send?"

"The person who comes." She stared at me another moment and then left.

I heard a motor start up, then the swerve of the car leaving the curb. Pascal took his time walking over to me and then, with a faint cry he jumped into my lap, curling himself on my open book. I stroked his head until he made that little motor purr that all cats make when they pretend to love you.

One day Montaigne went all the way from his home in Bordeaux to Italy for its famous physicians and for a change in diet, for that country's warm climate and healing sky. He went to soak himself in the mineral baths, which sometimes gave him relief—also noted in his journal. He recorded but never whined about the biting stones in his kidneys or the bedbugs in the mattress in a Florence hostel or complained about that city's summer heat, so great that he slept on a table pressed against an open window.

He traveled alone. Once, in Rome, Montaigne hired a translator, a fellow Frenchman, who, without notice or reason, left him without a good-bye. So, armed with maps and charts and curiosity, he went about the city with himself for company and guide. In that ancient city he witnessed horrific public executions of criminals, men drawn and quartered while still alive. He visited the libraries of cardinals and nobles, returning to his hostel to note in the same disinterested voice the books and the tortures he had seen and the hard stone that had that day passed through his urine.

I knew there was no hope in lifting Pascal up and dropping him on the carpet so that he would leave me alone to read. I knew he would just bound up again and sit on my book again and that he would do the same one hundred and one times before I gave up and left the room or left the house or left the city. So I took the string with a little ball attached to it that I kept tucked under the pillow and let it drop on the floor. He leapt off my lap and began pawing the rubber ball. I pulled it away and he followed with a one-two punch. Montaigne had once asked himself: Is it I who plays with the cat or is it he who plays with me?

The house seemed full now that she had gone, the rooms packed with me. I wandered about savoring the quiet, the solitude, the way my books, sleeping on their shelves, seemed to glow as I passed by—old friends who no longer need share me with another. I thought I would spend the rest of the day without a plan and do as I wished. Maybe I would sit all day and read. Maybe I would go out with my gun and empty the streets of all the noise. I would then at last have a silent, empty house surrounded by a tranquil, soundless zone. That was just a thought. I have no gun.

After his beloved friend died, Montaigne went into seclusion, keeping himself in a turreted stone tower at the edge of his estate. It was cold in winter and hot in summer and not well lit, the windows being small. He had had a very full life up to the point of his withdrawal, if fullness means social activity and a role in governing. He was a courtier in the royal court and the mayor of Bordeaux and was always out day and night doing things. But now in that tower Montaigne was determined to write, which he did, essays, which some think were addressed to his dead friend. His mind traveled everywhere, his prose keeping apace with all the distances and places his mind traveled. He wrote about cannibals. He wrote about friendship. What is friendship, he asked, and answered: When it is true, it is greater than any bond of blood. Brothers have in common the same port from whence they were issued but may be separated forever by jealousy and rivalry in matters of inheritance and property. Brothers may hate each other, kill each other, as the Old Testament so vividly illustrates. But friends choose each other and their intercourse deepens in trust, esteem, and affection; their intellectual exchange strikes flames.

He stayed in his tower for ten years, his world winnowed down to a stone room of books and a wooden table. Crows sat on his window ledge and studied him, imperturbable in their presence. His wife visited and in his place saw a triangle. Sometimes he would look at his friend's portrait on the table, a miniature in a plain silver frame, and say, "We've worked enough for now, let's go to lunch. What do you think?" Sometimes he just stayed in place until the evening, when he dined on cold mutton and lentils and read in the wintry candlelight. Once, as he climbed the stair to his bedchamber, he noticed his bent shadow trailing him on the wall. Just some years ago his shadow had bounded ahead of him, waiting for him to catch up. Now he grew tired easily; writing a page took hours and he was always in pain. He pissed rich blood. He howled. But he sat and wrote until he finished his book. Then he went on his extensive travels.

I went into the kitchen and made a dish of pears and Stilton and broke out the water biscuits; I opened the best wine I had ever bought, one so expensive that I had hid it from her, waiting for the right occasion to spring it. I sat at the kitchen table. Pascal leaped up to join me. I opened a can of boneless sardines, drained the oil, slid the fish onto a large, white plate, and set it beside me so that Pascal and I could lunch together. He was suspicious, sniffed, then retreated, and then returned to the same olfactory investigation until he finally decided to leave the novelty to rest. The bouquet rose from the wine bottle like a genie and filled the room with sparkling sunshine and the aromatic, medieval soil of Bordeaux. It pleased me to think that Montaigne might have drunk wine from the same vineyard, from the same offspring of grapes.

I went up to her bedroom and opened the closets. So many clothes, dresses, shoes, scarves, belts, hats. The drawers were stuffed with garter belts and black bikini panties that I had never been privy to seeing her wear. Soon the closet would be empty and I would leave it that way. Or leave it that way until I decided what to do with the house, too small for two, too large for one and a cat. She had left the bed unmade, the blankets and sheets twisted and tangled, as if they had been wrestling until they had given up, exhausted. I sniffed her pillow, which was heavy with perfume and dreams. Pascal came in and danced on the bed, where he had never been allowed. I left him there stretched out on her pillow and went down to my study.

It welcomed me as never before. My desk with its teetering piles of books and loose sheets of notes and a printer and computer and a Chinese lamp, little pots full of outdated stamps and rubber bands, an instant-coffee jar crammed with red pencils, green paper clips heaped in a chipped, blue teacup, a stapler, an old rotary phone, framed prints of Goya's *Puppet* and Poussin's *Echo and Narcissus*, Cézanne's *Bathers*, and Van Gogh's *Wheat Field in Rain* greeted and accepted me without any conditions. I could sit at my desk all day and night and never again be presented with the obligation to clear or clean an inch of the disorder. Now, if I wished, I could even sweep away every single thing on the desk and leave it bare and hungry. Or I could chop up and burn the desk in the fireplace. I would wait for a cold night. There was plenty of time now to make decisions.

I went back to the living room and turned on the TV and madly switched channels, finding I liked everything that flashed across the screen, especially the Military Channel, where I watched a history of tank battles and decided I would rather have been in the Navy if it had come to that. Montaigne, surprisingly, detested the sea, from where much contemplation springs. All the same, perhaps the swell of a wave and a splash of the brine might have made him a more dreamy man of the sky than the solid man of the earth, where he was so perfectly at home. Later, watching another channel, I bought four Roman coins, authentic reproductions of Emperor Hadrian's young lover, Antinous, whose death he grieved until his last imperial breath. On another channel, I ordered a device that sucked wax from the ears. It was guaranteed that my hearing would improve within days. But then, after it was too late to change my mind, I realized I did not need or want to improve my hearing. Except for the music I love, I thought I don't care to hear well at all. Most of what is said is better left unsaid and left unheard. It is the voices from the silent world of the self that matter, like the ones that Montaigne heard and wrote down in his tower room. I thought I might demolish the house now and build that tower in its place and live in the comfort of its invisible voices, and sit there and transcribe the voices as they came.

I grew bored with TV and realized that I missed reading my book of Montaigne's travels, that I missed him. Montaigne was someone I was sure that I could travel with, because he was someone whom I could leave or accompany whenever I chose. And there would be no recriminations, no arguments, no pulling this way and that about where to eat and how much to cool down or heat up the hotel room—or any room anywhere. I went back to my chair and opened Montaigne's book, sure that Pascal would soon arrive and jump up. But a half hour passed and he still had not come. I missed him and the game we played. So, after several more minutes, I went to find him. He was nowhere to be found. But the window to my wife's bedroom was open and I surmised he had left through it and to a world of his own making.

I was about to settle back to my reading when there was a strong knock at the door. I opened it to a man in a blue suit.

"Is she here?"

"Not presently," I said.

"Will she return presently?"

"Who knows?" I said.

"Well, I looked for her everywhere and thought she might have returned here," he said, peering in the doorway.

"Not here," I said, slowly closing the door.

"Do you mind if I come in a minute? Just to rest my feet."

"Have you been searching for her on foot?"

"Not at all," he said, nodding over to the cab standing before the house. "But I'm exhausted from looking for her."

"Come in," I said, not too graciously.

He went immediately to my favorite chair but before he could plunk himself down, I said, "That one's broken."

He sat down on the couch and gave me a sheepish grin. "Thanks buddy."

I pretended to be reading my book but I was sizing him up, slyly, I thought. I did not find him remarkable in any way.

"Is she a reliable woman?" he asked.

"Absolutely. And punctual too."

He looked about the room and folded his hands the way boys are told to do in a classroom. "Does she read all these books?"

"Some, but not all at once."

"That's very funny," he said, with a little sarcastic smile. Then, changing to a more agreeable one, he asked, "Got something to drink? Worked up a thirst running around town looking for her."

"I just opened a bottle of wine you may like."

"Is it from California?"

"No."

"From France?"

"No, from New Zealand."

"I'll pass then. How about a glass of water, no ice." I didn't answer. He stared at me a long time but I waited him out. I noticed he wore burgundy moccasins with tassels and was without socks. That he had an orange suntan that glowed.

"She has me drop her off at the mall and says to come back and get her in a an hour or two. But she never shows up."

"Was your meter running?"

"My Jag's in the shop. The cab's from my fleet."

"By the way, have you seen a cat out there in the street?"

"A salt-and-pepper one with a drooping ear?"

"Yes."

"No, I haven't." Then, in a shot, he added, "Is she your wife?"

"We're married," I said.

"She told me you were roommates."

"We do share rooms, though not all of them."

He stood up, pulled down his jacket, which seemed on the tight side, and came up close to me. "You're better off without her, pal. With all due respect, she's a flake but the kind that fits me,"

He went to the door and I followed, my book in hand, like a pistol. Would you still like that water?" I asked, in a most agreeable way.

"Don't tell her you saw me," he said.

"Cross my heart and hope to die," I said.

He gave me a long look, half friendly, half bewildered, half menacing. "You're not so bad for a dope."

He sped off in his cab—Apex. Twenty-four Hours a Day. We Go Everywhere. The street was empty. The sidewalk was empty. The houses and their lawns across the road were empty. The sky was empty. The clouds too. I shut the door and returned to my favorite chair and went back to my book.

Montaigne wrote brief notes to his wife describing his adventures with bedbugs and the summer heat, never referring to his urinary condition or to his pains, which worsened with each day. He noted that the Italians painted their bedpans with scenes from classical mythology, favoring those of Leda and her admiring swan. They were comforting, those bedpans, so unlike the severe white porcelain ones in France that never thought to combine art with excrement.

I was near the end of the book and that left me in a vacuum for the remainder of the day. I thought that now that I was at large, I would need to plan for the evening and the night ahead. I would leave tomorrow to itself for now. But then the door swung wide open and she appeared, fancy shopping bags in hand.

"Well, aren't you going to help me?" I relieved her of two of the larger bags and settled them on the sofa. "There's another one on the porch," she said, as if I had been malingering. I retrieved it and another one at the doorstep, a large, round, pink box.

She sat on the sofa and kicked off her shoes. She looked about as if in an unfamiliar place. "What have you done?"

"To what?" I asked.

"To the room! It looks different. Did you change anything?"

"Nothing."

She looked at me suspiciously then said, "Something's different."

"It knows you've left. Rooms always know when someone has left."

She pretended to yawn. "Sure."

"And they shift themselves to the new situation," I added. "Like when a person dies in a bedroom and the walls go gray and cold. Or when a child is born and the room goes rosy and roomier."

"Has anyone been here since I left? I can smell that someone has."

"Now that you mention it, yes."

"Was he wearing a blue suit?"

"I didn't notice."

"Let me show you something," she said, removing her dress. She fussed about the shopping bags and pulled out a red skirt and red jacket with large buttons. "Whataya think?" she asked, fastening her last fat button.

"You look like a ripe tomato."

"It matches my handbag," she said, waving it before me. "I realized after I left this morning that my bag needs something to go with it."

"Everything matches and matches your hair too."

"You've always had a good eye," she said.

"For you," I said, in a kind of flirty way that I wasn't sure I meant.

"If you don't mind, I'm going upstairs to pack some things."

"Let me know if you see Pascal up there, please."

"That's another thing. I cringed every time you explained to a guest that Pascal was named after some French philosopher," she said, turning from me.

"If you had ever seen Pascal stare up at the night sky and give a little shiver, you'd understand," I said.

She was already halfway up the stairs and I wasn't sure she had heard me. But then she shouted down, "Did he say when he'll come back?"

I pretended not to have heard her. She came down the stairs again and said, "Well?"

"He didn't say. But his Jag is in the shop."

"I don't care about the books. You can keep them all," she said. "They prefer you anyway, like the cat."

"I named him Pascal, after his namesake, who asked for the patience to sit. I named him Pascal because he sits quietly in the window box and I can see in his eyes that he is training himself against his nature to learn to sit."

She gathered up the red dress suit and the handbag and, without a word, went back up the stairs. I returned to my book but my heart was not in it. Montaigne was on his way back to Bordeaux to his wife and his old life of solitude and voices. To his old known comforts. For all its vaunted claims, travel is a deterioration, taking minutes off one's life with every passing mile. So, for all his bravery, his condition worsened with each jolt of the carriage, with each bug bite and bad meal. By the time he finally arrived home, the blood in his urine had grown darker, the pain stronger, the loneliness greater.

I returned to the kitchen and to the remains of my lunch, still scattered on the table like the flotsam of a minor wreck. I sipped a glass of wine. It tasted of damp nails forgotten in a dank cellar. I sat there as the dusk filtered through the kitchen window, softening the edges of the table and the chairs and the hulk of the fridge. My hand looked like a mitten. Montaigne should never have left his tower, I thought, and gave voice to it in the shadows, "You should have stayed home," I said, advice given too late to an old friend.

Then I went to the door, thinking that Pascal might be there sitting on the step, waiting for me to let him in after his adventures in the wide world. Or maybe he would be just sitting and waiting for the night and the chill of its distant stars.

—*For Edmund White*

Nominated by Conjunctions, Jane Ciabattari

HOW TO TRIUMPH
LIKE A GIRL

by ADA LIMÓN

from GULF COAST

I like the lady horses best,
how they make it all look easy,
like running 40 miles per hour
is as fun as taking a nap, or grass.
I like their lady horse swagger,
after winning. Ears up, girls, ears up!
But mainly, let's be honest, I like
that they're ladies. As if this big
dangerous animal is also a part of me,
that somewhere inside the delicate
skin of my body, there pumps
an 8-pound female horse heart,
giant with power, heavy with blood.
Don't you want to believe it?
Don't you want to tug my shirt and see
the huge beating genius machine
that thinks, no, it knows,
it's going to come in first.

Nominated by Gulf Coast

ELEGIES

by KATHLEEN OSSIP

from POETRY

AMY WINEHOUSE

All song is formal, and you
Maybe felt this and decided
You'd be formal too. (The eyeliner, the beehive: formal.)

When a desire to escape becomes formal,
It's dangerous. Then escape requires
Nullity, rather than a walk in the park or a movie.
Eventually, nullity gets harder and
Harder to achieve. After surgery, I had
Opiates. I pushed the button as often as I could.
Understood by music was how I felt. An escape
So complete it became a song. After that,
Elegy's the only necessary form.

STEVE JOBS

Say you lost all your money, or turned against your ambition.
Then you would be at peace, or
Else why does the mind punish the body?
Vengeance is mind, says the body.
Ever after, you're a mirror, "silver and exact."

Just like the bug in a string of code, the body defies the mind
Or looks in the mirror of the mind and shudders.
Better instruments are better because they're
Silver*ish* but intact.

TROY DAVIS

The clock is obdurate,
Random, and definite.
Obdurate the calendar.
You thump on the cot: another signature.

Did it didn't do it would do it again.
And if a *deferred* dream dies? Please sign the petition.
Very good. Let's hunt for a pen.
If you thump, there's another signature and
Signatures are given freely by the signer's hand.

LUCIAN FREUD

Lingering over
Unlovely bodies,
Couldn't help
Intuitively rendering
A whole
Nother angel.

Facts are
Relics—an
Effect worth
Undertaking: yes,
Dear daylight?

DONNA SUMMER

Discourse that night concerned the warm-blooded love we felt.
On the divan and in the ballroom and on the terrace, we felt it.
Now virtue meant liking the look of the face we lay next to.
Never mind the sting of the winter solstice.
All discourse that night concerned the warm-blooded love we felt.

Something lifted us higher. Her little finger told her so,
Untangling, with careless skill, the flora of the sexual grove.
Master physician with a masterly joy in wrapping up
Mud-spattered, coke-dusted wounds at midnight, when it's too
Early to stop dancing and go home. Our lily-minds soothed by her
Royalty concealed in the synthesizers in the flora of the sexual grove.

THE LAST DAYS
OF THE BALDOCK

by INARA VERZEMNIEKS

from TIN HOUSE

Given the chance, the more sentimental among them would probably return in summer. Summer was when it seemed as if all the residents of the Baldock threw open the doors of their homes to the bronchial, hawking churnings of the passing semis and wheeled coolers out to the picnic tables that had not yet surrendered to rot. There they would sit, cans clutched in cracked hands, as their dogs whipped smaller and smaller circles around the trunks of the Douglas firs to which they were chained. In those moments, it was possible for them to imagine that they had merely stopped there briefly on a long road trip, that they were no different from the men and women with sunglasses perched on the tops of their heads who trooped in and out of the nearby restrooms, mussed and squinting.

Sometimes they walked over to the information kiosk and collected travel brochures, and they would rustle the pages and pretend to plan journeys to state attractions they knew they would never reach. *Crater Lake is the deepest lake in the United States . . . Shop Woodburn Company Stores!* When it grew dark, they crumpled the sun-warmed paper in their fists and used it to start fires in the barbecue pits. After the flames died, they would toss whatever left-overs they had to the dogs, leaving them to thrash beneath the trees. Then they climbed inside their cars, stuffed blankets in the window jambs, reclined their seats, and let the freeway's dull squall, constant and never ending, gradually numb them to sleep.

Without any kind of written record or historical archive to consult, the question of who first settled the rest stop must be answered by one of its oldest former residents, a vast, coverall-clad man named Everett, who claims to have arrived in 1991, after years of wandering the bosky wilds along the interstate with his pet cat. Together, they set up house in the secluded farthest corner of a rest stop named for Robert "Sam" Baldock, "father of Oregon's modern highway system" and "honor roll member of the Asphalt Institute," first in the bushes in a rough hut assembled from scrap, and then in a ragged van that remained more or less parked in the same place as one decade turned into the next. In that time, dozens more joined Everett and his cat, drawn by stories circulating among those versed in a certain kind of desperation about how there was a place off Interstate 5, about fifteen miles outside Portland, Oregon, where someone with nothing left but a car or a camper and a tank of gas could stay indefinitely

Screened by thick stands of evergreens planted under Lady Bird Johnson's Highway Beautification Act, this back-lot settlement grew in relative isolation, its residents largely invisible to the outside world as they pursued the dystopian task of making a life in a place where no one was ever meant to stay. By the time I stumbled upon their community in October of 2009, they were a population of fifty, give or take. No formal census was ever attempted—or deemed necessary, for that matter—since they all knew perfectly well who they were and the myriad ways they passed their time. Seniors waited on social-security checks. Shift workers slept. Alcoholics drank. A single mother knocked on truck cabs. A one-eyed pot dealer trolled for customers. Others sat locked in their compacts, fingering sobriety tokens.

"We call each other Baldockians," said a woman who introduced herself to me as Jolee.

Jolee had been at the rest stop for going on three consecutive years when we first met, though she had lived there off and on for much longer, using the location as a winter retreat when it became too cold to pitch a tent in the foothills. When she was growing up, Jolee's dad had taken her to elk camp each year, taught her from the time she was just a little girl how to survive on her own in the woods. "And then he's all pissed off that I take that knowledge and use it to live like I do," she said. But in recent years, she had grown tired of testing herself for such long stretches, of being at the mercy of the elements, and so she and her boyfriend were residing at the Baldock in a rusting van that ran only occasionally and that periodically needed pushing across the parking lot to a new spot in order to appear in compliance with the rest stop's posted rule that a vehicle remain parked on the premises for no more than twelve hours at a stretch.

Jolee took it upon herself to keep an eye out for the strays, like me, people who needed the Baldock explained to them. Strays were different than visitors, like Jolee's kids, who came on Mother's Day or her birthday and sat for an hour with her at a picnic table, the grandparents who raised them waiting nearby in a running car. Strays were those who drifted into the community's territory by accident, but once they'd become aware of the Baldock's existence, they couldn't stop thinking about what they'd seen. The residents of the Baldock were used to strays, preachers, social workers, strangers with extra cans of kerosene and bags of groceries in the backs of their flatbeds, who kept coming back with questions and concern, but who never stayed.

I first came to the Baldock in an old school bus driven by a man whose job it was to bring hot meals to people living in the region's more rural areas, people for whom it is not an easy matter simply to drop by a soup kitchen or food pantry. I was a reporter at the time, working on a story for the local paper, shadowing the man's efforts. When he told me that our last stop of the night would be at a rest area, I could only imagine that he meant we would be taking a break, or perhaps offering food to down-on-their-luck drivers. But then we parked, and a crowd began to gather, and Jolee appeared. "Let me show you our home," she said.

And that's how I became the accidental chronicler of the Baldock's last days. In truth, it seemed as if they'd been waiting all along for someone to take an interest.

"People normally look right through us," Jolee told me. "Or they might ask, 'Where are you from?' like how people make small talk, and if we say, 'We're from right here,' they'll get this scared look on their faces, and then they'll rush away."

The access they gave me didn't seem to depend on my being a reporter, on any perceived authority that might have granted me; and, in fact, soon after I met them I signed paperwork accepting a voluntary layoff from that job. Instead, I suspect, they were judging me by a more subtle rubric, reading me for clues that would help them gauge my capacity to understand.

I came to learn that the orientation of all permanent arrivals was

242

typically left to a man everyone called "The Mayor." I could never get a fix on just what it was he had done to earn this title, whether it was due to a general sense of grudging respect for the fact that he was said to have once let a gangrenous toe rot in his boot because he was too cussed to see a doctor or the rumors that he kept a pistol in his RV. Either way The Mayor saw it as one of his principal duties to greet the incoming residents: "I don't have money, booze, or cigarettes to give you, and don't give me any shit. But I always have food to share. Ain't no one out here gonna starve."

Baldock etiquette discouraged questions, and this allowed most people to maintain a presence as blurred and unfixed as the reflections cast by the bathroom's unbreakable mirrors. No one asked about the swastika tattoo that crept just above a collar's edge. Or why a police scanner rested in the pocket of a car's door where insurance papers were sometimes kept. In his own more talkative moments, The Mayor liked to remind anyone who cared to listen that "you meet all kinds here, the bad and the good. Mostly good. Still, best advice I can give is to look out for yourself. Don't trust anyone." What he meant was that all the residents of the Baldock, himself included, had versions of the truth they preferred to keep to themselves, maybe even from themselves.

In Jolee's opinion, the most important person any newcomer could meet was the man who lived in a 1970s Dodge Vaquero motor home. "This here's Dad," she said as she motioned to a man of ashen face and hair who was trying to chase a tiny tawny-colored dog back into the battered rig. "Sweetpea, Sweetpea, come on now, sugar," the man coaxed as the dog jumped and nipped at the air, trying to catch circling flies with her teeth.

Addressing me, Jolee said, "I call him Dad because he's done the most to help us out here. He shared his knowledge about how things work, explained everything we need to know. He looks out for people."

What she meant but did not say, I would learn, was that Dad had once pulled her aside and pressed $100 in her palm. *Use it to leave him,* was all he said. And that had been the last of it. He never brought it up again and Jolee never told her boyfriend, who wandered over to the Vaquero every morning to suggest a run to the convenience store to get more beer. And Dad always obliged him.

Dad's name was Ray, and he seemed pleased that Jolee had mentioned him so prominently, over The Mayor. For as long as any one at the Baldock could remember, Ray'd been saying he had six months to live, smoking his days away beneath a sign that warned oxygen tanks were in use, while Sweetpea splintered bones on the floor of his motor home. Ray was born in Kentucky he said, but moved to Oregon when he was fifteen or sixteen and over the years had felled trees and labored as an auto mechanic. Somewhere along the way he had done irreparable damage to his lungs and now had emphysema. "All that asbestos in those brake pads," he figured.

Sometimes he would bring up wives, children. "Buried," he said, in a voice pumiced by all the years of smoking. But it was never clear what he meant by this, whether he meant them or his memories of them.

Sometimes he said he had fought in Vietnam. Other times he said he'd never been. He had lived at the Baldock for going on fifteen years. Twelve. Thirteen. He didn't seem to know anymore, one day so much like all the rest, mornings with the paper, coffee on the hot plate, and then when the shakes set in, a nip or two, on through the day, until his voice feathered at the edges and his eyes bobbed and pitched behind his glasses.

"It's not that we want to be here," he told me the night we met. "It's just we can't get out of here. I'm sixty-eight years old. I get $667 a month in social security and some food stamps. That's all I've got except for what I can make panhandling or rolling cans. Everyone here's the same, figuring out how to get by on less than nothing. But I'll tell you, I don't know how much longer I can make it. Last winter was a bearcat. It was hot dogs on Christmas. I was snowed in for three days. Icicles from top to bottom." He pulled out a pouch of tobacco and some papers and rolled a cigarette as he talked. "I'm too damn old for this anymore."

He'd been of a mind lately to light out for the coast—he was sure he could get a job as a park host somewhere—and so he was rationing gas, trying to save some cash. He'd even picked a day for his escape: "First of the month, I'm fixing to be gone."

He said this in October 2009. He said it again in November and in December and in January and in March and in April.

He was, in fact, among the last to leave the Baldock.

Jack was among the last to arrive, driving in the night after the Fourth of July, his gas gauge near empty, the trunk of his little white Ford four-door loaded down with what he had managed to take while everyone was gone, as his wife had asked him to do, so the kids wouldn't see: a Route 66 suitcase packed with clothing, including his good church suit;

an old camping cooler; a pile of books; a sleeping bag; a tent; and a scrapbook his wife had made that contained the boys' baby pictures and photos from the barbecue they threw in the backyard the day he got his union card.

He'd told himself he'd leave the rest stop come morning, but the truth was he had nowhere else to stay, not on $206 a week in unemployment, not with his wife and kids needing money whether he lived with them anymore or not and the debt collectors lining up. None of his family would take him in, and for a long time, he felt it was no less than what he deserved for what a fool he'd been. He'd known, after all, as someone who'd been raised in a strict family of Jehovah's Witnesses, and who had married a committed convert, that secret strip-club visits and hours of adult movies downloaded from the Internet rank up there on the list of the faith's most grievous sins, right along with lying about it all, repeatedly. Still, he couldn't stop. According to the church elders, who referee such matters, excommunication was the only fit punishment. "Disfellowshipping," they call it. And while a part of Jack wanted to believe that maybe it was a bit out of proportion to the offense, he did, as he put it in his more contrite moments, "regret the crap I put my wife through, and I really did put her through crap—it's not as if I was an angel, and then got kicked out." And so he accepted the elders' pronouncement of his exile, if only because he did not know of any other way to express his sense of humiliation appropriately, other than to make himself disappear.

At first, he pitched a tent at the state campground, but at fifteen dollars a day, the campsite fee added up quickly and he was left with less than one hundred dollars a week. It was there, in passing, that another man mentioned the Baldock.

He resisted the idea initially, but then, one day, driving along Interstate 5 on his way to a job interview, he decided to pull off at the rest-stop exit. He was stopping only to use the bathroom. That's the reason he gave himself. But when he still had some time to kill before his appointment, he found himself following the man's directions, guiding his car past the rows of mud-spattered semis and the volunteers dispensing Styrofoam cups of grainy drip coffee, until he reached the invisible line separating those who were simply passing through from those who had nowhere else to go. He sat for a few minutes and watched through the windshield, his engine ticking. He watched the dogs, running and rucking the earth beneath the trees to which they were tethered. He watched the people hunched around the picnic tables, sun-burned and knotty-limbed. Their laughter, loud and muculent, beat against the sealed windows like birds' wings.

It took three more days for his resolve to build, then take. His first night, he parked as far as he could from all the other cars, which were gathered close, fin to fin, as if in a shoal. For much of the night, Jack sat bolt upright, certain he could hear voices, the jangle of dog collars outside his door. But in the morning, he couldn't think of anywhere else to go and he wanted to conserve what little gas he had left. And so he'd remained there, just sitting in his car, in the oppressive heat, and tried hard to look as if he wasn't looking. He could sense everyone was looking at him, too, though not in an unfriendly way. Sometimes someone would wave. Or nod at him, like an unspoken acknowledgement of something shared. It made him uncomfortable, the way they seemed to recognize something in him before he saw it in himself. At the time, Jack didn't yet feel he had anything in common with anyone at the rest stop; he still believed he would be there only temporarily.

No one else thought he'd be long for the Baldock, either. "I get the feeling this place is going to blow his mind," Jolee told me. "Short-timer," Ray predicted. "You mean he's not another volunteer?" a visiting social worker asked me one night. Jack worked hard at cultivating the appearance of normalcy or what passed for it in the world beyond the rest stop, anyway. His clothes looked freshly pressed, though he had no iron. "If you take them out of the dryer and fold them just the right way while they're still warm, you can make it look like you've creased them," he later explained. He spit shined his shoes. Although he had only a high school equivalency degree, he regularly worked through stacks of books and in careful handwriting filled pages of a journal.

The childhood Jack described, when I asked about it, sounded isolated. Few friends. A life that revolved around the family's faith. At some point, though, he'd become possessed by the idea that he would like to live in a world that offered experiences more expansive than those he'd known. After years of working variously as a pizza delivery man and a swing-shift worker at the local dairy, he decided it might be wise to learn a trade, like carpentry, and had been fortunate enough to apprentice out just as a condo-building boom swept through Portland, industrial wasteland giving way to "planned urban communities." Suddenly, he was framing walls in million-dollar penthouses with Mt. Hood views.

He recalled how once, during that time, he had taken his wife to a restaurant near a development in downtown Portland that he was helping to build. Up until then, he and his wife had only gone out to places like Applebee's and, months later, Jack still remembered the white tablecloths, the white flowers, the way the food came out on white plates, "like paintings." Looking back, he realized it was the first moment he had allowed himself to think he might be different, that all along he had been living the wrong life. But then his work started slowing. Then the housing bubble collapsed completely, and the condos men like Jack had been working on were left to stand empty, their interiors an expanse of white.

The layoff came not long after he and his wife bought their first house. In response, Jack thought it made sense to enroll in school again, to learn another trade, like driving a truck, so he'd have something else to fall back on. The school told him he could take out loans, and he figured if he found work quickly he could pay them back before long. He graduated with his CDL at the time gas prices spiked and trucking companies started slashing their fleets. He'd added another $5,000 in debt to his name. Soon, they had to let the house go, the minivan, too.

Now, at the rest stop, he read Dave Ramsey's book *The Total Money Makeover* by flashlight at night, marking passages that seemed particularly relevant. On Ramsey's advice, Jack had started to portion his unemployment money into envelopes that he marked "bills," "gas," "savings," "fun," and "allowance" for his two boys, even if it was just a couple of singles. Later, he would make an envelope for "child support." By the time we met in October, he had been out of work for six months and had been living at the rest stop for three. He was thirty-six.

He carried copies of his resume in the front seat of his car, in case an opportunity arose to hand one out. Once, he flagged down a maintenance crew working at the rest stop and pushed a sheet in their hands, but that failed to yield any leads, as did the applications he filled out through the unemployment office. He did not have a criminal record or a problem with drugs or alcohol, though he had joined a twelve-step group, hoping, as he put it, it would help him "fix whatever's broken in me." He'd even tried to continue going to services at the Jehovah's Witness Kingdom Hall in the nearby town of Aurora, although, in keeping with what is expected of the excommunicated, he sat in the back and did not speak to anyone.

In the context of the Baldock—where a convicted pedophile with a habit of luring little boys into his vehicle, driving them to out-of-the-way places, then forcing them to have sex at knifepoint, happily lived out his last days; where, a few years ago, the decomposing body of a fifty-six-year-old man believed to have been murdered was found in the underbrush not far from where vehicles parked; and where, more than once, the grip of a pistol could be glimpsed peeping out from under a seat—Jack, with his resumes and scrapbooks and savings envelopes, seemed remarkably naïve, impossibly good, even. "Just a baby," Ray told me.

Of course, it all depended on your perspective. Jack knew his parents and his in-laws and, most importantly, his wife had plenty to say about him and what he'd done. Or not say. Sometimes when he called, they hung up on him. Once, his mom took a few whispered seconds to say that she shouldn't be speaking to him, not after what he'd done, that those were the consequences of his excommunication, and he shouldn't call again. And he couldn't argue with the opinion his family now held of him. He was everything they thought he was. He was nothing. He had tried to come up with a list of good things about himself in his journal. He wanted to be honest.

Finally, he wrote, "I am alive."

They had their own ways of measuring time. One month had passed when the medical delivery truck arrived to drop off a new set of oxygen tanks at Ray's Vaquero. It was fall when the school buses came to fetch the children. Saturday when the church group came round, offering pancakes and prayers. Thursday when the bus from St. Vincent de Paul pulled in with its onboard kitchen and cafeteria tables where the seats should have been, a place out of the cold where they could eat plates of fettuccini and turkey melts. Night when the jacked-up pickup came through the lot, its driver tapping his brake lights, waiting for one of the semis to wink its high beams back, the signal that he should park and climb inside to name his price.

They marked the persistence of loneliness by the frequency with which a knackered blue van appeared, groaning its way through the parking lot, the driver waving gently like a beauty queen on a float. It was Everett and his cat. A local social-service agency had managed to get him into a low-income apartment complex that allowed pets before he and the cat had to face a nineteenth winter at the Baldock. Still, the van coasted past nearly every day. "Too quiet in my new place," Everett would explain and then launch into his latest theories about the causes of unemployment and homelessness to anyone who stood outside his window long enough to listen—NAFTA, globalization, illegal immigration. He never required any kind of acknowledgment, except to be heard, engine idling, cat perched unblinking on the passenger seat.

Soon, they felt the weather turn, winds wailing cold out of the Columbia River Gorge and turning the condensation that accumulated inside their windshields while they slept into streaks of ice. Mornings, they followed each other's footprints through the frosted grass to the restrooms, where they washed and shaved beneath the industrial lights.

On one of those cold nights, after most of the other residents had retreated to their cars, Jolee stood with me in the wind by the picnic tables with an insulated coffee cup in her hands, watching the receding taillights of cars bound for the freeway on-ramp. "All any of us want is to get back over there one day," she said, her eyes following each car as it left. "We want to be over there with them, doing normal things. Like paying taxes. I'm serious. The day I pay taxes is the day I know I've made it back to the mainstream. That's what I want, to feel normal again."

By mid-November, she was gone. She gathered her things from the floor of the van and stuffed them in a backpack, then walked over to Jack's car to borrow his cell phone, which she pressed against her bruising cheek. "I'm sick—I need to go somewhere to get better," she said. Her boyfriend watched silently from the open door of the van with the dogs, his own face welted and swollen. Eventually, Jolee's father's pickup appeared and she climbed inside the cab. When it disappeared onto the freeway, her boyfriend got up and walked over to a sign directing patrons to the restrooms, and he drove his fist into the metal as hard as he could. Finally, he spoke. "Time to go to the store," he said. "Who's going to give me a ride?"

He went on a bender that lasted days, stumbled around in a fog. He accidently locked one of the dogs inside the van, the pit-bull mix who'd loved Jolee, and by the time he remembered and opened the door, the dog had torn the stuffing from the two front seats, shredded all the clothing strewn about, then snapped at his reaching hand. No one knew what to say, and one of the cardinal rules of the Baldock was that no one was in a position to judge, so they all kept quiet, and let him go on saying that the tears he wiped from his red eyes were because of the dog.

Jack for his part had given up his silent visits to the Kingdom Hall and had stopped talking about one day reconciling with his wife. He felt embarrassed when he thought about his uneasiness that first night at the rest stop, how he had imagined he could somehow hold himself apart. After four months at the Baldock, he'd seen enough of "what people do to survive" to realize that he had been deeply misguided ever to presume he'd known what it was to endure. Like the woman who often left her ten-year-old son alone in their motor home while she visited the rows of parked semis—and even the rigs of her neighbors—creeping back hours later, sometimes with what looked like bite marks on her chest. Or the people who stood by the low wall near the rest-stop bathrooms, which they called just that, "The Wall," flashing signs made from the cardboard backs of empty half racks at all the weary travelers emerging from the cocoons of their cars, road tired and bladder full, hoping to part some change from them. They organized their panhandling in shifts in an attempt to maintain some kind of order and equity, but there were often fights when they tried to chase off anyone who didn't live at the rest stop, the tweakers who had homes or hotel rooms, but who would parachute in just long enough to beg money off tourists for a hit. In the hierarchy of the Baldock, those who came to beg but who had somewhere else to stay were openly disdained, cursed as cheats and liars, not because of their habits, but because they presented themselves as homeless when they had somewhere else to go.

As a rule, the police tended not to bother the rest-stop residents, unless someone called in a specific complaint. Although officials had long been aware of the community living there, and the local district attorney's office certainly made its position on the matter clear when it began referring to the Baldock as "Sodom and Gomorrah," the unspoken policy, at least on the ground, appeared to be one of benign neglect, so long as the residents kept themselves out of the run sheets.

But then, one day, a particularly ambitious state trooper came through and ticketed a number of vehicles for lapsed tags, and rather than watch their homes disappear on the backs of tow trucks, those residents quickly disappeared. The whole scene had struck Jack as unbearably unfair, and he couldn't stop thinking about it, like a pawl clicking over and over again into the grooves of a gear. He sat at one of the picnic tables for hours, trying to organize his thoughts. Finally, he got in his car and drove to the local community center. There, in front of the public computer, he began to type.

Baldock residents often spoke about how much they feared breakdown—as in, "My car's broken down on me twice now and I don't know what I'll do if it happens again." Impounds were an altogether different matter, however, and represented perhaps the most frightening possibility of all for someone whose car was his final vulnerability, the one thing left tethering him to any illusions of stability. Losing a car to impound almost certainly meant losing that car for good. Or as Jack wrote at the computer that day: *How can we afford to get them out? . . . (W)e cannot pay for towing or impound lot fees. Even if we pull all our money together, this is an expense we cannot afford . . .*

He typed: *We have a very difficult time paying auto insurance, gas and food. Many of us are looking for work, and have to travel long distances in search of employment. Gas prices are high and food stamps are good but not enough people receive them. None of us can afford a home, an apartment hotel or even campgrounds . . .*

He typed: *We are homeless!*

And he typed: *All we seek is a safe place to live, until we find better options. The rest areas provide us a place to sleep, help each other out and have access to the rest rooms 24 hours a day . . .*

He kept going until he'd filled the whole page. He imagined it would be a letter of grievance, written on behalf of the entire community. He ended with the line *Thank you for your support.* Later, Ray read a copy at his dinette, holding it close to his glasses. "Boy can write!" he said, speaking as if Jack was not standing next to him. "Fancy. There's even semicolons!"

For Jack, the biggest declaration in the whole letter had come down to a single word.

We, he had written.

It was a word drawn from the nights they made communal meals, pooling their ingredients to stretch emergency food boxes and food-stamp allocations. Someone would always fix up plates for those who slept during the day and did shift work at night, balancing leftovers and thermoses of coffee on the hoods of cars for the drivers to find when they woke. From the way they bought each other presents from the Dollar Store, socks and singing cards (*Wild thing you make my heart sing*). From the time they climbed onto Ray's roof to fix the leaks that soaked his bedding, or when they helped Jack change his oil, or lent one another cooler space or propane. But also from the moments when the dogs wouldn't stop barking, and someone was screaming for them to shut the fuck up, and when the trash cans overflowed with all the garbage they'd dumped, and yet another person was asking if he could get a ride to the Plaid for more beer and smokes and only offering pocket change to cover the gas, and from the old-timers who would grouse about how the young had no work ethic, just wanted to smoke dope and have everything handed to them, and then they'd ask if they could take a shift at The Wall. It was Ray, pawing women's asses, braying and frothing at The Mayor that he was nothing more than an imposter, that he, Ray, had more right to appoint himself sovereign of the Baldock. And the boy who spent his nights alone in his motor home, waiting for the sound of his mother at the door—he did not go to school, but no one said anything, just as no one said anything about the abrasions on his mother's chest that turned purple, then green. In a single word, Jack had written himself into the Baldock, and he'd meant it unequivocally—the whole kind, desperate, resourceful, ugly truth of it—without denial or defense.

Thanksgiving marked the turning, the point at which time and memory began to pull away from them, though no one recognized it as it was happening. They were all too preoccupied with the planning of a Baldock-wide turkey feast; a list had been drawn up of ingredients to procure, and while everyone seemed to agree on mashed potatoes and gravy, some people disagreed over the value of stuffing and yams.

People decided to lose themselves in holiday preparations rather than focus on a disconcerting little story that had begun knifing its way through the populace. Apparently, a few days before Thanksgiving, one of the rest-stop cleaners told someone who told someone else that as of the first of the month, the Baldock would have a new landlord, and this one was not likely to be tolerant of the current laissez-faire living arrangements. Rumor had it there were all sorts of plans to spruce the place up—artist demonstrations, fancy coffee, solar panels, nature trails (Ray had harrumphed over this one: "Nature trails, my ass; if there was any nature to find here, we'd have killed it, gutted it, and eaten it by now, had a big old barbecue").

But disbelief gradually gave way to paranoia. Whether it was the maintenance-worker-cum-informant who was the first to mention the possibility of police sweeps and mass banishment, or it was the result of the residents' own grim future casting, soon the rest stop was frantic with speculation of an impending eviction. And so it came to pass that the inhabitants of the Baldock found themselves in a curious and unexpected position: after telling themselves for as long as they could remember that they couldn't wait to leave this place, they now realized they wanted nothing more than to stay.

They tried to talk about other things. On Thanksgiving morning, the early risers crammed into Ray's motor home, downing cups of coffee and taking turns putting the soles of their shoes on the propane heater until they could smell the scorched rubber, savoring the burn of their numb toes. "You know what I love most about Thanksgiving?" Jack said. "Football. It's been months since I've actually seen a game on a TV, not just listened to it on the radio." Everyone nodded and they talked about how luxurious it would be to sit on a sofa again, stupid with turkey, tasked with no other concern than whether to flick between the college or pro games. It struck them all as the height of decadence, of insanely good fortune.

And then the man who looked like a gnome and hardly ever socialized knocked on the motor-home window, face flushed. "Did you hear they're going to kick us out?" he shouted.

"You're late to the party," Ray barked through the window. "We've been hearing that for days now. All bullshit. Just scare tactics. They want to make the panhandling stop. I've been here for thirteen years and this one always makes the rounds, but it's all show."

He raised his cup of coffee to his lips, but his hand was trembling.

"Anyway, I'm leaving. Come the first of the month, I'm outta here. I'm sick of all the drama. The doctor tells me I got six months to live and gotdamned if I'm gonna die at the Baldock."

His face was red and the cords of his neck had stretched taut, and no one spoke for fear of winding him up even more. He reached down, took a beer from the case he kept under the motor home's dinette, and poured some into his coffee as though it were cream.

And at this, the day began its slow slide into drunkenness for everyone except Jack, who didn't complain when he was asked to make a run to the convenience store when provisions ran low. He came back with five dollars' worth of Powerball tickets, bought from his "fun" envelope. The jackpot had reached nearly $200 million. "I figured if we won, we could all buy houses, maybe even the rest stop," he said.

Eventually, the main rest area, which had been heaving with holiday travelers, slowed to a few scattered cars. Afternoon tipped toward evening. The food remained uncooked, the air inside the motor home brackish with smoke. Ray, who had been brooding over his mug for some time, finally spoke. "Some people would say they wouldn't be caught dead living like this, in this nasty old RV," he said. "But you know what, I consider myself so fortunate to have this. Because when you've had nothing—and I've been there—living like a no-good dirty bum, low

253

as you can go, in the streets, and people won't even look you in the face, like you're an animal or something and you don't have shit, you're thankful for whatever you can get. Let me tell you, I've never been so thankful."

He jabbed his face with his fists, trying to hide the tears.

"I don't know what I'll do if I lose this. I can't live like that again." No one spoke.

Abruptly, Ray collected himself and motioned for another beer. "You know, when I leave here on the first, I won't miss a single one of you fools, stuck in this place. Now if you'll excuse me, I need the pisser."

The dreaded December 1 arrived without incident. Outwardly, at least, each day resembled the next. Ray's Vaquero did not budge. The blue van traced its lonely revolutions. Jack dropped money into his envelopes. He had finally found a job, working the graveyard shift at a manufacturing plant for $9.30 an hour, making "plastic injection molded components." And while at first he was relieved to be receiving a paycheck again, he had been doing the math and it had dawned on him that it would never add up to the kind of money he needed to move into even a modest apartment, first, last, and a deposit. He'd toured a complex in Wilsonville—"They had microwaves built into the cabinets, it was beautiful; I'd give anything to live in a place that nice"—but they wanted to see proof of income of at least $1,400 a month. He made just under that. "It's like a merry-go-round you can't get off," he said. "I don't know how I'm going to get out of this."

So he continued to sleep in his car at the rest stop and hoped each day that it would not be his last. Everyone did. Some people urged a discussion of contingencies, the way some families speak of fire-evacuation plans or designated meeting places following natural disasters. What about forest-service land? Was there a remote wooded space where they could all caravan? Too cold this time of year, the pessimists argued. Think of all the food and propane and water you would need to stockpile.

Others, like members of any neighborhood group upon hearing rumors of possible planning changes, turned to the public computer at the community center for reconnaissance. As a result, they now knew the name of the new landlord: Oregon Travel Experience, a semi-independent state agency, as the online literature put it. It had been granted the go-ahead by the legislature to take over the operations of five rest areas that had previously fallen under the purview of the Department of Transportation. And though none of what they could find was written in what one would call plain, unadorned speech, one phrase in particular, about helping the rest stops achieve their "full economic development potential," seemed to them to translate as having something to do with money—be that making money or saving it. Either way, it was not a concept that they suspected would live comfortably alongside homelessness. Intuition told them that much.

Then one day, a woman appeared in the back lot. By the pristine condition of her vehicle, they knew she wasn't a new arrival. As it turned out, she was the new landlord, head of the OTE. Her name was Cheryl, she said. She'd stopped by because she wanted to personally reassure everyone that OTE was not just going to kick people out of the rest stop, but they should know things were going to change at the Baldock. She had been talking to people from the community center where many of them received assistance, and she hoped that over the next few weeks they all might be able to work together to find a way to help everyone move on to something more stable.

"We're not stupid," Ray said later, after she had left. "It was just a different way to say the same thing: you're out of here."

Jack was not ready to embrace Ray's cynicism. He wanted to believe that the promise made to them had been sincere, that no one would be kicked out of the rest stop until he or she had somewhere else to go. But where would that be? Whenever he tried to trace a clear path out of the Baldock for any of them, it always came out confused, occluded, unmappable. No sooner had he considered a possible exit route than his mind would throw up a fact that directly contradicted this option, and so it went, fact upon fact, one after another, like a thicket of construction barricades choking all conceivable ways forward.

Fact: There's not a single homeless shelter in this particular county.

Fact: What if you have a criminal record or are living with someone with a criminal record? What if you have an eviction in your past? No one rents to you.

Fact: Most RV parks won't rent a spot to rigs ten years or older, yet that's what most people at the Baldock owned.

Fact: Most one-bed-room apartments in the area rent for $750 a month.

He rehearsed his arguments on me, and on anyone else who would listen, and when there was no one to listen, he repeated them to himself, until he was losing sleep. It had reached the point where he was

255

reporting for his graveyard shift bleary, his thoughts smudged, sluggish. He blocked his car windows with sunshades to keep out the daylight, but still he winced and churned at the sounds of his neighbors, who seemed to be tuning their voices to a pitch that matched the collective anxiety level.

They grew irritated with each other. It was easier to cloak fear with anger. Ray, for one, announced that his motor home was henceforth off limits to any more coffee klatches. He locked himself inside and did not speak to anyone, though they could see him, glowering at them all through the blinds. He should have been happy. The Mayor had abdicated, putting the Baldock in his rearview mirror. As it turned out, he was not homeless, merely restless, prone to long cooling-off periods when confrontations arose at home. After carefully considering his options, he'd apparently found the idea of returning to the missus preferable to gutting out another day in the uncertain climate of the Baldock.

In this way, they welcomed spring, agitated and aggrieved. Finally in March, a meeting was called at a local church. Cheryl from the OTE promised to be there, along with the man she had recently appointed the rest stop's new manager, as well as local politicians, a deputy district attorney, a trooper from the state patrol. A good number of people from the Baldock showed up, even a few people who no longer lived there, including Jolee, whose new home was a camp trailer on her parents' property, and Everett. Ray had said he would boycott it.

"Ornery old fart," Jolee said, and she called him on his cell phone until he relented and showed up late, smelling of drink, his face gray. Jolee pressed a mint on him.

They sat at tables set with tablecloths and formal place settings for lunch and bouquets of lilacs and bulb flowers and bowls of paste-wrapped candy. Someone had set up a whiteboard at the front of the room. The Canby Center, the social-service agency that had worked most closely with the residents over the years, had organized the event, and the center's director at the time, a woman named Ronelle, spoke first.

"We're here so that you can have a chance to speak," she said. "Please be frank about the obstacles and the barriers you face so that the people here can understand what you are up against, and what might help you."

But how to make it all fit on a whiteboard? They each tried to tell a corner of the story, but it came out fractured, a chorus of elisions:

"A lot of places won't let you have animals and animals are part of our sanity."

"I had to sell my house and move into my motor coach."

"Your *motor coach*?"

"SHH!"

"You have no idea how scary it is trying to imagine where to go to next."

"I never thought in my life I would panhandle, but I've flown a sign to raise money for my tags, my insurance."

"A lot of us have jobs, but they aren't very stable or we don't have enough hours to make what it takes to get back in a place. I make just above minimum wage, and I have child support to pay too."

"Some of us just slipped through the cracks. We don't have alcohol problems, medical problems, or a mental illness. There seems to be no help for us."

"I've had times where I've worked double shifts, and then I need to catch up on my sleep all at once. I might sleep twelve hours straight in my car. I need a place where I can do that, so I can keep my job."

"You know, if you move us, you aren't going to get rid of us. We just go hide."

"We used to have movie nights in the summer. Jack had this portable DVD player and he'd set it on one of the picnic tables, and we'd all pretend like we were at a drive-in . . ."

Ray said nothing.

Finally, Cheryl rose and spoke. "We understand you're a community, a neighborhood." She respected that very much. She knew they were afraid, but she wanted to reassure them a "transition plan" was being developed. "We promise to keep you informed every step of the way."

So much said, and yet, in the end, it would be silence that told them the most. The phrase they most hoped to hear—*you can stay*—went unspoken and there was only the scrape of chairs all around, the rustle of skirts and suits departing.

It was time to go, but they dawdled. Everett shook the remainder of the candy into the front pocket of his overalls. Jolee went with her boyfriend off to a quiet corner to talk, their heads close together. And Jack stood off to the side, rehearsing one last speech: "What if I did some maintenance work for you, strictly volunteer. Could you let me sleep there during the day?"

Maybe, in those last days, if they had been different people, more like the people they saw on the other side of the rest stop, those so seemingly certain in their slacks and sedans, counting down the miles to home, maybe then they might have known how to reassure each other, how to spin this into a good thing, a fortunate thing, to be given the chance to leave this place and pretend it had never existed. Wasn't that what they had wished for all along? As it was, they hid their faces under propped hoods, screwdrivers clenched between their teeth, cussing recalcitrant old engines into cooperating for the drive ahead.

Proffers had been extended to each resident, elaborate relocation plans crafted by a committee of representatives from the county and state, police officers and social workers and housing specialists, assembled at the request of Oregon Travel Experience.

For Jack, and seven others, immediate slots in a six-week class offered through the county that would help him land low-income housing. For the more complicated cases that eluded immediate solutions, prepaid spots in campgrounds and motels. For one man, detox. For others, help navigating social-security applications and untangling veterans' benefits.

For Ray, a stall had been secured in an RV park willing to allow his old motor home, but he wasn't having it. "It's nothing but a drug den. Place is full of meth heads and thieves. Sweetpea and I won't go." He was convinced that everyone who agreed to leave the Baldock was just being set up for a fall. "Once they get you alone," he said, "you just become a number. We should hunker down, like a family."

He was still refusing to budge, right up until the last day in April, when everyone was asked to caravan to Champoeg State Park, where a block of adjoining campsites had been booked for the weekend, after which everyone would head on to whatever was next. True to its word, Oregon Travel Experience had not kicked anyone out, but now that all the residents had been offered someplace else to stay, that promise no longer held. From this day forward, anyone who remained at the rest stop, or who returned, was subject to trespassing charges should he violate the twelve-hour rule. Or as Ray translated it: "Once you leave, you leave. They've got you."

As the others made their last-minute preparations, packing and re-placing flat tires and loading squirming dogs into cargo holds, Ray hunkered down in his Vaquero. "This is gonna get nasty," he promised through the blinds.

His standoff lasted less than two hours. By late afternoon, he'd pulled into one of the empty berths at the state park, next to Jack, who stood shrouded in tent fabric. "Can someone please help me with the poles?" he called. This was the campground where Jack had first stayed when his wife kicked him out. It also marked the first time in nine months he did not have to sleep in the seat of a car.

The sun warmed the leaves of the ash trees and, together, they sat at one of the communal picnic tables, watching the dogs skitter through the underbrush and admiring the trailers of their new, if temporary, neighbors. It was a nice campground, everyone agreed, though they would never venture farther than their assigned row. They would not go where there were birding trails and pet-friendly yurts, or to the field reserved for disc golf. They kept close together, to what was familiar, working their way through their coolers, telling each other this wasn't so different from the Baldock, but then worrying all the while that their new neighbors might think them too loud, too uncouth ("DON'T PEE AGAINST THAT TREE!"), shushing the dogs, trying not to think about the checkout dates recorded on their receipts, when they would all head off into whatever it was that waited for them after this, alone.

Once, long ago, this had been a pioneer settlement, the last stop for those who had set off across the plains, drifting west until they couldn't drift anymore. Now, on special occasions, volunteers in period garb demonstrated for park visitors the difficulty of life for those who had once tried to settle on the frontier's edge. Each year, in "a celebration of Oregon's rugged pioneer roots," the curious and the masochistic could attempt the skills those pioneers acquired for daily survival, such as wheat threshing, butter churning, and wool carding. This particular weekend, however, happened to mark the occasion of Founder's Day, when, nearly one hundred and seventy years ago, the settlers had gathered and voted to establish a provisional government. The land where the park now sat was to have been its capital. Already, in preparation for the festivities, men in boots and braces were rigging draft horses to plow furrows in the earth as minivans puttered past.

Such re-creation was all that was left of what had once transpired there. Eighteen years after the historic vote, the nearby river tongued its banks, then surged. The settlement vanished beneath seven feet of water, and the pioneers scattered. They never rebuilt. Twelve miles away, for the first night in more than a decade, the back lot of the Baldock stood empty, like a stretch of back shore licked clean by the tide.

Ray disappeared first, pulling out of the campground in the middle of the night. No one heard from him for months, and everyone started to wonder if he might really be dead.

The rest of them tried to forget the Baldock as they moved into rent-assisted apartments and bought plants and hand towels and carefully positioned throws on the backs of donated sofas, where they sat, absorbing the quiet. Some of them found jobs, and some of them lost those jobs when they failed the drug tests. Those who had not been visited by their children in their car days practiced unfolding hide-a-beds, stored plastic cereal bowls in the cupboards.

They called each other, until they didn't.

Months passed.

They did not see the workers bent over the long-neglected flower beds of the Baldock, planting local bulbs of peony and iris.

Then Ray finally surfaced, alive, but rigless and grieving. "I did a dumb thing," is how he said it to me. "Had some drinks with a friend, drove off, cops stopped me. I'm not gonna lie, I had beer on my breath, so they gave me a DUI, took the motor home and I couldn't get it back."

He had been looking for a place where he and Sweetpea could stay—how he hated to beg—and for a while the joke was it looked like a Baldock reunion, because it was Jolee who offered to help. She had a couch of her own now—she'd managed to get a little rent-controlled apartment in Oregon City that she shared with her boyfriend, though since he'd left the rest stop, he was no longer being called a boyfriend but a fiancé—and she told Ray he was welcome to the living room. Just like old times, they'd said, and crammed into the little apartment. And it was true that it was just like old times, but that wasn't always good. Ray grew restless—"can't stand being cooped up"—and took to walking Sweetpea around and around the apartment complex, until one day he slipped on a patch of ice and shattered his hip—"broke the socket clean through"—sentencing himself to forty-five days in a hospital bed.

"I've got nothing," he said upon his release. "I'm seventy years old and not a damn thing to my name." He'd left Sweetpea with Jolee and he hoped to buy a van "come the first of the month, something less than $750, if I can find it." But even if he found a new vehicle, he had no idea where to go. He insisted he had no desire to return to the Baldock. "That's all in the past. Gone now. Buried." But the way he said it sounded as if he wished it wasn't true.

Jack was the one who went back.

"Yes," he'd said, and then he hung up the phone and set it on the coffee table of his apartment, where he now kept his journals and scrapbooks in a neat, angled stack. Then he'd picked it up again to quit his job at the manufacturing plant. On his last shift, his colleagues presented him with a sheet cake. They had scribbled a message onto the chocolate frosting. "Good luck Jackass!"

He pulled back into the parking lot of the Baldock on New Year's Day.

It was January 1, 2011, and he had stayed away from the rest stop for a total of six months.

They set him to work mowing the grass and emptying trash and erasing the graffiti that erupted in the bathrooms. He pruned the trees where the dogs once howled and paced. He made it his special project to tame the overgrown spinneys that romped the edges of the property, only to unearth in his sculptings a decade's worth of discarded liquor bottles, tattered condoms, needles, all carted away like evidence of an obscene archeological dig. He worked until no signs of the old settlement remained.

Also among his duties was to tend to travelers who might be stranded, who needed a jump or a tire changed or some gas. Sometimes, he gave directions. For all this he made ten dollars an hour and received benefits better than those he had known when he was with the union. It was the happiest he'd felt in a long time, but also, strangely, the loneliest.

For company, he sought the continued counsel of Dave Ramsey, who strongly advised a second job if one hoped to shed debt more quickly. And so, on his days off, Jack returned to the manufacturing plant and his cake-giving colleagues of the graveyard shift.

The borders of his life had now contracted to a simple triangulate: work, his boys, and the garden apartment where he hung his sons' framed school photos on the wall and taped a flier for a one-bedroom house for sale at the end of the road with an asking price of $129,000 to the refrigerator. He had been adding figures endlessly in his head, and although he was so tired he sometimes found his mouth refusing to form whole sentences, he was certain that, if he could keep this up and his car did not break down on him, he would be debt free within the year, maybe even build up an emergency fund.

Sometimes rumors reached him about his former neighbors at the Baldock. Ray had disappeared again and no one knew where he had drifted to this time. Jolee had lost her apartment and was briefly sighted living with her fiancé in the bushes at the confluence of the Willamette and Clackamas Rivers, where, according to the local parks and recreation department, "the beaches attract both the sun worshipper and the nature lover with sun, water, nature paths and wildlife!" A notice in the classified section of the local newspaper had recently announced the auction of all the possessions in her storage unit due to lack of payment.

Mostly, though, Jack lived in silence, quietly and deliberately tracing the same route each day, from rest stop to apartment, and at the end of it, the sound of his key in the door, then dinner at a small pine table with a single place setting and his manager's first review of his work at the rest stop, which he reread as he ate: "Keep up your consistently good attitude and strong work ethic and you'll do fine."

You'll do fine, he tells himself and tries not to think about those days at work when a car pulls into one of the rest stop's parking stalls, belongings strewn in the back, and how he prays it'll leave before he has to be the one to knock on the window and tell whoever's inside it's time to go.

Nominated by Tin House, Jessica Wilbanks

YOUR GHOST

by HILLARY GRAVENDYK

from SUGAR HOUSE REVIEW

Parted from the scene of old disasters
a magnet pulling one memory in two directions

the hand stilling the circles in a puddle
mind placed against the side of a stone

I guess we haven't offered up any new truths
turned your heart inside out for pennies

braided your hair into a soft basket
held nature's charms at arms length

wondering who sleeps where at night
where the imprint of your body goes when you
    rise

your ghost spilling like a lake into the hall
flash-flood of absence and promise

the sight of every angled enmity a kiss on the brow
the slope, the axis, three points in a bucket of lines

I know these roads by heart and all the ways back in
An arrow strung up like a party favor points the way

I want to hear your voice at the bottom of the stairs
I want to get drunk, hit rock bottom, kill something small

I want to break every heart in the room: your apparition
curled around my neck like an animal
made from clouds.

Nominated by Sugar House Review

LA PULCHRA NOTA

fiction by MOLLY McNETT

from IMAGE

> *Do not love the world or the things in the world. . . . For all that is in the world, the lust of the flesh and the lust of the eyes and the pride of life, is not of the Father, but is of the world. And the world passes away, and the lust of it; but he who does the will of God abides forever.*
>
> *—John 2:15*

> *Sing to him a new song; play skillfully on the strings, with loud shouts. For the work of the Lord is upright, and all his work is done in faithfulness.*
>
> *—Psalm 33:3*

My name is John Fuller. I am nine and twenty years of age, born in the year of our Lord 1370, the son of a learned musician and the youngest of twelve children—though the Lord in his wisdom was pleased to take five brothers and two sisters back to the fold. After a grave accident, I no longer possess the use of my hands. Any inaccuracies in this document are not the fault of the scribe, who enjoys a high reputation, but of my own mind. My pain is not inconsiderable. However, I will continue frankly, in as orderly a fashion as I am able, so that these words may accompany my confession to the honorable vicar of Saint Stephens.

My story begins as God knit me in the womb. There my knees pressed in to form the sockets of my eyes as they do in all men. However, my left knee—the cap of which has a sharp embossment—pressed upon the iris, pushing it to one side. While I am able to see clearly, it appears to others that the eye looks away from the place I have trained it. God be praised for this deformity, for it kept me close to him for the better part of my life.

My first memories are of two sounds—one ugly and one beautiful. As a child I lived in Oxfordshire in the northern Midlands. An old church stood in the center of the village, and in its demesne what I thought must be everything the world could possibly contain: a bakehouse, granary, pigsty, dairy, an assortment of dovecotes, and a malting house. Once I recall walking on the outskirts of this enclosure with my father when there came an ugly noise, dry and papery, as menacing as a snake's warning. My father quickly lifted me to his shoulders and ran toward our cottage. Looking back I saw a man whose skin bubbled up like a dark pudding—a leper, I later learned, required to wear a rattle to warn us of his coming. In one moment his eye caught mine from high upon my father's shoulders, and the look he gave me was so sinister that I have not forgot it. It seemed to say that only my father's body separated us, that in its absence the leper and I were one.

Our cottage was built at the edge of the village, along the banks of a tiny stream. One hot afternoon I awoke from a nap transfixed by the highest, sweetest sound I had ever heard. It was as if I could see, in my mind's eye, this sweet sound rapidly tracing the petals of a flower before plummeting down its stem. I learned later from my father that one capacity of the human voice had been described in such a way by Jerome of Moravia—as a vocal flowering. I went to the window. There my mother joined me, pointing to a nest in the bank-willow tree.

"That nest," I asked, "did you make it?" For my mother was skilled in weaving, and in fashioning all kinds of things.

"Of course not," she scolded me. "It is mother bird who builds it."

"How can she make it so?"

"God gave her the knowledge," she said. "Nothing perfect comes but it comes from God."

Then from somewhere in the tree the beautiful thick chirp came again, a trill and a sweet clucking. How I wanted to see the bird! But as much as I strained and leaned, she did not appear.

"How does she learn this song?" I asked.

"God puts the song in her breast," said my mother.

"And how can it be so sweet?"

"Tiresome boy," she smiled, "this also comes from God."

"And my eye?"

Her mouth twisted in irritation, and she dropped my hand. "From God," she muttered. "The good and the bad are from God. . . ."

And perhaps I remember this day so clearly because, soon after, it pleased divine providence to take my mother to the Lord, may he be praised for all things. This was in the year of our Lord 1376, in the month of June.

After my mother's death my father accepted a position as an organist in the town of Bishop's Lynn, in Norfolk. He explained to us that an organ was a wonderous and expensive piece of equipment, and only a church of good means could acquire one. We children admired our father greatly, and as the years passed he taught us whatever he knew of music and instruments.

At two and twenty I married a woman named Katherine, nine years my elder and the daughter of a well-to-do burgher. Her father accepted my appearance. Though thine eye may wander, he jested, see that thy heart does not. I assured him that because of my appearance, I was a devout man and had never been burdened with lust or pride. Katherine's inheritance was more than I might have hoped for, and we did not want for money. We had a cook, a maid, and a nurse; and Katherine was wise in shopping, never fooled by watered wine or the old fish sold at market, rubbed with pig's blood to make it look fresh. We enjoyed our supper over pleasant conversation, and in the evenings I would play the gittern or the psaltery, for my father had given me a small collection of instruments and I loved nothing more than music.

Katherine herself could not keep a pitch, and sometimes when I hummed a little tune without thinking, she might ask me to stop. But no wife is without such cavils, and she was gay in demeanor then, as middling comely as befit a woman of her years, and forthcoming in wifely duties. I was pleasantly surprised in my enjoyment of these, and called myself happy in life.

In the second year Katherine was with child, and when her time came she labored through the night. Never in my life had I heard such lamentation, and I wondered how the throat could bear such pressure unscathed. The midwife came out for the rose oil and sat on the stool beside me, her head in her hands, and when hours later she fetched some vinegar and sugar, she took bits of lambswool and tucked them in her ears before entering the birth room again. When finally the dawn came, I heard a small cry, but most of an hour passed before finally the midwife brought the child down the stairs to me. I was happy, although it was a girl. And as I held the babe, she brought another—twin girls.

I knew Katherine to be a good and honest woman, so I could not believe that twins must be sired by two fathers. But of course many did believe it. When the days of her purification were completed, Katherine was received, according to Leviticus, back into the church, made clean to make bread or prepare food. But on the way home that day some women tore the veil and wimple from her head so that she was made to walk home as bareheaded as a harlot. In the following week our neighbors spun a yellow cross to mark her garment and left it at our door, and spat at her as she went to market, and spat upon her babes. My old father the organist would no longer speak with her, and my sisters and brothers would no longer look upon her.

Was it out of sadness that Katherine refused me my marital rights, even as a year passed? I will never know. We did have a common devotion for the sweet creatures she had borne. We employed a nurse whose breasts were large enough for two, yet not large enough to flatten the children's noses, and we took joy as these two began to smile and babble and their curls were growing long. For my part, I felt a relief and pride at their smooth kneecaps and beautiful straight eyes. For though the woman carries the seed of the child, they may have shared my deformity. Together we looked and wondered at them as one wonders at the heavens and all the beauties of nature. They were so entirely alike that only a few tiny spackles on the nose could distinguish elder from younger.

But divine providence was pleased to take the life of our dear twins two days apart from each other, the first on the fifth of June at the hour of terce, in the year of our Lord 1393. Then I too was taken sick, and woke from my fever one morning to find that the second twin had been gathered back to the Lord on the seventh of June at 5 o'clock, in the year of our Lord 1393. For this may the Lord be thanked and praised, for every devout man knows the great mercy he shows us in taking a child out of the world. Yet had they stayed with us—had even one stayed—I believe I would not have this story to tell.

Katherine was a good woman, and, until this time, perfectly ordinary. But she began to weep all the day long and into the night, and no comfort I offered was of help to her. One winter's day I could not find my wife and, looking out the window, saw her sitting in the snow with her skirt spread round her. She wore no coat. I sent the nurse, who hovered over Katherine as she rocked back and forth on her heels.

"Sir, no coaxing could get her inside," she told me. "She says she is warm inside the body, and God tells her not to fear illness."

Then she leaned in and whispered, "She wears no knickers under the skirt."

Shortly after this incident, it pleased the Lord to take to paradise my father the organist, and for this may he be praised in his wisdom. I was given the tutelage of some of my father's students who lived across the canal in the old city where there were large stone dwellings of Roman style. I found these houses impressive, for our own was timber, post and beam, and so close to its rotting neighbor that the two dwellings leaned on each other at the top like a pair of *boureés*.

My pupils were young girls who lived in the old quarter, from wealthy families in which the boys studied chess and hawking and the girls embroidery and singing. Most of them did not sing well, yet the lessons were pleasant for me, a diversion from our home and its growing strangeness.

Katherine no longer did the shopping. Together we only went out to church, and there she would cry. The cries began softly, and then grew to sobs, and she fell forward to the pew in front of us, and then into the aisle writhing and groaning with a sound as great as the one she had poured forth in labor, so that it was only prudent to gather her and take her from the sanctuary. Then she smiled fiercely, her eyes gleaming in ecstasy.

"It is the Lord who makes me," she told me, later. "He speaks to me. And when I fall to the ground I cannot stop myself; it is because I hear the most beautiful music, that seems to come from heaven itself."

In truth I did not know if I could believe it. For we know of those who contract dancing fevers in the rainy season, when, for example, in Saint Vitus's dance, one town makes its way to another in a state of shivering frenzy. It seemed to be a madness of that sort. Indeed, Albertus Magnus has written that women who do not receive their husbands can become full of poisonous blood and it is better for them to expel the matter, but my wife dismissed this opinion when it was offered.

Still, she did seek the counsel of authorities, including William Southfield of the Carmelites, and Dame Julian, the anchoress, in her little cell. These agreed that God was speaking to Katherine through her fits. And so my wife had a new path to follow, this time as a woman of faith. And in time she was no longer shunned on the street. She had earned respect and her demeanor improved.

But though Saint Augustine tells us we might atone for any sin between married people by acts of Christian charity, our relations did not resume. At night we got in bed as usual, well-bedded in white sheets and nightcap. We took off our nightclothes under the covers. But when I turned to Katherine, she would feign sickness, or scratch herself.

"I have worms!" she would say, slapping my hand away.

"No," I assured her. "You have not scratched all day."

"They come out at night!"

"Let me see . . ." and smiling I would reach out to her nakedness. But she thrashed and spun away from me.

During this time I visited for the first time a student of my late father's who had recently recovered from illness. Her maid showed me to where she lay on the daybed still in a dressing gown of yellow silk. She looked to be sixteen, as dark haired as a Jewess, with large brown eyes and rather dark skin. I did not think of her as lovely. I suppose that those who were said to be beautiful had very white skin and light hair, so it did not occur to me to define the girl in this manner. Then, too, this dark girl covered her mouth in the manner of those with rotten teeth who have been trained not to offend others. So I sometimes covered my own sinister eye with my hand, or turned my face away, to avoid the onlooker's gaze.

"I am Olivia," she said meekly. "I am happy to meet you, and I know your father is with the Lord."

I thanked her, and asked her if she felt well enough to stand, for standing is the best way to sing. She nodded and, with some effort, hoisted herself up by the table stand.

"Let us begin with a recitation," I said, "for in this way I shall know what I need to teach you."

I do not remember much of the first song she sang, or even, exactly, my own reaction to it. My surprise was first that she sang a worldly song, popular in the courts of great men, and sung by troubadours. It made no mention of God.

But soon I had forgotten the song itself and marked the contrast between this girl and my typical student, who strained so on high registers, who, if she hit the note, often pushed into it like a German, or broke the tone in the manner of the French. Olivia's voice lifted to each note directly, holding on the tone without excess of ornament or vibration—the sweet sound of a child. In its simplicity there was something wondrous about it, and I wanted to laugh and delight in it, rather than find something to teach her. Yet her nurse sat embroidering on the settle, and she would report to Olivia's father. I had to begin with a suggestion, and so it came to me what I might add. For Isodore of Seville told us the voice should be "high, clear, and sweet" and indeed something was not entirely clear.

I asked, "You are aware of the epiglottis?"

Olivia shook her head. I asked the nurse to fetch ink and paper, and drew a small sketch of this leaf shaped part. "If the tongue, perhaps swollen from sickness, is sliding backward, it may be clouding the tone of what my father—working, as you know, on the organ as he did, and noticing its similarity with the human capacity for two kinds of sound—might call the lower register."

The nurse looked up attentively from her embroidery, while the student studied my sketch with a worried expression. I suppose that I wanted to lighten this expression, though I don't remember thinking so, only that my throat ached, as it did in the moment when as a child, I raced to the window to find that the bird was not there.

"In spite of this," I told her, "your voice at times comes close to a moment of perfection—what Jerome has called *la pulchra nota*. Let us begin to listen for it. Mostly it appears with no strain whatsoever. But be attentive, for when such a note comes, if you know it, you may ever after use its sound to guide you." Then I smiled, for her brows were still knit in a childlike concern.

"Do not worry," I said gaily. "It may be only a short while."

And at this she smiled back at me quite fully and naturally. "Oh!" she said. "Do you think so?"

"Yes," I said. "I'm sure of it."

That I should not have said, I thought later. I myself had never reached such a note in singing. Why should I praise so strongly? Was there another reason to do so? In fact I went over the entire lesson in my mind for some reason, retracing what I had said, and how I had said it, and I saw the image of Olivia's open face, her easy joy in singing. Perhaps I retraced our conversation only to protract the lesson in some way during the week. In this way I could avoid my circumstances at home.

For that night as I turned the psaltery, Katherine put her head in her hands and sighed, and said it would be better not to play at all. I changed my course and the next evening sang only plainchant, making my voice as soft and comforting as possible.

But she drew her shawl about her shoulders and came to sit next to me on my stool. There she repeated to me that the music she heard in her mind, whose perfection made her yell and writhe, was not of the world, but came directly from the Lord. So worldly music and sounds were only poor imitations, distracting from worship, as all worldly pleasures do.

There was quiet that evening in our empty house, empty of the sound of children and empty of conversation, empty of music. It was a place where sound became odious to both of us—the crack of a stool, the creak of our bed as we settled there.

I tried again to approach my wife in the night, for it was cold and we slept with our clothes off as always, tucked under the foot of the bed. But she turned to me and spoke softly:

"John, I have given you sorrow. But the Lord has a remedy. We must go to the anchoress, declare celibacy, and I will again wear white."

And she smiled, petting my face as if I were a child. This soft stroking of my skin, her face and breath held near to mine were so hateful to me that my jaw tightened and I fought an urge to strike her.

"No," I told her.

"No?" she asked, as if she did not believe my refusal.

And I repeated, "No."

The next day my wife did not eat. She couldn't bear the strength of mead, she said, or of meat. And all that week and into the next she would only sip from the broth of a boiled root. She no longer spoke to me, and though it was winter she walked with no shoes, placing her toes first so that the boards would not sound when she entered a room.

After a fortnight, she was so weak that she fainted daily. Yet leaning upon her maid she went to church, and to the anchoress in her cell, and when they had seen her the townspeople were drawn to this ethereal creature, including the neighbors who had shunned her. Some came to our house to ask her advice, and for prophecy. They were embarking on a pilgrimage, they said, and wanted to know if the day they had chosen was auspicious. Would she pray for a woman on the brink of death, would she find out if this woman might indeed recover? Was another woman's husband in heaven or purgatory? And though my wife seemed happy in this role, she continued to fast.

"Eat," I coaxed her.

I knew her silent answer: I will eat again when you come with me to the anchorite and take the vow.

Olivia's strength improved as my wife's waned. I had met with her three times over the course of that month. Often we talked at length before the lesson began, and if her nurse was in the room, she too might join in our conversation. These were easy, ordinary words, concerning the season, or the news of a birth or a neighbor's pilgrimage, for example, but because I had no companion with whom to speak at home, they seemed the more delightful to me. Perhaps in any event the girl's voice would have pleased me, so high was her laugh—it tinkled like a little bell.

Now she stood without grasping and did not need to clutch the table, and her singing had become so sweet and clear I could hear it in my head at night as I lay waiting for sleep. At those times, too, I sometimes found myself wondering if my own left eye was not very far off its course, after all. I had been observing it in the glass of late and it seemed to have improved. Or had I exaggerated its homely effect in the past? Was there any way I could be described as handsome? I had a large gap between my front teeth, but they were good. I was not tall, but strongly built. There was some pain caused by these thoughts, for I felt in some way that the Lord had removed me from his protection.

One day, on her last lesson of that month, Olivia was just in the middle of the *Rondel d'une Dame* à *son Amy*, from the *Chasse Départ*, in which a high *sol* was to be held for several measures. She smilingly ran the notes in the early section, with no strain on her face, but sometimes glancing at me, it seemed, to catch my eye:

Vivons toujours bien raisonnablement . . .
Let us always live justly
bearing our woes the most peacefully
that we can, without a single offense
to our love, for the first to fault
makes the other live inconstantly thereafter.

It was on the penultimate line, *En nostre amour, car le premier qui faut*—on its last syllable, *faut*—that Olivia soared over the high *sol*, lighting there delicately as the tone opened out into such exquisite vibrations that I cannot describe them, only that they seemed to fill the room and envelop us, so that we stood transported in their aftermath.

We rushed to one another, or really, the student to me. She threw her arms around my waist and I thought nothing of her nurse in the next room and embraced her, let myself gaze at her face turned up to mine, smilingly, and for this moment it seemed the most natural act in the world, so that there was no discomfort or thought of its being an embrace, and there was no need for words.

Still, she laughed and said, "I love you!"

I would like to end my story at this moment. I would like to linger here at the very crux of joy, where the note, and these words, were as one to me.

But I cannot. I then understood something about music that I had not learned from my father, or Jerome of Moravia, or Isodore of Seville.

La pulchra nota is the moment of beauty absolute, but what follows—
a pause, however small—is the realization of its passing. Perhaps no
perfection is without this silent realization.

The wind that had lifted the bird, and the room, and those hearts
within the room, drew still. I was as Adam in the garden—suddenly
naked, suddenly shamed. I released her and stepped back. I remember
that her smile remained, and then turned curious, so firm was her trust
in the note.

"This is a good beginning," I said. "But you have been ill and should
not tax yourself."

I suppose I said these words strangely. Later I wondered.

The student's head fell on its stem and she sank onto the bench as if
her weakness had returned. It pained me to see that she buried her face
in her hands, but I had no experience with love, and its offices, and
I did not know what to do. I turned and left without speaking more
to her.

In the streets of the old city—with its sturdy Roman buildings, its
flowerpots, its neat sewers—every young man I passed seemed a fitting
mate for a young nightingale. They wore short tunics with toggles
across the front, drawn tightly across their waists. I walked on into the
new quarter, past the tanners, where the offal stank in its pile near
the street and my house rotted and leaned against its neighbor. In a
puddle I saw the blurred vision of my form in its long shabby houp-
pelande, its stiff, high collar hiding my jaw, which I sensed now, in
comparison to these young men, was weak and undistinguished. How
I wished to be the beloved in the Song of Songs, whose eyes are like
doves beside springs of water, bathed in milk, fitly set; whose legs are
alabaster columns, set upon bases of gold! Even in youth I had never
been the object of admiration, and so I had not minded youth's passing,
but I was now full of jealousy for these fashionably clothed young men.
At the same time I was nearly delirious with joy. I replayed those words
to myself, words my wife did not speak: *I love you.*

You may not know, if you have not been called ill formed and ugly
from birth and a sweet young girl has never once looked at you in such
a way, how thirsty I felt for all that had been denied me! Suddenly Ol-
ivia's smooth face, dark as the curtains of Solomon, seemed very dear;
I thought of my wife and the slack skin of her neck, her visions and
writhing. I did not mind the vow of celibacy as much as I felt ashamed
that in exchange for a healthy dowry, I given up my right to love.

Of course, I wondered: had Olivia meant to say she loved me? In fact, did she love the music and the note itself, her ability to sing it? Or perhaps my small part in bringing it forth? And if I loved Olivia what did I love? The note? The girl herself? Or my own reflection in her eyes as someone worthy of such feeling?

So my thoughts crossed from happiness to unhappiness, and I could not sleep that night. I was bound for torture, it seemed, for love itself was a sin and promised the fires of hell; and lack of love a present torture. I suffered a kind of madness that could only be relieved by some act of goodness.

There my wife sat slumped in her rocking chair, and her bony shoulders from behind were those of an old woman. She had borne such sorrow; she was dying there in that chair, too weak to rise and take herself to bed.

"You must eat," I said softly.

"We must go to the anchoress," she whispered.

And so I answered, "Yes."

When I again crossed the canal to the old city to see Olivia the deed had been done. My wife was at home in her white robes. She wore a special mantle and ring, having taken the vow with me through the little window carved for the anchoress to receive the sacrament.

Olivia's nurse saw me into the study, and my hands trembled as I set down my music; as I spoke my normal pleasantries I stuttered. But when the student entered, her greeting was ordinary, and calm. Though she did not meet my eye, I wondered if I had imagined what had transpired just the week before as she began further on in the *Rondel*:

Desir mapprent telz regretz. . . .
Desire teaches me to know
such sorrows that I know not what can be born of them
And then suffering locks me in her prison
Vexation assaults me and beats me hard and fast
Alas, would you decrease my pain
Si vous pouvez. . . .

There it was, the beautiful voice, but the tone had become slightly reedy somehow. Or was it only when compared with *la pulchra nota?* But Olivia sensed a lack too, for she stopped singing and shook her head impatiently.

I hoped silently that I was responsible for her failure. For had I not been both happy and melancholy since her declaration of love? And

Jerome tells us that melancholy is an obstacle to perfection, that no sound has true beauty if it does not proceed from the joy of the heart. But I was not brave enough to console her with this information.

"I believe," I said, clearing my throat, "that you love the music because it comes from God. That is . . ."—here I began to sweat, and wiped my forehead with the long sleeve of my hoppelande—"that is, you are devout, and love God, and the music comes from God. All we do well is from God, every image, every sound, and we return the glory to him. And we will continue in that vein."

Here she stood and attempted the lines again, but her voice cracked and again she fell to the daybed heavily, shaking her head.

"I am sorry," she stammered, blushing darkly. "I have told you that I love you," she said, "and you did not reply. It is shame that causes my voice to weaken." Her eyes were shining with tears.

These were the words I wanted to hear! But could I erase her shame and sadness? Yes, I should tell her that I returned her love. And I should embrace her; I should sing from the Song of Songs:

Your teeth are like a flock of ewes
that have come up from the washing.
All of them bear twins;
not one among them is bereaved.

And then she would be happy; and in this way I might hear the note again. She would love me the more for that.

The devil spoke to me thus: The note is no harm. It is beautiful, and how can beauty be harmful, when it brings such pleasure? And worldly love is not a sin, but only pleasure, of which you have been deprived.

But the Lord said, If you love the girl, would you profane her? You cannot marry her, though your own marriage be celibate. And to come each week, drawing on her hope, would be to crush and ruin her.

I blinked and regarded Olivia as if from a great distance, summoning the hate of Amnon for Tamar. "You have regressed," I said. "Or, I may have misjudged your ability. You may be capable of again reaching such a note, but it is no longer within my province."

As in the beginning, before I had ever heard her sing, she lowered her head and covered her face in her hands, but this time her shoulders shook, and I saw that she hid her tears.

"I will find a suitable teacher to help you," I said.

I could hear her sobbing as I walked down the stairs, and as I walked out through the courtyard, that mournful sound carried from the open window. I tried to remember it, for I knew it would be the last I would hear that voice.

In my mind our lessons continue and I retrace every word and note and color of the voice, every dear ornament that rose naturally from her throat. I go back to the note, to recall its pitch and its perfection. Or sometimes in dreams the note comes to me, when through the open window a bird will trill and it lasts for what seems like an hour and then she rushes to me, and I wake to find that I can no longer stand or raise my hand to feed myself, and I remember.

I found that day a young minnesinger as dark as my dear student, and handsome, with good teeth and a good position. I sent him to her as a teacher, knowing full well what would happen. The note would sound, and the same feeling would well up in her heart; she would throw her little arms around this young man, and he would be free to respond. I do not know that this happened, of course. But it is written that jealousy is cruel as the grave, and that its flashes are flashes of fire. Over the bridge and crossing home I cried out in rage and frustration; at home my wife lay in her white garments, still weak though she had begun taking food. I told her I would lie with her.

"You shall not, John," she responded, still softly. And still full of that cloying gentleness, she petted my head, cooing at me and speaking as if I were a small child. "You know what you have vowed."

Heretofore I had accepted my marriage on her terms, and on her father's. I was deformed, and fortunate for such a dowry. Yet in that moment my wife seemed a humbug in her wailing and prediction and prophecy, and I forgot the sympathy I had for her.

"You have tricked me," I said. "Saint Paul wrote that the husband must render his wife what is due her, and the wife her husband."

"No," she said.

And she said no again and again as I took by anger and by force what I had sworn never to take again.

This was a great sin. I cannot hope to atone for it.

When it was done I pulled my clothes on and left her there crying. I was going out, I think; and if I knew where I planned to go, I never have remembered it. Would I have left for good? Would I have gone to Olivia, to proclaim my love honestly? I would like to think so. However, it was not to be. As I began to descend, I felt something at my back.

At first I thought the stair had given way—the stairs, too, were rotting in that house. But later I knew it did not give way. They told me I had simply lost my footing. The neighbors found me hours later, my head twisted under me and with such deep wounds they had to be plugged in five places.

A green sapling has sprung up by the window where I have been seated, and a finch has decided to make her nest here. I can't tell why she has chosen such a place, for the branch is thin and waves terribly in the wind, but whenever I come to the window to peer out at her, the nest remains, and that bright dot of gold I discern through the tree reassures me. I wait for my wife, who comes from her visit with the anchoress to lift the spoon to my lips. For her continued attentions, I am grateful.

She tells me of Sigar, the monk of Saint Albans. He dwelt at Northaw, in the wood, where the nightingales abounded, and their song was very sweet, and his enjoyment of it immense. And so he had them killed. For he should not joy in the warbling of the birds better than the worship of God.

Yet something has happened to me, so strange and wonderful that I must tell it here in the interest of the frankness I have promised. As my world narrows, I find ethereal music in the most ordinary of sounds. My wife does not suspect the delight I take in this.

If I tell you the world is beautiful, then close your eyes; it becomes more beautiful still. The tanner's wagon has a song, and cries of children are as sweet as the brook's, and the geese are strong and shocking; and in the market square the cry of the bull is full with breath and moisture and even, it seems to me, the strength of his bones.

I lie in bed, or I sit here. And it seems at times that heaven itself has seen me at the window, and comes to me before my time, as if it suspects I shall not reach it. The sun warming me, the little wind caressing my check, the green leaf of a katydid on the sill; these perfect notes sound everywhere, over and over again. For this, the Lord be praised. For all things praised.

Nominated by Image, John Bradley, David Libman

BLUE

fiction by RUSSELL BANKS

from THE YALE REVIEW

Ventana steps off the number thirty-three bus at 103rd and Northwest 7th Avenue in Miami Shores. It's almost 6:00 p.m., and at this time of year the city stays hot and sticky thick till the sun finally sets at 8:00. Everything's a trade-off: in summer you get the light late, but it stays hot till late, too. She walks quickly back along 7th, nervous about carrying so much cash, thirty-five one-hundred-dollar bills. She didn't want to pay for the car with a check and then have to wait till the check clears before she can drive it home—no way a used car dealer or any merchant who doesn't know her personally will accept a check from her or any black woman and let her take the goods home before the check clears. She wants the car now, today, so she can drive to work in Aventura tomorrow and for the first time park in the employees lot and on Sunday after church drive her own damn car, drive her own damn car, to the beach at Virginia Key with Gloria and the grandkids.

The credit union closes at four so she took the money—one hundred dollars a month secretly saved over nearly three years—out of her account during her lunch break and in the American Eagle ladies' room stashed the packet of thirty-five bills in her brassiere. She's wearing a high-necked rayon blouse, even though she knew the day would be hot as Hades and humid and the air-conditioning in the buses would likely be busted or weak. The number thirty-three at seven o'clock in the morning leaving from her block in Miami Shores to the number three in North Miami all the way out to Aventura Mall and then back again over the same route in late afternoon, early in the day or late, air conditioner working or not, it doesn't matter, she'd be in a serious sweat

279

just from walking from the bus stop across the long lot to the entrance of the mall and back. And the day is hot from early to late, and she does sweat more than if she wore a sleeveless blouse or tee shirt, but she got through the afternoon with no one at American Eagle Outfitters knowing about the money she's carrying and is relieved now to be walking up 7th and finally arriving at the gate of Sunshine Cars USA with the money still intact in her bra.

She's forty-seven years old and for twenty-five of those years has been a legally licensed driver in the state of Florida, but this will be the first car Ventana has ever owned herself. Her ex-husband Gordon when she was still married to him leased a new Buick every three years and let her drive with him riding in the back seat as if she was his chauffeur; her son Gordon Junior when he went into the navy bought a new Camaro with his enlistment bonus and parked it on her driveway and let her drive it while he was at sea until he couldn't afford to insure it anymore and had to sell it; and for a few years her daughter Gloria owned an old clunker of a van she let Ventana borrow from time to time to help friends move in or out, but then the finance company repossessed it. In all those years Ventana did not have a car of her own. Until today.

Well, she really doesn't own it; she hasn't even picked her car out yet. Most of the vehicles for sale by Sunshine Cars USA are out of her price range, but she knows from reading the listings in *The Miami Herald* that Sunshine Cars USA nonetheless has dozens of what they call pre-owned cars for $3,500 and under: cars with one previous owner, cars with low mileage, cars less than ten years old, cars still shiny and stylish; Tauruses, Avengers, DeVilles, Grand Vitaras, Malibus, Fusions, Cobalts, and Monte Carlos. Nearly every day for three years she has stopped on her way to catch the bus in the morning and making her way home at the end of the day and has peered through the eight-foot-high, spiked-iron fence surrounding the lot and checked out the rows of sparkling vehicles for sale. She almost never passes the lot without saying to herself, That Chevrolet wagon look about right for a woman like me, or, The black Crown Vic is more Gordon's kind of ride, but I could live with it, or, Those SUV-type vehicles are ugly, but they safe in an accident. In her mind over the last three years she has selected for herself hundreds of pre-owned cars and bought each of them on layaway, and until the car was actually sold off the lot to someone else, in her mind it remained hers. It's a trick she has played on herself. It's how she managed to accumulate the thirty-five-hundred dollars–pretending each month that she is not saving money, which is hard to do when you're always short of cash at the end of the month anyhow; no, she isn't saving up to buy a car, she's making a one-hundred-dollar lay-away monthly payment towards her car, that's what, and if she doesn't make her payment on time, she pretends the dealer will sell her car to a customer who has the cash, and all the money she paid on it up to now will be wasted and gone. So she makes her payment. Today, finally, Ventana is going to be the customer who has the cash.

The Sunshine Cars USA showroom is a peach-colored concrete bunker, windowless on three sides with a large plate glass window facing the street. The exterior walls of the building and the window are decorated with signs that shout, We Work With Any Credit Type! and promise, $1000 Down—You Ride! and brag, No Games, Just Great Deals! The spiked fence runs behind the showroom from one corner of the building to the other like a corral for a hundred or more pre-owned cars, closing off half the block between 97th and 98th Streets. Every ten feet droops an American flag the size of a bedsheet waiting for an early evening offshore breeze.

Ventana stops in front of the big plate glass window and looks into the dimly lit showroom beyond. A very fat black man in a short-sleeved white guayabera shirt sits behind a desk reading a newspaper. A red-faced white man with a shaved head in a black tee shirt and skinny jeans talks into his cellphone. Multi-colored tattoos swarm up and down his pink arms. Ventana has seen both men many times hanging around the showroom and sometimes strolling through the lot with potential buyers, and though she has never actually spoken with either man, she feels she knows them personally.

She likes the black man. She believes he's more honest than the white man, who is probably the boss, and decides that she will buy her car from the black salesman, give him the commission, when suddenly a woman is standing beside her on the sidewalk. She's a fawn-colored Hispanic girl half Ventana's size and age. Her lips are puffed up from the injections that skinny white and Latina ladies think makes them look sexy, but instead they just look like they got popped in the mouth by their bad boyfriend.

The girl smiles broadly as if she's known Ventana since their school days together, although Ventana has never seen her before. She says, "Hi, there, missus. You want to drive away with a nice new car today? Or you still just window-shopping? I see you walk by almost every day, you know. Time you took a car out on a test drive, don't you think?"

281

"You see me going past?"

"Sure. Ever since I started here I been seeing you. Time to stop lookin', girl, time to start drivin' your new car."

"Not a new car. Used car. Pre-owned car."

"Okay! That's what we got at Sunshine Cars USA, guaranteed pre-owned cars! Certified and warrantee'd. Not new, okay, but like new! What you got in mind, missus? My name's Tatiana, by the way." The girl sticks out her hand.

Ventana shakes the hand gently—it's small and cold. "I'm Ventana. Ventana Robertson. I only live two blocks off Seventh on Ninety-fifth, that's why you been seeing me before. On account of the bus stop at a Hundred and Third." She doesn't want the girl to think she's already decided to buy herself a car today and is carrying the cash to do it. She doesn't want to look like an easy sale. And she is hoping the fat black man will come out.

"Okay, Ventana! That's great. Do you own your place on Ninety-fifth, or rent?"

"Own."

"Okay. That's perfect. Married? Live alone?"

"Divorced. Alone."

"Okay, that's wonderful, Ventana. And I know you have a steady job that you go to every morning and come home from every night, because I see you coming and going, and that's very good, the steady job. So what's your price range, Ventana? What can I fit you into today?"

"I'm thinking something like under thirty-five hundred dollars. But I'll look around on my own for a while, thanks. The price tags, they on the cars?"

"Yes, they sure are! You just go ahead and kick the tires, Ventana. Check over on the far side of the lot, way in the back two rows. We've got a bunch of terrific vehicles right there that're in your price range. Will you be bringing us a trade?"

"Trade."

"A car to trade up for the new one."

"No."

"Okay, that's good too. We close at six, Ventana, but I'll be inside if you have any questions or decide you want to take a test drive in one of our excellent vehicles. It's still too hot out here for me. Don't forget, we can work with any kind of credit type. There's all kinds of arrangements for credit readily available through our own financing company. You have a Florida driver's license, right?"

Ventana nods and walks calmly through the open gate into the lot as if she's already bought and paid for her car, although her legs feel wobbly and she's pretty sure she is trembling, but doesn't want to look at her hands to find out. She knows she's scared, but can't name what she is scared of.

Tatiana watches her for a few seconds, wondering if she should follow her, the hell with the heat; then decides the woman isn't really serious yet. She strolls back inside the showroom and reports that the woman is a long-term tire-kicker, probably a month or more from signing away her firstborn, which makes the black man chuckle and the white man snort.

The black man checks his watch. "Yeah, well, she only got thirty minutes till we outa here."

Tatiana says, "She'll be back tomorrow. Early, I bet. The girl's decided where she's going to buy, now she just got to figure out what to buy."

"How much she got to spend?" the black man asks.

"She's sayin' three-five. I'll start her at five and work up from there."

"Too low. The '02 DeVille, start her with that. The bronze one. It's listed at nine. Tell her she can drive it home for six. Fifty-nine ninety-nine. Sisters like her, they too old for the Grand Ams but still hot enough to want a Caddy. She got the three-five?"

"Prob'ly."

"Gonna need financing. Forget the fucking Caddy. Go higher."

"For sure."

"Get her into the blue Beemer," the white man says.

Ventana makes her way towards the cars in the far corner of the lot, as instructed. She walks quickly past and deliberately avoids looking at the nearly new cars that she knows she can't afford. She doesn't want her car, when she finds it, to appear shabby and old by comparison, not pre-owned but used. Used up.

But when she gets to the far corner of the lot and walks past the cars that are supposed to be in her price range, most of them do look used up. Rusted, scraped, dinged and dented, they seem ready for the junk heap, just this side of the old cars sitting on cinderblocks or sinking into the weeds in the backyards of half the houses in her neighborhood, unsolvable mechanical problems waiting to be solved by the miraculous arrival of a pocketful of cash money from a lottery ticket payout, which will never come, and the vehicle will be finally sold for junk.

There is a black 2002 Honda Civic fastback that at first looks good to her, no dents or dings, no rust. The doors are locked, but when she squints against the glare and peers through the driver's side window she can make out the numbers on the odometer—278,519. End of the line, for sure. The sign in the window says Retail Price $4950, Special Offer $2950.

There is a blue 1999 Mercury Grand Marquis with half the teeth in its grill missing, bald tires, torn upholstery, trunk lid dented at the latch so she'll have to tie it closed with wire to keep it from yawning open when she drives it to work. A sign taped to the driver's side window says Retail Price $5950, Special Offer $2950.

Maybe she should go up a notch in price, she thinks. After all, even though they call it a "special offer," it's actually just an asking price, a number where negotiations can begin. That's when she spots a light blue 2002 Dodge Neon with a big yellow sign on the windshield that cheerfully yells, Low Mileage!!! The retail price is $6,950, and the asking price is $3,950. If she offers $3,000, they might settle on $3,500.

Okay, that's a car to test drive. But instead of driving just one car, she'll try to find two more, so she can intelligently compare three. In very little time she has added a 2002 Hyundai with 87,947 miles, clean body, no dents or rust, good tires, and has found a metallic gray 2002 Ford Taurus that she really prefers over both the Hyundai and the Neon. It's a large four-door sedan with a tan cloth interior, and this car too has a Low Mileage!!! sign, including the actual number of miles, 55,549. It's stodgy and boring, the kind of four-door sedan a high school math teacher or a social worker might own, nowhere near as sleek and borderline glamorous as the Neon and the Hyundai. It'll burn more gas than they, for sure. But the respectability and conventionality of the Taurus suit her. And unlike the Neon and the Hyundai, maybe because of its size, it does not feel used to Ventana; it feels pre-owned. Well cared for. By someone like her.

She takes another slow walk around the vehicle looking for scratches or dents she might have missed on her first pass, but there aren't any to be seen. When she steps away from the Taurus, intending to take another last look at the Neon and the Hyundai before heading for the showroom and Tatiana or maybe the fat black man, she hears coming from behind her the low rattling growl of a large animal and turning sees a gray dog coming toward her at full speed. It's a thick-bodied pit bull mix running low to the ground five or more car lengths away and closing fast, eyes yellow with rage, teeth bared, growling, not barking, a dog not interested in merely scaring her and driving her away. It's a guard dog, not a watchdog, and it wants to attack her, attack and kill her.

Ventana doesn't like dogs to start with, but this one terrifies her. She scrambles around to the front of the Taurus and climbs up on the hood and on her hands and knees gets up onto the roof of the car. The dog skids to a stop beside the car and circles the vehicle as if looking for a ramp or stairs. Finding none, it tries climbing onto the hood of the Taurus as she has done and falls off, which only increases its rage and determination to get at the woman on the roof of the car, a terrified and confused woman trying desperately not to panic and slip and fall off the car to the ground. "Help!" she cries out. "Somebody help me! Somebody, come get this dog away from me!"

She remembers that you aren't supposed to show fear to a dog, that it will only embolden the animal, so she carefully, unsteadily, stands up and folds her arms over her chest and tries to look unafraid of the beast as it circles the car, searching for a way up. She wishes she had a gun in her purse. A person is legally entitled to carry a concealed firearm in Florida, but she has always said no way she'll own and carry a gun, a mugger will only turn it against her or use it afterwards in the commission of some other crime in which a person gets killed. But now, forget all that liberal crap. Now she truly wishes she had a gun to shoot this dog dead.

She is a long ways from the gate where she came in, but the cars are parked side by side tightly enough all the way out to the gate that, jumping from rooftop to rooftop, she might be able to get over to where the Hispanic girl or the black man can hear her cries and call off their vicious dog. She's wearing sneakers, thank the Lord, and has good balance for a woman her age, and it hasn't rained all day and none of the cars appears to have been recently washed, so the metal roofs are not slippery. She slings the strap of her purse over her shoulder and across her chest, tries to calm her pounding heart, counts to ten and jumps from the roof of the Taurus to the roof of the Mercury Grand Marquis next to it.

She makes it across. The dog sees her land safely on the Mercury and snaps at the air in that direction, forgets about climbing onto the Taurus and races to the front of the Grand Marquis, where he leaps scratching and clawing onto the hood. But once again in his frenzy he fails to gain traction and falls off. She decides to keep moving as fast as she can, before she thinks too much about what will happen if she slips and falls or if somehow the dog manages to get onto the hood of one of the cars

285

and then to the roof so that he too can leap from roof to roof in pursuit of her, surely catching her and ripping into her flesh, pulling her to the ground where, just as surely, he will kill her.

She leaps from the Mercury to a white, high-topped 1999 Jeep Cherokee, from there to a 1997 Ford Expedition, the tallest and widest vehicle in the lot, the safest rooftop, impossible for the dog to get at her up there. But she decides to keep moving, to get to the fence and the gate and somehow attract the attention of one of the people who works for Sunshine Cars USA or somebody walking past on the street who will go inside the showroom and get one of the car people to come out and call off this animal.

She leaves the temporary safety of the big Ford Expedition and jumps to the slightly lower roof of a dark blue, sporty 2002 Mazda 626 LX, then onto a red 2005 Kia Sportage. Growling and drooling, the dog follows at ground level, not taking his eyes off her for a second. There is no way she can escape him, except by staying up on top of the cars, moving gradually closer to the high fence via the roofs of the fancier, pricier cars, genuinely pre-owned, not used, Mercedes Benzes, Cadillacs, Lincolns, and cars from more recent years, 2010, 2011, 2012, with lower mileage advertised in the window signs, 22,000 miles, 19,000, 18,000. As the mileage numbers drop, the price tags rise: Retail Price $15999, Special Offer $12999; Retail Price $18950, Special Offer $15950.

Eventually she arrives at the last row before the fence, and from the roof of a metallic silver 2012 Ford Escape spots the gate three car lengths in front of her, chained shut and padlocked. She looks at her watch, sees that it's 6:20 and remembers that the Hispanic girl said they close at 6:00. She is trapped in here, caged, imprisoned by a vicious, ugly dog that has nothing in its brain but a burning need to kill her solely because she accidentally entered his territory.

It occurs to her that she can call Sunshine Cars USA with her cellphone. She can explain her situation to whoever answers and get him to come back to the salesroom and unlock the chain, swing open the gate, put the dog on a leash and lead him away to wherever his cage is located so she can escape hers. From her perch atop the Ford SUV she can make out the web site, www.sunshinecarsusa.com, and phone number for Sunshine Cars USA painted on the big glittering sign atop the cinderblock salesroom.

She punches in the number and after a half-dozen rings hears the lightly accented voice of the Hispanic girl. Thank you for calling Sunshine Cars USA. Our hours are nine a.m. till six p.m. Please call back during business hours. Or at the sound of the beep you can leave a message with your number, and we'll call you back as soon as we can. Have a nice day!

Ventana hears the beep and says to the phone, "You locked me in with the cars by accident, and now your dog has me trapped, and I can't get out on account of the gate is locked. Please, I need someone to come unlock the gate and get this dog away from me. Please come right away! I'm very scared of this dog. Good-bye," she says and clicks off.

In less than two hours it will be dark. Maybe by then the dog will have gotten bored and wandered off or fallen asleep somewhere, and Ventana can climb over the fence and set herself free. She checks out the fence. It's nearly three feet taller than she. The spiked bars are too close together for her to squeeze through. She'll have to climb over the fence, which she is not sure she can do even if she has time to spare. She will first have to get from the rooftop of the Ford Escape down to the ground, run across the six or eight foot wide lane between the Escape and the fence and somehow in a matter of seconds pull herself up and over the fence. It looks impossible. There is no way she can do it without the dog hearing her and racing back from his doghouse or wherever the vicious beast hangs out when he isn't terrorizing humans.

She decides to call 911, but then stops herself. A rescue vehicle from the fire department will have a police escort attached. Things always get complicated when you involve the police. They'll want to know what she's doing inside a locked car lot anyhow. Maybe she hid there after closing time, intending to pop car doors and trunks and steal parts, hubcaps, radios and CD players, planning to throw them over the fence to an accomplice on the street. Didn't expect a guard dog to mess up her plans, did she? Maybe she hid in the lot after closing, intending to break through the back door into the showroom and steal the computers and office machines and any cash they stashed there. Before the police call off the dog and release her from her cage, she'll have to prove her innocence. Which for a black person is never easy in this city. Never easy anywhere. She decides not to call 911.

That leaves her daughter Gloria and a small number of other people she knows and trusts—her pastor, a few of her neighbors, even her exhusband, Gordon, whom she sort of trusts. Her son, Gordon Junior, who is more competent than anyone else she is close to, is stationed in Norfolk, Virginia. Not much he can do from there to help her. Gordon Senior will probably laugh at her for having put herself in this situation, and Gloria will simply panic and, looking for an excuse, start drinking again. She is too embarrassed to call on Reverend Knight or any of her women friends from the church or from the neighborhood, and she will never call on anyone from the store. Although, if she can't get free till nine tomorrow when Sunshine Cars USA opens again, she'll be hours late for work and will have to call American Eagle Outfitters anyhow and explain why she's late.

She thinks of hiding overnight inside one of the cars, sleeping on the back seat, but surely all the cars are locked, and in any case she is not going to climb down there and start checking doors to find out if one has been accidentally left unlocked. The dog will have her by the throat in thirty seconds. Her best option is to stay where she is until morning. It won't be painful or cause her serious suffering to curl up and lie here overnight on the roof of the Ford Escape and try to doze a little, as long as she doesn't fall asleep and accidentally roll over and tumble off the car onto the ground.

It's almost dark now and the heat of the day has mostly dissipated. She hopes it won't rain. Usually at this time of day clouds come in off the ocean bringing a shower that sometimes turns into a heavy rain that lasts for hours until the clouds get thoroughly wrung out. If that happens she will hate it, but she can endure it.

It's quieter than usual out there in the world beyond the fence. Traffic is light, and no one is on the street—she can see 7th Avenue all the way north to the bus stop at 103rd and in the opposite direction down to 95th Street, where her pink shotgun bungalow is located three doors off 7th, the windows dark, no one home. The narrow wooden garage she emptied out a week ago and where she planned to shelter her car tonight is shut and still emptied out, unused, waiting. Along 7th the streetlights suddenly flare to life. The number thirty-three bus, nearly empty, rumbles past. A police cruiser speeds by in the opposite direction, lights flashing like Fourth of July.

Using her purse as a pillow, she lies down on her side, facing 97th Street. She can't hear the dog's growls anymore or his heavy, wet, open-mouthed breathing and figures either he is lying in the dark nearby trying to trick her into coming down from the roof or he is just making his rounds and will soon come back to make sure that in his brief absence she hasn't tried to climb over the fence. She suddenly realizes that she is exhausted and despite her fear can barely keep her eyes open.

Then her eyes close.

She may have slept for a few minutes or it might have been a few hours, but when she opens her eyes again it's dark. On the sidewalk just beyond the fence someone in a gray hoodie is jouncing in place, hands deep in his pockets, looking straight at her. He's half-hidden in the shadow of the building, beyond the range of the streetlight on 7th, a slender young black man or maybe a man-sized teenaged boy, she can't tell.

"Yo, lady, what you doin' up there?"

She says nothing at first. What is she doing up there? Then says, "There's a bad dog won't let me get down. And the gate is locked tight."

She sits up and sees now that he is a teenaged boy, but not a boy she knows from the neighborhood. Mostly older folks live in the area, retired people who own their small homes and single parents of grown-up children and grandchildren like this one living in Overtown and Liberty City or out in Miami Gardens and the suburbs. He is younger than his size indicates, no more than thirteen or fourteen, probably visiting his mother or grandmother. He approaches the fence, when suddenly the dog emerges from darkness and rushes the fence, snarling and snapping through the bars, sending the boy back into the street.

"Whoa! That a bad dog all right!"

Ventana says, "Do me a favor. Go see if there's a watchman or guard in the showroom. They not answering the phone when I try calling, but maybe somebody's on duty there."

The boy walks around to the front of the building and peers through the window into the showroom. Seconds later he returns. "Anybody there, he be sittin' in the dark."

The dog, panting with excitement, has staked out a position between the fence and the Ford Escape—his small yellow eyes, his forehead flat and hard as a shovel and his wide, lipless, tooth-filled mouth controlling both the boy on one side of the fence and Ventana on the other.

"If you got a phone, lady, whyn't you call 911?"

"Be hard to explain to the police how I got in here," she says.

"Yeah, prob'ly would," he says. "How did you get in there?"

"Don't matter. Looking for a car to buy. What matters is how am I gonna get out of here?"

They are both silent for a moment. Finally he says, "Maybe somebody with a crane could do it. You know, lower a hook so you could grab onto it and get lifted out?"

She pictures that and says, "No way. I'd end up on the evening news for sure."

"I'm gonna call 911 for you, lady. Don't worry, they'll get you outa there."

"No, don't!" she cries, but it's too late, he already has his cell phone out and is making the call.

A dispatcher answers, and the boy says he's calling to report that there is a lady trapped by a vicious dog inside a car lot on Northwest 7th and 97th Street, and she needs rescuing.

The dispatcher asks for the name of the car lot, and the boy tells her. She asks his name, and he says Reynaldo Rodriquez. Ventana connects his last name to the tag worn by a hugely fat woman she knows slightly who lives on 96th and works the early shift at Esther's Diner on 103rd. You can't tell her age because of the fatness, but she's likely the boy's aunt or older sister, and he's been visiting her. Obviously a nice boy. Like her Gordon Junior at the same age.

She hears Reynaldo tell the dispatcher that he personally doesn't know the lady in the Sunshine Cars USA lot or how she got in there. He says he doesn't think there is a burglar alarm, he doesn't hear one anyhow, all he can see or hear is a lady trapped inside a locked fence by a guard dog. He says she is sitting on the roof of one of the cars to escape the dog. He listens and after a pause asks why should he call the police? The lady isn't doing anything illegal. He listens for a few seconds more, says okay and clicks off.

"Told me the situation not 911's job to decide on. Told me they just a call center, not the police. She said I was calling about a break-in. Told me to call the cops directly," he says to Ventana. "Even gave me the precinct phone number."

"Don't."

"Okay, I won't. Too bad you not a cat in a tree. Fire department be over here in a minute, no questions asked." He leans down and looks the dog in its small eyes, and the dog stares back and growls from somewhere deep in his chest.

She says, "Whyn't you go way over to the other side of the lot on 98th? Make a bunch of noise by the fence, like you trying to get in. When the dog runs over to stop you, I'll try to climb over the fence. Let's try that."

"Okay. But I could get busted, y' know, if it look like I'm trying to rob from these cars or break into the building. Which it would. They prob'ly have surveillance cameras. They everywhere, you know."

She agrees. She tells him to forget it, she'll just have to spend the night up here on top of this SUV, hope it doesn't rain and wait till they open the door of the dealership in the morning.

Reynaldo has his phone out again, has looked up a number and is tapping it in.

"Who you calling now?"

"If you see something, say something, yo. That's what they always telling us, right?"

"Who?"

"The television people. Channel Five News," he says. "I be seeing something, so now I be saying something." And before she has a chance to tell him to stop, he is talking to a producer, telling her there is a lady held prisoner by a vicious mean pit bull inside a locked used car lot on Northwest 7th and 97th Street. "That's right," he says, "Sunshine Cars USA. And 911, I called them for her myself, and they refused to help her. Re-fused! You should send a camera crew out here right now and put it on the eleven o'clock news, so this lady can get help. Maybe the people who own the used car dealership will see it on TV and will come unlock the fence and call off their vicious dog."

The producer asks him who he is, and he gives her his name and says he's a passerby. The woman tells him to wait there for the crew to arrive, because they'd like to tape him too. She says they'll be there in a matter of minutes.

He says he'll wait for them and clicks off. Grinning, he says to Ventana, "We gonna be famous, yo."

"I don't want to be famous. I just want to get free of this dog and his fence and his cars and go home."

"Sometimes being famous the only way to get free," the boy says. "What about Muhammed Ali? Famous. Or O.J.? Remember him? Famous. What about Jay-Z? Famous and free. I could name lots of people."

"Reynaldo, stop," Ventana says. "You're only a child."

"That's okay," he says, and laughs. "I still know stuff."

For the next fifteen minutes Ventana and Reynaldo chat as if they are sitting across a table at Esther's Diner, and indeed it turns out that the very large waitress at Esther's whose name-tag says Esmeralda Rodriquez is his mother. Reynaldo says he visits his moms once a week but lives with his father and his father's new wife over in Miami Gardens, because supposedly the schools are better there, though he is not all that cool about his father's new wife. Ventana asks why not, and he shrugs and says she is real young and disses his mother to him, which is definitely not cool. Ventana asks why he doesn't talk to his father about it, ask him to make her stop talking bad about his mother. He says they don't have that kind of relationship.

She says, "Oh." Then they go silent for a few moments. She likes the boy, but is not happy that he called the television station. Too late now. And maybe the boy is right, that somehow getting on television will set her free.

A white van with the CBS eye and a large blue 5 painted on the side turns off 7th Avenue onto 97th Street and parks close to where Reynaldo stands on the sidewalk. The driver, a cameraman, and a sound man get out of the van and start removing lights, sound boom, cables, battery, camera, and tripod from the back. Behind the van comes a pale green Ford Taurus, a lot like the one Ventana planned to test drive, driven by a black woman with straightened hair. The tall young woman in leather mini-skirt and lavender silk blouse looks like an actress or a model. Her face shines. She gets out of the car and speaks with the cameraman and his crew for a moment, then walks over to Reynaldo. She asks if he is the person who called See Something Say Something at Channel 5.

He says yes and points up at Ventana atop the silver Ford Escape. "She the one trapped inside the car lot, though. That dog there, he the one won't let her get down off the car and climb over the fence."

While the reporter touches up her makeup she asks him if it is true that he called 911 and they refused to help, and he says yes. They just told him to call the police in case it was a break-in.

The reporter says, "Was it a break-in?"

He laughs. "A little early in the night for robbing. Whyn't you ask her? Get it on camera," Reynaldo suggests. "You can get me on camera too, y' know. I recognize you from the TV," he says. "Forgot your name, though."

"Autumn Fowler," she says. When the cameraman has his camera set up with the high spiked fence, silver Ford Escape, and Ventana located in the central background, the reporter steps directly into the central foreground. The sound man swings his boom over her head just out of camera range. The driver, their lighting man, has arranged his lights so he can illuminate Autumn Fowler, Ventana, and Reynaldo each in turn simply by swinging the reflector disk. By now the dog has moved into the bright circle of light and is bouncing up and down, growling and scowling like a boxer stepping into the ring, demonstrating to the crowd that he will explode with fury against anyone foolish enough to enter the ring with him.

Several people have been hesitantly approaching along the sidewalk and edging up to the van. Others are emerging from nearby houses, and soon a crowd has gathered, drawn like moths to the lights, the camera, the tall, glamorous woman clipping a mike onto her blouse. One by one they realize why the camera, lights and mike, and the famous TV reporter have come to their neighborhood—it is the frightened middle-aged woman atop a silver SUV, one of their neighbors, a friend to some of them, and she's trapped inside a chained and locked used car lot by a pit bull guard dog. Several of them say her name to one another and wonder how on earth Ventana Robertson got herself into this situation. A couple of them speculate that because Ventana's so smart and resourceful it might be she's doing it for a reality TV program.

Autumn Fowler says to the cameraman, "Let me do the intro, then when I point to it pan down to the dog and up to the woman when I point to her. After I ask her a couple questions, come back to me, and then I'll talk to the kid for a minute."

"Gotcha."

"How long will I be on TV?" Reynaldo asks.

Autumn Fowler smiles at him. "Long enough for all your friends to recognize you."

"Awesome."

The reporter calls up to Ventana and asks her name.

Ventana says, "I don't want you to say my name on TV. I just want to get the people who own the dog to come put him on a leash so I can get down from here and go home."

"I understand. I may have to ask you to sign a release. Can you do that? You, too," she says to Reynaldo.

"If you can get me out of here, I'll sign anything," Ventana says.

"Me, too. But you can say my name on TV. It's Reynaldo Rodriquez," he says and spells Reynaldo for her.

"Thank you, Reynaldo."

"No problem, Autumn."

Autumn speaks to the camera for a few seconds, telling the viewers at home who she is and where she's reporting from. She briefly describes Ventana's plight, turns to Ventana and calls out to her, "Can you tell us how you got locked behind the fence, ma'am?"

"I was looking to buy a car. I guess they forgot I was here, the people who own the cars, and they locked the gate and went home. I tried calling . . ."

"And this dog," Autumn says, interrupting her, "this vicious dog has kept you from climbing over the fence and getting out? Is that correct?" she says and signals for the cameraman to start filming the dog, who on cue promptly lunges snarling against the fence.

"Yes, that's correct."

"You have a cellphone, I understand. Did you call 911?"

From behind her Reynaldo says, "I was the one called 911. She didn't want me to."

Autumn shakes her head with irritation. "I'll get to you in a minute," she says. Then, to Ventana, "Can you tell our viewers what happened when you called 911?"

"They said it must be a break-in so it wasn't their problem. It was something for the police," Ventana says, adding that she left a message on the used car dealer's answering machine, but that didn't do any good either. "They must not be checking their messages. I hope they watch the TV news tonight, so they can come leash up this dog and unlock the gate."

"Otherwise?"

"Otherwise I'll be staying up here till tomorrow morning when they come in to work."

Autumn turns to the camera. "There you have it. A woman alone, forced to sleep outside in the cold damp night like a homeless person, terrorized by a vicious guard dog, locked inside a cage like an animal. And when she calls 911 for help, she's turned away." She signals for the cameraman and lighting and sound man to focus on Reynaldo. "You were the one who called 911 for her, is that correct?" she asks him.

"Yes, m'am. That is correct. My name is Reynaldo Rodriquez. From Miami Gardens."

Autumn turns away from him and faces the camera again. "Thank you, Reynaldo. A good samaritan, a young man who heard something and then said something. Remember, folks, if you hear something, say something. Call us at 305-591-5555 or e-mail us at hearandsay@cbsmiami.com. This is Autumn Fowler in Miami Gardens."

She plucks the mike off her blouse and tells the cameraman she's done.

Reynaldo says, "Don't you want to ask me or the lady there some more questions? Maybe you could call 911 yourself, do it with the camera running. That'd be awesome TV!"

"Sorry, kid. This is sort of a cat stuck in a tree story. Not as big and exciting as you think." She chucks him under the chin and hands him the release to sign. He scrawls his name and gives the form back to her. She calls up to Ventana, "Don't worry about signing the release, hon, since we never used your name." She steps into her car and starts the engine. While the cameraman and his two assistants collect their equipment and cables and stash them in the van, she slowly parts the gathered crowd with her car and drives off. A minute later the crew and their van have departed from the scene too.

With the lights, camera, and the famous television reporter gone, the crowd of bystanders quickly loses interest. They're not worried about Ventana: now that she's been filmed for TV broadcast she's entered a different and higher level of reality and power than theirs. They drift back to their homes and apartments where they'll wait to watch the late news on Channel 5, hoping to catch a glimpse of themselves in the background, their neighborhood, the used car dealership they walk past every day of their lives, all of it made more radiant, color-soaked and multi-dimensional on high-definition TV than it could ever be in boring, flattened, black-and-white real life. The teenaged son of their neighbor, Esmeralda Rodriquez, will be remembered mainly for standing in the way of a clear view of the reporter. The woman trapped behind the fence by the guard dog, their neighbor, Ventana Robertson, her face and plight lost in the bright light of television and the presence right here in the neighborhood of the beautiful, charismatic reporter, will be all but forgotten. It's as if an angel has unexpectedly landed on Northwest 7th Avenue and 97th Street, and afterwards, when the angel flies back to her kingdom in the sky, no one tries to remember the occasion for her visit. They remember only that an angel was briefly here on earth, proving that a higher order of being truly does exist.

"You okay?" Reynaldo says.

"Of course not! I'm still up here, aren't I? That dog's still down there."

Reynaldo is silent for a moment. "Maybe when they show it on the eleven o'clock news . . ."

"You poor child! Not gonna happen. You heard her, this just a cat up a tree story to her and her TV people. You g'wan home to your daddy's house now. Takes a while to get across town to Miami Gardens by bus, and you prob'ly got a curfew."

He scrapes the toe of his left sneaker against the pavement. Then the right. "You gonna be all right?"

"Yes! Now git!" She's not angry at him, and in fact she's grateful for his kindness, but nonetheless is shouting angrily at him, "G'wan, now git!"

"Okay, okay, chill. I'm going." He takes a few steps towards 7th, then turns and says, "Hope it don't rain on you."

"I said git!" she yells, and Reynaldo runs.

Ventana is alone now. Except for the dog. He seems calmer since everyone's left. And he's no longer growling. He's curled up like a thick gray knot of muscle at the front of the Honda van parked beside her SUV and seems to be sleeping. Ventana wishes she knew his name. If she knew his name she could talk to him, maybe reassure him as to her good intentions. He must know already that she means no harm to him and his owner. For over four hours she's been his prisoner and has done nothing to threaten him. In the beginning when she ran from him and climbed up on the roof of the Taurus that she wanted to test drive and maybe buy and then hopped from roof to roof until ending here on top of the silver Ford Escape, he must have reasoned, assuming guard dogs in some way reason, that she was guilty of a crime or was about to commit one. She probably shouldn't have run like that, should have stood her ground instead, but he terrified her.

But that was a long while ago, and since then she's been his only companion here behind the fence, while on the other side of the fence, people have come and gone, they've stared at him and been scared of him, like Reynaldo, and have aimed lights and camera at him and mic'd him for a TV audience. The whole neighborhood has come by and looked at him and her, too, as if he and she were animals in a zoo. By now he must be used to Ventana's presence, as if they are cage-mates, not enemies.

Slowly she hitches her way to the edge of the roof and, more open-minded than before, carefully, calmly, almost objectively, examines the dog. She's still frightened, but the sight of him no longer panics her. He's large for a pit bull, maybe fifty or sixty pounds—she's seen many examples of the breed in the neighborhood walking with that characteristic bow-legged, chesty strut in the company of young men wearing baggy pants halfway down their underwear, tight muscle shirts and baseball caps on backwards, boys who are barely men and resemble their dogs the way people say dogs and their owners and husbands and wives over time come to resemble each other. She knows some of those young men personally, has known them since they were little boys. Inside they're not hard and dangerous, even the ones on drugs; they're soft and scared. Reynaldo has more spunk than they do. That's why they need to walk the streets with those hard, dangerous-looking dogs yanking on chain-link leashes.

She notices that the dog has been watching her with his yellow eyes half opened. He still hasn't moved, except for the rise and fall of his barrel-hooped chest—he's breathing through his nose, with his lipless mouth closed over his teeth like a giant python. A good sign, she thinks. She lets her legs dangle over the windshield of the vehicle, her feet almost touching the hood. The dog doesn't stir.

"What's your name, dog?" She almost laughs at the question. She can call him whatever she wants and that'll be his name, at least for tonight. She wonders if he belongs to the black salesman or the skinny white one. She doesn't know what a tattooed white man would name his guard dog, but if he's owned by the black man his name will be something country and southern, like Blue. She remembers a line from an old song, I had a dog and his name was Blue . . .

"Hey, Blue, you gonna let the nice lady come down?"

At the sound of her voice the dog lifts his massive head, looks up at Ventana for a few seconds, then lowers his head again, watching her with eyes wide open now, his small ears tipped forward, his forehead rippled as if with thought. Ventana remembers some more lines from the song and sings them to him. She has a thin, almost reedy singing voice:

You know Blue was a good ol' dog,
Treed a possum in a hollow log.
You know from that he was a good ol' dog . . .
Ol' Blue's feet was big and round,
Never 'lowed a possum to touch the ground . . .

No response from Blue, which she decides is a good sign, so she slides forward, and when her feet touch the hood of the car, she stands up. Feet apart, hands on her hips, shoulders squared, she believes she is the picture of self-confidence and good intentions. "Well, well, Blue," she says, smiling. "What do you make of this? I'm starting to think we gonna be friends, you and me."

Blue stands, squares his shoulders similarly and appears to smile back. He whips his tail like a piece of steel cable back and forth in a friendly seeming way and droops his ears in a manner that suggests submission to Ventana, as if he's decided that for the moment, until his owner shows up, she's the boss. Must be his owner is the black man, she thinks, since he's so relaxed around black people. Maybe the white man's not the boss, like she originally thought. She decided earlier that when she got out of here, whether it happened tonight or tomorrow morning, she would not come back and test drive and buy a vehicle from Sunshine Cars USA. But now she's thinking maybe she will.

She sits down on the hood and tells Blue face to face that she's going to walk over to the gate in the fence and try to climb over it. "Sorry to leave you, ol' Blue, but I got to get home," she explains. "I got to work tomorrow, and I need my sleep."

Keeping the silver Ford between them, still not taking her eyes off the dog, she slides her feet from the hood of the car to the ground and takes a short step away from the vehicle. Blue has watched her descent, and except to stand up and flip his tail back and forth has not reacted, has not even blinked. For the first time since she left the roof of the car, she takes her eyes off him—a ten-second trial. When she turns back he has not moved or changed his expression. He's watching her almost as if he's glad she's leaving, as if her departure will relieve him of duty and he'll be free to find a quiet spot in the lot to sleep away the rest of the night.

"Okay, I'm going now," she says. "Good-bye, Blue."

Ventana walks slowly along the fence towards the locked gate three car lengths away. She doesn't look back at Blue, and she doesn't walk tentatively; she walks like someone who is not afraid, faking it the same way she entered the lot hours earlier. She was afraid then, too, but only of buying a car, of being outsmarted by the salesman—or saleswoman, if she ended up buying it from the young Latina. She was afraid that the car would turn out to be a lemon, used up, rusting on cinderblocks in her back yard; that depositing one hundred dollars in the credit union at the end of every month for three long years would be wasted. Now she is afraid that she has dangerously mis-read a guard dog's intentions and desires. Though she walks with seeming confidence, she may be sacrificing herself to a set of obscure but nonetheless sacred principles of property and commerce. She is afraid of the blinding pain that will come if the guard dog attacks her. And for a second she lets herself imagine the awful relief that will come when only death can take away the pain. Her night has come to that.

She remembers another verse from that old song, but this time sings it silently to herself:

Old Blue died and I dug his grave,
I dug his grave with a silver spade.

The chained and padlocked gate is wide enough to drive a car through if it were open. Just below the top of the eight-foot spikes is a horizontal steel pipe that she believes she is tall enough to reach. She adjusts her purse so the strap crosses her chest and the bag hangs against her back. She reaches up and on tiptoes grabs the pipe. She pulls herself a few inches off the ground, then a few more, until she's high enough to work her right elbow through the spikes and over the pipe. Holding her weight with her upper right arm, she uses it as a fulcrum to swing her left foot up, above the pipe and through the spikes. With her left foot wedged between them, she is able to grab onto the spikes with both hands and pull herself high enough to see over the gate. She suddenly remembers the last lines of the verse:

I let him down with a golden chain,
And every link I called his name.

The empty streets and sidewalks out there, the darkened stores and warehouses and homes, the whole vast dark city itself, all seem to go on endlessly into the night. She is about to free herself from this cage. She is escaping into the city. Her right leg hangs in the air a few feet off the ground behind her. The dog doesn't growl or snarl. He doesn't even breathe loudly. He is silent and strikes like a snake. He clamps onto her leg with his powerful jaws and drags her backwards, off the gate.

Nominated by The Yale Review, Joyce Carol Oates

VISIT #1

by AFAA MICHAEL WEAVER

from PLOUGHSHARES

Your grandfather and I walk alike,
each of us counting the brittle spaces
in getting older. At the desk I explain
I want to see my son, and I see you
are now digits on a sheet. Black
men in black—the brothers—make sure
you obey the rules. It is like the times
I had to come to school to get you
for being bad. Being bad is the name
of this place and this place is the city
itself. Stars in the night are for escaping.
If you can touch one, you can crawl
out of this city, out of falling down.

In the doorway you come batting
back tears. It is the Detention Center,
not school, not the principal, but men
with violence as hope. My father
and I have come to see you, and we
so much want you to outlive us.
To bury you would pull us down
into the spiked pit of grief that kills.

So we laugh to make you laugh,
but you only cry because you know

we tried to teach you the good.
I pray for you. It is my only secret.
Black men in black count
the smiles we give you.

Nominated by Ploughshares, Martha Collins

HIPPIES AND BEATS

by EDWARD HOAGLAND

from NEW LETTERS

Being a little younger than the Beat generation writers (although my first book was published in the same year, 1956, as Allen Ginsberg's *Howl and Other Poems*) and yet older than the mainstream Hippie movement later on, I observed both with a certain skeptical affinity. I would leave their parties when the addled stoners started dropping acid but, like the Beats in a gray-flannel-suited America of the 1950s and the Hippies in Richard Nixon's realm, felt the country had been side-tracked. I preferred the earlier short-lived speed writer Thomas Wolfe, but did love Jack Kerouac's *On the Road* and had myself, by thumb or jalopy or railroad flatcar, seen three-fourths of the United States before being drafted into the armed forces for a couple of years. My favorite California writers were John Steinbeck, William Saroyan, and Wallace Stegner, not the Beats; but finding myself in San Francisco on a mission of mercy in 1958, I was interested, went to City Lights Bookstore, fount of *Howl* and its owner's *Coney Island of the Mind*, looked up Kenneth Rexroth, the learnedly aloof father figure who, unlike William Burroughs, another inspiration, hadn't shot and killed his wife, or even stabbed her, as Norman Mailer, still another, did to one of his, and went to parties I was invited to.

The Beats were patriarchal, for the most part. Women were crash pads where you showered, pigged out and got your ashes hauled, after driving night and day. Lawrence Ferlinghetti's *Coney Island* (also a haunt of mine back in New York) was published that year and Burroughs' *Naked Lunch* the next. Henry Miller, yet another influence, was puttering about the nearby Big Sur landscape at about this juncture, too, and it was a good time for Gary Snyder and Gregory Corso. I met Steinbeck and Stegner but not these Beat celebrities for another quarter-century (liked Snyder and Ginsberg), when their reputations had, as Vermonters say, "sugared off."

I love the strenuous hills and seafront seals, Jack London's storied Bay and John Muir's flower-meadows and Range of Light, but my mission was to assist an old girlfriend who had gotten pregnant by someone else to bear and keep her baby despite her Philadelphia parents' wish to have it aborted, which was why we'd driven west to live on Oak Street. But I went to Beat parties when invited, and later in New York knew people whose couches Kerouac slept on or Corso slept with as their lives unraveled. The definitive evening for me was in a warehouse that some trust-funder had rented to be part of the action. The roof lay under the scintillant lights of the Bay Bridge to Oakland with the city's sparkling diadem all around, and up there a bad acid trip eventually occurred, ending the festivities with sirens. A guy hallucinated that he could fly, stood on the ledge, flapped his arms, and jumped off. The event had also featured a blind girl lying on the bed where you dumped your coat in the living quarters one floor down. Her skirt was hiked to her hips, so anybody could stick his boner in—I didn't linger on the stairs to get in line. Of course, like the trust-funder, she was a volunteer, wanting to participate as best she could, not a slave girl. It wasn't the Old South.

The Beats had The Merry Pranksters of Ken Kesey, the Angry Young Men of Great Britain, James Dean motorcycling in *Rebel Without a Cause*, and the God-is-Dead French writers, as a rough parallel. Yet that blind girl for public use on the bed with the coats defines for me how the Hippies by contrast were sisterhood, matriarchal, and would never have countenanced that, but would have chosen partners for her if she wanted to hook up. In fact, at a commune near me in Vermont, a dozen years or more after that interlude on the West Coast, a woman who wanted a child would have a group of men she knew jack off into a salad bowl and stir the mix of jizzim with a turkey baster, so there would be no father as such, and fertilize herself. Another commune, being lesbian, simply imported an agreeable soul and had him impregnate everybody during the course of a month or two, so they could all experience pregnancy and childbirth at about the same time and raise their crop jointly. A rolling stone gathers no moss, and the Beats wanted no dependents; but the ladies in big earth-mother skirts, gardening bare-breasted to help their veggies grow, wanted place or moss and regeneration. They needed men to fix the cars, haul the trash, shoot a deer for protein, and scare off peeping toms.

The Beats didn't read very much that wasn't Buddhist or Beat, but they weren't anti-literate, like many Hippies, who seemed to regard reading as an Establishment activity. Mysticism like Carlos Castaneda's peyote/mescaline trips or Abbie Hoffman's (*Steal This Book*) Yippie calls to arms were okay, but otherwise dropping out of college had meant putting the glasses away. I knew an aspiring opera singer, a choreographer, a trading-post and newspaper publisher, a potter and chef, a target shooter who considered the tin cans he punctured works of accidental art, and a prison counselor, but nobody who owned and devoured books. Some were burnt out; some were Peter Pan. Some worked with locals and loggers in the woods; some peddled pot and pistols to Brooklyn or Boston. But none could just slam around like Beats on the road from Vermont to Oregon or Arkansas and expect their women to take them back—and women had veto power in any commune.

At the one, cunnilingus was the order of the day. The leader would even chat with me while a kneeling man performed the service at lunchtime. She'd kicked her husband out after she got tired of him sleeping between her and his mistress; they liked bed better with him gone. Men plowed their field with a horse and climbed up on the barn roof for dangerous repairs, but all the commune's clothes were kept in a barrel, and when you came down in the morning you were supposed to reach inside and wear whatever garment first came to hand, whether overalls or a dress, so that they'd wear dresses half the time. Electricity from the road was unhooked, and in the summer, holding hands around the rice and salad dinner table, each woman would announce where she would be sleeping that night—in the hayloft or upstairs, the pine woods or river meadow—for any member to visit her. But I saw one cruel scene, when a little girl ran to the leader to be put to bed and the woman told her exasperatedly, "Anybody here is your parent. Why come to me? Anybody here can brush your hair and tell you a story."

I was accepted as a visitor because I was known to live off the grid like them twenty miles away, as the crow flies, and would arrive with my goat and dog in the back seat, having climbed one of Vermont's fire-tower mountains for a story I was doing, and wasn't a drifter, a moocher, or known to hit on anyone. At another commune, where I also observed the goings-on without partaking of the pot, before departing about sunset when the women herded their kids off before any acid was dropped, a very pretty woman with black hair and white blouse offered me a beaker full of carrot juice as a sort of alternate initiation if I didn't want marijuana. I had conscientiously avoided ogling the women's breasts when they returned from gardening, but she still joked that I was there "for the tittie." My friend, a rocking-chair maker, defended me, and I turned down the carrot juice, desiring her but not an initiation. With his drawknife, he fashioned one Shaker-type chair per month, working by the phases of the moon, having learned during a year spent in a cave before joining the "Farm" that, apart from food, our central need is for a chair. I did find a hippie lover, at still a third commune, by bush-whacking forty miles over several days through the roadless forest south of Canada with her ex-husband. She then invited me into her sweat-house on an icy creek, an initiation I joyfully accepted. An artist in stained glass, she also made me love the smell of soldering and indeed of marijuana because she preferred to relax into carnality by smoking a toke. Her cabin, a mile walk up that tumbling brook from the highway, became a haven.

I'd been pent-up, pell-mell like *On the Road* and like another perambulatory, though broader-beamed book of the period, Saul Bellow's *The Adventures of Augie March*, during the 1950s. And we need that kite-flying spirit back, minus Beat inebriation. Our legislative quandaries—budgetary, immigration, same-sex marriage—could be resolved by a brief conversation with Walt Whitman. In the Beats' era, with the blind girl a public facility on the party bed, and the Beatles autographing their groupies' breasts, phrases like "maiden name," "losing your cherry," "your barn door is open," were still current. It took the hippies to help eclipse them, along with introducing the ubiquity of jeans, fresh-food ideas, androgyny, and being a burr under the saddle of American dumbheadedness abroad—with Vietnam, what else could you do but take to the woods.

Hipsters did not harbor worldly ambitions as a rule, so if they limped home to mom in Massachusetts after shooting for the moon, as Kerouac did, or back to Lawrence, Kansas, after having departed for a life of drugged expatriation, like Burroughs, nobody much noticed. Corso, disheveled, cadging drinks in Rome, bewailing that a long-ago wife had brought his daughter to visit him in prison, was more memorable than the black-bearded founder of our largest local commune getting himself into such addled straits his own car rolled over him. Hippies didn't thunder, out on a limb, or produce poets who weathered well like Gary

Snyder and Allen Ginsberg: not just Burroughs' putting an apple on his wife's head and shooting at it.

Nobody, so far as I know, has investigated how children conceived from semen in a salad bowl turned out, but probably okay; I once met a Navy Seal whose mother used to spit on the floor and make him lick it up. Freedom and ambivalence were what the Hippies sought. The winters were character-building and they learned carpentry, chainsaw-ing, latrine-digging if they stuck around, while their main stoner drug edged toward being decriminalized. But that was less romantic than hitting the road and spilling the beans in compulsive cadences, banging around, depending upon the kindness of strangers. My rocking-chair friend and my girlfriend both also died too young, perhaps from a shared distrust of doctors, or from smoking fungicided marijuana. Ginsberg intoned famously at the beginning of "Howl" that "I saw the best minds of my generation destroyed . . ." Dubious, but certainly people he loved.

Nominated by New Letters

PINE

by SUSAN STEWART

from THE PARIS REVIEW

a homely word:
a plosive, a long cry, a quiet stop, a silent letter
      like a storm and the end of a storm,
the kind brewing
        at the top of a pine,
              (torn hair, bowed spirits, and,
                    later, straightened shoulders)
who's who of the stirred and stirred up:
        musicians, revolutionaries, pines.

A coniferous tree with needle-shaped leaves.
Suffering or trouble; there's a pin inside.

The aphoristic seamstress was putting up a hem, a shelf of pins at her
                              pursed mouth.
"needles and pins / needles and pins / when a man marries / his trouble
begins."
A red pincushion with a twisted string, and a little pinecone tassel, at the
                                ready.

That particular smell, bracing,
        exact as a sharpened point.

The Christmas tree, nude and fragrant,
        propped as pure potential in

307

the corner with no nostalgia for
                    ornament or angels.

"Pine-Sol," nauseating, earnest, imitation—
    one means of knowing the real thing is the fake you find in school.
Pent up inside on a winter day, the steaming closeness from the radiators.
At the bell, running down the hillside. You wore *a. pinafore.*
The air had a *nip: pine*
                    was traveling in the opposite direction.

Sunlight streaming through a *stand of pines,*
                    dancing backward through the *A*'s and *T*'s.

Is it fern or willow that's the opposite of pine ?

An alphabet made of trees.

In the clearing vanished hunters
                    left their arrowheads
                    and deep cuts in the boulder wall:
                            petroglyphs, repeating triangles.

Grandmothers wearing *pinnies* trimmed in rickrack.
One family branch lived in a square of oak forest, the other in a circle
                                                of pines;
the oak line: solid, reliable, comic; the piney one capable of pain
                                                and surprise.
W-H-I-T-E: the white pine's five-frond sets spell its name. (Orthography of
                    other pines I don't yet know.)

The weight of snow on boughs, lethargic, then rocked by the thump of a
                                                settling crow.

Pinecones at the Villa Borghese: Fibonacci increments,
                    heart-shaped veins, shadowing the inner
                    edges of the petals.
Like variations at the margins of a bird feather.
                    Graffiti tattooing the broken
                    water clock, a handful
                            of pine nuts, pried out, for lunch.

Pining away like Respighi with your pencil.

For a coffin, you'd pick a plain
pine box suspended in a weedy sea.

No undergrowth, though, in a pine forest.

Unlike the noisy wash
of dry deciduous leaves,
the needles *blanket* the earth

pliant beneath a bare foot,
stealthy,
          floating,
a walk through the pines.

Silence in the forest comes from books.

Nominated by The Paris Review, Atsuro Riley, Richard Cecil

ANIMALS

fiction by MICHAEL KARDOS

from CRAZYHORSE

It's nearly lunchtime and the woman on the phone is getting snippy, so I intentionally flub a word. "I know this must be fistering for you."

"I beg your pardon?" she says.

"Fistering. Fisterating?"

"Do you mean 'frustrating'?"

"Yes—I mean that. I use the wrong word sometimes," I tell her, just as I've been taught to say. My confession will cause her temper to subside.

"But your English is really quite good," she says.

"Thank you," I tell her. "You are kind."

"It's the truth, Raj. Have you ever been to America?" She calls me Raj because she believes it's my name. Because I told her it is.

"No, Josephine," I tell her. That's her name—Josephine Sanders. "Though one of my cousin attends U.C.L.A. He likes America very much."

I know nothing about this woman other than her name, phone number, and computer model, but I sense she isn't a bad person. Certainly, her frustration is warranted. The CD-ROM drive on her new computer shouldn't already be failing.

"There's a lot to like," she says. "Not everything, but a lot. You should visit your cousin if you get the chance."

I thank her again and feel glad that we're being civil now.

"So tell me," the woman says, "where about in India are you guys located?" She's speaking to me as if to an acquaintance who might

310

someday become her friend. It wouldn't be hard to convince myself that she's lonely.

I tell her that the HCC call center is located in a small city named Veraval, on India's western shoreline. "It's traditionally a fishing port," I explain, "but we are attempting to modernize."

I would never have known about that distant city's existence had it not been circled in red marker on the map handed to us at orientation. The map is tacked to my cubicle along with various memos and reminders, a photograph of my parents, and another photograph of Pongo, the Doberman Pinscher I grew up with in Red Bank, New Jersey, and who is now buried in my parents' backyard.

"Everyone tries to modernize," the woman says. "It doesn't always lead to happiness."

"I know you're right," I tell her, because we're supposed to agree with the customer whenever feasible. I then repeat my feelings of personal sorrow that the CD-ROM drive on her Handel computer has stopped whirring, and I offer another apology for being unable to get it whirring again despite the twenty minutes we've spent together on the telephone, not to mention the thirty or more that she spent on hold prior to our conversation.

"I know this must be very . . . *frustrating*," I say, as if forcing my tongue into a new, baffling position, "but if you would hold for a moment, I'll transfer you to a scheduling agent, who will schedule an appointment for a service technician in your area to come to your home."

"I'd appreciate that," she says. "I'm in the middle of writing my doctoral dissertation, and I desperately need a working computer at home."

"Really? What's your subject?" Without meaning to, I've veered off-script and spoken way too informally. But I couldn't help it. A Ph.D. takes years to obtain, and I'm always bowled over by people with the luck and stamina to see their plans through.

"Sociology," she says, apparently unaware of my change in syntax. "I'm studying workplace stress in Memphis—that's a city in Tennessee—and the way that people react to it differently across gender and racial lines."

"I know where is Memphis," I say, overdoing it a little now. "Elvis Presley. Graceland."

"That's right," she says.

But Elvis holds no interest for me. "How long have you been writing your dissertation?"

"Six months," she says. "But I've been collecting data for years. It's become my whole life."

"Your study is very important," I tell her.

"I used to think so," she says. "Now I just want it finished. I've become a horrible person to be around. At night I dream about data files. Or about murdering my dissertation director." She laughs, but I can tell she doesn't think anything is funny. "And yes, I'm aware of the irony. Do you know what I mean by that, Raj?"

Because I find myself wanting her to like me, I answer her question the way I imagine a bright, bilingual man named Raj from Veraval would: "Irony? I believe so. You are studying workplace stress, and your work is causing you stress." When I get it right—the answer, the accent, the syntax—I *feel* like Raj, an optimistic upstart from Veraval, a young and ambitious cog in the wheel of international commerce. I imagine him carrying a briefcase to work. I feel glad for him.

"You got that right, amigo." She sighs into the phone. "Look, you sound like a nice guy, but I really need that computer to work. It's kind of a big deal."

"I understand," I tell her, disappointed to be getting back on script. But it's just as well. Today is Catfish Wednesday, and on Catfish Wednesday you have to beat the crowd. My bank of cubicles abuts the employee cafeteria, and my stomach is growling in response to the deep fryer. "I'm glad to help. Thank you for calling Handel Computers, Josephine. I'll transfer you now to a scheduling agent."

And because her problem is not a Critical Operating System Error, I do exactly what I've been trained to do. I hang up on her.

Training was a two-week affair in January. That was ten months ago, when I was desperate for work. To summarize: I'd come South for veterinary school, flunked out but didn't tell my family or friends back North, then decided to stick around so I could reapply the following year as an in-state resident. The dean said my chances for readmission were 50/50, which were about the best odds I'd ever been given for anything.

On our first day at Arihant, we twenty new hires followed our team leader to a windowless classroom deep in the bowels of the building, where we learned about the telephone system and call-tracking soft-

312

ware, and about the Handel Computer Corporation, the Seattle company that was outsourcing its customer service and tech support to us. The next two days, we received rudimentary training in PC support.

The following Monday morning began with a biscuit-and-gravy breakfast for the eighteen of us who'd made it successfully through the first week. A tall woman who looked a little like Christie Whitman rushed into the room, whammed the door shut behind her, and introduced herself as Margaret Lighthouse, our CEO. After presenting her brief biography—Wharton Business School, executive positions here and there—she handed out confidentiality statements for us to sign. Her eyes narrowed as she explained the severe repercussions of revealing company secrets—dismissal, criminal prosecution, the works.

Did she frighten any of us away? Not a chance. Not in this recession. We needed the work.

After collecting the forms, she smiled as if seeing us for the first time, shut off the lights, and began a Power Point presentation about the history of the American customer service industry. Projected onto the white screen were dry statistics about the loss of American jobs and the number of call centers being established overseas, where wages were low and employee motivation high.

"Riveting stuff," I whispered to the middle-aged woman beside me. She moved her chair away.

Margaret Lighthouse flipped on the lights, causing us all to blink and sit up a little straighter. "So now I have one of those company secrets to tell you about," she said, and winked.

Five minutes later, people were grinning. They tittered nervously. An elderly gentleman in a crisp suit muttered, "Holy shit," which caused more titters.

Fortified with an amazing secret, strong company coffee, and the knowledge that we were being paid for our time, we spent the next five days learning how to hide our natural dialects—Southern, East Coast, whatever—and to speak English with a proper Indian accent. Our teachers alternated between a retired TV meteorologist from Calcutta and a Mississippi-born linguist with a doctoral degree from Georgia State.

For eight hours a day, our instructors lectured us, grilled us, popped quizzes, and made us speak in front of the class. They assigned homework and expected us to do it. They taught us to drop our diphthongs and pronounce our W's like V's and our V's like B's. The three days devoted to phonology demanded tremendous concentration and practice. The final two days covered syntax and diction: applying plurals incorrectly, overusing gerund constructions and reflexive pronouns. And by the end of the week, my classmates sounded, to my ears anyway, less like residents of northern Mississippi and more like native Hindi speakers with an impressive command of the English language.

And if we could fool me, then surely we could fool some fed-up customer in the American heartland.

The con—there's no other word for it—went like this: The customer waits awhile on hold. And when he hears me say in my brand new accent, "Thank you for calling Handel Computer Corporation, may I please verify your name and computer model number?" he thinks: *Another goddamn foreign call center.* His expectations diminish. Rather than satisfaction, he expects courteous but ineffective service from somebody thousands of miles away. And a customer base with lowered expectations means that Handel computers can generally avoid paying for actual tech support and replacement parts.

What Arihant has done is to implement a key cost-saving service, heretofore handled beyond our shores, right on good old American soil.

I take thirty-seven calls today, seven above quota, before shutting off my computer terminal and heading for the parking lot. The sun has set and the evening is cool and pleasant, and for the briefest moment I feel as if I'm in the exact right spot in the universe. But as I begin to drive past residential streets and see the decorations—Santa on his sleigh, a blow-up snowman—I begin to feel nostalgic for those frigid northern winters. Unable to face my parents, I told them I had to stay here over Christmas to study.

"My son, the scholar," my old man said. "I'm sad, but impressed."

For decades, my father was an editor at the *Asbury Park Press* but recently got laid off. Now he's writing a book about the decline of print journalism. The man writes a great sentence, but I can't imagine who would want to read about anything so obvious. It's like writing a book about the wetness of water. "How about just for a few days?" he asked.

I can live a lie over the phone and in emails. But to stay in my parents' house over the holidays would've been too much. "Wish I could, Dad," I told him.

I know they're disappointed. Driving home, I try to tell myself that I did the right thing. Then I start thinking about the doctoral student,

314

Josephine. When she spoke about her dissertation, the phone line practically hummed with anxiety. I should have told her to take a day or two off. Drive to New Orleans and clear her head. That would have been good advice. But I'm not paid to give good advice. That's the job of the handful of actual computer techs on-staff, who handle only the most urgent problems. The rest of us, earning far less, run interference. We're polite. We ask the customer to reboot. To make sure all cables are plugged in tightly. We do our best, then we lose the call. Losing the call is pretty much the key part of my job.

Here's what I know happened the moment I hung up on Josephine: At first she wondered about the absence of hold music. Then, realizing the call had been disconnected, she became furious with me, with Handel Computers, and with the U.S. economy in general. This is the kind of service you get, she'd be thinking, when you ship all the jobs to Asia. Her instinct would be to call back immediately and demand a supervisor, maybe even the head of the whole damn department.

All part of the plan. Because then—and here's the important part—she looked at her watch and realized that she'd just spent thirty minutes on hold (our hold music is on a 15-second loop, making even the shortest hold-time feel endless) and another thirty minutes with me, only to achieve nothing. Screw it, she eventually decided. Her time was too valuable. For now, she'd use the computer without the damn CD-ROM drive.

If she ever calls back, it'll be weeks from now, late at night, when she's unable to sleep. Might as well give it one more shot, she'll think, and get out of bed. After another thirty minutes on hold, she'll speak with another compassionate but unhelpful member of the Handel customer service team who will, as trained, lose her call again.

Nobody ever calls back a third time.

I'm halfway home when I come across a small puppy walking along the shoulder of the road. I pull over and get out of the car to investigate. The animal is young—maybe eight or nine weeks. No collar. Malnourished. People in Mississippi have different relationships with their animals than they do in New Jersey, but still. A puppy is a defenseless creature, and somebody chose to dump it here at the edge of a residential neighborhood so it would become somebody else's problem. At times like this I fear for the human race.

I kneel down. "Hi, little puppy." A puppy should be happy to see you.

It should come over, tail wagging. This one glances up at me and looks away. It takes a few shaky steps in the other direction.

I scoop it up and place it on my passenger seat. A few miles away, at the vet school, is a 24-hour clinic. I could go there, but I won't. Applications were due two weeks ago, and I failed to send in mine. True, that application was my entire reason for staying in Mississippi this past year. But as the deadline neared, those 50/50 odds started to weigh on me. I couldn't stand the thought of getting rejected—or, worse, getting accepted and then flunking out again. I started thinking that when you only get accepted into one school out of twenty applications—which was what happened the first time around—maybe it means that the other nineteen schools knew what they were doing.

When I was flunking out last year, the dean called me into his office, where I flopped around like a hooked fish trying to save itself. "All I ever wanted was to be a veterinarian, sir," I told him. Just one semester living in the South and I'd already fallen into the habit of calling everybody "ma'am" and "sir." It's one of the reasons, besides the easy availability of cheap labor, why Arihant set up shop here. No one needs to be taught courtesy. "Ever since I was a little kid, when my dad brought home those two baby chicks for Easter, and they got sick and died. Ever since then, I've wanted to help animals."

The dean, a round-gutted Southern gentleman who smelled of spicy cologne and horses, had a habit of sighing deeply, as if he'd just finished a big meal and now felt guilty for it.

He sighed deeply. "I've always wanted to play shortstop for the Cardinals. Do you see what I'm saying, Charlie?"

That conversation kept weighing on me as the new deadline neared. It kept me from downloading the required forms, kept me from ordering my college transcripts and writing the entrance essay. I couldn't face the thought of another meeting with the dean. So I chickened out.

I'm not sure if it's chickening out now, too, or if it's the opposite— that maybe I'm showing resolve—but I head away from the vet school and toward home. When I arrive, I get the puppy crate out of the garage. I fostered several puppies the semester I was enrolled—lots of vet students do it—and accrued a lot of pet supplies.

I sit on the garage floor and examine the dog: short hair, big floppy ears, long tail. Probably a hound mix. She'd be cute if she weren't all ribs.

She doesn't appear to be injured—just malnourished and flea-ravaged. But my laundry room closet is filled with supplies: flea shampoo, antibiotics, pills for heartworm, tapeworm, cures for every ailment, courtesy of the vet school.

"You're gonna be OK," I tell her, running a flea brush through her matted fur. "I'm gonna make you well, little lady."

Unless she has parvo. Then she's finished.

I shouldn't have told the Easter chick story. I remember lying in bed after my meeting with Dean McKenzie—the blinds drawn, a cliché of depression—and thinking that I should have told him what mattered most, which is that when I was twelve years old, my family's Doberman Pinscher bit my friend Seth and had to be put down. It's a story I don't ever tell—I still ache over it a dozen years later—but my meeting with the dean would have been the right time. Especially since it was the truth. I believed that my becoming a vet might help to make up for getting our family dog killed.

I won't romanticize my relationship with Pongo. His bark rattled the windows. His chronic accidents on the dining room carpet put a constant scowl on my mother's face. He killed the occasional gopher or baby rabbit unwise enough to find itself in our lawn, and even though it was just the dog doing what he was hard-wired to do, the carnage always upset me.

Still. When I entered the house after school, he would follow me from room to room. He fetched a stick like it mattered, he had a belly that loved being scratched, and he was a licker, not a nipper. I taught him tricks, and my parents told me I had talent as a dog-trainer. What I had was patience, an even temper, and a smart animal. At two years old, though, the dog was still too energetic for his own good.

My friend Seth Hoberman was like an untrained dog, good-natured but mannerless. His voice was always twenty decibels too loud and he had no sense for how to respect an animal. One Saturday afternoon, my parents decided to go to a matinee and leave me at home unsupervised for a few hours—a new and wonderful development since my twelfth birthday.

Seth and I were in our small living room, sitting on the carpet in front of the sofa and watching professional wrestling on TV. During a commercial break, Seth turned to me and said, "Let's wrestle." I was never a physical kid, but Seth had three older brothers and no qualms about pinning me to the ground. I strained to get free but was too weak. Pongo watched us, lying flat on the ground and barking, and then Seth

317

got off me and began rousing the dog into a crazy state, teasing him with a sofa cushion, putting him in a headlock. I remember watching as Seth pinned the dog, same as he'd pinned me, and held him against the carpet. He started a slow three-count. The dog squirmed and whimpered. I knew I should tell Seth to ease up, but I was his friend, not his parent, and I was still annoyed that he'd pinned me so easily. I wanted to see if the dog would fare better than I had.

Seth had just shouted "Two!" when the dog bit his face. It was only a single bite on the cheek, not an attack, but it was no warning nip, either. Pongo immediately squirmed to his feet and, knowing he'd done wrong, scurried, tail down, to the corner of the room.

Monday morning at school, Seth was peeling back the bandage to show his six stitches to anyone who'd look. I trailed him, explaining word-for-word what my parents used to explain to me when the dog was still a puppy. *You have to be gentle with him,* I told Seth. *He's only an animal. Once you rile them up like that, it's not their fault.*

The hospital was required to notify animal control. Most family dogs are given a second chance, but the breed had a bad reputation then. Nowadays it's pit bulls. Before that it was Rottweilers. Back then it was Dobermans. Bad luck for us. Worse for him.

I'm still not sure whose fault it was. It might have been the dog's. Just because they're animals doesn't mean they're blameless. But I do know this: There are certain people in the world who have a knack for keeping the peace. And those people have a responsibility. I'm one of those people. I've always been one of those people.

Caring for a sick puppy, I remember too late, is no one-person job. When I was fostering those pound puppies, I had help from my girlfriend, Linda, a fourth-year with confidence and clinical experience. We didn't date long, just a few months. When I flunked out of school, her pity seemed to loom large, and I decided I couldn't be around her or our vet school friends. The last time she and I spoke, she informed me that she was staying an extra year for her internship and offered to help me with my application this time around. That's the kind of person she is. I told her I had it all under control, even though I didn't. That's the kind of person I am.

I'd sure accept her help tonight, though. I lie on the kitchen floor next to the crate and fail to guess when the puppy will suddenly squat and pee or, worse, excrete something truly awful. The night passes glacially—the puppy whimpers, a car passes out front, the refrigerator motor clicks on, then off. Every couple of hours, I turn on the kitchen light, let the puppy out of its crate, and measure out and administer various medicines.

I begin to think, as I'm prone to do late at night, about booking a flight and traveling halfway across the globe, all the way to Veraval, India. Except for coming south to Mississippi, I haven't traveled much, haven't ever left the country other than for one drunken spring break in Cancun, which reminded me an awful lot of Wildwood, New Jersey. So I wouldn't mind seeing the Eiffel Tower, or Big Ben or whatever. But what I'd really like is to walk the beaches of Veraval. I'd like to smell the fish as they're being gutted and talk to the people who are gutting them, even if we're speaking two different languages. I'd like to visit the ancient Nawabi summer palace, which, according to Wikipedia, is mainly ruined but still standing.

At some point I notice that the sky is becoming lighter, revealing a frosty December morning. I'm sweaty with exhaustion. I take the dog outside again, then crate her, take a long shower, throw on some clean clothes, and drive to Arihant. Carrying a full-to-the-brim coffee mug, I mumble hello to some co-workers and head to my cubicle. As I plug in my headset, I'm actually looking forward to the human voices about to come through my telephone extension, even if all they're doing is complaining.

Mid-morning, a group of new hires passes by. They're practicing their new accents on one another. A middle-aged woman wearing a Rudolf the Reindeer sweater gives me a friendly wave. Rudolf's nose is a red button. I wave back.

The real city of Veraval, I learned from the internet one sleepless night, is suffering from the global recession. Fish exports are down. The cement plant is producing cement just three days a week. The rayon manufacturer is close to bankruptcy. No business has gone unaffected. Men are leaving their families to seek out work. Raj, if there really were a Raj, would most likely be in a desperate situation.

But here at Arihant we're thriving. So is our little Southern town. There used to be no bowling alley. You had to drive to Meridian for decent Chinese food.

Before Arihant, we were a one-horse town. Now we have at least three horses.

❋   ❋   ❋

Her call comes a little past noon, the same time as yesterday. I was about to head home and let the dog out of its crate. But when I say, "Thank you for calling HCC, this is Raj speaking, may I ask for your Handel warranty code," and she says, "Is this the same Raj as yesterday?" and I say, "Josephine?," the dog slips my mind and I feel a small thrill.

"Yep," she says. "It's me."

And then I say something way out of bounds: "Buenos días, amiga."

Fortunately, her response is without suspicion. "You speak Spanish, too? My god, we Americans are provincial."

"I do not," I tell her. "Those are the only words I know. So how is your dissertation today?"

"We got cut off, you know."

"We did?"

Repeat customers are strongly discouraged. If a customer on my line tries to reconnect with Sanjay, for instance, then I'm supposed to say that Sanjay is home sick, or on vacation. If the customer is insistent, I'm supposed to say that Sanjay isn't actually at home or sick, but rather that he no longer works here. We're not supposed to say that Sanjay (or Bintu, or Leema, etc.) is deceased, but there are times when death is necessary.

What accounts for Josephine ending up on my line again? Pure chance. Her call was the next on the queue when I answered.

"When you went to transfer me," she said, "the call got screwed up. I was pretty fucking mad, pardon my French. But I feel a little calmer today."

"Yes, I deeply apologize," I tell her. At Arihant, we are always deeply apologizing. "But if you'll hold just a moment, I'll connect you now—"

"*Wait*," she says. "I mean, that'd be fine. But listen. I was wondering— what's it like in Veraval?"

Ah, I think. So you *are* lonely.

A surprising number of customers engage us in small talk. The human impulse to forge a connection runs deep. That, and the impulse to manipulate a situation—as if by getting to know us a little, we'll fast-track them toward a new computer. During orientation we were given a sheet titled *Facts About You*. I keep mine tacked to the wall of my cubicle.

- **Who Do You Work For?**: Never say that you work for Arihant. Instead, say that you work for the Handel Computer Corporation (You may also use the letters HCC).
- **Where Are You?**: Veraval, India. It is located on India's west coast.

320

- **Veraval's chief industry:** Fish exporting.
- **Have You Ever Been To America?** No. (Nor are you familiar with any part of American geography. If you must, say this: No, though I would like to someday. Or this: No, though my [relative] went to [name of major American university]).
- **Your first language:** Hindi. But you studied English in school from early on.
- **Type of fish caught/processed in Veraval:** Ribbon fish, cuttel fish, squid.
- **What time is it right now where you are?:** Add 10.5 hours to the current time.

I find myself giving Josephine an unusually detailed answer, telling her what I imagine to be true in my city-by-the-sea and what I imagine would be true about Raj—how he comes from a long line of fishermen, how his family and friends view him with admiration but also skepticism because of his education and indoor job. And because this life I'm describing is fantasy, I tell her that I have plans to travel to America one day to earn an advanced degree.

"Oh, you should," Josephine says. "I can tell you're ambitious. A lot more than I am, that's for sure."

"I don't understand," I say. "You are earning your doctorate."

"Yeah. About that—do you mind if I tell you something? It's kind of a confession. I wouldn't mind getting it off my chest."

The puppy has been in its crate for over four hours and needs me. I have to leave, but I can't help lowering my voice and saying, "Your confession is safe with me."

Last week, I overheard two co-workers talking at lunch about a caller who confessed to being involved in an extra-marital affair. Customer confessions aren't so rare. People need to unburden themselves, and they believe we're a world away.

I want to believe, though, that this conversation is different. Josephine's voice yesterday held a mix of desperation and camaraderie, which was why I decided to tell her my life story, fictitious as it was. Now that we've had these exchanges, isn't it at all possible that we're forming a bond, this stranger and I?

"I fabricated all my data," she says. When I don't say anything right away, she adds, "Do you know that word? Fabricated?"

I want to hear her say it again. So much so that I tell her, "No. I do not know this word."

"It means I made it all up. Five years of data. None of it's real."

"You are talking about your dissertation now?"

"Of course."

"What about your dreams of data files?" She is suddenly fascinating to me. "Are you not having those dreams?"

"Sure I am. I'm scared to death of getting caught. I've accepted a lot of grant money."

"Why did you make up your data?"

"You're a smart man, Raj. You can figure it out." Of course I can. But then she tells me anyway. "It wasn't coming out the way I wanted. This was easier. I got lazy."

"I see."

"*You see?* What are you, a therapist?"

"I mean, I get it," I tell her.

"You *get* it?" Her voice rises in pitch. "Jesus, don't you have anything to say that means anything?"

She's been holding her secret for so long that there's no way for my reaction to match her expectation. "What would you like me to—"

"Well, *I* don't know," she says. "I'm an American doctoral student who just admitted to fudging all her data. Be shocked or something. Call me a bitch."

The word jolts me back to standard protocol and broken syntax: "I am not calling you that. But if you will hold a moment—"

"Do you have a wife, Raj?"

Her question surprises me enough that I answer it truthfully.

"A girlfriend?" she asks.

"No."

"Are you gay? Do you have a homosexual lover?"

I tell her I am not homosexual.

"I'm naked, you know," she says. "I'm naked right now and touching myself."

I disconnect the call.

The puppy is worse. She has soiled her crate and barely lifts her head to look at me. She finally stands, shakily, tail drooping. I clean her with a damp towel, carry her out to the yard, and wait for her to do her business. This comes in the form of bloody diarrhea. No, not exactly. There is only blood. I run inside for a bowl of water and a can of wet puppy food. She isn't hungry or thirsty. I dip my fingers into the water and hold them up to her muzzle. She licks the water off them, but she needs more fluids. And I swear she's skinnier than yesterday.

I'm cursing myself for not getting home earlier, but the real mistake happened yesterday, when I decided to take her home and save her myself. She needs to be hydrated intravenously. Or maybe not. I'm in over my head. In fact, I know only two things for certain.

One: I've failed.

Two: The dog needs a vet.

The only animal hospital in town is fully booked for the day. There are only two vets working there, the receptionist explains, and Dr. Blinder is off buck hunting with his brothers in Missouri.

"Are you sure the other doctor can't make time?" Evidence that I'm no longer new to Mississippi: I'm unfazed by a vet who hunts.

"Sir," the receptionist says, "if it's an emergency, you should try the veterinary school."

And so I do what I must—I call Linda's cell—and when she answers we have a no-nonsense clinical conversation that ends with me carrying the puppy in its crate to the car and driving to the vet school's emergency clinic.

Linda is from New Jersey, too: Paramus. Shortly after we met, we learned that as teenagers we used to hang out at the same malls. She came to Mississippi to specialize in large animals—horses, cows—and there is something both rough and reassuring in the way she handles the puppy. Linda's hands are dry and raw from washing them all day long, but she looks pretty in her green scrubs, and I remember how she would sometimes wear a freshly laundered pair for pajamas.

She shakes her head. "We've got one sick patient on our hands."

I was right—the dog needs intravenous fluids, and I hold her still while Linda inserts the needle. This should be painful, but the dog doesn't make a sound.

"Good girl," Linda says.

While we wait for the bag of saline to drain, I ask Linda if she has nice holiday plans, and she tells me that she does. She asks me if I got my application off okay.

"It's out of my hands now," I tell her.

She inserts the IV into two other places on the dog's back, and the animal begins to look puffy from the sacs of water that have inflated under her skin.

Linda collects a fecal sample from the dog to test for parvo and heads off to the lab, which these days is off limits to me. I stand beside the examination table, pet the dog, and wait. When she returns a few minutes later, her expression reveals nothing. But when she says, "It's negative," I feel myself exhale.

"Don't feel too relieved," she quickly adds. "If she caught the virus recently, it might not show up yet on the test." She tells me to take the dog home, give her the meds, and hope for the best. "And no food," she says. "Not for a day or two."

"But she's so skinny already . . ."

When Linda looks at me, her face softens. "Look, Charlie—she's either going to perk up or she's going to get more dehydrated and die. Either way, it's going to happen fast."

"Don't you think she should stay here?"

"There's nothing we can do for her here that you can't do at home." Linda strokes the dog's head. "Trust me, she'll be better off with you." *I'm not the vet!*, I think. *They kicked me out, remember?* As if reading my thoughts, she adds, "If you want, I could come by later and help out."

I can feel it again, the pity, and tell her no thanks.

We ease the dog back into her crate, and Linda jots down a medication schedule. She loads me up with cans of prescription puppy food and more drugs. I can't decide if I should give Linda a hug, or a kiss on the cheek, or maybe just a handshake. In the end, I don't touch her at all.

"Thanks," I tell her.

She smiles. "It's all right, Charlie. It's what I do."

Back at home, the call to my boss goes fine. I haven't used a single sick or vacation day since taking the job, and my complete lack of a social calendar has been misinterpreted as dedication.

I carry the crate into my bedroom, shut the blinds, turn off the light, sit on the bed, and watch the dog sleep. Were it not for this animal, I would be fielding phone calls, smoothing ruffled feathers, making empty promises until five p.m., when I would go to the Tavern or maybe Big Daddy's for a burger and a few beers. I'd watch whatever game was on TV over the bar, soaking in the warmth of others' conversations, until at some point I'd feel tired and sober enough to drive home, where there is more TV and an internet that will connect me to absolutely anything, you name it, including pornography.

Some days, especially when the weather is warm and sunny, I imagine that my current life is rehabilitative. I'm off the grid, an explorer in this small town of crepe myrtles and catfish po-boys, working a secret job, almost as if I were C.I.A. I tell myself that someday I'll return to New Jersey a little worldlier than those around me, full of Southern yarns and witticisms. I'll be the life of the party.

I've been feeding this story to myself because loneliness, if you dwell on it, only gets worse. It makes a person do strange things. For instance, before I left work today, I jotted down Josephine's telephone number on a scrap of paper. And I find myself, now, taking off my shirt and pants, and then my boxer shorts, and when I'm lying completely naked on the unmade bed I use my cell phone to dial her number.

I'm wondering whether she'll pick up—she won't recognize my name on the caller ID—and what I'll say if she does. She answers on the second ring.

"Josephine?" I say. "This is Raj calling. From HCC."

"Oh," she says, her voice flat. "The caller ID said *C Falcone*."

I explain that I'm not calling from my usual extension. "I want to apologize for hanging up on you this morning."

"Really? No, I'm the one who needs to apologize. What I said earlier . . ."

"It's okay."

"No, it isn't," she says, her voice more animated. "It's fucking crazy. I mean, who says that? Don't answer. I'll tell you: a fucking lunatic, that's who."

"Please. Josephine." At first, I thought the reason I was calling her had to do with sex, but now I see it's something else. "You should cut yourself some slack," I tell her, and think: *forbidden diction!* I'm still keeping up the accent, still using my invented name. I take a slow breath. And in my full-on Jersey dialect, doing my best impression of myself, I say, "Anyway, I think it's time for me to make a confession."

I tell her everything: my company's Big Secret (Her response—"Holy shit!"—reminds me of the older gentleman I first trained alongside), and how I flunked out of vet school, and how nobody up north knows a thing about me anymore. I tell her that I've got a sick animal on my hands, and if the dog doesn't die on her own I'll probably find a way to screw up and kill her anyhow. Telling Josephine these things feels like when you've been holding your breath underwater for too long and then you surface and take that first greedy gulp of air.

The silence at the other end of the line makes me think that she's hung up the phone. But then I hear a sigh. "So 'Raj'—that's a bullshit name, isn't it? You're 'C Falcone.'"

"Charlie," I tell her.

"You really have some accent there, Charlie," she says.

"They trained us well. There was a linguist, and—"

"I'm talking about your New Jersey accent."

"Oh." I can't help smiling. It's human nature to fantasize, and what I fantasize is that we become friends. She lives in Memphis, just a few hours away. And if she's half as lonely as I am, and especially with the holidays so close. . . . "It sounds like we both have a few secrets, don't we?"

"Yeah. Well, about that. I should probably tell you something." Now, I assume, is when she'll mention the boyfriend or the husband, and I'll be quick to assure her that it doesn't matter. This is no longer about sex, if it ever was. I'll tell her that speaking to her, like this, means a lot. It doesn't solve everything, or anything, but that doesn't make it unimportant, this unburdening—even to a stranger. "The truth," she says, "since we're being truthful—is that I lied to you. About my dissertation. It isn't fabricated. Every bit of it is legit."

This isn't the confession I expected. "For real?"

"Of course," she says.

"Then why did you . . ." But I know. It should have occurred to me that our customers' confessions might be false. That maybe they're less interested in admitting a sin than in inventing a life.

"Let's just say that writing a dissertation isn't the best thing for one's mental health," she says. "You're in your own head all day long, except for when you meet with your dissertation director and she tells you that your methodology is wrong. Which means another six months in this hellhole. You can't imagine the neighborhood I'm living in, because my student stipend is so laughable. I'm not talking about roaches, either— I'm talking gunfire in the middle of the day. Heavy artillery, too, if you ask my landlord—who, by the way, sold me a .38 for protection and even showed me how to use it."

As I get this glimpse into her real life, I sympathize with her—how could I not?—but I feel betrayed. Her deep, dark secret, which led me to tell her mine, has ended up being no secret at all.

"But all this is temporary," I remind her. "Your dissertation will be behind you soon."

"Sure it will," she says. "Along with the last five years of my life." She is upset suddenly, her words sounding as if they're coming through tears. "And when I'm already feeling like shit, and then I call a customer service line for help and get jerked around, and hung up on . . ."

I decide to give her some actual, practical advice. "Do you have a flash drive? You know, for backup?"

"I don't know. I think so."

"Listen to me," I say, trying to sound soothing. "I want you to back up your dissertation. I field calls all day long from customers who've had their computers crash. Trust me, the computer you bought sucks."

"Yeah, I'm pretty bad at backing things up . . . but I just found one of those thingies here in my drawer while we were talking."

"Good. Back up your dissertation."

"Okay, Charlie. Point taken. I will."

"No, I mean do it now. While I stay on the line. Otherwise, you won't—I know what people are like."

She laughs a little into the phone. "You don't mind holding?"

I tell her I'm glad to—that it will be payback for all the customers I've put on hold. She says okay and sets her phone down. It's good to feel useful. I can't fix all of her problems, but I can make sure her data doesn't get lost. And just knowing that makes me feel a little better.

While I'm waiting, I think about whether I should stay at home tomorrow, assuming the dog lives through the night, or whether I should take her with me to work. With all the medication she's on, it would be easier to take her. She'd be safe in the crate, and I'd feel better being able to look in on her—

My thoughts are interrupted by a distinct "Fuck!" This is followed seconds later by "Jesus. Oh, Jesus."

"Josephine?" I say into the phone.

The expletives—distant, as if coming from across the room—keep coming and coming. It's a little frightening, as if she's been hurt somehow—electrocuted? Did something fall on her?—but then I listen past her words to the emotion behind them, the particular mode of anger. I've heard this before. I've sounded like this before, working late at night on a college paper, when I'm exhausted and not thinking as clearly as I should be.

It's the sound, I realize, of losing all your data.

"Charlie!" She's back on the line now. "Jesus, Charlie, I think I did it the wrong way." She's speaking very quickly. "I think I saved the old file over the new one. Oh, shit shit shit."

"How old is the old file?"

"It's . . . I don't know. A couple of *years*! Oh, Jesus, Charlie . . ."

"What about your old computer? Didn't you just buy this one?"

"I threw it away. It's gone."

The spit has dried in my mouth. "Don't do anything," I tell her, trying to maintain a calm voice. "Don't touch anything." I wish I knew how to help her, but all my training is in avoidance. "I'm going to call work right now and get one of the real tech guys to call you right away. These guys are good, Josephine. They'll be able to help you. They're going to walk you through this."

I don't know whether this is true or not. If the file's been overwritten, it's been overwritten. Gone is gone. Or not. I just don't know.

"Charlie. Oh, fuck. Oh . . . oh . . ." the sound she starts making then isn't English. It isn't even words. It's a horrible, retching sound, and I feel desperate to make it stop.

"Are you okay?" I ask. "Please, try to relax. It's going to be all right. I promise. Please. I'll get someone to help. They'll be calling your cell in just a couple of minutes. Can you hear me? This will all be fine."

I dial the direct extension for tech support and ask for Randy Adams, the supervisor. I don't like Randy. He drives a BMW and calls everyone "big guy." Still, he's the man to call, so I call him.

He listens to my predicament and says, "The girl's probably fucked."

"Are you sure?"

"No, that's why I said probably."

This is why I try to avoid Randy Adams. "But you have to call her and try to help. Or somebody does. She's really losing it."

He yawns audibly into the phone. "All right. It probably won't be until tomorrow, though."

"No, that's no good," I explain. "I told her somebody would be calling right away."

"Now why would you do that?"

No answer would satisfy him. And anything truthful—*Because it's the right thing to do. Because she knows all our secrets*—would get me reprimanded or fired. "Randy, *please*—do me a personal favor."

"Who did you say you were again?"

I repeat my name. Then I say, "I go by Raj," and describe where my cubicle is located. "Just have someone call her as soon as you can," I say.

"As soon as I can?" He laughs. "Now *there's* a promise I can keep."

Five minutes later, my cell phone rings. It's Josephine. I don't want to answer, but I do anyway.

She's discovered language again.

"Where's the fucking tech support, Charlie? You said they'd call."

I tell her it's imminent.

"It had better be—for your sake."

"It's coming," I say. "Guaranteed."

Another ten minutes goes by and my phone rings again. I don't answer. When a message is left, I delete it without listening and call Randy again. He's out on dinner break. I ask for another tech. I'm put on hold. After the hold music loops forty or fifty times, I hang up.

Ten minutes after that, Josephine calls again.

I shut off the phone.

A magazine is glanced at and returned to the bedside table.

The ceiling is studied.

Finally, I put on the television and settle on The Weather Channel— but The Weather Channel is playing cheery Christmas songs, so I shut off the TV and stare at the bedside clock until the numbers tell me it's time to administer the antibiotic. Then more ceiling-staring until it's time for the anti-diarrhea.

At some point long after the sun goes down, I remember that I haven't had any food since breakfast.

I make a sandwich, eat the sandwich. Then back to the bedroom. I flick on the bedside lamp to look at the schedule that Linda drew up, then flick the light off again. Between the frequent administering of medications and a fruitless attempt to keep the dog's crate clean, I know I'll be awake all night. The minutes and hours creep along as I wait for the next time to give a pill or squirt medicine or remove a soiled towel from the crate. By midnight, the dog has soiled so many towels that I can't keep up with the washing and decide to use T-shirts—first the cheap white ones, then whatever I happen to grab out of my dresser in the dark.

But here's the thing: Sometime after three a.m. I drop into a deep sleep, and when I awake again it's to the sound of the puppy walking around in her crate.

Despite the drawn blinds, the room is beginning to lighten. I'm shocked to see it's 8:05—I never expected to sleep so soundly, and now I'm late for work. I sit up in bed and take a look. The dog is perched on my Metallica concert T-shirt, looking up at me. Tail wagging.

She isn't a new dog, but all that medicine must have kicked in overnight, and when I carry her out to the yard she actually squirms in my hands like a real live animal. I won't understate the feeling: It's magnificent. She does her business, which is noticeably less disgusting than yesterday's. It's another frosty morning, crisp, a morning with possibilities, and it occurs to me what a difference even an awful night can make.

I decide that it is most definitely take-your-puppy-to-work day.

I give her water, then take the bowl away and crate her again while I get dressed—I'm running late and skip the shower—and then carry the crate out to the car. Most of the houses on my street have their Christmas decorations up. It's the sort of neighborhood I'd never be able to afford up north. In Hoboken I paid a fortune for a one-bedroom apartment with the shower in the kitchen. Now I pay half that for a house with a dishwasher and washer/dryer, with a yard out back where this dog, should she survive, would enjoy romping.

I head to work with Josephine on my mind, my guilt diminished somewhat by my motivation to get her some much-needed help when I arrive. She almost certainly did not receive a call from tech support yesterday. Her night must have been awful. But I'm going to help her today. I'll camp out in Randy Adams's office all morning if I have to. I'll plead with my boss. I'll get it done.

I turn on my cell phone and brace myself for the voicemails, but there are none—only missed calls: seven from Josephine, all in a two-hour span last night, and two from my mother this morning. I call my mother as I drive.

"Thank God," she says. "Are you all right?"

"Relax, Mom, it's only been a couple of weeks." Actually, it's been longer than that. We don't talk nearly enough, because of the lie. It's something I need to remedy. I know that. Hearing her voice, I'm transported to frigid New Jersey. I see mulled wine on the stove and a fire in the fireplace and every other damn Christmas cliché in the book—but I also see the puppy, peeing on their kitchen floor and pulling ornaments off the tree and getting into all sorts of trouble, and I want all of it. "Anyway," I tell her, "I think I'm going to—"

"The news," she says. "Isn't that your town? I've been watching all morning."

"Isn't *what* my town?" I ask.

I round the vast magnolia trees at the entrance to Arihant to find myself facing the flashing lights of emergency vehicles. Not just a few. The parking lot has been overtaken with police cars and ambulances and firetrucks, which have created a barrier between the building and the dozens of people—my co-workers—who must have been evacuated and are now gathered in clumps along the lot's perimeter. Away from the fluorescent lights of our cubicles, these people look strange to me, alien, but as I drive closer I see it isn't the light, but rather the sagging postures and contorted faces of the grieving.

This is no fire drill, no bomb scare.

"I have to go," I tell my mother.

Only when I get out of the car do I notice the news helicopters hovering overhead. Uniformed police are everywhere. Police tape blocks all the entrances to the building. I try to imagine what must be inside: the bodies, the blood.

The dog must not like being alone in the car, because she emits a piercing cry and begins to bark. So I open the back door, get her from the crate, and approach one of the police offers, a thick man wearing sunglasses.

"What happened?" I ask, though I already know. This is the new millennium, after all, and I own a television and a computer. I read the news. My entire life, I've grown up seeing this parking lot, these first-response vehicles flashing their harsh lights. I can easily decode this message.

"Do you work here?" he asks.

I tell him I do.

"There's been gunfire reported. That's all I can say."

"Was it the tech support people?" I ask.

He looks at me and frowns. "I don't know what you're talking about."

"It was a woman who did this, wasn't it?" When he doesn't answer right away, I say, "Listen, I think I know what happened. And why."

"Is this a for-real claim?"

I nod.

He removes his sunglasses. "What's your name?"

I tell him.

"Mr. Falcone, are you saying you know the perpetrator?" But the

331

answer isn't so simple, and when I hesitate the officer takes me by the arm. "We need to get you to a detective."

Just then I feel a tap on my arm. Standing beside me is a young woman whose cubicle is across the office from mine. I don't know her real or Indian name. All I know is that she always brings a mandarin orange to work, and for ten minutes every afternoon the air smells like citrus.

She looks up at me, eyes bloodshot. "Can I hug your dog?"

Her words make no sense, until I look down and notice what I'm carrying. So I hand the dog over. And what does this woman do? She hugs my dog. That's all. Just hugs her and then, without another word, hands her back to me.

One of the cafeteria guys sees us and comes over. Big guy with a crew cut and a dirty white apron. I don't know his name either. He doesn't know mine.

"Man," he says to me, "can I hug him, too?"

"Okay," I say, and hand him the dog.

"Mr. Falcone," says the cop, "you need to come with me now."

I follow him away from the building, toward one of the patrol cars where a group of officers is gathered. But I don't wait to start talking. I start saying things at a mad pace to this officer—I'm telling him about the secrets I never should have kept, and the secrets I never should have revealed—until he says to me, "Hold it a minute. I'm not the one who needs to know."

I keep talking.

But at one point I turn around and see that more and more people have gathered where we stood—new hires, upper management, the girl from the mailroom—and they're all waiting their turn to hug my dog, who doesn't squirm or protest at all as she's passed around from person to person. She lets herself be folded into each set of arms, remaining completely calm, either because she's sick or because of the cold or the strange surroundings, or, more likely, because that's the kind of animal she is.

Nominated by Crazyhorse, Terese Svoboda

ELEGY WITH
A CITY IN IT

by REGINALD DWAYNE BETTS

from THE KENYON REVIEW

There are men awed
by blood, lost in the black
of all that is awful:
think crack and aluminum. Odd
what time steals,
or steals time: black robes, awful
nights when men offed in streets awed
us. Dead bodies sold news; real
hustlers bled. The *Post* a reel
for Rayful: black death, awe,
chocolate city read
as accumulation: the red

of all those bodies. Red
sometimes a dark and awful
omen the best couldn't read.
Death almost invented when red
was the curse of men born black
and lost in a drama Reagan read
as war: crack vials and cash and red
in our eyes and we not still
with our pocket full of stones. Steel
in hands, and a god-awful
law aimed at stilling the red.
But ambition burns, makes all red

With a greed so damn real,
Fattened by all that others read
in the *Post* about how real
it is in the streets. This reel
is a flick that has awed
fools looking for something real
in bleeding streets, as if the real
is only what drowns: think Black,
Yusef, Moe; they all blackened
the inside of a casket, all real
flesh in that final moment, still
and nothing more, still

as men plotting on stealing
time from death and cold, reeled
in from the street like dead fish. Steel
assured mutual destruction; steel
should have kept us safe. I read
the obits, the map of death, still
as caskets holding men, still
as the bullet. Who is awed
by trouble? This awful
gristle and flesh torn by steel
turned into murder. Ask Black,
dead in nights' ruins. Bring out the black

ties the papers say. The black
hole is now the block. Steel
swallows men, spits them out black-
eyed, spits them out black-
balled. Reagan's curse might be real,
might be what has niggas black-
mailing themselves, dancing in black-
face. Chocolate city red
under the scrutiny. Asphalt red.
When we heard about Black,
there was this silence, awful
silence, like death was odd,
and still when I sing this awful

tale, there is more than a dead black
man in the center; there is a city still
as all the bodies that make '86 real—
a city still, and awful, still and stark red.

Nominated by The Kenyon Review

THE UNFOLLOWING

by LYN HEJINIAN

from LANA TURNER

51

Afloat in a glass-bottom boat, I see into the sea—a miniscule emerald
    memento
That the strongest social bonds are forged by language doesn't nullify
    the power that dancing around the puppet effigies of the men
    in power has
On the solemn face of the glinting belly is a button baby
You have to know how to roll on the horizon
Followers follow, possibles possibulate, coruscations consider, blood
    coagulates
An allegory is a depiction of something that can't be depicted
Mathias Madrid thrusts his fist toward his face in a mirror,
    Millicent Malcolm pets a faithful falcon on a perch, Margaret
    Mason makes fig jam to serve on cold toast with hard cheese
The pyrotechnical expanse, lacking azure, makes do with blatant
    blackness, unspoken light
Winter's cover's curled back by adjectives—whacking winter's roadside
    cover
Stained owls and up over the ill rabbits they fly
Several hours go by but hours are impossible to perceive
I market, am marketed, mark, remark
We walk down a street under windows that let in noise that might
    prompt someone asleep in the room to dream of drummers,

flautists, a man on stilts with a tuba, a sextet of giggling girls
What is it ghosts wonder?

56

It should not be strange to be a woman rewarded
Letters click as they wander, shift as they ascend, their altitudes attain
    autobiography
Next you are like dry steps' passing sound and fall, and then you are
    like sweetened grapefruit
Everything applies in the hyper-patterning that retrospect
    attempts and to which the irreverent response is "How
    splay!"
In the small houses of the children in the house there are always
    complex simplicities and one was a vast pink stuffed
    equine thing called Star
Wet Brahms
Revocation of harm
By moving from window to window and carefully recording at
    each what we see, we . . .
It is time you were told of the time I failed to defend the bull and
    indeed rejoiced in its murder
This is *not* hypocritical!
The statue at its fullest is emptiest of meaning
She speaks to another *not* about sex but about a particular game
    of truth
Sonorousness facilitates the descent of sunny motes from the
    ponderosa
Dancers have fleas—or, shall we say that fleas live on the planet
    of dancers?

62

Into the disordered shortening of a circle comes this little fury,
    this abdicated panic, this dirty Venus, this resemblance
    to nothing we know of the dead
Sky simultaneous bud, cavity contemporaneous slight
And from the tree a ripe peach falls and a puff of dust rises,
    gently circles, drifts, spreads, holds its shape, dissipates,
    and settles under the tree again and on the weeds nearby

Once there was a woman I'll name another day and in her care
    were eight well-matched strong pelicans who flew low
    over the sea in careful configurations that brought her
    aesthetic pleasure and more fish than she or they could
    eat
Life is rife with erasure and time is rich with delay
Immediately the eater spots some defects (bits of meat, scraps
    of green)
No, I did *not* forget the sad vagrant shuffling about in his red
    speckled secrecy and I will *never* do so *again*!
You've been boasting of your cantaloupe pottage, you've provided
    us with thin toast, your glory increases all about you
Hush—ssshh—what is it?
The ancestor wandered toward the horizon, he craved
    recognition, but eons went by and he landed in a circus,
    there being no other work for a man from the gloom of
    origins
Cousins are composite, constructed, compared
Quick, lively, assembled ripples monitor, mosquitoes spill, and
    the children dine on candy
The sky is another point, this time of ambiguous blue
Why didn't I think of that?

71
in memoriam Arkadii Trofimovich Dragomoshchenko
Feb 3 1946-Sept 12, 2012

A grasshopper singing of death laughs long—as if a heavy-
    hearted granny spoke a light word
A shadow scuds over glass, the glass stands still
Insects seethe and they say *that* is the dream of language but
    what is language if not what is threading through the
    veins of an insect's wings
What does it mean to say "now" now, as now surfaces in a gesture,
    as of a person pushing his eyeglasses up toward his
    brow
Our luggage is stacked sky-high, we are wearing twenty layers of
    clothes, every utterance is symphonic
I've never made curtains for these windows, stabbed by the mid-
    morning light

338

I pass with a broom, standing with a hose in my hand and my
    thumb against the nozzle
The loops of time droop, fall slack—and someone steps out of
    those that were his or hers, hers or his, his and hers, his
    and his, hers and hers—is it right, then, that we are left
    to hurtle alone
The girls danced in dead light, the cadavers lay in live light—but
    as for those girls, men with mouths like mare vaginas
    watched them
Every rough rupture demands elasticity of the imagination
The silver river is irreversible but you attentively watch its
    mouth
What you write achieves its independence though you are nimble,
    arrogant, sly and wise.
That is how you spend the day, which is itself a powerful force
    and raises the significant question "How did you get
    here?"
All suffering is in the egg—now suck it out of its shell and spit
    it away

72

Collective longer literature appeals to cloud variants over a
    crowd
See the gang, going to Alabama, tonguing cones, singing waka
    wasa bong
The robust thrush it is, stately as royalty, common as a
    pickpocket at a concert
I will not, I say, rest, I say, rotate
Let's go now to the very next neologism and term it
    fragmentarily
Desperate he was to cry out and couldn't, to say what he knew
    and know it
This takes adults—and very far indeed
The saxophonist breathes, takes a breath, inhales, gasps
Armadillo, yellow shovel, and empty oval
I sprawl across a bed strewn with breadcrumbs, ah ha!
At echo's edge, a rock wall rises, a monument to leisure
The mourner chortles, she's like a clown with sandpaper, at
    sorrow's involuntary humor

Her remarks, his remarks, their remarks, our remarks, my
        remarks, your remarks betray
Oh there is a blading in this gentle bend

Nominated by Lana Turner

HOW SHE REMEMBERS IT

fiction by RICK BASS

from THE IDAHO REVIEW

They left Missoula with a good bit of sun yet in the sky—what would be dusk at any other time of year. The light was at their backs, and the rivers, rather than charging straight down from out of the mountains, now meandered through broader valleys, which were suspended in that summer light, a sun that seemed to show no inclination of moving. Lilly's father had only begun to lose his memory, seemed more distracted than forgetful, then. He had been a drinker, too, once upon a time, though she did not know that in those days. It had been long ago, before she was even born. A hard drinker, one who had gone all the way to rock bottom, good years wasted, her mother would tell her later— but he was better now. Though recently those few memories he did still have—the reduced or compromised roster of them—were leaving. Even small things from the day before, or a week ago.

The pastures were soft and lush, the grass made emerald by May's alternations of thunderstorms and sunlight, and the farmers had not yet made their first cutting of hay. The rivers had cleared up and were running blue, scouring the year's silt from the bottoms, cleaning and scrubbing every stone. From time to time she and her father would see a bald eagle sitting in a cottonwood snag overlooking the river. There were more deer in the fields than cattle—occasionally they'd see a few Black Angus, like smudges of new charcoal amidst the rain-washed green—but mostly just deer, some of them swollen-bellied with the fawns that would be born any day, while others were still round with lactation, and with the fawns already having been dropped, simply not yet visible, still completely in hiding, in those tall grasses—and the

341

bucks with their still-growing antlers velvet-clad, so that they glowed like candelabras when they passed through shafts and slants of that lying-down light. Lilly was twelve, and her father was only fifty-two.

They rode with the windows down, the air still warm but not super-heated now, and in the brief curves of canyons they could detect a cooling that felt exquisite on their bare arms, with so much sun else-where, all around. It was only another four hours to the Paradise Valley, south of Livingston, where her father had friends, though he said if she wanted to get a room before that, they would, or if she wanted to stop and camp, they could do that, too. Lilly said she didn't care, and she didn't—it was enough to just be driving with the windows down, look-ing around, and thinking about things.

Now the tinge of valley light was shifting, the gold and green was becoming infused with purple and blue, and the touch of the air on their arms more delicious yet. Mayflies were hatching out along the river, drifting columns of them rising dense as fog or smoke and bounc-ing off their arms like little needles; and farther on, the larger stoneflies began to hatch, and were soon thudding off the windshield and smear-ing it with a pastel of the greens and yellows of insect blood, which the windshield wiper turned briefly into a slurry before wiping the way clean and clear again.

Nearing Deer Lodge at the beginning of true dusk, somewhere be-tween nine-thirty and ten, they saw the colorful lights of a tiny carnival, one of the portable setups that's able to fit all of its equipment onto a single long flatbed tractor-trailer, with the various parts for the five or six ancient rides so grease-cloaked and oil-blackened, and the hydraulic hoses so leaky and patched together with pipe clamps, that no self-respecting parent would let their child ride. And yet, in the summer, when a carnival suddenly appeared in the midst of such a small town, on a once-vacant lot, and knowing that in only two or three days the carnival would be gone, then what self-respecting parent could say no?

The highway that passed over Deer Lodge was slightly elevated and above the town, so that from their vantage they were looking down on the carnival. The lights of the fair, viewed through the canopy of fully leaved, summer-green cottonwoods—and in particular, the lights of the Ferris wheel, seeming to rise up into, and then somehow rotate through, the foliage—looked like slow-budding, continuous fireworks going off, never quite rising above the canopy. It resembled a secret, private fes-tivity, and they exited as if it had been their planned destination all along.

The carnival was so tiny that once they were on the downtown streets of Deer Lodge, they couldn't even find it at first. The streets were wide and dusty, and they could smell the June scent of the waxy buds of the cottonwoods, just opening. Both sides of the street were lined with the white fluff of cottonwood seeds, like drifts of snow. Up ahead, they could hear the grinding machinery of the fair, the squeak and rattle of the ancient gears, but there was no loudspeaker music, so that the atmosphere was not so much one of frivolity as dutiful, even lugubrious, labor.

Still, it was a fair, and when they rounded the last corner they could see the lights again, a sepulchral glow coming from the popcorn stand, and the rickety yellow iron gates set up all around the vacant city lot on which the carnival had set up shop.

The Ferris wheel had stopped in the time since they had turned off the highway, and there were no other children around, despite darkness only just now descending. They parked beneath one of the big cottonwoods and got out—the sweet scentedness of the buds and new leaves was almost overwhelming, and a strong dry wind was blowing from the west, sending the cottonwood fluff sailing past them—and they passed through the worn turnstile, where there was no ticket taker. They wandered around, looking at the little rides, marveling at the decrepitude of the infrastructure—rides that had been manufactured in the 1940s and '50s, and with puddles of oil already staining the dust of the gravel lot from where the rides had been standing for but a day or two, and with scraps and flanges of steel welded into patches, in places, atop the rest of the oil-darkened machinery, so fatigued now by time and the friction of innumerable revolutions that it seemed the wind itself might be sufficient to snap them off at their base.

A perfect summer run through the country, Lilly thought, would have had the carnival still be open, or the proprietors would have agreed to crank the rides back up one last time for her father. But the rides had closed at ten, and the workers, nearly as dark and oil-stained as the machinery, were smoking their cigarettes, and beginning to disassemble the carnival. The tractor-trailer on which it would all be folded and stacked and strapped down was already being revved up, rumbling and smoking—in no better shape than the rides—and as they went from one ride to the next, asking if each might still be open, the men who were busy with wrenches and sockets shook their heads and spoke to them in Spanish, not unkindly but in a way that let them know the momentum of their world was different from the leisurely pace of her and her father's. In a perfect world, she knew, she and her father would have ridden in the Ferris wheel up above the canopy of the summer cottonwoods, up high enough to look out at the last rim of purple and orange sunlight going down behind the Pintler Mountains, their crests still snowcapped; but in the real world it was darkening down in the dusty little town, and they were just able to buy a cotton candy cone before walking back out to their truck and continuing on their journey. And it was enough, was more than enough, to have the pink cotton candy, and to be driving on, and to simply imagine, rather than really remember, what it would have been like, riding the Ferris wheel around and around, with the whole carnival to themselves. It's been so long now that in Lilly's mind she almost remembers it like that—they were only a few minutes removed from having had that happen—and yet in a way she can't explain or know, it was almost better to not; better to miss, now and again, than to get everything you want, all the time, every time.

They stopped for gas at a Cenex convenience store—all those years later, her father still wouldn't shop at an Exxon, for what they had done at Prince William Sound, not the spill so much as the cover-up—and while he went inside to get a cup of coffee, having decided they would drive on through the night, all the way to the Paradise Valley, Lilly looked out her window at the woman in the car parked next to them.

She was driving an old red Cadillac, the paint so sun-faded as to be approaching more of a salmon color, and the fender wells were rust-gutted from decades of plowing through the salt-slurry of interstate winter slush. It was a soft-top, with a once-white vinyl roof stained greenish-yellow by the tassels and seeds from the maple tree beneath which it must have been parked, with no garage to protect it from the weather—even now, luminous green fragments clung to the chrome rainseams of the windows—and though the woman had not asked Lilly's counsel, Lilly found herself wanting to give her one piece of advice, which was that she should replace her tires, which were not merely balding, but mismatched in size and style. At least one of them was a radial, and worn so thin that the fraying steel wires of the undertread were springing out of the thin rubber. The car was an eyesore, but the tires themselves were an actual affront, and a hazard.

The woman, perhaps in her early fifties, though possibly simply hard-used, and much younger—or, just as possible, much older, and simply preserved, pickled somehow by toxins—had brittle orange-yellow hair and a sleeveless red T-shirt—what Lilly's father called a wife-beater shirt—and a weightlifter's shoulders, though with devastatingly sallow and flabbed-out arms. She wasn't so much fat—not really fat at all—as just loose; as if once, she had been hard, but no longer, and never again—and she was just sitting in her car smoking a cigarette, smoking it down to a nub. She labored at it further a short while, then flicked it out the window in Lilly's direction without even looking, or noticing that Lilly was looking, and then turned away from Lilly to murmur some endearment to her traveling companion, a nasty little rat-colored Chihuahua.

From her lap, she lifted a pink ice cream cone—which must have been her reason for stopping—and held it up for the little dog to eat. He scampered into her lap and began licking at it, fastidiously at first, but then really gnawing at the cone, wolfing it down, and she continued to hold it for him, fascinated and charmed by his nasty appetite, as the ice cream—bubblegum? strawberry?—began to splash and froth around his muzzle. She was still murmuring her adoration to him, fascinated by what she clearly perceived to be his singular skill, when Lilly's father came back out and got in the car.

He barely glanced at her, and as they backed out and then pulled away, the Chihuahua was still attacking the ice cream cone, had both sticky-damp paws up on the woman's chest now, laboring to get down into the cone, and still the woman beheld the little dog as if he was an amazement. And for all Lilly knew, when he had completed that cone, she was going to go in and get him another one. She looked like she had totally lost track of time and space: that stoned as she was, she easily could have remained there all night, slumping a little lower in her seat, settling, seemingly intent upon going nowhere. It was terrifying, and as they continued on through the night, satisfied for having simply gotten off the road briefly and having seen and experienced the fair, if not actually riding any of the rides, Lilly ate her cotton candy leisurely, slumping down in her seat and pretending, for a moment, and with a delicious thrill of horror, that she was that woman in the Cadillac, that that was where her life would or might end up—lonely, alcoholic, brain fried, lost, and needing to feed a nasty little dog ice cream, to have even that friendship.

As they drove, the stars blinked brightly above them—her father had cleaned the windshield again—and Lilly pulled loose stray tendrils of her cotton candy and released them out the window, into the wind, where she imagined birds up from South America finding them and, not knowing they were edible, weaving them into their nests.

345

She made up stories about the woman in the old red car. She had just gotten out of jail after serving twenty years and didn't have a friend in the world, or her husband had just that day been sent to jail for twenty or more years, perhaps her whole family. Or maybe she had just found out that her little dog was going to have to be put down—it had a tumor the size of a grapefruit, or at least a Ping-Pong ball, hidden in its stomach. Maybe the woman had been a great beauty once, in another life, another town, another state, forty or more years ago—back when her car had been new—and maybe, at times, she still believed herself to be. Maybe . . .

"What are you thinking?" her father asked.

"Nothing," she said.

They rode with the music still playing, putting safe and enormous distance between themselves and the woman with the dog. Driving on, peering forward into the night, and thinking about Yellowstone.

When she woke up, they had crossed over the Divide and it was the middle of the night, and they were in the Paradise Valley. They were driving slowly down a rain-slicked winding road, and hail was bouncing off their roof and windshield like marbles. The first thing she saw, and the reason she had awakened, was her father slowing to a stop, with the hail coming down so hard that he couldn't see far enough to continue on, and the roar on the roof so loud that even by shouting they could not make themselves heard or understood. They sat there for a few minutes with the engine running, and the hail streaming all around them, and then, like a fist unclenching, the storm began to release its hold, loosening back into drumming rain, and the road appeared before them again, steaming and hissing in their headlights, and paved with hail three inches deep.

They proceeded carefully, the mist clearing in tatters like smoke from a battlefield, and the road untraveled before them. They crossed the Yellowstone River, which was still running muddy, and which was frothy already with the quick runoff from the storm—green boughs of cottonwoods drifted past crazily, bobbing and pitching, so that Lilly knew the storm must have originated farther upstream, earlier in the evening, the high snowy mountains attracting lightning, like beacons, as soon as the evening first began to cool dramatically—and as they cracked their windows in order to clear the fog from the windshield, the iced-tea, summery scent of hail-crushed mint from along the river-banks was intense, as was that of the shredded green cottonwood leaves and fresh-churned black riverside earth, the loam ripped away by the rushing waters. It was like a stew of fresh scent, and felt as nurturing as any other stew.

The grass was tall along the narrow road, taller than the roof of their car, with bright white horse fences lining either side, and more cotton-woods grew close to the road, so that they formed a canopy above. In these places the road was covered with a mix of hail pebbles and leaves, some of the leaves with their bright green sides up and others with the pale silvery undersides showing. Several times her father had to stop and get out and clear the road of limbs. He dragged them to the side as if pulling a canoe, or dragging a deer he had shot, his breath leaping in fog-clouds from the exertion, and his tracks crisp and precise in the template of new hail.

It began to rain lightly, with a south wind stirring, sending the fallen green leaves skittering across the top of the snow and hail. They turned up a gravel side road and drove past a series of old red barns. Her father seemed surprised to see them, stopped and peered, then gestured to-ward one and said that he and Lilly's mother had slept there once when they first came into this country, but there had been an owl living in the barn, and it had kept them awake most of the night. And farther on, the road came to its end at a trailhead, where there was barely room, in the summer-tall grasses, for the car to turn around, and when they did so, the neatness and solitude of their tracks, revealing them to be the only travelers out and about in such a storm, and in such a world, was profound: as if the terrain and territory of all of the mountains, and all of the valley through which they had driven, was theirs and theirs alone, for that evening, at least. As if they were not exploring lands that had already been explored many times over, but instead territories that were entirely unknown, not yet dreamed or discovered.

The rain was drumming and blowing steadily past them now and Lilly stayed in the car while her father hurriedly set up the tent in the steaming blaze cast by their headlights. The rain appeared to be drift-ing in a curtain only along the foothills because she could see now in the valley slightly below them a few faint and widely scattered lights, farmhouses and ranches spaced far apart, but with their infrequent lights defining nonetheless the shape of the valley and the course of the river. When he finished putting the tent up he unrolled their sleeping bags, and Lilly raced from the car to the tent, crawled into her bag, as warm and dry as she could ever remember feeling, and slept without dreams or recollections of the day.

The green valley was gilded with light when they awoke in the morning. The air was cool and scrubbed clean from the storm and the hail had already melted. Other than the limbs and branches and leaves, there was no clue that the hail had been there in the first place. The sound sleepers in the valley would awaken and look out and think that they had mostly slept through a thunderstorm, and would know nothing of the winter scene they had missed completely: every bit as absent from their minds as if they had seen it, but then had it swept from their memory.

There was a rainbow over the valley and steam rising from the river far below. Lilly turned and looked behind them and was stunned to see the Beartooths right at their feet. She could feel the cold emanating from their glaciers as when one opens a freezer or refrigerator door. It made her laugh out loud to see such immense and jagged mountains rising right before them, and for her to have been standing there with her back to them, unknowing, as she stared out at the sylvan little valley.

She and her father were right at the gates of the mountains—that was what the trailhead was for, leading hunters up into the crags and ice fields.

Lilly kept looking out at the valley, then turning and looking back up at the Beartooths. How could any traveler decide which to choose? She chose both, and stared out at the Paradise Valley for a while, and then at the Beartooths, while her father stowed the sleeping bags and shook the water from the tent fly before spreading it in the back windshield of the car to dry in the morning sun as they drove.

They got in the car and drove down the winding road, away from the mountains and down into the surging fecundity of the valley, puddles splashing beneath them. They drove down to the little guest cabins and local diner along one of the side creeks that fed into the fast, broad Yellowstone. The lodge was really nothing more than a tiny mercantile with a gas pump, and he and her mother—back when they'd been exploring this country, just wandering around, being young—had stayed here some nights, if they had money for a room, in the series of tiny log cottages, painted dark brown, that lined the edges of the rushing, noisy creek.

A garish 1950s-style faux-neon sign, hugely oversized and illuminated by rows of individual brightly painted lightbulbs, had been welded to an immense steel post to hold its colossal weight, the kind of sign one might see outside a lounge advertising itself as the Thunderbird or the Wagon Wheel, but would generally not expect to encounter back in a quiet grove of trees far off the beaten track in south-central Montana.

It pleased her father to see that the sign was still there, by the rushing little creek, and he got out and took a picture of it to show her mother, though he said that to appreciate it fully, one needed to see it at night.

A hand-lettered cardboard sign, hanging on the door, said that the restaurant was closed for the day. As they left, they saw that the backside of the marquis advertised an upcoming outdoor concert the very next night—Martha Scanlan and the Revelators—and it was strange to see how quiet and isolated the hidden little grove was, in contrast to the garish ambition of the sign. Lilly felt badly for Martha Scanlan, whomever she was, and her Revelators. No one would ever find this place, and no one would ever see the spectacular illumination of her name in the colorful lights. A few cows from the pasture across the road, and the horses, on the other side of the creek. At least she would maybe get to eat breakfast in the diner. Lilly could imagine the cigarette smoke, and the dusty display case of Certs breath mints by the ancient cash register. She imagined Martha Scanlan tuning her guitar, beginning to prepare already, days ahead of time, for this bad idea of a concert. A barbecue was advertised to go along with it. Perhaps she was in one of the Dakotas at this very moment, hurrying on toward the lodge in an old Volkswagen bus, imagining a throng awaiting her, and a buzz building, rather than this quiet, secret grove of seven cabins. Perhaps the same storm that had washed over Lilly and her father the night before was now lashing her, out on the prairie somewhere, out in the badlands.

They stopped instead at a KOA along the river, where an elderly couple was just opening their store, still a few minutes before seven. They saw them walking over together to unlock the store, holding hands. There

349

were pink and yellow rosebushes planted out in front of the small log cabin store, already blooming—back home, the roses would not bloom for another week or two—and the storm had torn numerous petals loose, so that they were cast down on the damp pavement like alms. The bushes had surely been planted and tended by the old lady, or perhaps both she and the old man, but they appeared not to notice the spoilage, or if they noticed, not to mind. Their breath rose in clouds as they spoke quietly to one another, and perhaps they simply thought the storm's residue was pretty.

There were no other residents up and about. Perhaps a dozen or more behemoths—*Winnebangos*, her father called them—their silver sides as shiny as salmon, rested back among the old cottonwoods, but not even a generator was stirring, and Lilly imagined that it must have been a pretty rough night for all the old folks, no more able to sleep through the storm than had they been in a giant popcorn popper, and that after the storm had passed through, they must have wandered outside to inspect the damage, hoping for the best: that if the hail had caused any blemishes to their beloved, shining homes, they would not be visible to the larger world, but would be confined to the roofs of the travel homes, unseen by anything but the birds passing overhead.

Lilly and her father gave the old couple a minute or two to get the lights turned on and the cash register warmed up, and then they went inside and bought a breakfast bar each, some dry and unsatisfactory, crumbly little thing. Her father got a coffee while she got an orange juice, and then they were on the road again, driving early, through the greenest part of summer.

It is said that periods of deep emotional stress are sometimes accompanied by an increase in extrasensory perception, and inexplicable, startling connections or recurrences. Lilly believes it—has found it to be true—though she could not begin to guess the reason why this might be so. In a way, it could almost be seen as comforting, to realize that as the fabric and surface of a life begins to fray and disintegrate, and a traveler finds him- or herself in freefall, that there exists beneath the firmament of our relative unawareness the logic and order that is far more connected and interlocked. As if the truth—any deeper truth—can come easily, and quickly, when it needs to. When at long last it absolutely must.

Lilly has never heard, however, if such an increase in ESP, or such taut connectivity, can be linked also to periods of deep contentedness and extraordinary peace. As if there were also an equally ordered world above, to which the endings of one's nerves are more receptive, not due to their being frazzled or stripped bare, but stimulated, nurtured, by—what other word is there for it?—the condition of being loved deeply, and loving in return.

They were just riding, her father and Lilly. She didn't know then that something was wrong with him, and that he wasn't going to get better—though she did know that there was something wonderfully right with her, something gloriously good about the strange way the elements of one's world line up, sometimes—in times of duress, but also maybe during times of greatest ease: they had not traveled five miles before seeing the lady in the faded red Cadillac broken down on the side of the road, her hood elevated like the jaw-sprung maw of a shark awaiting its prey.

Despite the chill of the morning, smoke and steam boiled out from the engine's interior. It was not the simple gray-white steam of radiator boil-over, but was instead a black writhing column of burning oil, old oil. The fire of a two or three thousand dollar repair bill, or maybe no repair bill at all.

The woman with the dog was sitting on the side of the road next to the great ship of a car, like a detached hunter watching the last throes of an animal the hunter has just dispatched, or an old draft animal—aging plow horse, or downed heifer—to which the veterinarian has just administered the final injection.

The dog, which she held clutched in both arms like a teddy bear, appeared to be concerned by the situation, occasionally writhing and struggling, but the woman herself was the picture of reflective equanimity, save for the half-empty bottle of vodka sitting in the gravel beside her, which rested there as might a bottle of water sit beside a dehydrated triathlete pausing between events. She appeared so resigned, so accustomed, to this type of situation that her relaxed demeanor could almost be viewed, Lilly supposed, as a form of confidence.

She thought she understood why her father hesitated—why he was annoyed, even, that on such a perfect morning, there was this complication to their day, this unwelcome challenge or summons to Samaritanhood—but she was surprised by the anger she felt there in the car.

He actually drove on past the woman, not really deliberating—she and her father both knew he was going to stop and turn around, and go back—but instead allowing himself, she thinks now, the brief luxury of believing he could keep going. Of believing he was free to keep on going.

The woman watched him pass but made no gesture, no outreach or call for help other than to make a sour face briefly as she confirmed once again that she understood how the world was—that there was no mercy in it for her, and that people could not be expected to do the right things, could, in fact, be counted upon to do the wrong things—but then she quickly settled back into her I-don't-give-a-fuck beatitude, just sitting there and watching the western skies and holding tightly to the dog.

She was surprised, Lilly could tell, when her father pulled over and, checking for traffic, made the wide loop of a turnaround, and headed back. She was already a little drunk, a little unsteady, as she labored to rise from her cross-legged position, still gripping the dog, and whether her inebriation was the result of new work in that direction already begun that morning, or remnant from some further, more drunken place the previous night, Lilly had no way of knowing or guessing.

Where had she spent the night during the storm, Lilly wondered, *and what had she thought of it? Had she even noticed it?*

Lilly stayed in the car but with her window rolled down while her father got out and walked over to assess the smoking car. Even over the scent of the burning oil, she could smell the woman now—old sweat and salt and above all else stale alcohol—and she heard her ask her father in the predictable growl if he would like a sip. She held the bottle up to him as if it was a vintage of a particularly fine year. As if she had him spotted.

"I was going to go to Yellowstone," the woman said, staggering a bit. The dog was perched in her arms like a sailor in a crow's nest, ready to leap free should she topple, but with the practiced familiarity also of a veteran who had weathered many such tempests. "I wanted to go see the buffalo," she said. She made a small flapping motion with one hand. "Wooves, and all that shit." Danger. Excitement. Now she looked at the dying car, her pride and freedom, her other self. Her better self. "I don't guess you can fix it," she said to Lilly's father.

There was a pay phone back at the KOA. When she and the dog got in the backseat, Lilly turned and smiled at both of them—and hoped that the withering of her face did not betray her revulsion at the stench. The day was warming and not in their favor with her in the car. Her father drove quickly, and they each experimented with the window; it was hard to tell which was more unbearable: to have them

352

rolled down so that the scent molecules were stirred and swirled around, or to keep the windows up, where the odor was contained, and they finally settled on a combination that left each window cracked several inches.

Their passenger was getting all garrulous, even in that short distance, talking about—surprise—an unhappy relationship, a disappointing man, and now Lilly's father was pressing the accelerator so hard that the woman, none too steady to begin with, was pinned against the back-seat, pulling Gs, though still she kept talking, an occasional curse spilling from her lips followed by a surprised look in Lilly's direction—how did this child get here?—and an overwrought apology.

They fairly skidded into the gravel parking lot of the KOA—a plume of white shell-dust, a chalky breath of old limestone, swathed their arrival, and the old couple, who were out tending their roses, looked up with mild curiosity, prepared for some level of disapproval—and Lilly's father got out and opened the door for the woman, who was having trouble with the task. Lilly heard her father offer the woman twenty-five cents for the phone, but the woman declined, insisting with great protest that she had more than enough money for a phone call.

"Is that all you need?" Lilly's father asked. "Are you sure you'll be all right?" The woman now with the Chihuahua under one arm, like a purse, and the bottle in the other hand. The icy breath of the Beartooths—the mountains unobserved by the woman—and the rising lovely warmth of the day. The sound of the river.

"I'll be fine," she slurred. "Right as rain." Now the hostility swooped in over her like a harrier over a marsh, and she all but snarled at Lilly's father. With even a scornful glance in Lilly's direction, she said, "Y'all go on with your little vacation, don't you worry about me at all. I'll be just hunky-dory." The last two words took stupendous effort to pronounce, and she turned and shuffled and wove her way toward the pay phone, stopping now and again as if to ascertain whether it was retreating from her, seeming surprised, now and again, that she had not already reached it.

The old man and woman turned their hoses off and came walking over to see what the problem was.

"She is in a bad relationship," Lilly's father said—the truth, certainly, though also the closest Lilly would ever hear him come to telling a lie. He opened his billfold and handed the old man six twenty-dollar bills—enough for four nights' lodging in one of their cabins, along with hot running water, and some modest amount of groceries, assuming she didn't spend it all on beer. Lilly was surprised—flabbergasted—for they were not in the least bit rich, and it was a huge outlay for them.

"I don't know her," Lilly's father said to the old man and woman, and nothing more. They saw that the woman was not making a phone call—who really would she call and what was there to say?—but was instead only leaning against the phone box, housed in the warmth of the Plexiglas shell that half-encased her, tucked in out of the wind, and Lilly and her father left before she emerged from her reverie, fearing she might hail them, might seek to lay claim with some nebulous, moral obligation, or fearing, perhaps, that they might simply have to witness more humiliation, more desperation.

Lilly for one didn't feel at all bad about leaving her behind. She could stay and hear Martha Scanlan, could go to the barbecue. She might not get to see Yellowstone but she would be close; one never knew, it might work out somehow. And Lilly remained astounded at her father's generosity.

They started back in the direction they had already traveled. They didn't say anything about what had happened and it amazes Lilly now to consider that her father had the restraint and discipline to not try to put too fine a point on what they had seen. She knew—and knows—it would have been well within his rights to look over at Lilly and say even three words, *Don't drink, ever.*

They drove with the windows down, the clean valley winds scouring the new green fields and washing over them, and blasting away the lingering scent of their previous occupant. They drove past her car, which was still smoldering slightly, and then, not much farther down the road, her father got excited and pulled into the grass. At first Lilly had no idea why, thinking—fearing—he had spied another stranded motorist, another pilgrim. But instead he handed her the binoculars from the backseat and pointed out a yellow-headed blackbird not far from the road. The bird was in a clump of cattails in a sunken little wetland, where a few dairy cattle stood hock-deep, and beside which old metal barrels and an abandoned tractor rusted back down into squalor, while just upslope, a dingy mobile home perched so crookedly on an irregular stacking of cinder blocks that it appeared a single gust of wind, or even the wrong movement by one of the inhabitants, could send the trailer sliding down into the black-water pond—two white PVC pipes jutted from the earthen bank above the pond, no doubt overflow for various effluents—but it was the shocking beauty of the bird, with its incredible yellow head and boisterous, exuberant singing, head thrown back and trilling to the blue sky, having survived the storm, which fixed their attention.

"Would you look at that," her father kept exclaiming, handing her the binoculars so that she could see the bird's beauty close-up, and then, moments later, asking for them back, wanting to see it again—then growing more excited again, and passing them back to her, while the bird sang on and on.

A grizzled middle-aged man, probably no older than her father, but much worse for the wear, came out onto the porch, unnerved by their scrutiny, and Lilly began to imagine all the days that might have led him to this place—this downward slide, this destitution, this rendezvous with and embrace of failure.

What would it be like, to be him—the man in the stained T-shirt, porch-staggered and blinking groggily at the bright sunlight? It was only her own victory of being loved deeply that allowed her the luxury of such indulgent imaginings, such frightful considerations of slumber, detachment, escape.

They waved to the man—he did not wave back—and drove on, farther, through a gauntlet of the sleeping and storm-stunned, the unseeing, as if through ruminants standing in a field, awaiting the ax. She saw more pilgrims, some local residents and others tourists like themselves, traveling toward a landscape they had surely heard described as fantastic. They drove past them. Her father had something he wanted to show her, he said, a fantastic land of geysers and bears, ocher cliffs and cascading waterfalls, burbling mud pots and hot springs: a fantastic land, he said, something that she would remember always.

There was only one main road leading to the park, but he seemed tentative, kept looking at side roads as if lost, or unsure whether memories were attached to those stem-roads or not. He was wondering, she thinks now, if there were important or interesting stories at the end of each side road, and maybe he was trying—or bluffing—to remember things about them, even from the main road.

The blackbird had been good. It had been like fresh air through an open window after a long time of stifling air.

There was no way for him to tell her then in words the truth that he had to have been discovering each day: that to be isolate is better than to be numb, if it comes down to a choice. That even forgetting might be all right, eventually, after a long enough time.

She remembers stopping at the stone archway outside the park, so that they could take their picture: him setting the camera up on the hood, pressing the self timer, then running quickly to join her. Huffing, when he got there, having sprinted into the wind, as if into the past. His arm tight around her. How vast our brains must be, she thinks now, to remember even such tiny and essentially useless and fleeting things. How dare anyone sleep through even a moment of it?

Nominated by The Idaho Review, Frank X Gaspar, Philip Levine, Rachel Rose

"TOO MANY PIGEONS TO COUNT AND ONE DOVE"

by MARY SZYBIST

from INCARNADINE (GRAYWOLF PRESS)

Bellagio, Italy

—3:21   The startled ash tree
                alive with them, wings lacing
      through silver-green leaves—jumping

—3:24   from branch to branch
   they rattle the leaves, or make the green leaves
         sound dry—

—3:26   The surprise of a boat horn from below.
          Increasingly voluptuous
fluttering.

—3:28   One just there on the low branch—
          gone before I can breathe or
     describe it.

—3:29   Nothing stays long enough to know.
     How long since we've been inside
         anything together the way

—3:29   these birds are inside
   this tree together, shifting, making it into
          a shivering thing?

—3:30   A churchbell rings once.
             One pigeon flies
      over the top of the tree without skimming

—3:30   the high leaves, another
      flies to the tree below. I cannot find
        a picture of you in my mind

—3:30   to land on. In the overlapping of soft dark
        leaves, wings look
            to be tangled, but

—3:32   I see when they pull apart, one bird far, one
     near, they did not touch. One bird seems caught,
        flapping violently, one

—3:32   becomes still and tilts down—
         I cannot find the dove,
        have not seen it for minutes. One pigeon nips

—3:32   at something on a high branch,
      moves lower (it has taken this long for me to
        understand that they are eating). Two flap

—3:33   their wings without leaving their branches and
           I am tired
        of paying attention. The birds are all the same

—3:33   to me. It's too warm to stay still in the sun, leaning
        over this wood fence to try to get a better look
          into the branches. Why

—3:33   do pigeons gather in this tree
          or that one, why leave one for another
      in this moment or that one, why do I miss you

—3:33   now, but not now,
        my old idea of you, the feeling for you I lost
      and remade so many times until it was

—3:33   something else, as strange as your touch
                        was familiar. Why not look up
        at high white Alps or down at the

—3:33   untrumpeted shadows bronzing the water
                   or wonder why an almost lavender smoke
                hovers over that particular orange villa

—3:33   on the far shoreline or if I am
                        capable of loving you better
               or at all from this distance.

Nominated by Andrea Hollander, Rebecca McClanahan

MYSTERIES OF THOREAU, UNSOLVED

by REBECCA SOLNIT

from ORION

There is one writer in all literature whose laundry arrangements have been excoriated again and again, and it is not Virginia Woolf, who almost certainly never did her own washing, or James Baldwin, or the rest of the global pantheon. The laundry of the poets remains a closed topic, from the tubercular John Keats (blood-spotted handkerchiefs) to Pablo Neruda (lots of rumpled sheets). Only Henry David Thoreau has been tried in the popular imagination and found wanting for his cleaning arrangements, though the true nature of those arrangements are not so clear.

I got prodded into taking an interest in the laundry of the author of "Civil Disobedience" and "A Few Words in Defense of John Brown" in the course of an unwise exchange. Let me begin again by saying that I actually like Facebook, on which this particular morning I had sent birthday wishes to my Cuban translator and disseminated a booklet about debt resistance. I signed up for Facebook in 2007 to try to keep track of what young Burmese exiles were doing in response to the uprising in that country, and so I use it with fewer blushes than a lot of my friends—and perhaps even my "friends," since Facebook has provided me with a few thousand souls in that incoherent category.

And really, this is an essay about categories, which I have found such leaky vessels all my life: everything you can say about a category of people—immigrant taxi drivers, say, or nuns—has its exceptions, and so the category obscures more than it explains, though it does let people tidy up the complicated world into something simpler. I knew a Franciscan nun who started the great era of civil-disobedience actions against nuclear weapons at the Nevada Test Site that were to reshape my life so profoundly and lead to the largest mass arrests in American history, but remind me someday to tell you about the crackhead nun on the lam who framed her sex partner as a rapist and car thief. A private eye I know exonerated him, as I intend to do with Thoreau, uncle if not father of civil disobedience, over the question of the laundry.

It's because I bridle at so many categories that I objected to an acquaintance's sweeping generalization on Facebook that Americans don't care about prisoners. Now, more than 2 million of us *are* prisoners in this country, and many millions more are the family members of those in prison or are in the category of poor nonwhite people most often imprisoned, and all these people probably aren't indifferent. In my mild response I mentioned a host of organizations like the Center for Constitutional Rights, which has done a great deal for the prisoners in Guantánamo. I could've mentioned my friend Scott who was a pro-bono lawyer for the Angola Three for a decade or so, or my friend Melody, a criminal defense investigator who did quite a lot for people on death row. They are a minority, but they count.

Having ignored the warning signs of someone looking for people to condemn, I recklessly kept typing: "We were the nation of Thoreau and John Brown and the Concord Female Anti-Slavery Society when we were also the nation of slaveowners—and slaves." Which was a way of reiterating my sense that the opposite is also true of almost anything you can say about this vast messy empire of everybody from everywhere that pretends to be a coherent country, this place that is swamps and skyscrapers and mobile homes and Pueblo people in fourteenth-century villages on the Rio Grande. And 2.5 million prisoners. Truth for me has always come in tints and shades and spectrums and never in black and white, and America is a category so big as to be useless, unless you're talking about the government.

The poster replied: "And the nation of Thoreau's sister who came every week to take his dirty laundry." This was apparently supposed to mean that Thoreau was not a noble idealist but a man who let women do the dirty work, even though it had nothing to do with whether or not Thoreau or other Americans cared about prisoners, which is what we were supposed to be talking about. Or maybe it suggested that Thoreau's sister was imprisoned by gender roles and housework. It was also meant to imply that I worshipped false gods. I have heard other versions of this complaint about Thoreau. Quite a lot of people think that Thoreau was pretending to be a hermit in his cabin on Walden Pond while cheating by going home and visiting people and eating in town and otherwise being convivial and enjoying himself and benefiting from civilization. They think he is a hypocrite.

They mistake him for John Muir, who went alone deep into something that actually resembled the modern idea of wilderness (although it was, of course, indigenous homeland in which Muir alternately patronized and ignored the still-present Native Americans). Then, after his first, second, and several more summers in the Sierra, Muir married well and eventually lived in a grand three-story house in Martinez, California, and ran his father-in-law's big orchard business that paid for it all. Even John Muir is difficult to categorize, since he was gregarious enough to cofound the Sierra Club and complicated enough to labor as a lumberjack and sheepherder in the mountains he eventually wished to protect from logging and grazing. None of us is pure, and purity is a dreary pursuit best left to Puritans.

The tiny, well-built cabin at Walden was a laboratory for a prankish investigation of work, money, time, and space by our nation's or empire's trickster-in-chief, as well as a quiet place to write. During his two years there, Thoreau was never far from town, and he was not retreating from anything. He was advancing toward other things. The woods he roamed, before, during, and after his time in the famous shack, contained evidence of Indians; locals doing the various things people do in woods, including gathering wood and hunting; and escaped slaves on the long road north to Canada and freedom. He traveled with some of these slaves, guided them a little, and they guided him in other ways.

Slavery was very much on his mind during the time he lived at Walden Pond. His mother and sisters' organization, the Concord Female Anti-Slavery Society, met at least once in his cabin (for a celebration of the anniversary of the liberation of slaves in the Indies, shortly after he himself spent a night as a prisoner). This is how *not* a recluse he was: there were meetings in that tiny cabin that engaged with the laws of the nation and the status of strangers far away, and he also went to jail during that time, because he was fiercely opposed to the territorial war against Mexico and to slavery. The threads of empathy and obligation and idealism spun out from those people and those meetings. The Concord abolitionists chose to care about people they had never met; they chose to pit themselves against the most horrific injustices and established laws of their society; and they did it at a time when they were a small minority and the end of slavery was hardly visible on the horizon.

And the laundry? I did a quick online search and found a long parade of people who pretended to care who did Thoreau's laundry as a way of not having to care about Thoreau. They thought of Thoreau as a balloon and the laundry was their pin. Andrew Boynton in *Forbes* magazine observed in 2007 that his mother did his laundry; a cheesy website noted that he "took his dirty laundry home to mom!"; in 1983, a ponderous gentleman named Joseph Moldenhauer got in early on the accusation that he "brought his mother his dirty laundry"; a blogger complained that "he had someone else do his laundry"; another writer referred offhandedly to the "women who did his laundry."

A writer on an environmental website recently complained, "While philosophizing about self-sufficiency in his solitary shack, he would drop off his laundry at his mother's place back in town"; even Garrison Keillor got involved in the laundry question—"He wrote elegantly about independence and forgot to thank his mom for doing his laundry"; there's even a collection of short stories called *Thoreau's Laundry,* as well as a website that sells a Thoreau laundry bag. Search engines having a genius for incoherent categories, I also learned that Thoreau, New Mexico, a pleasant little town on Interstate 40, has four laundromats.

The standard allegation—the reader will note—is that Thoreau's mother, Cynthia Dunbar Thoreau, did his washing, not his sister, and no one suggests that she had to fetch it first. Besides which, he had two sisters, Sophia and Helen. The sneering follow-up message I got from the person who claimed that Thoreau was a man whose sister did his washing made me feel crummy for a day or so during an otherwise ebullient period of being around people that I love and who love me back. I composed various ripostes in my head. Having grown up with parents who believed deeply in the importance of being right and the merit of facts, I usually have to calm down and back up to realize that there is no such thing as winning an argument in this kind of situation, only escalating. Facebook's verb "friend" is annoying, but its corollary, "unfriend," is occasionally useful.

I decided against unfriending but for simply avoiding the person into whose unfriendly fire I'd strayed. The thing to do was to seek out more convivial company. I had dinner the next night with my friend Thomas, whom I've known almost twenty years and at whose wedding I was best man. A half-Burmese Londoner, he's only been in this hemisphere about five years, and he told me that reading *Walden* recently helped reconcile him to American individualism by exhibiting it as something energetic and eccentric as well as assertive. We began to correspond about Thoreau, and that dialogue deepened what was already a great friendship. I know two actual Thoreau scholars, one I met in the 1990s in Reno, and another who sought me out via Facebook (before the incident in question) and with whom I'd corresponded a little. I turned to them for more informed opinions on the washing. I wasn't going to argue about it; but I did want to know the truth for my own satisfaction.

The first acquaintance, Professor Michael Branch at the University of Nevada, Reno, was tired of hearing about the laundry: "The problem with explaining how much work the guy did is that you end up defending the wrong cause. I've stepped into this bear trap before." He listed some of the kinds of labor the shaggy Transcendentalist performed, including teaching, surveying, and running his family's pencil factory. But, he cautioned, "once you make this case, you've accidentally blessed the idea that paying attention to the world, studying botany, and writing a shitload of amazing prose isn't real work. Better to just say he never did a damned thing except write the century's best book and leave it at that. Lazy fucker."

Do we care who did the chores in any other creative household on earth? Did Dante ever take out the slops? Do we love housework that much? Or do we hate it that much? This fixation on the laundry is related to the larger question of whether artists should be good people as well as good artists, and probably the short answer is that everyone should be a good person, but a lot of artists were only good artists (and quite a lot more were only bad artists). Whether or not they were good people, the good artists gave us something. Pablo Picasso was sometimes not very nice to his lady friends, but he could paint. I was friends with the artist and filmmaker Bruce Conner for a quarter century, and his unreasonable insistence on perfection made his work brilliant and his company exacting and sometimes terrifying.

It wasn't as though if he hadn't made those seminal films and assemblages he would've been an uncomplicated good guy; it's not as though he was giving to art what he should have given to life; he was putting out what he had, and it was a huge and lasting gift on this impure earth, even if it came from an imperfect man. Thoreau was a moralist, a person who wrote about what we should do, whether how to walk or how to fight the government about slavery, and a moralist holds himself up to a higher standard: does he, so to speak, walk his talk? Or so moralists are always tested, but their premises are right or not independent of whether or not they live up to them. Martin Luther King Jr. was right about racism and injustice whether or not he led a blameless life. Digging into his dirty laundry doesn't undo those realities, though the FBI tried to blackmail and undermine him that way.

The second scholar I wrote to was also a Michael, Michael Sims, who is working on a book about the young Thoreau, and he was well primed for the question. "Thoreau did visit the village almost every day, and see his parents, and do chores around the house for them," he wrote. "While he was at Walden, they were in a house he helped build the year before he moved to the cabin—he and his father mainly—so he had considerable goodwill in the bank. During his entire adult life, he paid rent while at his parents' boarding house, and paid it faithfully, with records sometimes kept on the backs of poems or other writings. He worked in the garden, helped keep the house in good repair, provided foods from his own garden, and so on.

"People did drop by the cabin to bring him food sometimes, but people dropped by each other's houses with food all the time. It was the most common gift. He brought other people food, especially melons. (He was legendary for his talent in raising a vast array of melons.) I don't know if I have an actual record of the family doing his laundry, but I'll check as I go through some of that over the next month. But I would bet they did sometimes do his laundry. He was quite emotionally dependent upon his family, especially his mother, but he also contributed constantly. When his brother died young, Henry helped take up the slack in financial help. When his father died, Henry became not only the man of the house but the major force in the pencil business (which he had already almost revolutionized with his analysis of better ways to make pencils). So I think what I'm trying to say is that even at Walden he was very much a part of the family in every way."

After looking into the laundry question, I opened *Walden* again and examined the section where he does his accounts, which, as the historian Richard White points out, were a sort of parody of nineteenth-century preoccupations with efficiency and profitability, with the pettiness of keeping score and the souls of bookkeepers. He mentions "washing and mending, which for the most part were done out of the house, and their bills have not yet been received." It's not clear if that's out of his own cabin or his mother's house, during the Walden era, but it suggests that maybe his washing was done by strangers in a commercial transaction, or that maybe he thought that the question of who did the laundry was amusing and made an indecipherable joke about a bill his family wasn't really going to send.

He was, after all, the man who warned us against enterprises that required new clothes, often wore shabby ones, and was certainly not very concerned about having clean ones. He never married and did little to make work for women and did quite a bit of dirty work himself, including shoveling manure—of which he wrote, "Great thoughts hallow any labor. To-day I earned seventy five cents heaving manure out of a pen, and made a good bargain of it." He worked quite hard, often for his sisters' benefit, though he also played around with the idea of work, appointing himself inspector of snowstorms and proposing that his employment could be watching the seasons, which he did with such precision, describing what bloomed when and which bird species arrived on what date in his corner of Massachusetts, that his journals have been used to chart climate change in the present. We call that work, which was also so clearly a pleasure for him, science.

Intermittently, throughout his adult life, he was also struggling with tuberculosis, the disease that killed his older sister, Helen, in 1849 and sometimes sapped his strength long before it killed him in 1862. At the time of his death, he was lying in bed downstairs in a parlor with his younger sister Sophia at his side. Though we talk so much about the twenty-six months he dwelt at Walden Pond, he spent most of the rest of the forty-five years of his life at home with his family, as an intimate and essential part of what appears to have been an exceptionally loving group.

Labor was divided up by gender in those days, but it's hard to argue that women always had the worst of it in an era when men did the heavy work on farms and often the dirtiest and most physically demanding work around the house (in those days of outhouses, wood chopping, shoveling ashes and coal, handling horses and livestock, butchering, water pumping, and other largely bygone chores). Everyone worked around the home, until they became so affluent no one worked beyond the symbolic femininity of needlework. In between those two poles was a plethora of families who had hired help with the housework. I don't think women were particularly subjugated by domestic work in the centuries before housewives in the modern sense existed, though gender roles themselves deprived them of agency, voice, and rights. Thoreau's sisters resisted and maybe overcame them without their brother's aid.

Thoreau's mother ran a boardinghouse and yet another writer on Thoreau, Robert Sullivan, points out that, like a lot of nineteenth-century households, they had help—and that the Transcendentalists were uncomfortable with the hierarchy of servants and employers (Emerson tried having the maid sit at the dinner table with the family, but the cook refused to do so). Perhaps Thoreau, his mother, and his sisters all had their washing done by the same servant, or servants, who Sullivan suggests were likely to be recent Irish immigrants. Ireland's Catholics, fleeing the potato famine and British brutality, had started to arrive in the 1840s, and a torrent of desperate Irish would pour into this country for several decades; I am descended from some of them, and my orphaned Irish-American grandmother used to attribute her excellent figure to doing the washing (by hand, on a washboard) for the family that raised her. In his journal entry for June 9, 1853, Thoreau expresses sympathy for an Irish maid named Mary who told him she quit her position on a dairy farm because she was supposed to do the washing for twenty-two people, including ten men with two pairs of dirty overalls apiece.

The project of liberation is neverending, most urgent at its most literal but increasingly complex as it becomes metaphysical. Only free people can care about slaves or prisoners and do something about slavery and prisons, which is why the project of liberating yourself is not necessarily selfish (as long as you don't go down that endless solitary path marked After I'm Perfect I'll Do Something for Others, but stay on the boulevard marked My Freedom Is for Your Liberation Which I Must Also Attend to Now). On October 13, 2012, a few weeks after the unpleasant interchange about prisoners and laundry, I went to San Quentin State Prison to hear the prisoners read.

San Quentin was even more prisonlike than I'd imagined, with a patchwork of intimidating architectural styles: some crenelations like a medieval fortress, guard towers, sheer walls, razor-wire coils, warning signs, and entrance via steel gates that actually did slam shut with an echoing clang. We, the mostly female, mostly white audience for the reading, had been sent a long list of colors we were not allowed to wear: blue of course, but so many other colors that finally only black and purple and pink and patterns seemed safe for sure, so we looked as though we were going to a funeral or a punk concert. The prisoners were wearing various shades of blue, work boots or running shoes, and some jewelry. One had a Santa beard, one had dreadlocks, and the Latino murderer had a sharp pompadour and thick mustache. Only one of them looked young.

They read in the Catholic chapel, which was cold, low slung, made of cinder blocks, with a pure white crucified Jesus on the wall and grillwork visible through the fake stained glass. A lot of the stories were moving; some were unsettling, particularly the ones in which old rages and convoluted senses of causality (as evidenced by the passive tense used to describe killing a friend) lived on and women seemed more like possessions than fellow human beings. The category of maximum-security prisoner did not describe the range of these men. I was most touched by Troy Williams's straightforward account of weeping when he told his daughter, via telephone, that his parole had been denied. He was fearful of being seen to cry in a tough place like prison, but someone reached out to him, and he found a little bit more humanity than he expected.

"What kind of a prison have I put my child in?" he asked himself, expanding the idea of prison to include the way she was tied to his fate and locked out of his life. My friend Moriah had brought me to the event; she had been the year before and was moved not just by what she heard but by the fact that the small cluster of strangers from outside was about the most significant audience these guys were going to get. She had heard about it because her daughter was in school with a girl who lived in the same household as Zoe Mullery, the creative writing teacher who had for six years or more come once a week to work with these men. One of the men wrote in his biography in the handout we all received, "I picked up a book and was able to depart the brutal confines of the penitentiary, as well as the margins of my depressed mind. Reading became an escape without my actually escaping."

Zoe later told me that she had once looked at the history of the word *free* and it might interest me. According to the *Oxford English Dictionary*, *free* has the same Indo-European root as the Sanscrit word *priya*, which means "beloved" or "dear." If you think of etymology as a family tree, the dictionary says that most descendants of that ancient ancestor describe affection, and only the Germanic and Celtic branches describe liberty. The scholars say that the word may hark back to an era when a household consisted of the free people who were members of the extended family and the unfree ones who were slaves and servants. Family members had more rights than slaves and servants, so even though "free" in the United States is often seen as meaning one who has no ties, it was once the other way around. Which is another way of saying that freedom has less to do with that Lynyrd Skynyrd sense of the word (in which we don't care about prisoners or anyone else) and more to do with the idea of agency.

It doesn't actually matter who did Thoreau's washing, though I remained curious to see if we knew who that might be. We don't. But we do know quite a lot about the Thoreau family's values. The second Thoreau scholar, Michael Sims, had sent me an excellent essay by Sandra Harbert Petrulionis about the Concord Female Anti-Slavery Society that the writer's mother and sisters belonged to, along with Mrs. Emerson, and after the laundry issue was raised on Facebook, I read it again. "The influence they brought to bear on some of America's most noted antislavery speakers and writers had a pronounced and far-reaching impact," Petrulionis declares. "Thanks directly to eight women, six of whom lived in his home, Henry Thoreau had long been exposed to the most radical antislavery positions during his formative young-adult years."

The women seemed to find a kind of liberation for themselves in this movement for the liberation of others; they were able to act independently of husbands and fathers, to take public stands, to become political beings in a new way. The women's suffrage movement, the first feminist movement, grew directly out of the abolition movement: they went to liberate someone else and found that they too were not free. Thoreau's mother and sisters were more radical than he was initially; they even publicly supported the "disunion" position that would have had the North secede from the slave South long before the South actually seceded from the North. The Thoreau women were also participants in the Underground Railroad, and Henry David sometimes walked or drove the fugitives northward toward freedom. These Americans cared about prisoners enough to risk their own lives and liberty on their behalf.

A young abolitionist named Daniel Conway describes one such encounter, on July 27, 1853, thus: "In the morning I found the Thoreaus agitated by the arrival of a colored fugitive from Virginia, who had come to their door at daybreak. Thoreau took me to a room where his excellent sister, Sophia, was ministering to the fugitive. . . . I observed the tender and lowly devotion of Thoreau to the African. He now and then drew near to the trembling man, and with a cheerful voice bade him feel at home, and have no fear that any power should again wrong him. The whole day he mounted guard over the fugitive, for it was a slave-hunting time. But the guard had no weapon, and probably there was no such thing in the house. The next day the fugitive was got off to Canada, and I enjoyed my first walk with Thoreau."

In this vignette, brother and sister are collaborators in a project of liberation, and by this time, more than fifteen years after the founding of the Concord Female Anti-Slavery Society, Thoreau was wholeheart-edly recruited to the cause. A year later Thoreau wrote, "I endeavor in vain to observe Nature—my thoughts involuntarily go plotting against the state—I trust that all just men will conspire." Many just women already had. And so in my reply to Sims, I said, "Reading that superb piece you sent a month or so ago deepened my sense that his abolition-ist mother and sisters were political powerhouses in whose wake he swam. My position now is that the Thoreau women took in the filthy laundry of the whole nation, stained with slavery, and pressured Tho-reau and Emerson to hang it out in public, as they obediently did."

This is the washing that really mattered in Concord in the 1840s, the washing that affected not only the prisoners of slavery, but the fate of a nation and the literature of the century. Thoreau's writing helped twentieth-century liberators—Gandhi and King the most famous among them—chart their courses; he helps us chart our own as well, while also helping us measure climate change and giving us the plea-sures of his incomparable prose. His cabin at Walden was ten by fifteen feet, less than twice the size of a solitary-confinement cell at California's supermax Pelican Bay State Prison, though being confined to a space and retiring to it whenever you wish are far more different than night and day. In a sense Thoreau is still at work, and so are his sisters, or at least the fruit of Helen and Sophia Thoreau's work to end slavery is still with us, along with their brother's liberatory writings. Though there are other kinds of slavery still waiting to be ended, including much of what happens in our modern prison system.

Continuing my reply to Sims, I wrote, "Thoreau's relationship to his sisters reminds me a little of mine to my brother, who is a great activist and a great carpenter and builder, a support and ally to me in every possible way, and someone for whom I often cook and sometimes assist in other practical ways. (Of course in this version the sister is the so-cially inept writer person and the brother the more engaged activist who leads his sibling into the fray.)"

My brother David actually built me a home at one point. In that home in which he sometimes stayed and often ate (and usually did the dishes after he ate), we held political meetings as well as family gather-ings. In it, as before and since, I helped him with activist publications, because for almost all our adult life he has been a political organizer who seems to end up volunteering for publications. We've been through three books of his that way, and each of these projects for which I am an informal editor has drawn me deeper into political engagement.

David cares about prisoners and has worked on their behalf many times, most recently Bradley Manning. Sometimes I've joined him. He has often been arrested, spent time in jails from Georgia to Ontario, and is named after our grandfather, who was named after Thomas Davis, the Irish revolutionary and poet.

He has provided astute critiques of my writing and ideas, and without him I might be lost in the clouds, stuck in an ivory tower, or at least less often called into the streets. Though I am the writer, he taught me a word when we were building the home that was mine for a while. The word is *sister*, which is a verb in the construction industry, as in "to sister a beam." This means to set another plank alongside a beam and fasten the two together to create a stronger structure. It is the most fundamental image of the kind of relationship Thoreau had with his sisters and I with my brother: we reinforce each other.

It is what we are here to do, and to raise melons and build houses and write books and to free anyone who might possibly need freeing, including ourselves and the meanings of our lives in all their uncategorizable complexity. By this I don't mean freedom only in that sense that many Americans sometimes intend it, the sense in which we are free from each other. I mean freed to be with each other and to strengthen each other, as only free people can.

Nominated by Orion, Jane Hirshfield

THE STREETLAMP ABOVE ME DARKENS

by TARFIA FAIZULLAH

from NEW ENGLAND REVIEW

for this, I am grateful. This elegy
doesn't want a handful of puffed rice

tossed with mustard oil and chopped chilies,
but wants to understand why a firefly

flickers off then on, wants another throatful
or three of whiskey. This elegy is trying

hard to understand how we all become
corpses, but I'm trying to understand

permanence, because this elegy wants
to be a streetlamp dying as suddenly as

a child who, in death, remains a child.
Somewhere, there is a man meant for me,

or maybe he is meant merely to fall
asleep beside me. Across two oceans, there

is a world in which I thought I could live
without grief. There, I watched the hands

of a leper reach with hands made of lace
towards a woman who leaned into him.

There, I fingered bolts of satin I never
meant to buy. There, no one said her name.

How to look down into the abyss without
leaning forward? How to gather the morning's

flustered shadows into a river? To forget
my sister was ever born? Tonight, I will

watch a man I could have loved walk past,
hefting another woman's child. He won't

look at me. I won't have wanted him to.
This elegy wonders why it's so hard

to say, *I always miss you. Wait,* she might
have said. *But didn't you want your palms*

to be coated in mustard oil? Did you really
want to forget the damp scent of my grave?

Nominated by Dick Allen, Philip Dacey

DAYS OF BEING MILD

fiction by XUAN JULIANA WANG

from PLOUGHSHARES

It takes real skill to speed down the packed streets of Zhongguancun, but the singer with the mohawk is handling it like a pro. His asymmetrical spikes are poking the roof of his dad's sedan, so he's compensating by tilting his head slightly to the left.

We are meeting with a new band to talk about possibly shooting their music video. Sara is here to deal with the script details and she is leaning all the way forward to talk concept with the two guys up front. Sara's long blond hair is wavy and tumbling down her skinny back and Benji's got his fingers in her curls. His other hand is pinching a cigarette, arm out the window.

I'm staring at the women rhythmically patting their babies while selling counterfeit receipts, and I can hear taxi drivers asking about each other's families as their cars slide back and forth. Teenage part-timers are throwing advertisements in the air like confetti and somehow we're managing not to kill anyone.

The band's name is Brass Donkey and they're blasting their music from the sedan's tiny speakers. They sound a lot like Jump In On Box, the all-girl orbit-pop band that just got signed to Modern Sky Records. I'm digging the sound but nobody asks for my opinion.

We finally make our way to the singer Dao's apartment and more band members show up. He sits us down on the couch, and even though it's only noon, he offers us Jack Daniels and Lucky Strikes. There are piles of discs everywhere and stacks of DVD players that the bootleg DVDs keep breaking.

"So this video, we want it to really stand out. We're really into the Talking Heads right now, you know them? Talking Heads?"

The drummer turns on the TV and David Byrne appears, jerking his face back and forth to the beat of the music. All the band members are talking to us at once.

"We're no wave Funstrumental, but we sound Brit Pop."

"For this video we want something perversely sexual, like really obscene and perverse."

They look expectantly at Benji and Sara.

"Yeah, like really fucking sick, you know?"

"The more perverted the better!"

"Then we want this video to be blasting in the background during our big winter performance at Star Live, on the big monitors."

I smoke their cigarettes. "Aren't you afraid of the police coming in and shutting it down?"

"That would be spec-fuckin-tacular! It would be great to be shut down, even better if you could get us banned. Actually, let's make that a goal," said the singer, sinking back into his chair, turning up the music.

I watch Sara look down at her notes and then look up at me. I shrug whatever, and Benji stands up to leave and shakes everybody's hand. Then we're out of there. I can't wait to tell JJ and Ah Ming; they'd definitely get a kick out of this story.

As for the video, we'll do it if we feel like it, see how it goes.

We are what the people called *Bei Piao*—a term coined to describe the twenty-somethings who drift aimlessly to the northern capital, a phenomenal tumble of new faces to Beijing. We are the generation who awoke to consciousness listening to rock and roll, and who fed ourselves milk, McDonalds, and box sets of *Friends*. We are not our parents, with their loveless marriages and party-assigned jobs, and we are out to prove it.

We come with uncertain dreams, but our goal is to burn white hot, to prove that the Chinese, too, can be decadent and reckless. We are not good at math or saving money, but we are very good at being young. We are modern-day May Fourth–era superstars, only now we have Macbooks. We've read Kerouac in translation. We are marginally employed and falling behind on our filial piety payments, but we are cool. Who was going to tell us otherwise?

Five of us live in part of a reconverted pencil factory outside the fourth ring, smack in the middle of the 798 art district. We call our place The Fishtank, and it covers four hundred square meters of brick and semiexposed wall insulation. Before it became our home, it used to function as the women's showers for the factory workers. As a result, it is cheap and it is damp. The real Beijing, with its post-Olympic sky-scrapers, stadiums, and miles of shopping malls, rests comfortably in the distance, where we can glance fondly at the glow of lights while eating lamb sticks.

The roommates include JJ, the tall, dark-skinned half-Nigerian from Guangzhou, who is loud-mouthed and full of swagger. He keeps his head shaved, favors monochromatic denim ensembles, and is either drinking or playing with his own band Frisky Me Tender. The resident cinema-tographer is Benji, who is so handsome waitresses burst into fits of gig-gles when taking his orders. He is working on a series of migrant workers whom he dresses in designer labels. Benji, whose Chinese name we've forgotten, was renamed by his white girlfriend, Sara, a former research scholar who has since found it impossible to leave. Sara, with her green eyes and blond hair, spoke with an authentic marbled Northeastern Chi-nese accent, and somewhere along the line, she became one of us as well. There is Ah Ming from Xiamen, the photographer who shoots product photos of new consumer electronics, as well as an ever-rotating roster of models from Russia and Hong Kong. Some of them keep us company when they are sufficiently drunk. Then there's me and I'm short like Ah Ming, but based on appearances, sometimes I can't help but feel as though someone accidentally photographed me into this picture.

I'm a so-called producer, and what that really means is just that I have more money than the rest of them. Actually my dad does. My family's from Chong Qing, where my dad made a fortune on real estate and has more money than he can spend. Since I dropped out of Beijing Film Academy over a year ago, I've been hiding from my dad and am now living off the money I got from selling the BMW he gave me. I said I'd try to make it as a filmmaker, but I'm low on talent. Lately, I've been watching a lot of porn.

Our apartment is just around the corner from our new favorite bar See If, and that's where Benji, Sara, and I go after our meeting. See If is three stories of homemade wood furniture and Plexiglass floors. The drinks are named "if only," "if apart," "if together," "if no if," and so on. The alcohol is supposed to complement your mood, but it basically all tastes the same. JJ and Ah Ming and a bunch of part-time male models are all there with guitars strapped on. JJ is walking around suggestively strumming everyone's guitars.

Benji says to the group, "Hey, you have to hear the story about our meeting with the Brass Donkey guys. I think they want to get publicly flogged."

I get passed a pipe and I smoke something that makes me feel vaguely like I'm in trouble. I concentrate on looking at my friends and feel swell again.

JJ cuts in, "Dude, today a cab driver point-blank asked me how big my dick was." We listen to that story instead. Being a half-black Chinese guy, JJ is used to attention.

With the 2008 Olympics finally behind us, Beijing is getting its loud, open-mouthed, wise-cracking character back. The cops stopped checking identity papers on the street and all of us Bei Piao let out a collective sigh of relief. We were getting back to life as usual.

But then this thing happened. Last week I received an e-mail from my father. He was going to give me, his only son, the opportunity to make my own fortune. He purchased a dozen oilrigs in Louisiana and has hired an agency to get the L-1 investment visa ready for me to move there and manage it. It has been decreed that my piece of shit ass is going to move to the U.S. and make use of itself. In his mind, what was I doing drifting around in Beijing with hippies when there's an oil field in Louisiana with my name on it?

We test shoot the video on our roof, and even though it's a Wednesday, I make a few calls to modeling agencies and within the hour, half a dozen models are strutting across our tiles, wearing nipples and fishnets. Sara's the one posing them in obscene variations, asking them to take their clothes off. She can get away with almost anything because she's a white girl who speaks Chinese and everybody likes her. Benji's doing the actual filming while Ah Ming takes stills. Sometimes I load some film, but mostly I just drink beer and enjoy the atmosphere.

Just as the sun is whimpering its way down the side of the sky, the last girl shows up. She is a model from Hong Kong who renamed herself Zi Guang, The Light. She has a good face but like most girls who assume they deserve nice things, she is extremely unfriendly. Then, just as everyone is packing up to go, she emerges from the apartment naked and wrapped in Ah Ming's blue bed sheet. Her waist-length black hair licks at her face, her arms gather the bouquet of fabric against her small breasts, and the sheet clings to the silhouette of her long legs. Among our coffee cups and cigarettes, the rest of us hardly notice her, smile at her but not much more.

Not Ah Ming. He picks up his medium-format lens, ties his hair into a ponytail, and follows her onto the tile roof like a puppy.

He takes her hand, and helps ease her bare feet onto the chimney. With the sheet dripping down from her, she looks ten feet tall and glorious. She lowers the sheet and ties it around her waist, covers herself with her hair and looks away, purring like a cat, in a halfhearted bargain for attention.

So there's Ah Ming, between whose lips escapes a "My God," and he fumbles with filters and straps to get the perfect photo of her. The loose tiles creak underneath his feet.

"You're beautiful, too beautiful," he says. "You should father my children or marry me, whatever comes first."

Sara whispers to me, "I think this is going to be trouble." And I know just as well as everyone else that Ah Ming's falling for this girl, and it isn't going to be pretty.

If we could grant Ah Ming one wish, he'd probably say he'd wish to marry a tall girl. A very tall, very hot, girl. He claims that he wants to give his children a fighting chance. Can we really blame him though? Even if he only claimed to be of average male size, he's probably only 5 foot 3—in the morning, after he's taken a big breath and held it. Most of the time, the poor guy has to buy shoes in the children's department.

But all that is bullshit; it's just for show. Ah Ming, perpetually heartbroken Ah Ming, is the only one of us who can still memorize Tang Dynasty poetry, is always the first to notice if sorrow crosses any of our faces. I guess deep down we could all see that his wants were so simple—to be loved, respected, and not tossed away, for his meager holdings on this earth. It was all the wrong in him that made him so special, and we were all protective of him, and ready to hurt for him as we would hurt for no one else.

After the shoot is over, we go across town to D-22 to hear JJ's band perform. D-22 is the first underground punk rock club literally screamed into existence by foreign exchange students in the university district. JJ is opening for Car Sick Cars, whose hit song is a five-minute repetitive screaming of the words "Zhong Nan Hai," which is both the Beijing capitol building and the most popular brand of cigarettes among locals. Foreigners love it, and the audience throws cigarettes onto the stage like projectile missiles.

When JJ and his band hit the stage, it's obvious that he's wasted. He tips the mike stand over as he gyrates in his Adidas tracksuit. He is singing in English, "I trim girls all night long, white and black, I know how to trim those." These lyrics are new, they're probably bits of conversation he said earlier that day, grammatically Chinese and English, clauses that don't finish, lyrics that don't make sense. It's Cantonese slang for "hit on girls," coarsely translated to English, being yelled through a broken mike. We all know he kind of sucks, but so does everybody else and everyone's liking it. The Chinese groupies who took day-long buses into the city just to see the show are thrashing their heads back and forth as if they're saying, "No No No" when they're really saying "Yes Yes Yes." JJ finishes the set by jumping off the stage and feeling up a drunk Norwegian girl who doesn't seem to mind.

Like everyone else I know, JJ drinks a ton. Unlike everyone else, he doesn't seem to want to make it big. He says he just doesn't see the use of being a hardworking citizen. I certainly can't argue with that. I know most ordinary people will work their whole lives at some stable job and they'll never be able to afford so much as a one-bedroom in Beijing proper.

When the next band starts plugging in their instruments, Sara goes to mingle with the Canadian promoter, while JJ joins Benji and me by the bar.

"I am not writing for record labels. I just want to write music for the humiliated loser, the guy that gets hassled by the police, the night owl with no money, who loves to get fucked up," JJ says. I don't know if he knows that his description doesn't include someone like me, but we toast to that anyway.

Next we all go clubbing in Sanlitun at a place called Fiona. A once-famous French architect purportedly designed it in one hour. Every piece of furniture is a unique creation, and as a result, it looks like a Liberace-themed junkyard. Bamboo, an old acquaintance who runs a foreign modeling agency, is throwing a birthday party for herself.

"Can you believe I'm turning 29 again?" she says as a greeting while she ushers us into her private room. She kisses everyone on the mouth and presses little pills into our hands.

"Oh, to be young and beautiful, I can't think of anything more fabulous," she says, in her signature mixture of Chinese and English, as she drapes her arms around a new model boyfriend. His name is Kenny or Benny, and he looks like a skinny Hugh Jackman. He is obviously a homosexual, but that's just not something Bamboo has to accept.

The DJ spins funky house tracks, and the springboard dance floor floods with sweaty people who pant and paw at each other. Old businessmen drool at foreign girlfriends who lift up their skirts in elevated cages. Bamboo buys the drinks and toasts herself into oblivion, grooving around the dance floor, yelling at the foreigners to "Go nuts to apes and shit!"

I can't find Ah Ming or Benji, so instead I try striking up a conversation with skinny Hugh Jackman. He asks me to teach him Chinese, so I start by pointing to the items on the table.

"This is a bowl," I say.

"Bowa! Ah Bowl!" he says with a shit-eating grin on his face.

"Shot glass." I push it across the table toward him.

"Shout place," he slurs, laughing. "Oh yeaah, shout place!"

It's a good thing he's handsome, I think. I want to leave but I'm too high to wander around looking for my friends. I stick by the bar for a little bit and talk to the attractive waitresses who swear they've met me before, in another city, in another life, and I am sad that they have nothing to say to me but lies.

Beijing is a city that is alive and growing. At any given moment, people are feasting on the streets, studying for exams, or singing ballads in KTVs. Somewhere a woman with a modest salary is buying thousand-yuan pants from Chloé to prove her worth. Even though I couldn't cut it at Beijing Film Academy, I knew the city itself was for me. The dinosaur bones found underneath shopping malls, the peony gardens, the enclaves of art, these things were all exhilarating for me. I walk through new commercial complexes constructed at Guomao, which look at once like big awkward gangsters gawking at each other, as if hesitant to offer each other cigarettes, and I think, *I belong here.*

Tonight, I somehow end up crawling out of a cab to throw up by the side of the freeway. Traffic swirls around me, even though the morning light's not fully up. Then out of the blue, Sara and Benji appear, apparently because they happened to see my big shaved head projectile vomiting as their cab was passing. They pat me on the back and, on the side of the road, we eat hot pot from an old Xinjiang lady. I am so happy to be with them. It's at this moment I realize that what's going on is already slipping away, and while the cool air blows against my damp face on the taxi home, I can't help but miss it already.

One night, my last real girlfriend, Li Qiang, calls me.

"I'm moving to Shanghai next month, and I'm wondering if you could lend me some money to get settled. You know I'm good for it," she says. She knows more about me than anyone and there's not even a hiccup of hesitation in her voice.

That's just how Li Qiang did things. The girl couldn't just sit on a chair, she had to lie in it, with her head cocked to the side and a cigarette dangling dangerously. She is a sound mixer I met at the academy, and always dressed as if she had a Harley parked out back. Her playground was Mao's Live House, where she rejoiced in the last blaze of China's metal head scene.

There was never going to be a future for us; my father would have never accepted a poor musician into the family. Yet it was she who dumped me, simply saying, "I wish I could give you more. You should have more."

I meet her for coffee and hand her an envelope of money and she accepts it as though it's a book or a CD. She has cut her hair like a boy, but she is still fiercely beautiful and radiant as ever.

"We're doing well, you know," I say. "Benji's trying to get British art dealers to buy his photographs and Sara's in talks with a Dutch museum to exhibit her media installation. And Ah Ming just got published in a Finnish fashion magazine."

She goes, "That's impressive, but what are *you* doing?"

My throat is dry, and I'm not sure what to say, so I go, "I'm in between projects."

"Of course," she says, reaching over and messing up my hair.

Ah Ming's relationship with Zi Ying isn't normal either. Two days after they met, she moved into his room and began spending all her time on his bed. It is so weird in there even the pets stay away. For one, she would walk around topless, one minute laughing, the next waking us up with bawls.

"That girl should be taking antidepressants," Sara said.

In the mornings, Zi Ying tells Ah Ming she loves him, and he believes it. In the afternoons, she says he is disgusting to her and he believes that too. "You can't just pick and choose," he tells us. "When you're trying to get someone to love you, you have to take everything." When she sleeps with him, he marvels at all the soft places on her body he can kiss. It amazes him how easily he bruises when she kicks him away.

Ah Ming's website quickly becomes a shrine to Zi Ying's face. She is so crazy and beautiful it's as if she stole his eyes and hung them above her at all times. Gone are all the projects he'd been working on, and we hardly see him without her. It is only Zi Ying, her in the bathtub with goldfish, her on his bed with broken liquor bottles, lovingly captured and rendered over and over again.

We send each other his links over QQ. "This is kind of obsessive," JJ types.

"It's just a major muse mode," responds Benji, as he leans over to kiss Sara behind her ear.

More than Benji's girlfriend, Sara is the woman who helped all of us get over our shyness with and general distrust of white people. With Sara we learned many of her American customs, like hugging, and that took months of practice. "Arms out, touch face, squeeze!" We learn that Americans are able to take certain things for granted, like that the world appreciated their individuality. That they were raised thinking they were special, loved, and that their parents wanted them to follow their dreams and be happy. It was endlessly amazing.

We also learned English. We realized how different it really was to speak Chinese. We didn't used to have to say what we meant, because our old language allows for a certain amount of room to wiggle.

In Chinese we can ask, "What's it like?" because it can refer to anything going on, anything on your mind. The answer could be as simple-sounding as the one-syllable "men," which means, you're feeling stifled but lonely. The character drawn out is a heart trapped within a doorway. Fear is literally the feeling of whiteness. The word for "marriage" is the character of a woman and the character of fainting. How is English, that clumsy barking, ever going to compare?

But learn we did, useful acronyms like DTF (Down to Fuck), and Holy Shit, and we also became really good at ordering coffee. We learned how to throw the word *love* around, say "LOL" and laugh without laughing.

That afternoon, after coffee with Li Qiang, I buy her a parting present at an outdoor flea market. A *guoguo,* a pet katydid in a woven bamboo orb. They were traditionally companion pets for lonely old men, and the louder their voices, the more they were favored. Li Qiang picked out a mute one. The boy selling it to me says it lives for a hundred days.

"A hundred days?" she says as she brings the woven bamboo orb up against her big eyes. "This trapped little buddy is going to rhyme its own pitiful song for a hundred whole days?"

I tell her, "That's not so long, it's the length of autumn in Beijing. That's the length of a love affair." I realize I am giving away all my secrets. I think, *I want to roll you into the crook of my arm and take you somewhere far and green.* When she turns back toward me, I know the answer to my question before I even ask. I realize it is a mistake, the gesture, everything about me. She isn't going anywhere with me.

The only thing I have to offer her is money, and she has it already. I want to tell her that there's a lot of good shit about me that she would miss out on. But there's no art in me, and she sees it plainly in front of her. Instead, I kiss her fingers goodbye. They smell like cigarettes and nail polish, and I swear I'll never forget it.

By autumn, the trees shiver off their leaves and Zi Ying, too, becomes frigid and bored with Ah Ming. Our old friend Xiu Zhu comes back from "studying" abroad in Australia. She is a rich girl who looks like a rich boy. She has a crew cut, taped up breasts and a Porsche Cayenne, which she drives with one muscular arm on the steering wheel. Within an hour of meeting Zi Ying, we can all tell she is stealing her. By the time they finish their first cocktail, Xiu Zhu is already whispering English love songs into her ear.

We see less and less of Ah Ming after that. He still hangs out with the both of them, going to lesbian *lala* bars and getting himself hammered. The girls hold hands and laugh while he drinks whiskey after whiskey. He mournfully watches them kiss, as if he's witnessing an eclipse. Confused lesbians come up to him to ask where he got such a successful sex change operation, and he drinks until he passes out.

For my part, my father stops writing me e-mails asking about my well-being and just sends me a plane ticket. I don't tell anyone but I go to get my visa picture taken. The agency makes me take my earring out. Within the hour, the hole closes and now it's just a period of time manifested as a mole.

Winter, Zi Ying moves back to Hong Kong and breaks two hearts. Shortly after that, Ah Ming packs up his things as well. He tells us that under Beijing, beneath the web of shopping malls and housing complexes, lies the ruins of an ancient and desolate city. And beneath that there are two rivers, one that flows with politics and one that flows with art. If you drift here, you must quench your thirst with either of these waters, otherwise there is no way to sustain a life.

"I realize there is nothing for me here," he says, "no love here, not for a poor guy like me. It's waiting for me back in Xiamen, that's where it must be."

He sells his cameras, his clothes, even his phone.

"I don't want to leave a road to come back by," he says.

We all take Ah Ming to the train station, where he is leaving with the same grade-school backpack he arrived with. It's as if a spell has broken and suddenly we feel like jokers in our preripped jeans and purple Converses. We remember years ago, after having borrowed money from relatives, those first breaths taken inside that station. How timidly we walked forward with empty pockets and thin T-shirts. We had been *tu*, dirt, Chinese country bumpkins. And now one of us was giving up, but what could we have said to convince him he was wrong? What could have made him stay?

Everyone on the platform has their own confession to make, but when we open our mouths, the train comes, just in time to keep our shameful secrets, as trains are so good at doing. Someone is about to give away the mystery of loneliness, and then the train comes. The reason for living, the train comes, why she never loved him, the train comes, source of hope, train, lifetime of regret, train, never ending heartache, train, train, train, train, train.

Afterward, we huddle inside the station Starbucks, quietly sipping our macchiatos. Our cigarette butts are swept up by street sweepers whose weekly salaries probably amounted to what we paid for our coffee. The misty, mournful day is illuminated by the pollution, which makes Beijing's light pop, extending the slow orange days.

Out of nowhere JJ says, "I'm not sure if I actually like drinking coffee."

Sara says something about leaving soon to go home, and from the look on Benji's face, it is clear to me that this time, she might not be returning.

I want to say I might be leaving too, but instead I focus on an American couple sitting across the room from us. The woman holds in her arms a baby who doesn't look anything like her. They are an older couple, ruddy cheeked and healthy, and they order their organic juice and cappuccinos in English. As we sit together in those chairs, their Chinese baby starts screaming and banging his juice on the table. The couple is starting to look kind of despondent. The woman catches us staring, and the three of us look encouragingly at the baby. It's going to be OK, Chinese baby. You're a lucky boy. Such a lucky boy. Now please, please, shut up, before the Americans change their mind and give you back.

We somehow finish the Brass Donkey video and it's a semipornographic piece of garbage that gets banned immediately, of course. The band is happy because they're stamping "Banned in China" on their CDs and are being invited on a European tour. Without telling my friends, I go to the embassy to pick up my visa, secretly building the bridge on which to leave them. As I get out of there, I push back swarms of shabbily

385

dressed Chinese people just trying to get a glimpse of America, and it makes me feel lightheaded with good fortune.

The crowded scene reminds me of waiting at the ferry docks when I was a little boy, before my father had any money, when my life was ordinary. Our region was very hilly and in order to get any kind of shopping done, we took ferries to reach the nearest mall. The rickety little boats were always so overcrowded and flimsy that they would regularly tip over into the river, spilling both the young and old into the river's green waters. What I remember most were these brief moments of ecstasy, when the small overloaded boat gave in and the water was met with high-pitched screams. And we'd all just swim to shore, laughing at our rotten luck. Everybody would then simply get on another boat, dripping with water, letting our wet clothes dry in the breeze.

Brass Donkey's now banned song is playing loudly in my head. It's really pretty good; it's actually a protest song hiding behind a disco beat. "We have passion, but do not know why. What are we fighting for? Where is our direction? Do you want to be an individual? Or a grain of sand."

Nominated by Ploughshares, Sarah Frisch

LIKE A JET

SINA QUEYRAS

from MALAHAT REVIEW

> *Little streams passed all over their bodies.*
>
> —*Walt Whitman*

1

A hole in the sky where softness hung,
A crater where the world was, a moment
The size of Manhattan: amazed
We are not all sliding in.

I skirt abjection, drag my nails against
The hours. My eyes for one more glimpse,
Ochre (August, the rough tear of cotton,
The lace and wire, a harness of

Clinging). There is no shrugging off,
Weight, no exit ramp, no ease or release,
Perpetual shoulders on orange alert, jaw
Scraping the floor, the body contorts,

The body is fluid: I am leaking,
I no longer care who sees me leak.

2

I held her briefly at the end because finally
She could not scowl me away. Felt her unlatch,
A small mass, rocketing like helium, body
Already a swelling replicate of self.

I could see no verve, no after burn, no spirit
Lingering, just my empty reaching out:
How the dead can cower on the wing of
A plane or like a missile, shoot out of sight.

Muffled drum of heart, lungs like aging boxers
Swelling in a crow storm, hungry as Buck
Mulligan for her words: I chew them now,
Hollow seedpods clattering on my tongue.

Those whiskers of good intention: sad
Eliots' jet, as if hoarding, gorging, on pain.

3

Every last vein crammed with absence, hers
Yours, ours, I must return to the now. Two
Incompatible screens, the pixelated now,
The polyurethane grief, stuffed, animated,

Shrunken sweaters aping across an abandoned
Gym, Sexton's arms outstretched, smoky
Scotch a glass clinking across the honeyed floor.
I await your return and with it, futures

Uncorking. Hold tight, spray of time, we don't
Race to death it comes at us; there is no safety fence,
Once you drop, you walk into the forest as though
You owned it, you turn, wave, inhale black of day,

Exhale sight. Inhale death, exhale life, Ozymandias:
Everything that lives is light and she is now dark.

4

Time they say, time, and with it healing but also,
Recrimination and upset, my tumorette an airbag
Behind my eyes, blind me, my lack of patience:
Why is my exuberance rewarded? Hers snuffed?

Siblings crumble slow and unremarkable
As fences across the prairie. Who set the bar
So low? Who has tagged her foot? Mine?
Those red lines traced across a chest,

A lung split open: hard pebbles of light
Pelt your ease. Those high wire walkers vibrating
In the pain know something of loss's
Hammer, a persistent drum, a kit open under

The eave where pincers crack
A fly skull.

5

She is everywhere, the widening screen,
A surge in the weather, pages blooming,
Lines with animal movements, useless stalking.
I stare into the soup trying to ignite some memory

Of eating. Sweet rain where Raven, carrying summer
Storms, stomps the air: a bull, head ready to draw
The sky closed. The more death we know the closer
We are, and yes, the onward path, packed with guilt

And smart knots where pleasures show. I go to
August with her horses, to the clover path under
The power lines; there is no traceable reaction to
The arbutus's shedding while all else blooms, we

Upswing and trill, tunnel our emotions. No more death
Please: bite hard, I want to feel the future coming.

6

I felt something snap just now. It wasn't you parting
Your body—that was months ago, as if all this time
Grief has been spinning our heels and now we slow, steady,
Let it nestle into a fold with the lost coins and lint.

Where you were, the sawed-off limbs of a birch, a scorch
Of concrete, a hemline, shoulders wedged, socks like muffins
Oozing out of jeans, fashion is also exhausted, and who
Cares about whims, please save me from abstraction.

Who will sort the apples? Leonard. Leonard will sort the
Apples. Fredrick will drive the car. Jack will feel for you.
Describing is owning. Give me a woman with a lens
In her hand. Give me a woman with a will to read.

Give a woman a lost woman, an open vista, a stack of vellum,
Give me time, give me swagger, give me your ears.

7

All the gods know is destinations.[1] I have raised
A glass, my eye, your hook. Let's face it the world
Is a shrinking place and hungry: too much grief
To feed. I float away from you on hard

Covers. I step out on the stacked hours. Words
If they were soil how I would throw them back into the
Compost pile and wait for spring. Those "this is how
It is," speeches appear and later diamonds soft as bullets.

1 Sylvia Plath, "Getting There," Ariel

I went to the library looking to scaffold my thoughts.
Sure, now you say Lucretius. Intelligence is so often
Hindsight. Outside Holly Golightly's townhouse
There are taxis. The end of me, or you, is of no concern.

Frederick Seidel anoints me with the head of his penis.
It is soft as a chamois and spreads like egg across my scalp.

Nominated by The Malahat Review

THE DANCE CONTEST

by WELLS TOWER

from MCSWEENEY'S

MEN OF THE DARK

One afternoon at the start of the rainy season, Captain Surongporn, warden of Thep Moob Men's Prison, orders all inmates to the Zone B yard to hear some jolly news. Surongporn is only four months into his leadership; the prison, a former military fortification built in the reign of King Rama V, has been in operation since the end of World War II.

Surongporn's leading feature is a compact balloon of abdomen, proudly snugged in a brass-button shirt cut from lemon-colored cloth. He is a sway-backed little fellow built like a jellybean. The fourteen hundred men sitting or squatting before him all wear underclothes or cutoff pants. Nearly all are barefoot and shirtless. A few vain fellows, aristocrats for whom a suntan spells disgrace, hunch beneath broken umbrellas. Captain Surongporn looks shyly pleased with himself. His mien of coy potency resembles that of a gifted seven-year-old gymnast readying herself for her first public walk along the balance beam.

"My friends," he says, "I hope all of you are having a mellow and productive day. Perhaps you feel surprised that I say 'friends.' Well, you deserve to be called by that word. Three months ago, I came to you seeking assistance with several problems. Inmates doing bodily harm to each other was a problem. Drug casualties were a problem. Another problem was videos filmed on contraband phones, videos which referenced conduct that is unbecoming to you and unbecoming to this institution. One more problem was some chattering birds who told false stories to the BBC about conditions in our facility. Three months ago,

I asked for your help with these problems, and there has been no trouble since."

He smiles, showing beige teeth not much larger than the kernels of young corn.

"You have all cooperated in the suppression of bad elements, and we are now in a mellow time. And so I call you my friends."

A young man named Ter translates this information for Ron Tolenaar. "Yeah, a mellow time," brays Ron, Ter's patron and house boss of Dorm 23, Zone A. "Five men out the ghost door last month. Keep doing like this, the Moob will be a nice, quiet place. You won't hear a fucking sound but the waves and the birds going 'tweet.'"

Ron is 6'7", wears a size fourteen shoe. His lips, nose, and eyes bulge from his large crimson head, which looks like an infected thing that wants to be lanced. Ron is serving his first year of a forty-year sentence for exporting prostitutes stuffed with narcotics to Holland, his fatherland. Ter, his cellmate, is small and mantis thin. He is seventeen years old and serving no sentence at all. Before his death, Ter's uncle—Ter's last living relative—was a warder here, and he and Ter lived in an apartment off the seaside gun gallery. Pancreatitis killed the uncle in December of last year. In deference to the uncle's memory, the assistant warden has arranged for Ter to stay on in Thep Moob.

"Not five, I think," says Ter, his voice lowered to a whisper he wishes Ron would match.

"Yeah, five: three ODs, plus one AIDS, plus my man Julio, the Mexican faggot the yellow boys whipped," Ron intones at bullhorn volume, drawing the scrutiny of three yellow boys, high-ranking trusties kitted out with yellow shirts and white clubs. He meets their gaze sneeringly. The pineapple hooch Ron has been drinking since daybreak has put him in an heroic bent of mind. "They bashed his face to marmalade. I guess he is pretty mellow now."

"Would you be quiet, please," murmurs Declan Weyde, one of Ron's on-and-off roommates in A-23. "The Captains not talking in terms of reality. He's talking in terms of, 'Yeah, this summer was a mess, but no one said shit about it.' He's happy. It's a good thing. Shut up."

Declan has been in Thep Moob six years. When people ask him, he says, not very credibly, that he is serving an indefinite sentence for stealing a coffeepot. Declan's actual crime is a mystery of not much interest to other inmates, necessarily obsessed with their own survival. Ron's jabbering, he worries, will draw the yellow boys' attention to the elderly bronchial case who lies beside him, unconscious. Those caught napping during assembly are often made to run laps in the concrete courtyard on naked knees. This might kill the frail man, who is, after a fashion, Declan's friend.

"None of you people here has any balls," Ron says. "I really liked that faggot. Okay, he was a short-eyes—so what? People dig what they dig. He was a funny guy, the Mexican. Somebody give me a computer. I'll say shit to the whole world."

"Man, there aren't two people within a thousand miles who want to hear you talk," mutters Declan. The old man, who is suffering through the early stages of Pontiac fever, makes a sound in his throat like rock salt being flung against a chalkboard. He spits feebly. Rusty sputum darkens his moth-colored beard. The man is large and sickly pale, with a belly like a raw pork bun, rubbed to gleaming hairlessness by seventy years of textile friction. His only garments are a pair of maroon BVDs whose elastic is scalloped due to tensile breakdown. The leg welts swag away from the man's skinny thighs, displaying a crepey poundage of urological tackle. He is, in Declan's eyes, a man past all caring, and Declan worries that he will die very soon.

The old man himself is not frightened by the prospect of death. He is the Ralph D. Hepplewhite Distinguished Professor of Economics at Conant University, and he believes himself to be a rational person. By his own measure, he has lived a full and venturesome life, and it seems to him fitting that it should come to an end in a foreign land on a warm autumn day by the sea. The man is an American, and he is my father.

His name is Osmund Tower. The letter we will receive about his days in death's mudroom is not, as my mother puts it, "a masterpiece of earthly reflection." It will contain nothing much in the way of a fare-well, and no specific mention of us, his family. This will appall my mother and my brother, who will hear a passive cruelty in the blitheness of my father's tone. Let it go, I will tell them. Let us think the best of him.

At the assembly, Ron Tolenaar goes on voicing his drunken com-plaints about the death of Mexican Julio. A yellow boy waggles a trun-cheon at him. Ter pats Ron on the arm. "Yeah, maybe good shut the fuck up, Mister Ron," says Ter. "You stink like a party. You don't want they come to the dorm and take the fruit and jars and tubes."

Ron sees the wisdom in this. For the time being, he closes his mouth.

My father's mouth is open. Declan puts a hand to Osmund's face so that the yellow boys do not hear his moist, dragging snores.

Captain Surongporn turns his sallow, minuscule face to the gun-gallery wall on whose far side lies the sea. Mines bob in the near harbor against abettors of a marine escape. Farther out in the gulf, trawlers and pleasurecraft putter and glide. Today, a lucky wind from the south bears dim sounds of merriment from a yacht party miles out on the green deeps. Music is playing. Captain Surongporn can just make out "Dancing in the Moonlight" by King Harvest, a song he knows well. The windborne tune confers a felicity on the announcement the man is here to make.

"We have heard a wish for more recreation, by means of which to improve one's health and self-esteem," says the Captain. "Because you have respected my wishes and concerns, I will repay you with respect for yours. I am pleased to say that today we will grant this wish."

A roar goes up. The inmates want for much in Thep Moob, but more recreation is high on no one's list. They want a less repulsive daily meal, instead of their present ration—a ladleful of weevil-ridden rice topped with a few fish ribs to which crumbs of flesh rarely cling. They want improvements to the visitors' hall, whose telephones are so decrepit it sounds as though your loved one is speaking through a kazoo. They bawl for the lifting of the ban against intramural boxing, long forbidden as too generous a boon to the prison's bookies, who grow rich as it is. A spotted old man rises and roars for a ration of ice with which to soothe his gouty feet. "You pig fuckers won't give me medicine, you can give me ice, at least!" he says. A nearby warder takes issue with "pig fuckers." He knocks the gouty man square on the skull with the pommel of his steel baton. The man collapses neatly into a sitting position. The long truncheons of the trusties drub the concrete.

The thunder quiets the shouting. Captain Surongporn's high, flute-like voice can again be heard. "What I am happy to tell you is this," he says. The Captain pauses, uncurtains his tiny teeth, pans the hard hump of his belly from right to left. "We will have a dance contest here in Thep Moob. Every dorm will participate. Every man will dance. We will have transparency in the competition. The performances will be videoed, and these videos will be placed onto the internet. The winner will be determined by public vote. This is a wonderful opportunity to display your talent, and to show the world that our facility is a facility where fun and creative expression drive our process of reform."

"A wonderful opportunity for the Captain to fuck himself," growls

Ron Tolenaar. "Go ahead and shoot me. Put me in the Suitcase before I'll jump up and be a monkey."

This sentiment is general in the courtyard. The Captain looks out at fourteen hundred stone-faced men. Then he announces that an electrical outlet and a color television will be installed in the dorm that takes first prize. Second prize is a ceiling fan and an electrical outlet. Third prize is an electrical outlet.

"Piss in your outlet," Ron calls out, as a minor gleeful bedlam breaks out among the few dancers in the crowd. "Me and my men, we like to live in the dark."

"Sorry, but I would not piss on a little more splendor in our house," says Henri Permeuil, twenty-eight, a Frenchman strung with yoga sinew, Ron's best friend in A-23. "We could have music. A teapot. A thing for soups and stews. We could boil the beer and drink something very nice. And we could make some money, charging people's devices."

A contemplative suction draws the purple welt of Ron's lower lip into his mouth for an instant. He glances at the twin celebrations occurring among a crew of Nigerian smugglers and the transgendered prostitutes who run a brothel in Zone C. "Okay, an outlet would be nice, but we are still fucked," he says. Most dorms in Thep Moob house no fewer than fifty men. A-23 is a luxury cell, its six residents (save Ter) all Westerners who pay a high monthly bribe to hold the population to a comfortable half-dozen. They would make for a paltry choreographic spectacle.

"And who do we have who knows how to shake his ass? You can dance, Henri?"

Henri flutters a sophisticated hand at his temple, as though to say that dancing may be one of his undiscovered gifts.

"Declan?"

"Well, I guess I'm pretty aware of my body," Declan muses. "I've got pretty strong legs and my balance is pretty good. I don't often trip for no reason."

"And then this guy," says Ron, nodding at my father. "Professor Hippopotamus. Maybe we push him in a wagon. No, we totally are screwed."

The Captain has surrendered the microphone to the Director of Programs for a discussion of the contest's logistical details. The Director of Programs states once more that participation is mandatory. Each dorm will be randomly assigned, via bucket drawing, one of three songs around which to craft a routine. These are "Gonna Make You Sweat," by C+C Music Factory; "Ice Ice Baby," by Vanilla Ice; and "All My

Rowdy Friends Are Coming Over Tonight," by Hank Williams, Jr. These will be played over the public address system twice each during the daily recreation period. A line forms for the song draw, and the assembly is adjourned.

"If we get Bocephus, maybe we have a chance," says Ron. "I know a little bit the Texas Two-Step from my wife. If we pull Vanilla Ice, it will piss me off completely." He watches Declan Weyde cross the yard, burlesquing a little waltz across the broken concrete.

Through large and womanly plastic shades, Captain Surongporn, roving with his lieutenants, has an eye on Declan, too. The two have never met, but Surongporn pauses to say hello. "Mister Weyde," he says in English.

A flush rises in Declan's face. To be singled out by the Captain makes him feel dizzy and ill. He grins. "Yes, sir."

The Captain grins back. "Mister Coffee. The coffeepot man. You like dancing?"

"Yes, sir! I love it! Good for the body, good for the soul."

The Captain's smile goes even broader, showing a spot of beige gum where a molar fell out. "Good for the body, good for the soul," repeats the Captain, turning into the crowd of shirtless men stumbling rearward from his path. His heart drumming, Declan takes his turn at the bucket. He reaches into the dry, rustling salad of small paper strips. "Ice Ice Baby" is the song he draws for the men of Dorm A-23.

A LITTLE SIDE ACTION

When the syndicates draw up the odds, the famous transsexuals of C-5 Dormitory blow out the field. Not only are they Thep Moob's fanciest steppers, they own many small outfits to hurt a man's heart. Also, they have drawn for their number "Gonna Make You Sweat," an ideal match for their gifts. The bookies are nettled. No one will bet against C-5 for first prize. The bookies pay a visit to the Director of Programs; for a bribe of 3,000 baht, five pounds of dried fish, and two cartons of cigarettes, the Director agrees to ban women's clothing from the competition. The bookies pay this gladly.

In light of this dispensation, gamblers are now willing to look at the Nigerians of A-14 for first at eight-to-five. A good-size squad, three dozen men, share A-14, all of them convicted of muling heroin for the same Lagos importer, most of them living out death sentences that Thailand's capricious Justice Ministry rarely insists on carrying out. The

Nigerians are Christians. Their Sunday vespers service is a beloved spectacle in Thep Moob. At the conclusion of the liturgy, it is their custom to strike up a song, lay hands on one another's shoulders, and shuffle and sway in a graceful, hunkering ring. Among the general population, rare is the man so dead in spirit that his soul does not rise when the Nigerians dance. But can this power be harnessed to "All My Rowdy Friends Are Coming Over Tonight"?

The real excitement on the card is third place. Forty-eight teams will be vying for number three, all of them dark horses. One team that is not a dark horse is A-23, where my father and the others make their home. In the eyes of the gambling syndicate, A-23 is no horse at all.

Osmund Tower's illness is not helping the team's chances. Two days after the assembly, his fever has risen to 104. A colony of *Legionella pneumophila*, which started in his lungs, is franchising ambitiously throughout his body. Hundreds of bacterial lesions have sprung up on his palms and the soles of his feet. The lesions are tiny; the largest is smaller than an oat. Despite their modest size, each of these lesions is an open circuit to an arresting voltage of pain. This makes it impossible for my father to walk, or to wield a pencil or an eating utensil. His illness, dangerous only to the elderly and infirm, is easily curable. But a powerful gang of older Chinese inmates—also stricken with Pontiac flu—has bought up the infirmary's store of antibiotics, leaving nothing stronger than aspirin for the rest of the population until the next fiscal quarter. So my father lies on his mat, slipping calmly, pointlessly into death. Yet he is not in despair. The stupefying languor of his fever is pleasant in its way, a powerful narcotic. His roommates do not molest him. Their dorm's design recalls a '50s-style Holiday Inn, with a fourth, barred wall open to the air, allowing access along an exterior promenade; warm sea winds sough into the cell, drying my father's sweat without leaving him chilled.

My father is not the only dying man in A-23. On the far side of the dorm lies Oliver Fehar, twenty-eight, of Johannesburg. Last year, larking in Phuket, Oliver got drunk and drove a dune buggy over a pregnant bather, killing her. The baby survived, and will outlive Mr. Fehar. Oliver is dying of a systemic staph infection that entered his body through an ingrown toenail. His skin is the color of grape sherbet.

The two invalids do hold some interest for the prison's gambling community. The bookies of Thep Moob will offer action on which raindrop will first reach the bottom of a windowpane. They offer action on how many times Captain Surongporn will use the word *mellow* in his weekly addresses. And now there is lively action on whether my father or Oliver Fehar will be the first to die. Because of his age, and his visible speckling of sores, Osmund is the favorite in this contest, at three-to-two over the South African.

My father has been in Thep Moob awaiting trial for five weeks. Prior to his illness, he had gotten along well with his roommates; he is a natural follower of rules, and his fellows have yet to hear him utter a word of complaint. If Professor Tower had the dorm to himself, the area around his sleeping mat would resemble the detonation site of a bomb containing Kleenex, blood-pinkened frowses of dental floss kept for reuse, dirty laundry, coins, leaky pens, peanut shells, cockeyed reading glasses from the dollar store, magazine subscription cards, and splayed books. But here, out of respect for the commons, my father has kept his effects stacked and folded, neat as a pin.

As sick as he is, he is not wholly unresponsive. Late in the afternoon, when Ron and the others begin to complain that the sick men have dashed all hope of a good showing in the dance contest, Osmund is returned to the searing shame of a Boy Scout hiking trip fifty-some years before, when he fell in a creek and ruined his cargo of hamburger buns for the troop. "This is just terrible. I really do apologize," he murmurs now, rubbing phantom creek mud from his knees.

The dorms are unlocked between the hours of 5 a.m. and 8 p.m. Toward dusk, Declan Weyde shoulders past a knot of gamblers and Death Race spectators and into A-23. Declan is carrying a crock of lime yogurt purchased at the black-market grocery in Zone B. When the gamblers learn of Declan's plan for it, they say, in a babel of tongues, "Hey, get away from him, you rotten bastard!" and "Don't fuck me, Coffeepot, I've got money on that boy." Declan intends to feed Osmund the yogurt, queering the odds.

Whether spooning yogurt into my father will prolong the man's life is unclear, but Declan does not have much else to work with. To facilitate the feeding, he cradles Osmund's damp and fragrant head in the crook of his knee. My father is not a man to refuse a meal; he is a life-long licker of plates and a meticulous herder of tabletop crumbs. Now, though, as he loiters in death's lobby, angular cheilitis, a painful, scabrous breakage of the joint of the lips, prevents Professor Tower from opening his mouth wide enough to garage the laden spoon. So the yogurt's entry is a two-phase process: first my father slurps the mounded yogurt from the utensil, taking in about a two-thirds portion; then his gray tongue eels forth to polish off the unslurpable remnant. After each intake, a sensuous little air-brake sound of satiety—*auh!*—bursts from his lips. "Mm. Thank you, Declan! Man alive, this is just excellent," he murmurs.

"Take her easy, Professor," says the coffeepot thief. "You don't gotta *hoover it*. I'm not going anywhere."

My father does not hear this. He cranes avidly for the spoon, greedy as a newborn.

"Jesus, hey, cool it, man. Just let that settle for a second. This shit wasn't an easy score. If you puke it up all over the place, I'll be seriously pissed."

This rough talk is a show for the others. Declan has some skin in the Tower-Fehar Death Race game: in exchange for Declan's services as a fixer, my father has, since his arrival, been paying Declan's share of bribe-rent in the luxury dorm. This assistance has come at a time when Declan's finances are in some disarray. But even if Osmund's death did not mean Declan's eviction, I think Declan would be spooning the yogurt all the same.

At this moment Declan is fifty-five, a native of Vancouver, British Columbia. He has a kindly, squinting face, fringed by hay-colored hair through which a freckled pink scalp gleams. Many women have loved Declan Weyde, but he has no children. He wishes he'd had children. A physical expression of this desire is the fawn-colored, dime-size dimple on his forearm where an Amazonian botfly once laid an egg in his skin. Out of a sense of maternal duty, Declan attempted to carry the creature to term. When the boil finally split and the light of day broke upon a stillborn larva, Declan grieved. Emotionally twinned to the botfly scar is a tiny white line above the knuckle of his left thumb; this he received while driving across Mauritania with his then-girlfriend. Over her protests, he stopped to take on a pair of hitchhikers, teenage sisters, the elder extremely pregnant. The pregnant girl went into labor in the Fiat. Defying his girlfriend's hysterical objections, Declan delivered the baby. The umbilical cord he severed with his Leatherman tool, also lacerating his thumb. The wound caused Declan's girlfriend to worry that he had contracted a serious bloodborne illness (the young mother's blood had been everywhere), and the incident marked the end of their sexual relationship. This is all to say Declan is a man rich in a kind of patience and charity I'm not sure my own heart contains.

Why is it that water comes into my eyes, when I ponder this stranger's efforts to keep my father alive? Perhaps it is that the easy decency of Declan's yogurt kindness throws my own brokenness and selfishness into hard relief. I do love my father, but I am sorry to know that were I in Declan's place, the sight of the man, of the fat blind muscle of his tongue flexing and swanning for yogurt, would offend me. The impulse to rap the bridge of his nose with the spoon would be a low temptation I might lack the goodness to resist.

Ron Tolenaar has nothing against either man, but he wants both Professor Tower and Oliver Fehar to hurry up and die. The dance contest is only a month away. Perhaps a pair of ringers can be recruited to take the place of the dead men, and A-23 could make a viable bid for third place. Or perhaps it is time to make nice with the Portuguese book artists who toil in the prison glassworks. A book artist is a counterfeiter of passports. In the glassworks, ladders could be built and saw blades stolen. Then, some night, Ron and his accomplices could make for the dark stretch of fence in the citrus grove. The Cambodian border is only fifteen miles past the fence. Ron's loving wife and children are waiting for him in Breukelen.

The yogurt has no effect on the Legionella bacteria, which go on building grand cities in my father's lungs. But this spot of light grubbing ushers strength into his feeble frame, and Osmund's soul brightens, drawing vigor from the knowledge that Declan's promise to look after him was not the swindle he suspected it might be.

My father's first nights in Thep Moob were not pleasant. He'd been thrown into a sixty-man dorm whose only spot of unclaimed floor space was a small crescent of territory alongside the toilet hole, which was in constant use throughout the night. In the more crowded dorms, three square linoleum tiles (twenty inches on an edge) constitute one's allotted sleeping area, making the fetal position mandatory. No one clarified this code to my large father, who, to his terror and bewilderment, was anonymously cursed, kicked, punched, and, at least once, bitten in the black of the night. Declan had been enduring these barbarities for six months, since losing the last of his savings on a failed appeal. When he approached my father with the proposition of buying into A-23, Osmund, in his misery, did not hesitate to accept.

In addition to his own expenses, my father is paying two hundred and fifty dollars a month for Declan's protective companionship, which covers the younger man's dorm rent and canteen account. The thought has nagged at him that $250 per month for Declan's services is above fair market rate. Now, with his head in Declan's lap, he feels he has at last gotten some real value for his money, which unties a little knot of unease inside him.

The others in A-23 are not so pleased about the yogurt feed. Ron Tolenaar scowls at my ulcer-spangled father, sprawled like the pietà in Declan's lap. "You guys are really cute like this, but Declan, man, come on. This is stupid shit," the big man snarls from his hammock. "The Professor wants to die, give him respect and let him die."

"Except he obviously wants to live," says Declan. "Look at his appetite. He's practically eating the spoon."

"This yogurt is truly excellent," Osmund mutters through a cough.

Ron gestures at the dying men with the magazine he's reading, a publication called *Maximum Combat Aeronautics*. "I will turn him over to the hospital, both of these guys." Thep Moob's hospital is an ironical place, an amoeba zoo and diarrhea museum whose undisguised function is to hasten patients into death.

"You want to throw Oliver on the shitheap, go ahead. He's mostly furniture already," says Declan. "But nobody's going to fuck over my man here. Osmund is in my personal care."

"You care about your rent," says Ron, scowling now at Declan. "I care about electrification. I care about having tunes and stew and nice beer in the house. How we will do something competitive to your shitty 'Ice Ice Baby' is a hard thing, Declan. To do it with these guys is not possible. The team of two dead fuckers is not a winning team. I am making a new rule. In this house, if you can't feed yourself, no other man can feed you."

Henri Permeuil speaks up against this. So do Declan and Ter. The limits of Ron's authority strain against the far-reaching rules he has already put into place. These include prohibitions against chewing tobacco, harmonicas, durian, and masturbating while others are present. The residents of A-23 tolerate these restrictions, but to effectively ban a man from saving his cellie's life is a bridge too far.

"Okay, okay, but I don't give a shit if you are puking sick—you pull your weight in here. Hear me, guys?" says Ron. "A week. Oliver? Professor? Any man who is not on his toes next week, we send you to the hospital."

"The big man's bouncing back. He'll be shaking his ass in no time," Declan replies, plying Osmund with another mouthful. By way of testimony, my father sucks the yogurt down with a loud, vehement slurp. Ron glowers over his magazine, which is open to a photo essay of bikini women posed alongside combat drones.

"Tower, if you don't eat more quiet I'm going to tear off your head and pee in it. You hear me, man?"

"I heard 'peanut,'" says Professor Tower, who is slightly (and selectively) deaf. He owns a hearing aid, but it was so expensive he has been afraid to take it out of the box. He did not bring it to Thailand.

"Don't try to talk," says Declan. "It makes your mouth bleed."

"You heard me, man," says Ron. "You play dumb, but you hear me. I'm trying to look at my book, and some guy going *sluccch* isn't a very super thing to hear when I'm looking at bitches. You're making me really fucking nuts. I think maybe I'm going to have to smash you so I don't hear this *slurrch sluurch* anymore."

"I heard 'nuts.' I'm quite fond of nuts," my father murmurs. "And I expect I'll be able to manage nuts in a day or two, Ron. But for now, best to play it safe and stick to this delicious goop here. Declan, if you could fix me up with another bite, that would be great. Boy, the old head is really throbbing. There are some just extraordinarily vivid lights swirling and swooshing around behind my eyes right now."

Through all of this, Oliver Fehar says nothing. The five gamblers at the bars, all of whom have backed my father in the Death Race, are sick at heart. With rehearsal hour approaching, they make for the prison's citrus orchard, where a rapist from C-building with famously nimble feet is drilling a squad for the dance contest.

The familiar sixteenth-note overture pilfered from Bowie and Queen crackles over the PA system first. Henri Permeuil, who has taken on the role of A-23's choreographer, showcases for Ron, Declan, and Ter the latest revision of his routine. The cycle consists of jogging in place and madly gnashing one's teeth while slapping an invisible wall. Hostile confusion is the audience response.

"The dance is chewing?" says Declan. "Some kind of chewing fit?"

"It is very frightening," says Ter.

"This dance is garbage," says Ron. "I don't understand it at all."

Henri's miming palms wilt to his sides. "Hey, piss off, yeah? This is only concept number one," he says. "For your information, what I am doing, I am trapped in a freezer. Shivering in a freezer. What we do should have meaning. Not just be stupid, just hopping around like idiots. The world will see us. My idea is the world will see men who are dying, trapped in this place."

"The world will see some assholes biting around and slapping and looking pretty weird," says Ron.

"This is one idea. I have many ideas. We can win," says Henri, his chin tucked sullenly to his sunburned throat.

"Ah, motherfucker," says Ron, climbing back into his groaning hammock. "We all stay in the dark."

THE ANGEL OF THE GHOST DOOR

These, in ascending order of expense and preciousness, are the goods and services available on Thep Moob's healthy black market: laundry and housekeeping services, sexual services, haircuts, books and magazines (nonpornographic), rice, fresh-caught fish, dried fish, coffee, fruit, yogurt and hot menu items, clothes, loose tobacco, parasols, playing cards, prerolled cigarettes, knives, aspirin, books and magazines (pornographic), knifeproof vests and cod protectors, batteries, cannabis, opium, heroin, antibiotic ointment, hypodermic needles, narrow-spectrum antibiotics, anti-retroviral medication, anti-anxiety medication, cellular phones, broad-spectrum antibiotics—specifically, azithromycin, which is used to treat Pontiac flu—and laptop computers.

As I have mentioned, the Chinese clique has commandeered the prison dispensary's entire store of azithromycin. Declan Weyde understands that Professor Tower's life, and his own standard of living, can be saved only by appealing to a fat, walleyed warder named Sudrit Nut—the fickle angel of Thep Moob.

Sudrit's good works are diverse. When your letters are waylaid by Chokdee Boonma, the wicked guard whose industry it is to ransom inmates' mail, Sudrit can be petitioned to intercede in your favor. If you are an addict consigned to a term in the Suitcase—the refrigerator-size steel crate that stands in the wildflower meadow behind the glass factory—you pray to Sudrit as you broil. If you are lucky, Sudrit's hand will dim the air vent, and a life-giving cellophane bolus of brown heroin will parachute down.

Illiterates have successfully enlisted Sudrit's help in crafting applications for a King's pardon. Victims of rape, extortion, or secret slavery can make a case for relief to Sudrit. He does not hear every plea, and he does not side with even one of ten plaintiffs he hears, but once he determines to take your side, his aid is expeditious.

In his forty-three-year career at Thep Moob, Sudrit has saved the lives of an uncounted number of inmates, and he has killed forty-two. In the days when the condemned died by beheading, Sudrit decapitated eleven men. In the days when the condemned died by gunfire,

Sudrit's victims numbered nineteen. And in 2003, when the Thai penal authorities bowed to international pressure and decreed that men should die from a dose of potassium chloride injected by a licensed physician, Thep Moob's warden and the inmates were of an equal mind that in partial disobedience of the order, the job should be given to Sudrit Nut.

Since learning the art of the needle, Sudrit has put down twelve men. His touch is gentle and his observance of the last rites is scrupulous and performed in a soothing tone. He chants the sutra. He whispers the names of the Buddha. He anoints the forehead of the condemned with a cloth moistened in eucalyptus water, murmuring *ci, ce, ru, ni*—which means "heart," "form," "mental concepts," and *Nibbana*, letting go. Then he depresses the plunger with a heedful thumb. Only insane or unreasonable men curse Sudrit Nut as he stops their hearts.

The execution chamber is a block bunker down a white shell path from the glass factory. Beyond the bunker, the path winds to a gate of rusted iron plate. This gate is called *Pratuphi*, which means "the ghost door." It is only opened to admit a corpse. Through the ghost door, between the third and second walls of the prison, lies a cemetery for men whose bodies no one comes to claim. Marking each grave is an oblong of teak engraved with the inmate's number but not his name. Within a decade of each new burial, the Gulf's salt air will efface the wood to illegibility, and the useless marker can be uprooted and thrown out.

Executions are not announced in advance in Thep Moob. A condemned man is kept ignorant of his fate until, having been summoned from his cell on some false pretext, he finds himself being led down the shell path. The other inmates would not know with any certainty that one of their own had been executed if the prison administration did not believe in ghosts. Not long after a prisoner has been ushered through the ghost door, the hoarse and soothing tenor of Sudrit Nut is heard over the intercom. Softly, the prisoner's name is intoned, followed by these words: "We invite your spirit to leave us now."

You treat with Sudrit Nut in the Zone B yard on weekend afternoons. Sudrit owns a white plastic patio set stippled with green mildew. There he sits, under a ruined yellow parasol, playing checkers terribly. A goldfish could give Sudrit a run for his money in a checkers game; it is the petitioner's job to architect courses of triple jumps for Sudrit's pieces while you tell him of your troubles. His cocked eyes never meet yours, and there is no way of telling whether your story is working on him.

405

"Hello," "Move, please," and "Thank you" are the only words he tends to utter. At the end of the game he bids you farewell, and in a few days, your problem will be taken care of or else it will not.

Sudrit does not often help inmates with an aegis of money from home. Westerners regard his chaotic mercies with apprehension, bewilderment, and contempt. To the Euro-American mind, the obscure moral logic of Sudrit's interventions is something wanton and unholy. By what perverse divinity does this beady-eyed angel disdain, for example, to procure insulin for a falsely imprisoned diabetic, only to take up the case of a pederast whose cat has been abducted? And how could it be worth the humiliation to lay out your agony and helplessness before a grunting stranger who will likely do nothing for your cause—and, furthermore, to stage a credible loss to a man who, checkerswise, is nearly retarded?

The morning after Declan's administration of yogurt, my father's fever is nearing 105 degrees. Declan appears at Sudrit's patio set. He *waies* and winces and grins. He minces and murmurs in his Tarzan Thai, *I don't to disturb; I don't to annoy; yes, some minute of his time?* Sudrit, blinking froglike in the bright yellow shade of his parasol, invites Declan to sit. What is said? This isn't known; only that Declan defies suppliant protocol by thrashing Sudrit in eight straight games, and that both men laugh after each walloping. The day after Declan's visit to Sudrit, the executioner's errand boy appears at A-23 with a fourteen-day course of azithromycin. Twenty-four hours later, my father awakens, slick as a newborn, his fever broken.

RECREATION

For forty-eight hours after his fever's retreat, Osmund Tower lies on his mat, trying to will a revival of the lung infection. His is the futility of the sleeper who fights to remain in a dream as the white sunlight of morning and the concerns of the day haul him, like a whaler's spear, inexorably into consciousness. The matter of his disgrace is one of the larger buoys in the harpoon's cord. His name has not yet appeared in the international press, but it surely will when his case goes to trial weeks or months from now. He is being prosecuted for extreme foolishness. The American embassy in Bangkok assures us that a guilty verdict is a foregone conclusion.

The promise of romantic fulfillment pulled my father to Thailand. His aim was to meet a relatively beautiful Australian woman he had

406

gotten to know over the internet. In the course of a three-month correspondence consisting of email and video chats, a credible facsimile of human connection developed between them. Concupiscence held only a minor share of Osmund's interest in the woman. Age, and a long bout with leukemia five years ago, have diminished his sexual appetites. To pass entire hours untroubled by seizures of sexual desire, he has told me often in recent years, is a wondrous form of liberty.

The woman, who gave her name as Emily Hughes, had struck my father as kind and playful and undesperately lonesome. She said she was a travel agent in her early forties with a broken womb. The prospect of a romantic friendship, more than an unlikely coupling, had been thrilling to Osmund. And so, over Conant U's fall break, expecting nothing, he flew to meet Ms. Hughes in a resort town on Thailand's gulf coast.

She failed to appear. An intermediary with a face like an old-style ice bag appeared instead. She claimed to be Emily's older sister, Camilla. Camilla bore news that Emily, laid low with food poisoning, had been compelled to stay in Melbourne, but that she was keen to see him all the same. Camilla presented my father with a ticket to Australia and a pink suitcase containing bolts of Thai silk. At the airport, the police discovered in the case a false bottom that would have been obvious to anyone less abstracted than a Distinguished Professor of Economics. The false bottom held three kilos of opium, which, when unwrapped by the policemen, let a wonderful smell into the room.

After his arrest, Camilla came to visit Osmund in his holding cell. She told him that for $100,000, all would be put right with the authorities, and he would be on a plane home that evening. This upset him. By way of declining the proposition, he told her, "I feel very twitchy about entering into arrangements in which there are such obvious asymmetries of information. One hundred thousand dollars is a lot of money, and, I have to say, Camilla, where you're concerned, there ain't a real surplus of trust."

She departed, and the offer was not renewed.

The horror of the situation troubled my father less when he believed he was dying. Now he frets. He has always cut an eccentric figure among Conant University's economics faculty. He does not own a single tweed jacket, but instead layers Oxford shirts, as many as four on chilly days. He wears purple, iridescent Skechers sneakers, purchased because they were on sale at Walmart. He drives a twenty-five-year-old Toyota Tercel which he brush-painted shamrock green because that shade was on sale at Walmart. But neither his character nor his intellectual capacities have ever been in doubt. Now both of these things are in doubt. His department chair, who had already been gunning for Osmund's retirement, intends to strip my father of his salary, his tenure, and his pension plan. I have gone to plead with this son-of-a-bitch, unavailingly. An attorney friend of mine says we have grounds for a lawsuit against the university, but my father—my guileless, daft, loyal father—wrote in a recent letter that he "couldn't bring [him]self to muck things up for the department."

Osmund does not garden or turn wood on a lathe or read novels or cook. He teaches and produces scholarly articles. Without his work, life holds nothing for him. What of his Great Books in Macroeconomics class—has a substitute lecturer been found? If not, what damage has this inflicted on his students' academic careers? What of Marko Klyodz? He is Osmund's very promising Bulgarian thesis student, whose face is broken out in a half-dozen brownish cutaneous horns. My father believes the cutaneous horns, the longest of which is one-and-three-eighths inches, will be an obstacle to Marko's career. Marko lacks the money to have these removed, so before he left for his ill-fated vacation, my father offered to pay for the surgery. What has now become of Marko? Does he think my father made generous promises only to renege? And why does the possibility of a life sentence seem less frightening than excarceration from this cell, which seems a right and proper container for an unusually stupid man?

On the third day of his recovery, a small, slippered foot lightly kicking his ribs stirs my father from his sleep. A trusty stands over Osmund, jabbering in an unfriendly way.

"He says you stink, Tower. He's on solid ground there," Ron says from his hammock. Oliver is the only other man in the dorm. Declan is attending to a matter at the Activities Office. "He says you have to go have a wash."

The trusty leads my father to the bathhouse at the rear of the Zone A courtyard. He takes his place at the back of a queue of soot-blackened men, fresh from a day's work shoveling charcoal into the glass factory's kilns. At the far end of the line is a basin of water and a ladle, presided over by a trusty armed with a bamboo cane. Each man is afforded fifteen seconds of ablutions, which the trusty counts off. At "sixteen," if the inmate has not replaced the ladle, the trusty clouts his neck with the cane.

My father enjoys any game with such clear and easy rules. Even in his depressive languor, he washes lightning-quick. The ladle rings against the basin before the trusty gets to nine. Proud of this achievement, my father stands at attention for a moment, as though expecting a salute. With the bamboo cane, the trusty gently goads him toward the side door.

The door opens onto a small paved yard, where, to dry themselves, wet bathers promenade in a ring, holding their shorts in their hands. Osmund's wet skin thrills to the coolness of the air. The sensation so captivates his consciousness that he fails to notice a small, withered man making his way toward him against the current. In this man's hand is a parody of a knife made from a peanut-oil can. With a shrill cry, he flails for Osmund's throat. In a reflex of terror, my father swipes at the knife fortuitously, if unthinkingly, with the hand that holds his underpants. His parry bends the feeble blade.

The scrawny assassin does not give up. The man is a gambler in serious debt. His bookie—heavily leveraged in the Tower-Fehar ghost-door wager—has offered him amnesty in exchange for Osmund's murder. The debtor jumps onto my father's back, tugging at his head, attempting a bit of Hollywood business in which a deft jerk of the hands breaks a man's neck. He lacks the know-how for this feat, however, and the effect is mostly comic: my father howling and stumbling, the little gambler grappling and fumbling at Osmund's large, egglike head before a crowd of laughing men. The two are still conjoined when Declan Weyde rushes in upon the scene. Declan takes two fistfuls of the assassin's hair and pulls him from my father's back. He knees him several times in the face and stomach and balls. The miserable little man flees in a stumbling lope.

Declan hustles my father, still naked, down an opposite path toward the main yard. One of the assassin's bicuspids is lodged in the bone of Declan's knee. Grasping the tooth with the hem of his shirt, he works it free and puts it into his pocket.

"Ouch," says Declan, taking a seat on a concrete bench.

The surgery escapes my father's notice. He coughs, sniffs, blinks back tears of shock. "It isn't clear to me what that guy was so pissed off about," he says.

To Osmund's professional fascination, Declan spells out the statistical havoc the azithromycin played with the handicappers' forms. "So maybe the guy had money on you. Or maybe someone put him up to it. Fucking Ron, man. I can't believe he let you out of the dorm. You don't leave the dorm alone until this thing's sorted out."

"I'm not sure I understand how this industry functions. How can they calculate anything resembling a reliable market of probabilities if folks are just going to interfere and manipulate the outcome? Why would anyone pay out on an obviously crooked result?"

"The whole thing would have been a forfeit. Nobody would have to pay. People would have been pissed, but the guys covering your marker would have saved a shitwack of baht."

"Cripes. I haven't been in a fight since grade school, and I got the worst of that one. I'm extremely grateful for that guy's incompetence. You're fairly certain he isn't coming back?"

"I think he'll be under the weather for a while. You can put on your shorts now."

"Righty-o," says Osmund. A trio of heavily tattooed inmates, laboring at a garden plot, pause to grin at the sight of my father stepping into his underwear.

Punctured knee notwithstanding, the afternoon has been kind to Declan Weyde. While my father was en route to nearly being killed, Declan was in the office of the Director of Activities, receiving the glad news that his fishing license has come through.

Thep Moob is an aged prison. In the days when running water was considered too grand an amenity for felons, inmates bathed at a saltwater pool fed by a sluiceway running beneath the gulfward gun-gallery wall. The pool is now a recreational luxury. One cannot swim in it; to discourage escape attempts, two grids of one-inch rebar, stacked three feet apart, imprison the remaining water. The voids formed by the intersecting bars are approximately six inches by six inches. In an inadvertent mercy to fishermen, the voids of the two grids lie in alignment, allowing small fish to be hauled from the violet depths.

Fishing licenses are granted to fewer than thirty men a month, and Declan has been on the waitlist for five and a half years. He is eager to run his lines immediately to catch dinner for the dorm. My father wants to return to his mat.

"No one's going to get at you, Ozzie," Declan assures him. "We'll be right underneath the gun tower. It's safer than the dorm."

"I think I'd just as soon go lie down for a while," says Osmund. The bathhouse violence has renewed his melancholy.

"Is that a joke? All you do is lie down."

"Yeah, I'm just not feeling a tremendous surplus of energy at the moment."

"I don't give a shit," says Declan. "I can't carry you forever, Ozzie. You need to pull your fucking weight. I need help running lines. Getting those meds was a pain in the ass. I wouldn't have fooled with it if I'd known you were going to be such a waste of resources."

Here is proof of Declan's subtle wisdom. Of all the wrongs to detest in Thep Moob, Declan has heard my father lament nothing so vehemently as the fruit left daily to rot at the Buddha's knees in the Zone A yard. His acquaintance with my father spans only thirty-three days, yet he understands that above all things "a waste of resources" is what Osmund Tower most deplores. The phrase has a magical effect.

"I'd be delighted to fish with you, though skin cancer is an issue with me," my father says. "I'll need to go and get my hat."

Beside the sea pool stands a ramshackle structure made of salvaged plumbing pipe and minor lumber, clad in a patchwork of torn sheet plastic and canvas waterproofed with cooking grease. This is the prison restaurant. Guards and wealthy prisoners eat here. The restaurant's proprietor is a *kathoey* named Meena, an unpreened, square-skulled beauty in the Valerie Bertinelli mode. She does business under the sanction of Sam Wunon, a much-feared warder who has been Meena's faithful spouse for over a decade. They supply bait and loan tackle for a 50 percent tax of each fisherman's catch.

Declan knocks at the restaurant's window and displays his license. Meena, her face gridded with rope lines from a hammock siesta, passes him hooks, lines, a baggie of chicken skins, and, after some pleading, a fistful of old chopsticks.

At the sea wall, my father saws up the chicken skins, which behave under his plastic knife like a sort of durable mucus. Declan readies the tackle. Other inmates fish with the line wrapped around their fists, or else tied to the rebar, but Declan has a more cunning method in mind. From his pack, he takes a dozen or so of the wooden paddle-spoons that come free with an ice cream purchase at the prison canteen; using a knife made of sharpened bottle glass, he bores a hole through the center of each spoon's handle. He spits a chopstick through each hole, forming a little pile of crosses. In the spoons' paddles, he cuts a notch, to which he ties the lines.

These are tip-up rigs. The chopsticks sit on the rebar members of the sea pool's enclosure; when a fish takes the bait, a spoon will tip up, alerting the anglers that dinner is on the line.

"It's an old ice-fishing deal," Declan says. "I don't know if it'll work here, but I thought it would sit on the cage okay. I haven't done this since I was a kid. My father used to take me out on Dilworth Lake with him. He had a little trailer-cabin. I fucking hated it. He'd just sit in there getting plastered, which is basically what ice fishing is all about."

"You say it's about plaster," my father says. The assassin's forearm has left a raw place under his jaw. He rubs the spot with a palmful of sea-water.

"Getting shitfaced drunk."

"Drunk."

"Yeah, you know—you pass a frozen lake and see all those little sheds out there, it's basically a freakin' cirrhosis colony. Half of them probably don't even have a line in the water, but a hundred percent of the guys in there are blitzed out of their minds, just out there getting away from their wives. With me and my dad, it was kind of this unspoken thing that I'd handle the fishing stuff, and he'd handle the cabin—get the little coal fire going, get it staked into the ice and everything. And I'd spud out the holes and keep them skimmed and bait the hooks and do pretty much everything else, while he sat in a little camp chair pounding Molsons.

"One day we're in there—I'm maybe fifteen, sixteen, and suddenly the wind blows up and all hell breaks loose. Turns out, my dad didn't stake the fucking cabin, and the whole shack blows over onto its side. Of course it's the side with the door in it. So we're stuck, and not only that, the coal stove is spilling these fucking embers everywhere and the dog is going apeshit, and my dad's being totally useless, just kind of yelling. So I break out the window, which is now in the ceiling, haul myself up, and I'm going 'Dad, hand me Poxie, boost Poxie up to me,' but he doesn't know what the fuck he's doing, so he decides to just make a break for it. Climbs out the window and kind of falls on me, knocks me down on the ice. I'm just about to go back in to get the dog when another gust blows up and the cabin goes skittering off until it runs up against this island about a quarter of a mile away. 'Oh, jeez, oh jeez, oh jeez,' is all my father's saying. So I get in the truck.

"I just leave him standing there, freezing his ass off. I didn't care. I can see all this fire coming out the window of the cabin, so I know my dog's gotta be dead. But I drive after it anyway and I take the tire tool and I get a sheet of the plywood loose. A big wad of smoke comes billowing out, and then the damn dog trots through it like a little magician. She's coughing and her fur's burned in a few places, but otherwise, she's basically okay. Kind of a miracle. She was such a great little dog. So we drive back to where my dad's standing, watching the cabin burn. No apology, no nothing. Not even a, 'Hey, thanks for handling that there, fifteen-year-old kid.' I couldn't believe it. And usually I'm a pretty passive person. Or I was. I'm working on it. But I also have this real well of anger I can draw on, that sometimes gets me into trouble. I had to consciously put down the pry bar so I wouldn't hit him. I was that mad. And I was really lighting into him, verbally I mean. You know, just 'You're supposed to my father? You almost got us killed, just because you were so hot to get drunk you didn't anchor the fucking cabin? You're pathetic. If I ever have a kid and I do something like that, I hope I get locked up. I'd deserve it. Look at Poxie, you fucking asshole. You burnt up my dog!'"

Declan's story moves my father greatly. A tear comes to Osmund's eye, on a tide of feeling for fathers and sons. He thinks of me, and of my brother, and he feels that the guilt must be partly his that we have not grown into better men.

"Oh, Jesus, we do fuck them up, our children. Don't we, Declan?"

The tear falls. He clears his throat to make this confession.

"My boys couldn't have been older than six and eight when our cat had kittens. I told them to find homes for them, and when they didn't, I filled up a trash barrel with hose water and drowned the kittens while the boys watched. They cried and cried, which I didn't understand because I'd seen both my father and my grandfather do the same thing. But now I see how cruel this was, and perhaps this explains why my boys are furtive, solitary men incapable of forming meaningful human connections or even holding decent jobs." He closed his eyes. "My sons, I love you. I have failed you so."

Actually, I'm making this up. Not the part about the kittens. That really happened, but Osmund isn't thinking about that right now. It's good to be acknowledged for one's achievements, is the lesson my father takes from Declan's tale.

"It is important, isn't it? This sense that one is appreciated," my father says. "I remember very early on in my career, I just happened to be reading an article by George Stigler, who maybe you know, won the

413

Nobel Prize in 1982, and there in the footnote it said, 'For a pellucid investigation of symmetrical inflation targets, please read such-and-such,' and holy mackerel! There was a reference to the *first article I published* out of graduate school. I had to look up 'pellucid,' but boy, for a guy like that to just reach out and show that kind of appreciation for somebody just getting his start . . ."

"Must have been a real headfuck," Declan says.

"I still get warm fuzzies when I think of it. These things are important, to be recognized when we do something useful."

"Yeah, I guess on some level, everybody's kind of a fame hound," Declan says. "Which reminds me—you want to know something weird? With this stupid fucking dance thing, yeah, it'd be great to have a TV or whatever in the dorm. But more and more, I'm thinking it'll be kind of cool to have it on the Web—to know people out there are seeing me. Which makes no sense. We're going to look like a bunch of retards. Anyone who knows me and sees it, they'll either laugh or it'll depress the shit out of them."

He glances at his spoons. "When I first got in here, I just wanted to disappear. I'd have gone in the Suitcase before I'd have gone along with this Mickey Mouse bullshit. But you'll see, Ozzie. Or I hope you don't. Once people stop writing, stop making the trip to see you, you start to feel like a ghost." Declan frees a length of line snagged on a scab of rust. "I dunno. What the fuck."

The sudden bucking and hopping of Declan's rigs halts this gloomy line of talk. The men go into a panic of delight, hauling in their tackle. Bucking on the hooks are small, oblong fish with aristocratic, underslung jaws. A shifting aurora of yellow and blue plays over the fishes' flanks, colors that quench to dull dun the instant Declan dashes their brains against the wall of the sea pool. The two of them haul fish and bait lines as fast as they can. It is like a dream in which you keep finding money. They catch fifteen fish in eight minutes, but before ten minutes are up, the school has moved on.

As though to announce the end of the jubilee, a voice comes over the intercom. It utters a phlegmatic incantation in Thai that, uncharacteristically for public addresses here, does not suggest the imperative mood. My father fails to discern the name of Oliver Fehar in the stream of foreign jabber.

"Thank Christ," says Declan Weyde. "Oliver bailed."

"You say Oliver left," says Osmund.

414

"Sailed through the ghost door," Declan says. "He's out of here, man."

My father draws in a hungry lungful of wharf-scented air. His gaze registers the arrangement of salmon and slate hanging in the western sky.

"Boy," he says. "Being alive sure beats being dead."

THE ARIZONA DEAD ARM

Who is the new man grooving alone in the Zone C yard? A blindfold hides his eyes. His body is lean and chiseled. His groove device is a hula-hoop made from half-inch Pex plumbing conduit. He seems never to touch the hula hoop. No muscle in his body concerns itself explicitly with the revolving plastic O. The hoop, rather, wanders over him—his arms, his torso, his legs—taking the measure of some deep and powerful rotaryness, some strong orbital electron play within the gentleman. His feet seem to glide above the earth on a film of slick air. There are Balinese fancinesses of hand. No fooling: this man can get down.

Declan and Osmund encounter him on their way back from the sea pool. Declan says, "Hey, man, you're pretty good with that thing," and "Hey, excuse me?" and "Speak English, bro?" before the man pauses in his hoop work and lifts his blindfold. His name, he says, is Johnny Francis. Austin, Texas is his home. By way of friendly chitchat, my father describes Austin as "neat" and also "funky."

"No offense," Johnny replies, "but I'm trying to get through a workout here." He tugs the blindfold down. The hoop resumes its tour of the Texan's perfect frame. His routine is idle and meditative, the dance of a sleepwalker, the finning of a sleeping fish. Should Johnny Francis be persuaded to invest a little energy, it will be a motherfucker, dancingwise.

Declan fetches Ron Tolenaar. Ron sees what is at stake and attempts to recruit Johnny Francis to take Oliver's place in A-23. Nothing doing, says Johnny. He's already got a spot in a Westerners' dorm in Zone B. Say Ron covers three months of Johnny's rent in exchange for his directorship of the A-23 dance team? But Johnny's dorm drew "Gonna Make You Sweat." It would be a creative concession to have to craft a routine for "Ice Ice Baby." Five months' free rent plus laundry service? Ron has himself a deal. Johnny moves in the following day. Rehearsals begin that afternoon.

* * *

The autumn rains begin as well, and between midnight and dawn, the prison is a place my father does not want to leave. The susurrus of water on the lead roof is deafening, absolving. It drowns out all sounds of men crying in their sleep, of voices raised in fury, of the yard guard who, just to be obnoxious, bawlingly croons "New York, New York" at his audience of captives trying to sleep. The view from my father's mat is of the seaward rifle tower. Through the curtains of rain, the tower is a distant glow, an emblem of watchfulness as wholesome as a lit belvedere in a village church.

The choreography Johnny designs is complex and challenging. It calls for much lively ankling and swift pivot work. With only two daily broadcasts of "Ice Ice Baby," the lessons take place under a generous pressure. Declan, Ter, Ron, and Henri (despite his boasts) are not natural dancers, but after a few days' instruction, they have grasped the rudiments of the pivot step. My father has not. When the others shuffle left, he lumbers right, squandering precious rehearsal time.

"Fuckin', come on, dude, left!" Johnny roars at Osmund. Their common nationality makes him no gentler toward my father. "How hard is the concept of left?"

"Left, left, left, got it. Sorry," my father says.

"*Shuffle*, dude! Don't—I don't even know what to call what you're doing. Plant the right foot, T-step with the left. T-step. *T-step*! Are you shitting me, man? Jesus, this is really blowing my mind."

"I'm sorry," says my father. "But the tendons in my feet aren't in great shape. My ankles tend to swell, so the pirouettes are hard for me."

"*Pivot*, not pirouette, like this," says Declan Weyde, whirling slowly on the ball of one foot.

"How about you just stay the fuck out of everyone's way," says Johnny Francis. "Make that your priority."

"Stay the fuck out of the way," my father murmurs. "Got it."

At night, with the sound of the rain as a cover, Johnny Francis revolts against house rules by whacking off in the dark. This puts Ron Tolenaar in a bind: Johnny's gifts as a dancer and choreographer have raised his status in Ron's eyes, and so Ron feels not wholly entitled to rebuke Johnny over the violation. His wan wish is that Johnny will get it out of his system and desist on his own.

This does not come to pass. On the fifth night, Ron's tolerance

416

reaches its limit. Shortly after Johnny starts up, Ron turns on the light and storms over to the other man's mat. With his foot he nudges the blinking Texan, who still clutches a stiff prick in his hand.

"I told you, Johnny. You don't do it when other people are in the house. Now get your penis out of here, man. You do this some more, I'm gonna tear off your head and crap on it."

Johnny drags his waistband north of his erection. He grinds the palm of his hand against an eyesocket. "Look, Ron, I gotta tell you, man, the way you're running this house ain't sitting so cool with me."

"What? It is the rules. You need to get off, you come and do it before we get back from chow."

"Yeah, see, that doesn't really work with my deal," says Johnny Francis. "I'm an insomniac, which I've got ways of dealing with, one being I need to get empty before I can fall asleep. Plus, I work an Arizona Dead Arm, so it takes a while to get my hand to where I can do my thing."

"You Arizona what?" Ron asks.

Johnny Francis explains the Arizona Dead Arm, a practice of which he is surprised the others aren't aware. The notion is this: you lie for a time on your back in a self-administered "hammerlock" hold, in which the arm is wrenched upward toward the scapula. When the nerves have "gone to sleep," one can masturbate under the neural illusion that the hand on one's private parts belongs to a second party. This idea so intrigues Ron Tolenaar that the masturbation ban in A-23 is eased for a provisional, exploratory period.

Within a couple of nights, A-23's residents conclude that the benefits of the Arizona Dead Arm do not justify its procedural complexity. Neither my father nor Ron Tolenaar can compel his arm to fall asleep. Declan and Henri successfully clear that hurdle, but both find the benumbed arm too maladroit to deliver any satisfactions. Whether Ter has any luck with it is unknown; during the Dead Arm research, Ron remands Ter to the small areaway behind the toilet enclosure so as not to subject the young man to perversion.

Even after the experiment has been deemed a nonstarter the formidable yearning at the heart of the Dead Arm episode continues to suffuse the dorm. One evening, Ron Tolenaar can bear it no more. He seizes the hand of Henri Permeuil and puts it to his crotch. Ron will not return the favor, but under a quid pro quo agreement, Henri is able to persuade Johnny Francis to masturbate him in turn. By bedtime, Henri's forearms are sore.

Now, of an evening, the darkened cell is alive with the sounds of briskness and cooperation. *Schwitt-schwitt-schwitt.* A blind eavesdropper would believe he is overhearing the scrimmage of a lint-removal team.

So what of my father? He does not join in. Since being serially whittled by surgeons, his prostate is a sliver of its former self, reduced in size and shape to a lozenge of hotel soap in its last day of use. The lozenge is still technically operable, just as the old Bolens weedeater in his garage—with much priming and white-knuckled pull-cord jerkage—can sometimes be persuaded to start, but the reward rarely justifies the effort. The textile chorus inspires in him a complicated sort of envy akin to watching others gleefully gorge themselves on food for which you lack the appetite.

Tonight, he lies in the dark, manipulating a partial stoutness with no real clasmic ambition. Just showing his support for the spirit of teamwork and tenderness that has come into A-23, just tapping his foot at the edge of the dance floor. Beside him, Declan achieves manumission with what strikes my father as fearsome efficiency and dispatch. It is after the sounds of Declan toweling himself off desist that my father feels Declan's hand on his abdomen.

My father has not been touched by another person in this way in over a decade. The sensation he experiences is the equal and opposite of jumping into a freezing pool. His lungs bind up. Every cell in his body goes silent and hearkens to Declan's hand. His penis does stiffen, though perhaps less in venereal salute than sensual shock. Also connoisseurial curiosity. It is not necessarily that Osmund wishes to be masturbated by a man, but he does expect that a hand job administered by a fellow owner-operator of male anatomy will be first-rate.

But as the procedure wears on, my father is able to assess more clearly the quality of the experience. Declan's hand is clawlike, his motions jolting and importunate. Osmund is bewildered that another man should manage this familiar operation so clumsily; the vision of his father-stuff spilling onto Declan's cracked and calloused fingers is homely and impossible. My father's penis begins to wilt, which causes Declan to palp and wring it with renewed intensity. Not only is this awkward, it is quite painful. When he can stand it no longer, Osmund clears his throat.

"I don't know that this strikes me as being particularly effective," he says.

Declan's hand retracts. The men lie side by side on their mats, listening to the coursing rain.

A MORNING OF REFLECTION

The next day Osmund Tower rises and dresses at 5:35, shortly after the trusty unlocks the dorm. The morning is one of surpassing gentleness. The sunrise has not dispelled the rain-washed courtyard's atmosphere of predawn lavender. My father pauses on the catwalk and flares his nostrils for a maximum intake of fresh air. Far to the south, a merchant marine vessel creeps across the sea's Scope-colored breadth. The boat cheers Osmund as a happy augury. He considers the young man's fantasy of viewing the world from the decks of a container ship, and he is able to muster a warming delusion that his arrival at Thep Moob constitutes a fulfillment (though a denatured fulfillment) of a noble and swashbuckling dream. This delusion quickly abandons him. "Ree-diculous," my father says, smirking and shaking his head.

Behind him, he hears the tread of bare feet. Ter steps onto the walkway, delicately currying the sleep from his eye with a pinky nail.

"Good morning, Ter. You're up early."

"Johnny, man, he snore like a pig."

Ter and Osmund head down to the courtyard, where Meena is readying the coffeeshop for the day's trade. Osmund is her first customer. A slender hand parts the cloudy Visqueen that covers the service window. Meena's face is damp from her morning ablutions; even without her makeup, she is lovely, her beauty no trick of cosmetic art.

"Mm," my father says. "Your cheekbones are just extraordinary."

Amid the quick exchange of Thai between the warder's wife and Ter my father hears what sounds like "melon branding." Meena laughs, then vanishes behind the Visqueen to concoct a pair of coffees.

"What's this about melons?" my father asks Ter.

"Marlon Brando. Movie star. She think you look like him."

My father chortles his way into a bout of prodigious phlegm haulage. "I'm extremely flattered."

"Not young Marlon. Not *Streetcar* Marlon. *Superman* Marlon. The big guy."

The smile dims but does not vanish. "Fair enough. I suppose there is a resemblance there."

"No, you Peter Boyle. *Young Frankenstein*? Peter Boyle. He dead."

"How do you know so much about American movies, Ter?"

Ter's late uncle and guardian, it is explained, kept up a sizable video library, and he let Ter show films in the refectory on Saturday evenings. After his uncle's death, the library was plundered by the other guards, putting an end to movie night.

"Do Thai universities offer degrees in film, Ter?"

A lit cigarette falling from the rifle tower seizes the young man's interest. It strikes the pavement in a bloom of sparks. Ter has snatched it up before the second bounce.

Osmund persists. "You're a very good dancer, you know. Very artful and athletic. Maybe you'd like to study dance, or physical education of some kind. Your English is quite good. You could be an English teacher."

Behind a plume of dense blue lung smoke, my father's cellmate squints and shrugs.

"Let me ask you this: picture yourself in ten years, doing exactly what brings you the most pleasure. What would that be?"

With a moistened pinky, Ter smooths a rent in the rolling paper. "I don't know. Maybe I drive the bus."

"Okay, good. Bus driver is a fine profession. A city bus, or tours and things?"

"The prison bus. The bus take you to the court."

"Come on, man, you don't want to stay here. Talk about a waste of human capital. You're a bright guy. You ought to be out having adventures and enriching the world."

Ter pinches out the cigarette and puts it away for later. "My friends are here," he says.

The boy's complacency inspires in my father something close to anger. Mercifully, the coffees arrive and cut Osmund's line of questioning short. With Meena's miserly stub of a pencil, he signs for both coffees to be debited from his canteen account. Ter declines to drink his coffee, but instead thanks my father and carries it upstairs to Ron. Alone at the counter, Osmund downs his drink with many wet decibels, feeling curiously spurned.

But the morning air is sweet, and the coffee is, he tells Meena, "religious—just spectacular." He orders a second cup and a breakfast of eggs which he drowns with pepper vinegar and chili sauce. The meal is so delicious that Meena's disgusted scowl does not prevent my father's licking the plate. The bounty restores his mood. Osmund takes from his pocket a blank aerogramme and writes his weekly letter home.

My father has just sealed up the aerogramme when Declan comes am-
bling into the yard. He is making purposefully toward the bathhouse.
When his eyes meet Osmund's, they exchange a humiliated greeting:
partial wave, shallow nod. The trusty at the bathhouse door stands in
Declan's way; he has arrived too late for bath call. Declan pleads with
the trusty, to no success. He is desperate not for a bath, but to be spared
the discomfort of passing Osmund at the coffee counter. For an ago-
nized moment, he loiters, shamming interest in the graffiti on the bath-
house wall. The men's shared unease thickens over the courtyard like
smoke. The sole means of relieving it is for Declan to go and bid my
father good morning.

"Hiya."

"Morning, Declan. Let me fix you up with a cup of this excellent
coffee."

"All set, thanks."

"You sure? It's truly exceptional."

"I'm cool."

Osmund: *glurp, mm, gah!* "Man alive, you're missing out." At the
northern end of the courtyard, a troupe of shirtless teenagers covered
in bright tattoos cycle through some break-dance moves to razzing and
flatulent human-beat-box accompaniment.

"So, uh, yeah, I guess the scene in the dorm got a little too groovy
last night," says Declan, through a forced grin. "Just for the record, that
type of thing is really not my vibe. I was just, uh."

Osmund is not looking at Declan, but at the dancing boys. Under the
strain of his mortification, Declan's explanation of what is or is not his
vibe peters painfully out.

"Boy, those guys have a lot of energy. And their tattoos are marvel-
ously colorful," my father muses, apparently to himself. "I imagine the
pleasure of having a colorful tattoo is somewhat akin to the joy of pub-
lishing an elegantly written paper. It's about distinguishing oneself in
an artistic way."

"Yeah, I guess. But I mean, just to clear the air: I don't know where
your head's at this morning, but as far as that deal last night—"

"I feel good, I feel good," says my father, gazing off across the court-
yard. "The lungs are operating properly, and the pain I'd been feeling
in my ankle has diminished."

"Because, look, just so you know, I wasn't like, wanting, necessarily to—"

Osmund cuts him off: "Boy, being locked up ain't ideal, but it is nice to be around youthfulness and energy and this wonderful sea air. I don't think I'd last too long in an old folks' home."

Declan supposes Osmund is disgusted with him. With this fusillade of platitudes the professor seemingly wishes to silence, to annihilate the man who wrongly palped his cock. A helpless outrage mounts. Declan had only been following the mode of the moment. No big deal. But rather than discuss and void this minor mishap, my father has fled into abstraction. Declan begins to feel like Osmund's cranky wife, gassed up with unacknowledged feelings.

Osmund summons Meena for a third cup of coffee, which he drinks with noise and relish equal to the first. "I don't know what sort of coffeemaker it was that you stole, Declan, but if it made coffee half this good, I'd say the temptation was justifiable."

Declan's jaw distends to rake a patch of dry skin from his upper lip. "Are you fucking with me?"

"In what sense would I be fucking with you?"

"What, Henri told you?"

"Henri hasn't told me anything."

The tale is one from which Declan, until now, had striven to protect Osmund. But in his present state of mind, he is glad to have language that might do my father harm. The light of morning hardens in the yard, and Declan Weyde tells Osmund Tower the story of the coffeepot.

THE KETTLE THIEF

Sometime in his late forties, Declan Weyde became invisible to the women of North America. His descent into invisibility was not unforeseen—Declan's vision of a fulfilled life was one of constant travel, of knowing the world and its people and languages and lands, of fleeing the rat race for sporadic work as a handyman and spreader of mulch. What this life would cost him in comfort and respectability, it would repay him in illuminating experiences.

His voyaging had carried him to all of the planet's continents, Antarctica included. The only home he owned was an inherited hunting cabin that lacked indoor plumbing. In his twenties and thirties, women had seen past his penury and lack of ambition and beheld a kind and decent man who'd had many unusual experiences and who could talk about them amusingly. When Declan reached his middle years, though, women started to perceive him as an immature misfit or a potential

422

dependent. In time, they seemed to perceive him not at all. When he was at home at his cabin, which was miles from the nearest village, he could pass many months without so much as being looked at by a fellow member of the human race.

In his late fifties, Declan applied for work as an English teacher in Thailand. It had been his hope that his colleagues would be a campfire team of European backpack women with unshaven bodies and thick hair kerchiefed in bandanas. They would be the sort of women who would have an appreciation for a man who had traveled widely. They would not scruple over Declan's age or his composting commode.

He did not find these sorts of women. His posting was in the northern city of Chiang Rai. He taught not at a school, but at an experimental call center dedicated to the trading of latex futures with Western commodities markets. For the first time in his life, he had a job where he was expected to wear a necktie. The students in his classes were professionals with advanced degrees. Behind their politeness, Declan could sense their bewilderment at how a *farang* of his age should be working so lowly a job. On days off, he would journey to Bangkok or to the beach towns in the south. These he found too expensive, too young, too reverberant with confusing music. After a while, on the advice of a fellow traveler, Declan went to Ngop Na, which is where he got into trouble.

He found Ngop Na to be a town populated chiefly by prostitutes and their patrons. Declan was lonely, but not so lonely as to overcome a lifelong resolution never to hire a woman to sleep with him. He did not drink, so bars were out too. But he had paid ahead of time for a nonrefundable three-day hotel stay. He was stuck in Ngop Na with nothing to do.

"So I pretty much walked around and got massages. There was this one place on the corner near my hotel, with this one woman who gave me these great fucking massages—I got a three-hour massage from her every day. Feet, body, head. It was incredible. By the third day, we'd sort of gotten to know each other. Her name was Miaow. She had a couple of kids in Bangkok. She hated Ngop Na, but she got paid more there than she did in the city. So anyway, my last night, I took her out to dinner. We took a walk on the beach. And I guess we kissed a little bit, but nothing too heavy.

"I went down a few weeks later and saw her again, and it was really nice—we kind of got into a romance, that time, and it went from there. I met her kids, I met her mom. And I was really starting to think about setting up a life for myself in Thailand. The fucked-up thing was, right about then, my visa expired. I could have renewed it if I kept working, but Miaow didn't want to move her kids up to Chiang Rai, and I couldn't get anyone to hire me in Ngop Na. It's not a real education hub. So I told her, 'Look, I'll go back to B.C. I'll see if I can sell my cabin, and then I'll come back and we'll get married.' So that's what I did. I went home and I sold my place for sixty thousand bucks. I could live a long time on that in Thailand. In the meantime, I'd been talking to Miaow when I could, but she didn't have a computer, so she'd Skype me from the internet café a couple of times a week. Anyway, right after the closing, I head back to Thailand, and I go straight to Ngop Na, but Miaow's not at work. The other ladies at the massage place are saying, 'Oh, she stay home, she stay home. She sick.' I think, 'This is weird. I just heard from her. She knows I'm coming.'

"So I go to her apartment. She's not there, and I'm wondering what the hell is going on. I mean, I just sold my house, everything, to come and be with this girl. So that night, I'm walking past the bus station, and I see Miaow getting on a bus with this guy. I run over. I'm like, 'Hey, Miaow, what's going on?' She's with this weird-looking Thai dude. He's older than me, mid-sixties. Dressed like he's got a lot of dough, but in a Vegas sort of way. Shiny purple shirt and a bunch of gold chains.

"Miaow's all, 'Oh, Deck, Deck. Hi, hi, I'm so sorry.' She tells me her sister's been sick and that this guy here is her brother-in-law. They're going off to see the sister somewhere, and they'll be back in a few days. I say, 'Well, why don't I come along?' And she's like, No, no, her sister's a very private person, blah blah. Meanwhile the guy's on the bus, sort of huffing around, throwing their shit in the overhead thing, and looking daggers at me. For a second, I actually buy the story. That's how fucking stupid and gullible I am. I'm like, 'Fuck it, I'm coming with you,' just to see what happens. She's kind of pleading with me. 'No, no, no.'

"Anyway, I get on the bus with them. Turns out they're heading to this little string of resorts down the coast. The guy keeps turning around in his seat, looking at me, getting pissed off, and she's trying to calm him down. Was I upset? I mean, kind of. Though I guess I was also just kind of blown away that I'd been so dumb. Of course someone like Miaow's going to have a few guys on the side, and this guy definitely looked like a better bet than me, at least financially. But so now, I'm just like, you know what, fuck it. I came all this way and this asshole has

424

wrecked my scene, fuck it, I'll wreck his. So I do this sort of crazy thing. I follow them to the resort. I book a little cabana just down the beach from theirs. It's like a hundred fifty bucks a night, more money than I've ever spent on a hotel anywhere, let alone in Thailand. But, shit, I've got the cash, at least for now. And then I make it my daily thing to just sort of fuck with them.

"I'd get up early and tail them to breakfast. Like, 'Hey, guys, what're we doing today? Want to rent some jet skis? Want to go snorkeling?' I'd send them drinks and stuff at dinner. I'm actually having a blast. I'm sort of proud of myself for, like, letting this thing that could have really knocked my whole self-concept out of joint just turn into a kind of a joke. And I can tell it's working, the number I'm doing on their little deal. Like, they're not really talking. I can see them bitching at each other. She wants to just get the hell out of there to get away from me, but the guy's gotten territorial. Like, 'That *farang* asshole's not gonna run me off!' It was really pretty funny. She begged me to leave a few times, but when she saw I wasn't going to, she just started trying to ignore me.

"One thing I did: on one end of the beach, there was a kind of a hip little sunset cliff thing you could take a path to. The second night, after she sort of had it out with me, telling me she wouldn't see me anymore, she and that guy go off up the path. I'm actually a pretty good rock climber, so I do this thing where I go around to the other side of the little hill and scale up there really quick. I bust my ass doing it, so when they get to the top, I'm already there—like, 'Hey, guys, glad you could join me. Killer view!'

"By the third day, though, I was just about over it. I was going to head back to Ngop Na, and maybe go see if they'd take me on in Chiang Rai again, figure out how to get on with my life. I'm chilling on the beach in one of those chairs they have set up, checking on the train schedule. And Miaow and the guy are down the beach in their own little chairs, just carping at each other, having a fucking miserable time. I'm not even really paying them any attention by then. I've literally got my face in a train timetable, about to get the fuck out of their hair, when suddenly I'm out of the chair, in the sand, on my back. The guy must have been a black belt or something. I didn't see him coming. He just flipped me out of the chair, rabbit-punched me in the nose, and then he like grabbed me by the hinges of my jaw and hocks a fucking loogie into my mouth. I don't know where he learned that one, but man, it's a pretty

425

good way to humiliate somebody. I could taste the cigar he'd been smoking. And before I even know what the hell happened, he's on his way back up the beach.

"So I go back to my little cabana. I'm realizing the guy messed me up pretty good—I know it's bad, because when I get in there, there's this plumber in the bathroom. He takes one look at me, sort of goes pale, and he just hauls ass. My nose is totally broken and I'm coughing like I've been poisoned, trying to get this dude's lunger out of my throat.

"And you know, I'm really not a very angry guy. I'm not. I don't ever get so pissed off that I can't control it. Once or twice with my folks, but really, I've got a good handle on it. But something just kind of broke that day. And I don't know how I thought to do this, but do you know how they seal a joint in a cast-iron pipe? They tamp this stuff, this fiber stuff, oakum, down into the joint. Then they pour lead into it, which seals it off. That's what the plumber guy had been doing in my cabana, sealing a cast-iron pipe. And he'd left his little kettle there. I'd laid a little pipe before, so I knew what it was. This was a funny little third-world rig, not electric, but it had some, I dunno, sterno or magnesium in a little heating element in the base to keep the lead liquid.

"Anyway. Mr. Kung Fu had snuck up on me pretty good, but I got him even better. He was just lying on a chair, eyes closed. Miaow wasn't anywhere around. By then, she was probably thinking, 'Fuck both these guys. I'm done.' So I sneak up behind the dude, and when my shadow crosses his face, he opens his eyes. That's when I let him have it with the kettle. Probably there was a good pint of liquid lead in there. Man, what a freaky thing to see. His eye just sort went *fffff!* like a marshmallow in a campfire."

My father is not sure how to take this. The temperature of his bowels suddenly drops several degrees. "It killed him, I assume."

Declan coughs into his fist. The raconteur's brio that had briefly brightened the younger man's mood has departed. "He lived for a few months. It wasn't good. He couldn't really eat. The lead went through his sinus cavity. It messed up his tongue and his throat."

A sheeny black bird alights on the wall of the sea pool and makes a computer sound. Declan squints at it. A solid minute of silence passes.

Declan's story poses a challenge to Osmund's conscience. How does one respond to such a confession? What would his ex-wife, my mother, do? Perhaps she would condemn the man as evil and sever all contact with him. Or she would play at being the murderer's therapist. She

426

would buy Declan a journal and instruct him to chronicle his feelings and childhood hurts.

Osmund suffers an onset of spiritual exhaustion. For a time he is quiet. Then he says, "Funny, funny, this desire to transgress. When I was seven I became very preoccupied with trying to commit the perfect crime. One night, my parents had a party. I knew they would sleep in the following morning. So I got up very early. Downstairs, in a corner behind the radiator, were three nesting stools we rarely used. The smallest one was never used at all, so it struck me as an ideal victim. I took it outside, the dwarf stool, and got my father's hatchet from the toolshed. I loved that hatchet. Its size seemed to imply that I, as a child, was somehow sanctioned to destroy things. Anyway, I chopped up the stool with the hatchet, and I buried the broken parts under the pear tree in the backyard. The fruit of the tree was bitter. No one ever gathered the pears, so there was a sort of a haze of yellow jackets buzzing around its roots during summer and fall. The earth there seemed somehow evil and also off-limits. A good place to dump a body.

"As it turned out, it *was* the perfect crime. No one ever noticed that the stool was missing. About thirty years later, we stopped at my mother's on the way up to Maine. The pear tree had died and been cut down a long time before, but before we left in the morning, my mother asked me to dig out the stump. We were in a hurry and it infuriated Marian that I would delay our departure to truckle for my mother's favor by doing this menial chore. She always accused me of being tied to my mother's apron strings. Well, when I was rooting up the stump, I found the remains of that stool. I wanted to mention it to Marian, as evidence of my, I don't know, resistance to my mother's will. But I figured my wife would have a way of turning it on me, so I kept mum. Funny, funny."

Declan has nothing to say about my father's dismemberment of the dwarf stool. Already, his motives for making Osmund his confessor for the lead-kettle tale are obscure to him. A mild nausea of regret thickens his gullet. He watches the computer bird strut madly along the bars of the sea pool. Declan notices now that this bird is living with a serious injury. It has swallowed a fishhook. From its black beak curls a length of monofilament that takes an apricot hue in the day's young light.

THE DANCE CONTEST

It is the first Sunday in November, contest day. Thep Moob's general population waits outside the refectory, where the prisoners will dance for the video camera. To say that the inmates are stricken with dance fever would not be accurate. Most faces are leaden or asmolder with quiet rage. They are sacrificing a Sunday, a day of leisure in Thep Moob, to forced participation in disgraceful minstrelsy. The men are not even afforded the diversion of watching their fellow prisoners perform. Fearing that competitive passions might turn violent, Captain Surongporn has decreed that the teams will perform one-by-one, behind the closed doors of the refectory. The last team in the lineup will dance after a nine-hour wait in the yard.

The six men of A-23 slouch against the wall of the refectory, absorbing the bricks' banked heat against an unseasonable morning chill. "You hanging in there, Ozzie?" Declan asks my father. "We should have brought you a blanket or something."

My father is dressed only in a diaper, or rather, a towel swaddled around his midsection to resemble a diaper. He sniffs. "A little cold," he says. "If I'd been more organized I would have put on shorts or underpants so that I could have used the towel as a shawl. But there we are. It isn't unbearable."

Minutes before noon, A-23 is summoned to perform. "So, Johnny," my father is saying to Johnny Francis, as they pass through the refectory doors. "Just to be clear, I'm basically to stand there—"

"Don't just *stand there*. Move and shit. Do some baby shit."

"Sort of say, 'goo goo,' and things."

Johnny's eleventh-hour solution to the problem of Osmund's unfitness as a dancer has been to turn his liabilities—his unnimbleness and obesity—into, Johnny hopes, a winning gimmick. My diapered father is to portray a giant baby in A-23's now famous "Ice Ice Baby" video.

"I don't give a fuck what you say," says Johnny. "No one will be able to hear you. Just make sure you turn in the chorus."

"And the chorus is which?"

"When he says, 'Check out the hook while my DJ revolves it,' you just start turning around in a circle."

"And you'll say this?"

Johnny slaps his own temples. "The *fucking record, man!* Where the fuck have you been for the past month?"

"I'm very sorry, but my hearing—"

"Just listen for 'revolve,'" says Declan. "I'll tap you if you miss it."

"I'll stomp you on your prick," says Ron Tolenaar.

"Goo-goo, goo-goo, revolve," says Osmund. "Got it, got it."

Perhaps you are one of the four million online viewers of the "Ice Ice Baby " clip. I sometimes wonder if any of you four million has failed to ask me whether the video of my incarcerated father dancing in a diaper causes me pain. Yes, his imprisonment has been an agonizing ordeal for us, and yes, the first time I saw the video, I thought I would swoon and barf with shame. But beyond his letters (and the odd note from Ter, with whom I've struck up a correspondence), the video affords my only real glimpse of the old man's life in Thep Moob. Having now watched it dozens of times, I can honestly say that I'm grateful for it—it is a documentary testament to much of what I love and admire about my father. With the family resources under strain, I can't justify the time and expense of a trip to Thailand merely to speak with him through a Plexiglas window for twenty minutes once a week. So this brief film is what I have.

Even on the umpteenth viewing, the look of worry in his face in the opening moments makes my pulse hammer. He stands in the center of the shot, a pace or two in front of the other men. His nose and upper lip quaver, threatening a sneeze or a sobbing jag. His eyes swivel in their sockets, trying to glimpse his teammates, who crouch behind him, pumping haunchily in sprinters-at-the-starting-blocks attitudes. Naked terror distends his features, as though he expects the men to claw him to pieces. When they rise and boil out around him, his fear does not subside.

But a wise friend pointed out something remarkable about my father's performance here: he looks only at his fellow dancers. My father is the only member of his dance team with an entry in *Who's Who*, yet he is also the only dancer who glances not a single time at the camera, the eye of the world. His anxiety is not for himself, or for the certain harm the video will inflict on his reputation. His only worry is that he will be a bad baby and let down his team. No one can tell me that this is not a kind of valor.

The fellows move with a coherence and discipline that obviously took scores of hours to refine. It's hard to spot a false step. No one loses the beat. But despite each man's near-military commitment to the choreography, some impression of six particular spirits comes through. It stirs me to imagine how hard it must have been for this arbitrary association of variously damaged personalities to pull a routine together.

Ron Tolenaar seems to stand about seven feet tall—my father's letters have, if anything, understated his monstrousness. He looks like an enormous rubber pop-eye squeeze toy made in the likeness of that actor from the *Hellboy* movies. Ron's dance is sort of Mick Jaggerish, a fantail-pigeon strut. He jacks his neck, bugs his eyes, and works his lips in a burlesque that somehow transforms his grotesquerie into a kind of proud plumage. It's a weirdly sexy, mesmerizing sight. It identifies him beyond doubt as the leader of the dorm.

From what little I'd known about Ter up to my first viewing of the video, I'd expected his performative presence to be one of cautious near-invisibility. But he's a frenetic, hectic dancer, fiercely teenage in the viciousness with which he kicks his feet and swings the shaggy black blur of his hair. "Ice Ice Baby" vanished from the airwaves years before he was born, but he pumps his fists and mouths the lyrics with an arrogant, proprietary intensity. Watching him glide in and out of the chorus line, materializing and vanishing at his own whim, I feel reassured that Ter will make his own way in the world.

And there's Henri Permeuil, dogging the heels of Johnny Francis. He's sort of dancing *at* Johnny, moving with a vaguely vengeful fervency, desperate to upstage the Texan ringer. The glossy black do-rag knotted over his skull says, "I am the real artist here." During the breakdown, when the guys stridingly mill about before resuming their sprinters' squats, note Henri's two-second rendition of his stuck-in-the-freezer concept. Even if it does not transmit the suffering fullness of a captive soul, it doesn't look too bad.

Declan Weyde is confounding to watch. Nothing about him suggests a man capable of doing what he did. He's a shyly pretty man with strawberry blond hair and sturdy, Norwegian features. Hard muscle wraps his arms and legs. But where the other men violently buck and jerk— especially in the "arm-worm" and "give-me-elbow-room" sequences— watch the fluid, feminine economy of Declan's movements. He doesn't want to accidentally bash somebody, doesn't want even to bruise the air around him.

I love the choruses, especially the first one. You see Declan moonwalk past and touch my father's elbow to cue his revolving. Osmund begins to turn, one hand on his diaper knot, the other crooked over his head. He looks like a jewelry-box ballerina. I love it how he giggles while the other dancers steeple their arms about him, showering my father in handfuls of shredded toilet paper, a simulation of snow, of Ice-Ice. It's wonderful how he sort of gets lost in this moment, keeps revolving into the second verse until Declan touches him again. Watch his lips at 1:15, my favorite instant in the video. Declan touches him, and my father says, "Got it, thanks," and comes out of the turn. "Got it, thanks." All business. You can detect a new dignity in his manner here, a prideful awareness that he is the star of this show. The decency of Declan's vigilance and my father's obvious gratitude at being looked after—this does something to me. Also, other than that "Got it, thanks," I find it somehow winning that my father doesn't stop soundlessly murmuring "goo-goo" from the moment the action starts until he is led out of the frame.

PUBLIC RELATIONS

The contest ruins dozens of Thep Moob's gamblers and makes the bookies rich. The Nigerians do not place. The transgendered prostitutes of Zone C do not place. First prize goes to members of the Hard Snakes, a homicidal youth gang whose dancing talents no one suspected. Second prize goes to a team of heroin addicts whom the jackpot roused to a frenzy of choreographic dedication. The addicts swap the ceiling fan and the outlet to a drug dealer for a substantial amount of heroin. In the week after the dance contest, three members of their team die tranquilly of overdoses, which may be construed as compounding their triumph, or not.

An unqualified winner of the dance contest is Captain Surongporn. The outpouring of media comment on the contest establishes Surongporn as an inspired, liberal innovator in the science of rehabilitation, and blunts, somewhat, international outcries over abuses and overcrowding in Thai correctional facilities.

A-23's third-place victory is a double bounty for Ron Tolenaar, who, after recruiting Johnny Francis, laid a heavy bet on his own team's success. The purchase of a two-gallon slow cooker, a television, and a hot plate and kettle for the boiling of pineapple wort do not put a dent in his winnings.

The press attention begets mixed fortunes for the men of A-23. Neither the *New York Times* article about my fathers performance, nor the video's endless rebroadcast on CNN, helps Professor Tower's case with the Economics department. Though my father's guilt has yet to be determined in court, after reviewing the diaper footage, the provost agrees with the chair that my father is insane and possibly a deviant. Over the protests of a few loyal students and members of an internet fan site sympathetic to the straitened diaper man, Osmund's salary is halted and his tenure rescinded. I have initiated a lawsuit on his behalf, but the odds of success, I'm told, are small.

A reporter for the *Bangkok Post* uncovers Ter's astonishing story and, several weeks after the contest, publishes an article about the guiltless boy's lost youth behind the walls of Thep Moob. He is evicted and given a garret in Ngop Na, where he is employed, not all that happily, on a municipal landscaping crew. He makes the ninety-minute bus trip to Thep Moob on visiting days, once a week, ferrying to my father books, medications, fresh produce, and whatever other necessities can't be obtained inside. Six months after Ter's eviction, he impregnates a widow twice his age who lives in the neighboring apartment. They marry. Ter's visits to the prison taper off.

A-23 has lost another inmate by then, as well. Three days after the votes are tallied, a trusty escorts an electrician into the dorm to install the electrical outlet. While the installation is taking place, a second trusty comes to the cell to summon Declan Weyde. He is told that a man from the Canadian embassy awaits him in the visitors' area. Declan leaves the dorm at 9:45 a.m. By late afternoon, he has not returned. The men wonder what has become of him. Shortly after 7, the voice of Sudrit Nut comes over the public address system, inviting Declan's ghost to leave the prison grounds.

Declan Weyde's death by lethal injection is Thep Moob's first execution in two years, and the only execution of a Western prisoner in recent memory. Word in the prison is that the brother of the man Declan murdered is the politician Pechawat Phititommuphruak, lately appointed Minister of the Interior. Among conspiracy-minded inmates like Henri Permeuil, the timing of Declan's execution is grist for speculation.

"Do not be ignorant," says Henri. "The contest, the whole thing was a trick. The minister, this big man, he says to the Captain, 'Okay, that guy killed my brother. You have to kill him for me.' But a white guy? A Canadian? It's not so easy with the press. With the diplomats, with the tourist industry. You need some cover, doing this in The Land of a Thousand Smiles. So we were the cover. 'Everybody, look at the dancing monkeys while we put this poor bastard down.'"

Ron Tolenaar dismisses this theory, pointing out that Surpongporn couldn't have possibly known that the dance contest would develop the viral momentum that it did. "And be serious, if really, they are so worried, they'd have the Snakes hit Declan. They would hang him in the lime trees."

"Yes," says Henri. "And it was two little airplanes that brought the towers down. You don't like information you can't handle, so you put your hands over your eyes. Stay sleeping, Ron. I am awake."

BRUTAL BEANS

The loss of Declan Weyde sends my father into a confused depression. During the weeks following his friend's death, the distant grin into which Osmund's features lapse during moments of pain or bewilderment never leaves his face. My father's lifelong armor—his ebullience—thins, and his emissions of gnomic wisdom intensify. When Ter expresses his condolences over Declan's execution, my father's eyes go vacant and his grin stretches to the back molars.

"Yes, well, it is interesting, the importance of good judgment," my father says with musical elocution. "I'd say Declan demonstrated a pattern of extraordinarily poor judgment, both in his choice of a lover and in allowing his anger to get the better of him, so the outcome isn't terribly surprising. Ah, Ter, let us be grateful for our ability to suppress craziness and keep ones demons at bay."

But during insomniac hours before dawn, my father lies awake on his mat, plagued by two species of disquiet concerning his dead friend. The first lies in the purity of his affection for Declan's memory. In his secret heart, Osmund cares not at all that Declan killed a man. This seems proof of a kind of decline. Second, my father is haunted by a formless shadow-thought that he might have prevented Declan from killing the man, but out of laziness or cowardice chose not to. This thought is nonsensical and seems proof of another kind of decline.

His letters home make no mention of Declan's death, but dwell merrily on the quotidian details of his life in Thep Moob.

> There is a real satisfaction in attaining fluency with the system here. For example, during my first weeks, I was paying 70 thb for haircuts, which it turns out is outrageous. I now go to a fellow who does a reasonable job for 10 thb. I usually give him 11 or 12, and it's wonderful to see how much this little generosity delights him.

Or:

> This week's big news is that in place of the unsanitary toilet hole which is standard, we've had installed in our cell a proper

commode, to which is attached a hose for squirting one's butt. The butt-squirter is a great device. I don't know why American politicians are universally unwilling to propose anything in this line of innovation. The Thai save on paper and waste processing, and it turns out, there are really quite a number of nerve endings down there, so there is a good bit of pleasure to be derived from use of the butt-squirter. I would give my vote to any presidential candidate unafraid to say, *I am resolutely for saving resources and for stimulating nerves that don't otherwise get stimulated.*

In addition to the toilet fixture, mealtimes in A-23 mark an improvement in living standards. The men pool their money for groceries, and Ter prepares stews in the slow cooker that are the high point of the men's days. After Ter is sent out of Thep Moob, it is Ron Tolenaar who volunteers to cook the first meal, a dish he calls "Ron's Brutal Beans." This consists of kidney beans slow-cooked to paste and seasoned with ketchup, molasses, and whole chilies.

The dinnertime mood that night is somber. In their conscious hearts, the men of A-23 do not set much store by the fellowship of their dorm mates. Yet, with Declan and Ter gone, the unacknowledged tribal comfort of the dance-troupe days has gone, leaving a vacancy that cannot be discussed.

The men ladle out the beans in silence, and they would eat the beans in silence. But, as a queer mercy, Ron's stew is so revolting that the men have no choice but to talk about it.

"I've ate assholes that tasted better than this," says Johnny Francis. "Way better."

"Give me the knife," says Henri Permeuil. "Right now I will cut out my tongue."

"Fuck yourselves," says Ron. He takes a huge spoonful into his mouth but does not swallow it. For a moment, he goes still, panting through flared nostrils like a bull. Then he retches the beans back into his bowl. "Unspeakable," he says. The three men laugh.

Osmund does not, though he, too, finds the stew disgusting. Around a hot mouthful, he says, "I don't know what you guys are complaining about." His voice trills with a jolliness that is a form of fury. "I think these beans are very nicely spiced."

POSTSCRIPT

The personal letter is nearly extinct, and I think this is a loss. Digital communications are, I believe, subconsciously composed with a mass audience in mind. Even the direst, privatest sorts of emails professing love or requesting divorce betray the flavor of an interoffice bulletin or an entry for the Toastmasters prize. If one is lucky enough to get a personal letter these days, it's a thing to hold dear and keep confidential from the general public. That said, my father's recent messages have been somewhat stinting on intimate revelation, working mostly in the plumbing-and-haircuts line. When I am feeling hopeless about his situation, there is an earlier dispatch I reread for strange comfort. The letter is eccentric and probably more candid than a father should be with his son. Yet, if my father survives this ordeal, it will be his pliant nature and appetite for exploration (to which the letter testifies) that will guide him through. What follows is a transcription of the aerogramme Osmund wrote the morning after his confused episode with Declan Weyde, which confusion was never wholly resolved. I wish his friend had gotten a chance to read this letter before he was killed.

Dear Wells:

It is truly ridiculous to think back on how much psychological energy I expended over the years, worrying about the possibility that I might be a homosexual.

This wastage of energy began as early as sixth grade, and probably a good while before. There was a glade behind the school which my friend Miles Yoder and I would use to conduct these little experiments in preparation for the temptations and challenges awaiting us the following year, in junior high school. One of these researches involved smoking cigarettes stolen from Miles's mother. The thinking here was that we ought to familiarize ourselves with the experience of smoking, so that when older boys pressured us into using cigarettes we could do so without the risk of becoming nicotine addicts. (Totally absurd!) We also engaged in experimental "What if?" conversations about homosexual acts: "Hey, Miles, imagine me doing blank to you!" I would describe various deeds, and he would make retching sounds to prove that these things didn't appeal to him, and I would do the

435

same when he described these things for me. At one point, we did put our tongues into one another's mouths to prepare ourselves for our first opportunities to French kiss a girl. (In my case, this would be nearly a decade in coming.) It was my assumption that Miles and I would ultimately perform oral sex on each other. When this failed to come about, I did feel some disappointment and this terrified me.

In graduate school, I fell under the influence of Keynes, whose homosexuality was, for me, another source of confusion. I was just fanatical about his writing. I would walk around the Harvard campus reciting lines from his marvelous treatise *The Inflation of Currency as a Method of Taxation*, which, man, I thought was just wonderful. The limberness of thought and generosity of spirit with which Keynes accomplished his work seemed of a piece with the man's erotic fluidity. Yet, I worried that my fanaticism for Keynes's writing might be indicative of my own homosexuality, which, I know, sounds completely outrageous and idiotic. The other side of the coin was that perhaps I was *not* a homosexual, so therefore I constitutionally lacked the deep wellspring of creativity from which Keynes's intellectual genius flowed. Either possibility was agonizing to me. I went to see a therapist. I can't remember what he said.

At the time, there was a beer and hamburger joint in Cambridge called The Beef Station. Homosexual adventures were known to be available in the toilets of The Beef Station. When I was having difficulty getting going on my thesis, I had a cuckoo notion that it might help if I were to pay a visit there. Totally bananas. I never did it. Anyway, I was married to your mother at the time. All of this madness may in some way explain why I did not ultimately become a Keynesian, though his observation about the downward inflexibility of wages continues to inform my thinking on monetary policy.

My homosexuality was one of your mother's pet conversational baits. I remember one night, we were driving to a dinner party at the Kerners' house in Durham. I thought it would be faster to take Erwin Road and she thought it would be faster to take the bypass. I took Erwin Road, and this enraged her. "If Bill Larsh were with us, and he'd said 'Take the bypass,' you'd have taken the bypass. But anything I say, it's just so much white noise, isn't it, Ed? You don't hear a thing women say." My choice of Erwin Road, according to your mother, demonstrated a covert interest in sodomy. We did not enjoy ourselves at the Kerners'.

This argument, specifically as it pertains to Bill, got another airing more recently. You may remember Verla, the woman from USAID I was seeing during your freshman year of college. I was very much in love with her. She had an incisive mind, and she wrote a working paper on Sri Lankan rubber tariffs that was absolutely extraordinary. She had a tuneful laugh, and her calf muscles were extremely well formed. We took a vacation to Scotland one summer, and Bill, who was teaching in Paris at the time, came to visit us. He was absolutely gross with Verla. Constantly touching her and making very ugly and childish innuendos. We ate dinner one night at an Indian restaurant. He persuaded her to get up and dance with him there in the crowded dining room, though no music was playing. Bill, as you know, is phenomenally attractive and has slept with an astounding number of beautiful women. As much as I was disgusted by his behavior, I recall also feeling a little flattered that a sexual conquistador of Bill's high rank should be so taken with my girlfriend.

The following morning, I awoke to find myself alone in my bed. Verla had gone. At about half-past ten, Bill came and knocked. He said, "I had a visitor last night."

"Ah, did you?" I said.

"I did. Boy, oh boy. She's extraordinary, Osmund. Listen, I'm going skiing in Lucerne this weekend. I invited her to join me and she's accepted. Would you like to come along?"

Crushing is how this felt. Yet, I couldn't see how it would have helped to have discussed my feelings with Bill and Verla. (I never saw her again. At her request, Bill gathered her things from my room. She couldn't bear to face me.) So they went to Lucerne that day, and I climbed Arthur's Seat. I remember the air being very pure there. I remember wondering whether I might be the sort of nonessential person who would be wise to kill himself. You and I were not speaking at the time and I was at odds with your brother and suicide seemed like a possibility with general benefits. But I knew that this was a silly and self-pitying line of thought, and anyway, I couldn't find a good precipice, only very steep grades which would probably have left me badly contused but alive.

According to your mother, my failure to be violent with Bill or Verla was further proof of my homosexuality, specifically, of my hidden desire to make love with Bill. But it is not the case that I had erotic feelings for him. I haven't thought about the Verla stuff in years, and now that it occurs to me, I am appalled. I suppose the lesson is that one ought to be grateful that one is not phenomenally attractive, seeing as being phenomenally attractive, in Bill's case, appears to have assisted his belief that he can behave like a crook. It's some comfort that he is a third-rate scholar and I know he gets paid less than I do. A petty comfort.

But all this is to say that I am sorry for the time I hit you with the belt when you were seven. If you don't remember this, your friend Brendan was over at the house. I didn't like his shrill, nelly voice. On the afternoon in question, the two of you had taken a bag of cashews with you and climbed into the "way back" area of the old Datsun. I found you both there without pants. I believe you'd been inserting the cashews into your bottoms and playing some sort of snacktime roulette with the tainted nuts. I striped you with a belt, thinking it might discourage you from turning queer. This now strikes me as cruel and shameful. Maybe it is telling you too much to say that I have just recently, at the age of seventy, sampled gay sex (a mild, risk-free variety) for the first time in my life and I found it unappealing. It was with a man named Declan Weyde, a Canadian serving a very long sentence for the theft of a coffeemaker, which should give you some sense of the jurisprudential craziness I'm up against here. At any rate, Declan is a man I like and trust very much, and he is not physically unattractive. I mention this only to say that if I were inclined toward men, I think it's safe to say that I would have had a satisfying experience with Declan. Yet, I did not, which, I think, certifies me as a man of mainstream appetites.

What a lot of my life I've wasted on this issue. If I had it to do over again, I would have encouraged you and Brendan to do all you pleased with the cashews or whatever else. You could have learned a great deal. It is never a good or useful thing to diminish the scope of one's awareness or to restrict the flow of information.

At any rate, I am sorry for any harm I have done to you over these years, and though you were an unexpected addition to my life, you are a vital one. My love for you and your brother sustains me here. Know that I am safe and having good conversations with people. Ah, the absurdity of it all.

Love,
Dad

PS Months ago, I told my student Marko that I would reimburse him for a medical expense. I would be grateful if you could handle this for me. The procedure was to remove several prominent, hornlike growths from his cheeks and forehead. Please examine the bill from the doctor before paying, and if possible, do try to give him the check in person so that we can be sure he's had the surgery. Trust, but verify. If he still has the growths, do not give him the check.

Nominated by Don Waters

MINDFUL

by RACHEL ZUCKER

from THE KENYON REVIEW

jammed my airspace w/ an audible.com podcast
& to-do list Deborah lent me this pen better
make use of turn off it filled up inside dear friends
[*swipe again*] invite me to Brooklyn [*swipe
again*] I briefly [*GO*] hate them am rush rush &
rushing headphones never let me airways
I run & the running [GPS: *average time*]
[activity started] [GPS: *per mile*] then a snowstorm
no school I cried & said *Mayor Bloomberg
should be scalded with hot cocoa* when someone said
yay for snow I'm cutting it too close, Erin, if
a blizzard makes me [*too slow swipe again*]
cry I used to [*activity started*] long for snow
that quiet filling everything up what is time for
anyway? Jeremy says *It's funny how* [*Too Slow*]
[*same turnstile*] *'work' in your poems is a metaphor
for* [*Go*] [*Go*] [*Go*] [*Go*] [*Go*] *'free time'* [*same
turnstile*] 'free time' what's that? is it NY? *What
are you talking about?* asks Erin, *Seriously what
are you talking about?* [*1 X-fer*] [*total time*] [*average
time*] [*GO GO GO GO*] crammed in the tiny bed
Still I say *If you want me to stay, you need to lie still*
the toddler tries why? must he? [*X-fer*] [*X-fer*]

[*all service on the local track*] fall asleep fast I pray
to whom? [1 *X-fer OK*] is this what I was
waiting for: the one nap moment of silence?
if that's what I wanted should have made other
don't you think choices? *What do you mean by*
by 'dark'? asks Erin *What do you mean by 'intolerable?'*
'unhinged'? airways [*GO*] I give one son
a quarter for two or fewer complaints a day
& none for more the pediatrician confirms
they each have two testicles then shoots
the smallest boy in the arm that was the easiest
part of my day [*X-fer OK*] [*OK*] [*OK*] [*GO*] stroller
is it the lack of human [*X-fer*] contact? oh
please have no time for *that* got to go to sleep
by 10 p.m. or I'm up all night something about
circadian rhythms then it's toddler-early-waking
Still night! we tell him *Not time* timing time *Not*
time to wake up! we tell him *Go back* he won't
we're up it's dark is it too early to make lunch
or dinner? *What are you saying?* texts Erin *Can't*
talk I text back but want to say [*X-fer*] to ask
why is this life so run-run-run I run only thing
I can—free wasted time—control? long
underground F the train crosstown bus that
screaming is *my* son with his 50 small feet
kicking *Too slow bus!* screaming Meredith says
The breath is the only thing in your life that
takes care of itself does it? [*too fast*] [*same*
turnstile] Rebecca wanted us to do something
radical at this reading I don't have time did
wash my hair lifestyle choice I know time
isn't 'a *thing* you have' I meant to ask isn't there
some way, Erin, to get more not time but joy?
she's not home maybe running or at the grocery
or school [*X-fer*] can you anyone hear me? my
signal pen airway failed Deborah lent me
this one GPS *time left* or *time left*—two
meanings—I've forgotten to *oh!* left my *urgh!*
meat in the freezer or oven on so what? don't

make dinner—ha ha who will? the military?—
don't rush multi-stop stop checking the tiny
devices brain sucking the joy out here's the
[*too fast*] [*swipe again*] [*OK*] express

Nominated by David Baker

UNWILLING

by NANCE VAN WINCKEL

from THE GETTYSBURG REVIEW

Keeping her night light on—
that's new. *It's okay.* I lean
over the face. *Everything's fine.*
Her ninetieth birthday leered
like this, then licked. Passed.

As long as the clock ticks
the teeth in the glass
won't chatter. The china bluebird
won't chirp. Prayers
for my soul trail off . . .

as the wall with my picture on it
crumbles. So long: my eyes
still watching hers
may be the last to go.

Nominated by Gary Gildner, Christopher Howell

BOOK OF FORGET

by REBECCA HAZELTON

from AGNI

I made a stage out of an abandoned house, small
enough for me to look bigger, and I walked from end
to end in spangles, shaking what my momma
gave me in a symphony jiggling out over the dry
desert night. I danced after the knife thrower threw
his blades and before the velvet clown kicked away
his chair and hung himself, his tongue thick and purple,
urine dribbling down to the boards. There were
men in the audience, their hands hidden,
but mostly the darkness around me was oily
and the floods couldn't pool much further than the
    music
carried. Once a woman came and sat in the front row,
wife to one husband who stayed overlong in my dressing
    room.
She watched my entire act. I hope she went away
with some kind of answer, but these steps remain
the same regardless of who watches: one two, and I turn,
three four, I cock the hip. I wanted to be a contortionist,
to stand on my own neck before anyone else could,
but the world is full of women who can halve themselves.

My talent is in looking like someone you want
when the lights are on and like anyone who'll do when they're off.
There are other ways to dance but I never learned.
There are other ways to forget. This one barely works.

Nominated by David Hernandez, Robert Long Foreman, Alan Michael Parker

THE WEIRDOS

fiction by OTTESSA MOSHFEGH

from THE PARIS REVIEW

On our first date, he bought me a taco, talked at length about the ancients' theories of light, how it streams at angles to align events in space and time, that it is the source of all information, determines every outcome, how we can reflect it to summon aliens using mirrored bowls of water. I asked what the point of it all was, but he didn't seem to hear me. Lying on the grass outside a tennis arena, he held my face toward the sun, stared sideways at my eyeballs, and began to cry. He told me I was the sign he'd been waiting for and, like looking into a crystal ball, he'd just read a private message from God in the silvery vortex of my left pupil. I disregarded this and was impressed instead by the ease with which he rolled on top of me and slid his hands down the back of my jeans, gripping my buttocks in both palms and squeezing, all in front of a Mexican family picnicking on the lawn.

He was the manager of an apartment complex in a part of town where the palm trees were sick. They were infested by a parasite that made them soft like bendy straws, and so they arched over the roads, buckling under the weight of their own heads, fronds skimming the concrete surfaces of buildings, poking in through open windows. And when the wind blew, they clattered and sagged and you could hear them creaking. "Someone needs to cut these trees down," my boyfriend said one morning. He said it like he was really sad about it, like it really pained him, like someone, I don't know who, had really let him down. "It's just not right."

I watched him make the bed. His sheets were a poly-cotton blend, stained, faded, and pilly pastel landscapes. What was supposed to keep us warm at night was a spruce-green sleeping bag. He had an afghan he said his grandmother had knit—a matted brown-and-yellow mess of yarn that he laid asymmetrically over the corner of the bed as a decorative accent. I tried to overlook it.

I hated my boyfriend but I liked the neighborhood. It was a shadowy, crumbling collection of bungalows and auto-body shops. The apartment complex rose a few stories above it all, and from our bedroom window I could look out and down into the valley, which was always covered in orange haze. I liked how ugly it all was, how trashy. Everyone in the neighborhood walked around with their heads down on account of all the birds. Something in the trees attracted a strange breed of pigeon—black ones, with bright red legs and sharp, gold-tipped talons. My boyfriend said they were Egyptian crows. He felt they'd been sent to watch him, and so he behaved even more carefully than ever. When he passed a homeless person on the street, he shook his head and muttered a word I don't think he could have spelled: *ingrate.* If I turned my back during breakfast he'd say, "I noticed you spilled some of your coffee, so I wiped it up for you." If I didn't thank him profusely, he'd put down his fork, ask, "Was that okay?" He was a child, really. He had childish ideas. He told me he "walked like a cop," which scared off criminals on the street at night. "Why do you think I've never been mugged?" He made me laugh.

And he explained something he thought most people didn't understand about intelligence. "It comes from the heart," he said, beating his chest with his fist. "It has a lot to do with your blood type. And magnets." That one gave me pause. I took a better look at him. The texture of his face was thick, like oiled leather. The only smile he ever gave was one where he lowered his head, stuck his chin out, and pulled the corners of his mouth from ear to ear, eyes twinkling up idiotically through batting eyelashes. He was, after all, a professional actor. "I've been laying low," he explained, "waiting for the perfect time to break out. People who get famous quick are doomed." And he was superstitious. He carved a scarab beetle out of Ivory soap and mounted it with putty over the door of our apartment, said it would protect us from home invasions and let the aliens know that we were special, that we were on their side. Every morning he went out front and blasted the bird droppings, which were green and fluorescent, off the front stoop with a high-pressure hose. He hated those birds. They circled overhead, hid in the palm fronds when a cop car passed, screeched and cawed when a child dropped a lollipop, stood in thick lines on the electric wires, stared into our souls, according to my boyfriend.

"And also," he went on, putting his hands in his pockets, a gesture meant to let me know that he was defenseless, that he was a good boy, "I have to pick up a package at the post office." He made it sound like he was going on a secret mission, like what he had to do was so difficult, so perilous, required so much strength of character, he needed my support. He slid the pick-up slip from the postman across the counter as proof. "You'll do great," is what I said, trying to belittle him.

"Thanks, babe," he said and kissed my forehead. He looked down at the kitchen tile, shrugged his shoulders, then lifted his chin to show me a brave grin. I left him alone to clean the floor, which he did by picking up each little crumb with his fingers, then dotting out stuck-on dirt with squares of paper towel he wet in the sink. He had a theory about how to stay in shape. It was to tense your body vigorously during everyday activities. He walked around with buttocks clenched, arms rigid, neck and face turning red. When I first moved in, he ran up the stairs with my suitcase, then stared down at me as though I would applaud. And once, when he saw me glance at his arm, he said, "I'm basically an Olympic athlete. I just don't like to compete." He had a crudely drawn tattoo of a salivating dog on his shoulder. Underneath it was written, COMIN' TO GETCHA!

And he was short. I had never dated a short man before. The thought crossed my mind: Perhaps I am learning humility. Perhaps this man is the answer to my prayers. Perhaps he's saving my soul. I should be kind. I should be grateful. But I was not kind and I was not grateful. I watched with disgust as he unpacked a box of books he'd found in the trash, squatting down rhythmically to place each one on the shelf. These were his constant calisthenics. His legs were iron, by the way. His hamstrings were so tight he could barely bend at the waist. When he tried, he made a face like someone being penetrated from behind.

"When I get paid," he said, dusting the mantle, "I'm going to wear my yellow sports jacket and take you out on the town. Did I show you my yellow sports jacket? I bought it at a vintage boutique," he said. "It was really expensive. It's awesome."

I'd seen it in the closet. It was a contemporary, size 8 woman's blazer, according to the label.

"Show me," I said.

He ran, tucking his shirt in, licking his palms to slick his hair back, and came back with it on. His fingers barely poked out from the cuffs. The shoulder pads nearly hit his ears, as he had basically no neck. "What do you think?" he asked.

"You look very nice," I said, masking my lie with a yawn.

He grabbed me, picked me up, pinning my elbows, twirled me around, making pained faces from the effort, despite his Olympic strength. "Soon, babe, I'm gonna take you to Vegas and marry you."

"Okay," I said. "When?"

"Babe, you know I can't really do that," he said, putting me down, suddenly grave and uncomfortable, as though the idea had been mine.

"Why not?" I asked. "You don't like me?"

"I need my mother's blessing," he said shrugging, frowning. "But I love you so much," he confirmed, stretching his arms demonstratively above his head. I watched the plastic yellow button on the blazer strain and pop. He gasped, went on a mad search for the button on his knees, smushing his face against the base of the couch while he grasped blindly with his short arms under it. When he stood up, his face was bright red, his jaw was clenched. The look of sincere frustration was refreshing. I watched as he sewed the button back on with blue thread, grinding his teeth, breathing hard. Then I heard him in the bathroom screaming into a towel. I wondered who had taught him how to do that. I was slightly impressed.

He came back from the post office two hours later with a large, oblong cardboard box.

"I got hit by one of those birds," he said, turning his head to the side to reveal a bright green smear of bird shit along his face. "It's a sign," he said. "For sure."

"You better get cleaned up," I said. "Your agent called."

"Did I get an audition?" he asked. He came toward me with open arms. "Did she say what it was for?"

"A beer commercial," I said, backing away. "Your face," I pointed.

"I'll fix it," he said. "Babe, we're gonna be rich." I watched him peel off his clothes and get into the shower. I sat on the toilet and clipped my toenails.

"The trick to acting," he said from the shower, "is you really need to give it one hundred fifty percent. Your average actor gives maybe eighty, at most ninety percent. But I go all the way and then some. That's the secret."

"Uh-huh," I said, flushing my toenails down the toilet. "Is that the secret to success?"

"Yeah, babe," he assured me, whipping open the shower curtain. His body was a freckled mess of jerking muscles and stubble. He shaved his chest almost daily. He had a scar on his rib cage from where he told me he'd been stabbed in a bar fight. He had all kinds of stories. He said back home in Cleveland he used to hang around with gangsters. He spent a night in jail once after beating up a pimp who he'd seen kick a German shepherd—a sacred animal, he explained. Only his story of burning down an abandoned house when he was sixteen had a ring of truth.

"And you know what else?" he said, squatting in the bathtub and slathering the towel between his legs. His towels were all stenched with mildew and streaked with rust stains, by the way. "I'm handsome."

"You are?" I asked innocently.

"I'm a total stud," he said. "But it creeps up on you. That's why I'm good on TV. Nonthreatening."

"I see." I stood and leaned against the vanity, watched him wrap the towel around his waist, pull out his bag of makeup.

"I'm a face-changer, too," he went on. "One day I can look like the boy next door. The next day, a stone-faced killer. It just happens. My face changes overnight on its own. Natural-born actor."

"True enough," I agreed, and watched him dab concealer all over his nose.

While he was at his audition I walked around the apartment complex, kicking trash into corners. I sat in the concrete courtyard. There were birds everywhere, pecking at trash, lining the balconies, purring like cats between the succulents. I watched one walk toward me with a candy-bar wrapper in his beak. He dropped it at my feet and seemed to bow forward, then extended his wings wide, showing me the beautiful rainbow sheen of his jet-black chest. He flapped his wings gently, with subtlety, and rose from the ground. I thought maybe he was trying to seduce me. I got up and walked away, and he continued to hover there, suspended like a puppet. Nothing made me happy. I went out to the pool, skimmed the surface of the blue water with my hand, praying for one of us, my boyfriend or me, to die.

"I nailed it," he said when he came home from the audition. He shrugged the yellow blazer down his stiff arms, laid it on the back of the bar stool at the kitchen counter. "If they don't hire me, they don't know what's good for them. I really hit a home run." I kept stirring the spaghetti. I nodded and tried to smile a little. "And I saw the other guys that were auditioning, and man," he said, "they were all the worst. I'm a shoo-in. My agent call yet?"

"No," I said. "Not yet."

"I should go rub my crystal skull," he said. "Be right back."

I had a bad feeling about what my boyfriend had brought back from the post office. The box sat on the couch, unopened. He stood at the sink, vigorously scrubbing the plates from dinner, buttocks clenched and vibrating. "What's inside?" I asked.

"Open it up, babe," he said, turning slightly to make sure I caught sight of his devilish grin. It was the same grin he gave in his headshots. "Check it out," he said.

I licked my knife clean and cut through the packing tape. The box was full of Styrofoam peanuts. I fished around inside and found a long shotgun padded in bubble wrap.

"What's it for?"

"To shoot the crows," my boyfriend said. He held a plate up to the light and polished it frenetically with a paper towel. I thought for a moment.

"Let me take care of it," I said. "You need to focus on your career."

He seemed stunned, put down the plate.

"You do enough around here," I said. "Unless you would actually enjoy shooting those birds?"

He picked up the plate and turned his back to me.

"Of course not," he said. "Thanks, babe. Thanks for your support."

He slept that night with his phone next to his ear on the pillow and didn't touch me or say anything at all except "Good night, skully," to his crystal skull on the bedside table. I put my head on his shoulder, but he just rolled onto his side. When I woke up in the morning he was staring at the sun through the smog from the balcony, holding his eyes open with his fingers, crying, it seemed, though I wasn't sure.

I still hadn't cleaned the vacant apartment by the time the couple showed up to see it in the afternoon. I found them wandering around in back by the pool, sharing a huge bag of Utz potato chips. The man was younger, maybe midthirties, and wore a button-down shirt much too big for his wirey frame. The shirt had rectangular wrinkles in it as though it had just been taken out of its packaging. He wore jean shorts and sneakers, a red Cardinals hat. The woman was older, very tanned and fat, and had long salt-and-pepper hair parted in the middle. She wore a lot of turquoise jewelry, had something tattooed on her forehead between her eyes.

"Are you here to see the apartment?" I asked. I had my clipboard with the requisite forms, the keys.

"We love it here," said the woman frankly. She wiped her hands off on her skirt. "We'd like to move in right away."

I walked toward them. That tattoo on her forehead was like a third eye. It looked like a diamond on its side with a star inside of it. I stared at it for a second too long. Then her boyfriend chimed in.

"Are you the manager?" he asked, thumbing his nose nervously.

"I'm the manager's girlfriend. But don't you want to see the place first?" I jangled the keys for them.

"We already know," the woman said, shaking her head. She moved gently, like dancing to soft music. She seemed sweet, but she talked mechanically, as though reading off of cue cards. She stared resolutely at the stucco wall above my head. "We don't need to see it. We'll take it. Just show us where to sign." She smiled broadly, revealing the worst set of teeth I'd ever seen. They were sparse and yellow and black and jagged.

"These are the forms to fill out," I said, extending the clipboard toward her. The man continued to eat the chips and walked to the edge of the pool, stared up at the sky.

"What's with the birds?" he asked.

"They're Egyptian crows," I told him. "But I'm going to shoot them all."

I figured they were weirdos and nothing I said to them mattered. From the way the man nodded and dove his squirrel-like hand back into the bag of potato chips, it seemed I was right.

"Now listen," said the woman, squatting down with the clipboard on her knees, breathing heavily. "We're selling our estate up north and we want to pay for a year's rent in advance. That's how serious we are about renting this apartment."

"Okay," I said. "I'll tell the owners." She stood and showed me the form. Her name was Moon Kowalski. "I'll let you know," I said.

The man wiped his palms off on his shorts. "Hey, thanks a lot," he said earnestly. He shook my hand. The woman swayed from side to side and rubbed her third eye. When I got back to the apartment there was a message from my boyfriend's agent saying he got a callback. I went back to bed.

"I got you some ammo," said my boyfriend. He put the box right in front of my face on the pillow. "So you can shoot the birds." He seemed to have turned a corner. He seemed in high spirits.

"Call your agent," I told him. Then I turned my head. I could not stand to see him roar and pump his fist and dance excitedly, thrusting his crotch in celebration.

"I knew it, babe!" he cried. He pounced on me in the bed, flipped me faceup and kissed me. His mouth had a strange taste, like bitter chemicals. I let him peel my shirt up to my throat, twist the fabric until he could use it like a rope to pull me up toward him. He unzipped his shorts. I looked up at his face just to see how ugly it was and opened my mouth. It's true I relished him in certain ways. When he was done, he kissed my forehead and knelt by the bedside table, index finger on his crystal skull, and prayed.

I picked up the box of slugs. I'd never fired a gun before. There were instructions on how to load and fire the shotgun in the box it came in, with diagrams of how to hold the butt against your shoulder, little birds floating in the air. I listened to my boyfriend on the phone with his agent.

"Yes, ma'am. Yes, ma'am. Thank you very much," he was saying. "Uh-huh, uh-huh."

I really hated him. A crow came and sat on the sill of the window. It seemed to roll its eyes.

There were people I could have called, of course. It wasn't like I was in prison. I could have walked to the park or the coffee shop or gone to the movies or church. I could have gone to get a cheap massage or my fortune told. But I didn't feel like calling anyone or leaving the apartment complex. So I sat and watched my boyfriend clip his toenails. He had small, nubby feet. He collected the clippings in a pile by dragging his pinky finger neurotically across the floor. It pained me to see him so pleased with himself. "Hey, babe," he said. "What do you say we go up on the roof, try the gun out?" I didn't want to go up there. I knew it would make him happy.

"I'm not feeling well," I said. "I think I have a fever."

"Oh man," he said. "You sick?"

"Yeah," I said. "I think I'm sick. I feel terrible."

He got up and ran to the kitchen, came back chugging from a carton of orange juice. "I can't get sick now," he said. "You know this commercial is gonna be huge. After this, I'll be famous. You want to hear my lines?"

"My head hurts too much," I said. "Is that your new hairstyle?" He was always putting gel in his hair and he was always squinting, pursing his lips. "Is that gel?"

"No," he said, lying. "My hair's just like this." He went to the mirror, sucked in his cheeks, pushed his hair around, flexed his pectorals. "This time when I go in," he said, "I'm gonna be sort of James Dean, like I just don't give a shit, but sad, you know?" I couldn't stand it. I turned and faced the wall. Out the window the palms hovered and shimmied and cowered in the breeze. I didn't want him to be happy. I closed my eyes and prayed for a disaster, a huge earthquake or a drive-by shooting or a heart attack. I picked up the crystal skull. It was greasy and light, so light I thought it might be made of plastic.

"Don't touch that!" my boyfriend cried breathlessly, leaping over the bed and grabbing the skull out of my hands. "Great. Now I need to find a body of water to wash it in. I told you, don't touch my stuff."

"You never said I couldn't touch it," I said. "The pool's right outside."

He put the skull in a pocket of his cargo shorts and left.

The buzzer rang the next evening. I got on the intercom.

"Who is it?" I asked.

"It's the Kowalskis," the voice said. It was Moon's voice. "We couldn't wait. We're here with cash and a moving truck. Buzz us in?"

My boyfriend hadn't come home yet from his callback. He'd called to say that he was staying out late to watch the lunar eclipse and not to wait for him, and that he forgave me for touching his crystal skull and that he loved me so much and knew that when we were both dead we'd meet on a long river of light and there'd be slaves there to row us in a golden boat to outer space and feed us grapes and rub our feet. "Did my agent call yet?" he had asked.

"Not yet," I'd told him.

I put on my robe and went downstairs, propped open the gate with a brick. Moon stood there with a manila envelope full of money. I took it and handed her the keys.

"Like I said, we couldn't wait," said Moon. Her husband was unloading their moving truck, lugging black garbage bags off the back and placing them in rows on the sidewalk. Those damned crows flew across the violet sky, perched on top of the truck, cawed quietly to one another.

"It's late," I said to Moon.

"This is the perfect time to move," she said. "It's the equinox. Perfect timing." Her husband set down a moose head mounted on a shield-shaped piece of plywood. "He loves that moose," said Moon. "You love that moose, huh?" she said to her husband. He nodded, wiped his forehead, and ducked back into the truck.

I went back upstairs and started packing, stuffed the money Moon had given me at the bottom of my suitcase, cleared out my drawer, my boyfriend's makeup case, wrapped the shotgun in that terrible afghan, zipped it all up. Watching from the mezzanine as Moon carried in a large potted tree, her husband slumped behind her under a bag of golf clubs, I felt hopeful, as though it were me moving in, starting a new life. I felt energized. When I offered to help, Moon seemed to soften, flung her hair back and smiled, pointed to a woven basket full of silverware. I helped Moon's husband carry the old mattress out to the curb. We set it up against a tree and watched it veer back precariously toward the apartment complex. A cluster of crows sprang out from its leaves. "Gentle souls," the man said, and lit a cigarette.

When the truck was empty, Moon told me to sit down in the kitchen, rubbed the seat of a chair with a rag. I sat down.

"You must be tired," she said. "Let me find my coffee pot."

"I should get going," I said.

"No, you shouldn't," said Moon. Her voice was strange, pushy. When she spoke it was like a drum beating. "Be our guest," she said. "Want saltines ?" That third eye seemed to wink at me when she smiled. She found a plate and laid out the crackers. "Thank you for your help," she said.

I looked around at the walls, which were mottled and scratched and dirty.

"You can paint the place, you know," I told Moon. "My boyfriend was supposed to have painted already. Of course he didn't."

"The manager guy?" the husband called out from the brown velour sofa they'd set in the middle of the living room.

"How long have you two been a couple?" Moon asked. She laid her hands down flat on the kitchen table. They were like two brown lizards blinking in the sun.

"Not long," I said. "I'm leaving him," I added. "Tonight."

"Let me ask you one thing," Moon said. "Is he good to you?"

"He beats me," I lied. "And he's really dumb. I should have left him a long time ago."

Moon got up, looked over at her husband.

"I've got something for you," she said. She disappeared into the bedroom, where we'd piled all the garbage bags full of stuff. She came out with a black feather.

"Is that from the crows?" I asked.

"Sleep with this under your pillow," she said, rubbing her third eye. "And as you drift off think of everyone you know. Start off easy, like with your parents, your brothers and sisters, your best friends, and picture each person in your mind. Really try to picture them. Try to think of all your classmates, your neighbors, people you met on the street, on the bus, the girl from the coffee shop, your dentist, everybody from over the years. And then I want you to imagine your boyfriend. When you imagine him, imagine he's on one side and everybody else is on the other side."

"Then what?" I asked her.

"Then see which side you like better."

"You need anything," said her husband, "you know where to find us."

I went home and put on the yellow sports jacket. It didn't fit me any better than it fit my boyfriend. I put the feather under the pillow.

That night I had a dream there was a monkey in the tree outside my window. The monkey was so sad, all he could do was cover his face and weep. I tried handing him a banana but he just shook his head. I tried singing him a song. Nothing cheered him. "Hey," I said softly, "come here, let me hold you." But he turned his back to me. It broke my heart to see him crying. I would have done anything for him. Just to give that little monkey one happy moment, I would have died.

My boyfriend came home the next morning with a black eye.

"I can't talk to you," he said to me, rubbing the skull in his small, rough hands. I sat on the bed and watched him. His brow was furrowed like an old man's. "I can't even look at you," he said. "They're saying you're a scourge. A bad scourge."

"They?" I asked. "Do you know what a scourge is?"

He cocked his head. I watched his wheels grind. "Um," he said.

"You love me, remember?" I said.

"*Scourge* means you're going to ruin everything," he answered after a long pause.

"What happened to your eye?" I asked him, reaching a hand out. He blocked my arm with a swift karate chop. It didn't hurt. But I could see his heart beating through his shirt, sweat leaking down his arm.

"It's not good for me to talk to you," he said. He went into the bathroom. I heard the door slam, the shower run, and, after a moment, the nervous tapping of the razor against the tile. I sat on the bed for a while. The sun flickered harmlessly through the swaying palms.

I got my suitcase and lugged it up the two flights to the roof. I'd been there only once before, one night soon after I'd moved in, when I couldn't sleep. My boyfriend had come up and found me sitting on the ledge. We had talked for a while and kissed. "If you get torches and wave them up to the sky, it's like a signal to the aliens," he had said. He got up and twirled his arms around like propellers. "It's the light that calls them." He looked deep into my eyes. "I love you," he'd said. "More than anyone else on earth. More than my own mother. More than God."

"Okay," I'd told him. "Thanks."

Up on the roof I unzipped my suitcase, pulled out the shotgun. It was easy enough to slide the round into the magazine tube, as they called it, pull the action back. That's what the instructions said to do. But there were no birds around. I tried firing off a round, hoping it would startle the Egyptian crows, hoping something, anything would leap up in front of me, but my hand shook. I got scared. I couldn't do it. So I sat for a while and stared down at all the concrete, the palms flapping to and fro between the electric wires, then lugged the suitcase back down to our apartment.

After that he'd disappear a lot, call me from some windy alleyway, talk fast, explaining his regret, ask me to marry him, then call back to tell me to go to hell, that I was trash, that I wasn't worth his time on earth. Eventually he'd knock on the door with huge scabs all over his arms and face, body thrumming with methamphetamine, head bent like a naughty child's, asking to be forgiven. He always hid his shame and self-loathing under an expression of shame and self-loathing, swinging his fist back and forth, "shucks," always acting, even then. I don't think he ever experienced any real joy or humor. Deep down he probably thought I was crazy not to love him. And maybe I was. Maybe he was the man of my dreams.

Nominated by The Paris Review, Micaela Morrissette, Sarah Frisch

TRIM PALACE

fiction by ALEXANDER MAKSIK

from TIN HOUSE

When I ran into Joshua for the first time in nine years, I was working the Delta terminal and had just cleaned the men's room next to Malibu Al's. I can't remember why I looked up, but whatever the reason, there he was coming out of 58A.

It wasn't allowed, but I was taking my twenty minutes in the terminal rather than the break room—a windowless box I hated many times more than the job itself. Joshua was at the head of the line walking off the jet bridge wearing a black suit and a loosened tie the color of a good lime. At first I thought he was alone, but then a woman, mesmerized by her phone, glided to him as if guided by radar and gave him a little hip check. I was frozen and my adrenaline was going like I'd been caught doing something I shouldn't have been. Which, from a certain perspective, was exactly right.

I sat there waiting until he turned his head and looked right at me. Our eyes met for a second. He made no move and I thought, *Thank God, he doesn't recognize me.* And then I thought, *The fucker is pretending he doesn't recognize me.* And I started to feel all righteous, but I realized he was doing exactly what I was doing, and it made me sad to think we'd just let it go, that he'd keep on walking, I'd keep on sitting there, he'd keep on wearing suits and getting off airplanes with his pretty wife or whoever she was and I'd go on racking elephant rolls of toilet paper and scrubbing shit from white tile.

But he stopped and the woman, who was still gazing into her phone, took three extra steps before stopping too. I don't know what she did at that point, or what he did either, because I closed my eyes and pretended to be napping, as if sitting in front of 55B with that pink and purple sky behind me and my feet propped on a rolling bucket of dirty water and my fist around a mop handle was exactly what I wanted to be doing.

It was stupid and childish, and I was embarrassed twice—once for the job, once for the sleeping charade. Still, I'd committed to it, so I kept my eyes closed and waited for him to make his move. You close your eyes in public and time slows down and I thought, *Shit, he's changed his mind,* or maybe it wasn't *me* he saw. But then he was saying, "Petey? Peter?" so I opened my eyes and put on a whole show where I was a) suddenly awake and b) surprised as hell that Joshua, my old friend, my former roommate, after all these years, was standing right there.

I jumped up and got so into it that I nearly knocked over the bucket, sloshing water all over the place. He laughed but I could tell he was worried about his pants, or at least the shine of his shoes, which we both watched for one long second, before we really started into the whole dance of the thing.

"Petey," he said and hugged me. We were the same height, about five ten, five eleven, depending on the shoes, and built about the same— thin and neither of us very muscular. We'd never been shy, so it was always a good hug when it happened and I remembered that when he pulled me in.

"What the fuck, Pete," he said with both hands on my shoulders. He was looking at my gray coveralls and my boots and the bucket. Until that moment, I don't think he'd quite put it together.

"What the fuck is this, Pete? What are you *doing*?" He said it as if we were still living together, as if I'd just come home from the bar and it was three in the morning and we were sitting on the couch with our feet on the table, drinking beers. Like we still knew each other, were still friends and he had the right to ask me that kind of question. I was glad though. It was better than the alternative.

"What am I doing? I'm working, man. I'm doing my job. What are *you* doing?"

He moved back a step and gave me a squint and a half-smile to match mine. Then we both turned to look at the woman who was now standing in the middle of the concourse. She shrugged her shoulders and turned her hands out as if to say, *What the fuck?* Or more accurately, *Why the fuck are you talking to the janitor?*

Joshua gave her the one-minute finger.

"I got to go, Pete," he said. "She's tired."

I nodded.

"My wife," he said. "Sky."

"You're married."

"It was tiny. Hardly anyone there. Just family, really."

"Sure," I said.

"What's going on here, Pete? What the fuck?"

"What the fuck yourself."

He slipped a sleek black phone from his jacket pocket and it lit up blue in his hand. "Give me your number."

I gave it to him.

"I'll call. We'll catch up, okay? Maybe I can find you something." He slapped my shoulder, laughed, gave me one more look, and shook his head.

"Find me something?"

"Some work," he said. He'd already begun to walk away. "A fucking job."

"I have a job," I said as I watched him go, watched him wrap up his wife in his right arm, watched him lean down and press his mouth to her ear, each of them trailed by a silver suitcase on wheels.

I didn't expect to hear from him again.

Those nine years ago, we drove out to LA from Buffalo after we'd both just graduated from SUNY. It was, as his father said when he handed over the keys, a boondoggle. His parents had given him a yellow minivan and mine had given me $3,300. Enough, we thought, to start our lives. It was one of those clean, early moments when nothing is considered, a decision is made and you're in motion.

We found our way to Los Angeles and into Marina del Rey. We slept in the van for a week or so until we lucked into an apartment built to look like a schooner. It was a block from the beach. Nothing was difficult for us then, and perhaps that ease was what made us such fast friends—as if we both sensed that we were each other's luck, and that any complication might put an end to our fortune.

The landlord, Arnie Henry, was one of those guys in the seventies who'd made the Marina famous for coke and swinger parties, hot tubs and captain hats. He'd designed the apartment himself and was proud of the porthole windows, the rope banister, the brass fixtures, and, above all, the bow: a deck that swelled and jutted over the street,

461

complete with a hand-carved figurehead—a mermaid with green eyes and yellow hair and large, bare breasts whose chipped pink nipples pointed at our neighbors and their staid stucco buildings.

We'd bought some stolen black leatherette couches from a twitchy kid with a handlebar moustache who sold them to us new out of the back of his garage. When we got them into the apartment and had a beer together, it felt as if we were really home.

Once we were settled in and had the place furnished, Arnie came by to celebrate. I was leaning over the bow when Arnie pulled his rusted Porsche off Pacific and parked in front of the apartment, gassed it twice to announce his arrival, and killed the engine. He hefted himself out of the car with two bottles of champagne and pointed them at me like pistols.

"One good," he said. "One bad."

The apartment was built over a garage, so you entered from the street and came up some blue-carpeted stairs. When he got to the top he paused and looked around like he was seeing something beautiful for the first time. He swiveled his head from side to side, nodding in even increments like a sprinkler, each nod registering some other detail he approved of, and after a long pause said, "Boys, this place is a trim palace, a goddamned trim palace."

He put the good bottle on the coffee table—a heavy wooden cable spool we'd stolen from a construction site—and took us outside onto the deck. He handed Joshua the other bottle. There have been times I wondered if that was it right there: Arnie made him the lucky one.

"Go on, Josh. Christen this bitch," he said.

And Joshua did it without hesitating. Did it in one. Leaned way out over the railing. Gave a sure and solid swing, a good crack against the bow stem.

The bottle shattered and showered the asphalt below with glass and bad champagne.

I'll admit I was insulted that Joshua hadn't called me, but I wasn't surprised. So I let it go. I did my work, went home to my apartment, slept, read what I was reading, and went back to the airport.

Sometimes when our shifts overlapped I'd have my lunch with big Marco, a quiet guy my age but twice my size. We'd eat our sandwiches together and not say very much. He had a tattoo across the knuckles of his right hand. *Lucy*, it said. I asked all the time, but he'd never tell me who she was.

I lived in a studio across the street from the Westchester driving range, which was a step up from where I'd been, believe me, but still not the kind of place I'd want to bring somebody else. I was vain, I guess. Despite everything, I was still vain. You'd think it would have been blasted out of me by that point, but no.

The driving range was open until eleven some nights and I'd often fall asleep to the thin metal sound of golf balls being cracked out across the beat-up turf. Thwack thwack. Thwack. Into the night I could hear the clubheads crashing against those dead bucket balls.

I worked as often as I could. I covered for Marco when he was hung over, which was every Friday morning because of a dancer who wasn't Lucy and who worked Thursdays out at the Jet Strip, so Fridays I nearly always did doubles.

I burned whole years of my life there. Changing those giant wheels of toilet paper, mopping the tile, running a vacuum, refilling soap and paper-towel dispensers, emptying trash cans, picking up after the slobs.

You can't believe the things people do. What they leave behind for us in the sinks, on the floor, in the toilets, on chairs, in the plants, on top of vents. Blood and whiskers and shaving foam, phlegm and hair, vomit and snot, gum and bandages and condoms. Needles and finger-nails and dead skin. Half-eaten food. Half-empty cups. You'd clean one stall, move on, do another, and four minutes later, the stall you started with had paper all over the floor, piss on the seat, and a Frappucino sweating on the tile. Endless. The people surging through, the men grunting behind the locked doors, the sunsets behind glass, the smells of coffee and pizza, cleaning spray and floor polish, excrement and recycled air.

Still, I took pleasure in slapping palms with Marco, in our few jokes, in the illusion of somehow being under his protection. And not from anything in particular. Just protected, the way you feel when you're with someone so much bigger than you are, so much tougher.

But I knew what would happen with Marco. That we weren't really friends and one day, like so many other people, he'd fall off the earth. That I'd call him and he wouldn't answer and that would be it.

In those years at the airport, I'd imagine a panel of metal switches shaped like tiny baseball bats with a little light above each of them. One by one I snapped them off. Round red lights all in a row: love, outrage, lust, fury, longing, hunger. Day after day. Flipping those switches. Snap, snap, snap.

I had one of those prepaid mobile phones. It never rang except when it was Marco calling to get me to cover his shift, or very occasionally my father when he was sure my mother wasn't around.

And then two weeks after I'd run into Joshua, the phone lit up and flashed *Private, Private, Private* in rhythm with the trilling ringer.

"Petey," he said when I answered. "Petey, that you?"

"Who's this?" I said, knowing full well who it was.

"Petey, it's Joshua. Petey, my man. Listen, I want to catch up, okay? I want to go out, have a few beers, but I'm rushing today. I'm all over the place. Still I wanted to call because I have something for you. You there?"

"I'm here."

"Good. So here it is. Easy. Come up to the house, stay for the week. Take care of our dog. Simple."

I could hear him walking, could hear those shoes sounding against some polished surface.

"So that's it. You come up on Saturday morning. We're back a week later. Easy and we'll pay you two grand to do it. Good? Deal? All the food you need. Plenty of beer."

"This is why you called?"

"Petey, come on, man. We're stuck here. Our regular guy went MIA. We're leaving day after tomorrow. We're stuck."

"Take him to a kennel."

"Her. And we don't put her in kennels."

"Why not?"

"She's old and we just fucking don't." He sighed. "Look I'm offering you a vacation, man. A vacation plus two grand. You're telling me you can't use both?"

"I don't know if I can get off work."

"How long does it take you to make two grand doing that shit?"

"I don't want your money," I told him. "If I do it, it's a favor for an old friend."

"Sure, Petey. But we're still paying you."

"I'll let you know," I said.

"Good. As soon as you can? And Petey, man. I got to ask. Short version, okay, but, what the fuck happened?"

"With what?"

"Come on, man. How do you end up doing that job?"

"I'll let you know about Saturday," I said and hung up.

On Saturday morning, I watched from my window as Joshua stopped his BMW in front of my apartment.

I came down. I got in. We drove north.

Up to Sunset and east and east, no music on and everything hushed inside that car—the engine, Joshua's voice.

They'd been married for four years. No children. He was an advertising guy. She was a lawyer. The dog was a blue Great Dane. Her name was Juliette.

The car was hypnotic in its speed, its comfort, its quiet. I felt drugged by strangeness—the strangeness of being carried, the strangeness of Joshua so close, the strangeness of time.

We swung north off Sunset onto Kenter and drove up the canyon.

The fog was in from the ocean. It hung in the trees and the higher we climbed the closer to the street it hovered, so that soon we were breaking through it, driving nearly blind.

The canyon went on and on.

We slowed down. He reached up and pressed a button. A gate slid open. We pulled off the road and descended a steep driveway. When he'd stopped the car and killed the engine he looked at me.

"So you want to tell me now?"

I shrugged and opened the door. "When you're back," I said. "We'll get a drink or two."

The house—low and modern, all glass and concrete—rested at the bottom of a broad ravine. On all sides, grass extended outward to a perimeter of tall eucalyptus trees.

I followed Joshua from the car to the front door.

In the entryway, there were those identical silver suitcases, side by side.

He brought me to a guest room. There were towels stacked on a wide white bed. A robe hung on a hook in the bathroom, its belt tied in a loose knot. There were purple flowers next to the sink, and yellow flowers on the bedside table.

I left my old duffel on a chair and followed Joshua outside to a long rectangular swimming pool set in a concrete deck. There were gray lounge chairs in a neat line.

"All yours," he said and brought us back inside to the kitchen. He took two bottles of beer from the fridge, opened them, and handed me one. "Thanks for doing this," he said, tapping my bottle with his. "I'll be right back."

I waited and drank my beer. Nothing was out of place. There was a row of backless stools lined up at a counter. I slid one out and sat on it. I had no thoughts. It was as if the silence and all the order of that house had taken them.

I heard the sound of nails clicking on the concrete floor. And then Juliette came into the kitchen, stopped, and stared at me. She was enormous. The largest dog I've ever seen. She was the color of a storm. Amber eyes. For a moment, there was no sound at all.

Then there was the sound of footsteps. We watched as they came in together—fresh, dressed, and ready for travel. I stood up.

Joshua introduced me to Sky who was very pretty, smiled easily and thanked me and thanked me and said, "This is our baby." So I crossed the space between us and patted Juliette's chest. In return, she pushed her head against my hip. Everyone sighed at that.

Joshua opened a third beer for Sky and the three of us drank together while they went over the various instructions—food, pills, drops for her ears, drops for her eyes, her bed, her toys, her harness, her leash, what hurt, what she liked, what she didn't.

We slid one of the glass doors open off the kitchen and went outside.

"Thank you for taking care of her. She's our baby," Sky said, reaching for Joshua.

I could see the three of us holding our beers, Joshua and Sky hand in hand, looking on as Juliette limped across the lawn right to the very edge of the trees, where she turned and looked back at us, her cropped ears standing upright like a wolf's.

The doorbell rang and we returned inside. There was a thin man in a black suit with his hands behind his back. Sky introduced me and then he took their luggage to a sedan idling in the driveway.

"Call if you have any trouble. Any questions. Anything," Joshua said, studying me as if suddenly he'd had a second thought. His expression had changed. Something in his eyes.

The dog was leaning her head against my hip and I was scratching her ears.

"The smallest problem," Sky said. "Don't hesitate for a second." She was wearing a white straw fedora and when she bent down to kiss Juliette on the forehead, I could no longer see her face.

Once she'd slid into the car Joshua gave me a hug. "You're not some criminal now, are you, Petey?" He laughed, but I could see he was worried.

"Hope you locked away the silver," I said.

The dog and I stood in the doorway and watched as the sedan climbed the driveway, slipped through the gate, and disappeared. I closed the door and the two of us returned to the kitchen. I took another beer from the fridge and walked outside. The sun was beginning to burn through the fog and all the colors were coming on—the lawn, the leaves, the pool. I pulled off my shoes and socks and followed Juliette out to the trees. The grass was mown short and neat and flawless like the fairway of a good golf course. It was so even in texture and color that for a moment I worried I might ruin it with my bare feet. I drained my beer, let the bottle drop and began to jog.

I ran a quick hitch route.

"Hit me, Juliette," I said.

I ran a long post, made the turn, and clapped for the pass. "I'm open, Juliette."

She raised her big head and barked once.

I came back, bent over for the hike, and ran a buttonhook. She lumbered over and pushed her nose into my gut. I held her head. She gave me more of her weight.

I sat on the lawn while she struggled to lie down next to me, in pain with the effort. The fog had burned off completely. A breeze had come up. Juliette rested her chin on my thighs. I lay on the damp grass. All I heard were the leaves moving against each other and the faint creak of the branches. And then nothing.

I was thinking about the bar. The way my brain used to change. How I could see in ways I couldn't see anywhere else. How I moved so easily, with such speed and precision. How the more crowded the room the more in control I became. How I could see myself in the red, varnished ceiling. How I felt light and masterful and clear.

Juliette lifted her head from my legs and for a moment I was aware of her fading heat. I heard the leaves twisting against each other. Then the sound was gone.

The liquors were lined up in the well, glasses on the rubber runner, and I was flying a bottle across them—one-one-thousand, two-one-thousand, slide, one-one-thousand, two-one-thousand, slide. Green bills filling the tip jar. The soda gun in my hand, all the smiling, solicitous women, four, five, six deep, and I, night after night, their noble and sober king.

I was thinking about Joshua at the bar, sitting on a stool all the way at the end, leaning his shoulder against the window, the window giving onto the street. Joshua watching me work in the early days, drinking for free. Those nights when he was always there, coming in early after whatever job he was doing—working in mail rooms, working as someone's assistant, someone's gofer. Those early days before our impatience set in, before our fear.

I was thinking about the flickering fluorescent light, my palm against the cool white cinder block. My cheek. Sometimes my lips, my tongue. The constant noise. The screaming at night.

I opened my eyes. A jet drew a neat white line across the sky.

Juliette watched me, head bobbing in rhythm with her easy panting. I reached for her. She licked my hand.

I stood and waited for her to get up. It took several tries. She'd lead with her head and her shoulders, trying to get the momentum going, rocking back and forth. She was like a car with its wheels stuck in the mud. She rocked and rocked until she could get her feet beneath her and then pulled with her front legs. When she was up she was unsteady at first. You could see she didn't trust her body any longer. It had become unreliable, those legs refusing to do what they'd once done so effortlessly. I picked up the empty bottle as she struggled. I don't know why I didn't help immediately. Finally I reached beneath her, held on to her back legs just above the knees, right where the muscles flared to thigh, and I lifted.

I took another beer and a handful of treats for Juliette and the two of us went outside. I pulled off my shirt, sat on one of the lounge chairs, and fed her until she'd licked my hand clean. I drank half the beer, stood up, and let myself fall into the pool. From beneath the surface I could hear Juliette's muted barking. I stayed down and watched her through the rippling water, her dark form shifting on the deck. When I came up she looked like a puppy, moving her head from side to side, tongue lolling out. She licked water from my face until I dropped down and from beneath the surface I heard her far-off barking.

We slept through the afternoon in the breeze, in the sun—me on a chair, Juliette's pale and tender belly pressed to the warm concrete.

I woke in the cold and opened my eyes to the black branches breaking the low sun into a hundred hairline fractures.

After, we went for a walk. She was slow up the steps, and by the time we came to the street she was so tired we had to rest. We stood on the sidewalk watching the cars race past as the pink sky dissolved into darkness.

I waited for Juliette to shit, but she didn't, so we gave up and returned down the steps, the descent even harder on her legs. I locked the front door and gently removed her harness.

The outdoor lights had come on. The pool glowed the color of glass cleaner. The trees were lit from below—white and enormous in the night while everything around them was blackness.

We kept the great sliding glass doors open and the two of us lay on the soft living room carpet and watched the night. Nothing seemed to move. There was the bright blue rectangle. There were the trees stretching upward and arching toward us. Like fingers beginning to close. Like tar-stained skeleton claws. I drank beer after beer after beer. The air was cold and I liked the heat of Juliette's brittle ribs against my side.

There were noises out there, and Juliette was alert, her ears twitching, raising her head when a branch cracked, or something moved through the dry dead leaves beyond the light.

Later I closed the doors and got into bed. It was a bed unlike anything I'd ever known. I moved my legs across the bottom sheet as if I were treading water and laughed out loud. Juliette watched from the doorway, but when I switched off the light she swung around like a horse and left me.

I saw my father polishing his shoe. His sleeves rolled up, his left hand pressed against the insole, his right moving a chamois over the leather, a bit of gray hair fallen across his forehead. When I woke in the morning Juliette was at my door watching me.

I followed her to the living room, where she stopped, her nose at the glass.

Scattered across the white carpet were four dry turds.

"Oh, Juliette," I said as I slid the door open and she pushed out into the cold fog.

I cleaned up and walked outside where she crouched down and tried to pee as she staggered on her good back leg. She glanced at me. I turned away, imagining her humiliated.

In the kitchen, I hid her pills in her food. When she was finished, I kneeled, held her head in the crook of my arm, and put the drops in her eyes.

All day I lay in the sun—Juliette at the side of my chair, in my shade, my hand resting on her head while I watched the trees moving in the wind.

My father stood outside in his boots with a mug of coffee in his dry hand. I followed the ember of his Marlboro Red burn to his thick fingers. I could see his bloodied thumbnail, the dark street before him, the dimly lit house at his back. He dropped the butt into the dregs and walked a few steps down the path to the sidewalk.

From my bedroom window upstairs, I saw my mother's car stop in front of the house.

My father pulled the groceries from the trunk. Their lips moved. My mother smiled. She kissed his cheek. He wrapped one arm around her shoulder and held the bag of groceries in his other like an infant.

Juliette had gotten herself to her feet and was out at the edge of the trees, eyeing me, her head lowered, as if she weren't quite sure who I was.

I don't know why, but I called Marco. We'd never seen each other anywhere but the airport, but somehow I thought he might come up and have a few beers with me. I left a message, but he never called back.

That night I lay in their big Jacuzzi tub with a six pack beside me on the damp bathmat. I used their soap, their fragrant shampoo. I moved strands of Sky's blond hair along the side with my toe. There was a wedding photograph centered on the column between their sinks. From time to time, Juliette came in and licked my shoulder as if I belonged there. It made me very sad. It felt like a betrayal somehow, as if I'd burrowed too far into a life that wasn't my own. When I got out, I was too drunk and too tired to go for a walk. I passed out in the guestroom with a wet towel still wrapped around my waist.

In the morning I found Juliette trying to nose the door open. She'd shit all over the carpet again. "I'm sorry," I said, collecting the turds in a plastic bag.

Her leg seemed worse and on the lawn she nearly fell over trying to pee.

That afternoon we were sitting outside when the pool man came.

"I'm just taking care of the place," I said. As if I needed to make some excuse for lying in the sun on a Monday afternoon, an excuse for all that wealth that wasn't mine.

He moved his net slowly through the water.

At a far corner he scooped up a rat.

"Big motherfucker," he said, swinging the pole around to show us. Then he flung it into the undergrowth beyond the lawn.

"Coyotes will eat it."

"Yeah?" I said.

"Up here? Coyotes everywhere. Bobcats too now and then."

I nodded.

"They come down for the little dogs. The other day I found a Jack Russell floating in a pool just down the street."

He poured something into the water from a fat white bottle. "Wouldn't worry about that guy, though," he said, nodding at Juliette. "Nothing bigger than him out here."

When he'd gone, I got a beer and tried calling Marco again. It was such a beautiful house and it would have been nice to have someone around. Have a few beers, go for a swim. But he didn't answer.

Later, I took the house phone outside onto the lawn and dialed my father while the sun caught in the tangled lattice of branches, burned, and began to disappear.

"Dad. It's me."

"Peter," he said.

There'd been noise in the background, but whatever it was he stopped it. I could see him shifting the phone from between his ear and shoulder into his hand. I could see him frozen there, or maybe he was walking to the window, favoring his good hip, parting the curtain and looking out at the street, or combing his fingers through his beard.

"Hi, Dad."

"Pete," he said. "How are you?"

"I'm fine, I'm fine. How are you?"

"No complaints. You know, the world turns. Still got a job, still got a house."

"That's good," I said. A squirrel scrambled along a thin branch.

"Where are you, bud?"

"LA. Still in LA."

"And still at the airport?"

"Still there."

Juliette came outside, stood at the edge of the pool, and gave me her stare.

"Hey, you remember Joshua?"

"Sure I do."

"I ran into him the other night."

"So you're friends again?"

"Well, it's been a long time. You know. But right now, I'm up here at his house. I'm taking care of his dog."

"That's fantastic, Pete. Great that you're friends again. Happy to hear it."

"Yeah," I said. "It's nice. And what a beautiful dog. Beautiful house too."

"What's his name?"

"Her name. Juliette."

Juliette raised her head a bit. We held each other's eyes while I kept the phone tight to my ear, listening for some familiar sound—the radiators, the dishwasher, the back door, his hammered-spoon wind chimes, anything. I imagined him sitting down, moving his heavy frame into one of my mother's delicate kitchen chairs.

"Juliette," my father repeated. "What kind of name's that for a dog?"

"She's a Great Dane. She's really something else," I said.

"Well," he said. "I'm glad to hear you're doing so well."

I didn't say anything. I listened, but all I heard was his breath moving across the mouthpiece.

Then he said, "I miss you, son. I miss you every day."

"Me too," I said.

Again, both of us waited. I listened and I imagined him doing the same, as if some sound in the background might answer a question neither of us knew how to ask.

"I was thinking, Dad. I was thinking I'd like to come home for a while. Come see you."

"Oh, I'd like that, Peter. I'd like that so much."

"Me too," I said, beginning to speak more quickly, walking out to the trees. "I was thinking I'd come home next week and just, I don't know. I'd see you and Mom and, really, I don't know exactly. Just be home and get things together and figure out what's next. It would be nice to be home with you both."

"Peter," he said. "You know I'd love that."

Juliette was still watching me.

"I'd like that. You know I would. I'd love it, love it more than anything, but you also know I'm going to have to talk to your mother. I'll have to ask her. I'll have to find the right time and ask her. See what *she* says, see what she thinks about it." He paused and then said, "About you coming home," as if I'd forgotten what we were talking about.

I was walking back across the lawn to the house.

"Sure," I said. "Talk to her."

"I will, son. I *will* talk to her. You know, it's a matter of time. She'll come around."

"Sure," I said.

"Time will come. The time will come. It always does, bud."

"I'm going to go," I said. "I'm going to hang up now."

"I miss you, Peter. I miss you all the time."

That evening the fog came in and hovered thick between the trees. After I'd hidden the pills in Juliette's food, after she'd eaten, we lay together on our stomachs, in our place on the carpet at the open door where we listened to the strange night, pricking up our ears when the animals moved. We stayed inside, but we pushed our faces right up against the outside air.

I drank and drank and drank.

I thought of the coyotes coming down from the hills. I thought of the bobcats, of the Windex water going pink with blood. I thought of Joshua and a pair of red running shoes he used to wear when we were friends. I thought of Arnie Henry and the mermaid figurehead and the view of the ocean from the bow of his apartment and all those people in those days who came and went and came and went.

And then my knees drawn up against the smooth painted cinder-block wall.

We watched the fog drift in through the branches and into the bright clearing, where it floated above the grass. I kept my hand on Juliette's warm head and for a very long time we were still. Something heavy moved beneath the trees. Juliette worked herself up with a burst of strength, staggered for a moment, and then limped forward with her head down. Slowly she made her way across the short grass, sniffing the air. She found nothing. The animals went quiet and she waited, standing at the perimeter, gazing out into the fog, into the night.

And I waited flat on my stomach, chin on the backs of my hands, drunk.

We waited and waited.

Then Juliette swung around and made her way back, coming to rest at the edge of the pool, where, as if afraid she'd missed something, returned her gaze to the trees. There it was again, the scrape and crunch of the leaves followed by more quiet. And Juliette, in turning her head to me, lost her balance.

Her leg failed, and she collapsed sideways into the pool.

She went under and disappeared and then I was running. I slammed

473

my shoulder into the edge of the glass door but I kept on and there she was, her head breaking through the surface, her wide eyes on mine. I dove in and came up facing her. She was clawing with her front legs, but she was sinking. We were in the deep end. I was breathing hard. I swam to her. "Juliette, Juliette," I said. "It's all right girl, it's okay." She was making a terrible noise, snorting, and whimpering the faintest sound. I was dizzy with all the beer and already worn out before I got to her and when I did she tried to climb my chest, and beneath the weight of her, the weight of my sweatshirt, my jeans, the alcohol, I went under. Then her claws were moving, scratching at my neck, my cheek, driving me down. I swallowed water. Her nails were cutting at me and cutting at me. I could feel myself being dragged down and down. The cotton heavier and heavier. For a moment I stopped trying to swim, to return to the surface, to save her. Her claws were no longer on me, I no longer felt her weight, and somewhere through the water I saw Juliette's nearly useless legs beating like a windup toy.

I was touching the floor of the pool with my bare feet now, the rest of me suspended. I could have broken, could have stopped. I was warm with it. But I pushed hard with my feet and broke through and found her again, her regal head dipping beneath the surface, her bulging eyes. I worked myself behind her and held on and pulled and swam with the rest of what I had. I fought her and kicked and kicked and pulled and fought until we were to the shallow end, where I vomited and dragged her up over the steps and onto the concrete deck, where she tried and failed to stand, where she lay and shuddered and tried without standing to shake the water from her, wild, body trembling, where I lay behind her and held on with all my strength until she gave in and stopped fighting and the two of us began to breathe regularly and all we were doing was shaking together in the cold.

Later, I walked her through the kitchen and into the bathroom, where I wrapped her in all my fresh white towels and rubbed her dry. I stripped my wet clothes off and stood beneath the hot shower while Juliette stood on the bath mat, shivering and watching me through the fogging glass. After I'd used the hand towels on the sink to dry off, after I'd run the hair dryer over and over up and down her coat, after I'd gotten dressed and we'd walked to the living room, she was still shivering.

I helped her up onto the wide couch, where she lay at my side and rested her head in my lap. I unfolded a blanket and drew it up over our bodies.

I felt her shuddering beneath my hand. I felt my heart beating blood into the gashes on my neck, into the long scratch across my cheek, my forehead, across my soft belly.

The night went on and on. The fog moved through the trees and spilled out and out over the lawn, collecting like raw wool on the grass. Slowly, Juliette stopped shivering. Her eyes narrowed, she exhaled a long stuttering breath, and before long she was asleep.

Outside, the pool glowed its eerie blue and the water was smooth and still as if it were a solid thing.

Nominated by Tin House, Ben Fountain, Don Waters

CAPTCHA

by STEPHANIE STRICKLAND

from BOSTON REVIEW

cranium chambered cairn and passage grave
bulging Neolithic earth mound enclosing the vault

calibrated stone to this standard surpasses us
lost too inner touch on bone pale solstice beam

dervish Snow Queen covens of raven rim her platinum
cloak downed traces of her sledge paused print a fine grid

on the peregrine's pouring away world of no attachment
tilting wakes twisting falls sinking panes of land and water

dive-bomb raptor-force 200 miles per hour stoop!
copy and mod *her* aerial maneuvers map Northern core

rock extinct volcanoes lush with perforations cloak them
suspend them under numbers shadows from another place

•

—or site : the Emerald Viewer marks an avatar invisible
as it visits strolls beneath the lindens the lime honey bracts

in the log-on Lab World structured from permissions where
who hangs at your space from your space's erased from you

nor can you take your own movement for granted
earth and physics afterthought (interface) you install

an IM app in your dream equip folding but unfading
tutelary mesmerie with chat while *falling* as a peregrine

tinsel buttercup foil painted roof ruined roof of the Plaza
verdigris mansard copper slate rushing toward her she could tell

by a tension in the air wire-fine overhead—one rustling
shift—time to be swept back to sea so typed in mistakenly

(no peregrine eye) randomly assigned CAPTCHA squiggle
Turing test box of twisted-letter text to tag her

personhood denied

Nominated by Terese Svoboda

WATCHING A WOMAN ON THE M101 EXPRESS

by KAMILAH AISHA MOON

from SHE HAS A NAME (FOUR WAY BOOKS)

You sit in a hard, blue seat, one
of the ones reserved for the elderly
or infirm, a statue of need. Your mouth

open as if waiting for water or medicine, as if
mugged mid-sentence, or some ice age hit
right after terrible news.

Oblivious to the metro's bump and buck,
to the toddler begging in Spanish to be freed
from her stroller, to my ogling, you sit

embalmed, racooned, or moosed. You have
the kind of eyes that never quite close,
even in deepest sleep, lids

an undersized t-shirt that leaves belly
exposed. Tears navigate moles, veteran
swimmers of your creek-bed face.

I can't stop looking. You can't get over
whatever has happened, so shell-shocked
that birds could land and roost. I want to ask—

just so you know someone
is paying attention, but not enough
to know what ravages. It's rude
to stare. I'm from the South, a suburb
where Grief pulls the shades first,
stays home if indecent. But

your sorrow struts four rows down
from me, strands you an astronaut
on some distant, undiscovered moon.

Bodies to your left and right read papers,
nap, send text messages. You sit in a hard,
blue seat, mouth open. I study the pink

of your jaw, and wonder if you'll come back
before your stop comes.

Nominated by Four Way Books

BLACK PLANK

by NANCY GEYER

from THE GEORGIA REVIEW

Every few minutes, my father pushes out of his armchair to take a tour of his house. He stops at the desk I've made of the table off the kitchen and flips through my books. He asks me again what I'm working on, what sort of job I have these days. His curiosity is genuine; there's a lilt to his voice and light in his eyes. But the cumulative effect is such that it begins to feel like an interrogation. As if none of my answers pleases him. Eventually, even my own ears aren't satisfied.

And yet I appreciate my father's inquiries, because while I was growing up his career—which took him around the world—came first. The interest he's showing me now feels like a novelty. It's utterly free of preoccupation. The thought crosses my mind that maybe *this* is how I'll remember him: a single weekend will erase years of inattention. In any event, work is not what I'm doing. I've given up on trying to write in my father's home, which is just outside of Washington, DC, where I live, and am tackling my e-mail instead. Among the recent acquisitions at the National Gallery of Art, I learn from the museum's newsletter, is a 1967 piece titled *Black Plank* by John McCracken, a Minimalist artist with whom I'm only vaguely familiar. I mumble something to my father and he shuffles back to his cluttered study.

Black Plank. I come to a halt at these words as if I've been driving, not scrolling, and they are an obstacle in the road. Together they are inelegant, "unworkable in the literature of wonder or beauty," in G. K. Chesterton's formulation. They sound like the name of a disease—a mold that attacks the trunks of trees. They also evoke a human afflic-

480

tion: mind matter that's thick and dark, or—because the words are a bit of a tongue twister—blank.

The announcement includes no image, but one has already formed inside my head. A quick search confirms that the work is as I had guessed—as anyone might guess—a black plank. But not just any black plank. Made of plywood coated in fiberglass and polyester resin, it's "a rare black early plank in pristine condition," and one of the many planks that constitute the artist's "signature achievement."

McCracken, I learn, believes in UFOs and aliens. He feels that each of his planks "has its own personality, indeed its own being." He also believes in time travel and hopes the planks will function as time machines. The planks are displayed leaning against a wall, thereby bridging sculpture ("identified with the floor") and painting ("identified with the wall"). I'm weighing the profundity of this when my father comes to the table again to ask me what I'm working on. In this moment, whether the absurdities of the situation at hand have falsely implicated *Black Plank*, or the plank itself has contributed to the absurdities, the three of us become entwined.

A plank, if you visualize it upright, also has something of the signpost about it. It's what you hope to come across if you're lost in the woods. I set out to see *Black Plank* three days later, walking the twenty-five minutes from my home to the National Gallery. Washington was in the clutches of summer, with temperatures expected to approach ninety degrees, but the day was comfortable thanks to extensive cloud cover, which looked like unrolled batts of crimped wool.

Along the way I pondered the truism that "art is what you bring to it." I subscribe to this but at the same time find it suspect: it says nothing about getting anything in return. What was I bringing to *Black Plank*? A lifelong love of art, for one thing. A certain ruthlessness, for another. For example, I used to feel compelled to read an "important" book all the way through regardless of whether it was holding my interest. No longer: time is what's important. (How much of it would I spend on *Black Plank*?) There's also the independence of thought that comes with age, and an I-don't-give-a-damn attitude about how I'm perceived. Call me a sucker for loving *Black Plank*, or a philistine for hating it. I don't care. What else was I bringing? A trouble or two that tries my patience for the trivial and the meaningless, which would seem to bode poorly for the plank. But I also have a sensibility that favors less-than-monumental subjects. I fondly recall a movie I saw years ago in which the only action was a fight over a bicycle. And I delight in a quote from Annie Dillard: "Nothing is going to happen in this book."

Halfway to the museum, I turned north from Pennsylvania Avenue onto Second Street because I like to walk along the backs of the national landmarks, the tourists massed at their fronts and thus out of the way. Here it can be surprisingly quiet—deserted even—depending on the time of day. I passed behind the Library of Congress, its copper dome aged to green, the gilded Torch of Learning shining at its apex. To my right was the Folger Library, which has the largest collection of Shakespeare materials in the world. Crossing East Capitol Street, I had to my left a view of the Capitol a block away, its white dome topped by a classical female figure in flowing robes—the Statue of Freedom. She was facing me, for what we think of as the back of the Capitol was designed to be the front and is just as elaborate as the view from the Mall. I like this about the Capitol: say what you will about what goes on inside, the building itself shows no bad side. I passed behind the Supreme Court, the words JUSTICE THE GUARDIAN OF LIBERTY inscribed on its pediment. I walked by elaborate friezes and chiseled laurel wreaths and gigantic urns and Corinthian columns and Ionic pilasters and chandeliers ablaze in high windows and stone faces staring straight ahead from above arched windows and lion heads spouting water into marble basins. All of which is to say that if my errand seemed small at the outset, it now felt infinitesimal.

At Constitution Avenue I turned left and passed the Senate office buildings and the United States Court House. Glumly I walked by the Department of Labor, wondering if, after years of freelancing, I could ever again get a real job. I made a left onto Fourth Street NW, ignoring the entrance to the National Gallery's East Building, in which, somewhere, *Black Plank* leaned against a wall. I wanted to ascend the West Building's grand staircase. I wanted to take the pink marble steps because I fear that, in the name of security, the grand approach is becoming a thing of the past in Washington. The most recent casualty was the front entrance to the Supreme Court: now everyone, lawyers and visitors alike, must use a plaza-level side entrance that takes them *under* the stairs—prompting Justice Stephen G. Breyer to issue an impassioned reminder that the stairs "are not only a means to, but also a metaphor for, access to the court itself." By climbing the West Building's forty-one stairs and pushing through its massive doors, which are bound in leather and trimmed with brass nailheads in the manner of a club chair, I was showing respect for what was inside and elevating my spirits in the process.

One great thing about the National Gallery is that admission is free, so you don't have to cram lots of artworks into one exhausting visit. If you're in the vicinity—whether you live nearby or you're on your lunch break or are making a day of it on the Mall—you can drop in with the sole purpose of seeing *Black Plank* without feeling you must also swing by the Vermeers, say, or the Leonardo. And you can pass through the Rotunda and make straight for the underground passage to the East Building, as I did, without so much as a glance at Mercury-the-messenger-god atop the fountain, pointing with his index finger to Mount Olympus. "Next time," you tell yourself.

Hanging from a bookshelf in my father's study is a whiteboard on which is written

B—in Congo
Nancy here till Friday noon

To the immediate left of the board is my college photo, and although it's possible I've been in that position for years, I suspect that my father's wife, just before she left for Africa on business, moved it there to reinforce the connection between my name and my face. To the right of the board is a medium-size mirror. The third part of this book-blocking triptych, the mirror haunts me, though I can't figure out why. Eventually I decide that its placement serves a purpose as well: to reacquaint the inner and the outer selves.

Getting to *any* of the books on the shelves is difficult. Pictures hang from every edge. Framed newspaper articles that feature my dad. Photographs of him shaking hands with well-known people. Diplomas and letters and certificates of appreciation. This display looks for all the world like that of a man with an enormous ego. But there is no ego. My father had always hung a few mementos in his study, but the extravagance now is so that he might be reminded of what he had made of himself.

In the East Building at last, I went to the information desk for directions to *Black Plank*. The volunteer, a woman in her seventies, didn't know what it was so I described it: a black plank leaning against a wall. That didn't ring a bell, so she picked up the phone and called someone who reported that I had to go back downstairs. I quickly scanned the underground galleries for the distinctive shape until finally I was standing in front of it. And as luck would have it I pretty much had the plank to myself.

Photographs, I had to admit, don't do the piece justice: it's quite imposing—perhaps eight feet tall. And even more polished than I'd expected. It couldn't possibly be mistaken for construction site debris or for just another piece of wood in the lumberyard. Nor would you think it a "found object," elevated by virtue of being in a museum. You might not even guess it is made of wood, and certainly not of plywood. It looks pricey, slick. Even if you were invited to touch it, you'd be afraid to; it's so flawless you wouldn't dream of leaving fingerprints.

I had thought its blackness would be that of a black hole, whose point of no return sucks in color and light never to be seen again. But the ceiling lights shone in it like an assembly of suns, and the reflected hues of a Frank Stella collage in the room behind me gave it a bit of cheer. I felt awkward standing directly in front of it, unable to look at *Black Plank* without seeming to look at myself. You actually look *into* it, not *at* it, and therefore into yourself. This illusion of depth reminded me of Thoreau's lake-as-earth's-eye, "looking into which the beholder measures the depth of his own nature." Maybe our mirrors should be like this, I thought—a vehicle for soul-searching, just dark enough to be useless for applying lipstick or plucking gray hairs. The plank cast long, overlapping shadows on the wall behind it, narrow at the top and wider at the bottom, like an inverted paper fan beginning to open.

The front door opens and shuts quietly; my father has gone out. I finish the paragraph I'm reading, turn my book face down in my lap. I don't know what my father does when he's outside. I haven't wanted him to catch me spying from the window.

The house is suddenly quiet yet not silent. The clocks, the refrigerator, the air conditioning: they seal me off from the outside world, making me feel entombed. In my own home, I will suffer heat for an open window.

When my father returns after a few minutes, I flip my book right side up and call to him, "What's going on out in the world?" The words surprise me as soon as they leave my mouth. I hear in them a long-ago echo: "And what news of the world do you bring me, my lass?" my father would ask if he should encounter me coming in from play.

"I don't know," he replies. "I didn't look very far."

At 10:30 he goes out again, though we had agreed at 9:00 to lock the door for the night. Again, I turn over my book. And again he returns in several minutes.

"Are the stars out tonight?" I ask. He once was an amateur astronomer, and like many such fathers he occasionally set up the telescope on clear nights and arranged stars on bedroom ceilings. On my ceiling anyway, perhaps because they were one thing he could give me—a girl with three brothers—that didn't involve sports. How long was he up on the ladder, chart and ruler and pencil in hand, mapping the cosmos precisely?

"I don't know," he says gravely. "I didn't look up. But I'm *sure* they're out there."

Sometimes we must ask a question again and again to get to the heart of something. I returned to the museum several weeks later to attend a gallery talk about *Black Plank* because, though I wasn't sure what my question was, I wanted another go at it. The McCracken plank, I had to agree, was the mother of all planks, but so far I had neither liked nor disliked it—yet I wasn't ready to resign myself to indifference.

This time I took the metro, surfacing at the National Archives—home to the Declaration of Independence and the Constitution. I bypassed the West Building's grand staircase and went directly to the East Building's street-level entrance, which turned out to be a fitting gateway to my ultimate destination: the façade was undergoing repairs, so visitors had to pass through a plywood tunnel to get to the front door. But this wasn't just any plywood tunnel. It had been painted pearl gray to match the façade's marble veneer and had an overlay of bold geometric cutouts.

The discussion was conducted by Sally and Sydney, two of the museum's educators. I'd heard Sally before; she's an engaging lecturer who plays a not-insubstantial role in the lives of many middle-aged and elderly women. There were twenty of us in all, sitting on folding stools so small I was afraid I'd fall backwards into a Mel Bochner "language fraction": the words *over/in* painted on the wall.

Sally started out by introducing Sydney, a recent graduate of Princeton who, sadly for the Gallery, was soon bound for further schooling.

Sydney, added Sally, was "particularly crazy about *Black Plank*." And then Sydney, relaxed and immediately likeable, explained why she was attracted to it, and to all of Minimalism: because it's "hard" and "not so obvious." It's a very literal art, she said moments later, "it is what it is"—and I, remembering that one sign of a first-rate intelligence is the ability to hold two opposing ideas in mind at once, kept silent about the contradiction.

Minimalist artists were reacting against the gestural, Sydney explained, and in particular they had rejected Abstract Expressionism, in which the heart and soul of the artist are poured onto the canvas. Minimalism is cool, often making use of industrial materials. Whether or not the object is actually made by the artist doesn't matter. McCracken, however, makes his own planks, though he takes great pains to eliminate all signs of his handiwork. He coats the plywood in fiberglass to make sure the grain won't show through, and then he applies layer after layer of resin, sanding and polishing with power tools for days. He's a bit of a mystic, Sydney confirmed, beholden to the monolith, suggestive as that is of a supreme being.

I noticed as we were talking that we barely looked at *Black Plank*, even though it was right there in front of us. That neither Sally nor Sydney turned around to glance at it. This wasn't necessary, really. As Sydney had said, "You see it all in one go." Which doesn't mean there wasn't plenty to talk about. Someone in our group was quick to say that although Minimalism might be cool, she found *Black Plank* to be "very emotional and unpredictable." I almost looked down, as if this were an intimate confession. Someone else brought up the work's resemblance to hand-waxed surfboards—the West Coast Minimalists (of which McCracken was one until he moved to New Mexico) worked, after all, in a car-and-surfboard culture. Sally added that the LA Minimalists were derided by some critics for having a "finish fetish," a label that stuck. Someone else followed up on that, saying *Black Plank*'s reflectivity is very important, by which she seemed to mean that, without it, *Black Plank* wouldn't be *Black Plank*. Sally mentioned the importance of placement, stressing that *Black Plank* cannot be fully grasped unless it's "installed," and I had to keep from laughing out loud because to install *Black Plank* couldn't possibly mean anything other than to lean it against a wall, and as far as I could tell it didn't matter which side did the leaning.

A woman who described herself as a documentary filmmaker asked if narrative is embraced or eschewed by Minimalists. Should she keep trying to discern in *Black Plank* a story? (Answer: probably not.) Then a man sitting in the back said something about the narrative being re-pressed. The Freudian implications were taken up by the man next to him. Both men, I think, were curators. I strained to follow the conver-sation, but their voices didn't quite reach me; the room's acoustics bounced sound around. I thought I heard the second man say that anything made by a human being will have *something* of the human in it, and that narrative is there precisely by virtue of its not being stated. I had a hard time wrapping my mind around this while trying to hear what he said next. I leaned forward, even cupped an ear, but it was no use. His words trailed off. They got sucked out of the room or dissi-pated on the spot, or maybe they headed straight for the ether.

One fall afternoon, as we walk around the block, I try to engage my father in a conversation about all the places we'd lived before my par-ents' divorce: the cities and suburbs and small college towns we called home that never truly *felt* like home because we didn't stay in any of them quite long enough. I want to know where he was happiest, but he hesitates and then turns the question around. Not the tiny upstate New York town where I'd gone to high school, I say—not after living in Chicago.

Remind me again what I did there, he says. I tell him that he had taught at the college and had also directed a program there. Oh that's right, he says quickly, and I'm grateful he no longer feels the need to hide the gaps in his memory, though this means another layer has been peeled away and tossed to the wind. A thick layer—five years. If we're to be together we must go further back in time.

I don't know what my father had envisioned for his retirement, but *I* had hoped—we *all* had hoped—that although he might write a book, or continue to lecture now and then, he'd also finally have time to get to know his children, and his children's children. The more my ques-tions to him go unanswered, however, the more I understand that this time in his life might have been a chance to get to know *him*, without his heavy mantle of mission and responsibility. Or is this illness in some perverse way that chance? But what remains of a person after he's been stripped of what he had made of himself? After the ego has become disengaged and the accomplishments have been forgotten, but before all else is lost? Is there a core or essence, there from the beginning? Or is what's left more like fragments?

A small thing: after our walk, my father manages to find the fly swatter, and I am reminded for the first time in decades of how delighted I was as a child when a fly was loose in the house and he'd go after it with a vengeance. How could this be a grown man's battle, I recall wondering—a man the size of my father?

Because of their shape, and because to regard them is to be in them, it's almost impossible not to anthropomorphize McCracken's planks. The next time I peeked into *Black Plank*'s room I found a painting in its place. Sally happened to be there, having just completed a tour, so I asked her where it had gone. "I don't know," she said, eyes widening, and we both let out a giggle, for it was as if the plank had up and wandered off.

In the late 1960s, a lanky California artist named Scott Grieger began a series of fifteen "impersonations," one of which was of a McCracken plank. "It was a brainteaser to come up with an adequate impersonation of his sculpture," Grieger wrote in the text accompanying the black and white photographs that documented his work. "After ruminating about what to do for some time . . . it eventually became clear to me that becoming stiff as a board and simply leaning against a wall made perfect sense for a McCracken." A *New York Times* critic, finding the planks "so ready and yet so closed," felt they leaned in a way that evoked ladies of the night. Noting that McCracken was "physically plankish," an interviewer once asked him whether he was making *himself*. McCracken laughed and said, "Yeah, probably. You do something and it tends to be a self-portrait. I suppose if I were chubby I'd tend to do chubbier pieces." (The planks had to be about two feet taller than the human body, he said, to include the body's energy field.)

Maybe this simple recognition of—or longing for—like form explained why I couldn't help but look in on *Black Plank* whenever I happened to be at the museum, in the same way you might feel compelled to glance through an open door along an office corridor whether or not you know the person sitting at his desk. Whether or not that person might nod back.

Early in the New Year I catch up with *Black Plank* in a tiny, out-of-the-way room on the museum's third floor, now part of an exhibit titled *There is nothing to see here.* The title issues a challenge, but of the fifteen or twenty people who come and go inside of several minutes only a few appear to study the plank, or the piece of cardboard painted all-over white, or the dozen or so miniature all-black canvases distinguishable only by their frames, or any of the other similarly self-effacing works. Having already spent time with the plank, I too give it not much more than a glance—just enough to notice that it's lost the bit of cheer the Stella collage had given it, finding no colors to reflect in its new location, though "reflect" gives the wrong impression because the colors seem to come from within.

Still, I'm oddly glad to find it here, even in its more somber state. The plank is by now quite familiar, if no less mystifying. It's not *mystical*, not in the McCracken sense, but inscrutable all the same. If the plank were to function as McCracken said he wishes—if, by looking into it, you could glimpse the future—I would know that McCracken will not outlive this show, nor my father the year. But as it is, in this small, quiet room of nearly invisible works, in which (as the wall text has it) "the very difficulty of seeing them demands an extraordinary patience in viewing them," time seems to linger in the present, if not stand still. You can almost hang on to it. Only by leaving this room will you be pitched into the future.

Nominated by Judith Kitchen, Rosellen Brown, Jessica Wilbanks

BOY. CHILD WITHOUT LEGS. GETTING OFF A CHAIR

by OLIVER DE LA PAZ

from AMERICAN POETRY REVIEW

Photographed 1887, Eadweard Muybridge

The boy raises himself up by his arms
and follows a sequence of intentions.

Thrusts his hips out. In this action,
he is no longer a boy but a bell. The clapper,

the weight of his leg stumps. He rocks himself
and sets his body down on his haunches.

Then draws his arms slightly up and forward
again. Palms against the wooden studio floor. Perhaps

he feels the grit of sand between his fingers
or the lacquer blackening his nails. Regardless,

the intent to move is paramount because the line
between frames demands consecutive action.

Air on the bare and rounded ends of his legs
shears the speed of his movement. His bell peals

its silent toll. Rings a sound which is not a sound
but a heft. A series of sways this way and that.

His legs slow the swing of his pendular body to a
    wild
suspension aloft as the camera demands. Palms

against the floor as his trunk, again, thrusts forward
into the darkened wood. He sails, again aloft.

To mount the chair, the boy moves forward,
keeps his distance from the chair at arm's length.

He turns and raises his body up with one hand
on the ground, one on the chair. His absent legs

high in the air as if twirling a cartwheel.
The boy slowly wheels into the seat of the chair.

And slowly as if his body is the lip of a bell, done
ringing its one song, returns downward through

the will of gravity. And still, the camera snaps
while the chair has no intention or sequence. It is

idle and it is where the boy sits, turns to the camera,
and smiles. The shadows carve his muscled torso as

he contorts. As he turns himself again. Both arms
press to the floor and he lowers his haunches down.

Perhaps the black of the lens snaps its slow frame
audibly to usher the time. To urge the dismount from

the chair. And so the boy listens to his own peal.
The sound of his heart thickened

by the stress of such simple gestures. The reel
clicks its repetitions. While the breath of the man

behind the camera syncopates with the boy's own
swaying legs. In this frame, he is sitting still.

In this frame he flies.

Nominated by Ayse Papatya Bucak, Bruce Beasley

FOR BEDS

by MATTHEW VOLLMER

from NEW ORLEANS REVIEW

Merciful God, we humbly thank Thee for setting the earth on its rota-
tion around the sun, thus providing humanity with periods of light that
permit us, as we go about our daily business, to recognize with relative
clarity the things of the earth, and for the atmospheric changes and
angles of the sun that allow us to sense the progression of time and thus
acknowledge all manner of climatological differences. So too do we
thank Thee for creating a period of darkness during which our eyes
might find respite and our minds repose, and where we might also ex-
perience a reprieve from sense-making, most palpably experiencing, in
our dream-states, the joys and terrors of embarking upon adventures
much greater in scope than we would ever hope to undergo during our
comparatively prudent daytime excursions. But most of all, oh LORD,
we thank Thee for the beds upon which we sleep, and for which we too
often take for granted, failing to remember the hay-or-leaf-stuffed ani-
mal skin mattresses of yore, or the goat-skin waterbeds of Persia, or the
heaped palm-boughs of Egypt. We recognize now the discoveries of
vulcanized rubber and box springs, of memory foam invented by scien-
tists employed in our national aeronautics and space program. We
are thankful too, oh Heavenly Father, for the accoutrements that adorn
these beds, for the linens of silk or cotton or flannel, for blankets of
down, for pillows of goose feathers or micro-beads. We are thankful for
box springs, oh LORD, and that our beds are raised above the ground,
upon which roam the countless creatures that might do us harm, and
for the space below these beds, where, as youngsters, we imagined
monstrous, slobbering entities, and where now old socks and dust balls

have created a netherworld of forgotten things that, when spied upon, remind us that unseen spaces exist in our homes, and that these too deserve, from time to time, our attention. We therefore ask a blessing upon these our beds, that they may not do us harm but fulfill their promise in providing us a place to safely slumber, that they might be rafts upon which we lie to escape the storms of life, and that furthermore, they may remain a place where children are forbidden to jump—if only so that children may discover the joys of benign transgressions, so long as they do not fall and crack open their heads on our dressers or nightstands—and where lonely souls recline to read or bathe in the glow of television, and where couples unite in joyful lovemaking, a space into which children crawl when awoken from night terrors, and where poor souls who have lost loved ones might curl up into the positions they first took in the wombs of their mothers and, grasping wadded tissues, dab at their weeping eyes. Forgive us LORD, if we are to forget the luxuries afforded to us of our beds, and keep us ever mindful of those who sleep tonight upon surfaces that were not made with comfort in mind, those who, for reasons that are unknown to us, face conditions we cannot and therefore do not imagine, and should these poor souls die before they wake, grant them a final dream in which they lie with their lovers on a mattress of memory foam, the pressure-sensitive polyurethane surface molding to the shapes of their bodies, so that sleepers and beds, in the end, become one.

Nominated by New Orleans Review, Ed Falco

THE HUM OF ZUG ISLAND

by JAMAAL MAY

from THE KENYON REVIEW

In Windsor they blame it on machines
across the Detroit River. Residents can't ignore
the low frequency hum taking the shape of a sea-
serpent on oscilloscopes. Beyond gray snow,
plastic bags, and crushed hypodermic needles,
I know Zug Island is humming—waiting

the way the organs in me are waiting.
My body is a building full of machines,
some more complex than others: needle-
nosed pliers, pistols, a satellite—all ignoring
my commands to sit still. But the snow
wants to kiss us, I hear my skin say. The sea,

pouring from gutters toward the sea
that must be out there waiting—
eardrums covet the rushing. Just snow
melting, I say to the thrumming machines,
but my voice is easy to ignore.
So I find myself drawn again to needles

of light through drawn blinds, needles
of wind through a window's failing. A sea
of all the outside I try to ignore,
the hum that won't calm and won't wait.

This oscillating piston of a heart, the machine
that should know better, wants to see snow

tremble. It goes on about this rumor of snow
vibrating on that island where old factories needle
into the sky. You can hear it. A machine
that doesn't know it's dead sending a sea
of pulses across shore because it's tired of waiting
for someone to talk to. Tired of being ignored.

I know you want to answer it, I say. Don't ignore
what I told you about circuit boards and snow.
My jittery friends, I know waiting
is a hand closing slowly around needle
points, but we need the patience of a frozen sea.
Sometimes that quiets my machines,

the hum gets easier to ignore. But pine needles
still fall gold. Dead trees creak. A rain-gutter sea waits,
machine-gray, and my throat begs to drink the snow.

Nominated by Maxine Scates, David Baker

BY THE TIME YOU READ THIS

fiction by YANNICK MURPHY

from CONJUNCTIONS

"Dear Paul, by the time you read this, I will be dead. If you don't stop seeing that other woman, I will come back to haunt you. I will be the face in the mirror when you shave. I will be the wind you hear at night. I will be the creak in the stairs and the loud shudder of the settling roof beams that wakes us up from our sleep."

"Dear Cleo, I hope you never understand why your mother did this. If you ever find yourself close to understanding I want you to call and get help right away. Please promise me that. There are plenty of numbers to call in case of emergency on the fridge. (You might even consider calling Irving Propane; their staff has always been helpful and ready to come out to the house at a moment's notice if we think we hear even the slightest hissing sound of gas leaking from our lines.)"

"Dear Paul, have you ever noticed the birthmark on my labia? If not, you should look now. I'd hate to go to my grave thinking that I was married to a man all these years who didn't even notice such an intimate detail about me."

"Dear Paul, I'm doing this because I want you to respect my last wish, and that last wish is that you stop seeing that woman because I don't want Cleo to know the woman you left me for, even if she might be some amazing person you think Cleo should get to know, a choreographer, or symphony musician, or nuclear physicist. All that she'll ever be to me is a slut."

"Dear second-grade teacher Miss Debbie, thank you for always letting me come to class early so I could help you set up the classroom. Even though you were hugely overweight, I liked the way you looked and smiled at me. I liked the candy you would give us when we behaved well, and I am sorry that I told you that I thought you were bribing us. That was just something my father said, and I was repeating it. At times he takes things very seriously, and once, while watching election results, he threw our television out the window when a certain president was elected that he didn't like."

"Dear Cleo, I want you to throw away what you don't want, and keep what you want, of all that I owned. I think my pearl ring would look good on you, so don't throw that away, and don't throw away my mother's sorority pin, as there are little diamonds embedded in it, and it might be worth something someday. Also, even though the brown Creuset baking dish in the pantry looks old, it's French and very good for roasting new potatoes, and wipes clean easily, so I would say don't throw that away either. Don't throw away the handheld eggbeater, those are quite rare, ever since whisks became the rage, and you can't even buy one on eBay these days. Remember not to put the colored Pyrex bowls with the white interiors into the dishwasher, as their colors on the outside will fade. Definitely throw away all the boxes and boxes of colored slides your father's parents took on their trip to Alaska. They are just pictures of icebergs and flowers without any people in them."

"Dear Mom, I hope I did this right. My biggest fear is that I wake up in a hospital room and you are staring at me with fear in your eyes. The same fear you had when we were in that car accident and I hit my head on the windshield and there was so much blood you had to take off your shirt to stop the blood from flowing, and I was so embarrassed when the police came because you were wearing a white bra that looked dirty, like you had just come out from under the wheels of our car."

"Dear Dad, I hope I do this right, and really cleanly, because I want you to shake your head and say what you always used to say, which was, 'That girl can do anything once she puts her mind to it.' I want you to tell Mom that crying won't make me come back. I'm never coming back (well, if I do come back, it will just be to haunt Paul if he's still with that slut, so don't worry, I won't be coming back to where you and Mom are). Tell Mom something like the load of life was too hard for me to take, and now it's her job to hold it for me, just like when I was a girl and we would walk along the road back from school, and my backpack was too heavy and I would ask her to carry it. Make it sound like she still has a purpose in life."

"Dear Paul, tell me that you'll be so bent out of shape after my death that you'll fall into my grave after I'm lowered into it. Tell me you'll take out all of my pictures and put them on display on the dresser. Tell me you'll sleep with a pile of my clothes you pushed together to make look like a body and that's the only way you can fall asleep at night. Tell me you'll take Cleo to every place we've ever been together so you can say, And this is where we held hands, and this is where we kissed, and this is where I told her I loved her. Tell me you will remember that love more strongly than when I was alive so that it almost hurts, but not too much, of course, I still want you strong enough to take care of Cleo. Tell me you'll remember she has an appointment with the orthodontist in two weeks, it should take over an hour, so tell her to bring a good book to the office, and not one of those trashy YA books with the air-brushed covers. Tell me you'll bring her something good to read. She's almost ready for *The Lord of the Rings*; maybe they have redone the cover, and there's a trashy-looking YA cover with a swarthy, shirtless Frodo on it and you will have better luck getting her to read it than that old edition we have with its spine breaking off and thread hanging from where it was bound."

"Dear UPS man, thank you for all the years when you saw my car parked in town and decided to open the hatch of my unlocked car and put my package into it so that you could save time and gas by not having to drive all the way up the hill to my house. Thank you for always waving at me on any country road I ever saw you on, which was sometimes towns away from our town. (You certainly put in a lot of miles.) Thank you for always handing my dog a biscuit when she climbed into your truck, and thank you for not yelling at our chickens that also climbed into your truck and pecked the corrugated metal steps, and instead you just said, 'Shoo, shoo' in almost a whisper. I think we will see each other again someday. I really do. Don't forget to wave like usual. Maybe then I will find out your name."

"Dear Cleo, when you get your period, start off with tampons right away. Those pads can be uncomfortable, and with all of your swimming you'll want the tampons anyway. But of course, you probably know this, and you are probably saying, 'Geez, Mom' right now. Don't let your father get his panties in a wad about you dating boys. You've got good sense, and tell him you'll use it. He might bring out a baseball bat and sit on the front porch the first time a boy comes calling on you, but kiss him on the cheek before you leave on the date and tell him you studied a self-defense book at the library and you know how to rip the guy a new asshole if he tries anything on you."

"Dear sixth-grade English teacher Mr. Sun. Despite all of your grand teachings (I will never forget the meaning of 'hyperbole,' one of your vocabulary words, for example), I have not retained the knowledge of when to use 'lay' or 'lie.' They say 'lay' takes an object, but I still don't understand that. And the title of that book *As I Lay Dying* has screwed me up for years. Then there was that billboard when I was a kid, 'Winston tastes good like a cigarette should.' What was the matter with that grammar? I'd like to know. Anyway, I do thank you for a great sixth-grade class. I loved that short story called 'The Ledge' about the man and his son and his nephew who lose their skiff on a hunting trip to a small island and when the tide comes in, the father has to hold the boys aloft for as long as he can before they all drown from the freezing water that encroaches upon them from all sides. You might have known then that I would grow up to be the type of woman who would do this act now, which is what I will have done by the time you read this, since I loved those morose stories so much. (Was that just a run-on? I apologize if so.) You might have said then that I was a dead ringer for this kind of act I'm about to commit now."

"Dear Paul, I'm sorry I did this, in a way, I mean maybe all men are going to cheat on their wives eventually. You're certainly not the first. Maybe I'm just sorry I'm the type of woman who got upset enough about it to take her own life. I'm sorry you didn't marry the type of woman who just said, 'Fine, you want to fuck someone else, then I'll fuck someone else too.' I guess I should have gone out and found myself some other man, and then let it subside, and let us be together again. I couldn't do that, though; I couldn't stand to think about you with someone else. I think I did what was best. Don't you? Stupid how after all these years, I still want your approval. I should have been the type of woman who could just leave you, and wish you well, and feel sorry for you, and maybe, from time to time even stomach you and meet you for lunch and notice you were still wearing your hair in a ponytail after all these years, and recognize the sweater you were wearing as one I once gave you but that you've now forgotten where it came from. Listen, I'm going to throw that sweater out right now before I finish this note because, damn it, I don't want you wearing it in the presence of that slut. I've been thinking about that other lover I should have taken, instead of taking my own life. I mean, I don't know who I would have taken anyhow. There are all those fathers of the girls on Cleo's swim team. They're all smart and in shape, or at least they care about being in shape. I think I like one of the head lifeguards at the pool. He is younger than the rest of the fathers of the swim-team girls, but I have noticed him noticing me. I think you know him. He's the one with the big sparkling-blue eyes. He's tall. He's got a chest broader than yours, and he's got more muscle than you do. (Oh, did I just write 'got'? Yikes, I meant to say, 'He has more muscle than you do.')"

"Dear whatever your name is, of course, in my eyes, you are Dear Slut, but I should really take the 'dear' out anyway because 'dear' and 'slut' are probably too incongruous to appear one right after the other and there is probably some rule my sixth-grade English teacher, Mr. Sun, could tell me about placing two incongruous words right next to each other. So, Slut, I am writing this to let you know that even though I have never met you, I feel I should let you know that it's probably your fault I have taken all these pills because I know Paul and, really, I don't think he would have let himself go this far with you if you hadn't probably pushed yourself on him in some way. I wondered for a while what you looked like, but now I really don't want to know. I'm sure you're beautiful and thin, and have something unusual about you that Paul found irresistible. Maybe you have a lisp. Maybe you even have a limp, or one hand that is missing a finger. Has Paul taken you to the restaurant that's a house with the famous shepherd's pie and the jazz band whose drummer in the warmer months has to fit himself inside the massive fireplace because there is no other room for him, what with all the tables they try and fit in to accommodate the crowd?

"Has he held you the way he held me from behind at night where he is able to whisper in your ear? Has he told you about that dog he had when he was younger that followed him everywhere and then got killed by a tree his father felled and how his father chainsawed the tree into pieces to move the log off the dog, but it was too late, the dog was not going to make it, and a gun had to be used? Does he hold your hand when you walk to hurry you along the way he does me? Has he told you his favorite time of year is winter? Has he made you take long walks in the snow and pointed out the tracks of snowshoe rabbits and families of deer? Has he told you about Cleo? How beautiful she is and how when she was first born he suddenly became more frightened than he had ever been in his life because he realized he now had something he could lose and afterward he would never be the same? Has he told you how she inhales books and is really witty in a dry way you would not expect a girl her age to be? Has he told you she looks like me? She does. Our baby pictures are almost identical. Do you know Paul eats his chicken with two forks? I could never understand that, but the next time you see him eat chicken, notice how he will ask for an extra fork and not a knife. That is, if you really decide you are going to keep seeing him after I have killed myself and after he has grieved and realized I was his only true love. Are you really still going to want to be with him after all of that? I would think not. He might be somewhat of a basket case for a while. We've traveled all over the world together, and I know things about him that he hasn't told anyone else. He knows almost everything about me, except there are things, private things I am not going to discuss with you, that I think he has overlooked, but in the scheme of things, they are not so important after all. They are just minor blemishes, in a manner of speaking.

"Once we traveled to Spain and I fell off a moped that I was trying to start and I gave it too much gas and the moped reared and I fell on the ground, which was littered with big rocks, and I cut my knee terribly. He said he thought I was trying to show off when I did it. We didn't have disinfectant but we did have Grappa di Julia, a liquor that bubbled when it came into contact with my deep cut. He might tell you, after he finds me, how I was unstable anyway, and that it was not finding out that the two of you were seeing each other that made me kill myself. He might tell you how I hitchhiked while I was six months pregnant on the French island of Réunion and that I could have been kidnapped, but he would not be telling you the whole story because he does not know the whole story. The whole story is that I did not hitchhike anywhere, I just told him I did to make him feel bad that he had left me for the day to go to the caldera of a volcano. (I wasn't supposed to travel to high altitudes, being pregnant, so he went without me. I was jealous that he got to go see the active volcano and I didn't.) I came back to the house we were staying in with two very long baguettes I bought on my long journey home that did not involve my thumbs for hitching a ride, but only involved my legs with the swollen ankles from carrying a child curled like a pill bug inside of myself. So you see we cannot believe everything people tell us because sometimes they do not know for sure themselves."

"Dear Mom, you will probably react in the worst way to my death, and you are the one person I least feel like writing to. I bet you might have some advice for me now if you saw how I was thinking about killing myself. In this circumstance, you might have quoted some religious line you heard in *The Sound of Music*. If you were here with me you would say, 'Whenever God shuts a door, he opens a window.' And I would look around the room and say, 'The windows are already open, they've been open a while, and there are no more to open.' "

"Dear UPS man, Cleo is ordering a goose egg that she bought. She has an incubator for it. Please put the package inside the door. I would hate for the egg to become overheated and for the poor little chick to die before it has even had a chance to break free. I hope she has enough time to let the goose, when it hatches, imprint on her. She has little time these days since she is on the swim team, such a far drive away, and they practice so often and they go to so many meets. She is getting quite good, and just bought one of those Fastskin suits that are so tight I almost need a crowbar to get it on her. I wonder who will help her into the suit when I'm gone."

"Slut, if you are still with Paul after I've hung myself, do me this one favor, and make sure he compliments Cleo a lot. I believe there is nothing more valuable to a girl than a father who is able to tell his daughter how smart and beautiful she is. I think sometimes he doesn't want to tell her how beautiful she is because he doesn't want her to become full of herself and conceited. But I don't think there is a chance of that. If you haven't met her already somehow, you will realize when you do meet her (and of course I'm hoping you don't meet her and that Paul, in his grief over losing me, breaks up with you) that she is unassuming and forthright, and also very beautiful. She is one of those girls whose eyebrows you wish you had because they taper so nicely. She is tall and slender and can make you laugh easily. I guess I would be wrong to say I will miss her since I will no longer 'be' but I miss her right now, and she is just in the next room reading, only a plasterboard's thickness away. It is inconceivable to think that I won't miss her when I am dead, that's how much I love her. Do you have children? Probably not, since I have decided you are most likely young. I was kind of hoping that you did have children, or at least one child, and when trying to convince Paul to stay with you after I killed myself, you would have the monumental task of trying to sell not only yourself to Paul, but your child. Maybe he is a son, and has been having a hard time of it in school. Maybe he is a 'different kind of learner' and needs aides to go with him from class to class and take notes for him and give him the first lines of essays to get him started. Maybe someone holds the pencil for him and does the computation for math homework while he watches, wondering about what will be on the lunch menu that day. Maybe you don't tell Paul any of this, and what you tell Paul is that your son has the uncanny ability to tell who it is when you hear the phone ring. You make it seem like your son has some kind of powers the average child does not have. He can tell the minute he sees the color of a license plate what state it's from. I suppose you are questioning why, if I love Cleo so much, am I willing to leave her. I think maybe I have raised her too well. Let me explain. She can bake. Cream puffs and biscotti are in her repertoire at the tender age of twelve. She can sew, not just mend. A quilt she made that she tells me is the flying-geese pattern lays/lies on her bed. She quotes Shakespeare verbatim after just reading lines of him in one sitting. She can scoop up her pet goose in her arms and walk with it in the field and stroke its head and imitate the goose when it hisses. She is armed for the world, you see, and hardly needs me anymore, except of course for getting that racing suit on."

"Dear Paul, by the time you read this letter, I will have asphyxiated myself in the garage, but I did want you to know that I was thinking beforehand of the time we traveled to Madrid and you tried your hand at the Spanish tongue and kept asking the bank teller, 'Do I have a pen?' instead of correctly asking, 'Do you have a pen?' and I remember how I could not stop laughing, and when you realized your mistake, how you started laughing also, and the people on the line behind us were getting angry and started saying things we could not understand and throwing their hands up in the air, which we thought was very Spanish and made us laugh harder. I remember the time in Scotland when we were worried about waking up in time to catch our train back to London and the proprietor of the bed-and-breakfast said not to worry, he would come knock us up in the morning. Do you remember how hard we wanted to laugh then? We had to run up to our room while we covered our mouths to make sure we didn't laugh in front of him, and then after we made it to the room and slammed the door behind ourselves we fell onto the bed laughing, with tears streaming down our faces, and behind us a window with a breathtaking view of the Edinburgh Castle and black clouds sailing in the Scottish sky. Paul, I killed myself because I couldn't imagine those memories living alongside the more recent memories of you cheating on me."

"Dear coach of the swim team, I shot myself because my husband and I were having some marital infidelity problems, nothing more than that. I don't believe I'm insane, or that some kind of insanity or psychological neurosis runs in the family. I'm telling you this because I want you to treat Cleo as fairly as possible. Understand that she's no different from all of those other kids. She's not suddenly going to get so upset at not winning an event that she's been training for months for that you feel you have to put her on a suicide watch. (By the way, she has been telling me lately that she would like to improve her butterfly. I think she thinks she comes out of the water too high when she takes her breath, so maybe if you have time sometime you could work with her on her body profile.)"

"Slut, I slit my wrists because, well you know why. I don't want you to be a mother to Cleo, but maybe, once in a while, you could tell Cleo things a mother might tell her daughter. Things like, after changing into your swimsuit, don't forget to reach inside and to, one at a time, lift each breast up higher so it looks fuller and doesn't look like your breasts are silver-dollar pancakes."

"Dear UPS man, I ran in front of your truck because I got tired of waiting for a package that was never delivered. What I mean to say is that I was hoping my husband would fall back in love with me after having a torrid romance with a younger woman, and he never did. Did you ever have that package in the back of the truck and maybe it was undelivered? Maybe it is sitting in some holding facility in Maine where outside blueberries grow this time of year and seagulls alight on the rooftops. (Maybe you have seen Paul with his slut on your rounds, and you are shaking your head reading this, saying you could have told me all along that he would never leave the little hottie and that I was history long before the Christmas rush began last year.)"

"Dear Paul, I walked off into the woods alone one winter's night because you were the one who always told me that dying from the cold was probably the nicest way to go, that even right before I died I would not feel cold at all any longer and I would see everything around me more clearly than I ever had before. It was very Native American of me to do it this way. By the time you read this letter, you will have to imagine me leaning up against some maple tree having died feeling very alive, every leaf blowing past me sounding like a roar."

"Dear Mom, by the time you read this I will have jumped off the bridge over the falls. Please keep an eye on Paul in the future. After all, the women he dates will leave an impression on Cleo. Feel free to let Cleo know your opinion of these women. I won't be there to teach her the meaning of 'slut,' 'whore,' 'wanton,' 'cradle robber,' etc."

"Dear Mr. Sun, do you happen to know of any other expressions or words for women who would try to land a man at any cost? I would look those words up in a thesaurus or dictionary myself, the way you taught us to in sixth grade, but I am a little caught up right now, and it is more time-consuming than I thought. When you get them, would you please write them on a list and send them to my daughter Cleo at the following address:"

"Dear Cleo, I did this because I love you."
"Dear Paul, I did this because I hate you."

"Dear Mom and Dad, I wish there was a way you would never have to learn I did this."
"Slut, it's none of your business why I did this."
"Dear Mr. Sun, I did this to myself. I have done this to myself. I will have done this to myself. I shan't have done this to myself. I had to do this to myself. I have had to do this to myself. I will have had to have done this to myself. I myself have done this. I done did this."
"Dear Paul, just one last thing, I'm putting a roast in the oven, so by the time you read this letter, it will probably be done. I wanted to leave Cleo one last good meal. Don't make her eat that cube steak again, even if it is on sale; it was way too tough and bits of it got caught in her braces and every time she flosses she pops a spring and has to make a new appointment."
"Dear Death, here I come. Be forgiving, be swift, be the answer."
"Dear Death, you will have to take a rain check. I don't really want an answer. I can't really remember the big question anyway. All of my questions are small. Where is the hydrogen peroxide? I need to use some on Cleo because she has come down with swimmer's ear. Who has fiddled with the water heater, and why am I stuck in a lukewarm shower? If lightning, when it hits the air, is hotter than the sun, then why doesn't everything around the lightning bolt melt? Why aren't the nearby trees reduced to just puddles of sap? Can I pass a school bus on the road if it's stopped to drop off kids but the stop sign hasn't been extended by the driver? Besides, there are too many things going on here for me to want to kill myself right now. There is a goose egg coming that we will have to turn around in the incubator every morning and night. There is a storm coming, and I love how the lightning lights up the sky and the gray barn looks almost white. Also, there is a new barred owl in the tree by our window and I'd like to hear his call again tonight, as it is peaceful right to the bone. Also, the dog needs her second dosage of heartworm medication, and I better be around to give that to her. And one more thing, I am too tired right now to tie a noose/slit my wrists/pop pills/run the engine in the closed garage/jump off a bridge/pull a trigger/freeze to death/get run over. I think I just might lie/lay

down for a while and close my eyes and when I wake up I can decide what's the best thing to do, but right now, I am so tired and the bed looks so comforting and the sheets, just off the line, smell like flowers and sunshine."

Nominated by Conjunctions

PIGMEAT

by AMAUD JAMAUL JOHNSON

from DARKTOWN FOLLIES (TUPELO PRESS)

Come to this common fallow of bone,
This body, hulking—this billowing robe.

Midday & the moonlight across my face.
Come: these hands, this beat, the broad

Hiccup, a smile. Here, when all the heat
Has been washed & wrung clean from the body

When the men begin to open their leather cases
& hold their monocles a little closer to my heart

& the parable of the homegrown &
The parable of the artificial Negro

Will be told. Here, with the sweet broadax
Of history, the thunderous applause.

Here comes the first crystal stair.
Here, come Hell or high-water; Hell

Or some falter. All the ease in legalese.
Here comes my tautology—

A blackness of a blackness of a blackness.
My monochromatic rainbow,

Articulate as a single finger haloing the moon.
A generation, spun-out or spooling & I'm dancing.

Here. Step. Stutter-step, hush. I come.
Here comes the judge. Here comes the judge.

Nominated by Tupelo Press

JOHN CLARE

by MICHAEL DICKMAN

from BRICK

Now I remember
I wanted to talk to you
between your *Selected Poems*
and the punk rock music
playing on the radio

Between the blue irises and the Mexican lawn service

The skaters and the dragonflies

Do you know what it's like here

Scared beneath trees
the light on the one rose
is the one light

The sun keeps going

Tell me something between the yellowhammers and the leaf
    blowers

Between a worm getting pulled out of the dirt into the sky and
    a worm eating the dark

*

Children play in the past
in pastures and now I remember
7-Eleven parking lots
skateboarding through
black fields

Cows move through the fields to the fence and don't move again

Cows move
through the parking lot
toward a bike rack
in the heather

Black tongues
park out front and idle their engines

Daisies chain and unchain

In the morning someone hoses down the hot concrete and insects
     crawl through your name

*

The dogs are shy and snap
chew through chain-link
each other and now I remember fur
and won't let go or be beaten
to death by kids

Let the fur fly!

The boys ollie over the dogs
in their dreams

In dreams
some of the boys
kiss them on the mouth

Their mouths are clean and their noses are pink

All the dogs I grew up with are gone

They were someone's sweethearts shitting on the sidewalk
      in the sun

*

Flowers call you on the telephone
and the rain passes you notes
none of us will ever read
now I remember every line
a pine needle
falling at your feet

Can you name the flowers in your own backyard

Peonies drip onto the ground
making long-distance calls
person to person

The car alarms sound like roses

There are roses peonies and giant white papery things the size of
      your face and ferns

Ferns ferns ferns

The loves of my life

*

Birds are never lonely next to you
in neighbourhoods and wings clear the air
and are gone
into holes of sunlight
and leaves

Now I remember

There are holes all around

Holes in children
Holes in trees

Holes in the water and in the teeth of small animals if you can see
     that and can you see that

And wasps
eating entire families of deer

Here

I wanted to show you

Nominated by Brick, Mark Irwin, Joyce Carol Oates

FABLES

fiction by BENNETT SIMS

from CONJUNCTIONS

1.

The boy begs his mother to buy him a balloon. As they leave the grocery store and cross the parking lot, he holds the balloon by a string in his hand. It is round and red, and it bobs a few feet above him. Suddenly his mother looks down and orders him not to release the balloon. Her voice is stern. She says that if he loses it, she will not buy him another. The boy tightens his grip on the string. He had no intention of releasing the balloon. But the mother's prohibition disquiets him, for it seems to be addressed at a specific desire. Her voice implies that she has seen inside him: that deep down—in a place hidden from himself, yet visible to her—he really does want to release the balloon. Otherwise, why bother to forbid it? The boy feels stung by her censure. He grows sullen at the injustice. It isn't fair. He didn't do anything. They approach the car in the parking lot. The day is bright and all the car roofs glint. His fingers fidget, his palm throbs. Before, the balloon had been just a thing that he wanted to hold. Now, he cannot stop thinking about letting it go. He wants to release the string, to spite her. But he knows that this would only prove her right. By forbidding a thought he hadn't had, she has put that thought into his head; now, if he acts on the thought, it will be as good as admitting that he already had it. He glowers up at the balloon. Why had he begged her to buy it in the first place? What had he ever planned on doing with it, if not releasing it? Maybe she was right. For there is now nothing in the world that he more desires—has always desired—than to be rid of this balloon. The boy knows that it is the prohibition that has put this idea into his head, and yet, he can't remember a time before he had it. It is as if the prohibition has implanted not just the desire, but an entire prehistory of the desire. The second the thought crossed his mind, it had always already been in his mind. The moment his mother spoke to him, he became the boy she was speaking to: the kind of boy who releases balloons, who needs to be told not to. Yes, he imagines that he can remember now: how even in the grocery store—before he had so much as laid eyes on the balloon—even then he was secretly planning to release it. The boy releases the balloon. He watches it rise swiftly and diminish, snaking upward, its redness growing smaller and smaller against the blue sky. His chest hollows out with guilt. He should never have released the balloon. Hearing him whimper, his mother turns to see what has happened. She tells him sharply that she told him not to release the balloon. He begs her to go back into the grocery store and buy him another, but she shakes her head. They are at the car, and she is already digging through her purse for the keys. While she unlocks the door, he takes one last look above him, raking that vast expanse for some fleck of red.

2.

One day at recess, alone behind the jungle gym, the boy spots a crow perched on a low pine branch. He is used to seeing entire flocks in this tree. At dusk dozens will gather together on its branches, visible from across the playground as a cloud of black specks. They dot the treetop then, like ticks in a green flank. Even at that distance he can hear them cawing, a dark, sharp sound that they seem to draw from deep within the tree itself, their black bodies growing engorged on it. After school each afternoon, waiting for his mother in the parking lot, the boy will watch them, listening. Today, however, there is only the one crow, and although its beak hangs open, it does not caw. It is perfectly silent. It just sits there, cocking its head and blinking its beady eye in profile. The boy keeps expecting the crow to caw, to let the tree speak through it, in a voice infinitely older than it is. But its beak gapes and no sound comes out. If the boy listens carefully, he can distinguish the rustle of a breeze, some wind in the needles. And then it is possible to imagine that this hissing is emanating from the bird's beak, in steady, crackling waves, like static from a broken radio. That is the closest it comes to cawing. Maybe, if he startled it, he could get it to caw, the boy thinks. He kneels at the base of the tree, palming a pinecone from the ground.

It is pear shaped, and imbricated with brown scales, like a grenade of shingles. Rising, he readies the cone at his shoulder, the way a shot-putter would. The crow keeps cocking its head back and forth on its branch, oblivious. Its beak never narrows. The jaw's twin points remain poised at a precise and unchanging angle, as though biting down on something that the boy can't see: an invisible twig, or tuft of grass. Materials for its nest. The boy waits for the crow to blink, then lobs the pinecone. It misses by a foot, crashing through the foliage and landing behind the tree somewhere. The crow is unfazed. It retracts its head on its neck slightly, but it doesn't caw, and it is careful neither to open nor close its beak. It really is as if there is something in its mouth, something that it is determined not to drop. But its mouth is empty, and so the boy imagines that it is this very emptiness that it is bringing back to its nest: that it is building a nest of absences, gaps. The way it jealously hoards this absence between its mandibles, like a marble. Its beak must be broken, the boy decides, broken open. Or else, no: The bird is simply stubborn. It could caw if it wanted to. It is resisting only to spite him. He gathers four more pinecones. The longer the crow doesn't caw, the louder its silence becomes. The gap in its beak magnifies the stillness around them, until the boy can no longer hear any of the other playground sounds: teachers' whistles; the far-off squawks of his classmates on the soccer field. The boy feels alone with the crow, alone inside this quiet. He hugs the four pinecones against his stomach. He is determined to make the crow caw once before recess is over. He imagines that he is the teacher, the crow his pupil, and he remembers all the ways in which his own teacher calls on him in class: how the boy is made to speak, pronounce new vocabulary terms, say *present* when his name is said. Before recess is over, the boy will make the crow say *present*. He will pelt it with pinecones until it caws, until it constitutes itself in a caw, until the moment when—dropping that absence from its beak—the crow will finally announce its presence, say present, present its presence in the present sharpness of its caw. The crow looks up at the sky for a moment. Seizing the opportunity, the boy hurls another of his pinecones, this time missing its torso by a matter of inches. The crow spreads its wings and begins to bate on the branch. For a moment, it almost seems as if it is going to fly away. The boy grips a third pinecone tightly, until its spines bite into his flesh. Soon, he knows, the recess bell will ring. He squints at the crow, focusing its black body in the center of his vision. But just as he is about to throw the pinecone, the bird tucks its neck into its chest, looking down at him. It blinks its black eyes rapidly, agitatedly. Finally it closes its beak. And when at last it caws—rupturing the quiet around them, with a loud, sharp-syllabled *awe*—it is as startling as the first sound in creation.

3.

The boy walks his bike up a hill. In the middle of his street he sees a dead chipmunk, crushed evenly by the tires of a car. It has been flattened into a purse of fur. Around it, a red aura of gore. It makes a brown streak in the center of the lane, straight as a divider line. Ahead of him on the sidewalk he sees a live one. Only a yard away, a second chipmunk stands tensed on all fours, eyeing the boy and his bike. When it wrinkles its nose in rapid sniffs, the boy can tell that it is smelling the carcass stench, wafting in faint off the tarmac behind him. It must seem, to the chipmunk, as if the boy is its brother's murderer. He does not know how to correct this misunderstanding, or reassure the rodent that he means it no harm. He stands silent, trying to stifle any movement that might terrify it. It flees in terror anyway. In an abrupt about-face it dashes up the sidewalk, hugging the hill's concrete revetment; when it reaches a ground-level drainpipe—barely bigger than its body—it squeezes inside. The boy walks his bike up to the drainpipe. He moves slowly, so as not to startle. But his wheel spokes make a sinister sound as he approaches: Each bony click seems to close in on the animal, skeleton sound of Death's scythe tapping. When the boy reaches the drainpipe he bends to peer inside. Huddled into a ball, the chipmunk is shaking violently, its walnut-colored chest convulsing. It glares out at the boy, trapped. The rear of the pipe is backed up with gunk: mud, pine needles, dead leaves. The sight of the boy there, darkening the aperture of the drainpipe, must be a source of unbearable dread for the creature. He starts to back away, but it is too late. Inexplicably, recklessly, the chipmunk rushes forward. It reaches the edge of the pipe and leaps free, landing on the sidewalk at the boy's feet. There it freezes, locking its eyes on his shoes, as if awaiting the killing blow. The boy is careful to stand behind the bike's front tire. He gives the chipmunk a barrier, a zone of safety. He reassures it, by his very posture, that he means it no harm. The chipmunk cowers, catching its breath. The wheel casts a barred shadow over its body, a cage of shade in which the chipmunk trembles, frozen amid the many spokes. Indeed, the way that the tire's shadow encloses the rodent, it looks like a phantom hamster wheel. Like the kind of toy Death would keep its pets in—all the mortals who

517

are Death's pets. Maybe that is why the chipmunk dares not move, the boy thinks: because it already understands the nature of this wheel. To flee from Death is just to jog in place. Spinning inside one's dying. The boy takes the bike by the seat and rolls it back. As the front wheel withdraws, the shadow slides off its prisoner. Now the chipmunk is free to flee. But it hunkers to the ground, eyeing the boy's feet with coiled purpose. A second passes in which it does not so much as flinch, and the boy understands exactly what is about to happen: Feeling cornered, the chipmunk will charge him. In a brown blur it will scurry up his shoe and latch onto his pants leg, the way a squirrel mounts a tree trunk. As it claws at his pants for purchase, tearing through the cotton, the boy will be able to feel its bark-sharpened nails get a scansorial grip into his shinbone. The sear of skin tearing; the beading of blood. He cannot help imagining all this. He will kick out his leg—as if it were aflame, he imagines—but the chipmunk will hold fast to him, out of rabidness perhaps. Then the boy will have no choice. Above all, he knows, he will have to keep the creature from biting him. After trying so hard not to frighten it, he will be forced to kill it. With his free foot he will have to scrape it from his pants leg, onto the sidewalk, and stomp the life out of it, flattening it as dispassionately as that car had flattened the rodent in the road. In this way, he will become everything the animal mistook him for: its murderer, its personal death. The boy stares down at the chipmunk, which has begun to vibrate like a revving engine. Because it was wrong about the boy, it will prove to be right about the boy. Because it has mistaken the boy for a murderer, it will make the boy murder it. And so perhaps, the boy reflects, the chipmunk wasn't wrong after all: Maybe it could see clearly what the boy could not. That he had a role to play in its fate. The boy stomps his foot lightly on the sidewalk. Still the chipmunk does not run. It is ready now. It must have been waiting for this moment its entire life. Seeing the boy today, it recognized him instantaneously: He was the human who had been set aside for it, the boy it had been assigned from the beginning. *He* was the place it was fated to die. Now, at long last, it has an appointment to keep.

4.

On his walk home from school the boy pauses at the edge of his neighbors' yard. It is wide and well manicured and unfenced, and today their dog is out in it. A standard chocolate poodle—as tall as the boy's chest when standing—it is couchant now, in the middle of the lawn. It has not yet noticed the boy from where it lies. It pants happily in the midday heat, its long tongue lolling from its jaw. Some curls are combed into a bouffant on its forehead, where they seem to seethe, massed and wrinkled like an exposed brown brain. The dog's owners—the boy's neighbors—are nowhere to be seen. Far out of earshot, deep within their white two-story house. If the dog were to suddenly bark loudly and attack the boy—if the boy were to shout for help—they would not be able to hear. At least twice a week the boy passes the poodle in the yard like this. The sight of it always paralyzes him with fear. He will stop walking for a moment, then sidle slowly down the sidewalk, careful not to draw the dog's attention. What is to keep it from mauling him? The owners are never outside with it. Evidently they trust the poodle. It is allowed to roam unsupervised in the yard, which is not technically— but only appears to be—unfenced. In reality, the boy's mother has explained to him, it employs a so-called invisible fence: a virtual boundary of radio waves tracing the perimeter of the lawn. GPS coordinates are broadcast to the dog's shock collar, which is programmed to administer mild jolts of admonitory electricity whenever the poodle trespasses the property line. There is nothing—she reassured him—to be afraid of. After a few hours of behavioral training, the dog would have learned to obey the dictates of its collar. It would have internalized the limits of its prison. And so even if it noticed the boy one day—even if it bounded barking toward him—it would know to stop short at the pavement. As his mother was explaining this, the boy nodded to show he understood. But deep down he still does not trust the invisible fence. He wonders, for instance, how it is supposed to keep other animals *out* of the yard. All it would take is for a rabid bat, or raccoon, or chipmunk to crawl across the boundary line and bite and infect the dog. Then when the boy was walking home one day, he would see the poodle foaming at the mouth in the yard, with nothing but a symbolic cage of X/Y coordinates separating it from him. And what was to keep the dog—mindless with rage—from simply disregarding the fence, in that case? Assuming it could remember the fence at all. For the rabies might very well have wiped its memory clean, erasing its behavioral training. Then the dog would be incapable of recognizing symbolic cages, only real ones, and it would not think twice before bounding across the yard at the boy. He stares at the poodle. It is facing the house, panting. He does not know its name. Sometimes he imagines being attacked by the dog, and in these fantasies—which he indulges in involuntarily, standing motionless with fear on the sidewalk—he assigns it the name Gerald. He imagines the neighbors running across the lawn, calling, *Gerald, Gerald, get off him,* even as the poodle pins him to the pavement and snaps its jaws. This is always the most horrifying moment, for the boy, in the fantasy. How the dog can ignore its own name. How it can conduct this beast's balancing act, suspended between two minds: the mind that answers to Gerald and the mind that murders meat. For once it starts tearing into the boy's throat, it is not Gerald any longer: It has already regressed, passed backward through some baptism. Not only nameless now, but unnameable. That is what terrifies the boy. The name cannot enclose the dog forever. It is just a kind of kennel you can keep it in. The boy pictures all the flimsy walls of this poodle's name: the collar's silver tag, engraved *Gerald*; the blue plastic food bowl, marked *Gerald*; the sound of its owners' voices, shouting *Gerald*. Each of them is just another invisible fence, which the dog can choose to trespass at will. The poodle turns to him now, cocking its head sideways. At any moment, the boy knows, the animal could transform from a friendly house pet into a ferocious guardian: a Cerberus at the gates of the hell that it will make this boy's life, if he makes even one move toward its masters. From his place on the sidewalk, the boy reaches out his arm. He extends it over the lawn, as over a candle's flame. Unfolding his hand, he holds it palm down inside the dog's territory. The poodle rises, stretching its hind legs and shaking the tiredness from its coat. It begins to cross the yard. Every few steps it stops, eyeing the boy. *It* is afraid of *him,* he realizes. The dog must recognize the threat that the boy poses. That he could snap. Attack it. That he is wild, unpredictable, unconstrained. From the poodle's point of view, the only thing holding the boy back is a kind of invisible fence, or else system of invisible fences. The name his mother gave him. The school uniform he wears. The fact that he walks with his back straight, and hair combed, and that he knows better than to murder his neighbors' pets. This is all that protects the poodle from him now, the poodle must be thinking. He imagines himself enraged like the dog, rabid like the dog; he imagines himself punching the animal, in blind mindlessness. Yes, it is possible. He can see himself that way, one day: suspended over a void where no name reaches. The dog approaches the edge of the grass. It stops a foot back, looking up at the boy's hand. Suspicious, it sniffs. It curls back its lip slightly, revealing a white incisor. The boy's hand is cold with sweat. It is exactly as he always imagined. He wants to call the dog's name, in soothing tones—*There, Gerald. There, Gerald.*—but he remembers that *Gerald* is not its real name. And so, not knowing what to call it, the boy says nothing. He stands there on the pavement. The dog stands on the grass.

5.

Behind his house one afternoon the boy finds a chunk of ice. It is lying on the sidewalk, fist sized and flecked with dirt. Someone must have dropped it there from a five-pound bag or a cooler. Now it lies exposed to the summer. It is the clear kind, blue-gray all the way through, except at its core, where a brilliant whiteness has condensed: sunlight, locked inside. Tiny hairlines of trapped light radiate outward, veining the ice's interior from corner to corner, touching the edges and returning to center. The radiance seems to ricochet around in there, bouncing off the walls of its container. Even as the boy is considering this, the ice jerks toward him. The chunk shifts a centimeter across the pavement, then stops abruptly, as if thinking better of it. The boy can hardly stifle his surprise. He knows that there is some kind of glacial principle at work: that as the chunk melts, it lubricates its own passage, and is displaced across the pavement in a basal slide. But still, the way it had moved. Exactly like a living thing. Bending down, he can see the darkened trail behind the ice, where it has wet the pebbled concrete. While the boy is studying this, the chunk scrapes forward again, another centimeter. The light at its center glints, melting it from within. Where is it headed? The boy's shadow stops an inch or two away, and it almost seems as if the ice is trying to crawl inside. As if, stuck beneath the sun, it is seeking shelter in his shade. Dragging itself into his shadow. And it's strange too, the boy thinks, how what melts it helps it move. That is the paradox the ice has been presented with: this light at its core, the light that is killing it, is what enables it to escape. It has to glide along a film of its own dying. The faster that it moves, the more of itself that it melts, and so it is alive with its own limit, animated by this horizon inscribed in its being. There is a lesson to be learned in this, the boy thinks. He watches the chunk, waiting for it to judder forward again. The ball of light sits calmly at its center, like a pilot in the cockpit. It will steer the chunk forward by destroying it. Death is what's driving the ice. It collaborates with the ice's other side, the side that wants to survive, and together these twin engines propel the chunk to safety. As the boy watches, a line of water melts off one edge, trickling down the sidewalk in an exploratory rivulet. Paving the way for the glacier. The boy was right: It is headed directly for him. He watches the tendril inch into the shadow of his head, worming blindly forward. It punches deeper and deeper into the darkness. This is the track that the death-driven ice will travel, the boy understands. Gradually the glacier will slide into his head. One-way into the shade. One-way into the shadow that his skull casts. There has to be some kind of lesson in this.

Nominated by Conjunctions

MIMESIS

by FADY JOUDAH

from ALIGHT (COPPER CANYON PRESS)

My daughter
               wouldn't hurt a spider
That had nested
Between her bicycle handles
For two weeks
She waited
Until it left of its own accord

If you tear down the web I said
It will simply know
This isn't a place to call home
And you'd get to go biking

She said that's how others
Become refugees isn't it?

Nominated by Copper Canyon Press, Anis Shivani

WAKING LUNA

fiction by AISHA GAWAD

from THE KENYON REVIEW

My cousin Luna sleeps on a Super 8 motel bed in Jersey City, in a room that overlooks the Holland Tunnel toll plaza, next to a Home Depot that makes me sad because I can't imagine anyone in this place having a home for which they might ever need a hammer or some drywall or satin-finish paint. But there it sits, massively waiting, just in case. New York City is just eight dollars and ten minutes away.

On nights when she doesn't call, I picture Luna sleeping on beds like this—beds with sticky sheets, beds with scratchy polyester quilts and pillows that are yellow at the corners, beds that squeak and sing her to sleep. Mattresses that press her cheeks into lopsided sleep smiles. Air conditioners that make it rain dust all over her glittery body.

I have driven here in Baba's old Tercel all the way from Bay Ridge—that sliver of South Brooklyn that smells of lamb on a spit for blocks. I am eating hot grape leaves from a Styrofoam container when she calls—*Come get me*, she says, not a command, not a plea, just a statement of fact. It is a Friday afternoon and both our mothers are at the masjid for Jumaa prayers like the good Muslim women they raised us to be. I find my father smoking rose water shisha on a sidewalk corner with all two of the other Arab atheists. I tell him I am going to the library. He hands me the car keys.

I park the car next to a used tire shop and a sign that reads "Welcome to Jersey City: America's Golden Door." In the motel lobby Luna doesn't answer her phone, so I stand at a Plexiglass window and press the bell. After a few minutes, I can see the reflection of a man standing behind me—a sweaty, small man with half a black mustache on the right side of his upper lip. And I want to say, *Do you know you only have Half a mustache?* He is breathing heavily and standing too closely. He is saying something like, *Checkout was at 12 o'fucking clock, lady. Get her outta here.*

And I know immediately that he is in that rare category of men who cannot be charmed by Luna. Not like the time Baba went to bail her out of the drunk tank and found her perched atop a desk, thumb wrestling with some fat sergeant. Not like the time our high-school crossing guard let her direct traffic—Luna waving the neon stick around like Merlin the Wizard. I know immediately that mustache man is not going to make this easy on us. I wish I could find a way to seal her inside that motel room, to envelop her in pixie dust, to buy her time.

When we were eight and first learning how to pray, we used to think the world would pause for us until we had finished. We would slip our little white prayer scarves over our heads, kneel and bend and kneel and bend, turn our heads and say *peace be upon you and the mercy of Allah* to the right and then to the left, and when we stood up, yanking the scarves off, we were always shocked to find out that we had missed the first ten minutes of *DuckTales.*

Mustache man tells me to walk up a staircase along the outdoor courtyard. He tells me to turn right, then left. He follows a few steps behind me the whole way. At room 206, he tells me to stop. He reaches across me and puts a key in the lock. I can feel his breath on my neck and his eyes on my tits and I wonder what the imam is saying in his sermon today.

The door swings open and the two of us stand there a moment like Detectives Stabler and Benson surveying the crime scene. *We're gonna need a toxicology report,* Stabler says. *And a rape kit,* Benson agrees.

Thanks, I say to Mustache Man.

I can help you get her cleaned up, he says.

That's OK.

There's no prostitutes in my motel, you know.

She's not a prostitute, I start to say, but his hand is suddenly on my shoulder as if it had disconnected from his wrist and crawled up my body. *You smell like vanilla,* he says. I step inside the room and start to shut the door. I slide the chain across the bolt before he has a chance to follow me. *I'll be back in a minute,* he says through the door.

Luna is fast asleep on the bed, lying straight like a mummy. I lie down next to her and place my hand on her stomach so that I can feel it rise and fall because this is a luxury. There used to be a time when I didn't need to feel her breathing to know that she was breathing. So I feel light-headed now, with all her extravagant breath around me. I close my eyes and imagine that we are at the Waldorf Astoria, which is where Luna tells me she is whenever she does not want me to know where she is.

Like when she left her own birthday party last year—her mother just about to stick a single candle into the pistachio-dotted rice pudding—Luna's favorite. I found her three hours later on Flatbush Avenue, shoeless and inexplicably in a neon pink tube dress that her mother, my khala Mona, would have dropped to her knees in repentant prayer at the sight of. When she saw me, she started to skip with her arms out straight like a giant pink Teletubby. *Amira*, she said, *Roo-roo. Do you know what I did with my shoes?*

Where the fuck were you? I asked.

At the Waldorf Astoria, she said, nuzzling into my shoulder, standing on top of my feet. *I met Dave Chappelle's brother. He drives a yellow convertible. He took me to the Waldorf and when the waiter asked what I wanted for dinner I said 'one platter of bonbons, please.' I had to go with him, Roo-roo.*

My cousin Luna snorts a lot of coke. She spends her days watching Dr. Phil with her mother and her nights dancing in traffic-cop bikinis or pouring shots of Patrón from glow-in-the-dark test tubes down the throats of twenty-one-year-olds with business cards that read "risk management" and "Goldman Sachs," or golf dads in argyle socks escaping the scrutiny of bored Long Island housewives. In the VIP rooms, the twenty-one-year-olds enjoy activities such as spanking, barking, and simulated rape while the golf dads like the feeling of nubile bodies curled up in their laps and the sound of the word "daddy" whispered softly into their ears. If they aren't balding, they also enjoy the feeling of young, hot fingers running through their hair.

My khala Mona thinks her daughter has the overnight shift at a luxury kennel in Staten Island, and the thought of Luna spending so much time in such close proximity to dogs, haram beasts that they are, is bad enough in her opinion, but the cover story does explain the strange stench of sweat and semen clinging to her hair and skin each morning—it explains the red scratches along her collarbone, the bruises on her inner thigh, the constant pink itch around her nostrils. The truth would crush her almost as much as if Luna eloped with an Israeli settler. If her father, my khalu Ibrahim, hadn't been deported back to Egypt on suspicions that he had used his taxicab fare earnings to fund the Brotherhood, if he weren't still locked in a Cairo cell where each day he learned a new use for a wire hanger, he would most likely lock his daughter in the basement.

Lying next to her, watching her breathe, I close my eyes and pretend I can feel four-hundred-count-thread Egyptian cotton sheets underneath us. I imagine a bottle of champagne on the dresser and two glasses that bubble and fizz. There is a pyramid of truffles—ones with caramel and raspberry cream hidden inside. There is a black-tuxedoed waiter standing outside the door carrying a silver tray. And on the silver tray is a note on pretty Waldorf Astoria stationery for me and my cousin Luna. *Leave it under the door please, oh won't you please?* I say, because it's probably just the mayor calling again to tell me he hopes we can make it for tea.

When I open my eyes, someone is banging on the door. I have been lying here for too long. Baba will be wondering what books I am checking out—Marx or maybe Luxemburg. Mama will want me for tomatoes that need chopping. Khala Mona will want her daughter for the family's nightly call to a secret cell phone in a Cairo prison that goes through maybe once a week if they're lucky.

Open up, Mustache Man calls.

We'll be out in a minute, I say.

I need to inspect the room for damage.

Everything's fine.

I want to help you. I'll carry her out. She can sleep it off in the lobby. You and I can talk. You're not a prostitute, I can tell. Prostitutes never smell that good. You want a free room for the night? I won't bite. Please, open up. Open the door. Unchain this fucking door. I'll break it down. This is my fucking hotel. Open the door.

I give Luna a little shake, but she doesn't stir. If we had the whole day, I would let her sleep. And when she woke up finally to vomit, I would braid her hair while she rested her cheek on the cold, chipped toilet seat. I would pretend we were at a spa and fill the hair-clogged

527

tub with warm water so that she could soak her blistered toes. We would tune the alarm radio to Besos 99.1 and dance in front of the air conditioner like we do when Brooklyn is too hot even for the Arabs, our shirts billowing out in front of us like sails. I would help her gather the strings of her underwear off the floor. I would wait as she coughed and collected the scraps of her voice from behind the bed.

The banging on the door has stopped. He slips a note under the crack, written on a soiled Burger King napkin. It says, *I'm calling the cops, you bitch.*

I find a white washcloth in the bathroom that looks like maybe it was clean yesterday. I run it under warm water from the sink and bring it back to sleeping, breathing Luna. I press the cloth to her cheek, which is an angry purple color with a blood-crusted scratch curved around it like a parenthesis. Her eyes open into slits like a mole burrowing up into daylight for the first time. She isn't scared because she knows that the hand with the wet cloth is mine. *Hi,* she says. I wipe the blood away from her cheek with a corner of the cloth, and I use the clean part to pat her forehead and collarbone. *Hi,* I say.

I rinse the cloth in the sink and soak it in water again, this time rubbing it with a bar of half-used soap. I wrap the cloth around first one foot, then the other, wiping the dirt off and soothing the big screaming blisters. She curls her toes toward me, and I imagine that this is like the time that we were seven and took off our shoes at the park even though Mama told us not to. And Luna got a splinter the size of Texas in her foot and had to hop all the way home on one leg and didn't cry at all. I wrap her toes in strips of toilet paper and wish I had thought to bring Band-Aids and maybe a gun.

Luna is looking at me, watching me walk back and forth between the bathroom and bed. *I've never been to the Waldorf Astoria before,* I say as I work. *While you were sleeping, I took a bath in the Jacuzzi tub and then I sat around for hours in the plush white cotton robe waiting for you to wake up and split a bonbon with me. I watched a marathon of Bridezillas on TV. Did you know they have cable here?*

I keep talking as I pull her up to a sitting position and slip her dress off her head. It has little spots of blood on it and I remember when she bought it—at the same Wet Seal where we once found a used tampon in the dressing room. But Luna is a loyal customer, a lifetime's worth of loyal-enough loyal to earn her a hundred Girl Scout badges.

I have brought a Fort Hamilton High hooded sweatshirt, terry cloth sweatpants, and a pair of flip flops because that is all she would tell me on the phone, over and over again, *My feet hurt, Roo-roo. My feet hurt so bad.* She leans on me, her naked breasts dangling over my forearms as I help her into the pants. She sits back on the bed while I wedge the flip flops between her toilet-papered toes. Last is the hoodie, which I put on her from behind so that she can lean against my knees when I lift her arms up and pull the sweatshirt over her head, pulling the hole wide so that it doesn't drag against her bruised cheek. *There is breakfast waiting for us in the lounge,* I say. *They offered us caviar and French pastries, but I said, 'What do we look like, a bunch of fucking pussies? Give us some Eggo waffles and don't make me tell you twice. Good help is so hard to find these days, I swear.*

I stuff her dress and panties and her five-inch stilettos into the plastic bag I brought the sweats in and survey the room. *Did you bring anything else?* I say, and she shrugs. So I look under the pillows and the quilt; I duck my head under the bed and check the bathroom. On the floor next to the air conditioner, I find a man's gold pinkie ring with a capital "Z" embossed on it like a wax seal. *Friend of yours?* I ask, holding the ring up to her and then wishing that I had dropped it into the toilet and flushed it without a word, so that I didn't have to hear her try to tell me who Z is and why he isn't as bad as he seems.

Ziad, she says, pressing her thumb into the gold Z because Luna never has enough markings to remind herself of where she's been. *I pretended to throw it out the window because he had a hickey on his neck, and you know hickeys aren't my style. So he got mad.*

So he got mad, I think. So a man named Ziad got mad, and now I am standing in a Super 8 motel room where another man with half a mustache is calling the cops, telling the dispatcher, *There are two prostitutes in my hotel. Two Spanish chicks, probably shooting up right fucking now.*

I remember when we were sixteen she lost her virginity to the captain of the soccer team, a Yemeni guy who dumped her the next day because she was no longer "pure." I remember when she started at the club, begging me not to tell, and how for the first couple of weeks she kept her tips in a Tinkerbell wallet under her bed—*for Baba's lawyers,* she said. And she really believed it.

I remember how last Ramadan she fasted even though she was already chasing snow by then, building herself an igloo and shutting me out. *A sacrifice is a sacrifice,* she said. Those were fifteen-hour days and she was faithful, waiting until after sunset to arrange a line, pour a nice cold glass of Hennessey and Coke, open a bag of Gummi Bears—Luna's perfect iftar meal. One week in, she fainted on the pole, her body slid-ing down to the stage like a great oiled disco ball.

I never told her—never told anyone—that I cheated that summer. That I had cheated every Ramadan for the past three years, taking big, desperate gulps of water when no one was looking. And while the clock ticked toward sunset, I watched Luna's face so I would know what thirst looked like.

I remember when we were ten in Qur'an school—Luna raised her hand and said she wanted to be reincarnated as A'isha, the prophet's wife, because she dreamed of riding her own camel into battle. I re-member how she was made to stand in the corner because Muslims don't believe in reincarnation and how she stood there, holding the reigns of her invisible two-humped steed. I remember when I still felt like there was a bungee cord running from my lungs, dragging along the streets of Brooklyn and up into her mouth, no matter where she was, every breath connected, my inhale dependent on her exhale. I don't remember when it snapped.

I know what you re thinking, she says. *But he's not that bad.*

His name is Ziad Abbasi, the club owner's son, a thirty-five-year-old Iranian with a wife, two kids, and a healthy drug trade on the side. I vaguely remember her telling me about him. Luna has lots of men on rotation, but they usually fit one of two categories: men who offer to pay her phone bill after one lap dance and men who spend months ignoring her and then buy an entire night's worth of dances just so he can feel like he saved her. Ziad is the second kind of man. For the first few months, he hardly glanced at her. She was just another girl on a pole. But then he gave her two weeks' paid vacation and two dozen red roses and suddenly she was special. On their first date, he took her on a picnic, popping wine corks under the glow of the old train station lamps in Liberty State Park. But after a couple weeks, when he's zip-ping up and bored already, he's the kind of man who sniffs the air and tells her to change her panties for fuck's sake.

What happened? I ask, even though I already don't want to know.

She shrugs. *I think he's fucking one of the other girls.*

I wonder when he punched her, before or after sex. Luna is full of forgiveness. I imagine him walking out to the parking lot, swinging the keys to the Beemer, vowing to stick with nice and easy white women from now on instead of Muslim girls gone bad, never once considering how she would get home, no money, miles away from our post 9/11 paradise, our A-rab self-exile, the land where every woman in a niqab is your auntie and every man in a black tie is an FBI agent, the land where you always know what to expect.

I imagine her slipping Ziad's ring into her box of treasures, still nestled between polyester thongs in her underwear drawer. For her seventh birthday, our grandmother sent her a small wooden keepsake box from Egypt—dark wood with tiny mother-of-pearl tiles. Luna and I would spend all day searching the park and Khala Mona's bedroom for treasure—a shell-shaped bath bead, one fake diamond stud, a Canadian penny. At the end of each day, we'd sort through our findings and decide what was worthy of the treasure box—she'd veto the miniature tea cup I found, I'd refuse even to look at the dead hornet she found. We always had to agree. It only occurred to me years later to wonder why I never made a treasure box of my own. It seems hers was enough for the both of us.

Ready? I ask her.

She nods through a yawn. When she smiles, the parenthesis on her cheek curves into a half moon. Half a Luna.

We have to run, I say.

She nods like this is normal.

We're half way down the block when I hear Mustache Man shriek, *I can see you, you whores. I can see you.*

Luna turns her head to look back. *He's like an evil Keebler Elf,* she says. She grabs my hand and we run faster. At the car, the key gets stuck in the lock. While I'm slamming my body into the door and jiggling the lock, Luna looks around her like a hunted gazelle. Inside the car, with the doors locked, the ignition purring, we laugh that crazy cackling witch sisters' laugh that makes strangers move away from us on the street.

I remember that we still have to stop at the library before going home, and I imagine Luna sitting cross-legged on the floor reading Shel Silverstein poems while I check out a stack of Baba-approved books that will one day turn me into leftist pussy. I imagine little girls with their mothers staring at her, this beautifully bruised woman with skin the color of weak tea and gray-green eyes like a Palestinian. They

531

will watch her laughing over a poem about a boy who eats the entire contents of his refrigerator, and they will vow with their tiny pink lips never to forget her. Because women, young and innocent or educated and bitchy, will always crave the kind of beauty that Luna wears like an old sweater.

The next time she calls, I will consider not answering. I will heed the warning of the club bouncers when they say, *You still cleaning up after her crazy ass?* Or my college friends when they tell me she's *irresponsible*, that she puts me in *dangerous situations*. I might even study for a test or have dinner with my parents, my phone glowing silently, insistently. I think about it every time. But who am I if I don't answer, if I don't go? I'm nobody, just a girl who used to sleep curled up with my cheek pressed against the cool skin of her back.

In the car, Luna adjusts the passenger seat so that she's practically lying down and lays a palm across her eyes to shade against the sun like she's the Queen of Sheba and not a battered stripper. We pull out of the parking lot and into standstill-Friday-rush-hour-tunnel traffic. It will cost eight dollars and ten minutes until we enter the dark cool mouth of the tunnel, and I don't know about Luna, but I will hold my breath, I will hold it until I see New York opening up before us, I will hold it until we are home.

Nominated by The Kenyon Review

RAPE JOKE

by PATRICIA LOCKWOOD

from THE AWL

The rape joke is that you were 19 years old.

The rape joke is that he was your boyfriend.

The rape joke it wore a goatee. A goatee.

Imagine the rape joke looking in the mirror, perfectly reflecting back itself, and grooming itself to look more like a rape joke. "Ahhhh," it thinks. "Yes. A *goatee*."

No offense.

The rape joke is that he was seven years older. The rape joke is that you had known him for years, since you were too young to be interesting to him. You liked that use of the word *interesting*, as if you were a piece of knowledge that someone could be desperate to acquire, to assimilate, and to spit back out in different form through his goateed mouth.

Then suddenly you were older, but not very old at all.

The rape joke is that you had been drinking wine coolers. Wine coolers! Who drinks wine coolers? People who get raped, according to the rape joke.

The rape joke is he was a bouncer, and kept people out for a living.

Not you!

The rape joke is that he carried a knife, and would show it to you, and would turn it over and over in his hands as if it were a book.

He wasn't threatening you, you understood. He just really liked his knife.

The rape joke is he once almost murdered a dude by throwing him through a plate–glass window. The next day he told you and he was trembling, which you took as evidence of his sensitivity.

How can a piece of knowledge be stupid? But of course you were so stupid.

The rape joke is that sometimes he would tell you you were going on a date and then take you over to his best friend Peewee's house and make you watch wrestling while they all got high.

The rape joke is that his best friend was named Peewee.

OK, the rape joke is that he worshiped The Rock.

Like the dude was completely in love with The Rock. He thought it was so great what he could do with his eyebrow.

The rape joke is he called wrestling "a soap opera for men." Men love drama too, he assured you.

The rape joke is that his bookshelf was just a row of paperbacks about serial killers. You mistook this for an interest in history, and laboring under this misapprehension you once gave him a copy of Günter Grass's *My Century*, which he never even tried to read.

It gets funnier.

The rape joke is that he kept a diary. I wonder if he wrote about the rape in it.

The rape joke is that you read it once, and he talked about another girl. He called her Miss Geography, and said "he didn't have those urges when he looked at her anymore," not since he met you. Close call, Miss Geography!

The rape joke is that he was your father's high-school student— your father taught World Religion. You helped him clean out his classroom at the end of the year, and he let you take home the most beat-up textbooks.

The rape joke is that he knew you when you were 12 years old. He once helped your family move two states over, and you drove from Cincinnati to St. Louis with him, all by yourselves, and he was kind to you, and you talked the whole way. He had chaw in his mouth the entire time, and you told him he was disgusting and he laughed, and spat the juice through his goatee into a Mountain Dew bottle.

The rape joke is that *come on*, you should have seen it coming. This rape joke is practically writing itself.

The rape joke is that you were facedown. The rape joke is you were wearing a pretty green necklace that your sister had made for you. Later you cut that necklace up. The mattress felt a specific way, and your mouth felt a specific way open against it, as if you were speaking, but you know you were not. As if your mouth were open ten years into the future, reciting a poem called Rape Joke.

The rape joke is that time is different, becomes more horrible and more habitable, and accommodates your need to go deeper into it.

Just like the body, which more than a concrete form is a capacity.

You know the body of time is *elastic*, can take almost anything you give it, and heals quickly.

The rape joke is that of course there was blood, which in human beings is so close to the surface.

The rape joke is you went home like nothing happened, and

laughed about it the next day and the day after that, and when you told people you laughed, and that was the rape joke.

It was a year before you told your parents, because he was like a son to them. The rape joke is that when you told your father, he made the sign of the cross over you and said, "I absolve you of your sins, in the name of the Father, and of the Son, and of the Holy Spirit," which even in its total wrongheadedness, was so completely sweet.

The rape joke is that you were crazy for the next five years, and had to move cities, and had to move states, and whole days went down into the sinkhole of thinking about why it happened. Like you went to look at your backyard and suddenly it wasn't there, and you were looking down into the center of the earth, which played the same red event perpetually.

The rape joke is that after a while you weren't crazy anymore, but close call, Miss Geography.

The rape joke is that for the next five years all you did was write, and never about yourself, about anything else, about apples on the tree, about islands, dead poets and the worms that aerated them, and there was no warm body in what you wrote, it was elsewhere.

The rape joke is that this is finally artless. The rape joke is that you do not write artlessly.

The rape joke is if you write a poem called Rape Joke, you're asking for it to become the only thing people remember about you.

The rape joke is that you asked why he did it. The rape joke is he said he didn't know, like what else would a rape joke say? The rape joke said YOU were the one who was drunk, and the rape joke said you remembered it wrong, which made you laugh out loud for one long split-open second. The wine coolers weren't Bartles & Jaymes, but it would be funnier for the rape joke if they were. It was some pussy flavor, like Passionate Mango or Destroyed Strawberry, which you drank down without question and trustingly in the heart of Cincinnati Ohio.

Can rape jokes be funny at all, is the question.

Can any part of the rape joke be funny. The part where it ends—
haha, just kidding! Though you did dream of killing the rape joke
for years, spilling all of its blood out, and telling it that way.

The rape joke cries out for the right to be told.

The rape joke is that this is just how it happened.

The rape joke is that the next day he gave you *Pet Sounds*. No
really. *Pet Sounds*. He said he was sorry and then he gave you *Pet
Sounds*. Come on, that's a little bit funny.

Admit it.

Nominated by John Bradley, Diane Seuss

GHAZAL

by MARILYN HACKER

from LITTLE STAR

Across the river, in the orchard on the hill, a woman
said, sometimes a handful of red earth can fulfill a woman.

She remains a speaker, although silent;
remains, although invisible, a woman.

I loved a man, I loved a city, I loved a language.
I loved, make of it what you will, a woman.

No one spoke up against the law forbidding speech,
until a schoolboy, until a monk, until a woman . . .

Who might have thought they'd hesitate to kill a child,
who might have thought they'd hesitate to kill a woman?

Rita shoulders her rifle in front of the looking-glass.
There's more than one way a uniform can thrill a woman.

The hakawâti with grey hair and no breasts
writing words and crossing them out is still a woman.

Nominated by Little Star, Grace Schulman

UNMOVING LIKE A MIGHTY RIVER STILLED

fiction by ALAN ROSSI

from THE MISSOURI REVIEW

Blake's SUV wound along the highway, and in the distance the Sierra rose gray and snow-specked against the horizon. Blake was driving, rarely watching the road, and talking about the new helmet camera he had bought. Kieran sat in the backseat and watched the back of Blake's long, ponytailed red hair, wondering if Blake noticed how often he was correcting for left of center, while Blake continued talking about the helmet cam, his head bobbing while he spoke. Kieran occasionally glanced at the back of Ian's head, shotgun, a clean-shaved-bald head, to see how he was responding to Blake, if he was as annoyed as Kieran. He didn't think Ian was. Blake was going to use the helmet cam on the climb up the Dome, he was saying, correcting left of center, and then hop into a canyon right behind Kieran with the helmet cam on to record the entire thing, POV. Ian could take the pics, but Blake wanted to hear the fear, was how he put it.

All you're going to hear is a lot of wind, Ian said. But you go ahead, little buddy. Watch the road.

The little Sierras were fuzz covered in a morning mist, the clouds a whitish growth against the rock. Higher up were darker cumulus, snow.

It's supposed to clear up, Ian said. He was checking his phone. You guys should be able to do the jump.

We're doing the jump no matter what, Blake said. The helmet cam'll get through this shit.

The highway was riding clean of other cars, and Kieran did not want to be with either of these people. He did not want to hear Blake talking about his helmet cam another minute, and he did not want to hear

Blake explain what was going to be captured on the helmet cam, but Blake kept discussing the helmet cam. Helmet cam, he said. Helmet cam, helmet cam, helmet cam. The red-haired ponytail flapped with his bobbing head. They had found more and more elaborate ways to record and be recognized for their climbs and jumps: first two high-powered, high-pixel cameras, one with a long exposure to capture the entire route up a wall, like a slug's trail against rock, the other for more precise action shots. Next came a digital handheld video camera, so that whenever one of them wasn't climbing, one of them was filming. And now the helmet cam, so that no one had to film, exactly, and yet the entire trip would be recorded and later be recognized. And Kieran was sick, sick with them, with himself, with whatever it was they were doing or no longer doing.

Ian said, That sandbagging bastard better wake up.

He was talking about Kieran. He had let his eyes close to feel this deep, penetrating sickness.

There were pictures of them in magazines: *Climbing World*, *Climbing*, *Rock*, *Gripped*, *Vertical Jones*, etc., all years ago now. Blake squatting against the snow near nude; Ian hung on a bouldering problem; Kieran stretched to a good crimper like a primate stuck in pose. All years ago, when they had worked nothing jobs only to climb. Now—Kieran with a family and working as a client relations manager at an insurance company, Ian adjuncting full-time hours at a local university, Blake still not really doing anything—now they wanted video of highly regulated, banned sites (everything was banned in the U.S., Kieran always said), possibly a documentary of themselves. A documentary of themselves! Already all these pictures and videos were posted to a website Blake had begun: there were injuries, broken fingers, sprained ankles, sprained wrists, cuts, bruises, falls, and there were successes, on-sighted routes, solos, simul-solos, swift pulls and cranks, hops off into canyons, tracking Ian in his wingsuit going down steep, steep, head up yet coming in close to the wall and then opening up and over the talus and his body a flying squirrel gliding along the canyon floor. Kieran could not look at the website, the photos. He could not look at himself in the photos, particularly. He did not know why they needed to be displayed. He did not like looking at himself. At first, when he was first in a magazine all glossy and himself sort of airbrushed, probably, and his hair long and under a beanie, which was his signature, sure, that was nice, and people knew him and talked to him, and that was nice. No, it was more than nice: he wanted only to be honest and accurate;

it was exactly what he wanted. He had wanted to be in magazines and have his name printed and for people to recognize him, glossed out and his name there in black, and himself hopping into a canyon or hanging from a headwall, certainly, yes, he had maybe even dreamed of these things, desiring it maybe too much, wanting it all too much. Now, now, though, now he hated it, hated looking at himself. He did not see what putting up the photos and videos did for anyone, especially himself. Everyone else had done everything anyway; every spot they had been to had been recorded before; every recording was really a re-recording. Nothing original. So when a new set of photos went up, a new vid, a new route they'd tried (which had been tried before, utterly and completely), other groups they knew posted response videos: nice whipper, but check this peel; reaching like a grandma for a dropped penny, pretty, but watch this one; awesome moonrise, what kind of exposure you use? I used a Nikon D5100 16.2MP Digital with a 55–200mm zoom on these shots in Moab. Always a competition. What the fuck happened to Chuck Pratt? *I don't want to write about climbing; I don't want to talk about it; I don't want to photograph it; I don't want to think about it; all I want to do is do it.* All these sandbaggers didn't know shit about what climbing really was, everything made to show off, as a performance, to be better than everybody else. What it had become was what Kieran had wanted to get away from: selfish, vain, showing-off-playacting. This, in all, everything considered, *this* was what he believed to be the end for him. As soon as the photos began showing up in magazines and Blake began that website and became more concerned with *showing* others what they had done rather than actually *doing* the thing: the end. It bled into his whole life.

Hey, dicklicker, Blake said. I have to piss. You drive a minute. He pulled a Big Gulp from the backseat and dumped the remaining contents, a rush of cold wind through the open window, then unzipped himself, waiting for Ian to take the wheel.

No no, fuck no, Ian said. Just pull the fuck over.

I'll just do it here. I don't want to pull over.

Pull the shit over and piss, Kieran said.

Blake yanked the jeep.

Kieran knew it was unfair to say that the videos and/or photos and/or website itself was any kind of *cause*, per se. He understood that he was the cause of the feelings of emptiness and meaninglessness, yet he could not help but seek an outside cause and, therefore, the pictures, the videos. He watched Blake angle stiffly down into the ditch off the high-way to pee, not actually watching him, his eyes seeing him but Kieran not actually paying attention, not observing. Yet, Kieran thought, after thinking of these things being posted and published and really seeing what they were, which was more than mere recording of vanity or a showing-off, what he really saw them as was a series of attempts to make the climbs and the hops all the more thrilling, difficult, and therefore impressive, dramatic, by adding a kind of meta-aspect to the climb, by forcing himself, Ian and Blake to have to be that much more astute, that much better, that much more impressive during their climbs and hops, turning them into actors. What they had become were actors. He was certain Blake and Ian felt it because he saw it in the way they climbed: making a problem look more difficult, dramatizing by psychically convincing themselves that a particular move or a particular route was more difficult, near impossible, deadpointed; all of this near unconsciously done, but still, with those cameras, they were aware. He was aware of the slightly louder grunts he made. The roars Blake let go when he peeled or cranked were louder, the muscles in his arms flexed, perhaps, rather than simply being used, the breath he took a bit more rapid, the shakeout of hands and arms more exaggerated and grimacey. Kieran himself was aware of grunting more. He did not know if he had ever grunted on a climb before. The grunts, the pictures, the cameras, all were symptoms of the climb losing its *it*-ness, the simple thing of *doing it* (it was not a simple thing, but doing, simply *doing it*, was). And now it was as though he was not simply climbing but watching himself climbing and, further, watching what others might see when they saw him climbing.

Blake shook off. The grass in the ditch waved in the wind. Ian took the spot as driver. A semi passed them and gave a long, blaring honk, which from the ditch Blake flicked off. He jogged around the jeep. When he opened the door, a gust of cold whushed in again, and Ian said, I thought it was supposed to be warmer today.

Nada, Blake said. One of my balls froze off out there. Plopped right down. Rolled away. And a badger ate it.

All show. It bled into his life, is how Kieran thought of it. It was as though he were bleeding this sickened self everywhere. Though, again, he tried to be open and mindful and aware enough that perhaps he was reading into the cameras too much and perhaps it was something else in his life that had bled and sickened and made empty and meaningless the climbs and flys, not the cameras alone. It was not possible to know which way the thing worked: whether the cameras and the feelings of being an actor bled into his life and ruined the climbs and flys and therefore his life, or whether his life at home, which he often saw as stagnant and mundane and boring and also somehow as a theatrical thing, had made meaningless the climb. He could no longer separate the two worlds. He had to admit either as a possibility. Above all, he was determined to be fair.

The SUV, filled neatly with camping and climbing gear, with a kayak on the top rack in case they wanted to ride rapids the next day, rode onto an off-ramp, which looped, then led into Yosemite. This had once been Kieran's favorite part of the ride. A stream rode along the road, down through boulders; you could hear it from the car. Ian opened Kieran's window because this was what they had learned of one another. Ian knew that Kieran liked to hear the rush of the meltwater through the stream as they rode up. It was a signal of the beginning of the journey, the window opening, the sound of the rushing stream's meltwater, the smell of wet forest and sequoia and cool moss. Kieran thought of rolling the window up now because it was cold and because who cared? It was just a stream. He did not know, could not understand, why he had wanted to hear the stream before. Yet the window was down and the water was rushing and Blake said, Titties, which was a thing he often said to jokingly ruin or perhaps only lighten what Ian and Kieran thought were profound or otherwise spiritual moments. Sometimes he said, Jesus titties, but this time he didn't. Before his year-long step into the meaninglessness of the climb or fly, which was devastating to Kieran's peace of mind, to his ability to function in the world, he would easily laugh and close his eyes at Blake's titty comment or Jesus comment, and they would all go quiet, but now he was just thinking of the ways in which everything had been lost and become meaningless and stupid, and now the entire situation, meaning his mind, turned on him so that he saw himself as a terribly self-pitying person, even more sickeningly so than a vain actor on a rock or a pretender living in a suburban home.

One of the main reasons for self-pitying: he worked as a Client Relations Manager for an insurance claims unit. He could not see himself as an Insurance Claims District Manager. Yet he was one, chatting and approving or disapproving claims and making small talk, the whole time watching himself, sickened by it, doing this chatting and small-talking. His voice mail had become a point of great disturbance and dis-ease in his life. He often thought "dis-ease" and then "disease" and then "dis-ease." Titties, titties, titties, Blake was going. On the voice-mail mes-

543

sage was his voice saying that if he was not in his office answering his phone he was either in the backcountry, solving some rock, or hitting the rapids. It was a voice-mail message he had made nearly four years ago and which he now regretted for its narcissistic manners and strategies, aiming to highlight that while he was certainly going to get back to and cared about whoever was calling, he had this other life that was not only important to him but also more unique, challenging and therefore rewarding than the life of whoever was leaving the message. He had no idea if he had seen this intention to one-up the message-leaver three or four years ago. He thought he'd possibly had an awareness of the narcissistic nature of the message but had felt it socially acceptable, believed that he was simply sharing something with the message-leaver. Four years ago, when he first started as a Client Relations Manager, and now—which he was not as ready to flaunt—was actually a Client Relations District Manager, having been promoted, he did believe he saw the solipsistic nature of the message but felt it was more an expression of personality or an expression of passion—he believed, possibly, it made him more human and real and therefore caring and concerned to the potential client message-leaver. Now, though, he believed this expression on his voice mail to be highly calculated toward vanity and narcissism, toward making a favorable and leaning-toward-the-awe-inspiring impression on clients, so that the client understood that he was both a real person and a person who was interested in challenging himself and pushing himself to new, if somewhat abstract, for the listener/leaver, limits. Thus making himself less real, less authentic by way of the idea that he obviously was trying to impress a client on a phone message. The entire past year he had wanted to delete the message and record a new one. However, recording a new message meant that the few clients who knew him well would most likely comment on the new message and the erasure of the old message. Quite possibly they would remark that the new message was blander, more business-like, more neutral in terms of personality. The really astute ones, or even just the fairly astute ones, might even ask whether he was still climbing and hopping and kayaking. They might ask him this in a sarcastic or cynical tone of voice, revealing that they'd known all along that he was just showing off. Which was what he now believed he was doing. When, four years ago, he'd believed he was sharing a personal interest and even conveying something about his spirituality (for at the time he deeply believed that climbing contained something of spiritual experience for him—at least the rush after the climb or hop: that good fading of fear and hard work and connection with a thing, the thing, every-thing), now he could not even think of broaching the subject of spiri-tuality or some collective universal experience derived from the act of climbing because that, along with just plain climbing or flying, seemed ever increasingly more like showing off and playacting, while at the same time being the same routinized constant as work: every other weekend, every other weekend, every other weekend. It was like he was in a child custody battle with what had once been the most important part of his life.

The SUV went up a series of switchbacks, the air becoming colder, the distant rushing sound of the river becoming more echoey and quiet. This was how he had noticed himself experiencing the world recently: thinking for an overlong period of time about some past event or the state of his life and forgetting that he was actually sitting or standing somewhere doing something; he did not know what had been happen-ing in the car for the past few minutes. Then he remembered what had been happening, which he always found strange: that while stuck in his head he could still register what was actually happening as if watching a film and not really caring to watch it. What had happened in the car was Ian had asked for a piece of gum. Ian wanted some gum. Blake, from the passenger seat, produced a joint, and Ian said, Wrong Answer, and then a piece of gum was produced. Blake took a hit of his joint anyway. This, Kieran realized now, was strange. They never smoked before a climb or hop. He heard himself saying now, as Blake pulled the car lighter from the lighter plug, Are you planning on peeling today?

To which Blake replied, All right, Judge McGee.

I'm just saying, the Domes nothing to scoff at.

That's why I'm buying life insurance from you today, Blake said, pull-ing down a long drag. He handed the joint toward Ian, and Ian waved it off a second time. And I know you don't want any, either. Right, right? Am I right?

Kieran knew he didn't have to reply to this, and he didn't, mainly because he wanted to get back to thinking about what he was thinking about, which, even while conversing, he had been thinking about: the spiritual nature of the climb and the memory that that had caused to surface about his wife. The notion of climbing as a spiritual act, of los-ing self and becoming what he'd read years prior as the one that is without a second (all after the climb, of course, upon reflection), had been the key element in his granola-girl wife falling in love with him.

545

What had happened he now saw as eerily manipulative: he had been on a rock in northern Utah with someone named Brennan, who had, four years ago, with Kieran, broken his tibia for the third time and was now, with a family and medical bills and work, essentially done climbing. He had been with this Brennan on a very difficult headwall. And what had happened on the headwall was that Brennan fell while lead-climbing. Falls happen. Climbers peel out daily. What was frightening about this particular fall was that Brennan had advanced far up beyond Kieran, and he was just about to clip in, high up on this huge, overhanging headwall. They were almost two hundred feet up, and Brennan was about to clip in, Kieran remembered, and there were people below. Hikers had stopped to watch. And there was Brennan high against the wall, Kieran lower, kind of edging along in order to reach a tough crimper, Brennan on this impossibly beautiful red rock which just chimneyed out and up through the trees into the sky. Brennan lost a foothold. He was reaching, trying to get the rope secure, and his foot slipped out of its hold, Kieran remembered. His toe—when he was pushing up to reach and clip in to an old climbing bolt to secure himself and Kieran on this lead climb—slipped out of the hold, and he was not ready for the slip. His hands reached and caught nothing, and Kieran remembered seeing all this happen impossibly slowly, saw that Brennan was definitely peeling and that he was going to fall, and fall far, and because the wall suddenly went steep where Brennan was but because it wasn't near as steep where he'd last clipped in, Kieran immediately knew Brennan was going to hit the wall—all this Kieran saw before it happened, all of it was happening very slowly yet impossibly fast. Brennan's toe slipped; his hands, which were trying desperately now to clip in, reached and tried to hold, crimping on a crack, Brennan's feet going panic bear and wild and his fingers losing their crimp, and one of his feet was able to push himself off the wall, but at an awkward angle, not straight back but to the side, and his body then came off the wall not straight back but to the side, right, and because his feet were panicked as a newbie, they failed to push off properly, and his body fell first right, then swung hard left, and his left leg caught against the less steep part of the wall, this overhang that neither of them had given any real attention, and stayed stuck. His left leg got stuck, somehow, on the overhang, while his body was still moving relentlessly to the left. Panic bear, panic bear, panic bear was going and going in Kieran's head. While the rest of Brennan's body continued to fall, his left leg stayed in place and stuck in this overhang, almost a kind of bucket hold, his left leg stuck and his right leg panic-bearing, and while his body fell past and got lower than that leg, the leg wrenched strangely, and Kieran could hear a horrid and nauseating crack, which turned the fall into a full-on screamer. As suddenly as his leg had stuck and wrenched and cracked, it let go and fell with the rest of Brennan. The rope finally caught; Brennan's body jolted to a stop at his waist and he swung there screaming in his harness, with his left leg, which was now free, bent hideously with a bone protruding from his skin, seeming to dangle like a broken limb hanging hard from a tree and waving in a gentle wind. Kieran rappelled so fast off the wall he didn't even realize he was doing it. He rapelled in no time, almost a hundred feet in what must have seemed to other people to have been seconds. He then, with Brennan's semiconscious help, belayed him down and got him onto the forest floor. The two hikers who had been watching were now on cell phones, calling for help. Brennan lay on the forest floor beyond pale, bloodless and eyes wide and head lolling around, and anytime his leg with the dangling part of the limb seemed to move, a bolt shot through Kieran as though it was he himself who was injured. Brennan, on the other hand, was not even there: his body had shot him with so much adrenaline that he was no longer in pain. He was, understandably, in shock, and a white foam gathered at the corners of his mouth. There was his leg, of course, with protruding bone and little blood, strangely, as though the bone had burned the skin when it came through, as though it cracked hot and came through skin on fire, and the sharp edge of a bone sticking out now was like a kind of perforated tusk, but there were also his hands grabbing at his midsection: when Kieran lifted his shirt there was a darkening bruise around his harness, along his abdomen, from the long fall and the harness whipping when it caught him. The two hikers, one of them a cute blonde girl in pigtails (how could he have even noticed such a thing?), wearing shorts and hiking boots and a plaid shirt, very attractive and very concerned, who would later become Kieran's granola-girl wife: neither could get cell-phone service. Kieran did not have a cell phone. He didn't even bother to ask Brennan. What he did was, he told the blonde granola-girl with pigtails and her friend, a man named Kyle, to walk behind him. Walk behind him and steady Brennan's leg. He was going to carry him down. At least until they got into cell-phone range. And this was what he did. He carried Brennan, who was thankfully in shock, down the mountain, with Kyle and the granola-girl, later Anne or Annie, she liked both, walking behind and trying their best to steady Brennan's leg—it wouldn't have worked, but Brennan was in shock and there was so much adrenaline coursing through his body that he seemed less in pain than simply gone. Until he wasn't gone, and the screaming began again, but a kind of low-mewled screaming, not a groan or moan but a low-cat-mewling from deep deep deep inside Brennan. After some hiking, though, they had gotten their cells working, so they set him down like setting down a porcelain doll. And so this was part one of how Kieran got Anne: the pigtailed granola-girl. How Kieran got Anne part two was much more sinister and manipulative and narcissistically motivated. Forget that the entire event now seemed terribly clichéd and filmic to Kieran; all of that was out of his control. It was what happened after, Kieran knew.

After they got Brennan down, some twenty minutes of hiking, they were able to use their cell phones. After this, after Brennan was carted away, they went back and got their gear and got down the mountain and followed Brennan's ambulance to the hospital, where they sat in the waiting room: after all this, Anne asked how Kieran had done all that so fast. I would have panicked, she said. How did you keep such a cool head? And what he said! What he said! What he said was, You have to have one. *You have to have one?* You have to have one! You have to have one. Her eyes were like widened tunnels, like blown holes in a mountainside. He felt she was eating him in, sucking him in. Then something caught in him, and he said, I wasn't cool, I was just doing it. *Just doing it, just doing it, just doing it.* It was a commercial, he'd felt, and then the width of those eyes like deep vortices in the sea, caving in, and he revised again and said, You would have done the same thing. Anybody would've. No, Anne had said. Not anybody would have been able to do that.

The car crunched the rocks to a stop, and they began to unload and burden themselves with the packs. Blake was in the haze Kieran expected him to be in, Ian was munching on the gum and then suddenly spit it into the woods, and Kieran had got his pack on and was dreading the hike. He didn't want to hike.

Pouty Panda, Blake said. No reason. Blue sky blue mind.

Suckfull of soul and let them ghosts go, Ian said. He slung his pack on and pulled a beanie with a big tufted pink fluffball over his bald head.

Drop down and let the wind make you drown, Kieran said.

Eh, Blake said.

They walked. Ian in front, Blake next, then Kieran. The trees grew on steep ground and were moss covered on all sides, not that lie of north only, and rain began to fall in a sick fit, drizzling now, now raining hard, now stopped or only misting, mixed with a quick-melting sleet. Clouds moved in the tops of the trees, and on the switchbacks they gained views of valleys laid across the floor of the world reaching back toward the invisible and distant city. Kieran liked to picture it: a grid of Lego-like rectangles just visible beyond the floor of the valley. Before the city was the town, set on the undulating foothills, old bungalows and squatters' two-stories and finer homes on the opposite side. Kieran's house was there, on the historic side of the city, which was actually a side of the city with no zoning, the houses either renovated and well kept or dilapidated sleepers or imploding crackhomes or merely boarded squatters. They lived near a cemetery, which rose above the city. A place he and Anne had once slept in to test their fears or to simply look down upon the city blinking at night; he liked watching the city from the cemetery hills; he liked the cars making light over the highways; he liked watching the planes winking red in the sky above the sleeping city; he liked sitting with Anne. You could see the freeway wrap around the city buildings, and being up high in the cemetery had a similar effect, though muted and quieter and closer to all things, as being upon rock and looking and sensing and feeling the curvature of the great world. Upon rock you were alone. In the cemetery, even with Anne, there was a different kind of aloneness. That quiet burning of being in the cemetery after dark with someone else who was not simply a person Kieran chose to be with because they had the same mutual obsession or addiction or whatever-it-was-maybe-religion, just this other person sitting there breathing, sitting on her butt, her knees brought up to her chest, her arms wrapped around her legs, her head rested on one knee, looking either down at the blinking city or at Kieran. Not saying anything. And how beautiful was that? No talking. For once. Just sitting. Not doing anything, nothing at all. This was the person, and there were moments when she reached out and put a hand on his hand, and an electricity went between them. The world rolled on. Sirens clamored for attention in the distance. Cars passed among the houses and buildings. Those moments were incomprehensible, still, unrecognizable. They would then begin their walk down among the great headstones and shadowed mausoleums beneath a white, over-bright moon, which lit their necessary journey. Yet, or again, soon, after all that, that which was mysterious eventually gave way to the ordinary. No touch worked, no city-view sparkled, no silent commune occurred. What he did now was he lived with his Anne and their daughter in their house among all the other houses and other lives, which seemed, without close inspection, to be exactly alike, though Kieran realized this wasn't the case, though yes it was the case, and all because of this climb with Brennan who would never climb again. Without Brennan, no Annie. Brennan who would never boulder again. Who would probably have a hard time hiking anything too steep. And fuck, no way to still, no getting out, no way away, not only from this one stuck world, but from himself. Poor Brennan. These necessary tools and packs and foods were merely ancillary to the climb or the fly. The climb was the rock itself. The jump was the jump itself. Being on the rock itself. Flying the fly. Kieran and the rock, one conquering the other, which is of course a beginners notion, a climber's most clichéd notion, that one actually conquers anything. Yet Kieran knew there was no other way to put it except that way, "conquering," though if pushed to come up with another way of saying, which he often did to himself, it was you and the rock, Kieran and the rock. And after the climb, that cleanness of mind, with the Sierra riding along the horizon, stepping into sky, the valley below pulsing with green and brown and the river coursing through it all aglisten across the land. The memoryless mind now open and receiving all.

Come all ye faithful, Ian said.

Come all you angels, lets eat everything bagels, Blake said. Seriously, I'm hungry.

When one is hungry, one eats, Ian said. But when one is eating, is one hungry? The hunger is all that is the case.

And when the head is fed, the case is closed.

Shut up.

He's a megalomaniac, megalomaniac on the floor. And he's dancing like he's never danced before.

Kieran laughed, though the joke was stupid. Wait. Where was he again? Annie. No, no, something else. Oh, yes, Kieran and the rock. When he had once believed in Kieran and the rock, being on the rock itself, part of what he understood himself to mean was that he disappeared into the rock, became the rock. Or if he were to engage with Ian on such a subject, which they often did early on: becoming the climb, becoming the fly. Kieran understood this idea of becoming the climb, though he preferred to think of it as becoming the rock, but that was only a little difference and not one worth arguing over because it seemed as though they were meaning the same thing: that they lost themselves out there. Which was a terribly powerful and addicting paradox. That a thing which took so much discipline, control, focus, to mention nothing of skill, strength (not only arm and leg strength but finger strength—even more, digit strength, power in the tip of a finger), stamina and an almost ballerina-like agility along with a clean mind to see the moves—that this physical act also contrived to rid one of one-self. Not anymore. Not again, either. That was very clear. Not again. What he thought of on the climb now or on a hop steepening along the side of a mountain wall, steepening until letting go and flying was: I'm climbing this wall again why? I'm trying to fly again why? I'm going down this river again why? Then there would come the thought of the photos being taken above or below him or of the video camera Blake always had to hold and now the helmet cam, helmet cam, helmet cam. Everything recorded, digitized, made for others, and when they went out as groups, what people said were things like: What kind of lens do you have on that thing? You make Blake look like a better skier, sicko. Kieran doesn't take the pics because he's the star, right? And Kieran could never, even after however many beers, say that he didn't take pictures because he despised the recording of these climbs or flys or downrivers or whitewaters; he couldn't say he didn't take a picture because so much of him was being recorded. He couldn't say that the thing was the thing and the picture was pointless, not even worth a memory, that what had become most important to them, beyond the fly or the climb, was the choreographing of it, he couldn't say any of that because he was in all the fucking photos, he was the one being photo-graphed, and Blake had even started to tell him how to climb: Reach here, this is a good shot. Try to get that left leg swung up. Wait, wait, let me come around to get you from here. Ian never did this. Ian climbed and didn't bother about it either, but they had both spoken and said, Blake is taking this shit too far. He's making us pose. I don't want to pose, Kieran had said, as if opening himself up, finally, to someone. I don't want to be a thing. It was the same with Anne, just her being known as Anne the granola-girl, she was Anne this thing, and already Maddie, their child, was known as Maddie the hatter, because she al-ways wanted to wear hats like her father wore beanies.

Snow now, higher up, the Sequoia thinning out and taken over by lodgepole pines, the needles brown and slipping underfoot. Over that stream he'd slipped on the ice once and sprained his ankle and worse than any whipper: out for two months, in a boot, fucking around the house. Breath visible in front of Ian, Blake too far ahead singing a song which the wind couldn't quite wipe from the world, its stupid droning falling back. Shut the fuck up, Kieran yelled. Blake turned and paused, thirty yards up, and said, Pouty panda pouts onward and upward. The burn in quads and calves, the land rising and steady breathing in of cooler and thinner air.

What the fuck, his four-year-old girl was already now not known as a little being but as this thing, this labeled thing, just as all things were labeled: Maddie the mad hatter and her mommy Annie the granola-girl and then Kieran the brave, they say, ha ha, let's take a picture of the fam, the fam all smiling, happy fam always happy. When first with Annie there was a whirlpooling freedom to everything: her riding rapids as a first-timer with only him as her guide, and good she was gone into it and loving; putting on a squirrel suit and jumping down for flying, again only him as her guide; and the promises they made, not to speak more of the events, of sex in his office or sex almost anywhere they pleased, not to speak of that, so as not to corrupt or lose it, they always ended up overtalking it, overshowing it to themselves so that they made it flicker out or simply burst out, burned out, like a firecracker smacking out on pavement, leaving a burned black scar.

They stopped and ate. Snow fell whisperingly, and they sat beneath a pine and ate sandwiches and drank coconut water and ate cookies Annie had made. Soon there was a layer of snow on the ground, two inches. Then the white lay on the trees like a mother's quilt. Blake lay back, his head propped on a rock, and he kept his eyes closed, envisioning. He always liked to see the climb or see the jump before he did it. Nothing could get fucked up if he made his mind like his body, he said. His eyes moved behind closed eyelids. Ian tossed his sandwich crusts away, and they sat stark brown on top of the layer of snow. Kieran saw their footprints that walked up behind them and ended where they were sitting, overlapping one another.

What'd you have to promise to get her to give us these? Blake said about the cookies. He was sitting up again, munching. Jesus titties, these are great.

She is the devil's baker, and he has promised her his firstborn child, who she is currently indoctrinating in the ways of baking.

She hates baking, Kieran said.

Oh, god, the promises: him promising her some type of life, some incomprehensible life, some child and garden, and a house with tatami mats and bamboo carpet and a battery-powered car, certainly that car, and cutting each other's hair and giving it to the cancer kids altruistically but showing off the bags of hair, posting the pics, the hair pics, them both bald a month, posting the bald pics, the pics of the kids who would get the hair, endless pics of their own kid, Maddie, kid pics, kid pics, in the water, there's our daughter, in the sand, Maddie holding our hand, sleeping, eating, vomiting, crying, smiling, walking, talking, laughing, all over that kid everywhere, her own little reality TV-life. The promises coming out of him like a waterfall: when had he really ever wanted a garden? It was not possible to know now, and he was certain he'd never wanted a child but was also certain he knew she did, so he'd promised and promised, knew that the first years were going to be their free years and then he'd have to give up some things, he said he'd be willing, certainly, to give up some things, not so many risks, not with a child, not so many jumps or climbs or treks fifty miles in freezing temps just because, just because, not with a child, there were no just becauses with a child because there couldn't be. Even in their idea of the kid's freeness, how there wouldn't be rules, they wouldn't be authoritarians, wouldn't force the kid to sleep or tell it when to eat, that they would do things free of any rules, even then the rules came of their own accord. And then, forget letting the kid be whatever it might be: it becomes what they were and what they were and are, are, are two people stuck in the middle of a frozen lake, right before spring, taking care to not make a crack, to not cause the ice to break, to fall in. And so that's how our lives go, like that, upon ice and ready to fall through: The milk is fucking gone. It wasn't me. Then who was it? It wasn't me. Maddie, did you finish the milk? No, I saw Daddy having some yesterday. I didn't have any yesterday. Kieran? It wasn't me, for fuck's sake. Not in front of Maddie, and on and on like a bad movie. And then what's even worse, even worse is the way she comes running to me in the evening, after I work, the way she comes running to me after a climb or fly, the way she stands on my feet and then wants to be marched around, mini-soldier: Mini-soldier march, she says. Mini-soldier march. She holds on to my legs, and I walk around like a giant, and shouldn't this be fun, shouldn't this be warming-house fun, a warm house filled with a little light and fucking joy, but instead Annie whispers to me when Maddie's down: She loves you more. She doesn't love me more. She does, she never does that with me. She sees you all the time. No, she loves you more, just like the dog loves you more. The dog doesn't love me more. Everything loves you more because you let everything do whatever it wants to do, while I have to be the disciplinarian. No, everything loves me more because everything can see I don't have a stick up my dick, and also, she told me you scare her. She said that? She said Mommy's

553

eyes scare me sometimes, and she thought you were the one who took her PolarPaul away. She lost her PolarPaul at the zoo, and we agreed to say that he ran away, that he wanted to go back to the North Paul, remember? I remember, I do, but she still thinks you took her. I told Annie this, and what is worse, what is worse, when Maddie told me about being scared of Mommy because she took PolarPaul, I had said, I don't think so, I don't think Mommy did that, and when Maddie said, No, I know she did, I decided to make her laugh and said, Mommy steals my socks, she steals my shoes and my socks and my hat, and I began tickling her. Believe that? But I was lying, lying and manipulating the whole thing, turning her against her mother. And there I am, just playing, just tickling, but really I was, so easy to see now, turning her against her poor mother in small yet accruing ways, using PolarPaul as a weapon, not only turning her against her mother but also making her see me as the one, the bestest, the greateseightest dadest madman ever. Am I the greateseightest dadest madman ever? Yes, you are. Yes yes yes.

It wasn't quite a whiteout. Off a cliff's ridge, you could see the surrounding mountains through cloud momentarily, like the glimpse of a lighthouse through fog. They did the climb, a shortened version. Two walls coming together at one-eighty, a thin gripper and a good whipper, and they all took their falls, the snow caking to the rock and bits of ice beginning to slip into cracks and holds. It was difficult, but they got up, shaking out arms and stretching their necks. Another hike up to the tip-top and then on to the drop zone, and nobody or everybody or whoever decided to jump. Then no jumping today. Not in a near whiteout, too white, too much snow and wind, the cliffs in the distance becoming harder and harder to see. They got their gear on, Ian in a canopy, Blake and Kieran in wingsuits, and Ian kept saying, I thought you weren't bringing the wingsuit to Kieran, but Blake thought he was talking to him.

Yeah, right, Blake said. I'm strapped in.

They went to the exit point and did gear checks there: almost a plank some BASErs had made years ago, dropping down into the valley. One foot off and gone. It was the quiet time before. Suddenly everything came to a point, like a wide-horizon landscape sucked of all color and object into one impossible, glowing dot.

Let's do a twoer, Blake was saying, the helmet cam propped on top of his bulbous and red helmet. I've never done it in this weather.

It's a bad idea, Ian said. You get caught on a swirly or Kieran's burble

554

or something. It's a bad idea. We should wait a bit. I want to get good separation on you two. I can't see shit in this.

A moment later Blake had his helmet off and was saying he was glad he brought the dope after all 'cause at least they could do some flying on the ground, to which only he laughed, infuriating Kieran even more, and he stepped to the exit and said, A twoer, let's do it.

And we both took one big hop into the valley, though Blake a second behind me, and I felt my body turn and kept my head up and arms wide and legs together and then in three seconds, opened my legs up and the rush pushing my face back on my skull, then steep almost straight down, diving, steepening against the wall, I could see the dark of the wall parallel to me, both going down, and the etchings of snow collecting on cracks and ledges tracking by, and then widening, opening my body, ending the dive, toward the talus and body spread around the invisible ball in the middle of me and in a quick instant of full spreading the dive ends and I'm slow falling, almost horizontal with the ground now, the wall long behind me, flying the fly now, the wind against my chest and little flecks of ice against my cheeks and flicking noiselessly on my goggles and that insane, slow falling flying rush in a sudden, pure white, the land below gone, only white, the pressure on calves and thighs and pulling on the small of my back, like someone pulling my vertebrae out and the hard hot pressure on shoulders and the rush into nothing, pure white and then the pure white cloud breaking and darts of dark and then dark green and then the forest floor darkening along, unmoving like a mighty river stilled, and ranging for my site, searching for that opening and the stream we passed earlier in the day motionless and whitecapped, as if the world below was just a photograph, a still frame, and I flip onto my back to watch the lowered ceiling of white I've just fallen through and in dreamlike glimpses the shadow of Blake in his suit a second above me scurries across and behind the white ceiling and I flip again, ranging, following the river between the valley walls, always following the river and the trees coming closer to other trees and then the opening in the distance, and the landing site is almost sunny, a sun-clean cut swatch of angling beams hitting the grass and high boulders in the valley, and I give Blake the signal that I'm opening, at maybe seven hundred, I open the chute and feel myself sucked up, stopped, unfailing, yet falling vertically now, more slowly down, and then I'm suddenly and unexpectedly ruggedly spinning down and down in a whirling tumble, falling even faster, as quickly as my pc stilled my horizontal fly, I'm falling faster and faster straight down, and I think the throw didn't clear the burble and look up to see my chute cluttered with legs, Blake's legs kicking, killing and tangling my canopy, and I seem to no longer be moving, but it is the landing site moving both horizontally and vertically toward me at once, as if the earth were moving toward me, as if, for once, it's not me moving or doing, but instead it, the earth, acting upon me, and I'm praying he gets his legs out by pulling his own canopy so he'll get off mine, hoping he's not in flail or tumble, hoping he hasn't *already* pulled his canopy. I'm envisioning him pulling off and up, his canopy letting him float up, up. How I envision it is like this: trying to see it all to make it happen, but all I'm really seeing is what's happening while I'm thinking, which is the earth rushing up.

Nominated by The Missouri Review

SUPERWHITE

by JIM WHITE

from RADIO SILENCE

I.

This all started back in 1983 in Amsterdam, Holland. I was living in a sort of self-imposed exile. It was one of those depressing, gray winter days. I was trudging past a world-famous nightclub called the Melkweg when, through a clouded plate-glass window, I noticed a music video playing. Normally this wouldn't have been cause for stopping, as the place typically aired a fare of affected British New Romantic groups like Spandau Ballet or The Human League. But this was different. It featured a palsied young man struggling through a series of disembodied, dyskinetic posturings. I ventured within earshot and, from what I could gather, this strange person was singing something about burning down a house.

At that time I was truly lost, displaced in every way—physically, spiritually, psychologically, culturally. Day in and day out I'd sit and think, mostly about Jesus and the mess I was in because of Him. I'd given up on the End Times Christianity that had been the centerpiece of my existence for most of my life, and in the process I'd painted myself into a weird existential corner.

I'd brought an old guitar to Holland to pass the time. I'd sit in my sparsely furnished room and write song after song detailing the various landmarks of my confusion. These were erratic, disjunctive odes to unhappiness that, on the rare occasion when I shared them with others, were seldom met with a positive response. A Scandinavian cruise-ship worker once said upon hearing them, "It sounds like being in a small room with many shortwave radios playing all at once."

The shortwave radio analogy was apt, considering the constant clatter of disorganized thoughts coursing through my mind—the infernal static, the meandering fragments of meaning randomly interweaving with the flotsam and jetsam of years of poor mental housekeeping. So imagine my surprise when, as I stood there watching this video, the clatter momentarily abated. I felt a shadow of peace pass over me, followed by a surge of kinship with that weirdo singing about burning down his house. This notion of kinship was, at that moment of my spiral into self, so profoundly welcome that I burst into tears.

The next day I forced myself to go to a record store to find out more about this person. The clerk directed me to a section devoted to a band called Talking Heads, then reverently uttered the singer's name: "It's David Byrne." I purchased a cassette and over the ensuing months listened to it dozens of times. Eventually the tape began to drag and slur, then one day it broke. That was the last I heard of David Byrne for a long while. It never occurred to me to replace the tape or seek out other examples of his work. I was lost. Gradually the memory of him faded into the ever-shifting quicksand of my mind.

I drifted from place to place, back home to the South for a while, then to New York City where I landed an illegal sublet in a tough Puerto Rican neighborhood in Lower Manhattan. Just days before I left north Florida I'd purchased a white, Western-cut suit to wear during my inevitable job hunt in the city. As I tried it on in the St. Vincent de Paul thrift store, I thought it made a real statement about who I was.

Once in the Big Apple, the futility of buying such an offbeat garment became abundantly clear. I couldn't find a job anywhere, much less in an office where a suit might actually be appropriate. Week after week I looked for work, but nobody was interested in hiring me.

Eventually I ran out of money and took to eating out of restaurant dumpsters. I was deeply depressed and on the verge of becoming homeless when I finally found a job making sandwiches in a SoHo cafeteria. Minimum wage and one meal a day. Being destitute and not having much of a wardrobe, the white suit became an all-purpose garment that I wore in my leisure time. I cut quite a figure as I rode my old bike around the downtown area, imagining myself immune from the filth flying at me from every direction.

A few weeks into my New York tenure I noticed a puzzling dynamic. Wherever I went, passers-by seemed to do double-takes, the expressions on their faces conveying a sort of favorable appraisal to which I was unaccustomed. I could only guess that they must have been attracted to the exotic suit. This was in part the case, although the full explanation was far more complicated than I imagined.

At this time I was trying to shed my dour Pentecostal ways and become more worldly, so several nights a week I donned my white suit and forced myself out into the world. I discovered a scattering of edgy dance clubs near my apartment. Slipping ignominiously through their doors, I'd guzzle down a few shots of overpriced whiskey, wait for the booze to take effect, then try my hand at modern dancing.

I was terrible—wild and unrhythmic, unfamiliar with the fashionable steps of the day. You'd think I would have been universally shunned in such places, but, to my surprise, hipster-types would come prancing up to me, flashing huge greedy smiles. They'd dance with me, often inexplicably slapping themselves in the forehead and making chopping motions on their arms as they undulated to the mind-numbing beat. Thinking this to be some popular new dance, I aped their movements, much to their delight.

One day while passing an artsy movie theater on Eighth Street I was startled to discover a photo of my white-suited self in a movie advertisement. The poster was for a film called *Stop Making Sense*. Examining it more carefully, I saw that in fact it wasn't me at all. It was that palsied guy, David Byrne. He, too, wore a white suit, although his didn't fit quite as well as mine. I studied the image, deciding he and I looked a bit alike—his hair was cut in a fashion identical to mine, his build was slight and rangy, and he wore that same vexed expression I'd been told I had.

It was a discount matinee, so I paid my two dollars and sat down in the empty theater. Through the opening scenes I felt a further sense of kinship with this lunatic who sang and sputtered about burning down his house. I was burning down my house, too, after all, albeit in a symbolic, circuitous, and oblique manner.

The sense of kinship vanished when David Byrne began his quirky, emblematic dancing. He commenced to chop on his arm and slap his forehead and suddenly all those grinning, dancing hipsters made sense. They thought they were dancing with the legendary David Byrne and were thrilled when he did his signature moves for them. But in fact nothing could have been further from the truth. They were dancing with a minimum-wage nobody, a clinically depressed sandwich maker, an illusion. The idea of participating in illusions may be alluring to some, but it wasn't to me. I was engaged in an epic struggle to become myself, not David Byrne. As such I left the theater and threw the white suit in the garbage.

The sandwich shop closed down so I took a job driving a cab. One night I picked up the lead singer from a popular band called Gaye Bykers on Acid. He was utterly wasted and was accompanied by a garish Asian woman who I assumed was a groupie. After commenting favorably on my hyper-aggressive driving style, he began to soliloquize about how cab drivers and rock stars were essentially practicing the same art form. He riffed on that line of horseshit until we arrived at his ritzy Midtown hotel.

As he was disembarking, he invited me to his concert the next night at Madison Square Garden. "Oy mate, what's the name? Put you on the guest list."

I pointed to my name, clearly listed on my hack license.

"No! That ain't right, is it now? You're not him—you're . . . you're . . . fucking Travis Bickle! Right?" He scowled, flashing his best punk-rock sneer.

I offered no response.

"Yeah, that's you, mate. Right, Travis?"

I looked away. The groupie giggled nervously.

"Right then. Travis Fucking Bickle. No worries, you're on the list!" he said, slamming the door and staggering off.

I suppose he was trying to be helpful, but I resented his remark and so did not attend the Gaye Bykers on Acid concert. The last person in the world I wanted to become was Travis Bickle, the homicidal schizophrenic stalker from Martin Scorsese's film *Taxi Driver*. And yet over the coming years, the taint of that worrisome persona began to settle on me like coal dust falling on a doomed, impoverished, West Virginia mining town.

II.

Not long after the Travis Bickle incident, I had a peculiar dream about a black woman I knew from a writing class I was taking. A radical feminist from the South, she was a lovely collision of contradictions—rural yet highly educated, self-assured yet vulnerable, full of hard-won dignity and salt-of-the-earth humor. I crossed paths with her a few days later and told her about the dream.

The action began on a boat landing at the edge of a vast, murky swamp. I was myself, but she was a yellow bulldozer. Her motor was running, and I climbed into her cockpit, put her in gear, and drove her into the swamp, jumping off as the slimy green water pooled around my waist. I swam back to shore as she plowed ahead driverless, disappearing into the mire

I thought, being a writer, she would appreciate the absurdity of the dream, but she didn't. Instead she lowered her brow and sternly informed me that I was not to have any more dreams about her. There was an awkwardness in the ensuing silence so I apologized, blaming my indiscretion on the fact that I was too pathetically white.

She seemed both puzzled and accepting of my confession, so I launched forward with an elaboration, hoping to put the unfortunate rift behind us. I explained that I'd recently seen performances by black musicians such as Don Cherry and John Lee Hooker and that I envied their connection to the rhythmic world. Their performances seemed so much more integral and compelling than the shows of parallel white musicians such as jazz pianist Monty Alexander and Joe Jackson, whom I'd also seen recently. It was clear I had no such rhythmic connection to the universe, but I deeply desired one. The catch was that whenever I tried to emulate the mannerisms of these black epitomes of soul, instead of becoming more soulful and rhythmic and, well, black, I became the opposite—more pathetically white.

She listened with something approaching interest, so I continued.

It occurred to me that if there was a spectrum between—for lack of better terminology—blackness and whiteness, soulfulness and soullessness, that by all appearances I was situated so far into the realm of white that no amount of effort would get me anywhere near the other end where the zone of soulfulness apparently existed. It was just too far to go. The physics clearly suggested I would never be able to remake myself into a black man.

"Oh, honey, no. Don't try that," she said. "White folks trying to act black? You know what we call them? Perpetrators."

Yes. Amen. There was nothing more pathetically white than a "perpetrator." Still, I explained, I was unwilling to accept a fate of mediocre whiteness. It occurred to me that instead of making feeble attempts to cross that vast expanse of whiteness to get to the realm of soul, I'd be better off going in the opposite direction, endeavoring to become more and more white.

"Oh, right," she said, "like that Jung thing. Enantiodromia." I stared blank-faced until she continued. "You know, where a person takes some aspect of personality so far that it becomes its opposite."

"Actually, yes." My theory was that if I ventured far enough into the realm of white, I might actually reach the end of whiteness. There, my being would become so suffused with whiteness that something transformative might happen, perhaps a form of blindness would befall me, and then I might accidentally stumble into a rhythmic, soulful black modality.

There was a moment of formulation on her part. Then, instead of rejecting the paradigm, she went with it. "So correct me if I'm wrong here," she said. "What you're trying to do . . . you're trying to become *superwhite*?"

Superwhite! As soon as she uttered the term a halo of definition formed over the whirlwind of thought-projectiles that had been crashing around in my mind for years. I was trying to become superwhite! It was that simple.

"Exactly!" I told her. "I'm trying to become superwhite!"

She patted me on the shoulder and in parting said, "Well, honey, if anyone can become superwhite, it has got to be you."

Superwhite. That's what I was aiming for, and as she said the word a second time a face materialized in my mind's eye—David Byrne's. I hadn't thought of him in years. But of course! David Byrne is so white that he's black. He's superwhite! No wonder I felt that mysterious kinship with him all those years ago—we were both on the same path. Clearly he was far ahead of me in his metamorphosis, but we were fellow transcendence seekers in the far-white spectrum. There and then I understood—somehow, someway, I would eventually come face to face with David Byrne, and I would neither introduce myself, nor offer any preamble or apology, I would simply, boldly, with a knowing smile, speak the word "superwhite." And if the universe was the place of mysterious order and meaning that I so desperately needed it to be, he would instantly both understand and embrace my declaration.

My realignment with self was nudged in a distinctly superwhite direction a few days later. My hair had grown long and floppy, like a collie's, so I decided to go for a more anachronistic look to accelerate the transition.

I dug out my electric hair trimmer, aiming for one of those haircuts from the '50s—thin on the sides and a little stylish wave on the top. Things were going well enough until I jerked a bit and, an inch or so above my left ear, gouged out a huge chunk of hair, right down to the scalp.

There was no covering my mistake. By the time I'd smoothed the bald spot the entire left side of my head was shaved clean. There was only one solution—I'd have to shave the right side in a similar fashion. I did so, but much to my dismay the line between skin and stubble was much higher than on the left. There followed a series of reductive mis-calculations, and by the time I put the trimmer down, there remained only a scruffy patch of hair down the center of my head. I'd given my-self a de facto Mohawk. This was not an improved self, not even a David Byrne. This was a Travis Bickle. Perhaps the Gaye Bykers on Acid singer was on to something.

When I showed up at the taxi fleet the next day, several of the veteran drivers guffawed, offering up the obvious catcalls. I'd been suffering from increased bouts of depression and had withdrawn completely from the friendly daily dialogues of the drivers as they waited for cabs to come in. I sulked in a corner of the shape-up room, waiting for my name to be called. The teasing continued, but I couldn't really argue—I not only looked like Travis Bickle, I was starting to feel like him.

About an hour later I heard the dispatcher call out "Bickle. Travis Bickle, your cab is ready." Further hilarity ensued. I refused to budge. Finally he called my name, then, smirking, handed me my trip sheet and keys. Out into the wilderness of New York City I hurtled.

It was a crisp, blue, early fall afternoon. Customers came and went. An average day guided by the random gods of transportation. Here takes you there. There takes you somewhere else. Every ride redefines your shift. Just near sunset I found myself hunting fares downtown. At the corner of Houston and LaGuardia Place, an angular, odd-looking fellow sporting a coonskin cap and mirrored sunglasses jaywalked in front of me as I sat in traffic. There was something familiar about his gait. He turned and looked my way, and who was that jaywalker? It was David Byrne, of course. Less than a week after my superwhite epiph-any, there he was.

The moment was laden with myriad ill-defined portents. Obviously this was no coincidence. I knew I had to convey the word "superwhite" to him, then something pivotal would happen, but what? I turned the corner and followed him. What should I do? Park the cab and approach him on foot? Or just shout "superwhite" from behind the wheel? That was better, more dramatic, more cinematic. And what would he do in return? Break into a palsied dance on my behalf? Or maybe bark out some equally surreal non sequitur, some corollary to superwhite that only he and I would understand? It would be like Einstein bumping into Edison in a doughnut shop. We'd share communion in the secret language of superwhite. This was going to be a defining moment in my life, a meshing of disparate threads, a miraculous nexus between obscurity and fame.

I followed at a safe distance as David Byrne walked ahead at a leisurely pace. I found myself waiting, but for what? I simply wanted to make sure I did this the right way. I took a breath and relaxed, letting my mind clear, studying him as he walked. He was shorter than I was and had eschewed the white suit for some kind of postmodern cowboy outfit. Suddenly he seemed to realize someone was following him. He stopped and shot a furtive look over his shoulder. Eye contact. It was time to shit or get off the pot, so I lifted my chin, smiled confidently, and called out, "Superwhite."

There are those magic moments in life that you dream of, when opportunity intersects with desire and preparation. This was certain to be one of those occasions. But unfortunately my voice was somewhat louder and more aggressive than I'd intended. David Byrne flinched. I waited for some welcoming reply, but none came. Was he simply triangulating the significance of my message? His mirrored sunglasses made it difficult to read his expression. He turned back around and continued on his way

I sped up. Drawing nearer, I shouted more emphatically, "*Superwhite!*" fighting the urge to contaminate the message with the burden of explanation. If I had to explain superwhite to him, it would invalidate the power of the term.

"SUPERWHITE!" I shouted a third time, and now he reacted. But instead of turning around and addressing me as a brother, he quickened his pace to a speed somewhere between a canter and a trot. I hit the gas, matching his increase and further closing the gap between us, shouting over and over the word that he, and only he, should have both understood and welcomed.

Suddenly he broke away from the curbside and sprinted toward the open doorway of a photo store, disappearing inside. I could see him peering at me from behind a circular rack of instruction manuals. I called out "superwhite" a few more times, but to no avail.

Somewhere in the growing abandonment of my calling, in the plate-glass window of the photo store I caught a blurry reflection of myself leaning out the taxi's window as I furiously shouted to my world-famous doppelgänger. The sight of Mohawked me stopped me dead in my tracks. It took a moment before I realized that this was some garbled inversion of my first encounter with David Byrne all those years ago in Holland, when I watched him through a window as he ranted about burning down his house. But this time I was the person ranting. I looked less like David Byrne and more like Travis Bickle. Oh, the indignity of it. My house was certainly burning down, and there wasn't a damn thing I could do to stop it. I sped away, defeated, demoralized, and furious that the mechanics of the universe had failed me so miserably.

III.

After the superwhite debacle I sank further into depression. Over the next few years more and more went wrong with my life and mind. Following several failed romances I began to contemplate suicide with regularity and intensity.

Eventually I settled upon a convoluted plan for ending my life. I'd heard of yogis who could slow their heartbeats, rendering themselves comatose simply with the power of their minds, and of old people who, after suffering some great tragedy such as the loss of a beloved spouse, simply willed themselves to die while doctors helplessly stood by. Perhaps I could do the same.

Initially my plan seemed to work. I fell ill with a fever and was taken to bed. The fever persisted for days, then weeks. Unable to work, I was forced to leave New York and return home to the South, presumably to convalesce, but if all went according to plan, to wither away and perish.

Once home, the mysterious illness worsened. Relatives began to worry, prompting a forced visit to a local country doctor. He prescribed antibiotics. Once the medicine had run its course the fever returned redoubled. I resisted any further urgings to consult doctors, privately vowing to just lie in bed and die.

To pass the time, after putting down the guitar for many years, I started to write songs again. My mom's boyfriend, an airplane mechanic from Knoxville, loaned me a strange purple electric guitar with a marginally functioning whammy bar. He'd purchased it as a teenager. It was an obscure brand called Prestige and came with a small, inexpensive amp that, after sitting unused in a closet for three decades, miraculously still worked.

I was bedridden. The days crawled by. Songs of sorrow and regret were written. Landmarks of confusion were wearily revisited then abandoned. There was a shift in these new compositions, a plaintive simplicity. The songs sounded tired and worn out, much less complicated than those I'd written years before in Amsterdam. It was as if my ability to express myself was failing alongside my internal organs.

Word spread back to the few friends I had in New York that I was gravely ill, perhaps dying. There were some hushed whisperings that I had AIDS. A devoted, longsuffering schoolmate from college, who believed there to be some kernel of talent hidden in the chronic clutter of my mind, learned of my spiral and actually traveled to north Florida to pay me a surprise visit.

As he approached my house he heard someone singing and playing guitar through the open window; He recognized my voice and, knowing how shy and skittish I was about attention, listened from outside. He'd never heard me sing before, as by the time I met him I'd learned to keep that part of my creative life a secret. After I finished moaning five or six melancholic dirges and laid down the Prestige, I was startled by the sound of applause wafting through the open window My friend came in, sat down on the bed, and made me promise to do two things: find a better doctor and make a recording of those songs for him. It was a touching gesture.

Despite my promise, I never looked for another doctor. Months passed and I simply waited to die. No such luck. Instead, slowly, incrementally I began to recover, to be able to move about, to walk short distances, and even to drive a car again. Spring was in the air. I sighed, packed my belongings, and returned to New York and cab driving.

Once there I dug out my old half-busted tape player and recorded those songs for my friend. It was the least I could do, considering I hadn't kept my word regarding the doctor. He'd relocated to L.A. to work in the film business. Once he got the tape he played it for his girlfriend, who was some sort of artistic prodigy with, among other accomplishments, an advanced degree in music. Struck by the odd arrangements and lyrics, she borrowed the tape and played it for a friend, Melanie Ciccone, who allegedly worked in the music business.

Melanie was likewise puzzled and intrigued. She contacted me. Imagine my surprise when she said she not only liked my songs but suggested that I send the tape to various luminary record companies for commercial assessment.

After our conversation I sat in my room and worked over the details. Who was this lady who wanted me to send my crappy homemade tape to huge, world-famous record labels? And why? It was a miserable recording done in my kitchen with a RadioShack microphone that I'd picked up at a yard sale for a buck. There were no drums, no bass, no keyboards—no players other than myself. The recording was done in mono, and something was broken inside the machine so that sound only came out of one speaker. You could hear my Puerto Rican neighbors arguing in the background.

It all seemed so hilariously absurd that I went along with it. I figured it was a prank, that she was a kook who was going to lure me to a motel in Wisconsin and stab me to death. That's how my luck had been running. I sent ten tapes out to major labels and was none too surprised when they began to come back in the mail, each one bearing a stamp over the address that read, UNSOLICITED MATERIAL: RETURNED UNOPENED. Ultimately all the tapes were returned unlistened to, save one—the one that had gone to Warner Brothers. They listened to my tape. There was a letter enclosed attesting to that fact. It read:

Dear Sir,

We have received your tape and listened to it. We feel the material herein is very weak. We have no interest in having any further contact with you. Please do not contact us again. Your tape is returned herewith.

Sincerely,
XXXXXXX

In a way it was a relief. Between the "herein" and the "herewith" it was clear this masquerade was over.

I went back to cab driving. A few weeks passed and Melanie Ciccone called to see how the labels had responded. When I broke the news she was furious. "They're wrong!" she said, promising that she was going to find me a record deal. Twenty minutes later she called back and instructed me to send my tape to a certain address on Twelfth Street in New York. "The label is called Luaka Bop," she said. "David Byrne runs it."

I could hardly say goodbye. I laughed for days.

And then I sent the tape. I included no return address, nothing explaining who I was. The only message attached was a Post-it note that read: "Melanie said to send this, so I did." I included no further elaborations because, quite frankly, I knew that no one, particularly David Byrne, was going to listen to it.

So imagine my surprise a few days later when I found myself on the phone with Melanie. She wanted to know why I hadn't included any contact info with the tape. I was in the middle of inventing a lame excuse when it occurred to me that the tape had reached its destination in New York and someone had apparently listened to it. This was a bigger hoax than I realized—now people in New York were involved. She instructed me to contact someone named Yale Evelev, the label head of Luaka Bop. I called, and in his terse, staccato style of communicating, Yale Evelev said, "Okay Got the tape. Let's talk. When can you come by?"

I walked into the Luaka Bop offices a few minutes later. Various beautiful women were milling around, filing papers, talking on phones in hushed professional voices. A secretary eyed me warily and asked me to take a seat as she notified someone that I'd arrived. A moment later David Byrne appeared.

Well, he didn't exactly appear. He came bursting down the hallway holding out his hand like an excited schoolboy. When it became clear that he was moving toward me, that he was about to speak, I rose to greet him.

"Wow, what an honor to meet you!" he said. "Wow! I really love your music! Wow!"

I was dumbfounded. Before I could muster a response, David Byrne spun on his heels and, with the back of his head just a few inches from the end of my nose, asked the receptionist in the same excited tone, "Any good mail for me today?" She passed him a stack of letters and, seemingly unaware of my presence, he began to read.

Minutes passed. Eventually I sat back down and took stock of the situation.

There are those moments in life when events became so surreal that you suspect you've crossed over to a bizarre alternate universe. That's how this was. A world-famous musician, a celebrity of the highest order—someone who'd been on the cover of *Time* magazine—had just spoken strange words to me, words that were said in the exact order and with the exact enthusiasm that *I* should have said them to *him*.

Eventually he spun back toward me. "What about pedal steel?"

Pedal steel? I was a reclusive hermit who'd never played in a band or sang in public. I didn't even know there was a conventional tuning for guitar. I had no idea that the term "pedal steel" described the device that made those weepy sounds you hear on country-and-western records, so I just smiled blankly.

"How about singing saw?" he added.

"I'm not sure what you're talking about," I told him.

"On your album," he said. And with that he trotted back to his office, leaving me in a state of bewilderment.

A moment later, Yale Evelev appeared. Like any capable label head, he was much more cagey than David Byrne. He invited me into his office. My raggedy little homemade cassette tape was sitting on his neat, professional-looking desk. It looked so out of place. I'd drawn a picture of an army of angels carrying a coffin on the cover.

We began an innocuous conversation—where was I from, how old was I—and then it happened again: the word "album" was mentioned.

"What album?" I asked.

He paused, seemingly puzzled by my question. "Well, your album, of course—if everything works out. There's not a big budget, but we're partners with Warner Brothers, so you'll have a great label behind you." Warner Brothers. It took every fiber of my being to suppress the mad laughter welling up inside me.

As I unlocked the door to my apartment an hour later the phone rang. It was Melanie. She shouted, "They want to make an album with you!" I was beyond bewildered.

I called my sister for advice. She teaches law on the West Coast and leads an eminently sane, sensible life. As best I could, I had shielded her from my psychological troubles. But now I needed her help, so I launched into the saga, starting with Holland and the music video, then the white suit and being mistaken for David Byrne. I told her about the bulldozer dream and the black woman's wisdom, the Gaye Bykers on Acid singer and my de facto Mohawk, stalking David Byrne and shouting "superwhite" at him, and how I worried I was turning into Travis Bickle. Finally I explained about the tapes being returned and the interview at David Byrne's record label.

She took it well enough, listening silently Then at the end of my harangue, in true lawyerly form, she disregarded the innumerable indicators of mental instability and calmly advised me to do exactly as she said: "Under no circumstances are you to say 'superwhite' to David Byrne or anyone else at that label until you have a signed contract in your hands."

Something about the dry certainty of her response made this suddenly seem real. It was a simple business transaction, and she was offering a viable tactic to close the deal. It felt dazzlingly comforting. Of course! I would withhold information, play things close to the vest, like a true businessman. And should things go wrong, the superwhite story would be my ace in the hole.

IV.

Some weeks passed. One afternoon I was at home working on a song that was going nowhere, beating my head against the wall over a line of lyrics:

Busy in the head, I'm busy in the head.
Got a skull full of half-baked hillbilly bread.
I wish I was a stump. I'd be better off dead.
'Cause Lord have mercy I'm busy busy busy in the head.

The phone rang. Yale Evelev said, "Look, can you come over? We gotta talk." His tone worried me.

It was late in the day. I got to the Luaka Bop office just as Yale was locking up. He asked if I minded taking a cab with him to Brooklyn where he was supposed to meet someone for dinner. We could talk along the way, and he'd cover my subway fare home.

We weaved our way downtown. In addition to the disorientation of being in the back seat of a cab after spending ten long years in the front, it was equally confusing pretending to be both a musician and a businessman with Yale. He was a real businessman, after all, and he talked a good game. The outstanding issue with him was my lack of experience as an entertainer. I'd never been on a stage or played to an audience. Possibly ten people in the world had ever heard my music. He'd suggested weeks earlier that I book some shows so he could see me perform, telling me he couldn't really offer me a contract until he'd seen my "show." I'd been to music venues all over town and was laughed at when I inquired about bookings. Beck used to busk on the streets back then—that's how hard it was to get a real gig in Manhattan.

I explained that none of the hip clubs were interested. I had no experience, no real demo tape, no band, no following, no connections or music buddies who might put in a good word for me. Hell, I didn't even do drugs. Yale listened to all this, then shook his head, asking me how, if I couldn't even get a simple gig, was I going to become a professional musician?

He brainstormed aloud. Maybe I needed to find another label to release my first album, then Luaka Bop could release my second one if the first did well. Maybe I needed to join a punk band and tour relentlessly for a few years, learning how to perform. It suddenly sounded very much like this was the kiss-off, the thanks-but-no-thanks that I was so familiar with. But I still had my secret weapon. I hadn't told them about superwhite. Was it time?

The cab exited the Williamsburg Bridge, banked south on Broadway, and pulled up to Peter Luger Steak House. I'd driven high rollers there before—Mafioso-types, celebrities, and what-have-you. I figured I'd bolt before he could break the bad news, so as the cab rolled to a stop, I threw open the door and said, "Okay, Yale, see you later."

"Where're you going?"

"Home," I told him. "We can finish this later."

"No. We're not done talking. Come inside. Maybe join us for dinner?"

I tried to politely beg off, telling him I had errands to run, but he would hear none of it. To complicate matters I'd become a vegetarian that morning. That very morning I had vowed never to eat meat again. And here I was being offered a free meal at one of the best steak restaurants in the world. Goddamn. I started to get out of the cab, but Yale grabbed me by the arm. "Really, come inside."

"No, I gotta go," I insisted.

"Look." Yale was getting pissed. "Everybody's waiting. Get it?"

Everybody? He dragged me into the restaurant.

At the nearest table sat David Byrne. The rest of the label staff was there as well. Beautiful women, hip young men, all smiling at me.

"Congratulations!" Yale said, huffing a bit. "You're now a recording artist with Luaka Bop. We drew up the contracts this morning. Now take a seat and enjoy a nice big steak."

I, a vegetarian for roughly twelve hours, sat at the table across from

David Byrne and studied the menu. Meat, meat, and more meat. I surrendered and ordered the best steak I would ever eat. And as I ate, I flashed back to years earlier, to the moment when I first called out "superwhite" to David Byrne. I remembered how disappointed I'd felt when he didn't seem to accept or comprehend the message.

But here I was, wasn't I? Sitting down to an elegant dinner with Superwhite himself. So maybe he did hear what I shouted so long ago, after all. Maybe the mechanics of hearing are more complicated than I'd imagined. Maybe at times we hear in ways so incremental as to elude understanding. Maybe we burn down our houses, sliver by sliver, nail by nail, until we find ourselves sitting atop a mountain of astonishing ashes that we can truly call our own.

Two years later I found myself back in northern Europe. Another dismal, gray winter day. This time it was Hamburg, Germany I'd just finished watching a David Byrne show for the twenty-third time in twenty-eight days. Despite having no performance experience, he had generously invited me to be his opening act in Europe. I slept in a bunk on the tour bus just a few feet from him. We became friends.

At the end of the show, I noticed an attractive woman sitting alone at a table, clutching a huge teddy bear. A security guard passed by and informed her that the club was closing. I walked backstage and packed up my gear. Ten minutes later, as I passed David's dressing room, he called out to me. There was a hint of desperation in his voice.

I entered to find he had a guest. He always had some exotic celebrity visiting him—Brian Eno, Debbie Harry, Adrian Belew. This time it was the woman with the teddy bear. She was staring at him intently, sadly, whispering something. He introduced me to her then hastily exited, moving away at something between a canter and a trot. The woman looked crestfallen. We spoke briefly. It was clear that she was mentally ill. She told me that she just *had* to give the giant teddy bear to David. She just had to. A moment later several security guards arrived. It took all three of them to carry her, kicking and screaming, out the door.

EPILOGUE

I'm not sure when it was that I relayed the story of superwhite to David. I remember that he laughed when I described the spectrum between soulfulness and soullessness and how I was trying to become so white that I was soulful, like him. He appeared to understand the crackpot physics of which I spoke.

To his further credit he seemed unperturbed by the revelation that I'd once stalked him. In fact he had no memory of the incident. After touring with him extensively, I now know why. For in every town, in every city in the world, there are incarnations of me—sad, lonely, lost souls, deliverers of giant teddy bears, legions of accidental Travis Bickles who believe with all their hearts that they are communicating with someone important, someone connected, someone who will help them undertake a magical leap from the furthest-most reaches of nowhere to the center of somewhere.

Nominated by Radio Silence

SPECIAL MENTION

(The editors also wish to mention the following important works published by small presses last year. Listings are in no particular order.)

POETRY

Refrain — Gregory Maher (Spillway)
The Ring — Alan Williamson (Yale Review)
Patience — Ross Gay (Solstice)
A Nickel On Top of a Penny — Stephen Burt (Virginia Quarterly)
Accident — Sophie Cabot Black (Paris American)
Wreck — Erin Mullikin and David Wojciechowski (Birdfeast)
August On The Coast — D. Nurkse (Ploughshares)
So Come — Brian Henry (Virginia Quarterly)
The Parallel Cathedral — Tom Sleigh (Poem-A-Day)
Explanation (Hiroshima) — Andrea Cohen (Threepenny Review)
from Sabbaths 2013 — Wendell Berry (Threepenny Review)
Rolling Deep — Amy King (Clockhouse)
Poem On The End of a Lure—Kara van de Graaf (New South)
Aftermaths — R.A. Villanueva (Ninth Letter)
When I Was A Straight — Julie Marie Wade (Bloom)
The Shape of It — Wendy Xu (Black Warrior)
Moonset — Andrew McFadyen-Ketchum (Iron Horse)
Litany for my Father's Guns — Bruce Snider (Pleiades)
Young People Will Have White Hair — Carson Cistulli (Smartish Pace)
Akhmatova's Ashtray — David Roderick (Indiana Review)

Origin of Difference — Marcelo Hernandez Castillo (Construction)
Is There Still A Betty In This New Life? — Diane Seuss (Blackbird)
The God of Numbers — Danusha Laméris (The Sun)
Trappist — T.R. Hummer (Codex)
Bomb Threat — Karyna McGlynn (Sixth Finch)

NONFICTION

A Catalogue of Possible Endings — Rick Moody (Salmagundi)
Death Will Abide — Ellen Lambert (Raritan)
Voice and Hammer — Jeff Sharlet (Virginia Quarterly)
You Gotta Have Heart — Lynne Sharon Schwartz (Agni)
The Top Shelf — Floyd Skloot (Sewanee Review)
Masters In This Hall — Melora Wolff (Normal School)
A Coat of Armour — Robert Hass (Brick)
Let Nothing You Dismay — Joan Murray (The Sun)
Love Is Here and Now You're Gone — Garret Keizer (Virginia Quarterly)
Notes From A Nonnative Daughter — Abigail Greenbaum (Ecotone)
A Brief and Necessary Madness — Kirk Wilson (River Teeth)
On The Inner Lives of Ghosts — Antonio Muñoz Molina (Hudson Review)
The Circus Train — Judith Kitchen (Georgia Review)
The Lives of Strangers — Paisley Rekdal (Broad Street)
Ammunition — Bruce Snider (Iowa Review)
The World of Coca-Cola — Anton Barba-Kay (The Point)
Strip — Marya Hornbacher (Fourth Genre)
Be Strong, Be Brave — B.A. Newmark (Boulevard)
Shadow Animals — Julie Riddle (Georgia Review)
Crimes Against A Wrecker Driver — Bonnie Jo Campbell (Southern Review)
Telling Who I Am Before I Forget . . . — Gerda Saunders (Georgia Review)
Little X — Elizabeth Tallent (Threepenny Review)
Letter From Williamsburg — Kristin Dombek (Paris Review)
The Running of the Brides — Jessamyn Hope (Colorado Review)
Making Friends — Susann Cokal (Broad Street)
Dark Matter — Susanne Antonetta (Fourth Genre)
Unlikely Magic — David Wojahn (Blackbird)
Loving Kip — Jamie Johnson (Brain, Child)

Burning Bushes — Dan DeWeese (Oregon Humanities)
Strapped — Hal Stucker (Boston Review)
Charity: A Memoir — L.E. Kimball (Natural Bridge)
Hourglass — Julie Marie Wade (Hunger Mountain)
Bruised in a Manner Fitting — Matthew Nye (Chicago Review)
The Half-Life — Annie Penfield (Fourth Genre)
The Manly Arts — W. Todd Kaneko (The Normal School)
My Cousin's Face — Rachel Kadish (American Athenaeum)
When Enough Is Enough — Lynn Freed (Narrative)
Whose Story Is This? — Barbara Hurd (New Ohio Review)
Adopt A Bench — Rebecca McClanahan (The Sun)
The Moving Face (for Roger Ebert) — Riva Lehrer (TriQuarterly)
Year of The Dogs — Caitlin Horrocks (Southern Review)
Writing My Way Home — Ron Capps (Delmarva Review)
Still, God Helps You — Melissa Pritchard (Wilson Quarterly)
Something Borrowed in the Berkeley Hills — Heather Kirk Lanier
    (Southwest Review)
Someone Else — Chris Offutt (River Teeth)
Sixty-Eight — James Nolan (Boulevard)
A Brown-Skinned Lady and Her Sunblock — A. Sandosharaj (River
    Teeth)
William Stafford's Boot Camp for the Seriously Bewildered — James
    Moore (Tavern Books)
Council of the Pecans — Robin Wall Kimmerer (Orion)
The Black Saint And The Best-selling Writer — Joe Miller (Missouri
    Review)
Seeing Is Believing . . . — Anand Prahlad (Fifth Wednesday)

FICTION

Sons — Michael Coffey (New England Review)
The Neighbor — Mary Gordon (Image)
The Hut — Katie Chase (Joyland)
Going Across Jordan — James Lee Burke (Southern Review)
Breeding Grounds — Amy Bitterman (Chicago Quarterly)
Church Time — Ashlee Adams Crews (Southwest Review)
Père David Speaks of the Panda — Molly Patterson (Image)
Crow Fair — Thomas McGuane (Granta)
La Luz de Jesús — Don Waters (Idaho Review)
The Black Book of Conscience — Chris Adrian (Zoetrope)

Saturdays He Drove The Ford Pickup — David Brendan Hopes (Ruminate)

Girl X — Daniel A. Hoyt (Witness)

Do Not Use Quotation Marks to Indicate Irony — Anthony Wallace (Cleaver)

Long and Oval — MK Ahn (Noon)

The Wedding Visitor — Elizabeth Spencer (ZYZZYVA)

My Beautiful Life — Paul Christensen (Agni)

Transfer Station — Elise Juska (Ploughshares)

Einstein's Beach House — Jacob M. Appel (Sonora Review)

Careful, Don't Slip — Jane Delury (Yale Review)

The Lonely — Holly Wilson (Narrative)

The Drowned Maidens Club — Jaclyn Dwyer (The Pinch)

The Derrotero Method — Emily Nemens (Gettysburg Review)

The Captain — Rattawut Lapcharoensap (Granta)

Prodigal Sister — Pamela Painter (Five Points)

FM 104 — Kathryn Schwille (Memorious)

Long Tom Lookout — Nicole Cullen (Idaho Review)

Nu — Josh Emmons (Ecotone)

The Private Room — Merritt Tierce (*Dallas Noir*, Akashic Books)

Suicide Woods — Benjamin Percy (McSweeney's)

Raw Edge — Alice Mattison (Threepenny Review)

The Memory of Bones — Tegan Nia Swanson (Ecotone)

This I Believed — Matthew Vollmer (The Sun)

Karl — Alois Hotschnig (Hudson Review)

The Circle — Leslie Pietrzyk (Gettysburg Review)

Vigilante — Aimee Bender (Black Clock)

Jubilee — Michael Knight (Ploughshares)

Arlene In Five — Jerry McGahan (Ploughshares)

Next to Nothing — Stephen O'Connor (Conjunctions)

Forbearance — Charles Baxter (Michigan Quarterly Review)

Listening To Angels — William Kittredge (Narrative)

To A Good Home — Bret Anthony Johnston (Virginia Quarterly)

Wall-To-Wall Counseling — Jim Shepard (Tin House)

Ugly — Tamara Schuyler (CutBank)

The Escort — Richard Burgin (The Hopkins Review)

Antarctica — Laura van den Berg (Glimmer Train)

What Remains — Jennifer Haigh (Five Points)

Water and Oil — Michael Knight (Southern Review)

In Need of Assistance — Daniel Story (Ninth Letter)

Predator II — Michael Rose (Epoch)

The Mission — Joy Williams (Little Star)

Sonnet 126 —Douglas Trevor (Michigan Quarterly Review)

The Gatecrasher of Hyboria — Ron Austin (Natural Bridge)

The Fireside Poets — Kelsey Ronan (Michigan Quarterly Review)

The Mountain Man's Relativity Theory — S. Brady Tucker (Iowa Review)

Big Eyes, Wide Smiles — Andrew Brininstool (Third Coast)

The Disappearing — Joyce Carol Oates (American Short Fiction)

Natural Resources — Matthew Neill Null (Baltimore Review)

Frère Clément — Samuel Klonimos (Raritan)

A Hole In The Sky — Henry Bean (Black Clock)

Renters — Peter Orner (World Literature Today)

Quitting Time — Caleb Crain (Little Star)

Grief Bacon — Selena Anderson (Agni)

The Immigrant — Chaitali Sen (Colorado Review)

The Curse of the Davenports — David Gates (Paris Review)

Decorum — Edith Pearlman (Antioch Review)

Galaxies Beyond Violet — Melanie Rae Thon (Five Points)

Promotion — Michelle Latiolais (Santa Monica Review)

from *Vox Populi* — Clay Reynolds (Texas Review Press)

The Debt — Ann Beattie (Virginia Quarterly Review)

Charybdis — Cole Becher (Iowa Review)

from *I Am Not A Hero* — Pierre Autin-Grenier (Brooklyn Rail)

The Blind Pig — Jen Beagin (Juked)

Three — Jean Thompson (Southwest Review)

from *The Dark Burthen* — Michael Ives (Seneca Review)

Palace of the Brine — Kerry-Lee Powell (Malahat Review)

Harold's Problem — Max Ross (New Orleans Review)

Travelers — Landon Houle (Beloit Fiction Review)

Sunk — Gerri Brightwell (Redivider)

Last Tour — Sam Martone (Lumina)

Lexa Flying Solo — Katie Cortese (Gulf Coast)

PRESSES FEATURED IN THE PUSHCART PRIZE EDITIONS SINCE 1976

A-Minor
The Account
Agni
Ahsahta Press
Ailanthus Press
Alaska Quarterly Review
Alcheringa/Ethnopoetics
Alice James Books
Ambergris
Amelia
American Circus
American Letters and Commentary
American Literature
American PEN
American Poetry Review
American Scholar
American Short Fiction
The American Voice
Amicus Journal
Amnesty International
Anaesthesia Review
Anhinga Press
Another Chicago Magazine
Antaeus
Antietam Review
Antioch Review
Apalachee Quarterly

Aphra
Aralia Press
The Ark
Art and Understanding
Arts and Letters
Artword Quarterly
Ascensius Press
Ascent
Aspen Leaves
Aspen Poetry Anthology
Assaracus
Assembling
Atlanta Review
Autonomedia
Avocet Press
The Awl
The Baffler
Bakunin
Bamboo Ridge
Barlenmir House
Barnwood Press
Barrow Street
Bellevue Literary Review
The Bellingham Review
Bellowing Ark
Beloit Poetry Journal
Bennington Review

Bilingual Review
Black American Literature Forum
Blackbird
Black Renaissance Noire
Black Rooster
Black Scholar
Black Sparrow
Black Warrior Review
Blackwells Press
The Believer
Bloom
Bloomsbury Review
Blue Cloud Quarterly
Blueline
Blue Unicorn
Blue Wind Press
Bluefish
BOA Editions
Bomb
Bookslinger Editions
Boston Review
Boulevard
Boxspring
Briar Cliff Review
Brick
Bridge
Bridges
Brown Journal of Arts
Burning Deck Press
Cafe Review
Caliban
California Quarterly
Callaloo
Calliope
Calliopea Press
Calyx
The Canary
Canto
Capra Press
Carcanet Editions
Caribbean Writer
Carolina Quarterly
Cedar Rock

Center
Chariton Review
Charnel House
Chattahoochee Review
Chautauqua Literary Journal
Chelsea
Chicago Review
Chouteau Review
Chowder Review
Cimarron Review
Cincinnati Review
Cincinnati Poetry Review
City Lights Books
Cleveland State Univ. Poetry Ctr.
Clown War
CoEvolution Quarterly
Cold Mountain Press
The Collagist
Colorado Review
Columbia: A Magazine of Poetry and Prose
Confluence Press
Confrontation
Conjunctions
Connecticut Review
Copper Canyon Press
Cosmic Information Agency
Countermeasures
Counterpoint
Court Green
Crawl Out Your Window
Crazyhorse
Creative Nonfiction
Crescent Review
Cross Cultural Communications
Cross Currents
Crosstown Books
Crowd
Cue
Cumberland Poetry Review
Curbstone Press
Cutbank
Cypher Books
Dacotah Territory

Daedalus

Dalkey Archive Press

Decatur House

December

Denver Quarterly

Desperation Press

Dogwood

Domestic Crude

Doubletake

Dragon Gate Inc.

Dreamworks

Dryad Press

Duck Down Press

Dunes Review

Durak

East River Anthology

Eastern Washington University Press

Ecotone

El Malpensante

Eleven Eleven

Ellis Press

Empty Bowl

Epiphany

Epoch

Ergo!

Evansville Review

Exquisite Corpse

Faultline

Fence

Fiction

Fiction Collective

Fiction International

Field

Fifth Wednesday Journal

Fine Madness

Firebrand Books

Firelands Art Review

First Intensity

5 A.M.

Five Fingers Review

Five Points Press

Florida Review

Forklift

The Formalist

Four Way Books

Fourth Genre

Frontiers: A Journal of Women Studies

Fugue

Gallimaufry

Genre

The Georgia Review

Gettysburg Review

Ghost Dance

Gibbs-Smith

Glimmer Train

Goddard Journal

David Godine, Publisher

Graham House Press

Grand Street

Granta

Graywolf Press

Great River Review

Green Mountains Review

Greenfield Review

Greensboro Review

Guardian Press

Gulf Coast

Hanging Loose

Harbour Publishing

Hard Pressed

Harvard Review

Hayden's Ferry Review

Hermitage Press

Heyday

Hills

Hollyridge Press

Holmgangers Press

Holy Cow!

Home Planet News

Hudson Review

Hunger Mountain

Hungry Mind Review

Ibbetson Street Press

Icarus

Icon

Idaho Review

Iguana Press

Image

In Character

Indiana Review

Indiana Writes

Intermedia

Intro

Invisible City

Inwood Press

Iowa Review

Ironwood

Jam To-day

J Journal

The Journal

Jubilat

The Kanchenjunga Press

Kansas Quarterly

Kayak

Kelsey Street Press

Kenyon Review

Kestrel

Lake Effect

Lana Turner

Latitudes Press

Laughing Waters Press

Laurel Poetry Collective

Laurel Review

L'Epervier Press

Liberation

Linquis

Literal Latté

Literary Imagination

The Literary Review

The Little Magazine

Little Patuxent Review

Little Star

Living Hand Press

Living Poets Press

Logbridge-Rhodes

Louisville Review

Lowlands Review

Lucille

Lynx House Press

Lyric

The MacGuffin

Magic Circle Press

Malahat Review

Manoa

Manroot

Many Mountains Moving

Marlboro Review

Massachusetts Review

McSweeney's

Meridian

Mho & Mho Works

Micah Publications

Michigan Quarterly

Mid-American Review

Milkweed Editions

Milkweed Quarterly

The Minnesota Review

Mississippi Review

Mississippi Valley Review

Missouri Review

Montana Gothic

Montana Review

Montemora

Moon Pony Press

Mount Voices

Mr. Cogito Press

MSS

Mudfish

Mulch Press

Muzzle Magazine

N + 1

Nada Press

Narrative

National Poetry Review

Nebraska Poets Calendar

Nebraska Review

New America

New American Review

New American Writing

The New Criterion

New Delta Review

New Directions

New England Review

New England Review and Bread Loaf
    Quarterly

New Issues

New Letters

New Ohio Review

New Orleans Review

New South Books

New Verse News

New Virginia Review

New York Quarterly

New York University Press

Nimrod

9X9 Industries

Ninth Letter

Noon

North American Review

North Atlantic Books

North Dakota Quarterly

North Point Press

Northeastern University Press

Northern Lights

Northwest Review

Notre Dame Review

O. ARS

O. Bl k

Obsidian

Obsidian II

Ocho

Oconee Review

October

Ohio Review

Old Crow Review

Ontario Review

Open City

Open Places

Orca Press

Orchises Press

Oregon Humanities

Orion

Other Voices

Oxford American

Oxford Press

Oyez Press

Oyster Boy Review

Painted Bride Quarterly

Painted Hills Review

Palo Alto Review

Paris Press

Paris Review

Parkett

Parnassus: Poetry in Review

Partisan Review

Passages North

Paterson Literary Review

Pebble Lake Review

Penca Books

Pentagram

Penumbra Press

Pequod

Persea: An International Review

Perugia Press

Per Contra

Pilot Light

The Pinch

Pipedream Press

Pitcairn Press

Pitt Magazine

Pleasure Boat Studio

Pleiades

Ploughshares

Poems & Plays

Poet and Critic

Poet Lore

Poetry

Poetry Atlanta Press

Poetry East

Poetry International

Poetry Ireland Review

Poetry Northwest

Poetry Now

The Point

Post Road

Prairie Schooner

Prescott Street Press

Press

Promise of Learnings
Provincetown Arts
A Public Space
Puerto Del Sol
Quaderni Di Yip
Quarry West
The Quarterly
Quarterly West
Quiddity
Radio Silence
Rainbow Press
Raritan: A Quarterly Review
Rattle
Red Cedar Review
Red Clay Books
Red Dust Press
Red Earth Press
Red Hen Press
Release Press
Republic of Letters
Review of Contemporary Fiction
Revista Chicano-Riqueña
Rhetoric Review
Rivendell
River Styx
River Teeth
Rowan Tree Press
Ruminate
Runes
Russian *Samizdat*
Salamander
Salmagundi
San Marcos Press
Sarabande Books
Sea Pen Press and Paper Mill
Seal Press
Seamark Press
Seattle Review
Second Coming Press
Semiotext(e)
Seneca Review
Seven Days
The Seventies Press

Sewanee Review
Shankpainter
Shantih
Shearsman
Sheep Meadow Press
Shenandoah
A Shout In the Street
Sibyl-Child Press
Side Show
Sixth Finch
Small Moon
Smartish Pace
The Smith
Snake Nation Review
Solo
Solo 2
Some
The Sonora Review
Southern Indiana Review
Southern Poetry Review
Southern Review
Southwest Review
Speakeasy
Spectrum
Spillway
Spork
The Spirit That Moves Us
St. Andrews Press
Story
Story Quarterly
Streetfare Journal
Stuart Wright, Publisher
Subtropics
Sugar House Review
Sulfur
The Sun
Sun & Moon Press
Sun Press
Sunstone
Sweet
Sycamore Review
Tamagawa
Tar River Poetry

Teal Press
Telephone Books
Telescope
Temblor
The Temple
Tendril
Texas Slough
Think
Third Coast
13th Moon
THIS
Thorp Springs Press
Three Rivers Press
Threepenny Review
Thunder City Press
Thunder's Mouth Press
Tia Chucha Press
Tikkun
Tin House
Tombouctou Books
Toothpaste Press
Transatlantic Review
Treelight
Triplopia
TriQuarterly
Truck Press
Tupelo Press
TurnRow
Tusculum Review
Undine
Unicorn Press
University of Chicago Press
University of Georgia Press
University of Illinois Press
University of Iowa Press
University of Massachusetts Press
University of North Texas Press
University of Pittsburgh Press
University of Wisconsin Press

University Press of New England
Unmuzzled Ox
Unspeakable Visions of the Individual
Vagabond
Vallum
Verse
Verse Wisconsin
Vignette
Virginia Quarterly Review
Volt
Wampeter Press
Washington Writers Workshop
Water-Stone
Water Table
Wave Books
West Branch
Western Humanities Review
Westigan Review
White Pine Press
Wickwire Press
Wig Leaf
Willow Springs
Wilmore City
Witness
Word Beat Press
Word-Smith
World Literature Today
Wormwood Review
Writers Forum
Xanadu
Yale Review
Yardbird Reader
Yarrow
Y-Bird
Yes Yes Books
Zeitgeist Press
Zoetrope: All-Story
Zone 3
ZYZZYVA

THE PUSHCART PRIZE FELLOWSHIPS

The Pushcart Prize Fellowships Inc., a 501 (c) (3) nonprofit corporation, is the endowment for The Pushcart Prize. "Members" donated up to $249 each. "Sponsors" gave between $250 and $999. "Benefactors" donated from $1000 to $4,999. "Patrons" donated $5,000 and more. We are very grateful for these donations. Gifts of any amount are welcome. For information write to the Fellowships at PO Box 380, Wainscott, NY 11975.

E. S. Bumas
Richard Burgin
Skylar H. Burris
David Caliguiuri
Kathy Callaway
Janine Canan
Henry Carlile
Fran Castan
Chelsea Associates
Marianne Cherry
Phillis M. Choyke
Suzanne Cleary
Martha Collins
Ted Conklin
Joan Connor
John Copenhaven
Dan Corrie
Tricia Currans-Sheehan
Jim Daniels
Thadious Davis
Maija Devine
Sharon Dilworth
Edward J. DiMaio
Kent Dixon
John Duncklee
Elaine Edelman
Renee Edison & Don Kaplan
Nancy Edwards
M.D. Elevitch
Failbetter.com
Irvin Faust
Tom Filer
Susan Firer
Nick Flynn
Stakey Flythe Jr.
Peter Fogo
Linda N. Foster
Fugue
Alice Fulton
Eugene K. Garber
Frank X. Gaspar
A Gathering of the Tribes
Reginald Gibbons
Emily Fox Gordon
Philip Graham
Eamon Grennan
Lee Meitzen Grue
Habit of Rainy Nights
Rachel Hadas
Susan Hahn
Meredith Hall
Harp Strings
Jeffrey Harrison
Lois Marie Harrod
Healing Muse
Alex Henderson

Lily Henderson
Daniel Henry
Neva Herington
Lou Hertz
William Heyen
Bob Hicok
R. C. Hildebrandt
Kathleen Hill
Jane Hirshfield
Edward Hoagland
Daniel Hoffman
Doug Holder
Richard Holinger
Rochelle L. Holt
Richard M. Huber
Brigid Hughes
Lynne Hugo
Illya's Honey
Susan Indigo
Mark Irwin
Beverly A. Jackson
Richard Jackson
Christian Jara
David Jauss
Marilyn Johnston
Alice Jones
Journal of New Jersey Poets
Robert Kalich
Julia Kasdorf
Miriam Poli Katsikis
Meg Kearney
Celine Keating
Brigit Kelly
John Kistner
Judith Kitchen
Stephen Kopel
Peter Krass
David Kresh
Maxine Kumin
Valerie Laken
Babs Lakey
Linda Lancione
Maxine Landis
Lane Larson
Dorianne Laux & Joseph Millar
Sydney Lea
Donald Lev
Dana Levin
Gerald Locklin
Linda Lacione
Rachel Loden
Radomir Luza, Jr.
William Lychack
Annette Lynch
Elzabeth MacKierman
Elizabeth Macklin

Leah Maines
Mark Manalang
Norma Marder
Jack Marshall
Michael Martone
Tara L. Masih
Dan Masterson
Peter Matthiessen
Alice Mattison
Tracy Mayor
Robert McBrearty
Jane McCafferty
Rebecca McClanahan
Bob McCrane
Jo McDougall
Sandy McIntosh
James McKean
Roberta Mendel
Didi Menendez
Barbara Milton
Alexander Mindt
Mississippi Review
Martin Mitchell
Roger Mitchell
Jewell Mogan
Patricia Monaghan
Jim Moore
James Morse
William Mulvihill
Nami Mun
Carol Muske-Dukes
Edward Mycue
Deirdre Neilen
W. Dale Nelson
Jean Nordhaus
Ontario Review Foundation
Daniel Orozco
Other Voices
Pamela Painter
Paris Review
Alan Michael Parker
Ellen Parker
Veronica Patterson
David Pearce, M.D.
Robert Phillips
Donald Platt
Valerie Polichar
Pool
Horatio Potter
Jeffrey & Priscilla Potter
Marcia Preston
Eric Puchner
Tony Quagliano
Barbara Quinn
Belle Randall
Martha Rhodes

Nancy Richard
Stacey Richter
James Reiss
Katrina Roberts
Judith R. Robinson
Jessica Roeder
Martin Rosner
Kay Ryan
Sy Safransky
Brian Salchert
James Salter
Sherod Santos
R.A. Sasaki
Valerie Sayers
Maxine Scates
Alice Schell
Dennis & Loretta Schmitz
Helen Schulman
Philip Schultz
Shenandoah
Peggy Shinner
Vivian Shipley
Joan Silver
Skyline
John E. Smelcer
Raymond J. Smith
Joyce Carol Smith
Philip St. Clair
Lorraine Standish
Maureen Stanton
Michael Steinberg
Sybil Steinberg
Jody Stewart
Barbara Stone
Storyteller Magazine
Bill & Pat Strachan
Julie Suk
Sun Publishing
Sweet Annie Press
Katherine Taylor
Pamela Taylor
Elaine Jerranova
Susan Terris
Marcelle Thiébaux
Robert Thomas
Andrew Tonkovich
Pauls Toutonghi
Juanita Torrence-Thompson
William Trowbridge
Martin Tucker
Jeannette Valentine
Victoria Valentine
Hans Van de Bovenkamp
Tino Villanueva
William & Jeanne Wagner
BJ Ward

Susan O. Warner
Rosanna Warren
Margareta Waterman
Michael Waters
Sandi Weinberg
Andrew Weinstein
Jason Wesco
West Meadow Press
Susan Wheeler
Dara Wier
Ellen Wilbur
Galen Williams
Marie Sheppard Williams

Eleanor Wilner
Irene K. Wilson
Steven Wingate
Sandra Wisenberg
Wings Press
Robert W. Witt
Margo Wizansky
Matt Yurdana
Christina Zawadiwsky
Sander Zulauf
ZYZZYVA

SUSTAINING MEMBERS

Agni
Betty Adcock
Anonymous (2)
Dick & L.N. Allen
Russell Allen
Carolyn Alessio
Jacob M. Appel
Philip Appleman
Linda Aschbrenner
Renee Ashley
Jean Auel
Jim Barnes
Catherine Barnett
Ann Beattie
Joe David Bellamy
Madison Smartt Bell
Beloit Poetry Journal
Linda Bierds
Bridge Works
Rosellen Brown
Fran Castan
David S. Caldwell
Dan Chaon
Chelsea Associates
Suzanne Cleary
Martha Collins
Linda Coleman
Ted Conklin
Bernard Connors
Daniel L. Dolgin & Loraine F. Gardner
Elaine Edelman
Dallas Ernst
Ben & Sharon Fountain
Eagene Garber
Robert L. Giron
Emily Fox Gordon
Susan Hahn
The Healing Muse
Alexander C. Henderson

Bob Hicok
Kathleen Hill
Helen & Frank Houghton
Mark Irwin
Diane Johnson
Christian Jara
Don & René Kaplan
Edmund Keeley
Judith Kitchen
Peter Krass
Maxine Kumin
Wally Lamb
Linda Lancione
Sydney Lea
Thomas Lux
William Lychack
Norma Marder
Michael Martone
Peter Matthiessen
Alice Mattison
Robert McBrearty
Jane McCafferty
Deirdre Neilen
Neltje
Daniel Orozco
Pamela Painter
Horatio Potter
Jeffrey Potter
David B. Pearce, M.D.
Barbara & Warren Phillips
Kay Ryan
Elizabeth R. Rea
James Reiss
Stacey Richter
Sy Safransky
Valerie Sayers
Maxine Scates
Alice Schell
Dennis Schmitz

CONTRIBUTING SMALL PRESSES FOR PUSHCART PRIZE XXXIX

A

aaduna, 144 Genesee St., Ste. 102-259, Auburn, NY 13021

ABZ Press, PO Box 2746, Huntington, WV 25757-2746

Able Muse Review, 467 Saratoga Ave., #602, San Jose, CA 95129

Accents Publishing, P.O. Box 910456, Lexington, KY 40591-0456

The Account, 4607 N. Campbell Ave., Apt. 2, Chicago, IL 60625

Acorn, 115 Conifer Lane, Walnut Creek, CA 94598

The Adroit Journal, 1223 Westover Rd., Stamford, CT 06902-1037

Agni Magazine, Boston University, 236 Bay State Rd., Boston, MA 02215

Airlie Press, P.O. Box 434, Monmouth, OR 97361

Airways, P.O. Box 1109, Sandpoint, ID 83864

Alaska Quarterly Review, 3211 Providence Dr., Anchorage, AK 99508-4614

Aldrich Press, 24600 Mountain Ave., #35, Hemet, CA 92544

Alice James Books, 114 Prescott St., Farmington, ME 04938

Alternating Current, P.O. Box 183, Palo Alto, CA 94302

American Athenaeum, P.O. Box 2107, Lusby, MD 20657

American Arts Quarterly, 915 Broadway, Ste. 1104, New York, NY 10010

The American Scholar, 1606 New Hampshire Ave. NW, Washington, DC 20009

American Short Fiction, P.O. Box 4152, Austin ,TX 78765

Ampersand Books, 5040 10th Ave. So., Gulfport, FL 33707

Anaphora, 5755 E. River Rd., #2201, Tucson, AZ 85750

Animal, 264 Fallen Palm Dr., Casselberry, FL 32707

Annapurna Magazine, 4408 Sayre Dr., Princeton, NJ 08540

Anomalous Press, 98 Rock Island Rd., Quincy MA 02169

The Antioch Review, PO Box 148, Yellow Springs, OH 45387-0148

Antrim House Books, 21 Goodrich Rd., Simsbury, CT 06070

Any Puppets Press, 6065 Chabot Rd., Oakland, CA 94618

Apeiron Review, 1173 Ridgeview Dr., Waynesboro, PA 17268

Appalachian Heritage, P.O. Box 599, Shepherdstown, WV 25443

Apple Valley Review, 88 South 3rd St., #336, San Jose, CA 95113

Apryl Skies, 13547 Ventura Blvd., Sherman Oaks, CA 91423

apt, 2643 Maryland Ave., #3, Baltimore, MD 21218

Arcadia Magazine, 9616 Nichols Rd., Oklahoma City, OK 73120

Arizona Authors, 6145 West Echo Lane, Glendale, AZ 85302

ArmChair/Shotgun, 377 Flatbush Ave., No. 3, Brooklyn, NY 11238

Arroyo Literary Review, C.S.U. 25800 Carlos Bee Blvd., Hayward, CA 94542

Arts & Ideas, P.O. Box 1130, West Tisbury, MA 02575

Ascent, Concordia College, 901 8ths St. S., Moorhead, MN 56562

Ashland Creek Press, 2305 Ashland St., Ste. C417, Ashland, OR 97520

Asian American Literary Review, 1110 Severnview Dr., Crownsville, MD 21032

Askew, P.O. Box 559, Ventura, CA 93002

Asymptote Journal, 40 Butler St., 3rd Floor, Brooklyn, NY 11231

At Length, 716 W. Cornwallis Rd., Durham, NC 27707

Atelier26 Books, 4207 SE Woodstock Blvd., #421, Portland, OR 97206

Atlanta Review, PO Box 8248, Atlanta, GA 31106

The Atlas Review, 54 India St., Apt. 3, Brooklyn, NY 11222

Atticus Books, 39 Longview Ave., Madison, NJ 07940

Augury Books, 305 E. 12th St., Apt 1, New York, NY 10003

B

The Backwaters Press, 3502 North 52nd St., Omaha, NE 68104-3506

The Bacon Review, 19 S. Emerson St., Denver, CO 80209

Bacopa, P.O.Box 358396, Gainesville, FL 32635-8396

Ballard Street Poetry Journal, 124 Alvarado Ave., Worcester, MA 01604

The Baltimore Review, 6514 Maplewood Rd., Baltimore, MD 21212

Bamboo Ridge Press, PO Box 61781, Honolulu, HI 96839-1781

Bartleby Snopes, 20741 Hampshire Circle, Lakeville, MN 55044

Bat City Review, 208 West 21st St., Stop B 5000, Austin, TX 78712

Bayou Magazine, U.N.O., 2000 Lake Shore Dr., New Orleans, LA 70148

Beaten Track Publishing, 11 Manor Crescent, Burscough Lancashire L40 7TW, UK

Belle Reve Literary Journal, www.bellerevejournal.com

Bellevue Literary Review, NYU School of Medicine, 550 First Ave, OBV-A612, New York, NY 10016

Bellingham Review, MS-9053, WWU, Bellingham, WA 98225

Beloit Fiction Journal, 700 College St., Box 11, Beloit, WI 53511

Beloit Poetry Journal, PO Box 151, Farmington, ME 04938

Bennett & Hastings Publishing, 2400 NW 80th St., #254, Seattle WA 98117

Big River Poetry Review, 4550 North Blvd., #220, Baton Rouge, LA 70806

Big Table, 383 Langley Rd., #2, Newton Centre, MA 02459

Birch Brook Press, P.O. Box 81, Delhi, NY 13753

Birdfeast, 656 Old Lincoln Highway, Ligonier, PA 15658

Birmingham Poetry Review, English Dept., UAB, Birmingham, AL 35294

BkMk Press, UMKC, 5100 Rockhill Rd., Kansas City, MO 64110-2446

Black Clock, CalArts, 24700 McBean Parkway, Valencia, CA 91355

Black Hills Writers Group, P.O. Box 1539, Rapid City, SD 57709

Black Scat Books, 930 Central Park Ave., Lakeport, CA 95453

Blackbird, P.O. Box 843082, Richmond, VA 23284-3082

Blacktop Passages, 15420 Livingston Ave., Apt. 3009, Lutz, FL 33559

blink-ink, P.O. Box 5, North Branford, CT 06471

Bloodroot, P.O. Box 322, Thetford Center, VT 05075

Bloom, 5482 Wilshire Blvd., #1616, Los Angeles, CA 90036

Blue Cubicle Press, P.O. Box 250382, Plano, TX 75025-0382

Blue Fifth Review, 267 Lark Meadow Circle, Bluff City, TN 37618

Blue Hour Press, 640 NE 10th St., McMinnville, OR 97128

Blue Lyra Review, 2305 W. Horizon Ridge Pkwy, Apt #424, Henderson, NV 89052

Blue Mesa Review, UNM, MCS 03-2170, Albuquerque, NM 87131-0001

Blue Scarab Press, P.O. Box 2803, Pawleys Island, SC 29585

Blue Unicorn, 22 Avon Rd., Kensington, CA 94707

Bluestem, English Dept., Eastern Illinois University, Charleston, IL 61920-3011

Bodega Magazine, 468 Smith St., #3, Brooklyn, NY 11231

Body, Mezivrsi 87/17, 147 00 Praha 4, Czech Republic

The Boiler Journal, 1818 Leicester St., Garland, TX 75044

Book Thug, 260 Ryding Ave., Toronto ON M6N 1H5, Canada

Booth, English Dept., Butler Univ., 4600 Sunset Ave., Indianapolis, IN 46208

Border Crossing, Lake Superior State Univ., 650 W. Easterday Ave., Sault Sainte Marie, MI 49783

Border Senses, 1500 Texas St., #up, El Paso, TX 79901

Boston Review, P.O. Box 425786, Cambridge, MA 02142

Bottom Dog Press, P.O. Box 425, Huron, OH 44839

Boulevard, 6614 Clayton Rd., PMB #325, Richmond Heights, MO 63117

Bound Off, P.O. Box 821, Cedar Rapids, IA 52406-0821

Box of Jars, 453 Washington Ave., #5A, Brooklyn, NY 11238

Boxcar Poetry Review, 630 S. Kenmore Ave., #206, Los Angeles, CA 90005

Brain, Child, 341 Newtown Turnpike, Wilton, CT 06897

Brevity, English Dept., Ohio University, Athens, OH 45701

The Briar Cliff Review, 3303 Rebecca St., Sioux City, IA 51104-2100

Brick, P.O. Box 609, Stn. P, Toronto, Ontario, M5S 2Y4, Canada

BrickHouse Books, 306 Suffolk Rd., Baltimore, MD 21218

Brilliant Corners, 700 College Place, Williamsport, PA 17701

Broad Street, P.O. Box 842010, Virginia Commonwealth Univ., Richmond, VA 23284

Broadkill Review, P.O. Box 63, Milton, DE 19968

Brooklyn Arts Press, 154 N. 9th St., #1, Brooklyn, NY 11211

The Brooklyn Rail, 845 Hancock St., Brooklyn, NY 11253

Bull City Press, 1217 Odyssey Dr., Durham, NC 27713

Burntdistrict, 2016 S. 185th St., Omaha, NE 68130

Burrow Press, P.O. Box 533709, Orlando, FL 32853

C

cahoodaloodaling, 1802 W. Maryland Ave., #3067, Phoenix, AZ 85015

Caitlin Press, 8100 Alderwood Rd., Halfmoon Bay, VON 1Y1, BC

California Quarterly, P.O. Box 7126, Orange, CA 92863

The Camel Saloon, 11190 Abbotts Station Dr., Johns Creek, GA 30097

Camera Obscura, P.O. Box 2356, Addison, TX 75069

The Carolina Quarterly, Box 3520, UNC, Chapel Hill, NC 27599-3520

Cartagena Journal, 3727 Monroe St., Columbia, SC 29205

Carve, P.O. Box 701510, Dallas, TX 75370

Casa de Snapdragon, 12901 Bryce Ave. NE, Albuquerque, NM 87112

Catamaran Literary Reader, 1050 River St., #113, Santa Cruz, CA 95060

Cave Moon Press, 7704 Mieras Rd., Yakima, WA 98901

Cave Wall Press, PO Box 29546, Greensboro, NC 27429-9546

Cease, Cows, 20300 Burr Oak Dr., #B, Coupland, TX 78615

Cerise Press, 10510 Parker St., Omaha, NE 68114

The Chattahoochee Review, 555 North Indian Creek Dr., Clarkston, GA 30021

Chatter House Press, 7915 S. Emerson Ave., Ste. B303, Indianapolis, IN 46237

Chautauqua, UNC Wilmington, 601 South College Rd., Wilmington, NC 28403

Chelsea Station Editions, 362 West 36th St., #2R, New York, NY 10018

Chicago Poetry, 2626 W. Iowa, 2F, Chicago, IL 60622

Chicago Review, 935 E. 60th St., Chicago, IL 60637

Cider Press Review, P.O. Box 33384, San Diego, CA 92163

Cimarron Review, Oklahoma State Univ., 205 Morrill Hal, Stillwater, OK 74078

Cincinnati Review, Univ. of Cincinnati, PO Box 210069, Cincinnati, OH 45221-0069

Cincinnati Writers Project, 79 W. Broad St., Hopewell, NJ 08525

Citizens for Decent Literature Press, 5 Morningside Dr., Jacksonville, IL 62650

Citron Review, 933 Pineview Ridge Ct., Ballwin, MO 63201

Cleaver Magazine, 8250 Shawnee St., Philadelphia, PA 19118

Clockhouse, 900 W. 190th St., #2M, New York, NY 10040

Coal City Review, English Dept., University of Kansas, Lawrence, KS 66045

Codex Journal, English Dept., Eastern Illinois University, 600 Lincoln Ave., Charleston, IL 61920

Codorus Press, 34-43 Crescent St., Ste. 1S, Astoria, NY 11106

The Collagist, Warren Wilson College, PO 9000, CPO 6205, Ashville, NC 28815

Colorado Review, Colorado State Univ., Fort Collins, CO 80523-9105

Columbia Poetry Review, 600 South Michigan Ave., Chicago, IL 60605-1996

Comment, 185 Young St., Hamilton, ON Canada LN8 1V9

The Common, Frost Library, P.O. Box 5000, Amherst College, Amherst, MA 01002

Confrontation, English Dept., LIU/Post, Brookville, NY 11548

Conium Press, 4753 Eagleridge Circle, #302, Pueblo, CO 81008

Conjunctions, Bard College, Annandale-on-Hudson, NY 12504-5000

Consequence Magazine, P.O. Box 323, Cohasset, MA 02025

Constellations, 127 Lake View Ave., Cambridge, MA 02138

Conte, AAB 321 32000 Campus Dr., Salisbury, MD 21804

Copper Canyon Press, PO Box 271, Port Townsend, WA 98368

Counterexample Poetics, 13 Sixth St., Englewood Cliffs, NJ 07632

Court Green, 600 South Michigan Ave., Chicago, IL 60605-1996

Cowfeather Press, P.O. Box 620216, Middleton, WI 53562

Crab Orchard Review, SIUC, 1000 Faner Drive, MC 4503, Carbondale, IL 62901

Crack the Spine, 29 Park Place, #1506, Hattiesburg, MS 39402

Crazyhorse, College of Charleston, 66 George St., Charleston, SC 29424

The Cream City Review, UW-Milwaukee, P.O. Box 413, Milwaukee, WI 53201

Creative Nonfiction, 5501 Walnut St., Ste. 202, Pittsburgh, PA 15232

Cross-Cultural Communications, 239 Wynsum Ave., Merrick, NY 11566-4725

Cultural Weekly, 215 S. Santa Fe Ave., Studio 19, Los Angeles, CA 90012

Cumberland River Review, 333 Murfreesboro Rd., Nashville, IN 37210-2877

The Curator, 227 16th St., Seal Beach, CA 90740

CutBank, 1626 Mason Lane, Charlottesville, VA 22903

Cutthroat, A Journal of the Arts, PO Box 2414, Durango, CO 81302

D

Daniel & Daniel Publishers, P.O. Box 2790, McKinleyville, CA 95519-2790

Dark Moon Books, 3412 Imperial Palm Dr., Largo, FL 33771

Deadly Chaps, 32 Union Square East, #1212-A, New York, NY 10002

december, P.O. Box 16130, St. Louis, MO 63105

decomP, 726 Carriage Hill Dr., Athens, OH 45701

Deep South, 203 Iris Lane, Lafayette, LA 70506

The Delmarva Review, PO Box 544, St. Michaels, MD 21663

The Destroyer, 3166 Barbara Court, LA., CA 90068

Divinity Press, 1203 Hurlock Court, Bear, DE 19701

The DMQ Review, 16393 Bonnie Lane, Los Gatos, CA 95032

The Doctor T. J. Eckleburg Review, 1717 Massachusetts Ave., NW, #104, Washington, DC 20036

Dos Gatos Press, 1310 Crestwood Rd., Austin, TX 78722

drafthorse literary journal, Lincoln Memorial University, P.O. Box 2005, Harrogate, TN 37752

Dragoncor Productions, 12530 Culver Blvd., #3, Los Angeles, CA 90066-6622

Dragonfly Press, P.O. Box 746, Columbia, CA 95310

The Drum Literary Magazine, 19 Pelham Rd., Weston, MA 02493

Drunken Boat, c/o Shankar, 119 Main St., Chester, CT 06412

E

ecotone, UNCW, 601 S. College Rd., Wilmington, NC 28403

Educe Journal, 7 ½ W. Franklin, Boise, ID 83702

Edwin E. Smith Publishing, 199 Clark Rd., McRae, AR 72102

Ekphrasis, PO Box 161236, Sacramento, CA 95816-1236

El Zarape Press, 1413 Jay Ave., McAllen, TX 78504

Eleven Eleven Journal, 1111 Eighth St., S.F., CA 94107

Emby Press, 3675 Essex Ave., Atlanta, GA 30339

Encircle Publications, P.O. Box 187, Farmington, ME 04938

Enizagam, Oakland School for the Arts, 530 18th St., Oakland, CA 94612

Epoch, 251 Goldwin Smith Hall, Cornell University, Ithaca NY 14853-3201

Escape Into Life, 108 Gladys Drive, Normal, IL 61761

Evening Street Press, 625 Edgecliff Drive, Columbus, OH 43235

Event, PO Box 2503, New Westminster, BC, V3L 5B2, Canada

Every Day Publishing, P.O. Box 2482, 349 W. Georgia St., Vancouver BC, Canada V6B 3W7

F

The Farallon Review, 1017 L St., #348, Sacramento, CA 95814

Faultline, English Dept., UC Irvine, Irvine, CA 92697-2650

The Feral Press, P.O. Box 358, Oyster Bay, NY 11771

Fiction International, SDSU, San Diego, CA 92182-8140

Fiction Week Literary Review, 887 South Rice Rd., Ojai, CA 93023

The Fiddlehead, P.O. Box 4400, Univ. New Brunswick, Fredericton, NB E3B 5A3

Field, 50 North Professor St., Oberlin, OH 44074-1091

Fifth Wednesday, P.O. Box 4033, Lisle, 1L 60532-9033

Finishing Line Press, P.O. Box 1626, Georgetown, KY 40324

The First Line, PO Box 250382, Plano, TX 75025-0382

5 AM, Box 205, Spring Church, PA 15686

Five Chapters, 387 Third Ave., Brooklyn, NY 11215

Five Points, Georgia State University, University Plaza, Atlanta, GA 30303-3083

Flash Frontier, P.O. Box 910, Kerikeri 0245, New Zealand

Fleur-de-Lis Press, 851 So. Fourth St., Louisville, KY 40203

Flint Hills Review, Campus Box 4019, 1200 Commercial St., Emporia, KS 66801

The Florida Review, P.O. Box 161346, Orlando, FL 32816-1346

Flycatcher, 5595 Lake Island Dr., Atlanta, GA 30327

Flying House, 1622 Hatch Pl., Downers Grove, IL 60516

Flyway, English Dept., 206 Ross Hall, Iowa State Univ., Ames, IA 50011

Folded Word, 79 Tracy Way, Meredith, NH 03253

Fomite, 58 Peru St., Burlington, VT 05401-8606

Four Chambers Press, 1005 E. Moreland, St., Phoenix, AZ 85006

Fourth Genre, 235 Bessey Hall, East Lansing, MI 48824-1033

The Fourth River, Chatham University, 1 Woodland Rd., Pittsburgh, PA 15232

Free State Review, 3637 Black Rock Rd., Upperco, MO 21155

Freelancelot Publishing, 7001 Seaview Ave., NW, #160, PMB 527, Seattle, WA 98117

The Freeman, 600 Merrimon Ave., Apt 18B, Asheville, NC 28804

Fugue, University of Idaho, 875 Perimeter Dr., MS 1102, Moscow, ID 83844-1102

Full Grown People, 106 Tripper Ct., Charlottesville, VA 22903

Full of Crow, P.O. Box 1123, Easton, PA 18044

Full of Crow Fiction, 2929 Nicol, Oakland, CA 94602

G

Garden Oak Press, 1953 Huffstatler St., Ste. A, Rainbow, CA 92028

Gargoyle Magazine, 3819 13th St. N., Arlington, VA 22201-4922

Gaspereau Press, 47 Church Ave., Kentville, Nova Scotia, Canada B4N 2M7

Gemini Magazine, PO Box 1485, Onset, MA 02558

The Georgia Review, University of Georgia, Athens, GA 30602-9009

The Gettysburg Review, Gettysburg College, Box 2446, Gettysburg, PA 17325-1491

Ghost Ocean Magazine, 5234 N. Wayne Ave., #1, Chicago, IL 60640

Ghost Town Literary Review, 1516 Myra St., Redlands, CA 92373

Gigantic, 496 Broadway, #3, Brooklyn, NY 11211

Gigantic Sequins, 2335 E. Fletcher St., Philadelphia, PA 19125

Gilbert Magazine, 4117 Pebblebrook Circle, Minneapolis, MN 55437

Gival Press, PO Box 3812, Arlington, VA 22203

Glass Lyre Press, P.O. Box 2693, Glenview, IL 60026

Glimmer Train Press, P.O. Box 80430, Portland, OR 97280-1430

Glint Literary Journal, Fayetteville State Univ., 1200 Murchison Rd., Fayetteville, NC 28301

Gold Man Review, P.O. Box 8202, Salem, OR 97303

Gold Wake Press, 5108 Avalon Dr., Randolph, MA 02368

Good Sheppard Press, 110 Landers St., #2, San Francisco, CA 94114

Grain, Box 67, Saskatoon, SK, S7K 3K1, Canada

Granta, 12 Addison Ave., Holland Park, London W11 4QR, England

Gravel, University of Arkansas at Monticello, Monticello, AR 71655

Great River Review, PO Box 406, Red Wing, MN 55066

great weather for MEDIA, 515 Broadway, #2B, New York, NY 10012

Green Bay Group, 793 E. Foothill Blvd., San Luis Obispo, CA 93405-1615

The Greensboro Review, UNC Greensboro, Greensboro, NC 27402-6170

The Greensilk Journal, 1459 Redland Rd., Cross Junction, VA 22625

Grey Sparrow Press, P.O. Box 211664, St. Paul, MN 55121

Grist, 301 McClung Tower, Univ. of Tennessee, Knoxville, TN 37996

Grolier Poetry Press, 6 Plympton St., Cambridge, MA 02138

Gulf Coast, University of Houston, Houston, TX 77204-3013

H

hack writers, 7 Cromwell Rd. Cleethorpes. DN 35 0AL, UK

Haight Ashbury Literary Journal, 558 Joost Ave., San Francisco, CA 94127

Hamilton Arts & Letters, 92 Stanley Ave., Hamilton ON, L8P 2L3, Canada

Hamilton Stone Review, P.O. Box 43, Maplewood, NJ 07040

Hand Fashioned Media, 300 South Central Ave., #C55, Hartsdale, NY 10530

Hand Type Press, P.O. Box 3941, Minneapolis, MN 55403-0941

Harbour Publishing Co., P.O. Box 219, Madeira Park, BC V0N 2H0 Canada

The Harlequin, 2001 Westheimer Rd., #255, Houston, TX 77098

Harpur Palate, PO Box 6000, Binghamton University, Binghamton, NY 13902

Harvard Review, Lamont Library–Harvard University, Cambridge, MA 02138

Hayden's Ferry Review, A.S.U., P.O. Box 870302, Tempe, AZ 85287-0302

Headmistress Press, P.O. Box 275, Eagle Rock, MO 65641

The Healing Muse, 618 Irving Ave., Syracuse, NY 13210

Heavy Feather Review, 4416 Grayson St., Kettering, OH 45429

Hedgerow Books, 71 South Pleasant St., Amherst, MA 01002

Heron's Nest, 476 Guilford Circle, Marietta, GA 30068

Heyday, P.O. Box 9145, Berkeley, CA 94709

Hippocampus Magazine, 222 E. Walnut St., #2, Lancaaster, PA 17602

Hobart, PO Box 1658, Ann Arbor, MI 48106

Hobble Creek Review, PO Box 3511, West Wendover, NV 89883

Hobblebush Books, 17A Old Milford Rd., Brookline, NH 03033

The Hollins Critic, P.O. Box 9538, Roanoke, VA 24020-1538

Home Planet News, PO Box 455, High Falls, NY 12440

Homebound, P.O. Box 1442, Pawcatuck, CT 06379

The Hoot and Hare Review, 309 Sarabande Dr., Cary, NC 27513

Horror Society Press, 6635 W. Happy Valley Rd., Ste. A104, #218, Glendale, AZ 85310

Hot Metal Bridge, University of Pittsburgh, English Dept., 4200 Fifth Ave., Pittsburgh, PA 15260

Hotel Amerika, Columbia College, 600 S. Michigan Ave., Chicago, IL 60605

The Hudson Review, 684 Park Ave., New York, NY 10065

Huizache, UHV University Center, #130, 3007 N. Ben Wilson, Victoria, TX 77901

Hunger Mountain, 36 College St., Montpelier, VT 05602

Hydeout Press, 1262 Fry Ave., Lakewood, OH 44107

I

I-70 Review, 5021 S. Tierney Dr., Independence, MO 64055

iARTistas, 604 Vale St., Bloomington, IL 61701

Ibbetson Street Press, 25 School Street, Somerville, MA 02143

The Idaho Review, Boise State Univ., 1910 University Dr., Boise, ID 83725

Illya's Honey, PO Box 700865, Dallas, TX 75370

Image, 3307 Third Avenue West, Seattle, WA 98119

Immagine&Poesia, C. Galileo Ferraris 75, 10128, Torino, Italy

India Currents, 1885 Lundy Ave., Ste. 220, San Jose, CA 95131-9983

Indiana Review, 1020 E. Kirkwood Ave., Bloomington, IN 47405-7103

The Inflectionist Review, 11322 SE 45th Ave., Portland, OR 97222

Interim, UNLV, 4505 Maryland Pkwy, Box 455011, Las Vegas, NV 89154-5011

Intranslation, 85 Hancock St., Brooklyn, NY 11233

The Iowa Review, 308 EPB, University of Iowa, Iowa City, IA 52242

Iris G. Press, 1716 Swarr Run Rd., J-108, Lancaster, PA 17601

Iron Horse, English Dept., Texas Tech Univ., Lubbock, TX 79409-3091

J

J Journal, 524 West 59th St., 7th fl, NY, NY 10019

Jabberwock Review, Mississippi State Univ., Drawer E, Mississippi State, MS 39762

Jacar Press, 6617 Deerview Trail, Durham, NC 27712

Jaded Ibis Press, P.O. Box 61122, Seattle, WA 98141-6112

Jelly Bucket, 521 Lancaster Ave., Case Annex 467, Richmond, KY 40475

Jewish Women's Literary Annual, 40 Central Park So., #6D, New York, NY 10019

jmww, 2105 E. Lamley St., Baltimore, MD 21231

The Journal, Ohio State Univ., 164 West 17th Ave., Columbus, OH 43210

The Journal of Experimental Fiction, 12 Simpson St., #D, Geneva, IL 60134

Joyland, 302-3R Nassau Ave., Brooklyn, NY 11222
Juked, 3941 Newdale Rd., #26, Chevy Chase, MD 20815

K

Kartika Review, API Cultural Center, 934 Brannan St., San Francisco, CA 94103

Kelsey Review, Mercer County Community College, 1200 Old Trenton Rd., West Windsor, NJ 08550-3407

Kenyon Review, Finn House, 102 W. Wiggin St., Gambier, OH 43022

Kestrel, 264000, Fairmont State Univ., 1201 Locust Ave., Fairmont, WV 26554

Kin, 425 S. 5th St., Brooklyn, NY 11211

Kind of a Hurricane, Press, 1817 Green Place, Ormond Beach, FL 32174

Korean Expatriate Literature, 11533 Promenade Drive, Santa Fe Springs, CA 90670

Kweli Journal, P.O. Box 693, New York, NY 10021

KY Story, 2111B Fayette Dr., Richmond, KY 40475

L

The Labletter, 3712 N. Broadway, #241, Chicago, IL 60613

Lake Effect, 4951 College Drive, Erie, PA 16563-1501

Lalitamba, 110 West 86th St., #5D, New York, NY 10024

Lamar University Press, 400 MLK Blvd., P.O. Box 10009, Beaumont, TX 77710

Lascaux Review, Parrish, Lessingstr 27, 55543 Bad Kreuznach, Germany

Lavender Review, P.O. Box 275, Eagle Rock, MO 65641-0275

Leaf Press, Box 416, Lantzville, BC, V0R 2H0 Canada

Ledgetop Publishing, P.O. Box 105, Richmond, MA 02154

The Lindenwood Review, 209 S. Kingshighway, St. Charles, MO 63301-1695

Lips, 7002 Blvd. East, #2-26G, Guttenberg, NJ 07093

The Literarian, 17 East 47th St., New York, NY 10017

Literary Juice, 511 Travers Circle, Apt. C, Mishawaka, IN 46545

The Literary Review, 285 Madison Ave./M-GH2-01, Madison, NJ 07940

Little Fiction, 728 Willard Ave., Toronto, ON M6S 3S5, Canada

Little Star, 107 Bank St., New York, NY 10014

The Lives You Touch, P.O. Box 276, Gwynedd Valley, PA 19437-0276

Livingston Press, Station 22, Univ. of West Alabama, Livingston, AL 35470

Local Gems Press, 408 7th St., East Northport, NY 11731

Lookout Books, 601 South College Rd., Wilmington, NC 28403

Loose Leaves Publishing, 4218 Allison Rd., Tucson, AZ 85712

Los Angeles Review, PO Box 2458, Redmond, WA 98073

The Louisville Review, Spalding Univ., 851 South Fourth St., Louisville, KY 40203

Loving Healing Press Inc., 5145 Pontiac Trail, Ann Arbor, MI 48105-9279

low key/slate, #262, Street 31, F-10/1, Islamabad, Pakistan

Lowestoft Chronicle Press, 1925 Massachusetts Ave., Cambridge, MA 02140

Lumina, 1 Mead Way, Bronxville, NY 10708

Lunch Ticket, Antioch University, 400 Corporate Pointe, Culver City, CA 90230

M

The MacGuffin, 18600 Haggerty Rd., Livonia, MI 48152

make/shift, PO Box 2697, Venice, CA 90294

The Manhattan Review, 440 Riverside Dr., #38, New York, NY 10027

Manic D Press, P.O. Box 410804, San Francisco, CA 94141

Marin Poetry Center, P.O. Box 9091, San Rafael, CA 94912

The Massachusetts Review, South College 126047, Amherst, MA 01003-7140

The Masters Review, 1824 NW Couch St., Portland, OR 97209

Matchbook, 31 Berkley Place #2, Buffalo, NY 14209

Matter Press, P.O. Box 704, Wynnewood, PA 19096

Mayhaven Publishing, P.O. Box 557, Mahomet, IL 61853

The McNeese Review, Box 93465, McNeese State University, Lake Charles, LA 70609-2655

McSweeney's, 849 Valencia, San Francisco, CA 94110

Memorious, 409 N. Main St., 2A, Hattiesburg, MS 39401

Menacing Hedge, 424 SW Kenyon St., Seattle, WA 98106

Metazen, Ulrich-von-Huttenstr. 8, 81739 Munich, Germany

Michigan Quarterly Review, 915 E. Washington St., Ann Arbor, MI 48109-1070

Mid-American Review, Bowling Green State Univ., Bowling Green, OH 43403

Middle Gray Magazine, 88 Washington St., Brighton, MA 02135

Middlewest, 5821 N. Winthrop Ave., #25, Chicago, IL 60660

Midway Journal, 8 Durham St., #3, Somerville, MA 02143

Midwestern Gothic, 957 E. Grant, Des Plaines, IL 60016

Mina-Helwig Company, 8732 Nottingham Place, La Jolla, CA 92037

the minnesota review, Virginia Tech, ASPECT, Blacksburg, VA 24061

MiPOesias, 604 Vale St., Bloomington, IL 61701

Miramar, 342 Oliver Rd., Santa Barbara, CA 93109

Misfit Magazine, 143 Furman St., Schenectady, NY 12304

The Missing Slate, #262, Street 31, F-10/1, Islamabad, Pakistan

Mississippi Review, 118 College Dr. #5144, Hattiesburg, MS 39406

The Missouri Review, 357 McReynolds Hall, Univ. of Missouri, Columbia, MO 65211

Mobius, the Journal of Social Change, 505 Christianson St., Madison, WI 53714

mojo, WSU, English Dept., Box 14, 1845 Fairmount St., Wichita, KS 67260-0014

Moonrise Press, P.O. Box 4288, Los Angeles—Sunland, CA 91041

Mount Hope, Roger Williams Univ., One Old Ferry Rd., Bristol, RI 02806

Mouse Tales Press, 19558 Green Mountain Dr., Newhall, CA 91321

Mouthfeel Press, 15307 Mineral, El Paso, TX 79928

Muddy River Poetry Review, 15 Eliot St., Chestnut Hill, MA 02467

Muse-Pie Press, 73 Pennington Ave., Passaic, NJ 07055

N

n + 1, 68 Jay St., #405, Brooklyn, NY 11201

NANO Fiction, P.O. Box 2188, Tuscaloosa, AL 35403

Narrative, 2443 Fillmore St., #214, San Francisco, CA 94115

A Narrow Fellow, 4302 Kinloch Rd., Louisville, KY 40207

Natural Bridge, English Dept., One University Blvd., St. Louis, MO 63121-4400

Naugatuck River Review, PO Box 368, Westfield, MA 01085

Nazar Look Journal, Luntrasului 16, 900338 Constanta, Romania

Neon, 8 Village Close, Wilberforce Rd., Norwich, Norfolk NR5 8NA, UK

New American Writing, 369 Molino Ave., Mill Valley, CA 94941

New Delta Review, English Dept., 15 Allen Hall, L.S.U., Baton Rouge, LA 70803

New England Review, Middlebury College, Middlebury, VT 05753

The New Guard, P.O. Box 866, Wells, ME 04090

New Letters, UMKC, 5100 Rockhill Rd., Kansas City, MO 64110-2499

New Libri Press, 4230 95th Ave., SE, Mercer Island, WA 98040

New Michigan Press, 8058 E. 7th St., Tucson, AZ 85710

New Ohio Review, Ohio University, 360 Ellis Hall, Athens, OH 45701

New Orleans Review, Loyola University, 6363 St. Charles Ave., New Orleans, LA 70118

The New Orphic Review, 706 Mill St., Nelson, B.C. V1L 4S5 Canada

new south, Campus Box 1894, Georgia State Univ., Atlanta, GA 30303-3083

New Verse News, Les Belles Maisons H-11, J1. Serpong Raya, Serpong Utara, Tangerang-Baten 15310, Indonesia

Newfound Journal, 3506 Manchaca Rd., Austin, TX 78704

Night Ballet Press, 123 Glendale Court, Elyria, OH 44035

Nimrod, 800 South Tucker Dr., Tulsa, OK 74104

1966: A Journal of Creative Nonfiction, One Trinity Place, San Antonio, TX 78212-7200

Ninth Letter, 608 S. Wright St., Urbana, IL 61801

Niteblade, 11323-126 St., Edmonton, Alberta, Canada T5M 0R5

noisivelvet, 2057 W. Berwyn Ave., #3, Chicago, IL 60625

Nomos Review, 28900 Lakefront Rd., Temecula, CA 92591

Noon, 1324 Lexington Ave., PMB 298, New York, NY 10128

The Normal School, 5245 N. Backer Ave., M/S PB 98, Fresno, CA 93740

North American Review, Univ. of Northern Iowa, Cedar Falls, IA 50614-0516

North Carolina Literary Review, ECU Mailstop 555, Greenville, NC 27858-4353

North Dakota Quarterly, 276 Centennial Drive, Grand Forks, ND 58202-7209

Not One of Us, 12 Curtis Rd., Natick, MA 01760

Notre Dame Review, 840 Flanner Hall, Notre Dame, IN 46556

O

O-Dark-Thirty, 5812 Morland Drive No., Adamstown, MD 21710

Ocean State Review, University of Rhode Island, 60 Upper College Rd., Kingston, RI 02881

Off the Coast, PO Box 14, Robbinston, ME 04671

Ofi Press, 4821 Calz. Tlalpan, Tlalpan Centro, Tlalpan, CP 14000, DF, Mexico

Old Mountain Press, P.O. Box 66, Webster, NC 28788

1/25, (one of twenty-five), 151 Applegate Lane, East Brunswick, NJ 08816

One Story, 232 3rd St., #E106, Brooklyn, NY 11215

One Teen Story, 232 3rd St., #E106, Brooklyn, NY 11215

One Trick Pony Review, 42540 W. Bunker Dr., Maricopa, AZ 85138

Orchises Press, P.O. Box 320533, Alexandria, VA 22320-4533

Oregon Humanities, 813 SW Alder St., #702, Portland, OR 97205

Origami Poems Project, P.O. Box 1623, E. Greenwich, RI 02818

Orion Magazine, 187 Main St., Great Barrington, MA 01230

Osiris, PO Box 297, Deerfield, MA 01342

Outside In Literary & Travel Magazine, 1475 SW Charles St., Dundee, OR 97115

Overtime, PO Box 250382, Plano, TX 75025-0382

Oxford American, 201 Donaghey Ave, Main 107, Conway AR 72035

Oyez Review, Roosevelt Univ., Literature & Languages, Chicago, IL 60605-1394

P

P.R.A. Publishing, PO Box 211701, Martinez, GA 30917

PANK Magazine, 1230 W. Polk Ave., Apt. 107, Charleston, IL 61920

Parcel, 6 E. 7th St., Lawrence, KS 66044

The Paris-American, P.O. Box 167, Tomkins Cove, NY 10986

The Paris Review, 544 West 27th St., New York, NY 10003

Parody, P.O. Box 404, East Rochester, NY 14445

Passages North, English Dept., N.M.U., Marquette, MI 49855-5363

Paterson Literary Review, 1 College Blvd., Paterson, NJ 07505-1179

Peg Leg Publishing, 1612 NW 20th St., Oklahoma City, OK 73106

Penduline Press, 14674 SW Mulberry Dr., Portland, OR 97224

PEN America, 588 Broadway (Ste 303, New York, NY 10012)

Permafrost, Univ. of Alaska, P.O. Box 755720, Fairbanks, AK 99775-0640

Perpetual Motion Machine Publishing, 152 Dew Fall Trail, Cíbolo, TX 78108

Perugia Press, PO Box 60364, Florence, MA 01062

The Petigru Review, 4840 Forest Dr., Ste. 6B, PMB 189, Columbia, SC 29206

Philadelphia Stories, Sommers, 107 West Main St., Ephrata, PA 17522

Phrygian Press, 58-09 205th St., Bayside, NY 11364

Pilgrimage, Colorado State University, 2200 Bonforte Blvd., Pueblo, CO 81001

The Pinch, English Dept., 467 Patterson Hall, Memphis, TN 38152-3510

Ping-Pong, 48603 Highway One, Big Sur, CA 93920

Pinwheel, 2265 W. Leland Ave., #1, Chicago, IL 60625

Pirene's Fountain, 3616 Glenlake Dr., Glenview, IL 60026

Pithead Chapel, 121 Heritage Dr., Apt. 3, Negaunee, MI 49866

Plain View Press, 3800 N. Lamar Blvd., Ste. 730-260, Austin, TX 78756

Pleiades, Univ. of Central Missouri, English Dept., Warrensburg, MO 64093-5046

Plenitude Publishing Society 102-2507 Wark St., Victoria, BC V8T 4G7 Canada

Ploughshares, Emerson College, 120 Boylston St., Boston, MA 02116-4624

Poecology, 109 McFarland, #418, Stanford, CA 94305

Poems and Plays, MTSU, P. O. Box 70, Murfreesboro, TN 37132

Poet Lore, 4508 Walsh St., Bethesda, MD 20815

poeticdiversity: the litzine of Los Angeles, 6028 Comey Ave., L.A., CA 90034

Poetry Magazine, 61 West Superior St., Chicago, IL 60654

Poetry Northwest, 2000 Tower St., Everett, WA 98201

Poetry Pacific, 1550 68th Ave. W., Vancouver, BC V6P 2V5 Canada

The Poetry Porch, 115588 Hollett St., Scituate, MA02086

Poetry South, MVSU 7242, 14000 Hwy 82 West, Itta Bena, MS 38941-1400

The Poet's Billow, 245 N. Collingwood, Syracuse, NY 13206

The Poet's Haven, P.O. Box 1501, Massillon, OH 44648

Poets and Artists, 604 Vale St., Bloomington, IL 61701

The Point, 732 S. Financial Place, #704, Chicago, IL 60605

Pool, 11500 San Vicente Blvd., #224, L.A. CA 90049

Post Road, Boston College, 140 Commonwealth Ave., Chestnut Hill, MA 02467

Postcard Poems and Prose Magazine, 14605 Lafernier St., Baraga, MI 49908

Postscripts to Darkness. 144-195 Cooper, Ottawa, ON K2P 0E6 Canada

Potomac Review, 51 Manakee St., MT/212, Rockville, MD 20850

Prairie Journal Trust, 28 Crowfoot Terrace NW, P.O. Box 68073, Calgary, AB, T3G 3N8, Canada

Prairie Schooner, UNL, 123 Andrews Hall, Lincoln, NE 68588-0334

Presa Press, PO Box 792, Rockford, MI 49341

Prick of the Spindle, P.O. Box 170607, Birmingham, AL 35217

Printer's Devil Review, 74 Park St., Apt. 2, Somerville, MA 02143

Prism International, UBC, Buch E462—1866 Main Mall, Vancouver BC V6T 1Z1

Progenitor, Arapahoe Community College, Campus Box 27, 5900 S. Santa Fe Dr., P.O. Box 9002, Littleton, CO 80160

Prospect Park Books, 969 South Raymond Ave., Pasadena, CA 91105

Provo Canyon Review, 4006 N. Canyon Rd., Provo, UT 84604

A Public Space, 323 Dean St., Brooklyn, NY 11217

Puerto Del Sol, N.M.S.U, P.O. Box 30001, MSC 3E, Las Cruces, NM 88003

Q

Queen's Ferry Press, 8622 Naomi St., Plano, TX 75024

Quiddity, Benedictine University, 1500 N. Fifth St., Springfield, IL 62702

Quiet Lightning, c/o E. Karp, 734 Balboa St., SF, CA 94118

Quill and Parchment Press, 1825 Echo Park Ave., Los Angeles, CA 90046

The Quotable, 520 W 21st St., #230, Norfolk, VA 23517

Qwerty, UNB Fredericton, P.O. Box 4440, Fredericton, NB, Canada E3B5A3

R

R. L. Crow Publications, PO Box 262, Penn Valley, CA 95946

Radio Silence, PO Box 40626, San Francisco, CA 94140

Radius, 65 Paine St., #2, Worcester, MA 01605

The Rag, 11901 SW 34th Ave., Portland, OR 97219

Ragazine, Box 8586, Endwell, NY 13762

Raintown Review, 5390 Fallriver Row Ct., Columbia, MD 21044

Raleigh Review, Box 6725, Raleigh, NC 27628

Rappahannock Review, UMW, 1301 College Ave., Fredericksburg, VA 22401

Raritan: A Quarterly Review, Rutgers, 31 Mine St., New Brunswick, NJ 08901

Rattle, 12411 Ventura Blvd., Studio City, CA 91604

The Raven Chronicles, 12346 Sand Point Way, N.E., Seattle, WA 98125

Read Short Fiction, 249 Great Plain Rd., Danbury, CT 06811

Red Bridge Press, 667 2nd Avenue, San Francisco, CA 94118

Red Hen Press, PO Box 40820, Pasadena, CA 91114

Red River Review, 4669 Mountain Oak St., Fort Worth, TX 76244-4397

Red Savina Review, 305 S. Nickel, Deming, NM 88030

Redactions, 604 N. 31st Ave., Apt D-2, Hattiesburg, MS 39401

Redivider, Emerson College, 120 Boylston St., Boston, MA 02116

Referential Magazine, 21B Morton Rd., Bryn Mawr, PA 19010

Revolution House, 516 N. 6th St., #3, Lafayette, IN 47901

Reworked Press, 3215 Windshire Lane, #415, Charlotte, NC 28273

Rhino, P.O. Box 591, Evanston, IL 60204

River Otter Press, P.O. Box 211664, St. Paul, MN 55121

River Styx, 3547 Olive St., Ste. 107, St. Louis, MO 63103-1024

River Teeth, Ashland University, 401 College Ave., Ashland, OH 44805

Rock & Sling, Whitworth Univ., 300 W. Hawthorne Rd., Spokane, WA 99251

Rose Red Review, 13026 Staton Drive, Austin, TX 78727

Ruminate, 1041 N. Taft Hill Rd., Ft. Collins, CO 80521

S

Sakura Publishing, P.O. Box 1681, Hermitage, PA 16148

Salamander, 41 Temple St., Boston, MA 02114-4280

Salmagundi, Skidmore College, Saratoga Springs, NY 12866-1632

Santa Monica Review, 1900 Pico Blvd., Santa Monica, CA 90405

Saranac Review, SUNY, 101 Broad St., Plattsburgh, NY 12901-2681

Sawyer House, 721 Dean St., Floor 3, Brooklyn, NY 11238

Scars Publications, 829 Brian Court, Gurnee, IL 60031

Schuylkill Valley Journal, 240 Golf Hills Rd., Havertown, PA 19083

Scribendi, MSC06-3890, 1 University of New Mexico, Albuquerque, NM 87131

Sea Haven Books, P.O. Box 61, Tolovana Park, OR 97145

2nd & Church, P.O. Box 198156, Nashville, TN 37129-8156

Seems, Lakeland College, PO Box 359, Sheboygan, WI 53082-0359

Sein und Werden, 9 Dorris St., Manchester M19 2TP UK

Sewanee Review, 735 University Ave, Sewanee, TN 37383

Shabda Press, 3343 East Del Mar Blvd., Pasadena, CA 91107

Shenandoah, Washington & Lee University, Lexington, VA 24450-2116

Sibling Rivalry Press, 13913 Magnolia Glen, Alexander, AR 72002

Silk Road Review, 2043 College Way, Forest Grove, OR 97116-1797

Silver Birch Press, P.O. Box 29458, Los Angeles, CA 90029

Sinister Wisdom, P.O. Box 3252, Berkeley, CA 94703

Six Three Whiskey Press, 1234 6th St., #403, Santa Monica, CA 90401

Sixfold, 28 Farm Field Ridge Rd., Sandy Hook, CT 06482

Sixteen Rivers Press, P.O. Box 640663, San Francisco, CA 94164-0663

Sixth Finch, 95 Carolina Ave., #2, Jamaica Plain, MA 02130

Skive Magazine, 86/1 Laman St., Cooks Hill NSW 2300 Australia

A Slant of Light, SUNY New Paltz, 1 Hawk Dr., New Paltz, NY 12561

Sleet Magazine, 1846 Bohland Ave., St. Paul, MN 55116

Slice, P.O. Box 659, Village Station, New York, NY 10014

The Sligo Journal, Montgomery College, Takoma Park, MD 20912

Slipstream, Box 2071, Niagara Falls, NY 14301

Small Print Magazine, P.O. Box 71956, Richmond, VA 23255-1956

Smartish Pace, P.O. Box 22161, Baltimore, MD 21203

Snail Mail Review, 1694 Augusta Pointe Drive, Ripon, CA 95366

V

Vallum, 5038 Sherbrooke West, PO Box 23077 CP Vendome, Montreal, QC H4A 1T0, Canada

Vector Press, 226 Ella St., #2, Pittsburgh, PA 15224

Versal, 334 Oxford St., #2, Rochester, NY 14607

Verse Wisconsin, P.O. Box 620216, Middleton, WI, 53562-0216

Vine Leaves, c/o Jessica Bell, Konopisopoulou 31, Athens, 1152, Greece

The Virginia Quarterly Review, 5 Boar's Head Lane, P.O. Box 400223, Charlottesville, VA 22904

VoiceCatcher, P.O. Box 6064, Portland, OR 97228-6064

The Volta, 1423 E. University Blvd., Modern Languages Bldg. 472, Tucson, AZ 85721

vox poetica, 160 Summit St., Englewood, NJ 07631

W

Wag's Revue, 313 Sackett St., #3, Brooklyn, NY 11231

Wake: Great Lake Thoughts & Culture, 1 Campus Dr., Allendale, MI 49401-9403

War, Literature & the Arts, HQ USAFA/DFENG, 2354 Fairchild Dr., Ste. 6D-149, USAF Academy, CO 80840-6242

Washington Square Review, 58 W. 10th St., NY, NY 10011

Water-Stone Review, MS A1730, 1536 Hewitt Ave., St. Paul, MN 55104-1284

Waxwing Magazine, 220 S. Humphreys St., Flagstaff, AZ 86001

Wayne State University Press, 4809 Woodward Ave., Detroit, MI 48201-1309

The Weeklings, 43 N. Manheim Blvd., New Paltz, NY 12561

West Branch, Stadler Center for Poetry, Bucknell Univ., Lewisburg, PA 17837

The Westchester Review, Box 246H, Scarsdale, NY 10583

Whispering Prairie Press, P.O. Box 410661, Kansas City, MO 64141

Whistling Shade, 1495 Midway, Saint Paul, MN 55108

The White Review, 243 Knightsbridge, London SW7 1DN, United Kingdom

White Violet Press, 24600 Mountain Ave., #35, Hemet, CA 92544

Wigleaf, 2609 Johnson Dr., Columbia, MO 65203

Wild Goose Poetry Review, 838 4th Avenue Dr. NW, Hickory, NC 28601

Wilderness House Press, 145 Foster St., Littleton, MA 01460

Willow Springs, 501 N. Riverpoint Blvd., Ste 425, Spokane, WA 99202

Wings Press, 627 E. Guenther, San Antonio, TX 78210

Wiseblood Books, P.O. Box 11612, Milwaukee, WI 53211

Wising Up Press, P.O. Box 2122, Decatur, GA 30031-2122

Witness, Box 455085, Las Vegas, NV 89154-5085

WMG Publishing, P.O. Box 269, Lincoln City, OR 97367

The Worcester Review, 1 Ekman St., Worcester, MA 01607

Word Palace Press, P.O. Box 583, San Luis Obispo, CA 93406

Wordgathering, 7507 Park Ave., Pennsauken, NJ 08109

World Literature Today, 630 Parrington Oval, Ste. 110, Norman, OK 73019-4033

Write Bloody Books, 2306 E. Cesar Chavez, Ste. 103, Austin TX 78702

Writecorner Press, PO Box 140310, Gainesville, FL 32614-0310

The Writing Disorder, P.O. Box 93613, L.A., CA 90093

Writing Knights Press, 7406 Kingston Ct., Mentor, OH 44060

Writing on the Edge, Writing Program, UC Davis, Davis, CA 95616

Written Backwards, 1325 H St., #11, Sacramento, CA 95814

Y

The Yale Review, PO Box 208243, New Haven, CT 06520
Yarn, 26 Hawthorne Lane, Weston, MA 02493
Yellow Flag Press, 224 Melody Dr., Lafayette, LA 70503
Yellow Medicine Review, English Dept., SMSU, 1501 State St., Marshall, MN 56258
Yemassee, English Dept., USC, Columbia, SC 29208
Yes Yes Books, 1232 NE Prescott St., Portland, OR 97211-4662
Your Impossible Voice, 820 26th Ave., #4, San Francisco, CA 94121

Z

Zephyr Press, 50 Kenwood St., Brookline, MA 02446-2413
Zoetrope: All Story, 916 Kearny St., San Francisco, CA 94133
Zone 3, APSU, P.O. Box 4565, Clarksville, TN 37044
Zymbol, 21 Conant St., Ste. 3, Salem, MA 01970
ZYZZYVA, 466 Geary St., Ste. 401, San Francisco, CA 94102-1262

CONTRIBUTORS' NOTES

RUSSELL BANKS' latest book is published by Ecco Press. He lives in upstate New York and Miami.

RICK BASS is the author of thirty-one books of fiction and nonfiction, including most recently a novel, *All The Land To Hold Us*. He lives in Montana.

REGINALD DWAYNE BETTS's next poetry collection will be published by Four Way Books in 2015. He is the author of a memoir and a previous poetry gathering.

KARA CANDITO wrote two prize winning books—*Spectator* (University of Utah Press, 2014) and *Taste of Cherry* (University of Nebraska Press, 2009). She lives in Madison, Wisconsin.

HENRI COLE teaches at Ohio State University and is poetry editor of *The New Republic*. He has published eight poetry collections.

OLIVER DE LA PAZ lives in Deming, Washington.

MICHAEL DICKMAN was born and raised in Portland, Oregon and now resides in Princeton, New Jersey.

EMMA DUFFY–COMPARONE lives in Portsmouth, New Hampshire. "The Zen Thing" is her first published story.

TARFIA FAIZULLAH is visiting professor in poetry at the University of Michigan. She is the author of *Seam*, winner of the Crab Orchard first book award.

MARIBETH FISCHER founded the Rehoboth Beach Writers' Guild in 2005 and currently serves as Executive Director. She authored two award winning books from Dutton and Simon & Schuster.

AISHA GAWAD received an MFA in fiction from Cornell. She is at work on a novel about the police and the Arab community in Bay Ridge, Brooklyn.

NANCY GEYER is working on an essay collection. Her nonfiction has received awards from *The Iowa Review, Iron Horse* and *Terrain .org.*

LOUISE GLÜCK lives in Cambridge and teaches at Yale. Her *Faithful And Virtuous Night* is just out from Farrar, Straus and Giroux.

HILLARY GRAVENDYK (1979–2014) taught English at Pomona College in Claremont, California. Her poetry has appeared in many journals and in a chapbook published by Achiote Press (2008) and a collection from Omnidawn (2012).

MARILYN HACKER has authored twelve books of poems and won numerous prizes. She lives in Paris.

REBECCA HAZELTON teaches at the Wisconsin Creative Writing Institute. Her poems have appeared in *The Southern Review, Agni, Pleiades* and elsewhere.

LYN HEJINIAN is a poet, small press publisher and translator. She has authored over twenty books including most recently *The Book of A Thousand Eyes.*

BOB HICOK's *Elegy Owed* (Copper Canyon, 2013) was a finalist for the National Book Critics Circle Award. He is a past guest co–editor of poetry for the Pushcart Prize.

EDWARD HOAGLAND's most recent novel in *Children Are Diamonds* (Arcade, 2013). He is a member of The American Academy of Arts and Letters.

MARY HOOD is the author of a novel and two collections of short stories. A story collection and a novella are forthcoming in 2015.

REBECCA GAYLE HOWELL's *Render/An Apocalypse* won the Cleveland State University Poetry Center's First Book Prize. She lives in Lexington, Kentucky.

PACIFIQUE IRANKUNDA moved to the United States from Burundi and graduated from Deerfield Academy and Williams College. He is working on a book about his Burundi childhood.

AMAND JAMAUL JOHNSON is a former Stegner Fellow at Stanford. His two books are *Darktown Follies* (2013) and *Red Summer* (2006), both from Tupelo Press.

FADY JOUDAH is a Palestinian-American poet, translator and physician of internal medicine. His first book won the 2007 Yale Younger Poets Competition. *Textu* is just out from Copper Canyon.

MICHAEL KARDOS' new novel, *Before He Finds Her,* is forthcoming in 2015. He co–directs the writing program at Mississippi State University.

THOMAS E. KENNEDY's latest book is *Kerrigan in Copenhagen* (Bloomsbury). He lives in Denmark.

PHILIP LEVINE's most recent book is *News of The World* (Knopf). A book of essays is due in 2015.

SANDRA LIM's *The Wilderness* is just published by W.W. Norton. *Loveliest Grotesque* came out from Kore Press in 2006.

ADA LIMÓN's new poetry collection, *Bright Dead Things,* is soon out from Milkweed Editions. She is also the author of *Lucky Wreck, This Big Fake World,* and *Sharks In The Rivers*.

PATRICIA LOCKWOOD is the author of *Balloon Pop Outlaw Black* and *Motherland Fatherland and Homelandsexuals*. She lives in Lawrence, Kansas.

ALEXANDER MAKSIK is the author of two novels. His work has appeared in *Harper's, The Atlantic, Harvard Review* and elsewhere.

JAMAAL MAY is a Kenyon Review Fellow and the author of *Hum* (Alice James Books). He co–directs the Organic Weapon Arts Chapbook and Video Series with Tarfia Faizullah.

DAVID MEANS authored four story collections including *The Spot* and *Assorted Fire Events,* winner of the *Los Angeles Times* Book Prize. In 2013 he received a Guggenheim Fellowship.

MOLLY MCNETT's stories have appeared in *New England Review, Best American Short Stories, Crazyhorse* and other journals. She lives on a farm with her family in Oregon, Illinois.

LINCOLN MICHEL's debut collection, *Upright Beasts,* is due from Coffee House Press. He is co–editor of *Gigantic* and online editor of *Electric Literature.*

KAMILAH AISHA MOON is the author of *She Has A Name* (Four Way Books) which includes her Pushcart winning poem. She has taught at Medger Evers College, Drew University and Adelphi University.

OTTESSA MOSHFEGH's first book, *McGlue,* is just out. She lives in Oakland, California.

YANNICK MURPHY's latest novel is *This Is The Water* (Harper Perennial).

KATHLEEN OSSIP's *The Do–Over* was one of *Publishers Weekly*'s best books of 2011. She teaches at The New School, New York.

D. A. POWELL's current book is *Repast* (Graywolf, 2014). His *Useless Landscape, or A Guide for Boys* won The National Book Critics Circle Award in poetry.

SINA QUEYRAS books are published by Coach House press.

ALAN ROSSI's work has appeared in *Ninth Letter, The Florida Review, Ohio Review* and elsewhere. He lives in South Carolina.

RACHEL RUCKER's nine books include a memoir, MOTHERS, and a double collection of prose and poetry. *The Pedestrians* (where "Mindful" appears). She teaches at New York University.

KAREN RUSSELL is the author of a story collection and the novel *Swamplandia!* which was a finalist for The Pulitzer Prize.

MICHELLE SEATON teaches at Grub Street and lives in Boston. Her stories have appeared in *Sycamore Review, Harvard Review* and elsewhere.

BENNETT SIMS' novel *A Questionable Shape* (Two Dollar Radio) won the 2014 Bard Fiction Prize.

REBECCA SOLNIT is the author of seventeen books about place, politics and "wandering around in thought and on foot." She lives in San Francisco.

SUSAN STEWART's most recent book of poems is *Red Rover.* Her prose book is *The Poet's Freedom: A Notebook on Making.* She lives in Princeton, New Jersey.

STEPHANIE STRICKLAND's "Captcha" appears in her volume *Dragon Logic* (Ahsahta Press). She lives in New York.

BARRETT SWANSON's essays and fiction have been published in *The Point, American Short Fiction, The Millions* and elsewhere. He lives in Madison, Wisconsin.

MARY SZYBIST's *Incarnadine* won The 2013 National Book Award. She teaches at Lewis and Clark College in Portland, Oregon.

JONI TEVIS has published two books of nonfiction. She teaches at Furman University in Greenville, South Carolina.

DANIEL TOVROV lives in San Francisco. He is a reporter, editor and student.

WELLS TOWER is the author of *Everything Ravaged, Everything Burned.*

FREDERIC TUTEN has published five novels plus a collection of short stories, *Self Portraits: Fictions* (Norton). He lives in New York.

INARA VERZEMNIEKS is a graduate of The University of Iowa's writing program. She was a finalist for the Pulitzer Prize in 2006.

SHAWN VESTAL is the author of *God Forsaken Idaho.* He lives in Spokane.

ELLEN BRYANT VOIGT's *Kyrie* was a finalist for the National Book Critics Circle Award. She has published seven volumes of poetry.

MATTHEW VOLLMER edits the University of Michigan's 21st Century Prose series. He is the author of two story collections, an essay collection and co–editor of an anthology of fake documents.

XUAN JULIANA WANG was a Wallace Stegner Fellow at Stanford and holds on MFA from Columbia University.

LATOYA WATKINS is a Ph.D. candidate at The University of Texas. Her stories have appeared in *Specter, Lunch Ticket, Kweli Journal* and *Potomac Review.*

AFAA MICHAEL WEAVER received The 2014 Kingsley Tufts Award for his 12th book of poetry, *The Government of Nature* (University of Pittsburgh). His new play is GRIP.

JIM WHITE worked as a model in Milan, a professional surfer and a cab driver. He has released several records on Luaka Bop and independently.

JOE WILKINS wrote the memoir *The Mountain And The Fathers: Growing Up On The Big Dry.* He lives in Oregon.

NANCE VAN WINCKEL has just published her sixth collection of poems and her fourth book of linked stories. A photo-collage novel, *Ever Yrs,* is forthcoming.

RACHEL ZUCKER is the author of nine books, most recently a memoir, MOTHERs. She teaches at New York University.

INDEX

The following is a listing in alphabetical order by author's last name of works reprinted in the *Pushcart Prize* editions since 1976.

621

623

627

629

630

632

633

643

644

645